MASTERS

MASTERS

THE ARCHERS
OF SAINT SEBASTIAN III

JEANNE ROLAND

NEPENTHE PRESS

Copyright © 2023 by Jeanne Roland

All rights reserved.

No part of this publication may be reproduced, distributed, or transmitted in any form or by any means, including photocopying, recording, or other electronic or mechanical methods, without the prior written permission of the publisher and the author, except in the case of brief quotations embodied in critical reviews and certain other noncommercial uses permitted by copyright law. For permission requests, contact the author at xaire@jeanneroland.com.

This is a work of fiction. Any resemblance to actual events or persons, living or dead, is entirely coincidental.

Cover art and interior design created in Canva Pro for Nepenthe Press. *Background image: "Flowers by a Stone Vase,"* Peter Faes, ca. 1786, in the Metropolitan Museum of Art, Public Domain image; *Inset: "The Martyrdom of Saint Sebastian,"* Workshop of Gerard van Honthorst (Netherlands ca. 1623), in the Centraal museum, Utrecht, Public Domain image.

For a full citation of the source files for all of the artwork used herein, see the illustration credits page at the back of the book. Our press logo and Jeanne Roland's author logo were created by Miblart.

ISBN 978-1-7378870-7-2 (Paperback)

ISBN 978-1-7378870-6-5 (ebook)

ISBN 978-1-7378870-8-9 (Hardback)

Published by Nepenthe Press
Beavercreek, Ohio

NEPENTHE PRESS
WWW.NEPENTHEPRESS.COM

FOR MIMI
WHO SHARES AND FUELS MY PASSIONS

AND FOR SAM
WHO NEVER LETS ME GIVE UP ON THEM

OUT OF THE WOODS

PART ONE

CHAPTER ONE

Do you have any idea what it's like, to find out everything you thought you knew was a lie? At the memory of that scornful look he cast down at me, I'm resolved. I'll not watch him be the one to win the competitions, nor sit idly by and let his trick work. I swear I'll find a way to beat him. It can't be too late to win.

I step into the little clearing in Brecelyn's woods as alert and as cautious as a deer. My quick breath is coming out in visible clouds of mist like a deer's, too, and after a long trek alone through the dark woods, the half-day glow in the open space is almost blinding. A light snow must have fallen sometime earlier in the night, unnoticed by us all in our preoccupation with the evening's more dire events, and before me now stands a perfect circle of white bathed in the light of a full moon. I've only seen a moon like the one that's out tonight once before, on the night I led the squires on an outing to the convent of St. Genevieve to ask for a kiss. A witching moon the boys called it then, and I guess they were right; at least, with the icy foliage and the snow-strewn ground gleaming in the moonlight the place is so transformed from what it was during the day that I hardly recognize it. Now it's an inviolate druid's circle or the forbidding haunt of a faery queen, and I suppose it should be beautiful. But this place can never be anything but ugly to me, and if anyone had told me when I stumbled blindly away from here this morning that I'd ever come back willingly, or that it would now seem to me to be a place where things made sense, I'd have said he was crazy.

I pluck up my courage and pick my way across the open ground, lifting each foot high and placing it down deliberately again as I go. A nervous tick has started pulsing away erratically against my wrists and behind my temples at being back here again, but when I pause to lean the bow in my hand against my leg and adjust the shooting bracer carefully on my arm, I'm not stalling. It's just my usual routine, before taking any shot.

When I've got the bracer positioned, I pick up my bow again. It's a long clean, line, and holding its smooth wood feels good. It feels right. It's something I understand, something that makes sense. *I* make sense, when it's in my hand. I'm a boy again, Tristan's squire Marek and an archer of St. Sebastian, the boy I want to be. It's about the only thing that's made any sense today, and right now I need to do something that makes sense, something I can know exactly how I'm supposed to feel about it.

I slide an arrow out from the quiver slung across my shoulder, and roll it between my fingers. It's one I made myself, and I don't think I'm bragging when I say it's as beautiful as any work of art. I'm good with my hands and I never do anything but my best work on Tristan's equipment, and a squire always shoots with his master's arrows. It's a little thing, but it feels good, too, moving in my hand. I watch the thin red whipping swirl through the feathers of the fletching as I twirl the arrow, and the red bands around the shaft that are Tristan's mark blur until they could be a smear of blood.

With a deep breath, I slip the nock of the arrow onto the bowstring. Then I step to the place where Tristan fell, an unmarked arrow in his side. I know the exact spot where it happened, on the day of that fateful hunt here so long ago. I recognized it right away this morning, didn't I, when Remy and I came out of the woods across it, by some extraordinary chance? A lucky chance for me, as it turns out, although I felt anything but lucky, then. Now even with it covered in snow I couldn't miss it. Not after the wretched scene that followed our discovery, when all the boys spilled into the clearing behind us, to find me with a broken arrow clutched in my hand.

A fresh wave of frustration and rage washes over me, although after all that's happened since I'm no longer sure who or what it is I'm so angry at.

Myself, maybe.

How could I have been running thoughtlessly through the woods to Tristan's *rival*, bent on betraying Tristan, and myself? I was about to throw away everything I'd worked so long and hard to achieve for the both of us, and why? Because I'd let the girl in me be seduced. And how easily he did it! Just by letting a hawk land on my hand. At the thought of how I felt standing in Brecelyn's field as that bird of his swooped down toward me, a flush of shame floods my cheeks.

Who am I kidding? I know exactly who it is I'm really furious at.

I give myself a shake. I didn't come here to think about this morning. I came here to forget all about it. It's time to take aim and focus on what it is I really want. So I force my mind further back, to the day Tristan was shot, and I lift my bow slowly. As I do I sight across the clearing, along the path the arrow that struck Tristan must have come in its flight. My eyes search out the hiding place where his shooter would have been concealed, waiting for his prey, and I find it easily: a fallen log, with the tall stump of a tree rising next to it, its arms outstretched. It's not hard to imagine it's the boy who must have stood beside it then — an archer in St. Sebastian's garb, dressed all in black, without a spot of color to relieve the midnight of his costume.

I bend my bow, and as I rise into my shot, I focus all my concentration on that stump, just as though it really were that treacherous boy, that day. As I do, in my mind I picture Tristan's enemy and mine as he would have looked then: tall and strong, his head held high, the huge yew bow in his powerful hands trained on Tristan. He throws back his broad shoulders, and those incredible arms of his eagerly stretch his bow, straining it to the breaking point for the kill. There's a murderous scowl blazing on his handsome face; his thick, black hair falls in a wave across his brow, his dark eyes flash with fire; his mouth curls into a triumphant sneer, as his breath comes out hot and fast through parted lips that ... uh ... his lips ... *warm, hungry lips, pressing mine ...*

"Oh, *damn it all!*"

With an exasperated cry I squeeze my eyes shut and let my arrow fly, sending it with shaking arms in a perfect shot, straight for his eye.

The arrow strikes the stump with a loud thwack. It's a very satisfying sound. To me, it sounds like finality.

Okay, maybe it's an empty gesture. But I do feel better. A little.

"*Gads,* Marek! *What a remarkable shot!*" a languid voice suddenly exclaims behind me, and I jump about two feet straight into the air.

I clutch my chest and stagger backward, more from shock than from fear. I'd know that impeccably accented voice anywhere.

It's Gilles, and I'm caught.

I can't believe it! I've managed to make a complete fool of myself on the exact same spot, twice in one day.

My eyes fly open, and I whirl around. Sure enough, an elegant boy is lounging up against a tree a few feet behind me, dressed to the nines despite the hour and casually examining the fingernails of one hand in the moonlight.

"But whatever *do* you have against *stumps?*" he drawls, amused. "Why, you've positively *emasculated* the poor thing!"

I look back over my shoulder, to see with dismay that he's right. My arrow *is* sticking out of the stump. But it's much, much lower down on it than where anyone could picture a boy's eye to be.

I turn my back on the stump with an embarrassed grimace.

"What are you doing here, Gilles?" I demand flatly.

"I should think that was perfectly obvious," he replies smoothly, and it is. How Gilles got into the elaborate get-up of silk and lace he's wearing in time to follow me out here from the castle I don't know, though, since he's notorious for sleeping in the nude. And how he managed to catch up with me without me hearing him is even more of a mystery, since I now see that he's got a mount tethered to the trunk of a tree a few yards away. I must have been even more wrapped up in my own thoughts as I snuck out here than I'd thought not to hear him on the path behind me, on horseback.

"More to the point, I should think," Gilles is continuing, "Just what exactly might *you* be doing here?"

5

As I flounder to think up a convincing response, he pushes off from the tree and saunters over.

"Returning to the scene of the crime, eh?"

He doesn't say whose crime he means, and I don't ask. I don't want to know. But I have the unnerving feeling I often have with Gilles that he thinks he knows exactly what *I'm* thinking, and what really brought me here. Even worse, maybe he does.

"I couldn't sleep, that's all," I grumble.

"Ah, but of course!" Gilles trills, slinging an arm conspiratorially around my shoulder, and pointing up at the sky with a wink. "You were drawn out by Mistress Moon, no doubt! You do know what they call a moon like that, don't you?" he adds, and before I can stop him, he exclaims happily,

"A *lovers'* moon!" and I cringe, even though I knew it was coming. Needless to say, I remember that epithet from the night of our convent run, too — all too well.

"Why Marek, you sly devil!" he chuckles, slapping me on the back. "Don't tell me I've interrupted a *lovers'* rendezvous?!" He looks around exaggeratedly. "Who is she? Some lucky kitchen maid? Or serving boy, perhaps, if that's more to your taste? Well, well, I am sorry, dear boy, if I've scared off your paramour. Far be it from me to come between *lovers* …" He drags out the word teasingly, for some reason looking off toward my arrow in the stump with an arch expression on his face.

"Don't be ridiculous," I huff, cutting him off. If he says *lovers* one more time, I think I might throttle him, even if he is a master. And the Marquis de Chartrain, to boot.

"More ridiculous than midnight target practice?" he replies shrewdly, and I blush. "I do admire your diligence, of course, Marek, but if you're hoping to start a fad of moonlight archery, I'm afraid it will never catch on."

I'm just opening my mouth to spout some lie that might explain my odd behavior when he suddenly stiffens, and slips a silencing hand over my mouth.

"*Ssshhh!*" he hisses, cocking his head to one side and peering off intently into the woods.

"*Mmmph! WhazizitGlles?*" I whisper, my words coming out garbled under his hand.

"Up ahead, through those trees," he whispers back, gesturing in front of us. "A lantern, or a torch. There!"

I look in the direction Gilles is pointing, but at first I don't see anything. Then Gilles takes my head between his hands and turns it at the proper angle, and I see it. There is a light moving between the trees ahead in the distance, winking in and out of sight and bobbing around so much I can't tell whether it's coming from one source, or two.

"Oh, Gilles! Do you think it's *marauders?*" I ask anxiously, louder than I intend, and the word echoes around the clearing. Even in the best of times armed bands of scavengers are always roaming around the countryside, and since the onset of the plague lawlessness of every type has only gotten worse. Brecelyn's reputation for strength of arms usually keeps his lands pretty safe, but nobody's immune.

"Don't be silly, Marek," Gilles scoffs, shushing me again. "It's only one or two men, at the most. Poachers, most likely, taking advantage of the moonlight to set their traps." He elbows me in the ribs teasingly. "Or *another* pair of lovers, looking for a trysting place!"

Before I can protest, he's continuing thoughtfully,

"Then again, I suppose it could be a thief. Isn't Brecelyn's chapel of St. Sebastian off in that direction? Surely there are all sorts of tempting things a thief could want to pilfer from in there. Come on, squire! We'd better investigate."

Now I really try to protest. I have no intention of plunging through the woods in pursuit of criminals with Gilles. It's completely insane, and I certainly don't want to do it on horseback. I hate horses, even in full daylight. But Gilles is already pulling me by the arm, dragging me across the clearing toward his horse.

"*Pfft.* Don't fuss so!" Gilles clucks, brushing aside my suggestion to go back to the castle for help. "There's no time for that. Whoever it was, they were moving off at a rather quick clip. It's probably already too late to catch them, more's the pity. And besides, we're both armed — you with your bow, and me with my trusty rapier. What could possibly happen to us?"

I didn't notice it before, but Gilles does have his long, thin blade slung through his belt. Even so, it seems to me that quite a lot could happen to us; as far as I can tell, the sword is mostly for show. But there's no point in saying so. There's no arguing with Gilles. Particularly not after he stops briefly to look me in the eye and add deliberately,

"I'm afraid I'm going to have to insist, dear boy. I can't leave you here alone, and I have absolutely no intention of letting you out of my sight," and I know he doesn't just mean to keep me safe. He thinks I came out here planning to run away.

There's nothing for me to do but hang my head and follow him reluctantly, and this time I don't try to protest. Maybe Gilles is right. Maybe I kind of was running away.

"I was going to go back, before dawn," I mumble, mostly to myself, as Gilles untethers his horse. I've started to twist my hands together nervously; it's not really at the thought of what we might find at the chapel. I don't have any taste for setting off on another fool's errand now, but Gilles is probably right and we'll be perfectly safe. It's that Gilles's pointed comment has dredged up unwelcome thoughts, of all the reasons why he might well think that I would want to run away tonight.

Once he gets the horse untied, Gilles swings himself lightly up into the saddle. The creature is unusually high-spirited; it's been prancing and snorting, jangling its bridle and stamping in a way that's worrisome enough while Gilles mounts up, so I've been keeping my distance. But I haven't really been paying much attention. Gilles is an experienced horseman, and I've been preoccupied, trying to keep my thoughts from straying into dangerous territory. When Gilles reaches a hand down to me, though, I have to step in close.

It's not just my own nervous fear of horses that sets the creature off. As I'm reaching my hand up to take Gilles's, I get a good, close-up look at the huge beast he's seated on. And to my utter astonishment, I recognize it. The horse in front of me isn't Gilles's.

It's *his*.

Taran's.

I recoil with a sharp, involuntary cry, and in that instant the horse seems to recognize me with displeasure, too. It rears up wildly over me and I cringe back in terror, because of the real hooves poised above me, and because of the vivid flashbacks the sight brings on: a sickening thud, a blinding pain, and the crack of my nose breaking, the sounds of me being ruined as a girl — followed fast by a flash of this very horse, rearing up in front of me on this same spot, in exactly this way. And just like that, I'm reliving this morning, all over again.

Before my battered face can sustain fresh damage, Gilles plucks me lightly off the ground and up onto the horse beside him, but it's too late. As Gilles calms the horse and urges it forward through the trees, inevitably the sound that fills the forest around me isn't that of our own progress through the woods, but the sound of Taran riding away, back to the waiting arms of his fiancée.

Taran.

Each dull beat of the horse's hooves against the wet snow beneath us seems to pound out his master's name. *Taran, Taran.* The name opens the floodgates of memory, and all of Remy's awful revelations tumble out and crash around me in rhythm with the beating hooves — the ugly truths that brought my reckless flight through the woods this morning to a disastrous end: it *was* Taran who wounded Tristan. He'd never broken off with Melissande. He just let me believe it, and the fragile thing I'd thought was growing between us was all the subtle deceit of a cold-hearted villain, just another attempt to bring Tristan down. A boy who prefers a defiant look? There's no such thing. It was a cruel lie, and while I was busy constructing an empty fantasy around the image of a noble boy who doesn't exist, Taran was urging Brecelyn to move his wedding *closer*, because he couldn't wait. Because he *didn't* wait. Because Melissande was already carrying his child.

Something clenches painfully in my own belly, and I let my head fall back heavily against Gilles. The frilly lace on his collar tickles the back of my neck and the hilt of his rapier pokes me uncomfortably in the side, but I hardly notice. I try to force the thought of the baby away, but more memories crowd

MASTERS

forward in its wake that aren't much better: me, throwing myself against Taran's stiff, impassive back. Pounding my fists against him ruthlessly and gouging at him with that traitorous arrow of his while the boys looked on in confusion, shocked that I'd detain him with old accusations when he was trying to rush to his ill fiancée. Taran's cold, imperious look down at me from his perch atop this very horse. Then me thrashing away blindly through these woods to the very chapel of St. Sebastian where we're headed now, to swear an oath there that I know to my shame was less a heartfelt renewal of my squire's vow to Tristan than a cry of pain and rage. All of that is bad enough.

But it's nothing compared with what happened next.

I'm jolted out of my thoughts by Gilles's arm jerking me back against him harder, as I start to slip off the horse.

I struggle to compose myself, and I sneak a hand up to wipe away a tear, not wanting to give myself away. I think I'm being pretty furtive about it but I must sniff, since soon an immaculate square of white cloth materializes under my nose.

"Don't fret now, there's a good lad," Gilles says softly. "It'll all come right, in the end. See if it doesn't."

I don't bother to correct him, or even to reply. I just take the cloth and wipe my face dutifully.

Gilles must sense some of what I'm thinking, since he adds lightly,

"Don't worry about the boys too much either, son. You had every right to be upset by that arrow. They'll forget all about it soon enough. Why, they probably already have."

"But the wretched *timing* of it, Gilles," I say miserably. "While I was yelling foul names at him, the ... the ... the..."

I can't bring myself to say it. But Gilles apparently has no such compunction.

"Yes, the *baby*," he drawls, almost sarcastically, and I'm taken aback. I'd never have thought Gilles could sound so callous.

"The *timing* of it, indeed ..." he continues musingly. "Damned convenient, wouldn't you say?"

My whole body bristles with shock. Surely Gilles can't mean to imply that the loss of a baby conceived out of wedlock is convenient, or that anyone could be happy about it? Surely he, too, saw the look on Taran's face — that terrible look, when at last Sir Brecelyn had descended from his daughter's sickroom to give the rest of us boys below in the great hall the welcome news that Melissande herself was out of danger, and for a split-second Taran appeared behind him on the landing at the top of the stairs.

When I stiffen in outrage under him, though, Gilles just says mildly,

"Mark my words, Marek. Things aren't always what they seem."

At the irony of Gilles telling this to me of all people, I roll my eyes in the dark. But I don't make any response. In part, because I actually have no idea

9

what Gilles is getting at. And in part, because before the old, familiar feeling that I'm missing something crucial yet again can fully settle over me, the outline of a stone building appears through the trees in front of us.

We've arrived at the chapel.

"JUST AS I SUSPECTED," GILLES SAYS, AS WE COME OUT IN FRONT of the chapel door and he reins the horse to a halt. "Someone's been here tonight, all right. There's light coming from inside."

Gilles slides easily to the ground. Then he pulls me down after him, thoughtfully plopping me down rather far from the big horse.

"Are you sure we should go in?" I ask, not very hopefully.

"Positive," Gilles replies, pulling out his rapier and striding toward the door. "Nock an arrow, Marek," he adds. "And cover for me, as I open the door."

"You can't be serious!" I demand, but Gilles is unperturbed.

"Okay, then," he says, slipping his rapier back into his belt. "Give me your bow, and I'll cover for you," and it's not much better. But by now Gilles is bending my bow and jerking his head at the door, so I step up bravely, and try the latch.

It's unlocked, unfortunately. Gilles gives me an encouraging nod, and so I fling the door open and jump back hastily, just as Gilles leaps forward through the door, sweeping the bow around in front of him and peering into the chapel.

Nothing.

"Empty," he proclaims, sounding disappointed, and as he disappears further inside, I follow him in, relieved.

Finding no danger within, Gilles flings my bow down on a pew and starts looking around, rubbing his hands together, and I follow suit by unburdening myself of my quiver to warm my hands, too. Even through my thick shooting gloves my hands are frozen stiff, and it's considerably warmer inside the chapel than it was outside. It feels as though the small space has been warmed up naturally, by the heat of bodies that have only recently vacated the place, and that someone's been in here recently is obvious, just as Gilles said. Somebody's lighted the little oil lamps that hang under the chapel's icons and left them burning. It's safe enough, since the wicks are stuck into corks that float on a layer of oil suspended over water. Once the wicks draw up all the fuel, the water below douses the flames. But the little vessels can't hold enough oil to have been lit more than a few hours ago.

"Look here, Marek, what did I tell you?" Gilles exclaims, wandering over by the altar and pointing down at a rickety table set up next to it, on which two cups, an almost-empty bottle of wine, and the crust of a loaf of bread are lying.

"The remains of a midnight supper! Yes, it's just as I suspected," he repeats, pulling back one of a pair of wooden chairs pushed up to the table and sprawling himself down onto it. "A pair of lovers out for a tryst, nothing more. And they've thoughtfully left us just enough wine to toast their health."

Just enough for *one* of us, I think, as Gilles pours himself the dregs of the wine, tipping back in the chair far enough to cross his long, booted legs up on the table.

"Might as well linger a moment, and warm up for the ride back," he declares, settling in.

I've been wandering around, too, looking at everything but not daring to touch anything, and feeling rather strange about being in this place at night. It would be odd in any event, but after having been here in the brilliant light of day so recently, the cold stones and the murky glow from the swinging lamps are downright eerie. A dozen pairs of eyes are following me, as painted saints stare down from the walls all around me.

"Young lovers, wherever you are, I salute you!" Gilles exclaims annoyingly, lifting his cup to drink as I come up beside him. He looks up at me expectantly over his cup. "Well?"

"Well what?"

"Aren't you going to suggest some other scenario?" he demands.

"What do you mean?"

"You disappoint me, Marek," he says, shaking his head sadly. "Aren't you going to accuse our generous host of some new *skullduggery*?" He draws the absurd word out exaggeratedly, inflecting it as only Gilles could. "No? What a shame. And here I was, sure you'd have gotten some notion into your head by now, and that you'd regale me with a preposterous theory about how Brecelyn and his henchmen must be coming out here in the dead of night, to hatch another dastardly plot against the crown. You know. Something outrageous. The sort of melodramatic excess that's just in your line."

I don't dignify this with a reply. It's hardly fair, since no one is more self-dramatizing than Gilles. I know exactly what he means, though, of course. He's ribbing me about my interpretation of the events at Thirds last year, when I foolishly thought Sir Brecelyn had ordered his huntsman to use our competition as a cover for assassinating the prince. Embarrassingly, it turned out that the man was just a disgruntled employee, and the prince wasn't even in the royal box at the time the man was shooting down into the crowd. I know Gilles is just teasing me, trying to lighten my mood, even, and I guess it is sort of funny. But I'm in no mood tonight of all nights to hear any of my old accusations rehearsed, or to think about how far I still am from figuring out what it really was that got my father killed.

When I don't rise to his bait, Gilles doesn't take it amiss. Needing no audience, he simply returns to his earlier theme and starts waxing lyrical about lovers again in a most grating fashion. When he starts to sing an old love ballad that echoes crazily around the hollow room I move away, not wanting to let Gilles suspect how much all his talk of lovers is getting under my skin. For some reason, I find myself gravitating over to one of the alcoves, to the place where I dragged Tristan to tend to his wound here after the hunt; to the place where I pulled the arrow out of Tristan's body that *Taran* shot into him.

I kneel down, and maybe it's my imagination, but even in the low light I think I can still see a faint stain on the floor, where Tristan's blood gushed out under my hand. I stare down at it for a while, and then I don't know why I do it. I lie down on the floor on the spot, and I try to call up everything about how I felt that day: how terrible that arrow felt shuddering through Tristan's flesh. How afraid I was that I'd lose him, just like I lost my father. How desperately I loved Tristan then, and how much I still love him now.

In the background, Gilles is chatting away, drinking and not paying any attention to me.

"Really, though, it is rather curious, I'll admit," he says after a while. "Do you know, my boy, if you were to suggest some plotting here tonight, I might even be tempted to agree with you."

He takes another sip of wine. "Can't have been a thief, at any rate," he mutters thoughtfully. "Nothing obvious is missing. Rather pious lovers, too, I must say," he adds, looking around at the lit lamps. "And not just pious lovers. Lovers, with a *key*."

He pauses dramatically, as though giving me the opportunity to jump in and expound some theory about the mysterious visitors. When I don't contribute anything, after a while he continues with a shrug in his voice,

"I daresay, this isn't much of a place for a tryst, either, come to think of it. All this hard stone and wood. So chafing! It would hardly be comfortable. Just imagine it!"

And before I know it, I am imagining it. I'm not just remembering how Tristan and I lay concealed here on the day of the hunt anymore, but what followed quickly thereafter: Taran leading Melissande inside, for their first private interview. Melissande, breathlessly inviting Taran to kiss her. And how she later told all the girls at the convent that he *did* kiss her passionately in this chapel, and I'd thought it was a lie.

Lovers, using this place for a tryst. Lovers, with access to a key.

At the sudden vision of just which pair of lovers probably did use this chapel for their amorous encounters, and of what else might well have happened on this very spot, there's another sharp jab low in my belly. I roll over, clutching myself and willing the sensation to pass, while Gilles launches into a long list of unlikely places where he's supposedly enjoyed dangerous liaisons with lucky ladies of his own. It takes him quite a while to exhaust his imagination and I'm glad of it, since it takes even longer for me to force the horrible feeling away.

I press my cheek against the stone of the floor, imagining it's Tristan's cheek cool and pale under my own, and I know it's just exhaustion. I shouldn't give in to it. But it's been a long, hard day and I'm bone cold and tired. I don't know what I thought I was going to accomplish, skulking around in the woods in the middle of the night. I was a fool if I thought I could control what I was feeling by doing something as ridiculous as shooting at trees. Even the voice reverberating through the little room isn't Gilles's anymore. It's my own, the words of the brash oaths I swore here just this morning ringing mockingly in my ears.

Avenging my father? What a joke! I'll sooner be shaking the hand of the man who killed him, and thanking him for his hospitality. *And what of helping Tristan?* I don't have any idea how I can hope to do that, either. For all my bravado this morning, I don't really have a plan. Stuck out here at Brecelyn's the guild has seemed far away, but that's just an illusion. The trials will be starting up again sooner than we know, and unless I think of something, and fast, Tristan won't be ready. I used all my father's training methods on him last year, and beating out the best of the Journeys has always been a longshot for him, even under the best of circumstances. But as it is now? He's in *last* place. Helping Tristan win won't just take a brilliant idea — a brilliant idea I don't have. It'll take a miracle.

A tear of frustration slides down across the bridge of my nose, and I let it form a little pool on the dusty floor under me. How could I have let Taran sidetrack me from thinking about the competitions all winter, when figuring out how to get Tristan ready for them should have been my first, my only priority? How can I still be letting my emotions undermine me, when so much is at stake? It's not just that I can't bear to see Tristan lose now or stand the thought of it being Taran who beats him. I've finally seen what I should have right away, that day in barracks when the other squires told me exactly why it is that Remy doesn't care about making Journey. There *is* a good way my story with Tristan can end. One improbable, impossible way — and it's been there all along, right under my nose. What I *should* have been doing all these months is trying to find some way to make it happen. But how? Shooting all the trees in Louvain isn't going to help me figure out what to do about that.

"And let's not forget behind the rosebushes, back at dear old St. Sebastian's!" Gilles laughs, coming to the end of his list. "What a thorny place for an encounter *that* was! Well worth the inconvenience of a few prickles, however, as I remember it. Goodness, Marek, you lazy boy! Whatever are you doing down there? Don't tell me you've fallen asleep," he exclaims indignantly, apparently only just noticing that I've been lying on the floor throughout his recitation.

I hear his boots scrape across the table as he gets to his feet, but I don't move. What's the point? I have no idea what my next move should be. How easy it would be, if I could simply ask Taran what it is he thinks he knows about Tristan's chances in the trials that made him bother to seduce me! But I can't do that, and I can't even summon the will to beg Saint Sebastian to help me; if he were to send me a sign, I doubt I'd recognize it, let alone be able to figure it out. I've thought too many things were signs today and been proven wrong to trust in my ability even to do that.

"Come on, then. The wine's gone, and it's dreadfully late," Gilles says, with a yawn and a stretch. "We've been up most of the night as it is, and I do hate missing my beauty sleep. I shudder to think what I'll look like in the morning."

Gilles always looks as fresh as a rose, but I don't say anything. I don't get up right away, either. As I've been lying here motionless, curled up and staring off blankly into the gloom under the pew in front of me and feeling sorry for myself, I've only just realized that I've actually been staring unseeingly at *something*.

For a while now, my eyes have been resting on a spot up under the pew, where the bench's thick leg meets the seat and supports it from below. Someone's gouged away the wood right at the joint, to make a little shelf-like cavity underneath the bench, a hidey-hole of the kind a tippling priest might use to conceal a secret stash of wine, or a woman to hide some illicit memento from the prying eyes of a father or a husband. It's so cleverly positioned I would never have noticed it if not for my extreme angle, lying as I am with my head on the floor, almost under the pew. Even so, the interior of the hole is in deep shadow. As Gilles bustles around gathering up his belongings, I put out a hand to feel around in it, curious.

There's something there.

My hand comes away with a little book, no bigger than my palm, and I prop myself up on one elbow gingerly to inspect my discovery.

It's nothing more than a dozen or so small sheets of parchment, crudely stitched together and bound in a little leather case. It looks like the sort of thing a girl might carry to chapel, a daybook of illuminated prayers, or maybe a small ledger of some sort, although I'm not sure why anyone would bother to conceal either of those things.

When I flip it open, I see right away that it's neither. My reading isn't what it should be, but even in the dim light I can tell that the cramped writing on the pages is too amateurish to be the work of a monk or a scribe, and there are no columns of numbers or dates. It's more like a compilation of letters, or a private journal. *Love letters*, I'm sure Gilles will insist, or silly personal jottings someone was at pains to keep hidden. From the thick layer of dust on the book's cover, the hiding place did its work well. The book must have been concealed here for a very long time.

"Take a look at this, will you, Gilles?" I say, jogged out of my mood by the unexpectedness of the find, and sitting up. I can't read the thing easily myself, but there might be something amusing in it we can talk about on the ride back — something to distract Gilles from harping on lovers, anyway.

Even if it is love letters, at least they're surely too old to have belonged to anyone we know.

Gilles is busily adjusting his rapier at his waist, and so I'm just about to get to my feet to take the little book over and show it to him. I've already got my mouth open to describe it, in fact, when in idly turning over one of its pages, my eyes come to rest on something that stops me in my tracks.

I clamp my mouth shut and dart a glance at Gilles, but he hasn't looked up.

I shift around on the floor and hold the book protectively close against my stomach. Thus hunched over, I squint down at the page again, and blink.

It wasn't my imagination. It's really there.

In the center of a block of text, there's a simple illustration. It's nothing more than a hasty sketch, a scribble, even. It's so childishly done, I doubt I'd have been able to make much of it, let alone tell what it was supposed to represent. That is, if I hadn't recognized it instantly, the moment I saw it.

As well I should. Until quite recently, a much better copy of the same thing was my only possession. It's a sketch of the portrait of Lady Meliana Brecelyn that hangs in Sir Brecelyn's study, the very painting reproduced in the illumination Father Abelard once gave to me.

I sit immobile for a moment looking dumbly down at the face of Melissande's mother as it stares up out of the book at me. From the knowing smile on her face, she could be remembering a secret tryst of her own here in the chapel with her lover.

Her lover, who was probably my own father.

On impulse I shove the book down into a fold of my tunic, just as Gilles finishes fussing with his sword and turns inquiringly to me.

"Take a look at what?" he demands, coming over.

I cast a quick look around. The cloth Gilles lent me earlier is lying discarded next to me on the floor; I must have still been holding it when I wandered over, though I really don't remember it.

I snatch it up hastily, and I hold it out to him apologetically. Quite a bit of dust from the book has come off onto it from my hand.

Gilles wrinkles his nose.

"Keep it, dear boy, keep it," he says dismissively, waving it away with hardly a glance. So I shove it down into my waistband, too, where it can help conceal the little book further. As I do, an erratic beat starts pulsing along inside my wrists again. This time, it's not nerves drumming through me. It's the stirring of excitement.

There could be any number of explanations for how the painting of Lady Brecelyn came to be sketched in the notebook now tucked down inside my tunic, and for who might have thought to copy it there. But I can't think of many, and all of them lead me to the same conclusion: the book *is* old, but not as old as I'd thought. It can't date back further than Meliana's engagement to Sir Brecelyn, since in the painting she's depicted as Helen before the walls of Troy, with Brecelyn's castle standing in for the fabled city destroyed by her beauty. The book must have belonged to someone we know after all, or at least someone we know *of*, since whoever wrote it was intimate enough with the current Sir Brecelyn to have had access to his private apartments, where the painting hangs.

Either that, or the sketcher saw the painting where Brian de Gilford told me it was first on display, before Lady Brecelyn was married:

at St. Sebastian's.

That the book contains secrets is obvious enough from the efforts taken to conceal it. It's awfully hard to resist the conclusion that like the sketch, those secrets involve Sir Brecelyn's wife; that the dainty little book belonged to her, in fact. And I don't try. I just squeeze my hand against it tighter, my head reeling. That this picture should find its way to me *again*, here in the Saint's own chapel, when I'm in need of inspiration the most and almost a year to the day after Father Abelard first gave me his stained copy of the very same thing — well, that can't be a coincidence either, can it? I don't have to be as superstitious as Armand or as my old friend Brother Benedict to guess what this little book must be. *This* is the answer from the Saint to my pleas this morning, the one I've been waiting for all day — the very thing I need to fulfill my vows and accomplish my purpose in coming to St. Sebastian's in the first place. Somehow, this little book must be the key to my father's past. I'm sure of it.

I can't believe it. After a year of finding nothing but more questions, I'm finally going to get some answers. It's about time.

I give myself another shake, and rein in my imagination. There's really no way to know who wrote the book, or what it contains. Exhaustion is making me hysterical; it probably is just a coincidence, another in a long string of bitter coincidences I've suffered through today. Putting too much stock in it is just going to set me up for more disappointment. But I can't quite still the erratic pulse my discovery has stirred up, and even if the book isn't really a sign, it is a timely reminder. It may be too late for my father, but Tristan is counting on me. I'll never solve our problems by lying around on the floor, feeling sorry for myself.

Just as I'm thinking this, however, Gilles exclaims,

"Gads, Marek. At the rate you're moving, it'll be daybreak before we get back. Are you planning to lounge around here all night? Think of poor Tristan! He's had quite a shock tonight; more than you know. And we masters do *worry* so, when we don't know what our squires are doing. Here," he says, extending an arm down to me. "I'd better give you a helping hand. You obviously need it."

I stare up at him, my mouth hanging open stupidly.

"What? You needn't look so surprised," he says, sounding offended, and I suppose it is rather rude. I can't help it, though. Standing over me and looking down his aristocratic nose at me, Gilles's pale skin is as smooth and as flawless as marble in the lamplight, and with his loose hair flowing around his shoulders like a flood of molten bronze, he's as beautiful as the epiphany of any saint. But Gilles always looks incredible, and I'm not surprised that he'd offer me his hand (well, maybe I am a little, since my own hands are filthy and Gilles is usually so fastidious). It's that in a flash of inspiration as bright as an epiphany, too, Gilles's words and the sight of him reaching down to help me have given me an idea.

Not a brilliant idea, admittedly. Only the kernel of one, really — more of an old, nebulous thought, dredged back up to the forefront of my mind. But an idea, nonetheless.

I'm still in a daze as I put up my hand and let Gilles pull me to my feet.

Once I'm up, before he lets go of my hand, as Gilles steadies me for a moment he leans in to inquire meaningfully,

"So, did you find what you were looking for out here, son?" and I wonder if he's seen the notebook. But I know he doesn't mean here, in the chapel.

"Not really," I say, and it's true. It's going to be a long time before I can really hope to master my emotions, or to lay the events of this day to rest. But with the little book pressing against my waist and Gilles's hand still clasped in mine, when Gilles asks,

"Ready to go back, then?"

I find to my surprise that I am.

As soon as we emerge from the chapel and out under the night sky, Gilles predictably starts up his chatter about the moon again. Either I'm numb to it or I really am feeling better, because it doesn't bother me as much as it did earlier. When he exclaims,

"We're in luck, Marek! Our *lovers'* moon may be setting, but we've still got it to guide us for a little while," I simply retort,

"The moon never helped anyone, or hurt them, either," only remembering too late where I heard *that* phrase before. But I don't let it bother me overmuch, either. I just snort, and as I let Gilles lead me over to the place where the horse is waiting, I lift my arms in imitation of shooting down the moon, the way Taran did on the night he first said the exact same thing.

"Never disparage the moon to me, Marek," Gilles says reprovingly, swinging himself up into the saddle, and pulling me up after him. "You see, I'm a terrible romantic! I want the happy ending, for myself, and for all my friends."

Only Gilles could possibly be thinking about happy endings, tonight of all nights. But I'm feeling in more of a mood to banter with him, so I say dryly,

"I doubt my idea of a happy ending and yours would be the same, Gilles."

"Why ever not?" he demands. "Try me."

"Tristan, winning Guards. And me, going to Meuse with him, as his squire."

"Hmm. I see what you mean," Gilles concedes, urging the horse under us into a walk. "Since I did rather plan on winning myself. Ah well, not to worry! You'll come up with something else. You'd do well to remember, Marek: there's always more than one possible happy ending."

Not for me, I think. But I don't say so, and I don't let it discourage me. And when he's silent for a moment, and then says quietly,

"They're wrong, you know, when they say women are the ones who draw down the moon. Women are fickle creatures, Marek. It takes more than the little thing *they* feel to bring out a moon like the one that's shining tonight. When there's a moon like that, it's because somewhere there's a *man* whose heart is heavy enough to have pulled it down to him. Somewhere, there's a *man* who's suffering; suffering, from unrequited love," it really should bother me most of all. But Gilles's voice sounds so uncharacteristically serious, so devoid of its usual foppish tones, that instead it occurs to me wonder just what it is that's put Gilles so in mind of lovers tonight.

I was too preoccupied before to think about it beyond finding it annoying, but it is sort of odd. Almost as odd as how I failed to hear his approach through the woods earlier, on this massive horse. As we're riding along now crashing through the icy bracken, it's making a terrible racket.

"Gilles," I demand, suddenly suspicious. "You weren't *already* in the clearing when I showed up there tonight, were you?"

"What a notion!" he scoffs, not really answering.

"Well, if you did follow me out from the castle," I press, "how could you have possibly known the boy you were following was me?"

"One St. Sebastian's squire does look much like any other, from a distance," he concedes. Before I can question him further, though, he breaks into an exaggerated fit of coughing.

"Gads, Marek, *phew!* Is that ghastly stench coming from *you?*" he exclaims, and I can't help but laugh. I guess I was too preoccupied to notice it earlier, too, but the little cloth Gilles gave me is drenched in scent, and it's letting off a powerful odor.

"Don't you even recognize it? It's your own perfume."

"Not *my* perfume, I assure you," Gilles declares with a shudder, so I pull the handkerchief out carefully, making sure not to dislodge the little notebook, and I wave it back over my shoulder at him.

"Just as I said," he says, without taking it. "I use only the best stuff. And wherever *did* you get that horrid rag? *Do* stop waving it under my nose. That's not mine, either."

"What do you mean, it isn't yours? It has to be."

"And yet it's not," he insists.

I take the cloth in front of me again and peer down at it, turning it over in my hands, confused. "But it's got your monogram. A capital G for Gilles, in red thread, in one corner."

"That proves it, then," he says smugly. "*Embroidered handkerchiefs.* Whoever heard of such a thing?! So *gaudy*." He sniffs. "Besides, my monogram is C for *Chartrain*, not a G."

There's a pause.

"Just how did you say you came to have that in your possession, Marek?"

"I picked it up off the floor in the chapel, just now."

"How extraordinary!" he exclaims, after a beat. "Why, my boy, I do believe you've found what they call 'a *clue.*' Surely it can only have gotten there one way. It must have been dropped there tonight, by one of your nefarious midnight chapel-plotters."

It's a little overdone, and I wonder if Gilles isn't just trying to keep me from returning to my earlier questions. But when I try to suggest that the cloth could have been lost in the chapel on any number of previous occasions, he scoffs.

"Don't you know the first thing about perfumes?!" he demands scornfully. "Goodness, remind me to instruct Pascal to remedy that. A good squire should know everything about his master's proper toilette. No wonder Tristan always smells so *natural*. Not even scent as cheap and as tawdry as the stuff on that rag can linger indefinitely. Take my word for it. That cloth's been doused, and recently."

I can't argue, since it's true that I don't know anything about perfume. And that I rather like the way Tristan smells. With the little book in my waistband and my little idea rattling around in the back of my mind, though, I'm more in the mood to play along with Gilles's games now than I was earlier, and so we spend the rest of the ride back entertaining each other by making up increasingly outrageous theories about just who might have been out in the chapel tonight, and what they were doing. By the time we reach the lawns, we've gone through all the Gs we can think of: Aristide (Guyenne), Master Guillaume, and absurdly enough, even the boys' perennial favorite, Guillaume Tell. And why not? We don't know any women whose names start with G, and anyway there's no reason to think that whoever dropped the cloth was really someone we know.

"Ah, Marek! Rosy-Fingered Dawn, just as the poet says," Gilles exclaims dreamily, gesturing dramatically in front of us as we come out onto the open fields. The moon's been down for a while now and behind us the sun is just peaking up through the trees. It's sending long rays of pinkish-orange light across the lawns that do look a lot like fingers reaching out to caress the castle, and its walls now shimmer ahead in the gentle morning light like a beacon. It's a scene of such beauty that without meaning to I hear myself asking Gilles in a small voice,

"Do you really believe it, Gilles? That a happy ending is possible?"

"It's my personal philosophy that anything's possible," he laughs back. "A happy ending? Why, my boy, I positively guarantee it."

He whips the horse into a run beneath us, and as we fly across the snow-strewn fields, I start laughing, too, at Gilles's ridiculous statement, and at the exhilarating feeling of leaving the dark woods behind. Tristan's ahead, waiting for me, and Gilles was right. We've been away too long. Right now, it feels like I've been away from Tristan all winter. It's high time I was getting back to him.

CHAPTER TWO

As we race along with Brecelyn's walls looming ever larger in front of us on the horizon, it's not long before I begin to get a little worried about how Tristan's come through the night, and nervous at the thought of having to face the inhabitants of the castle again. By the time we burst into the yard, eliciting an indignant yell from the sleepy guard perched atop the gate and sending chickens and pigs and men waking to the chores of the day scattering out of our way, exhilaration isn't the only emotion coursing through me anymore.

It doesn't help that as soon as we cross through the wall, the inner keep of the castle rises up over us like a sentinel tower, strong and silent. And when we're plunged into its shadow and I know that somewhere within its cold, sheer walls Taran is shut in tight, then one emotion threatens to rise up in me and overshadow all the others, too. But I push it determinedly away. I don't let myself glance up at the dark windows of the west wing, or think about just how far away a happy ending really seems.

Pascal is waiting for us at the top of the steps outside the entrance to the main hall, his arms crossed and a sour expression on his face. When he catches sight of us charging into the yard, he squares his shoulders and starts bustling purposefully down the stairs toward us. Although I'm sure Gilles has noticed him, too, he doesn't slacken our speed until we're almost on top of him, and even then he reins in the horse so sharply that it skids to a stop with a flourish, kicking up a great flurry of dust right in Pascal's face.

"*There* you are, master!" Pascal exclaims, coughing and waving away the dust. "Wherever *have* you been? I've been looking everywhere for you."

"Just out for a little excursion in the woods with *Marek* here," Gilles drawls silkily, sliding effortlessly off the horse. He plops the reins into Pascal's hands and adds,

"You know what *those* are like, I'm sure," and marches off inside without so much as a backward glance. Pascal's left with no choice but to help me awkwardly down from the big horse alone, and he's got such a puzzled frown on his face as he helps steady me on my feet that I assume I'm going to be stuck explaining to him where we've been. But when I look up at him, he just demands,

"What in the world were you two doing, on *Taran's* horse?" and I can't answer.

It's such an obvious question. It's the first thing I should have wondered myself, if I'd been thinking clearly. It just never occurred to me to ask.

When all I can do is shrug, Pascal leads the horse away back to stables, grumbling under his breath. I feel a little guilty watching him go, but I'm not going to offer to help take care of *that* horse, and I can't worry about Pascal, or Gilles either, right now. It's time to find Tristan. I turn and sprint up the steps and into the great hall, eager to look for him.

I spot him right away, sitting alone in front of the big fire, and I hasten over to him, positively bursting to tell him about the idea that came to me out in the chapel. Tristan's sure to be as excited about it as I am, and once we put our heads together, I know it won't take us long to work it up into a practical plan.

When I come up silently next to him, I see instantly that now is not the time to launch into an incoherent ramble about gazing up at Gilles from the chapel floor, since up close Tristan looks like hell. There are dark circles under his eyes, and I doubt he got any more sleep last night than I did. His expression is so glazed over and he's staring down in front of him so unseeingly he could be sleeping now, with his eyes open. I guess it's better than I was expecting. I didn't think I'd find him up and dressed.

"You up early too, kid?" he says without looking up, and he catches me by surprise. I didn't think he knew I was there.

"I never went to bed, actually," I confess.

"Couldn't sleep either, huh?" he says, straightening up enough to flash me the ghost of a grin.

It comes out more of a grimace. He looks quite sheepish, actually, and I suspect we're both thinking about a little melodramatic excess of his own here last night, when he leaped up from this very stool to pace around the room like a madman, tearing out his hair and moaning out curses as we awaited word of Melissande. I wonder very much how he's feeling about Melissande this morning, now that the danger to her is past. And about Remy's revelations, now that they've had a chance to sink in. But I don't ask.

Instead, I bend down to pick up a little folded piece of paper lying neglected on the ground by Tristan's feet. He must have been holding it earlier, and it's slipped unnoticed from his hand.

I know what it is, even before I've straightened up with it. It's the little square of parchment Father Abelard gave me with his marred illumination of Meliana Brecelyn on it, the one I was just thinking about out in the chapel. The one Tristan appropriated from me, because of the resemblance between mother and daughter.

I give a little start, although I'm not really surprised that Tristan still has it, or that he's obviously been sitting here brooding over it. I already knew Tristan's been secretly carrying it around with him as a memento of Melissande, despite supposedly having given her up. I'm just surprised it's cropped up again so soon, and the book with the picture's twin amongst its pages grows heavier at my waist. I'd almost forgotten about it, and now my hand starts itching to pull out my discovery and show it to Tristan.

One glance at him is enough to decide me not to do it. If the book does prove to be the diary of Lady Meliana herself, as I'm hoping it will, the secrets it promises to hold might not be just those of my own father, but of Tristan's father, too. And of Melissande's. Until I'm absolutely sure what the book is and what it contains, I'm not going to tell Tristan anything about it. He's been through enough.

As I've been thinking, I've idly opened the illumination up and smoothed it out, and Tristan's begun watching me curiously. So I hold it out to him. I don't mean anything by it; I know he wants it, and I'm just giving it back. Maybe it is a little accusingly, though, and Tristan hesitates. It's the slightest of pauses, but I find I'm disappointed when Tristan can't resist reclaiming it, and he plucks it out of my hand.

That is, until instead of tucking it into his tunic as I thought he would, he gets purposely to his feet and takes two long strides over to the hearth with it. I come up next to him, just as he tosses my old treasure into the fire.

We stand side by side for a long time, watching it burn in companionable silence.

THE LAST CURL OF SMOKE IS STILL RISING FROM THE WISP OF paper in the hearth when Falko comes stumping down the stairs and over to the sideboard behind us. His hair is standing up at odd angles, and although he's mercifully got on an exceptionally long tunic, he doesn't seem to have on anything below it at all. Barefoot, bare-legged and bleary-eyed, he grabs up two big fistfuls of sausage and shoves them both into his mouth, demanding loudly,

"Any of you lot seen Pruie? I can't find one blasted pair of clean tights."

At least I think he does. It's a little hard to tell.

Without waiting for an answer he stumbles right out the front door, mumbling under his breath in a voice impeded by enough sausages to feed a small village, *"what's the world coming to, when a man's got to bare-ass it through a chicken yard to find a pair of pants?,"* and with that, the mood that had settled between us is broken. Tristan turns to me with a laugh and clasps me on the shoulder, and with a heartiness that's only a little forced, he says,

"Damn it all, Marek! What with the plague, and, *er*, well, other things, I can't believe I let myself get so distracted all winter. I've lost precious time."

"I know exactly what you mean, master!" I exclaim, gratified at hearing him voice a sentiment so close to my own. I knew we'd be in perfect sympathy. "Luckily, it's not too late. No one else is ready for the competitions either, and if we put our heads together, we can come up with a strategy sure to get us into Guards, I know it! In fact ..."

Before I can get any further, Tristan puts up a hand to cut me off.

"*Guards?!*" he snorts. "Don't be absurd. I'll thank you for not to mention *that* to me again, Marek," and I blink. If he's not talking about getting ready for the trials, what is he talking about?

Seeing my flummoxed expression (and no doubt sensing that I'm about to argue with him), he looks back into the fire and says shortly,

"We both know I never stood a chance of winning Guards. I'll not have anyone thinking *I* think any differently, or that I'm pining over impossibilities. I won't be made to look a fool again."

I shouldn't say anything, since I now see just how dark the circles under his eyes really are, and I know he's probably thinking mostly about Melissande. I mean, he did rather make himself look a fool over her, and I know better than most how that humiliation feels. But I can't help it. I've finally started to see a way forward for us and I can't let it be stymied — not even by Tristan.

"But the *competitions*," I sputter. "Surely you're not going to just *give up?*"

"Of course not," he says indignantly. "I'm no *quitter*. And I have no intention of making anything easier, for *him*. Besides, it's crucial that we stay at St. Sebastian's as long as possible. We've got unfinished business there."

"Unfinished business?" I don't like the sound of that at all.

He turns to me with a wicked grin. "You didn't really think I'd let us leave St. Sebastian's without exposing your father's killers, did you? That would be a poor way to repay you, after what you did for me on the tower."

I open my mouth, but no words come out. Tristan can't really be going to do this to me, *now*.

Finally I manage,

"Don't you remember convincing *me* to drop the whole thing, just a few months ago? You said it yourself, there's no way to find out what happened at Thirds. Trying can only get us into trouble."

My words have no effect. He's got a worrisome gleam in his eye that I know past from experience means he's entirely serious. So I say just as seriously,

"Listen to me, Tristan, please. I lost my father. I can't lose you, too, and our future is at stake. Can't we leave the past alone?"

I feel the little notebook tug guiltily against my waist again, but I ignore it. What Tristan's talking about is entirely different.

"Aren't *you* forgetting something, Marek? It's not just about your father. If someone really tried to assassinate our prince at Thirds, isn't it our sacred duty to our country to bring the crime to light, and to make damned sure nothing like it ever happens again? *You* said it yourself, and I should have listened to you." His voice takes on a sarcastic edge. "We've recently had it demonstrated to us quite vividly, haven't we? Villains who fail with their first shot always take another." He fixes me with a challenging look. "Or are you going to try to tell me you no longer think it was a plot against the crown that got your father killed?"

There's nothing I can say to that, and he knows it. I feel another guilty tug at my waist; this time it's the handkerchief from the chapel floor. There's no way I'm going to show him *that* now, either. The last thing I need is for him to get wind of any of Gilles's conspiracy theories about it. But I stop trying to dissuade him. And I don't bother to mention the obvious — that it's only now after all chance of winning Melissande is gone that Tristan's willing to pursue exposing her father. Anything I might say now would surely just entrench him further, and although I don't doubt that Tristan sincerely wants to repay me, I'm pretty sure I know what this is really about.

He must genuinely believe he has no shot at Guards at all, and he's looking for another way to beat Taran. What better way to outshine his rival, what part would suit his ideal of himself better, than to be the single-handed savior of all Ardennes?

All I can do is stifle a noise that's part a groan and part a sigh of frustration. I don't dare ask Tristan to help me turn my idea into a strategy now; in his present mood, he would surely shoot it down.

"Just promise me one thing, won't you Tristan?" I finally say, and my voice must sound awfully small, because Tristan puts a protective arm around me. "Promise me you'll be careful."

"Aren't I always?"

When all I do is frown, he adds more gently,

"Cheer up, kid! There's not much we can do until we get back to St. Sebastian's. If you've been right about this thing all along, that's where the plot was hatched, and that's where our real work will be. But while we wait it out here, surely there's no harm in gathering what additional information we can about our host, *subtly*. Nothing that will arouse any suspicion."

"How?" I demand, hardly mollified.

"The usual methods," he says, and I suppose he means seducing the maids.

"I do believe, Marek," he declares with a stretch, "it's high time I started taking an interest in politics."

As if *that* wouldn't be entirely suspicious.

"Don't look so glum," he exclaims, reaching down to ruffle my hair. "You'll thank me, when we've gotten justice for your father."

"Not if it's at the price of your head," I grumble. "Besides, vengeance isn't really my style," but I feel myself blush as I say it, thinking guiltily of some of my own wilder sentiments this morning.

"I know, kid. That's one of the things I love about you," he says, and in that easy way of his he disarms me and I can't stay annoyed at him. Not even when his next statement is the most alarming one of all:

"That's why when the time comes, Marek, *I'm* going to take vengeance, for you."

I don't mean to encourage him, I really don't. But he delivers the line so superbly and the sentiment behind it is so gallant, I can't help myself. I throw my arms around him, and I hug him tightly. I mean, it really has been one hell of a day, and besides, I know Tristan well. He's just gotten caught up in his role, and he isn't really serious.

At least, I don't think he is.

A DOOR BANGS OPEN BEHIND US AND ARISTIDE COMES STAMPING in from outside, up unusually early for him and unaccountably looking as though *he* never went to bed last night, either. With no word of explanation he goes past us with a grunt and disappears up the stairs to the west wing, just as Gilles comes strolling down in the opposite direction, freshly attired in one of his more startling outfits. The castle's starting to come to life, and it's business as usual again for the Journeys.

"Say Marek," Tristan asks, catching sight of him. "Just what were the two of you doing, up and out so early?"

"The kid had a date with a stump," Gilles drawls, irritatingly enough, as he saunters over to join us in a silk tunic of a hue so rosy it would make dawn blush. But thankfully he doesn't elaborate. And when instead he gives Tristan an appraising look up and down and says,

"Come on, old man. Let's scrounge up some real food. It'll do you a world of good," and starts leading him off toward the kitchens, I get the impression Gilles is no more inclined to divulge our whereabouts last night to Tristan than he was to Pascal.

I'm a little surprised; I'd rather expected Gilles to make one of his performances out of describing our trip to the chapel to Tristan and to all the boys, and that he'd make speculating about the identity of the midnight visitors who lost a handkerchief there into a recurring theme, something to pass the time at meals or to debate out in the garden on afternoons back at the guild. But if he's ready to drop the joke then so am I, since I would surely end up being the butt of it.

Tristan resists Gilles's hand long enough to ask,

"Coming, Marek?," and I shake my head. I'm too tired, and I don't care to elaborate about last night yet, either. Besides, Tristan's mood must be starting to lift already, if he's hungry again.

"I don't know about you," I declare, "but before I do anything else, I'm going back to bed!"

As Tristan and Gilles disappear together in search of enough breakfast to

MASTERS

satisfy appetites the size of theirs, I snag up a wayward sausage or two that Falko overlooked from the sideboard and I head off to finally get some rest.

I must be even more exhausted than I'd thought, since the thing that's flitting through my mind as I trudge up the stairs after one of the longest and hardest days of my life isn't anything about yesterday's disasters in the clearing or last night's adventure in the chapel, or about my father, or the upcoming competitions, or even about Tristan or Taran and Melissande, but this:

A perfumed handkerchief, gaudily embroidered in red thread? It actually sounds a lot like something Gilles would own, to me.

I ONLY REMEMBER ABOUT THE LITTLE BOOK WHEN I'M ALREADY almost back to my room. So I circle wearily back along the corridor and down the steps again, to the suit of ceremonial armor belonging to Brecelyn's father that stands in an alcove at the foot of the stairs. After a quick glance around confirms that Tristan and Gilles haven't returned and that the hall is momentarily empty, I slip the notebook out of my waistband. Then I shove it neatly down into the fist of one of the heavy metal gauntlets where it can't be seen.

I'm dying to read it, of course. But I'm much too tired to tackle trying to make heads or tails of it now, and deciphering it isn't going to be easy for me. Puzzling it out is going to take considerable time and effort, and I'm going to have to figure out where I can do it without fear of interruption, and not just by Tristan; after almost being branded a thief back at the guild, I don't dare run the risk of being caught with it up in my room. If St. Sebastian's punishes its own, I hate to think what a man as vindictive as Sir Brecelyn would do if he thought I'd stolen his wife's private diary — which I suppose from one point of view is essentially what I'm hoping I've just done.

Besides, it wasn't only Tristan's potential reaction to the contents of the book that kept me from pulling it out earlier. I'm still reeling from one set of revelations; I'm not sure I'm quite ready to face another, particularly not of the kind I suspect are waiting for me in the notebook's pages. The thought of finding out now that Melissande really is my sister is understandably unbearable to me. There's only one thing that would be worse, given the circumstances:

finding out that she's Taran's.

As I throw myself heavily down onto my cot back in my room, I try not to let having to leave the book temporarily out of my possession bother me. An opportunity will come to retrieve it, I'm sure. And if I'm to succeed this year, I've got to learn a lesson from my enemies. This year, I'll be the boy who knows how to bide his time.

CHAPTER THREE

When I wake up the next morning, I'm disoriented. It takes me a while to figure out that I must have come straight upstairs and slept for an entire day and night. Tristan thoughtfully didn't rouse me for meals or chores, and I've slept off the worst of my exhaustion. Outside, dawn is already breaking again.

I swing my legs tentatively over the side of my cot and sit up, and although I can't say I'm exactly as fresh as a rose, I do feel better. It's a new day, and it's time to put the past behind me and start looking forward. After my gesture with the stump and Tristan's with the parchment, I think maybe we're both ready. It's time to cast off the empty dreams of winter, and get up again.

Before I try, though, I rest my head down on my hands for a moment, and mutter to myself:

"Just don't think about him. Just don't think about him." And it works. It really does. Sort of.

I get up to dress, and on a whim, instead of putting on the same old brown pants I was wearing when I undressed, I rummage around in the bottom of my bag and pull out my best black shirt, tunic, and trousers. It's my squire's costume. I've been so listless while hanging around Brecelyn's that I've gotten into the habit of wearing my rattiest clothes — hand-me-downs from Gilles, or old tunics that don't fit Tristan across the shoulders anymore, anything to keep from having to do any washing — so it's been a long time since I had it on. Pulling it on feels good, and once I'm dressed in it, I feel like my old self again; not some lovesick girl, but a squire with a job to do. It *is* time to look ahead, and I've got a lot on my plate.

Once I've pulled on my boots and I'm out in the corridor, I hesitate outside Tristan's door, trying to decide whether to let him sleep or rouse him for practice. It's not just to get our minds off recent events or to keep Tristan out of trouble that I'm anxious to get him back into a regular training regime. Rumor really does have it that we'll be heading back to St. Sebastian's soon. Of course, rumors of our return started up almost as soon as we arrived at the castle, but lately they aren't just coming from kitchen boys or staff, or even from the Journeys. The vets have started talking about it, too, and anyway it's logical enough.

It's already March. Last year Firsts were in May, so if Master Guillaume intends to get us settled back at the guild in time to keep to our ancestral schedule of competitions, we've got to be returning before long. And when we do, Tristan has to be ready — mentally *and* physically. He's fared better than some of the others; he at least didn't catch the plague or get bashed by a giant with a hammer in the market square, and I'm actually not entirely sure where Tristan stands in the rankings after Thirds last year. But wherever he is, it's not at the top; his stellar performance at the final competition may have been enough to squeak him through to veteran status, but considering how far he'd plummeted after his disastrous wounding for Seconds, it can't have pulled him up much past the lowest slot. With only the six best Journeys left and two set to be cut at each trial, the competition is going to be extremely tight, and now more than ever I want Tristan to win.

I give Tristan's door a tentative rap, and when there's no answer, I decide to let him sleep in. I guess one more day won't make any difference. So I head downstairs alone. With Tristan asleep, now might be a perfect time to sneak a look inside my purloined notebook, or to start giving the notion that came to me out in the chapel last night some serious thought. I'm going to have to make it into something pretty good if I'm to get Tristan enthusiastic about it, and I suspect that's going to be a more daunting proposition than I bargained for, since as I amble down the steps in the cold light of day, I find it's more of a feeling than an idea, really; just a vague sense that I've been thinking about the competitions in entirely the wrong way.

Downstairs, I find the hall strangely empty. It must be even earlier than I thought, and I'm the only one up. I'm just wandering over to the sideboard to see if anything's been left out for us and casting a surreptitious glance over at the suit of armor in the alcove when there's a low rumbling from somewhere nearby. I assume it must be the sausages from yesterday morning, still tumbling around in my stomach, until Frans emerges from the shadows, pulling a little toy across the floor on a string. He and Pip have been playing with it in a corner by the fire, and at the sight of me Frans has come scurrying over with the thing still in tow, clattering over the stone floor behind him.

"Master, there you are!" he exclaims brightly. "Feeling better?"

I must still be feeling a bit delicate, actually, because I grumble back,

"What an infernal racket you're making, Frans. You'd better not let the others catch you, if you end up waking them with it."

"Waking them!" he chirps. "Everyone else is already up and out, master. They're all already out on the field."

It's not early. Quite to the contrary, as Frans soon informs me. Master Leon's called an unexpected mandatory practice for this morning, and it's already underway. In predictable fashion, although this is the first I've heard of it, I'm already late.

"Why in the world didn't you fetch me?!" I cry, uncomfortably aware I'm not making the best start on my new resolve to be St. Sebastian's most diligent squire.

"Master Tristan told me to wait right here for you, in case you came down," he replies. He looks so crestfallen I regret being short with him, and Frans isn't really what's bothering me. It's that while we've been talking, Pip's come up and taken the string out of Frans's hand, and out of the corner of my eye I can see him dashing about the room, pulling the wretched toy behind him. It's a small wooden horse on wheels, impeccably carved. The kind of thing a man good with his hands might make as a gift for a little child. For a newborn son.

I can still hear its hollow rattle echoing behind me as I hustle out the door.

I'm understandably feeling a little rattled myself as I bustle around to the armory to get my equipment. On top of everything else I'm hungry again, since the boys had picked the sideboard clean; after the lean days of the plague, none of us has gotten used to having enough to eat, and the Journeys in particular fall on any offering like a pack of wolves on a sheepfold. And even after my long sleep I'm not sure I'm really up for a hard morning's retrieval, particularly not with the sadistic Master Leon in charge. And let's face it. I'm not eager to face all the boys again. Particularly one of them. But as I dust off my bow and swing it up onto my shoulder, I manage a smile. We've been left to our own devices for so long that if the masters are calling for mandatory drills again, it can only mean one thing. The rumors must be true. The masters are gearing up for our return to St. Sebastian's.

We're finally going home. And soon.

I hasten out onto the field, and even from a distance out I spot Tristan in the middle of one of his beautiful shots. To my relief he looks much better than he did yesterday morning; he's in fine form, and all the boys look to be in good spirits. They've obviously made the same assumption about the significance of the drill as I have, and there's an energy out on the range that hasn't been there since our arrival at Brecelyn's. Tristan and I aren't the only ones eager to put the long, sad winter behind us.

When I approach the line and the boys greet me casually enough, my tentative smile broadens. It's just as Gilles predicted. They've already forgotten all about being annoyed at me for the unfortunate timing of my accusations of Taran the other day.

Even better, Taran himself hasn't shown up.

Best of all, nobody seems to expect him to.

As I'm trying to slip up and unobtrusively take my place next to Tristan, Master Leon catches sight of me. He pauses mid-bark in his calling out of the boys' shots just long enough to put up his hands in a mock salute and say sarcastically,

"Well, well, well. Look who's deigned to join us, boys! If it isn't hotshot. I thought you were supposed to be suffering from some pox or other."

It's not one of Tristan's better lies, but he's covered for me and I'm so pleased by the scene in front of me that I just beam back,

"It seems to have miraculously cleared up, master."

Master Leon's already not paying any attention to me, and I'm too busy surveying the field with satisfaction to take any more notice of him, anyway; at the sight of the drill the master's running, my smile has transformed into a positive grin.

In front of me, targets have been set up for the boys at about 75 yards from the line. Since Pascal's been doing double duty and retrieving for my master and his own, Tristan and Gilles are set up right next to each other.

It's perfect.

The thing is, the little spark of an idea that came to me out in the chapel may still be hopelessly vague, and I may not be ready to risk telling Tristan anything about it — and not just because I can't quite see the final shape of it; what I've got in mind is pretty unorthodox, and it goes against everything I've been telling him. That's not the only flaw. It's also going to require convincing Gilles to go along with it, and on top of everything else, I can't be sure it's going to work. But if I'm going to get Tristan into Guards I've got to get creative, and Tristan and Gilles drilling at butts side-by-side? It's a good start.

I just don't let myself dwell on the reasons why it's taken me so long to see what's been right in front of me all winter. Or that even to me, the scheme that's now beginning to form in the back of my mind sounds less like a plan to help Tristan win, than a plan to cause Taran to fail.

"Ah, a squire who knows how to dress for the occasion," Gilles exclaims, turning to me at Master Leon's gesture and leaning casually on his bow as he waits for Pascal to return from a retrieval.

"You're a sight for sore eyes, squire," Tristan agrees, looking me over approvingly. Before I can respond to either of them with more than a grin, Pascal bustles back to the line, his arms full of arrows. A few spill out onto the ground at my feet as he shoves a fistful into my arms, exclaiming sourly,

"*There* you are, Marek. Thank Heavens."

"The poor boy is all butterfingers today," Gilles sniffs, and I'm surprised — and not only at his mildly insulting tone. Pascal is usually the most efficient of squires. Then I see that Gilles has shot an inordinately large number of shafts in a single flight, and since Pascal has been filling in for me and retrieving for Tristan, too, he's been having a devil of a time carrying them all back at the same time and keeping them sorted. Gilles seems to be enjoying Pascal's discomfort immensely.

"What's up with them?" I whisper, once Pascal's back is turned. Gilles and Pascal are usually as thick as thieves.

"Pascal's gotten wind of a rumor some stable boys have been circulating, that Gilles took out a horse at midnight the other night and didn't bring it back until dawn," Tristan replies, shooting me a questioning glance. "Gilles has refused to explain, and Pascal's upset about it."

I grimace. I don't want to be responsible for a falling out between friends, so I just nod, resolving to straighten everything out as soon as practice is over. It will be embarrassing admitting that Gilles was actually just keeping a watchful eye on *me*, but I was going to have to tell Tristan something about my moonlight foray into the woods anyway, and I figure it should be easy enough. That is, until Tristan adds,

"Pascal's assumed Gilles must have gone to St. Genevieve's, and that he doesn't want him to know about it."

"He doesn't think he went to visit *Lady Sibilla*, surely?!" I exclaim, louder than I intend.

"I rather imagine Pascal's more afraid Gilles was visiting Sibilla's younger, more beautiful twin."

So *that's* it. I remember thinking at the time that it would mean trouble, when Pascal saved a lovely village girl by pulling her up onto the guild wall who did bear a striking resemblance to Lady Sibilla, then Gilles stole his thunder by gallantly whisking her off to the convent to safety — particularly after Gilles went out of his way to describe the spectacular kiss he gave the girl in the process. I'm pretty sure Gilles was just paying Pascal back for his previous pursuit of Sibilla, but if Pascal thinks Gilles has been sneaking off for some midnight visits to the girl, I doubt he's going to accept any counter explanation from me. I can tell just from the smug look on Gilles's face that he's been thoroughly enjoying fueling Pascal's erroneous assumptions. He's going to be no help at all.

"If I were you, I'd stay out of it," Tristan says shrewdly, guessing my thoughts, and I'm sure he's right. But it's a problem, and not just because I feel guilty. I was rather hoping to make Pascal an ally, to get him to help convince Gilles to fall in with my plans. It's all going to be that much harder, if Pascal gets annoyed with *me*, thinking I'm trying to cover for his master.

WE'VE ONLY BEEN DRILLING FOR A LITTLE WHILE BEFORE Master Leon gets thoroughly fed up with us. The boys are all too keyed-up to concentrate, and we're all so out of shape that the practice has been something of a fiasco. Gilles is more interested in giving little sighs and suggestive stretches designed to irritate Pascal than in hitting the target, and Taran isn't the only Journey missing from practice entirely. Jurian's not bothered to show up, either. But it's only when Falko eventually wanders up about an hour late that the master decides he's had enough.

Falko's wedged into a pair of tights so small and short for him that he could have borrowed them from Pip, and Jurian's squire Rennie is following along in his wake, wearing a scowl and carrying Falko's quiver over his shoulder; Falko's own squire Pruie is nowhere to be seen. Not only does Falko look ridiculous, but when he starts shooting his shoulder is still such a mess (or maybe his circulation so impeded by his tight pants) that his shots go so far wide as to be downright dangerous. After narrowly ducking a particularly wayward shot, with a few choice oaths the master stalks off the field in search of a stiff drink and he leaves us to our own devices, which suits the boys fine. Everybody is really much more interested in talking about getting ready for the competitions again than in actually doing it. Well, everybody but me.

Before he disappears from sight, Leon pauses at the edge of the field just long enough to shout back to us,

"What a waste of a perfectly good morning! I'd have been better off overseeing certifications for the regent's latest quota of conscriptions than squandering my time on a pampered pack of *amateurs*."

"Certifications, master? *Here?*" Aristide calls after him incredulously.

"Just where do *you* suggest we hold them, Guyenne?" the master barks back. "In the rubble of our guild? Or maybe we should set up shop at that delightful brothel of yours — '*The Retching Rooster*,' or whatever it is. At least *there* I hear you actually exert yourself! Oh, but I forget. That *glorious* institution is sadly all in ruins, too, isn't it? So I guess we're all stuck here."

As soon as the master's gone, the boys dissolve into laughter almost immediately. But Aristide stands looking back to where the master disappeared from view with a frown on his face, and I don't blame him. I wouldn't be too happy, either, knowing that my profligate habits were the joke of the masters' quarters.

After a while, he too turns back to join us as we all start to congregate together, drifting toward the center of the field until we're gathered around the station that was originally Gilles's. The Journeys start taking turns making lazy shots at Gilles's target, but nobody's really practicing anymore; everyone's joking around, at first imitating the master or teasing Aristide, but mostly we're all talking excitedly about the possibility of an imminent return to the guild.

Before long, though, what the boys are really doing isn't gossiping about going home, but just gossiping in general. I'm listening in carefully, curious to see if Gilles is going to break down and say something about our trip to the chapel the other night. But he seems as disinclined to mention it today as he was yesterday, and to my dismay, instead what the boys are all soon gossiping about isn't anything to do with me or Gilles, or Aristide. It's about Taran and Melissande.

I guess I should have anticipated it. After all, the shock of recent events has begun to recede for them, and in its place the boys' curiosity is resurfacing. Taran isn't here. Melissande is sure to be fine. And admittedly, the surprising situation between them is pretty juicy. So it's only natural that the boys would soon start in on some good-natured speculation about it. In particular, it's the timing of it all that's caught their attention. It isn't the baby *per se* that's on their minds, though. It's the timing of the commencement of the necessary activity between Taran and Melissande required to produce one.

It all starts with an innocent enough comment from Rennie.

"I can't say *I'm* that happy at the prospect of leaving," he complains, trying to remind us all that he's been holing up for a little activity of his own with his fiancée every afternoon. Having found himself in the unlikely position of being the squire with the most experience with girls, he never misses a chance to rub it in. He's become quite insufferable about it, actually.

"Yeah, I guess there'll be a lot more grass growing around here, once we're gone," Falko says, picking up the theme, and when he looks out toward the woods in a way that suggests he's remembering de Gilford's crude comments about Taran 'not letting the grass grow' out in the clearing the other day, pretty soon the others cast off all reticence, too, and start gossiping about Taran and Melissande like fishmongers' wives. Well, everyone but me.

"Frankly, I find it all rather incredible," Gilles exclaims.

"Could have knocked me over with a feather," Falko agrees.

"I guess we know *now* where the old boy was going, every afternoon after Thirds," Aristide chuckles. "And to think, at the time I thought he was out riding around, upset about what happened to *Woodcock* here, if you can believe it."

"I didn't think he was even that interested in girls," Pascal muses. "Not until the *convent* outing, anyway," he adds, shooting a sidelong look at his master.

None of the other squires are willing to believe things had progressed very far between Taran and Melissande before the night of our squires' outing to the convent either, when we witnessed Taran give Melissande an impressive first kiss. And when Armand turns to Aristide and insists (no doubt remembering the rather impressive kiss between Melissande and *Tristan* at Thirds that he himself witnessed),

"Come on, master! You can't convince me she was already keen on Taran, way back then!," pretty soon the boys have all agreed that it must have been at some point later, during our first winter stay here, that Melissande's baby was conceived. But when? Nothing seems to fit.

"I can't understand it. I could have sworn she preferred you, Tristan," Armand muses.

"Maybe it was the poetry contest that did the trick, and she was whipped into a passion by Taran's *blank* verse!" Rennie laughs, and it's not long before Aristide is cackling,

"Nah, it was the wall-scaling challenge! I bet he impressed her with his *virility*, when he was prying open her portcullis!"

"It must have been the night of the fire," Falko crows back. "She couldn't resist the *swish* of his axe!"

Long before Falko illustrates this comment with a gesture ruder even than the one Aristide used to punctuate his, I've already heard plenty. With Aristide and Falko dominating the conversation it's only destined to deteriorate, and next to me Tristan's been standing stock still, trying hard to look aloof, disinterested. But his neck is bright red, and I know he's finding the whole thing as excruciating as I am. I doubt it's the crudity of the boys' comments that's upsetting him, though. He's used to it. It's that everyone seems convinced it was actually one of Tristan's own schemes that gave Taran the opportunity finally to win Melissande over.

"What do *you* say, Marek?" Rennie demands, turning to me suddenly and catching me off guard, just as I'm closing my eyes and starting to chant to myself, *just don't think about …* "You always have an opinion. When do *you* think the old man stormed the castle?"

Before I can stop it, at the phrase I have a vivid flash of being back in Taran's hot little room, standing behind him with my arms wrapped around him. He's leaning back heavily against me, groaning *"I can't, I can't"* as I slide my hands hungrily over his bare chest.

"Careful there, dear boy," Gilles says mildly, giving me a nudge. "That's not a *stump*, you know. If you squeeze that bow any harder, it's going to break."

The worst of it is, I probably know the answer. Unlike the others, I have the benefit of de Gilford's information — about seeing Melissande all hot and bothered outside Taran's door on the night *before* the fire — the day he tried to tell me Taran was a master of the 'reluctant method' just like his father, and I wouldn't listen. But I'm not sure how much stock to put in anything de Gilford has to say, and I wouldn't mention it, anyway. It's not just that I have no stomach for joining the conversation. I'm also sure Tristan wouldn't appreciate hearing it one bit.

Throughout this whole thing I've been subtly trying to get Tristan's attention, tugging on his sleeve and trying to lead him away, and he's been obstinately ignoring me. I don't understand it, until Tristan can't contain himself any longer and he finally breaks into the conversation, just as Falko is making a comment about Taran's wooden unicorn so obscene, it makes me seriously reconsider whether we did Roxanne a favor by saving her from a stoning if it was only to end up with him.

In a voice that's studiously casual but that's not fooling anyone, Tristan says,

"It's damned odd, though, isn't it? Why bother to hide Melissande away from us like that? Surely she couldn't have been showing much *yet*," and I figure it out. The timing of it all has started to bother him, too, naturally enough. Even if it weren't for the pain of it, it's got to be a matter of some vanity with him. He'd hate to have to think that Melissande had already succumbed to Taran before he'd sworn her off himself.

"Indeed," Gilles agrees soothingly, stepping up past him to take a turn at the target. "But perhaps hiding the fact that Melissande was showing too much was not her father's intention at all. Perhaps it was quite the opposite."

"Don't tell me you mean she was sequestered away to *draw* our attention to her, and to pique our curiosity?" Aristide replies sarcastically.

"Well ... it's possible, isn't it?" Gilles considers. "After all, that's precisely what happened."

"Just what are you hinting at, Gilles?" Tristan demands.

"Me?" Gilles replies innocently. "I'm not hinting anything. Just musing about possibilities."

"Ignore him," Aristide snorts. "He's always trying to sound mysterious, just to annoy us."

I wonder, though. Gilles clearly thinks he knows something; that much was apparent the other night. I'm in no mood to ask Gilles to elaborate, however, even if I thought he would. Next to me Tristan's finally started to unravel, and I've been getting increasingly annoyed, too, though probably for a different reason. Well, maybe partly for the same reason. But it isn't just because I'm eager to change the subject that I cut in crossly over Aristide. It's also because as the boys have been talking, the shock of more recent events has started to recede for me, too, and my anger at Taran has started to resurface.

"Aren't you all overlooking the most important thing?!" I demand hotly.

The boys have all been acting thrilled to find that Taran isn't quite the boy *they'd* thought he was, that he's turned out to be something of a smooth operator, a stud. They're all talking about him now like he's some kind of hero. Have they all forgotten the *other* revelation of yesterday? That Taran *shot* at Tristan? That he tried to kill him, in fact? Nobody seems to care about that anymore, but me. If the boys are ready to congratulate Taran for his conquests, it seems to me they should be ready to hold him accountable for his crimes.

"The *arrow*," I say, when the boys pause their babble long enough to turn to me. After a beat, they all turn back and start gossiping again, as though they didn't hear me. Only Gilles pays any attention to me at all.

"Oh, pshaw!" he trills airily. "Not back on that again, are you, Marek? Didn't I say it at the time? That arrow could have gotten into the woods any number of ways."

"He *shot* Tristan, Gilles!" I insist. "You heard him. He practically admitted it! Why would he do that, if it weren't true?"

"I can think of several reasons," Gilles scoffs. But I can't think of any. And Gilles doesn't know what I know.

"Remy *saw* him, Gilles. He told me so."

I feel a little guilty as soon as I say it, since Remy begged me not to tell. But Remy isn't here, and Gilles just waves this off dismissively anyway.

"Oh, *Remy*. Who knows *what* that flighty boy thinks he saw."

I can tell the others all agree. Even Tristan doesn't seem very interested in it anymore. But they didn't see Remy's face, or hear him in the clearing when he accidentally let the truth slip out. Remy knows what he saw, I'm sure of it. There can be no question that Remy knew exactly what he was saying to me in the clearing that day.

"Oh, so what if Taran took a shot at him?" Aristide puts in lazily. "In my book, he'd have been justified in killing him, after the way he went after his fiancée. No offense, Tristan," he adds, and Tristan sneers back,

"None taken, naturally."

"We all know Taran doesn't miss, Marek," Armand adds more diplomatically. "If he'd really intended to hurt Tristan, he'd be dead."

"An unfortunate fit of jealousy, that's the thing," Falko blusters. "Hot-blooded bastard. All in the past though, surely. No sense in holding it against the old boy now. Holding a grudge never does anybody any good."

There's no point trying to convince them. Nobody wants to listen to anything that's going to ruin the first fragile good mood they've enjoyed in weeks, and I guess I can't blame them. I'm not sure if even I can really believe Tristan's in any new danger from Taran now, and something in Armand's comment is bothering me, so I let it drop. Temporarily. But I think back to the feel of forcing that bloody arrow through Tristan's side, and I know Taran's arrow did hurt Tristan. A lot. And just the fact that it was Taran who shot it probably ended up hurting me even more. I have no intention of giving up my anger over it. Even if Falko is right, and it isn't doing me any good.

CHAPTER FOUR

By the time things finally break up and Tristan and I are making our way back inside in stony silence, I don't want to think about the arrow anymore either. It doesn't help my mood any that as we're trudging along next to Gilles, Aristide falls into step beside us. I'd been just about to suggest to the boys that they meet up for a private training session this afternoon, and the last thing I need is Aristide horning in. He must want something, too, to be so obviously tagging along with Tristan and Gilles, since usually he can't stand them.

It doesn't take him long to come out with it.

"Did it strike either of you that Master Leon was holding out on us earlier?" he blurts out suddenly, and I'm surprised. I wouldn't have thought he'd want to remind the boys of his humiliating exchange with the master. "*You* heard him. He was being purposely evasive. I mean, doing certifications *here*, when we're surely headed back to St. Sebastian's? What's the rush? And all those new conscriptions he was talking about. Why is the regent calling for them now?" he demands.

Behind Aristide's back, Tristan shoots a glance at Gilles. Although I do see it (and the slight incline of the head that Gilles gives Tristan back in response), I quite fail to catch the significance of the gestures. I'm too caught up in replying confidently,

"That's obvious, isn't it? What with losses to the plague and all, our units must be hurting. The regent must simply be refilling the ranks."

I'm pretty proud of myself that this logical answer has occurred to me faster than to the others; I've promised myself to pay better attention when the boys are talking, and it's paying off. So it's gratifying when Aristide concedes,

"I suppose that *could* explain it," for once not bothering to jeer at my ignorance. He sounds uncharacteristically thoughtful, actually, and it's curious enough that even the stagey way Tristan is now clearing his throat behind me doesn't fully register. So I'm completely suckered in, when Tristan answers in a grave voice,

"It must be exactly as we've feared, then, don't you agree, Gilles?" and Gilles agrees seriously (well, seriously, for him),

"Indeed, my friend. The terrible rumors! They must be nothing but the truth."

"Rumors? What rumors?" I cry, taken aback, as Aristide snaps, "What is it? Just what do louses think you know?"

Tristan just shakes his head, while Gilles makes a clicking noise against his teeth with his tongue. Before I can ask anything, Aristide is saying accusingly,

"It's *Calais*, isn't it?! I thought so. We're preparing to send more reinforcements, for the damned *English*! That place is going to be the ruin of us. I've said so all along."

"Cal*ais*!" Gilles sniffs dismissively, sidling up on one side of Aristide, while Tristan circles around to squeeze in between me and Aristide on his other side. They're surrounding him, but Aristide is too het up to notice.

"Calais will be the least of our problems, if the reports we've heard through Gilles's connections are true," Tristan declares, slipping an arm confidentially around Aristide's shoulders. "I'm sorry, kid," he adds, turning to me with a meaningful look, and when he continues, he's choosing his words so carefully that I begin to feel really anxious. It doesn't occur to me he might be buying himself time to improvise. Or that the odd way his eye is fluttering might be a furtive wink. "I didn't want you finding out this way, Marek, but ... well ... er, the French —" he's saying, and Aristide is barking impatiently, "What? What? Out with it, damn you, DuBois," when Gilles breaks in almost gleefully,

"The French are planning a full-scale invasion, of *Ardennes*! That's what!"

"What?" I squawk, in perfect unison with Aristide. We both stand there dumbfounded as Gilles continues silkily,

"Regrettable, but true. Reliable reports have it that they're slowly amassing troops on our borders. Oh, they're being subtle about it — beefing up a border garrison here, installing a temporary camp there, but the signs are unmistakable. They've wanted to do it for centuries, and with us siding with England and the English now suffering from plague themselves and too weak to help us, they've got a perfect opportunity, and a perfect excuse."

"It could come any day now," Tristan confirms darkly, while Gilles says pointedly to Aristide: "Based on troop movement and so forth, their intended point of entry is just west of Tournai. Oh, goodness, Ari! Aren't most of your family's holdings right around there? *Tsk, tsk*. What a pity. I suppose they'll be the first things to go."

There's a beat of complete silence as I digest this horrible piece of information, and as Aristide's face registers a look close to pure shock. I'm in shock, too; I can't believe Tristan's been withholding from me something as momentous as an impending invasion. Then there's a sound from the other side of Aristide, like a little whoosh of air.

It's Gilles, stifling a laugh.

All at once, with a loud oath Aristide shakes Tristan's arm off angrily and explodes,

"*By all the confounded Saints in Hell!* I should have known. *Is nothing sacred to either of you?!,*" as it dawns on him that the boys have been having him on. The whole thing has been one of their little performances, payback for Aristide's snide comments about both of them earlier during practice. They've done such a convincing job of it, too, that I think I don't fully realize they've made the whole thing up just to annoy Aristide until Gilles turns to me and elaborates,

"And just how do you suppose those slippery Frenchies plan to succeed, dear boy? To know our weaknesses? *Collaborators.* Just picture it, Marek! On estates all across Ardennes, greedy, unscrupulous aristocrats are sneaking out for secret assignations at *midnight*, in stables, or in lonely *chapels ...*" and I snort. I see Gilles can't resist teasing *me*, too.

Aristide has already started to stalk off fuming, but without missing a beat Gilles stretches out one long leg and steps adroitly in his way. So he's no longer really talking to me when he says only inches from Aristide's nose,

"If and when our dear country falls, Marek, it'll be the work of her own countrymen, turned informant for French gold. Which does rather make one wonder, just why it is *you're* so interested in finding out what the regent's up to, Ari. And just where *you've* been spending *your* midnights lately."

"Of all the bloody cheek!" Aristide sputters, his face suddenly turning livid red. "Just what do you think you're accusing me of?!"

"Being a traitor, of course," Gilles replies smoothly, and it's not long before the two of them are embroiled in one of their more vicious arguments and Tristan and I have slowed our pace to fall back and leave them to it. They continue quarreling hotly the rest of the way back to the armory (or rather, Aristide is all hot and bothered. Gilles is thoroughly enjoying himself). The last I hear of it, Gilles is saying,

"Wasn't your family's land mostly all gifted them by the French? I bet you'd be willing to sell a few state secrets if you thought it'd get you some more," and Aristide is sneering back, "What about *your* midnight whereabouts, and *your* family!? You got all your land from the French, too, if I recall," to which Gilles just trills happily, "True. But *my* family *stole* it from them!"

Once they're out of earshot, Tristan exclaims with satisfaction, "That went beautifully, don't you think?"

"Was it *wise*, though, Tristan? To antagonize Aristide like that?" I reply petulantly, embarrassed at having fallen for the ruse myself. "The last thing we need now is another enemy. And did you have to make up such an extravagant rumor? You really had him going. Me, too, at first, I'll admit. He was really upset."

At the idea of worrying about Aristide, Tristan just scoffs. "And besides," he declares casually, "the rumors are all true enough. Didn't I tell you I was going to start paying more attention to politics?"

Beside him, I freeze in my tracks.

Tristan continues on a few paces before he notices. When he turns back to see me standing stock still with my mouth hanging open and my eyes wide, he laughs.

"That's *all* they are, Marek. Idle rumors," he says confidently, coming back and putting a hand affectionately on my shoulder. "The sort of stuff that's always circulating, if you'd ever bother to listen." When I still don't move, he says seriously, "We've not seen warfare on our soil for decades, kid, and for good reason. The reputation of our archers is too feared to allow for it! Trust me, Marek: an invasion will never find us, here in Ardennes."

I do trust Tristan, and I'm sure he knows what he's talking about. But his words fail to reassure me as much as they probably should, since this is exactly what everyone said about the plague.

"What do you say, little brother?" Tristan says, as he prods me back into motion beside him. "If the French ever do dare to invade, shall we join up?"

"Join up what?" I ask, putting my hand up to my temple; Aristide isn't the only one the boys have flustered.

"The army, of course."

"Join the army?" I repeat stupidly. "As what?"

"As *archers*, obviously!" he laughs, and it is obvious. I don't know why, though, but it never occurred to me that Tristan might someday want to seek a military commission. I thought he couldn't stand the sight of blood.

"And the *competitions*, Tristan? Remember? You said you were going to *try*," I object, rather foolishly I suppose, since if our country were ever under direct attack, I doubt even Master Guillaume would go on with the trials.

"I'm talking about '*after*,' of course," he says dismissively. "It's nowhere near campaigning season yet; if the French do make a move, it won't be for months — well after I'm likely to be out. Oh, I almost wish they *would* invade! Just think how thrilling, to be out on the front lines, knowing you were risking all for your prince, and for your country."

From the faraway, wistful look that comes over Tristan's face, I'm pretty sure it's not his prince he's thinking about. He's picturing taking a tearful and repentant Melissande into his arms and giving her some flowery goodbye speech before rushing off to die nobly for her in battle, so she'll have to spend the rest of her (married) life mourning him in chastity, with some token of his stashed under her pillow, or more of his love letters. He's said it off-handedly enough, but I know Tristan well; this isn't the first time he's considered the possibility.

"Tristan," I say sternly, cutting through his reverie. "Being on the front lines would *not* be romantic. It would be drudgery and disease, starvation rations and putrid, disfiguring wounds, and that's if you're lucky! And besides," I insist, even though he probably won't like it. "You forget. You won't be *'out'* in a few months. You'll be in Guards. *We'll* be in Guards, together."

"Have it your way, little brother," he just shrugs indifferently, seeing my worried expression. "No army for us," he declares lightly, and I feel relieved. But he still looks a little wistful. And then he adds,

"If by some miracle everything *does* go your way, Marek, and I make Guards; if an invasion ever comes to Ardennes, just where do you think the Black Guard will be other than on the front lines?"

I'm saved from having to contemplate this unpleasant pronouncement by the return of Gilles; he's tired of toying with Aristide and he's circled back around to gloat over the success of their trick with Tristan.

"Where will the Black Guard be?" he drawls, joining the conversation. "When *I* make Guards, boys, I can assure you I do not intend to be found anywhere near any 'lines' at all — front, back, or center. I'll be lounging around on a parapet high over L'île de Meuse, drinking, flirting, bossing Pascal around, and looking fabulous. The only danger our country will be in from the French is if they spontaneously combust on our borders, out of sheer envy."

With that, the three of us head inside together laughing, all fear of the French effectively dismissed and the boys' idle talk of traitors temporarily forgotten. But the little incident leaves me feeling apprehensive, though not for the most obvious reasons that it might. It doesn't bode well that Tristan's already so focused on what can come after St. Sebastian's for us, before the competitions have even started up again. Or that it's pretty clear if I leave the matter up to him, he's going to come up with something I don't much like. I've got to get Tristan positive about the trials again, and fast — at the rate he's going, the next idea he comes up with for outshining Taran is likely to take him straight past losing with style, to dying with it.

It only occurs to me later to wonder just why it was that Gilles's absurd accusations succeeded in disturbing Aristide so much. I doubt I'd have given it a second thought, if it weren't for the fact that when Tristan steps forward to hold the armory door open for us, he gives Gilles a mock bow, and with a grin he says,

"*M. le Marquis*, my old friend. Wouldn't it be fair to say that *you're* a greedy, unscrupulous aristocrat?"

And Gilles agrees just as happily, "Indubitably! Possibly, the greediest."

OUT IN THE ARMORY, WHEN A LONG LINE OF BRECELYN'S servants files in carrying steaming bowls of water and fresh towels ordered up for us by Gilles, I see an opportunity. I hurry through stashing Tristan's gear, and in the commotion as the others start eagerly stripping down I slip away unnoticed, foregoing my own chance to wash up. I'm used to being dirty, and the thought of the concealed notebook has been in the back of my mind all morning. If I'm quick there should be just enough time to get a look inside it while the boys are safely occupied, since primping usually takes them quite a long time.

The main hall isn't empty, but I didn't expect it to be at this time of day. There are a few servants coming in and out, and an occasional man-at-arms of Brecelyn's wanders through, but it's nobody who's likely to pay me much mind. So I sidle over to the suit of armor casually, and when the coast is clear, I fish the book out of the gauntlet and I duck into a dark corner behind the armor with it, where I'm partially concealed from view. I'm going to have to examine the book right here, where I can replace it at a moment's notice.

I don't waste time trying to read it. I know it's risky, but I tell myself I'll just take a quick peek inside, enough to satisfy my curiosity about the book's author, if I can.

Infuriatingly, there's no identifying inscription inside the book's front cover. So I rifle through its pages indiscriminately, keeping an ear open for the sound of the boys' return.

I see right away that the book is indeed a private diary of sorts. Although there aren't any dates, the writing is in long, discrete blocks like entries, and there are enough tall, solitary 'I's to show that it's written in the first person. It's easier to make out these capital letters, so I scan across the pages, looking for ones that might start a proper name. I'm not looking for *I*, or *M* for Meliana, or even *G*, for the mysterious chapel visitor. I'm looking for *J*, for Jakob Mellor. And *J*, for Jan.

Ironically enough, it is a big, bold *G* much like the one on the handkerchief from the chapel that first catches my eye. And it's at the beginning of a name I recognize. I know I don't have much time, but after a glance behind me I force myself to work systematically back through the line in which the name appears.

When I'm done, there's no nervous pulse beating inside my wrists. My breathing is still. I think my heart may have literally stopped, and I'm strangely calm.

I guess I'm in shock.

Unless I'm very much mistaken, the line I've just struggled through reads as follows:

It wasn't my father who let it slip to Mother and me that the Brecelyn boy is one of his Journeymen at St. Sebastian's this year, but Guillaume.

I gaze down at the sentence for a moment in wonder, trying to process it. I don't think I fully believed it before, but there can be no question about it. This diary really did belong to Lady Meliana Brecelyn. Brian de Gilford told me she was one of the previous guild masters' daughters, didn't he? And that she met Sir Hugo during his Journeyman year at the guild. And Guillaume — that has to be Master Guillaume, doesn't it? A young Meliana Brecelyn wrote this diary, and in it she's going to talk about

43

Hugo Brecelyn's Journey year. The year he was a Journey, along with my father.

So the impossible can happen, and one of my wild, improbable assumptions has proven to be nothing but the truth.

I've got my father's past, right in the palm of my hand.

I'm so flabbergasted, I throw caution to the wind. I forget everything: that I'm standing in broad daylight with Brecelyn's dead wife's book in my hands, that the hall is filling with servants laying out our noon meal on the sideboard, and that the boys are sure to be coming back inside to eat that meal at any moment. I even forget that whatever is written in this book about my father and Meliana is probably something I don't really want to know. I turn wildly back through the pages, and I bend my head down to start reading the book right from the beginning, at first slowly as I pick through the scrawled print, and then faster and faster as I become more accustomed to it, on pins and needles at the thought that I'm about to read something of my father's past.

Instead, to my dismay what I read is this:

How good it is to be back in my old room, and to have some privacy again! It feels like ages since I had the luxury of committing my thoughts to writing, without having to worry about one of the nuns' 'little inspections,' or another girl rifling through my things. Oh, the others were all content to sit around in that convent sewing and giggling, dropping hints about the fantastic matches their fathers were sure to arrange for them and pretending to think my rank comes only from Father's position. They were all jealous of me, and I wasn't the least bit tempted to confide any of my secrets to them. But now I have a fresh little book, a pen in hand, and a secret I am dying to tell, to you, dear friend — the secret of how I liberated myself from that dismal place. It was really quite clever of me.

As soon as I stepped foot inside St. Genevieve's I knew I had to get away. The place was deadly dull, the nuns were tyrants, and I wasn't going to let those other girls lord it over me indefinitely. Besides, I knew why Father had sent me there. He was planning to arrange a marriage for me, too, and he wanted me out of the way so that I couldn't have any say in it. But it wasn't going to be any 'fantastic match,' at least not in my opinion. He was going to stick me with some dreary old cloth merchant's son, or one of the local wool dyers; I'd heard him talking often enough about what an asset my looks would be in helping him forge a bond between St. Sebastian's and one the other powerful guilds in town. That's all Father cares about; using my looks to his advantage. Well, I don't intend to let him. I plan to use them to my own.

Sometimes being so beautiful can be a real burden. It's a lot of work, and I've had to make sacrifices. Everyone wants something from me, and it's so tedious having to endure the attentions of every dolt and loser who thinks he's flattering me by his clumsy flirtations, who thinks I should be thrilled to be nothing more than an object of men's lust or of other women's envy. But I'd be a fool not to admit that it has its advantages, and I've come to see my beauty as my weapon. I haven't had much choice. It's the only one a girl is allowed to wield.

I knew my looks were my ticket out of there as soon as I laid eyes on the fool of a priest who came in twice a day to give us mass. I saw the expression on his face when he caught sight of me coming in for chapel with the other girls on that very first afternoon, and I knew that look. It was the look of a starving man who's been shown a joint of plump, juicy beef. I met his gaze, and when he was the first to look away, I knew I had him. It was all too easy. Whoever thought it was a good idea to put a grown man like that in charge of educating adolescent girls, I'm sure I don't know. Celibacy. What a joke! It's a disaster waiting to happen.

I softened him up first a bit, of course. For a man old enough to be my father he wasn't bad looking, so it wasn't an unpleasant task, though he was a little thin for my taste. Ascetic. You know the type. I prefer a man with meat on his bones. He was a likable enough old rascal, but I couldn't afford to feel sorry for him, and for all his vows he proved to be no different from the rest. I launched my assault that very day, and with the equipment at my disposal it wasn't hard to get him all worked up.

I'd make sure to wear my tightest dresses to chapel, unlacing the high bodices when the nuns weren't looking so I could pull them down precariously low as we filed in through the side door under the portico. Then when I knew he was watching, I'd linger at the font, brushing holy water down over my cleavage with a lingering hand. But I did my real work at communion, and in the confessional. An artfully low bend over the cup and a deep breath gave him a clear view down over my breasts, and when I'd let my hair fall forward to brush against his forearm as he held the communal chalice up under me or let my tongue peek out between my lips to lick up a wayward drop, his hand would tremble so hard it's a miracle he didn't slosh out half the wine. And what fun it was, making up 'impure thoughts' sure to get him sweating in that hot little confessional box! I quite outdid myself, punctuating my descriptions with a well-placed moan or two, and I never left the cubicle until I could hear his heavy breathing coming through the screen. It was so entertaining I even stayed on at the convent longer than I'd intended, and I knew it was time to make an end of it when I found myself starting to get a little too fond of our game. So when I judged I'd sufficiently primed the pump, as it were, I made my move.

I timed it impeccably to coincide with one of Father's pre-arranged visits. I waited until I saw the priest go in to robe in the vestry. Then with a word to that dimwitted neophyte Agnes who was supposed to be chaperoning me to send my father into the chapel upon his arrival, I followed my target inside. I was waiting for him, leaning invitingly back against the altar, when he came out. I had a story ready to explain myself: a fit of hysteria, a demonic urge in need of exorcising through a vigorous 'laying on of hands.' But I needn't have bothered. As soon as I yanked down my dress and the lecherous old goat got an eyeful of round, quivering flesh, he jumped on the bait like a lion on a gazelle. Imagine the scene, as just when he reached out and grabbed my bare breast as eagerly as Adam plucking at the apple, my father walked in, followed by the

Mother Superior. Sadistic old cow, was she ever embarrassed! It was a struggle not to erupt in a gale of laughter.

That was it for the priest, and the end of my stay at St. Genevieve's. He got the boot and was disgraced into the bargain, and the Mother Superior got an earful about the whole scandalous affair from my father. But Father must have suspected something. He took pity on the poor man and offered him a post giving mass back at St. Sebastian's, saying he'd be kept out of temptation's way ministering to a pack of boys. I've seen him periodically since then, on those rare occasions when we've joined Father for mass in the guild chapel. Papa never said a word about the incident to my mother, but the first time I attended mass 'en famille' at the guild afterward, Father first pulled me aside and asked if it would upset me unduly to see the man again.

"I expect I'll manage," I replied archly, to which my father simply raised his eyebrows and said,

"Yes, I expect you will. You always do. Just go easy on him, won't you, Meli?"

He knows me awfully well.

"What on earth are you doing back here, Marek?" a loud voice booms, right in my ear. "Tristan running you so ragged, you've taken to hiding from him, have you?"

It's Falko, and he's come around the suit of armor to stand right behind me. I was so caught up in a gruesome fascination with the story on the page in front of me that I didn't hear his clumping approach. It's only when his huge hand slaps me jovially on the back that I come back to myself with a jolt, and I realize what I've done. I've let myself get caught red-handed with the book, by the boy with the biggest mouth of the bunch. I should have remembered that left to his own devices, Falko has an unusually high tolerance for being dirty, too.

I startle violently, and for a horrible moment the book bobbles around in my hands. Then with a ruffle of pages it falls to the floor at my feet, just as Falko leans inquisitively over my shoulder.

"Say, whatcha looking at there so intently?" he demands. "Got yourself another little *illu-minated* gem?" he chortles, stretching out the word suggestively and giving me a nudge in the ribs.

I lean forward, too, cursing myself, and hoping against hope that Falko hasn't noticed the book, although I don't see how even someone as unobservant as he is could miss it. It made an audible thud, and it's lying splayed open on the ground right in front of us.

"Back here drooling over another blonde, what?" Falko continues hopefully, craning his neck to see down around me.

I step lightly on top of the book, covering it with the toe of my boot. The memory of Falko grabbing my now-burnt manuscript page out of Aristide's hand back at the guild and reading its smudged text out delightedly to all the boys scrolls miserably through my mind.

"I was just, *uh*, admiring the inlay work on this visor," I stammer.

It's one of my worst lies, since I was obviously hunched over in the other direction and Falko must know it. But my hiding spot turns out to be a lucky break for me. Falko can't resist an opening to talk about knights and their paraphernalia, and he falls for it.

"Ah, a fellow connoisseur!" he exclaims happily, launching into some long-winded blather about the forging of arms, but I'm not listening. I'm racking my brain trying to figure out what I'm going to do when he inevitably pulls me along with him, either to inspect the armor from another angle or to join the boys now starting to wander in for mess over at one of the long tables. One of the others is sure to come over to see what we're doing any minute, and I can't count on any of them being as easily side-tracked. Obviously, I can't stand back here on the spot, obstinately refusing to budge throughout the entire noon meal, either.

As Falko drones on and I struggle to keep my foot over the book under his jostling, the full magnitude of my folly settles over me, as heavy as any suit of armor. If the book is discovered publicly like this, there are only two possible outcomes, both of them disasters: it'll be turned over to Brecelyn and I'll never see it again, or Falko will read its unseemly secrets aloud to everyone over supper, and my efforts to spare Tristan the book's contents will have all been in vain. And if I'm pegged as a thief into the bargain, I won't be the only one to pay a heavy price. Why didn't I think about it sooner, that Tristan would surely share in my punishment? At the least we'd be separated, before our second year together has even begun. All my plans for us would be over.

I'm just wondering if I can manage to kick the book unobtrusively into a dark corner when there's a discrete little cough somewhere beside me. In my anxiety I hadn't noticed it before, but Falko's got Frans with him. Falko's own squire Pruie must still be eluding him and Rennie's bolted, so Falko's pressed the lad into service. He's got one big arm draped around the boy's neck, and he's been using it to herd him reluctantly along.

I look down at Frans, to find his intelligent little face looking up at me. We share a look for a moment. Then Frans squeaks,

"Bit of dirt on your boot, master!" and in a deft move, he ducks down from under Falko's arm as though to give my boot a quick wipe. I shift my weight, and Frans slips the book out from under my foot, palming it like a pro. When he straightens up with it, I put a hand behind my back and wiggle my fingers for it, and as I'm nodding my head vigorously at Falko in the other direction, to all appearances enthralled by what he's saying, Frans passes it smoothly back to me.

Once I've got the book again, I waste no time in dropping it back into concealment under the guise of running my hand along the armor in

47

appreciation of some point Falko's making. Fortunately for me, Falko's enthusiastic voice and my own sigh of relief are so loud, they effectively cover the hollow ring the book makes as it plops back down into the fist of the glove.

By the time Tristan finally strolls in to rescue us, smelling suspiciously like Gilles has taken it upon himself to further Tristan's education in perfume out in the armory, the book's back in its hiding place and Frans and I have suffered through such a long lecture by Falko that my nerves have had a chance to recover, some. As I settle myself on the bench for mess next to a very sweet-smelling Tristan, though, I feel unclean from missing my own chance to wash, and even more from reading that other girl's private thoughts. What I just read wasn't the sort of thing I was hoping to find in the journal at all; it was distinctly unpleasant, and as I try to choke down my stew what I really should be doing is saying a silent word of thanks to Frans for a narrow escape and swearing off the blasted thing for good.

Instead, I'm thinking furiously about how I'm going to manage to read the rest of it without getting caught. Because for those few moments when the book was lying open at my feet, two words in bold print stared up at me from one of its pages, and I see them swimming before my eyes for the rest of the meal:

Jan Verbeke.

As we're all making our way upstairs later to rest before taking the field again for the afternoon, I fall into step beside Frans.

"*About what happened earlier, behind the suit of armor ...*" I begin casually, but Frans just looks up at me innocently and says,

"Whatever *can* you be referring to, master?" and I know I don't have to explain.

I've never been so glad I decided not to kick Frans out of barracks. We continue up the steps side-by-side behind Tristan, and as we go, I reach a hand down lightly to ruffle Frans's hair.

CHAPTER FIVE

Any hopes I might have been harboring that Tristan's words in front of the fire were a passing whim are frustrated later that very day, when I discover to my chagrin that he's already started in on his self-appointed task of investigating Sir Brecelyn. As always Tristan is as good as his word and he *is* being subtle about it, though; so subtle, in fact, I doubt I'd have noticed if he hadn't told me himself what he intended.

As it is, when I come downstairs after our noon siesta to find him in the middle of a game of chance with some of Brecelyn's men, I think nothing of it — except to hope that he's winning, since as far as I know he doesn't have any money. And when he then waves off my suggestion of an afternoon practice session, choosing instead to invite half the garrison to join him in a drink to celebrate his winnings, all I am is annoyed. It's not until I spot him strolling across the courtyard later that afternoon with a bucket in each hand and a milkmaid on each arm that I figure it out. As predicted, his preferred investigative method is going to involve flirting his way through a wide swathe of Brecelyn's serving staff.

He's got one of his old, lazy smiles on his face, the kind that could charm the birds right out of the trees, and he looks like he's thoroughly enjoying himself, so I convince myself maybe it's a good thing. It'll keep him safely occupied with his mind off Melissande until I can figure out how to get him back on track, and I don't see how he can get himself into too much trouble, since there are no rules against consorting with girls *here*.

It's not until later that night, though, when some of us are sitting around the big fire in the great hall and digesting another whopping meal, that I get firsthand confirmation of Tristan's activities. Most of the boys have already gone upstairs to bed, but Falko's slumped in a drunken stupor on a big chair next to a drowsy Jurian, Armand is teaching Frans to play knucklebones on the hearth, and Gilles is sprawled out beside them on the floor. Someone's spread out the pelt of some unfortunate animal in front of the fireplace as a rug and Gilles is lying on it, his arms folded lazily behind his head and his long legs crossed and resting on top of what's left of the animal's head. The

49

boys have been having a desultory conversation, but I've only been half-listening. On his own way upstairs Remy ducked past Gilles to position a pair of big boots to dry on the hearth, and I've been sitting here ever since trying hard not to stare at them — or to kick them straight into the fire. But when Tristan leans back on his stool to say leadingly,

"It's mighty strange, boys," I know what he's doing. He thinks he's found out something *already*, and he wants the boys to confirm it. I know what *I* should do, too — I should clear my throat or make some other noise to discourage him. Instead, I lean in closer, curious despite myself.

"All right, I'll bite," Jurian drawls. "Entertain us. What's up, DuBois?"

"I was talking with some of the men this afternoon. Sir Hugo's personal retainers," Tristan says casually. "They were doing a lot of grumbling. Seems Brecelyn's got them all pulling double or triple shifts."

"Well of course," Gilles exclaims. "Servants are *always* grumbling. And nobody likes standing guard."

"And you may have forgotten that the whole country's recently been ravaged by plague, but I can assure you *I* haven't," Jurian puts in languidly. "He probably doesn't have that many men left."

"That's just it, Jurian," Tristan replies. "The plague is over, and Brecelyn's made no move to hire more men to replace the ones that died. The regent's refilling the ranks; why not Sir Hugo? With things so unsettled, this is the worst possible time to let his defenses slacken."

"No doubt putting up all of us from St. Sebastian's for so long is beginning to take its toll," Gilles says reasonably. "It must be costing him a fortune."

"That's another thing," Tristan insists. "According to the servants, they were on Spartan rations around here before we showed up — wages cut, no meat served. Certainly no lavish meals like the ones we've been enjoying."

"What?! No *sausages?!*" Falko belches, coming out of his stupor for a moment at the mention of meat.

"Just what do *you* make of it, Tristan?" Gilles inquires, reaching down to stroke the fur under him indulgently.

"Brecelyn's seriously strapped for cash, and from what I can tell, his troubles began before the plague ever hit."

"If he's hurting financially, why wouldn't he just say so? Why make such a show of wealth?" Armand asks, looking up from his game. "And why agree to put us up in the first place, if he can't afford it?"

There's a pause, as Tristan waits to ensure he's got everyone's full attention. Then he declares with a flourish,

"Boys, Sir Hugo Brecelyn is *broke* — and he doesn't want Master Guillaume or anyone at St. Sebastian's to know about it!"

This is met by the boys with a polite but profound silence. It's all rather far-fetched; I mean, that a man should need to economize after suffering through a plague that decimated his flocks or that he'd treat his guests more lavishly than his own staff is logical enough. But Tristan's sounding so pleased with himself and his bright good humor is so brittle that nobody wants to deflate him, and I know I shouldn't either.

I hear myself demanding anyway,

"If Brecelyn's so broke, Tristan, then just where is the money coming from that it's costing him to host us?"

If I thought to discourage him, I'm disappointed. Instead, as Gilles catches my eye and purrs "*Gee*, Marek," in a way that's surely meant to sound like the capital letter G to me but just like one of his usual exclamations to the others, Tristan replies emphatically,

"Where is the money coming from? I don't know, Marek. But I can tell you this. I fully intend to find out."

<hr />

I DON'T THINK IT'S SURPRISING I'D HAVE TROUBLE SLEEPING that night and on the nights which follow, and not only because of Tristan's pronouncement or Gilles's insistence on teasing me about the handkerchief, or even because I'll never really rest until I've read more of Meliana's journal, now that I've seen my father's name in it. With the resumption of regular drills we've entered a countdown to leaving Brecelyn's castle, and I'm filled with an anticipation for going home that's rivaled only by my anxiety over what's going to happen when we get there.

As soon as we're back at St. Sebastian's, the trials that have seemed so far off for so long will suddenly be upon us, and I can't stop worrying about our chances. I can't shake the feeling that the timing of this, too, is crucial: I've got to have a winning strategy all worked out and ready to present to Tristan as soon as we get back to St. Sebastian's, or I'll have missed my window of opportunity and I'll never convince him. Oh, Tristan's been practicing diligently enough, pounding himself with brutal clout drills every afternoon that leave us both exhausted, and I try to take it as a positive sign — that underneath it all he'd still dearly love to win, if only he thought he could do it. But I don't like it. Anger and resentment aren't what Tristan needs to see him through this year, and neither are clouts. Yet as I lie awake, tossing and turning and examining the inspiration that came to me out in the chapel from every angle, it remains frustratingly vague, no more than the certainty that somehow or other, making Gilles our ally is the key to Tristan's success this year.

At least, it's this worry for the future that I always start out thinking about. In the pitch blackness of my room, it's harder to keep as tight control over my thoughts as I do during the day, and inevitably an old worry steals over me. It's embarrassing to admit it, but alone in the dark I can't help fearing that I'll see my dream of the hawk again. I'm pretty sure I'm done with it. But I don't think I could stand having to suffer through it again now, and despite my resolve to look forward, each night I find my thoughts drifting back — sometimes to the urgent voice that whispered through that dream, and sometimes to my father — but more often, to Melissande.

Maybe it's partly because Gilles's cryptic comments about the baby are still preying on me. But given her terrible ordeal, I can't help imagining how she must be suffering, and feeling sorry for her loss. I know I should be philosophical about it. The infant mortality rate is shockingly high, and we've all had plenty of exposure to it. Losing a baby early in pregnancy is commonplace enough, and as soon as Melissande herself was out of danger, the other boys were content to put the episode behind them and to count it as more of a setback than a tragedy. But I can't put it behind me so easily.

It's not just the baby that's on my mind, though. Maybe I should be angry with Melissande for hurting Tristan, and I am, a little — irrationally enough. It's not her fault she's engaged to Taran; I doubt anybody ever asked her opinion about it. But I guess I've never really thought about things from her point of view before, and it's started to occur to me that perhaps Melissande hasn't had much of an easier time of it all than I have.

She grew up without a mother, too, and her relationship with her father can't have been any less complicated than mine was. I can't quite bring myself to think of her incredible beauty as a burden, but even I have to admit she hasn't used it as a weapon, and being beautiful herself hasn't kept her from falling victim to the boys' charms. If nothing else, I wonder how Melissande would feel if she knew how many representations of her have been chucked into her father's fire.

I picture her lying idle and bereaved up in her room somewhere above me, and I know Fate *has* put a terrible burden on Melissande, only it's not the beauty her mother lamented. It's one I've escaped so far, thanks to St. Sebastian: the burden of just being a girl.

Sometimes, too, without intending to I find myself sliding my hand down across my own belly, for once not imagining it's a boy's hand. It feels smooth and hard. And empty. Yet there's a soft swell in the center of it. It's slight, just the faintest hint that somewhere underneath it all, I really am a girl. I don't know why I've never thought it before — that there's something more than companionship I'll be giving up, if I stay a boy forever. But I always pull my hand away and roll over before I can dwell on it. Or on other reasons why the whole thing might be hitting me so hard. I certainly don't let myself think of Taran's expression as it was that night at the top of the stairs.

Despite Tristan's dramatic gesture with the parchment, it's perfectly obvious that he hasn't really been able to stop thinking about Melissande, either — even before I catch him one evening, brooding over her in an alcove of the corridor to the west wing. I come upon him on my way down to dinner, standing at the same window where I found him staring out the night of the fire, after he said his goodbye to her. He's wearing much the same faraway expression he wore then, and sure enough, as I come up behind him, without turning around he says,

"Do you know what the devil of it is, Marek?," and I guess he's finally gotten around to feeling bitter towards her. It was bound to happen, after the things the boys were saying. After all, the unpalatable truth of it is that while he was pining away for her, Melissande was disporting herself with Taran. But just like that night, I've underestimated Tristan, again.

"Upstairs somewhere, she's hurting and I can't go to her. I've no right to comfort her, or even to speak. No right at all. Do you know what it is, to know someone you care for is suffering, and to be unable to do anything about it? I can't even tell her how I feel."

I can't reply. I do know exactly what that is.

"But I suppose *he*'s comforting her," he adds, a bitter note now creeping into his voice, and before I can stop myself, I picture it.

It's bad enough, even before he continues,

"If I know anything about human nature, Marek, mark my words. Before long, the way they'll be comforting each other is by trying to produce another child. If they haven't gotten started already."

We both hurry downstairs, before we can let ourselves picture *that*.

As we go, I search around for something to say to comfort him, even though I know just how useless it is; neither of us will really be able to put this episode behind us until we leave the castle. There's no point in telling him just to forget about her, either, even though she was always something of an impossibility, and surely now she's hopelessly lost to him, as lost as ... well, just lost.

I suggest it anyway. I only realize I must be a little annoyed at him, too, when I hear myself add,

"You know, it's not like you really know her all that well. You've hardly ever even talked to her."

Tristan doesn't take it amiss. With a look meant to convey how much worldlier he is than I am, he sighs,

"When it's right, you just know, Marek," and I roll my eyes. It's a little hypocritical, I suppose, since I fell in love with him just from seeing him sitting on top of a wall.

"I guess I was fooling myself," he continues. "I thought we didn't need words, that we understood each other. I don't know how to describe it, but it was like there was something between us — an unspoken *sympathy*. I guess that sounds ridiculous to you."

I don't answer. I'm already feeling unsteady, actually, when he adds,

"You know, sort of like the one between the two of us. Only not as strong as *ours*, of course. Nothing's as strong as that," and he ruffles my hair, and continues on down the stairs.

Behind him, I've come to a full stop. It's an opening if I've ever heard one, and God help me, I almost take it. I can feel irrevocable words forming on my lips, words that would tell him right then and there, in the middle of the hallway, that I'm a girl. A girl who loves him. But luckily, I catch myself back. When it's right, I guess you do just know. And everything about the timing of this is completely wrong.

◆―――――◆

AFTER THAT CONVERSATION ON THE STAIRS, TRISTAN NEVER mentions Melissande again directly. Instead, he throws himself into his pursuit of the domestic staff with such gusto that it isn't long before I manage to convince myself he's already well on his way to forgetting all about her with his usual practicality. When I notice the girls he's singling out for attention are all ones directly involved in serving Melissande in one capacity or another, I even assume he's enjoying getting a little subtle revenge on her into the bargain. Then I figure it out. He's not forgotten about Melissande — far from it. Whether he'd admit it to himself or not, Tristan's been targeting Melissande's maids because what he's really been hoping for with all his questioning of them isn't to learn anything about Sir Brecelyn. It's to hear some word of their mistress.

That's why when I come down for breakfast one morning a few days later to find him with a chambermaid backed up against the wall on the landing between the west and the east wings (having obviously waylaid her as she was on her way down directly from Melissande's room), it's not because I'm at all curious to hear what Tristan's finding out that I find myself leaning closer. It's something else entirely that catches my attention.

Tristan's slouched lazily against the wall, with one elbow propped above the girl's shoulder. He's fiddling absently with a lock of her hair and bending down to whisper something into her ear that's making her erupt in a cascade of high-pitched giggles; it's a singularly grating sound, but boys seem to love it. The girl's got both hands clasped primly behind her back in a pose that seems more destined to show off her ample figure than to preserve her modesty, since her cleavage is jutting out under Tristan's nose and she's wearing a flimsy dress with no more than a loose drawstring to hold it all in, the sort of thing men always seem to insist on dressing their female servants in. Her breasts were already overflowing out the top, but with each giggle the string's been slipping open further and now it's threatening to give way entirely.

None of that is very surprising. Nor is the fact that at first Tristan doesn't pay any attention to me as I approach, intent as he is on worsening the plight of the string. But as I'm ducking past, head down, my averted eyes happen to flit to the girl's hands — only to see to my surprise that she hasn't been wriggling and simpering simply to flirt with Tristan. Her pose is no accident, either. She's got something concealed behind her back and she's doesn't want him to notice it.

When I pull up short and take an unintentional step closer, Tristan glances up at me and drawls,

"'Lo, Marek," with absolutely no shame and without moving from his slouch against the wall (or against the *girl*, I might add). And in that moment, when Tristan's head is turned, the girl darts her hand up as quick as a flash and shoves something down between her breasts under cover of pulling up her slipping dress. By the time Tristan's turned his attention back to her she's firmly tying the string again and giving him a coquettish look that says she's now ready to enjoy herself fully, having gotten the item safely secreted away. I continue on my way and leave them to it, lost in my own thoughts, for once glad that boys seem incapable of seeing past the chest of a girl in a low-cut dress.

It's true I didn't get a good look at what the girl was concealing. I only got the briefest of glimpses of it, actually, before it disappeared into her bodice. But it was enough to recognize it: a tiny blue glass bottle with a cork stopper, identical to the ones I once saw Sir Brecelyn carrying in a little wooden case. If I was right in what I thought then and the bottles contain tonics belonging to Melissande, for her to still be secretly taking one can only mean one thing. Melissande's not recovered from her fever as well as her father's been letting on. She must still be dangerously ill, and the last thing Tristan needs now is to get wind of it. He'll never get over her, if he gets caught up in worrying about her all over again.

Having left Tristan so engrossed, I'm hardly expecting him to join me for breakfast. So it takes me by surprise when he comes up behind me only moments later and slaps me vigorously on the back as I'm looking over the lavish array of pastries on the sideboard in front of me with a worried expression.

"Well, that tears it!" he declares triumphantly. "You scoffed, Marek. But surely you must agree with me now."

"I'll admit, it is a suspiciously ostentatious spread," I concede, and Tristan laughs.

"Not the *breakfast*, kid. The *bottle*. Not even you can have missed seeing that girl shoving it down the front of her dress."

So he did notice.

"I suppose there could be any number of explanations for it," I venture, but Tristan shakes his head.

"There's only one that makes any sense," he says confidently, and I know he's right. I can't see why he sounds so happy about it, though. I'd have expected him to rush upstairs to break down Melissande's door and throw himself across her sickbed, or at least to start pacing around the room and tearing out his hair again. I never would have thought Tristan so vindictive that he'd wish Melissande ill, just because it's turned out she prefers his brother.

"Brecelyn must be cutting his staff's wages back even more than I'd imagined, Marek, if the maids have been reduced to stealing perfumes right out of their mistress's chambers," Tristan declares, and I feel mighty foolish. Of course.

The girl is simply a petty thief, and there's nothing more to it. It's so obvious, I almost burst out with a giggle of my own. Gilles was right about me; I have gotten ridiculously melodramatic. No wonder he's made a game of it to tease me.

"Er, Tristan. A light-fingered maid, pilfering from her mistress — that can't really be very unusual," I say, trying hard not to think about the fact that technically speaking, *I* was probably the last light-fingered girl to pilfer from Melissande, when I took her veil.

"Maybe not. But it all fits," he insists. "And it's not just the bottle. Believe me, I've talked to *a lot* of maids in the past few days," he says, and I roll my eyes, picturing it. "And if the girls can be believed, these economies of Brecelyn's started long before we got here, Marek. And not just before the plague ever hit. *Before* our *first* stay here, even, for the hunt! You do see what that means, don't you? Brecelyn hosted us once, when he could ill afford it — and an attempt on the prince followed soon after. For him to be hosting us *again*, and when he can afford it even less, it must be for the same reason. Sir Hugo and his accomplices from within our own guild are using our visit as a cover, so they can plot how they're going to try it again."

There are holes in Tristan's theory so wide, even I could shoot an arrow through one of them from a distance of 300 paces. It unnerves me anyway. Not because I believe it, exactly. But Tristan clearly wants to, and I know finding out he didn't really save the prince at Thirds last year has always rankled. If the blazing look on his face is anything to go by, he's so enamored of the idea of having a second chance at it now that I shudder to think what he might do, if he thought he saw the opportunity. There's only one thing about it that gives me comfort: the fact that I'm pretty sure Tristan doesn't really believe any of it, either.

Still, it gives me a funny feeling that he's hit on a theory uncannily like some of the wilder ones Gilles has been needling me about — even though we never told Tristan about the lamps we found lit out in Brecelyn's chapel at midnight.

⸻⊸⊷⊶⊷⊸⸻

PERHAPS IT'S AS ARISTIDE SUGGESTED, AND OUR MENTAL preoccupation with Melissande during this time is partly fueled by the fact that for most of it she herself never actually appears. I'm grateful for it, but a little apprehensive. Just as in the days leading up to that fateful morning in the clearing, her failure to materialize even after she should have fully recovered begins to feel ominous.

It's a strange time for all of us, caught in limbo as we are between the anticipation of leaving and the reality of still being stuck here, and with everything that's on my mind, there are really only two things that make it at all bearable for me.

The first is that Melissande isn't the only one who rarely appears. Taran, too, is nowhere to be seen. He never comes to any of Master Leon's practices and if he's training at all, it isn't with the others — something that would be remarkable enough for any of the Journeys but is unheard of for him. He's not to be found lurking in the corridor of the west wing anymore, either, since Brecelyn soon moves him up to a room on the second floor where he can be closer to Melissande in her recovery (there being no point any longer in keeping up the pretense that they're being kept chastely apart). He doesn't show up for any meals, and Remy is kept so busy mothering him that I'm largely deprived of his company, too. If we're not busy together with our squires' tasks, the most I see of Remy is when he casts me soulful little glances from across the room as he hurries by on some errand or other for Taran, or when he's furtively scurrying from the kitchen up to the second floor carrying plates of food to try to tempt his master, and jugs of wine. The plates all come back untouched.

The jugs of wine, empty.

It's not because there's little opportunity for conversation, though, that Remy and I never speak directly about finding Taran's arrow. I desperately want to question him about it, of course. Sometimes it's so frustrating knowing there's someone standing right next to me who knows exactly what happened the day of Tristan's wounding so long ago that I want to climb right out of my skin. But I know Remy'd just try to lie, and I can't really blame him for being loyal. We're both so anxious that the enmity between Taran and Tristan not spill over and ruin our friendship, too, that we come to a tacit agreement:

Remy's willing to overlook the fact that I hate his master, if I'm willing to overlook the fact that he loves him.

The closest we come to mentioning what happened in the clearing that morning between us is one evening when Remy squeezes in next to me at evening mess. I'd only arrived myself moments earlier with Pascal, and as we sat down we were so engrossed in a lively discussion of some mildly pornographic manuscripts we found when assigned the task of sorting through deceased old Master Gheeraert's things that at first I don't notice what's right in front of me. It's the little wooden horse. Someone's left it sitting on the table.

"Isn't it clever?" Remy exclaims, when he sees me eyeing it with disfavor. "Do you know what it is, Marek?"

"It's a horse."

With a laugh, he slings an arm around my shoulder and picks the horse up, holding it out for my inspection much as he once did the ill-fated unicorn. I appreciate the gesture just about as much.

"It's not just any horse, silly!" he laughs affectionately, giving me a squeeze and turning the toy over admiringly. "It's the *Trojan* horse! See its swollen belly?"

He prods the thing, running his finger over the curve of the horse's abdomen. Something slick slides in my own belly, just as it did back in the clearing.

"It's *pregnant* ... with Greek soldiers! Such a sad story, don't you think?" he says, happily enough. "How *low*, how *cowardly*, to sneak into such a venerable place under false colors," he continues. "Those poor Trojans, welcoming the enemy within their walls, disguised as a friend! But I guess it isn't always easy to spot an enemy, is it? Particularly not a subtle one. Not until it's too late."

He shoots me a meaningful glance. "It just goes to show, doesn't it, Marek, not to judge on appearances. You know, things aren't always what they seem."

He's said it casually enough, but I know what he's trying to tell me. I would, even if it weren't for his unnerving echoing of Gilles's phrase about it. He's trying to backpedal, to take back what he said about seeing Taran shoot Tristan without opening the discussion directly again. And when he adds,

"But you know what I am to *you*, don't you, Marek? At least, what I want to be," and under the table he puts his hand firmly on my knee, I know what he's telling me, too, even before he starts to slide it up the inside of my thigh. So much for not being 'bold.' Remy's finally getting around to making good on his threat to woo me.

Instead of answering, I clamp my knees together and I take the horse out of his hand. And with a vigorous push, I send it rolling down to the opposite end of the table. I don't know why it disconcerts me that when it comes to a stop, it's directly in front of Tristan.

THE SECOND SAVING GRACE OF THAT LAST WEEK AT BRECELYN'S is that we soon get certain confirmation of our assumption about the significance of resumed drills, and we squires are kept so busy preparing for the big move back to St. Sebastian's that I don't have time or energy to spare for anything else.

The news comes one evening during dinner. When Master Guillaume rises up from Brecelyn's table and gestures us to our feet, it's been so long since I snapped to attention I feel almost out of shape. It's also been so long since the master addressed us formally that we all know what he's going to say. When a spontaneous cheer goes up before he can even open his mouth, I'm cheering loudest of all.

"Gentlemen, I can see you have heard the rumors!" he barks, slapping his tankard down on the table in front of him for silence. "So let me make it official. The time for our triumphant return to our glorious guild is indeed drawing near! If all goes as planned, we should be saying our goodbyes to our generous host and heading for home by the end of the week. Crews of veterans stand organized and ready to be sent ahead, to begin making the necessary arrangements for the reconstruction work, and to start, *er*, preparing the way, for the return of our Journeys."

"I suppose he means disposing of all the dead bodies," Gilles interjects in a loud whisper, and I hope he's right. Usually we squires are made to do the dirtiest work, and carting away the bodies of our men and of the villagers who were left where they fell on the night of our departure is just the sort of task the masters enjoy inflicting on us. We're probably only being spared it now because there aren't enough of us left. Just clearing out the gully beyond the wall where we threw our own men is going to take a small army. I don't even want to think about the abandoned infirmary.

"I won't deny we've got our work cut out for us," the master is continuing soberly. "It's not just our walls that will need rebuilding. It is also our numbers, and our reputation. To this end, I myself will be leaving you first thing tomorrow morning, for Meuse."

At the loud murmuring that's started to fill the hall, the master slaps the table with both palms so suddenly I jump, even though I see him do it. "We've suffered grievous losses, men! And I won't hide from you that there are those in the capital who would seek to use our setbacks to undermine us. Those who have in the past thought St. Sebastian's too strong, too influential." He twists his lips in disgust, and I think I know who he's talking about. I remember his dislike of the prince's constable Hieronymous. "But I can assure you I have no intention of letting that happen. Not only do I plan to remind the regent personally of his promise that the prince's upcoming coronation be timed to coincide with the induction of our winner into Guards this year —"; he pauses, rather obviously looking around the room to nod at Taran, annoyingly enough. Momentarily nonplussed at being unable to find him, he twists his lips sourly again before resuming,

"*Any*way, I will also be bringing back reinforcements with me, since our membership has been seriously depleted. You can expect to see many new faces around the guild this year, and some old ones, too. *Desperate times call for desperate measures*, that's our watchword this year, men."

He pauses, letting the phrase hang over us just long enough for it to begin to sound like one of his threats. Then he slams his fist down on the table again.

"Don't get me wrong, men! We must be bold and forge this setback into an opportunity. Think of it this way: the old has been cleared away, to make room for the new. Now is the time for vision! St. Sebastian's will rise again, bigger and better than ever. We're at a critical juncture, for our guild and for our country. Our enemies may be circling," Guillaume exclaims, and when he then pauses dramatically again for a breath, I miss what he says next, distracted by the toe of a boot jostling my shin. I look up to see Gilles grinning at me from across the table, silently mouthing the letter 'G' and motioning exaggeratedly with his head down the table toward Aristide. I ignore him. When I tune back in, the master's already winding down:

"... and I expect every man to do his part. Unfortunately, this all means that I will not be making the return trip with you. I'll be sending you back to the guild in the tender care of Master Leon and joining you there as soon as I can. The next time I address you, I trust it will be back in the bosom of our joyous little family, reunited again at our beloved St. Sebastian's. Oh yes, and any Journey or squire who fails to turn up promptly for practice in my absence is to be flogged within an inch of his life!"

We meet this speech with wild approval, even though the master is surely serious. He always is. As our stomps and shouts ring out, instead of sitting down again Master Guillaume excuses himself directly and strides out of the hall, as though stalking off to begin on his vigorous program right away.

"What do you suppose the master meant by *old faces?*" Pascal shouts in my ear, over the noise.

"Word is, he's bringing back a new trainer with him — and it's going to be *old Poncellet!*" Armand shouts back.

From across the table, Rennie laughs,

"Nah, it can't be *him!* Don't you remember? De Gilford told us his '*member*'ship had been seriously depleted!," and it's true. We do need a new trainer, since both Royce and Baylen are dead, and I'm sure Master Leon is already tired of training us himself. But I seriously doubt it's going to be that infamous rake from before my father's time, even if he's still alive — and intact.

Around me, the boys keep up a steady stream of eager babble as we settle ourselves back on the benches, all talking over each other to retell off-color stories about Poncellet or to speculate wildly about what Master G intends to do in Meuse and the likely state in which we'll find St. Sebastian's. I can feel excitement building in me, too, about all these things (well, except maybe about old Poncellet), but I don't really hear much of the rest of the conversation. Instead, as the meal progresses all I can hear over the hum of the boys' excited voices is Meliana's notebook, calling out to me with increasing urgency from its hiding place across the room.

I can't be anything but thrilled by the master's announcement, but I know what it means. I've got precious little time to complete my own projects before we leave the castle, and in particular, my time to read Lady Brecelyn's journal is about to run out.

If I'm really going to do it, I've only got a few days left, since the one thing that's absolutely certain is that the book can't come back to St. Sebastian's with me. I can't risk taking it out during daylight again, either.

That would be the height of foolishness — an act of recklessness almost as desperate and idiotic as sneaking down after dark to read it at night, when if I were to be caught lurking around downstairs and reading it, there could be no innocent explanation for my actions. My stealth alone would be proof of guilt, and all my fears of repercussions for myself and for Tristan would surely come true.

So I'm going to have to make damned sure I don't get caught. Because of course, by the time our meal is over, sneaking down to read the journal after everyone else is asleep is exactly what I've decided to do.

CHAPTER SIX

Staying awake until I'm sure the castle is enveloped in slumber is easy, since I haven't been sleeping much these days anyway. By the time I judge it to be late enough to venture forth, though, my candle's gone out and I've been lying in the dark for so long that I've worked myself up into a state of high nervous tension. When I fumble around on my bedside table for my flint and tinder to light the candle again, my fingers are so cold and my hands trembling so hard that at first I think I'm not going to be able to manage it.

I'm not just anxious about the possibility of getting caught. By now I have had a chance to start thinking about what I'm likely to find in the journal's pages. I've been lying here for hours with not much else to think about, in fact — or at least, not much that's any better. The idea of reading a story as ugly as the one I've already read that has *my father* in it is bad enough. If I'm about to find out now that he, too, wasn't quite the boy I'd thought he was, well, I'm just not sure I can bear it.

When at length I get the candle lit, I pad to the door without putting on my boots. I ease the latch open silently, without letting the slightest creak escape; it's a little disconcerting just how adept I'm getting at skulking around this place at night.

The hallway outside is empty and eerily quiet; even the footfalls of my stocking feet against the flagstones resound in the hollow corridor, and so when I've crept my way along to come even with Tristan's room, I hesitate. It's probably my imagination, but I think I can hear his gentle snoring and the sound of him shifting around on his cot coming from inside the room. I step closer and hover there a moment, sorely tempted to open the door and go in. I picture nudging him awake, explaining everything to him in a low whisper, and begging him to come with me. Tristan could read the book easily, and we could make it into one of our adventures, a story for Tristan to embellish with his usual flair for the boys tomorrow.

But I don't do it.

A little further on, I come to another stop, even with another door. This time I don't move toward it. I don't turn my head to look at it, where it's looming on the periphery of my vision. I just stand immobile in the middle of the hallway, staring into the darkness straight ahead of me, my mind a blank. With the shadows from my candle cast across its recesses, the door seems bigger and stronger than the others, its latch shut tighter, and the room beyond it colder and more silent. But maybe that's because I know it's empty now.

In my mind, I picture stepping over to the door and letting my head rest heavily against it, and pressing my cheek up against its rough wood. But I don't do it, either. And after a moment, when a drop of hot wax dribbles down the side of my candle and onto my hand, I start moving again, alone down the long, silent hallway.

Once I've made my way down into the hall below and fished the journal out of its hiding place, I hasten over to the hearth with it, to settle in among the sleeping castle dogs in front of the glowing embers of the great fire. What faint light is still coming from the dying coals on the grate will help illuminate the book for me, and if anyone should happen to catch me downstairs, I can claim to have wandered down from my frigid room in search of some heat. If I really get desperate, I can always send the book the way of the parchment and chuck it straight into the fire.

I wedge myself in on the hearthstones between the warm bodies of two oversized but friendly mutts, and I fix my candle next to me in a pool of molten wax. Then I prop the little book precariously against a drowsy canine head that's come to rest on my knee. I carefully open Meliana's journal with hands that are shaking so hard now with equal parts anticipation and fear that it takes all my concentration just to get it balanced, and I bend closer, peering down to find my place.

As I start to read, the scrawled words swim and I find there are tears in my eyes. I'm not entirely sure how long they've been there, exactly — if they began back up in the hallway, or when they started to form, or why. But now I let them fall, overwhelmed by too many emotions to name them all at everything that's happened to me since I last saw my father. And at the knowledge that ready or not, after fifteen long years of waiting, I'm about to meet my father as I never knew him, at last:

When I awoke to the sun streaming in through the slats of the shutters, I let out a curse and rolled out of bed. I usually don't get up early, if I can help it. There are servants to do the work, and I need my beauty sleep. But this morning I had a task to do, and it was already getting late. Tomorrow is Firsts at St. Sebastian's, and I was determined to get an advance look at the field.

I'd heard all about the boys for weeks, of course. Father talks of nothing but the Journeys on the rare nights he takes a meal with us in our house in town and not at the guild. It's tedious, as I couldn't care less about archery, though I think if I'd been a boy, I'd have made a fantastic Journey. As it is, with the equipment I've got I'm as sure a shot as any archer, and I had no doubt I could bring my quarry down. All I needed was to pick out my target. I already had a pretty good idea of who it was going to be.

Imagine my satisfaction, when I found out that Sir Maurice Brecelyn's son Hugo is one of the Journeys this year. I'd been back for over a month from that wretched convent school on the edge of town where my father tried to dump me before I found out about it; Father never mentioned it, the cagey old despot. He's always trying to keep me away from 'his boys,' as he thinks of them.

I'd been in no hurry, though, thinking from his conversation at mealtimes that it was just a bunch of paupers and peasants at St. Sebastian's this year, nothing to interest me, and I'd turned my attentions elsewhere. I was already working on a few rather unpromising prospects of my own around town, but once it all came out about Brecelyn's boy being within my grasp, I dropped all my other projects. Hugo Brecelyn, at St. Sebastian's! I couldn't believe my luck.

It wasn't my father who let it slip to Mother and me that the Brecelyn boy is one of his Journeymen at St. Sebastian's this year, but Guillaume, during one of his accustomed Sunday suppers at our house. He's one of the trainers at St. Sebastian's and Father's favorite, the only one ever invited into our home. I've known Guilly all my life, of course, and I imagine Father thinks he's something like an older brother to me, though he can't be that much older than I am. But I've got other plans for Guilly. I always do.

It's funny, but we don't really know that much about him. He just showed up outside the guild one day, a serious, self-contained little boy, and Father took a shine to him. He took him in, first to the kitchens, then to the stables. He had a thirst for archery and he was a natural shot, and it wasn't long before he was squiring for some of the boys. Even before he was old enough to stand for apprentice he was already better than most of his masters, and it was a foregone conclusion that he'd end up a Journeyman himself. I used to follow him around, dogging his steps and telling him I'd marry him one day, and at the time, I really believed it. Guilly pretended it annoyed him, but he liked the attention. He was fond of me, I could tell, even though I hadn't come into my beauty then, yet.

I've outgrown all that now, of course. Can you imagine it? Me, married to an ex-stable boy? It's laughable. But I saw the flash of surprise in Guilly's eyes when I wafted into our drawing room to greet him a few months ago on my return from a temporary exile in Mons, no longer the gangly thing I'd been when I left, all teeth and knees and elbows. I'd missed Guilly's own Journey trials, having been sent to my aunt's house to keep me out of trouble right before he was to stand in the competitions. It took me a few years of concerted effort to get into enough mischief to cause the tough old bird to throw up her hands and send me back home again, and then as soon as I was back, I found myself shunted off to St. Genevieve's, 'where I can keep a firm eye on you myself, my girl,' as Father said. By the time I was settled back in at home Guilly was done, and it's his own squire who's in the competitions now. I was sorry to have missed seeing Guilly in action; from all accounts he put on a real show and I'd have liked to have seen it for myself, even though I usually find the actual shooting part of the trials quite boring.

Yes, it was very gratifying to see the look on Guilly's face the first time he saw me again, in all my glory. After the way he used to turn up his nose at me, it was very gratifying indeed, particularly now that's he's such a bigshot around the guild and all. You just don't forget your first crush that easily either, do you? So although he doesn't know it yet, I've decided to let him suffer for a while; then when the time is right, I plan to take him as a lover. I think that will be quite interesting. There's something about him that makes me think he'll be pretty good at it, once I get him going. Something unusual. I mean, I've never heard of anyone else who actually made Guards and then chose to stay on at St. Sebastian's as a trainer instead.

I was just shimmying into my second-best gown, a pink silk shift that's so light and tight it fits me like a second skin, when there was a scuffling in the hall that could only mean one thing. My little sister Madeleine was awake, too. In a moment she was bursting into the room, way too bubbly for so early in the morning. Or noon, rather.

"Oh, Meli! Are you going out?" she demanded, catching me putting on the dress.

"Of course not," I lied. I couldn't risk having her tagging along. "I'm just trying on outfits, for tomorrow. Trying to decide what I'll wear at Firsts."

"Do wear that one, Meli. You look so lovely in it," she said prettily, coming around behind me to help me fasten it up. "I can hardly wait, can you?" she asked, eagerly riffling through the wardrobe in search of a dress of her own while I ran a brush through my hair. "I've been dying to see that boy Father's been talking about so much. You know, the one who was Guillaume's squire. Jan Verbeke."

"Oh, him." I snorted, pausing with the brush in midair. "Frankly, I'm sick of hearing about him."

He's all Father and Guilly want to talk about these days. It's all Jan Verbeke this, Jan Verbeke that with them. They were salivating over him so much at dinner the other night, it was disgusting. I'll admit I was a little curious about him, too, at first. But it turns out the boy's a peasant. His father was a fletcher, for God's sake.

"If I have to hear his name one more time, I think I'm going to scream!" I said, and I meant it. Father is usually pretty tight-lipped about the boys and their chances, and I've had a devil of a time getting any information out of him about Hugo, but neither he nor Guilly seem able to shut up about this Verbeke boy. They think he's some kind of prodigy.

"He's sure to win, Meli," Madeleine continued, deciding on a dress and pulling out its heavy skirts from the wardrobe with a grunt. "Father says so. According to him, he's even better than Guillaume. Even Guilly says so. He's been bragging about him all over town. He's ever so proud of him. And the competition tomorrow, it's in his best skill."

"Pshaw," I replied airily, snapping my fingers dismissively and plying the brush again. "Jan Verbeke. He's a nobody. Take it from me, 'blood will out.' If anybody's going to win, it will be Hugo Brecelyn."

"Have it your way, Meli," she laughed, and I didn't bother to reply. I simply surveyed my reflection in the mirror with a satisfied smile. Let Father and Guilly say what they will. They may know archers, but I know breeding. Hugo Brecelyn will never let a fletcher's son beat him.

 I slipped out of the room while Maddie was pulling her own dress on over her head, and I was out the door before she knew I'd gone, wanting to be away before she could catch up with me or question me, and I didn't need any busybody servants tagging along to spy on me, either. I only tarried on the front step long enough to pluck a single white rose from the climbing vine outside our door. Having thus armed myself, I was ready to take the field.

 When I'd made my way across town and arrived outside the guild wall, I let myself in through the little side door that leads directly into the garden. Technically speaking I shouldn't have been inside the wall at all, at least not by myself. Women are allowed inside the chapel and in the garden, as long as they're properly chaperoned, and Father's even been known to let girls out onto the training grounds from time to time. But I'd never tried to visit the guild by myself, and it felt a little odd. Naughty, even. As long as I didn't go inside the guild hall proper, though, and if I could avoid that snoopy dolt François and his creepy little minion Albrecht, I assumed I'd be fine. If caught, I could just lie and say Father had given me permission. Nobody would doubt it.

 Still, I hesitated for a moment and looked around. I could hear the sound of men's voices out on the butts, beyond the wooden gate that leads out to the practice range. But in the garden, no one was around. So far, so good. I relaxed and took a moment to compose myself and tidy up after the dusty walk through town. I needed to make my best impression. That was the whole point, wasn't it? I meant to give Brecelyn's son an advance glimpse of what he was competing for, and although I'm confident I can outshine any girl in Louvain, I'm no fool. I know what boys are, how easy it is to infatuate them. So I knew the importance of getting to Brecelyn first, before he could have his fancy turned by someone else. But I didn't want to appear too eager. I had to play it just right.

 I shook out my skirts, and as I was smoothing them down again, I'm not sure what it was that made me turn and look back over my shoulder, to the place where the guild chapel of St. Sebastian stands in the corner of the garden. Maybe it was the feeling of eyes on me, or maybe it was just nerves. But for a moment I thought I saw the shadow of a long, thin face staring out at me from behind the rippled glass of the chapel window. It was probably my imagination. But if someone was there, I knew who it was.

 I smiled to myself, remembering that fumbling grapple against the altar at St. Genevieve's, and the memory gave me courage. It reminded me of how I always win the day, in the end. So I plucked the rose out of my bodice and raised it toward the window in a coquettish salute, just in case the poor old fool of a priest really was watching me. Then with a flounce of my skirts I turned away, ready to face the much more appealing prospect of the boys on the other side of the garden gate. I tucked the rose back into its place and I pushed through onto the butts, suitably girded for sport. Those Saint Sebastian boys wouldn't know what had hit them.

 To my great annoyance, Guillaume was right on the other side of the gate.

 He was lounging next to one of the boys' cabinets, and when he caught sight of me, a furious scowl creased his brow and he leaped to his feet. I turned away and pretended I hadn't seen him, quickening my pace, but in two long strides he'd cut me off and taken up a stance right in front of me, arms crossed, barring my way.

"Just what do you think you're doing here, Meliana?" he demanded. "I'll not have you poking around, distracting my boys," he added sternly, sounding so like a little version of my father that I laughed.

"Your boys, Guilly? From the way you talk, anyone would think you already fancy yourself a master here!" I teased, putting out a hand to arrange the collar of his tunic, but he wasn't having any of it. He shrugged me off, his frown deepening.

"I'm warning you, Meli —" he started, and I cut him off.

"No, I'm warning you, Guilly! Father knows I'm here, silly. He asked me to come himself, to, uh, choose one of the horses out in the stables for my own. I'm to meet him there."

I sounded so confident that Guillaume hesitated, unsure, so I added, "Not even you'd disrespect the wishes of a master, would you?"

It's so easy to get them all in a twist, just by saying the word 'master.'

"I think you're lying, Meli," he said evenly.

"Possibly," I replied. "Shall we go to the stables together, and tell father of your suspicions?"

When I wouldn't back down, Guilly finally pursed his lips and said,

"I'll let you by, this once. But don't let me catch you sneaking back onto the butts again, or there'll be hell to pay," and as he turned angrily to make his way inside, he added,

"When I'm master here, I can promise you this. I'll not allow girls on the butts, or in the garden. I won't let a girl within ten yards of the guild wall!"

"When you're master here, Guilly," I laughed back, smiling at my victory, "I'll roll over in my grave." And as he passed me, I leaned in quickly and gave him a moist kiss low on the corner of his mouth, before he could pull away. I know he hates it when I do that. Probably because despite himself, he likes it, too. And I know it.

As he stalked off, I heard him grumbling under his breath,

"Careful, Meli, or I might just hold you to that."

With Guillaume out of my way, I was at my leisure to scan the field. At first, I was afraid I'd lingered over my toilette too long and I was too late. Morning practice was over, and it must have been almost time for noon mess. But I soon saw with relief that although only a few of the boys were still out taking shots on the range, others were lounging by their cabinets with their squires or cooling off at the water barrels lined up along the archive wall. Most of the Journeys looked to still be hanging about somewhere, and most importantly, Hugo Brecelyn was one of them.

I spotted him right away. There was no mistaking him. As I said, breeding will tell. Everything about him screamed aristocrat.

When I first saw him, he was alone. He was leaning up under the eaves of the archives, a little ways away from the other boys, his back against the wall and one leg bent up so that his booted foot was resting flat against the wall under him. His head was bent slightly to look down at something he was doing with his hands — a bit of whittling, or the like. He was dressed more casually than I'd have dressed him, in a soft, dove-gray tunic, and his trousers of the same color were tucked down into the top of his short, black boots. But the simple attire suited him. He had an athletic grace that was apparent even in repose, and a natural authority that didn't need the trappings of his rank to assert itself. He was bigger and more powerful looking than the others, but not bulky; everything about him was in perfect proportion. He was a long, clean line, and in his pose against the wall his form was a sinuous curve that accentuated his lean, elegant body, and his long, strong legs. His profile was a beautiful line, too, under a thick shock of wavy black hair.

I expected him to be attractive, of course. He's a Journey, and the boys are always good-looking. But I never expected anything like this. This boy was the total package. It was quite an exciting turn of events, and I smiled a little to myself, as the appeal of becoming Lady Meliana Brecelyn started taking on a whole new dimension.

I'd been standing rooted in place and staring at the boy for too long. So with a squaring of my shoulders, I proceeded forward slowly, determined to play it cool. I made sure to sway my hips gently as I walked haltingly along, and I looked around as timidly as I could manage, as though I was scanning the field for my father. I knew exactly where he was, of course. I wouldn't have been there if I hadn't known he was safely away on an errand in town.

I made sure not to look at the Brecelyn boy directly, but it was awfully hard to keep my eyes off him. As I approached, I felt a jump in my pulse that grew more erratic the closer I got to him, and an unfamiliar and not entirely pleasant sensation began to steal over me. I knew what it is, though I'd rarely felt it myself. It was the response I usually elicit, in men. I clasped my hands together, only to find that my hands were trembling, and beads of sweat were forming at my temples that were only partly the result of the heavy fabric of my skin-tight dress.

Even more annoyingly, the boy hadn't looked up. He'd been whistling softly under his breath as he plied a small knife against the piece of wood in his hand, and as I came nearer, all he did was modify his whistle slightly, so one long note rose, then fell in a teasing manner. I suppose it would have been flattering, if it hadn't sounded so much like he was laughing at me.

I cast a quick look over at him. There was a smile playing at the corner of his lips, but all he did was raise his eyebrows slightly, and keep whittling. He was playing it awfully cool, too, I could see, and I guess I shouldn't have been surprised. A boy like Hugo, with his upbringing and position, he must have met plenty of girls. Society girls, ones who knew how to play the game. He was an experienced flirt, but I didn't mind. I didn't let it bother me, much. I was up to the challenge. And he might have been playing it cool, but he'd noticed me, all right. It was just a matter of playing out the charade, and we both knew it.

I came to a full stop and looked around me helplessly. By this time some of the other boys had noticed me, and they'd started to amble over in the guise of joining their friend. One big one without a tunic on at all who really was all bulging muscles stumped over and plopped his massive, sweating body heavily against the wall next to Hugo. With a lascivious grin, he slung one arm casually around Hugo's shoulders. But he was looking straight at me. Ogling me openly, actually. He was a damned fine-looking piece of meat himself, but about as subtle as a rutting pig.

He was obviously one of those big, dumb clouters. From the moment he caught sight of me, he'd been making chuffing noises and hitching up his breeches in a way I found quite disgusting, and although he had a singularly handsome face and a fine head of hair with one wayward lock that hung down fetchingly over his eyes, the effect was ruined by the insipid look on his face. And by the fact that I think he really was drooling. Ugh.

A few others followed hot on his heels, all falling over themselves to make their way over before I moved away, but I noticed they gathered around Hugo as though he was the natural focal point of their group. It was obvious they all looked up to him as their leader. A tall, thin one with a dopey smile was looking at him with a particularly fawning expression, and the obsequiousness of them all would have been quite nauseating, if it wasn't so gratifying. After all, why shouldn't the other boys look up to Hugo? His father's titled. He's loaded. He's magnificent. And he's going to be mine.

Yes, it's going to be very pleasant indeed, being Lady Meliana Brecelyn.

All the boys were clearly waiting on Hugo, watching him to see what he was going to do, but frustratingly he hadn't made any move. So I slowed to a stop, looked around me in confusion, then lifted up my hands toward the group in the helpless little gesture of a woman in need of a man's assistance. Only a cad would have ignored such an obvious cry for help, and it had the desired effect. Sort of. The big, stupid one draped over Hugo cleared his throat loudly, and giving the top of his trousers a few more tugs, bellowed,

"Lost there, little lady? And what's a fine filly like you doing out here in the pasture, all alone? Why, I'd offer you a stall in my stables, any day!"

I managed a tight little smile, but really. Again, ugh.

"She's the master's daughter, Jakob," Hugo laughed, shaking his head, but still not looking up from his whittling or moving from his casual slouch against the wall. The big lout next to him at least had the grace to flush with embarrassment, and too late to make an attempt to pull himself together and look presentable. He tried to wipe some of the thick sweat off his chest with the back of his hand, only to leave a smear of dirt across his belly. What a swine.

"Guilty as charged!" I trilled, forging on. "Can any of you boys tell me where I might find my father?"

The boys all turned to Hugo; they couldn't seem to answer a simple question for themselves when he was around.

"He'll be in his office at this hour, I expect," he said. Then he added pointedly, sounding amused again, "inside the guild."

I didn't let him rattle me. "A pity," I replied, shaking my head and turning as if to go. But I wasn't done. Not by a long shot. So I turn backed around suddenly, as though a thought had just occurred to me.

"Oh!" I exclaimed prettily. "How rude of me!," and all the boys made dismissive noises, like I could never be rude. Except for Brecelyn. I could tell he was waiting to see what my next gambit was going to be.

"I'd be remiss, if I didn't wish you boys luck tomorrow. It's all so exciting," I added breathlessly. Before I could continue, Hugo asked calmly,

"A big archery fan, are you?," and it threw me off. I scowled. He'd said it quite sarcastically.

It was a slip, but I recovered quickly. Ignoring him, I asked,

"So, who should I be rooting for tomorrow, boys? Which one of you do you think is going to win?"

"You're looking right at him!" the tall, thin boy exclaimed, nodding at Hugo, while the big boy slapped Hugo on the chest and crowed, "No question about it!"

Hugo didn't demur. He just grinned and shook his head, while the others fell all over themselves congratulating him in advance. But I knew he was going to win, too. And I liked his easy, unassuming confidence. It was terribly attractive.

"Don't feel too bad, boys," I said lightly. "Hugo's had advantages, I'm sure. Trainers and the like, on his estate. Breeding will out, I always say."

There was a confused shuffling as I was talking, and some of the boys starting snickering and poking each other. Too late, I saw I'd made another mistake. I shouldn't have let on I already knew who Hugo was. It was an amateur's mistake, and I cursed myself. I'd let the boy get under my skin, and they'd all figured out that I'd come over purposely to meet Brecelyn, but it couldn't be helped.

"Breeding will out," Hugo was repeating musingly, while the other boys grinned. "Yes, yes, I suppose it will. Eventually," he added.

And they all laughed. I couldn't see what was so funny about it. They'd all started snickering again, jostling him and slapping him and saying, "Yes, old Brecelyn here's sure to win," or the like. From the way they sounded, you'd think they were looking forward to losing to him. Boys.

"So, it's a foregone conclusion, is it?" I said archly, in my best flirty voice, taking the situation in hand and struggling to keep a coy smile plastered on my face. And finally, my efforts paid off. Hugo looked up, right at me.

"Nothing's a foregone conclusion," he said levelly, and I knew he wasn't talking just about archery.

It was all I could do to keep from scowling again. But I refused to leave the field the loser. I was going to beat him, if it killed me. So I pulled out my secret weapon: the white rose, tucked down into my bodice. All the boys' eyes went wide, watching it emerge.

When I'd pulled it all the way out, I twirled it in my hand, and said,

"I've heard you boys sometimes carry tokens into the competitions with you, for luck," and I let the suggestion hang there, waiting to see if Hugo would take the bait. When he just stayed there resting against the wall and contemplating me steadily from under partially lowered lids, after a moment or two in which I felt my temperature slowly rising despite my efforts to remain cool under his gaze, the big stupid one gave his shoulder a shake and exclaimed,

"She's offering you a token, man!"

"Really? I didn't hear anything like that," he said, infuriatingly. "I suppose I must be a little slow. You know, just a country boy," and his lip curved into a secret smile at his little joke. A country boy. Ha. A boy whose father owns half the country around here, more's like. But before I could reply, he was adding deliberately,

"Is that what you were doing, miss? Offering me a token?"

Of all the gall! He was going to make me say it, in front of all of them. From his tone, you'd have thought he expected me to beg him to take it.

"You may have it, if you want it, of course," I said, trying to sound offhand, but to my dismay my voice wobbled slightly. "From the sound of it, though, you don't think you need it!"

"On the contrary," he said smoothly, plucking the rose lightly out of my hand, "If Brecelyn's victory tomorrow is a foregone conclusion, I need all the help I can get."

Before I could try to figure out this witticism, he'd taken hold of my hand and bent to brush my fingertips with his lips, and I couldn't think about anything else.

With a quick nod over my hand that was distinctly like a dismissal, he turned and sauntered toward the stables without a backward glance, whistling again carelessly under his breath. As he went, the boys scrambled off after him, grinning at me and jostling each other as they made their own hasty gestures of farewell. It was probably just because they knew they were all late for mess already, but they looked just like courtiers following their king, and from his posture as he moved off, I could tell that Hugo Brecelyn thought he'd won that round.

I knew better. He may have left me there with a trembling slowly climbing up my limbs from the place where his lips had grazed my fingertips, but my rose was right where I wanted it to be, tucked down into the waistband of his tunic, and I knew its gentle fragrance would start doing its work. He'll be thinking of me all night, and tomorrow when he takes the field and sees me shining in the stands, I'll be the prize foremost in his mind.

So after a moment spent pulling myself together, I sauntered off myself, pleased with my morning's work.

As I went, I wondered idly just which of those slobs trailing along slavishly in Hugo's wake was the infamous Jan Verbeke.

... *Goddamned Bloody, Lying Bastard! Of all the lowdown, dirty tricks. If I never attend another Firsts at St. Sebastian's, it'll be too soon.*

I was all set to enjoy myself. I was looking ravishing in my best green dress, and when we settled ourselves in the box Father had reserved for us in the front row of the stands, all eyes in the crowd were on me. It isn't often I have the chance to bask in that kind of public attention around here, and I was almost looking forward to what I usually find a most tedious task: sitting through a long day pretending to be enthralled by watching boys play with their toys in the hot sun. It was going to be worth it, to watch my Hugo win.

I didn't even let it bother me, much, when I saw that one of the Guardsmen in attendance was that lech Brian de Gilford, and that he'd stationed himself right in front of our box. He's usually good for a laugh, actually, and he's quite attractive, for a man his age. I'll confess I've even let him get a grope or two in the past, out around the booths or under the bleachers, so I had no doubts about what was on his mind. But I didn't need him around getting in my way.

When the competition finally started and the boys filed out onto the field, I didn't have to pretend to be excited. My Journey looked absolutely fantastic. He was so regal in his pure black regalia, he didn't need any flashy lining on his cloak or gaudy color to stand out. He was the obvious class of the competition, and I couldn't resist elbowing Madeleine in the ribs and saying to her confidently,

"He's going to win it all, see if he doesn't," as the trumpet blared and he stepped forward.

"Well, duh," she responded, but I wasn't listening. My father had risen, and he was announcing the boy's name.

Imagine my confusion, my complete humiliation, when the name my father called out wasn't Hugo Brecelyn's name at all! As the stands erupted in applause around me and the boy took his bow, I was burning with outrage. I wanted to slide right under the bench, to hide the flush flaming on my face. To make matters worse, as though acknowledging the approbation of the crowd, that horrid boy had the gall to pull out my rose in a sweeping gesture, kiss it, and with a dazzling smile, throw it back to me in the stands, much to the audience's entertainment.

It came right at me; a perfect shot, and I had to reach up and catch it. It was either that, or be hit in the face with it. And as soon as I had it in my hands and fresh applause was ringing out around me, that's when he did it. That infuriating, gorgeous boy cocked his head in my direction and raised his hand in a rakish salute, and as his name reverberated through the exposition grounds around me, he gave me a great, big, exaggerated wink.

Jan Verbeke. The bloody, magnificent bastard. I could have died of embarrassment.

To add insult to injury, the other Journeys already on the field all started laughing, even that big oaf of a friend of his, Jakob Mellor. All of that would have been bad enough, but that tall, thin boy — Verbeke's obsequious little toady — he was laughing hardest of all, even though it turns out, he's really the one who's Brecelyn's son! All my plans were in ruins, and all I could do was sit there and fume, while my father and the other judges looked on in confusion. They had no idea what was going on, of course, but that the whole thing was somehow a joke at my expense was clear enough to all of Louvain.

He went on to win easily, of course. He was incredible, he could do anything. And when he did an exhibition he'd cooked up with one of the older veterans that was simply impossible to believe, he was unbeatable. Even I had to admit it was thrilling to watch him. And over the course of the competition, my good mood was eventually restored, more or less. I started rooting for him, just as hard as everyone else. Because after suffering that wink, I decided right then and there that I was going to get the last laugh. I'll win, in the end. Nobody's ever gotten the best of me.

Oh, I'll marry that insipid Brecelyn boy, make no mistake about that. I'll be Lady Meliana Brecelyn if it kills me. But I'll have Jan Verbeke, too. I'll bring him to his knees, and I'll make him my lover, just see if I don't. I've never wanted anything as much. I have to have him, really. And what I want, I get. Make no mistake about that, either.

I'm not sure I would have heard the low, warning growl emanating from the furry head under my hand if at just that point one of Meliana's entries didn't come to an end.

As it is, I'm clumsily flipping the page, absorbed in my father's story and eager to find out what happened next, when I become aware of three things all at once:

Something's woken the dogs around me.

There's a presence in the hall not far behind me and the room is noticeably colder, as though someone's let in a gust of freezing air from outside.

And further away, from the opposite direction, the sound of heavy hobnail boots is ringing out in one of the long corridors leading from the back of the castle. One of Brecelyn's men is approaching, making his way out for a turn at watch on the wall.

"*Sshh!*" I whisper to the snarling mass of fur next to me, as I hastily shove the book under its belly and hunker down next to it.

But the dog doesn't shush. Instead, it growls louder. Then maddeningly, it starts to bark.

"For God's sake, shut that thing up, will you?!" an angry voice hisses in the dark from disturbingly close, seconds before I'm kicked in the side, hard, by the toe of a highly polished boot.

A boot I recognize.

Of all people, it's Aristide.

That he's just come in from outside is obvious from the fact that the boot he's kicked me with is wet and muddy, and the heavy cloak he's wearing slung around his shoulders is beaded with dew.

"Ugh, *Marek*," he groans, apparently just recognizing me, too. "Of all the rotten luck. What in the devil are *you* doing there?" he demands, his voice an exasperated stage-whisper as he leans over and peers down at me with a scowl on his face.

I admit it. I panic.

I start hyperventilating, and I think I probably really would have cast the little book straight into the fire, if I so weren't busy clutching my side in pain and trying to catch my breath, and if the dog weren't now lying on top of it. Before I can pull myself together, Aristide's clamped a clammy hand over my mouth and crouched down next to me, as the sound of big boots approaching grows louder. It would be pretty funny if I weren't so genuinely scared, and if I could breathe, since Aristide's now hunched over in an awkward way that gives me the impression he's trying to look like he's one of the dogs.

Unfortunately, as he shifts around, one of his slick boots comes down heavily on my companion's tail.

There's a loud howl from the dog, an oath from Aristide as the dog bites him, and a grunt from me, as both of them fall into my lap in a snarling heap, and a second later a voice over my head is demanding loudly,

"*Hark! Who goes there?*"

It's not very original, but it's effective.

Terrifying, actually. Because it's coming from a massive man who's now towering threateningly over us, a man the size of a mountain, a man with a cruel, brutal face … and an unnaturally high-pitched voice.

A voice I recognize instantly, too.

So does Aristide, because I hear him grumble under his breath,

"Just *great*. Thanks a lot, *Marek*."

It's one of Brecelyn's toughest men. His staunchest yeoman. His fiercest fighter. It's Hardy the Hammer Hardouin, the giant of a man who fought against Falko in the market square.

There's a bit of a scuffle, as Aristide attempts to right himself and adopt a semblance of his usual aristocratic dignity. Wisely, I stay huddled on the floor with my head down, as Aristide extricates himself from the dog pack and draws himself up, squaring his shoulders and tugging on the bottom of his jerkin. When he's composed himself, he drawls as arrogantly as he can manage,

"Top of the evening to you, my good man," but he sounds nervous. I can't say I blame him. Even at his full height, Aristide doesn't come up much past Hardouin's navel.

"Ain't nobody supposed to be down here'n the hall at this hour," is all Hardy says, though I think I hear him spit.

"Yes, yes, *quite*," Aristide replies, giving a most unconvincing chuckle, and I really wish it were Tristan who was here instead. Aristide is even worse at this sort of thing than Taran. "But you see," he continues, babbling, "As chance would have it, I was, *um*, just up *in my own room*, of course. And, *erm*, I found myself, *ah*, a wee bit *peckish*. Yes, that's it. And so I was just on my way to the kitchen, to scrounge up a bite."

"In a traveling cloak?" the big man asks sarcastically. Apparently he's not as stupid as he looks.

"Drafty things, castles," Aristide replies.

"What's that, then?" Hardy says, gesturing down at me. "Your dog?"

"*This?*" Aristide says, prodding me again with his foot. "Oh, that's just, ugh, *my* squire," he croaks, sounding strained at having to claim me. From the tone of his voice, I can picture his eyes rolling. "I can vouch for him."

"That so? And just *who* can vouch for *you*?" Hardy demands, and there's nothing Aristide can say to that.

It's a fair catch, and we both know what's coming. Hardouin is going to rouse the household, and pretty soon we're both going to have to explain exactly what we've been doing slinking around at midnight out on the grounds (in Aristide's case) and down in the great hall (in mine) to Sir Brecelyn, and probably to Master Guillaume as well. From the sound of Aristide's knees knocking together, he's got no better explanation than I do.

"Hell, I can vouch for 'em, *both!*" a hearty voice suddenly replies, echoing through the hall from the direction of the west wing. For a crazy moment, I think the voice is coming from the suit of armor. But it's even better. It's coming from a knight in shining armor, a champion come to save us from Hardouin in the nick of time. Again. It's Falko.

"Yo there, Hardy!" he booms happily, stumping down the stairs and pulling up the bottom of his tunic to rub his hairy belly. "'*Lo*, Ari. Whazzup, Marek? Fancy meeting you boys all down here. So, you guys all as hungry as I am? After that thin excuse for a stew tonight, am I ever famished!"

If the impressive growl that emanates from Falko's gut at this pronouncement is anything to judge by, louder even than any previously heard from the dogs, Falko at least really did come downstairs looking for something to eat.

"These friends of *yours*, DeBruyn?" Hardy asks, frowning dubiously.

As chance would have it, there's nothing a big brute loves better than a man who can best him. And so ever since one afternoon not long after our evacuation, when Falko and Hardouin ran into each other going in opposite directions down one of Brecelyn's long corridors only to take one look at each other and fall into each other's arms, they've been fast friends. Hardy's been teaching Falko the subtle art of the war hammer, and in exchange Falko's been introducing the previously temperate Hardouin to the joys of wine, women, and profanity; it's a friendship made in heaven (or maybe a little to the south), and the big man treats Falko just like his long-lost son. He might as well; after the way Falko's mace connected, he's not likely to have any more of his own.

"More than friends! Why, they're friends, of the *bosom*," Falko crows, making a rude sweeping gesture in front of his chest as he comes over, and the two of them dissolve into snickers.

They're both still laughing as Aristide and I follow along behind them to the kitchens, to play out the charade that we're all downstairs because we're hungry. But Aristide and I are both silent. Aristide is probably fuming over the indignity of being rescued by Falko; I'm thinking hard.

As I scrambled to my feet, I snatched up Meliana's notebook, of course. I couldn't just leave it sitting in the middle of the floor, and between Falko's jokes and Hardouin's appreciation of them, I don't think either of them noticed me slip it into my waistband. As I was hastily trying to tuck it in, however, for a moment it flipped open, right to the page with the sketch of Meliana on it identical to the one on my old parchment square. When at that exact moment, with a crackle and a pop of its embers, the fire flared up to illuminate the drawing and I heard a grunt of surprise from Aristide, I knew he'd seen it, and that he'd recognized it. So I'm already wondering what I can possibly say to Aristide later to put him off and what I can hope to do with the book now, even before Hardy pauses as we're coming back out of the kitchens, arms full of scavenged bread and baked meats, to fix us with a menacing stare and say pointedly,

"I'm looking the other way *this* night, boys, for the sake of my good buddy Falko here. But be warned. I'll be seein' to it that Sir Hugo posts a sentry down here'n the hall at night from now on. For your own protection, mind. In a place this size, a man might easily lose his way in the dark and find himself *accidentally* in the wrong room. And I don't think I have to tell you just how dangerous that'd be."

"Say, thanks, old man! You are so right! I'm *always* getting lost around here," Falko exclaims, as oblivious to tension as ever and his mouth already stuffed with meat.

I'm pretty sure Hardy's comment is directed more at Aristide than at me, but I get the message, loud and clear. I'd already ruled out reading the book by day. There will be no more reading it at night now, either.

Once Hardy's said his goodnights and the rest of us are about to mount the stairs to the west wing, I put a hand on Falko's arm to forestall him. It's much too late and I'm too tired to think of anything original; I'll have to use my old trick, one last time — and hope I can get up before everyone else and think of something better to do with the book tomorrow.

"Uh, Falko," I say, stepping over to the suit of armor and putting my hand with the book in it up under its forearm. "Remind me again. Just what did you say this piece was called, the vambrace, or the rerebrace?"

"It's *damned* funny you should ask —!" Falko replies gleefully, as predicted showing no surprise at all that I'd be interested in the nomenclature of armor at this time of night. He starts in on an animated discussion, and I drop the book back into its resting place with a clunk, not really caring anymore if Aristide notices. There's nothing I can do about it anyway, and he's got his own secrets to worry about.

That much is clear, even before he shoves me up against the wall not much later, once we're alone in the corridor together a few steps beyond Falko's door.

"Breathe one word of tonight to that meddling master of yours," he hisses, his weasel nose quivering inches from mine, "and I can guarantee you'll regret it! At the *very* least, I'll tell him where you've taken to squirreling away your pornography from him!"

When I throw myself down on my cot back in my own room, at first I feel a little hysterical at the narrow escape downstairs, and at the absurdity of circumstance that's led Aristide to leap to a conclusion about the journal's contents so convenient for me. He's dismissed the book as just another one of my embarrassing possessions, and from the sound of it, he was offering to buy my silence with his own. That suits me fine, since I have no intention of mentioning anything about tonight to anyone anyway, and frankly, I don't care what Aristide's been up to. So it's not long before I've forgotten all about him.

I suppose what I should be feeling is upset that Hardy's warning has made finishing the journal a practical impossibility now, and I am, a little.

But the book's surely already told me everything I most wanted to know: Meliana was irresistible, and she wanted my father. She wanted Brecelyn's title, too. And what she wanted, she always got. She said so herself. So I know what happened. She got engaged to Brecelyn, and then she took my father as a lover, just as she planned. When Brecelyn found out she was pregnant, he lashed out and rigged my father's saddle.

It *is* ugly, but it's understandable. It's a predictable pattern, even, and one I know all too well: the beautiful girl, the charming rival, and the brutal boy who takes a cowardly shot in revenge. It's Tristan's and Taran's story exactly, isn't it? Yes, it was all exactly as I'd already thought. It's all so obvious, such a perfect fit, I don't let the few little discrepancies between the two stories bother me, or the details of each one that don't quite add up — that from the sound of it, Brecelyn and my father didn't start out as rivals. They were friends. Or that despite the nasty names I was yelling at Taran as I gouged at his back, the one thing I can't really believe of him is that he's a coward. And most crucially, of course, that Tristan never took things too far, with Melissande.

I suppose I should be feeling pretty upset, too, by some of what I've just read in the journal, and by the full ramifications of it. And I probably am, underneath it all. Later I'll feel it, when I let myself picture my father together with that awful girl, and when I finally have to accept the hard truths about him that I've long suspected but never wanted to believe: that he really is Melissande's father, too, and that in the end, he proved to be no better a man than 'that oaf of a friend of his,' Jakob Mellor.

But I don't want to think about any of that right now. Something else much more important is demanding all my attention, something that shone out so brilliantly from the book's pages that I still feel dazzled by it. It's here in the room with me now, welling up from within me, filling the darkness around me with warmth and light: it's the vision of my father, as a radiant and triumphant young man.

Sure, he was cocky, and vain. A posturing boy like all the others, and maybe even something of a jerk, as Royce once said. But he was also charming, gorgeous, invincible. Once he was the best of the Journeys, a boy with 'that certain something,' in spades. He was exactly the boy I've always wanted him to be.

I lie back on my cot and I close my eyes, and I picture him: my father, leaning up against the guild wall under the archive eaves, a long, clean line all in dove gray. With this image in front of me, I let go all my questions about the past and my fears for the future, and my bitter disappointment over what followed for him after. For this one night, I let myself bask in that moment long ago, content in the knowledge that once my father was a beautiful, carefree boy, the pride of St. Sebastian's and its greatest archer; that once Jan Verbeke was the most glorious boy of them all.

I drift off into sleep still picturing him, and before long I'm soaring, flying

77

high over the walls of St. Sebastian's on swift wings. With searching eyes I scan the field below for a big, beautiful boy dressed all in dove gray, and when I spot him I let out a triumphant cry; with an answering laugh of pure joy, he raises his arm to me. Soon I'm circling down toward his outstretched hand, and before unconsciousness can fully overtake me, I've come to rest safely back home inside the guild again, with him.

CHAPTER SEVEN

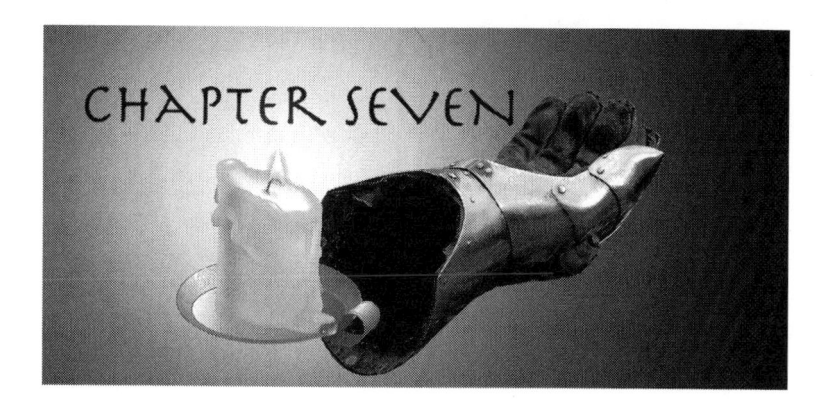

I don't make my usual early start of it the next morning. It's hard to rouse myself from the first deep sleep I've had in days, and when I wake I feel out of sorts, almost like I've got a hangover. And maybe I do. It was a late night last night and I was so drunk on the image of my father in Meliana's journal that there was bound to be some fallout; as predicted, this morning some of the book's unpleasantness has started to sink in. Even the glow of my beautiful dream is gone. All that's left of it is a disturbing impression that must have already been there last night, lurking somewhere in the back of my mind, biding its time. Now it's clinging to me like a greasy film that the dream's left behind.

By the time I get myself pulled together and downstairs, a bunch of the other boys are already lounging around at one of the long tables, eating breakfasts they've scrounged up off the sideboard. Tristan's there, digging into a big pile of pastries he's got lined up in front of him, and as soon as I see him, as always my mood lifts. Some of the glow of last night returns, too, when he catches sight of me and flashes me a big welcoming grin, waving a honeyed bun over his head at me in a rakish salute. I grin foolishly back, for a moment seeing him in my mind as my father at Firsts, waving a white rose flirtatiously to his girlfriend in the stands. When he tosses it to me in a perfect shot and I catch it, I even have to quell a silly urge to tuck it down inside my tunic as a token instead of eating it.

Gilles is already sitting on one side of Tristan and Jurian on the other, and the three of them are right in the middle of composing a particularly vivid apocryphal story about Poncellet and a butcher's block, using sausages as props. So it's for a number of reasons that I decide it would be prudent of me to sit at the other end of the table, with the squires. My head feels fuzzy as I squeeze in next to Pascal, like I'm still caught up in a haze left over from last night. There's something I should be remembering, some reason I wanted to get up early, but I can't remember what it was.

Before I can clear my head or finish a single bite of the bun in my hand,

Master Leon comes up behind me and taps me on the shoulder. I didn't even know he was in the hall.

"Master's asking for you, hotshot," he drawls, when I look up at him in surprise. "He's waiting for you up in his office. Better hurry; you're already late. *Again.*"

Master Leon's typically wandered off before giving me any hint at what the master wants of me, but it's not hard to guess. Now I remember what I was going to do this morning. I was going to figure out what to do with Meliana's journal, before it could get me into trouble. I guess it's too late for that.

I should have known Aristide's curiosity would get the better of him and that he'd make a point of getting to the book before me. I'm a little surprised he'd let his piece of leverage over me out of his hands, though, after the way he was acting about it last night; if nothing else, I'd have thought it more his style to enjoy holding it over my head. But he must have taken it straight to the master as soon as he saw what it really was, and I'm finally going to pay a price for all my midnight skulking. Even if the master actually wants to see me about something else entirely, for him to be bothering with me this morning when he was to make an early start of it for Meuse, it can't be anything good. It never is.

"Good luck, Marek," Pascal says, giving me an encouraging slap on the back as I climb reluctantly off the bench. Down the table, Tristan leans back inquiringly when he sees me getting up, but I don't meet his eye. I'm afraid he might offer to come with me, and that wouldn't do either of us any good. I'm reasonably sure by now the master can't stand him, and I certainly don't want him implicated in last night's crimes, if that's what's coming.

By 'his office,' I assume Leon must mean Sir Brecelyn's private study. The master's appropriated it for his own use during his stay, and why not? It's virtually an exact copy of his own office, back at the guild. So I hastily trot off upstairs alone, trying as I go to force down the half-chewed lump of bun that's now sticking in my throat, and I've worked myself up into a mass of nerves by the time I've managed to find the room again. It doesn't help that when I walk through the door after giving it a tentative knock, it is eerily just like facing the master in his den back at the guild.

He's seated as always behind a big wooden desk, and as always a single candle is burning that casts ghoulish shadows across his face, just as they did on the night I first met the master — and thought him my father's killer. But there is one difference: the huge painting hanging on the wall behind him.

As I step nervously into the room, Meliana Brecelyn leers out of the darkness at me, looming down over the master's head with a gloating look and competing with him for dominance of the room. Before I can stop myself, my eyes flicker up to her. I force them back down quickly, but the master's seen my reaction, and I don't think it's my imagination that the corner of his mouth twitches.

I wonder wildly if he's remembering the night he caught me in here and we stood next to each other, looking up at the painting — and he kissed me. Or maybe what he's remembering is Meliana herself, kissing the corner of his mouth. I know *I* should be thinking about my father and hating her right now, or at least trying to look a little less like I'm guiltily remembering reading her diary last night. But with that picture suspended above the master's head, what I'm really doing is wondering just what it is that the master himself actually felt about her. He doesn't look much like a man who's uncomfortable about sitting under the image of the dead girl he loved. He seems to be rather enjoying it.

"So, used the whip yet?" Guillaume says, with no preliminaries.

"Sorry, master?" It's so not what I was expecting, I must not have heard him correctly.

"Training the squires, Vervloet!" the master bellows at my confusion. "It hasn't escaped my notice that you've been slouching around the castle, neglecting your duties to your club."

The way he says it, you'd think squires' club was all his idea, not something he ruthlessly punished me for. Before I can figure out how to respond, he gets up and comes around from behind the desk and drapes an arm around my shoulder. It feels heavy, like a hunk of meat.

"There's no point pretending our popularity in Louvain isn't likely to be at an all-time low," he says confidentially. "Luckily, everyone inclined really to hate us is likely to be dead. And the survivors — they'll all have deluded themselves into thinking they're St. Sebastian's favorites, that our Saint went out of his way to save *them* from the plague, the idiots." I shift uncomfortably; this was exactly what I thought myself. "But what with relatives and loved ones, there's bound to be some resentment," he continues sourly. "We're going to have to pull out all the stops this year, to win them over again. I need every man ready, even the squires, in case we need to resort to more cheap pandering. If we've got to appeal to the lowest element with more empty shows and frivolous exhibitions, so be it. I'm counting on you for that."

I suppose it should be insulting. But by now I'm so relieved that I'm apparently not in trouble, and the master has raised a hand out in a sweeping gesture that's so seductively inviting, as though we're standing side-by-side envisioning a vista of possibilities opening up in front of us, that despite myself I start to feel excited at being included in his plans for the guild like this.

Unfortunately, what we're both really staring at in front of us is Meliana Brecelyn. She stares back at us, an unrepentant Helen before the walls she's destined to raze.

As though reading my thoughts, Guillaume says unexpectedly,

"A girl, inside the walls. It's always fatal, Marek. Remember that. Letting even one in was a serious mistake. And that one, she was the worst of them all."

He shoots me a shrewd glance. "Know the story?"

I don't know how to respond. I'm not at all sure which woman's story he means. So I'm not entirely sure what I'm confessing to when I admit,

"I've heard some of it, yes."

But the master just nods thoughtfully, thinking back over the story of the fall of Troy (at least, I *hope* that's what he's thinking about), and continues,

"They should have killed her on the spot, when that charming bastard brought her inside the walls with him. I can tell you, that's exactly what *I'll* do, if I ever catch DuBois sneaking another one in."

He says it matter-of-factly, as though there's no question that it was Tristan who snuck a girl into the Journey corridor on the eve of the Saint's day, even though the master knows full well it couldn't have been him. Wisely, I don't say anything. But unfortunately, the master isn't ready to drop the unpleasant subject of catching girls inside walls yet.

"Yes," he muses, looking up at the picture. "*'Helen of Troy.'* How appropriate! She brought the place down around her ears and reveled in it. A good, old St. Sebastian's style death by bludgeoning is just what she needed, as our ancestral rules require — I'm sure *you* agree with me."

"A good bludgeoning, right," I repeat, not sure who or what we're talking about again. Whatever it is, it isn't good. If I hear another allusion to Troy, I think I'm going to scream.

"And do you know what *did* happen to her, Marek, for her *crimes?*" he asks. When I just shake my head, beginning to wonder if I'm not about to find myself in trouble after all, after a beat he crows gleefully,

"Absolutely nothing!!!," and he starts laughing maniacally, as though this was the most uproariously funny thing he'd ever heard. I'm just debating whether I should take this as my cue to leave when he stops as abruptly as he started. He resumes his former topic so smoothly, we might never have been discussing the unnerving topic of punishing girls at all.

"Now's not the time for us to hide behind *our* walls, son!" he exclaims. "We've got to think big. Seize the day! Expand! So I've been thinking. We've been missing an opportunity with crossbows. You've shown me that. They went over a treat with the crowds, particularly that monstrosity of yours. So I've instructed Master Leon to set up some extra tutorials, once you're all back at St. Seb's, while I'm gone. You'll be checking out all the boys individually on crossbows and bringing everyone up to speed on the repeating bow. Can I count on you for that, too, Vervloet?"

I'm so flattered, I reply enthusiastically,

"Yes, master! I've already been working with the squires on crossbows, of course, but I can always do more," and the master just laughs.

"Who said anything about *squires*, son?!" he says, shaking his head.

With that, the master goes around and sits down behind his desk. When he looks up at me again, it's with an expression that says *"are you still here?,"* so I take my leave of him, as perplexed as ever after an interview with him.

It's not just that I must have misunderstood him; he can't have meant that I'm to have a hand in training the Journeys, can he? *'Desperate times call for desperate measures'* indeed, if I'm to be one of them. It's also that I get the distinct impression that despite what Meliana herself thought, Master Guillaume was never fond of her.

It could just be what Tristan's always said: there's a difference between love and lust. And I suppose I know better than most that there's a thin line between love and hate. But the master's opinion of girls in general seems depressingly low. Even more disconcerting, though, is a fact I can't deny any longer: that in his own way, the master does seem to be genuinely fond of *me*. And there can only be one reason for that.

I wander downstairs, feeling more confused than ever about what the master knows, which is saying something. By the time I've come back down into the west wing, I've even started feeling a little glad that Guillaume must by now suspect I'm the son of Jan Verbeke, and not only because it's apparently made me popular with him. He's just made it abundantly clear that if he ever finds out I'm Jan Verbeke's *daughter*, I will be in serious trouble.

When I run into Pascal on the landing as he's bustling back from some errand or other for Gilles and he falls into step next to me, asking,

"So, what did the master want with you?" and I reply,

"I have absolutely no idea," it's really nothing but the truth.

Just as we reach the bottom of the stairs, there's a resounding crash and I have to jump back up onto the step behind me to avoid being hit by a cup that comes flying out of nowhere.

"Bullseye!" Falko cries, off to my left somewhere.

He's crouched in the shadows with Jurian, where the two of them have gotten hold of Pip's toy. Boys can't resist anything with wheels, and they've built a ramp for it out of an old shield snatched off the nearby suit of armor. As they finish their breakfasts, they've been taking turns rolling the little horse down the inclined shield at some metal mugs stacked up to form a precarious tower, and Jurian's just made a direct hit. Amid mugs skittering across the floor, the little horse wobbles to a stop directly at my feet.

I stare down at it, and it shivers up at me accusingly. As I step carefully over it, all I can think is:

We can't be getting out of this place soon enough for me.

Pascal's continued on without me, and when I catch up with him again, he's lost in his own thoughts and muttering under his breath,

"Masters can be a real pain sometimes, can't they?"

I know he's not thinking about Master Guillaume anymore, and I should probably keep my mouth shut. But Pascal looks so glum I can't help it. I try to explain to him about Gilles and the chapel, and how Gilles was just out that night with me and not with any girls (or at least, not with any *other* ones). But Gilles has been having too much fun exacerbating the situation, and as a result Pascal isn't in a mood to listen to anything I have to say.

"Who's to say that redheaded girl is even at St. Genevieve's anymore?" I finally demand, exasperated.

"Oh, she's still there, all right," Pascal says grimly. Then to my surprise, he blushes.

"Don't tell me, Pascal!" I exclaim, guessing that Brecelyn's stables at midnight has been a busier place even than I'd imagined. Sure enough, he confesses.

"Armand and I *may* have borrowed Gilles's horse, and ridden past once or twice. Just to make sure she was all right, of course," he adds hastily. "And we did see her, out in the courtyard. But I didn't even get a chance to talk to her. It was a bit awkward, actually."

He doesn't elaborate, and he doesn't have to. No doubt Lady Sibilla was with her, since rumor has it she's taken the girl under her wing as her personal maid. After the way Pascal and Armand were both chasing after Sibilla this winter, it would have been awkward indeed. I just hope Armand doesn't take it into his head to throw Sibilla over and fall in love with the new girl, too. But he probably will.

Before I can think of something to say, Pascal's shoulders slump, and he sighs,

"Who am I kidding, Marek? I couldn't hope to compete with Gilles, even if I were willing to try."

I know he's right. Gilles is rich, flamboyant, gorgeous, skilled — unbelievable, really. And with his rank, if we weren't all at St. Sebastian's together, we'd be bowing and scraping to him and he'd be having his servants beat the likes of us out of his way with a stick. Or at least, he'd be having Pascal beat *me* out of his way. But I've never seen Pascal so down, and it gives me an idea. On impulse, I say,

"Pascal, why don't you let me train you, for Journey, once we're back at St. Sebastian's? I mean, seriously train you. You're a great squire, the best. But you don't always want to play second fiddle to Gilles, do you? Wouldn't you like to be the hero yourself, just once?" It's something I've wanted for myself, of course. But it didn't work out for me. Pascal just might be another matter, and the more I think about it, the more I think getting it for him would be sweet indeed. "With a little work, I can get you in, I'm sure."

I'm actually not sure at all; I mean, Pascal is handsome and athletic enough, but he's got terrible aim. I'm determined to get at least one of the squires in, though, and Remy's not interested (annoyingly enough, since he's sure he's off to Guards with Taran), Rennie's too ugly, just like me, and I doubt Master Guillaume wants a Journey who can't say more than the name of his chicken. That leaves Pascal and Armand, who's an even worse shot than Pascal is. Pascal's my best bet.

Pascal frowns, considering my proposition. Finally, he asks, "Do you think Gilles would mind?"

"Possibly," I admit, worried this will put him off. Instead he grins, "All right then, that settles it. I'm in!" and I know Tristan was right. I really should have minded my own business.

<hr>

BY THIS TIME MOST OF THE BOYS HAVE ALREADY DISPERSED, since it's getting late and everyone has taken Master Guillaume's warning about being punctual for practice to heart. Behind me Jurian and Falko are drawing their game to a close and I've naturally assumed that the other Journeys must be out in the armory by now, so Pascal and I are already halfway across the room on our way out to catch up with them before I notice that Tristan's still in the hall waiting for me. He's half-sitting on one of the tables, lounging with his hip hiked up against it to let one long, booted leg swing back and forth beneath him. I hasten over to him, and after reassuring him that all was well with the master (as far as I could tell), I ask, "Ready to go out?"

"Not yet," he says, without stirring from his perch against the table. To my inquiring look, he replies,

"I'm waiting for one of the others. So we can line up for practice, together," and I nod. I start looking around for Gilles, pleased that Tristan's falling in with my plans so nicely without me having to convince him. That is, until Tristan says, "And here he comes now," and I turn, and I see who it is.

"Falko?!" I demand, incredulous.

Sure enough, Falko's just hung the shield back on the suit of armor. Cramming a last pastry into his mouth and wiping his hands on his pants, he grabs up his bow and starts making his way over.

"I'm surprised it hasn't occurred to *you* yet, Marek," Tristan says, using the studiously casual tone of his that always makes me apprehensive. "I'd have thought it was obvious that what we need this year is a new ally."

"Falko?!?" I repeat, even more alarmed. It's not very charitable, I suppose, after the way Falko saved me last night. But Tristan and Falko have never been particular friends, and there can only be one reason Tristan would want him as an ally: Falko is the only pure clouter left. Well, the only *other* one.

"Look Tristan," I say quickly, before Falko can reach us. "After training with Baylen, you can't really think Falko is going to be much help to you on clouts, can you?" I think back to the day Falko tried to take me through his clout motion and we ended up in a heap out on the field. "He's not a very good trainer."

"No, he isn't," Tristan concedes. "But *you* are," and when he won't meet my eye, I get it — even before he adds, "And Falko's got to pass the *other* skills too, remember?"

I suppose Tristan could simply want to help a friend; after Falko's beating in the marketplace, all the boys have taken a hand in trying to rehabilitate him. But I doubt it. Tristan must be more pessimistic about his own chances than I feared, to be plotting to have *me* train Falko. If counting on Falko with his shattered shoulder to beat Taran out is the best plan for Guards that Tristan can come up with, our troubles are even worse than I'd thought.

I'm saved from a long morning worrying about how to keep us from becoming embroiled in some scheme with Falko (before I can win Tristan over to a scheme of my own) when one of the veterans appears in the hall with last-minute orders from Master Guillaume. The Journeys are to retrieve for themselves today, since the master isn't the only one set to leave Brecelyn's this morning. The first advance crew is scheduled to head out for St. Sebastian's, and we squires are needed to help get it ready.

When Tristan and Falko accordingly head off for the armory arm-in-arm without me and Pascal strides off to round up the other squires, I find myself temporarily alone in the hall. It's an opportunity I didn't expect, an extraordinary stroke of luck, actually: I'm to have a chance to retrieve Meliana's journal this morning after all, before it really can get me into trouble.

After my scare with the master, I know what I should do with it. The book holds no more secrets for me, and with Tristan out on the field cultivating Falko, it's time to call my duty to the past done and to concentrate on the more pressing problem of Tristan's future. There's a roaring fire blazing in the hearth; it'd be the work of a moment to throw it in, and sending the whole thing up in flames seems like a fitting end for it.

But I can't bring myself to do it. Instead, I nip over to the suit of armor, casting nervous glances around the room as I go. I'm distracted looking about for a new place to hide the little book as I shove my hand down into the glove, and at first my fumbling hand finds nothing but air. Assuming the journal's simply fallen further down into the gauntlet, I stretch out my fingers, straining them as far as they'll go, and I feel around against the cold, curved metal. I wiggle them down into each individual finger. Then I wiggle them some more.

Then I detach the glove entirely and shake it upside down.

Nothing comes out.

It's empty, and the little book is gone.

I replace the glove carefully, lost in thought. I suppose the journal could have fallen out unnoticed and gotten lost, at some point during Falko's and Jurian's game. But I know that's not what happened.

I guess I was wrong. About a lot of things.

My luck, for one.

And about the book not coming back to St. Sebastian's. It'll be coming back to the guild with me, all right — just not in my possession.

I stand there immobile in the shadow of the armor for a long time. And eventually, I manage to convince myself it's a good thing. The book is gone, as surely as if I had thrown it straight into the fire. I could never have voluntarily left off reading it, but this way I'm to be spared the sordid details of my father's story, just when it was surely about to get really ugly. Now I'll never have to read any more of the diary, and I know I'll never see it again, as long as I keep my mouth shut. And that's precisely what I'm going to do. Because to get it back, I really would have to become a thief at St. Sebastian's — and from the one boy most likely to enjoy proving that the old rumors about me were nothing but the truth.

I have only one regret about the little book, actually. I really wish Meliana had described the butts trick she saw my father do at Firsts, the one that was unbeatable. I know it sounds crazy, but Tristan and my father have gotten so tangled up in my mind, I think I really was expecting to find something in my father's past that would help me get Tristan through the trials. Butts is Tristan's specialty, too, and he won once doing a trick of my father's. It would have been sweet if he could have done it again. Besides, I've racked my brain and I *have* made progress, but I still haven't managed to transform my idea of winning Gilles over as Tristan's ally into a brilliant strategy; at least, not one Tristan's likely to find extraordinary enough for him. An unbeatable trick would have solved all my problems.

There's nothing I can do about it now, and so I square my shoulders, and I head off to look for Pascal and the others. And as I go, I keep telling myself it's all worked out for the best. But with each step I take down the long corridors, I feel myself going slower and slower, and getting more and more depressed. By the time I reach the short flight of stairs leading to Brecelyn's storerooms, I'm not moving at all.

I lower myself heavily onto one of the stone steps, and I rest my head in my hands.

It's not just that I can't really feel happy about losing control of the journal, or about the thought of it in Aristide's hands. Now that the book's quite literally been closed for me on my father's Journey days, something has started to dawn on me — something I must have known all along but been unwilling to admit, even to myself.

I *have* wanted to know about my father's past. I've been dying to know about it my whole life. That wasn't a lie. But just like Tristan and his investigations, I've also been using finding out about my father's youth as a distraction, to keep from having to face harder tasks. Tristan's been right, all along: knowing why Sir Hugo hated my father can never be enough. I won't have done my duty for my father until I've found out why Brecelyn killed him.

And that's not all. Gilles has just been teasing me with all his talk of plotting in chapels. But I guess his insinuations have done their work, all too well. Oh, I'm not gullible enough to have fallen into the trap of suspecting *Aristide* of treason. But I do know one aristocrat I'd be more than willing to believe is a traitor, and one I know for a fact to have already plotted against the crown. Tristan's been spinning idle theories simply to keep his mind off Melissande, and I've done my best to resist them. I really have. But the truth is he hasn't said anything I hadn't already thought myself. This is Brecelyn's estate, and his chapel out in the woods. If there is a new plot afoot Sir Hugo's surely in the thick of it, and I can't shake a growing certainty now that the plot that got my father killed isn't over yet. Not by a long shot.

In fact, I have a horrible premonition it's only just begun.

I allow myself one moment of pure and utter anxiety and despair, and I let out a howl of frustration that echoes endlessly down the empty hall.

Then I get up and shake it off, and I start down the corridor again.

By the time I join the boys out in the armory, I've managed to pull myself together, more or less. But I feel distinctly like a man who's taken up some old, familiar burdens, and funnily enough, with all the more serious things that are hanging over my head, it's actually something I haven't mentioned yet that's making me feel the most this way.

It's such a small thing. A trifle, really. But it's proving hard to ignore, and since I'm being brutally honest with myself, I may as well admit it. There *is* one thing about the notebook that's still bothering me.

It's nothing to do with losing it, or about any of its revelations, exactly. It's just something about the image of my father in it as Meliana described him — the very thing that's been bothering me all morning, since waking from my dream last night.

The thing is, I was expecting my father to sound a lot like Tristan. To be exactly like him, in fact. That's why I fell so hard for Tristan in the first place, isn't it? Because I thought him like my father, as a young man.

And my father *did* sound like Tristan. A lot.

But he also sounded a little like Taran.

And I wasn't at all prepared for that.

CHAPTER EIGHT

It's on a night exactly one week later that my dear sister Melissande finally makes her reappearance, on the very eve of our departure for the guild.

After days spent in a flurry of packing, we squires have gotten the wagons all loaded and ready; it's been a big job, since Master Leon insisted we do an organized job of it, and we've spent countless hours sorting through the jumbled piles of paraphernalia grabbed up randomly during our evacuation and dumped unceremoniously into Brecelyn's storerooms, with some pretty interesting results. Old Master Gheeraert's secret stash wasn't the only surprise, but a combination of modesty and fear prevents me from listing some of the things we discovered.

With these items discretely returned to their owners and everything else packed up we're ready to roll, and we're scheduled to head out for St. Sebastian's first thing in the morning.

Anticipation is running high; all week, we've been waylaying vets from the advance crews, anxious to hear their reports.

"Bodies everywhere!" one of them declared, his mouth full, when we convinced him to sit with us at mess one evening and give us all his news. "Men, women, dogs, rats, you name it. And don't even ask me what we found under the master's desk."

But no two reports are the same, and none of us really has any idea what to expect. So we've all been sitting around at table after supper, digesting our last whopping dinner at the castle and arguing for a long time about what we're likely to find back at St. Sebastian's, though the boys' opinions are all more a reflection of their own dispositions than of real information.

"Razed to the ground, for sure," Jurian exclaims, sounding rather pleased at the prospect.

"Nonsense. Hardly a stone's out of place, I'll wager," Gilles drawls, but since none of us really knows anything, eventually the conversation dwindles.

By now most everyone else has wandered upstairs for bed, and the hall is empty except for us boys. At first Tristan tries to start up one last half-hearted debate about Sir Brecelyn, but as predicted his enthusiasm for the topic has been noticeably waning with the approach of our leave-taking, and it's not long before he, too, falls silent. The big fire is burning low and a mellow atmosphere has fallen over us, the sort of contemplative mood that comes with any departure, even from a place one is desperate to leave. It's made worse tonight by our uncertainty about what we'll find back at the guild on the morrow, and by the fact that for some of the boys, our departure from Brecelyn's has to be tinged with some regret. Even before what happens next, I'm all too aware that unfortunately enough, Tristan is one of them.

It's at just this moment that Melissande suddenly appears on the landing, silhouetted against the darkness of the empty corridor beyond. She couldn't have timed her arrival better to catch our full attention, and I'll give her this: she knows how to make an entrance. Poised timidly at the top of the stairs, in the gentle firelight she's glowing with such exquisite beauty that she's positively ethereal. She looks pale and drawn, but it suits her. She's as delicate as a painted saint, a poignant Madonna deprived of her child. She's completely alone; not even Pip is with her, and she looks more fragile and vulnerable than ever.

As she pauses there, twisting her hands together and darting her eyes around the room as though trying to work up the courage to join us, she looks anxiously around for something. Or someone, rather. It doesn't take much to see who it is. As soon as her eyes meet Tristan's, she freezes, eyes locked on his. Her expression is so bereft and pitiful, and Tristan's staring back with a stricken look that so mirrors hers, it makes me think uncomfortably that maybe Tristan was right. They do look for all the world like two people who share an unspoken sympathy. With a sinking feeling, I can't help noticing that as always, the two of them together make a picture that looks right. And right now, what they look like is a perfect picture of star-crossed lovers, just as Tristan once envisioned them. Only now there's nothing glamorous about it. They both look unbearably sad.

Regrettably, it's also at this exact moment that Taran decides to rejoin us.

He staggers in on the opposite side of the room, from down a dark corridor entering the hall near the big fire. I have no idea where the hallway leads or what he can have been doing there, and his appearance is so unexpected, we all recoil just as though he were a stereotypical stage villain making a dramatic entrance. I can almost hear ominous music starting up in my head. Next to me Remy's making nervous little noises, and the boys have all started shuffling uneasily on the benches. Somewhere I think I hear Falko choking on something, and at the sudden sight of Taran after so long and when I'm so unprepared, my blood starts pounding in my ears and my heart leaps up violently in my chest. It's not just that nobody expected Taran to turn up. It's also that nobody could have expected him to turn up like *this*.

He looks so unlike his usual self, in fact, that at first I don't even recognize him.

Taran's never been a snappy dresser, like Gilles. But he's always crisp and clean, and he's certainly not one to go around in a state of undress or to remove his shirt at the drop of a hat, like the other boys. Tonight, though, his once-white shirt is soiled and stained, and it's entirely unfastened. It's hanging open so wide and it's slipping off his shoulder so far it looks about to fall off, and for some reason the fact that one corner of it is still tucked into the back of his trousers just makes him look even more disheveled. A vast expanse of his impressive chest is exposed, and it's gleaming in the firelight in a way that makes me think of Tristan, the first time I was ever alone in a room with him, and I swooned. Or Jurian on the night of Baylen's wedding, with an alcohol-fueled sweat diffusing through his pores. And Taran's exuding *something* mighty powerful, all right. But he looks so dark and dangerous, so like a man and not a boy, that to my dismay it's Aristide's awful word *virility* that leaps disturbingly to mind. His thick, dark hair is disheveled, too, both tousled up erratically and hanging down in a wave over his eyes, and he looks completely wild. I've never seen him this way. It's terribly sexy, really.

He's stinking drunk.

The temperature in the room seems to have suddenly gotten significantly hotter, and I don't think it's just me, although I know my own cheeks are flaming. If I thought Tristan was impressive when he's inebriated, it's nothing to Taran. He's absolutely petrifying. Almost as much as he's absolutely gorgeous.

Taran looks capable of anything, and at the sight of him a nervous tension fills the hall. Up on the landing Melissande's eyes go wide, and she looks as paralyzed as a doe caught in an open meadow. Just when I think she's about to turn tail and flee like a deer, too, Taran's eyes focus, and they come to rest on her with a glassy but malevolent stare.

"Ah, if it isn't the little woman!" he slurs, lurching forward. "Don't you have a *warm* greeting for your fiancé?"

In three long strides he reaches her. With a swift grab, he pulls her by the arm down the steps and into the middle of the room with him. The boys have all come to their feet, but we're all still so surprised (and they are engaged, after all) that all we can do is stand there watching them as though they really were part of a show being staged for our benefit.

By this point Taran has whirled Melissande around to face him, and for a moment he looms over her, swaying slightly. Then he reaches out and grabs her head between his hands, gripping her temples like a vise and tilting her face up to his. Dark, raw bruises stain his knuckles, as though he's been smashing his fists repeatedly against a wall, and the expression on his face as he stares down at her looks like he could be contemplating crushing her skull. I don't doubt he could do it.

Just as Tristan stirs beside me and I'm afraid he's about to leap forward and object, Taran suddenly jerks Melissande's head back, not hard enough to hurt her really, but fast and hard enough to make her cry out in surprise. And while her mouth is still wide open, he bends down swiftly and covers her mouth with his own, and he gives her a huge, sloppy, voracious kiss.

With one hand still pressed hard against the back of her head, he slides the other hand down her back, pulling her against him until her body is molded against his, and he keeps kissing her, so vigorously that he looks like he could be trying to eat her alive. The kiss is so rough and raw, so brutally deliberate, it seems to be fueled more by anger than desire.

Even so, it looks pretty damn good.

Somewhere next to me, one of the boys says *"Golly,"* in a small voice; everyone else is too stunned to do anything but keep gaping at them, and after a moment or two Melissande abandons all pretense at indifference. I can't say I blame her; Taran's so hot he's about to catch fire, and I know from experience what it is to be faced with the onslaught of that incredible body and those burning lips. With an embarrassing little noise, she flings her arms around him, and before long she's pressing herself up against Taran so hard and wrapping her arms and legs around him so enthusiastically she looks like she's trying to climb him like a tree. The whole shocking display goes on for so long and Taran's kiss is so vulgar and insistent, after a while I fear he's going to lower her to the ground and they're going to consummate the marriage again on the floor right in front of us before anyone can come to their senses enough to figure out how to stop them.

Then as quickly as he grabbed her, Taran drops Melissande flat. She's so off balance and he lets go of her so suddenly that she falls to the floor at his feet with a thud. Without looking down, he steps right over her and stumbles off across the hall, wiping his mouth with the back of his hand.

"Wow!" Falko exclaims enthusiastically, slapping me on the back. "If that's how he greets her when she's his *fiancée*, I can't wait to see how he greets her when she's his *wife!*"

Needless to say, that's not what I'm thinking at all. It's a good thing Sir Brecelyn doesn't have a rose garden. Otherwise, I'm sure I wouldn't be the only one running straight out of the hall and into it, jostling for a prime spot to vomit quietly behind a rosebush.

Remy hurries after Taran with a squeak, as Gilles and Pascal rush forward to help a very embarrassed and humiliated Melissande shakily to her feet. Next to me Tristan is fuming, torn between storming after Taran to demand satisfaction, and running to Melissande. But he can't really do either, and after a moment in which steam looks ready to come out of his ears, Tristan also stalks off, simmering with frustration, to disappear up the stairs to the west wing.

As he goes, I can't help but notice he's clenching and unclenching his fists.

None of the rest of us says anything as we help a thoroughly flustered Melissande back to her room, and afterward we finally disperse for the evening, having had about enough entertainment for one night. I'm not sure what the other boys make of it all, and I'm not entirely sure what I make of it, either. Taran's as drunk as a skunk, and I'm pretty sure that unlike Tristan, he's not going to have to pretend tomorrow not to remember anything that happened tonight. Even so, in some vague way at least, I'm sure he knew what he was doing. It didn't escape my notice that just before Taran disappeared from sight, he paused at the edge of the room and cast a glare of pure hatred back over his shoulder that took in all three of us: Melissande, Tristan, and me. And there can be only one explanation for that. He must have seen the look Melissande was giving Tristan when he stumbled into the hall. Even through his haze of intoxication, it had to have been as clear to Taran as it was to everyone else that despite having conceived a child with *him*, underneath it all it's still Tristan Melissande really loves. Why *I* should have come into it, though, is beyond me.

We've got an early morning and a long day ahead of us tomorrow, but as I lumber back to my own room I know that as usual, sleep won't come. Sure enough, when I throw myself down heavily on my cot in my dark little cell I'm far too agitated to sleep. I'm not thinking about the upcoming competitions, or about the fact that we're leaving in the morning, or even about Melissande — at least, not directly. I'm sure it's perfectly obvious what I am thinking about, or rather, what I'm trying not to think about — without much success. But I'm also thinking about going back to St. Sebastian's tomorrow with a fear that's almost as sharp as my longing for it. If that's all destroyed, too, I don't think I'll be able to stand it.

When at last exhaustion overtakes me and I slip into troubled sleep, inevitably I am back at the guild again. But not in barracks, or high over the field. I'm in Taran's hot little room. He's pulling my head back, his mouth closing over mine in a voracious, obliterating kiss. Just as his lips meet mine, he demands hoarsely, *"Tell me! Tell me you're not thinking about Tristan right now,"* and horribly, there are three of us in one embrace again. But there's nothing sensual about the feeling it gives me. Instead, something slides sickeningly through my belly, because this time, the one who is there in the embrace with us is Melissande.

I WAKE UP RIDICULOUSLY EARLY THE NEXT MORNING. I'VE SLEPT badly, and I'm in no mood to spend another minute in this room or anywhere in this castle. So I get up and out as quickly as possible, ready to do anything I can to hasten our departure along. After dressing hurriedly and bustling downstairs, I find that this morning, I really am the first one up. At least, the first of those who actually went to bed at all.

As I'm passing a window in one of the long corridors, I stop to take a look outside to get a sense of the time. The sun isn't even peeking over the hills yet; there's only a faint glow above the distant line of trees to suggest that daylight is on its way. The gloomy pre-dawn light is so dim, it takes me a moment to realize with surprise that the narrow window overlooks the little garden where the white gazebo stands. It's the place where Tristan gave Melissande her kiss at Thirds, and the place where I sat what was only a few days ago, after working the merlin with Taran. The place where I realized I was in love with him.

To my even greater surprise, Taran is there, sitting on the gazebo steps. He must have been there all night. He's still dressed in the same rumpled clothing he was wearing yesterday, and he's hunched over with his elbows on his knees, his bent head resting heavily in his hands. When I see him, I come to a stop. I stand there immobile at the window watching him, for a long time. Then I don't know what comes over me. I go straight into the kitchen and whip up an approximation of the concoction Albrecht used to make for us after we'd been on a bender, and I take it out to him. Maybe it's because he's sitting in almost the exact place and position I was in, that day. Or maybe it's because after last night, I'm having a hard time thinking of Taran as subtle.

At first, I don't think he even notices it when I sit down gingerly on the gazebo steps next to him. I don't say anything. I just hold the drink out under his nose, and after a while he reaches down one big hand and takes it from me. Without a word, he tosses it back in a single gulp. Then he drops the cup onto the ground in front of him and kicks it into the corner of the garden.

He's still in a foul mood, I see.

I really should go. It's not just foolish to stay; it's probably dangerous. Taran's hands are hanging limp and empty in front of him, and they look as big and powerful as ever as I stare down silently at them. I'm sure he could strangle me easily if he tried, and maybe that's what he's thinking about right now, from the way he's staring down at them, too. But they're also beautiful. I don't know why I never noticed it before. His fingers are long and tapered, and they look every bit skilled enough to carve the exquisite little animals he makes. For some reason, the painful bruises on his knuckles just make them look more sensitive. Vulnerable, even. And when I think of those hands carving the little horse, I can't help it. A tear trickles down my cheek, and I guess I do know why I came out here, after all. Why I can't leave, yet. There's something I have to say to him — if only to clear the air. If only so I can go back to safely hating him again.

"Taran," I say, my voice cracking a little, and not only because it's the first time I've spoken today, or even because it's the first time I've spoken to him since I attacked him in the clearing. "Taran, I'm so sorry."

I don't know what reaction I expected. Maybe none. But I've had my say and I'm about to get up and go, when Taran does something that shocks me more than anything he's ever done. Maybe more than anything's ever shocked me in my whole life.

Suddenly he looks up right at me. His searching expression is unreadable, and for a moment I feel as frozen as Melissande was last night. And when those big hands do shoot out for me, I recoil reflexively, and my hands fly up in alarm and surprise. But he's not reaching for my neck.

His hands clutch at my waist.

He throws his head down heavily, straight into my lap.

And starts crying.

At first I'm so stunned, I just sit there stone still staring down at him in bewilderment, my arms still raised in the air. Then without thinking I fold my arms around him, and I bend my own head down on top of his.

"Oh, Taran, I'm so sorry!" I whisper roughly, as I weave my hands through his hair. "I'm so sorry, about the *baby*."

The word has an immediate effect. Taran comes to his senses in an instant, and with a gurgled oath, he leaps to his feet and about a full yard backward away from me. He stands there snorting like a bull and looking down at me furiously, while a parade of grimaces crosses his face as though he's struggling to find something bad enough to say to me. He looks so disgusted with me I can hardly believe his head was resting in my arms just a moment ago. Eyes blazing, he sputters incredulously,

"You're sorry, about the *baby*?!"

Then he snarls, curls his lip, spits — and he's gone.

I'm left sitting there reeling, shaking like a marionette that's been jerked around violently on its strings. Unbelievable! What in the hell just happened?! How in the world did I let him get to me, *again*? I could kick myself, or tear out my own hair; how could I have let him past my defenses so easily, after I swore I'd never let myself get sucked in by him like that again? For once I'm not the one who's been acting melodramatic and hysterical, but I still feel like Taran's made a fool of me anyway. How dare he lure *me* into consoling *him*, after all he's done to me, and then have the audacity to be furious at me for it! Well, I'm plenty mad, too. At him, but even more, at myself.

Okay. Maybe I shouldn't have mentioned the baby. But I'm glad I did. I got it off my chest, and at least now I won't have to pity him anymore. I can go back to hating him without feeling guilty about it, and from now on, I fully intend to. After the horrible scene last night and the equally bizarre one now, it should be easy. Particularly since Taran's made it more than clear that he's back to hating me, too.

Yes, it should be very easy. But somehow, I can't seem to get up off the gazebo steps.

The place on my lap where Taran's head was resting feels heavy, like I can still feel the weight of it, pressing me down. Under me, the boards of the

95

gazebo are hard and scratchy. Around me, the thick air is close, cloying, and I can't get a breath. No insects crawl, no birds sing. Nothing stirs, nothing moves in the garden. This place that was so vibrant only days ago is dead, a decaying tangle of weeds. All the life's gone out of it. There's nothing left, but the unbearable weight of emptiness.

I'm still sitting there immobile on the gazebo steps much later, when Armand comes bustling around the corner looking for me.

"Oh, *there* you are, Marek," he exclaims. "I've been looking for you for over half an hour! Pascal's getting antsy. You'd better come along, if you want to have any place for Tristan's stuff."

It must be well past dawn by now, and as Armand soon informs me, the other boys are already out in the armory getting the last of their masters' equipment and their own loaded into the wagons. Although we packed the boys' bows in their cases yesterday, we didn't want to risk leaving our archery gear out in the open overnight. I know Armand's right; if I wait around here any longer all the prime spots in our wagon will be taken, and I still haven't packed up my own things. Even so, I don't know how much longer I would have remained there unmoving, if at just that moment there weren't a bloodcurdling scream.

"What on earth was *that*?" Armand cries, jumping backward in alarm and crossing himself. The sound's brought me to my feet, too, even though I know exactly what it is.

"It's a bird," I reply, my voice cracking on the word.

"Ugh," Armand says, shivering. "It sounds like someone's strangling it."

"No," I say, looking out over his shoulder into the sky. "I think, somewhere out in Brecelyn's woods, a hawk has caught a mouse in its claws."

"Funny," Armand exclaims with a shudder, as I let him lead me away. "It sounds more like it's the mouse that's caught the hawk."

The image this comment conjures up is so absurd, as I hasten inside with Armand it never occurs to me at all that he could be right.

ONCE INDOORS, AFTER ASSURING ARMAND I'LL BE QUICK ABOUT it, I make a hasty detour back to the west wing just long enough to grab up my own things and Tristan's out of our rooms, shoving everything into the old traveling bag Father Abelard once gave me. In particular, I make sure to stuff in the embroidered handkerchief I found out in the chapel, thrusting it way down into the bottom of the bag next to Baylen's whip, just in case there really is anyone back at the guild who might recognize it. As I do, there's a little crunching sound, like a bit of parchment crumpling. I've not bothered to clean out the bag since our last visit here, so I suppose it must be a remnant from Tristan's ill-fated poetry contest, probably the love letter of Jurian's about Baylen that I picked up off the floor that night. I can't bring myself to fish it out and toss it away now, and with Baylen dead it's too depressing to think about. So I just cram it down in further, and before long I'm shouldering the bag and heading out to join the boys.

To buy some time, I take a shortcut to the armory. A little-used stairway at the far end of the west wing gives access directly onto a warren of corridors at the back of the castle; it's mostly used by the servants to move unobtrusively between floors so we boys rarely use it, and it'll mean taking a route past the guards' barracks, which I usually like to avoid. But at this time of day the bowels of the castle should be virtually empty and it'll be quicker, and I've taken Armand's warning about space in the wagons to heart. So I scurry down the narrow steps into the twisting, turning passageways below at top speed, pleased that I was right; everyone's already up and out and busy with the preparations for our departure, and there's no one about to get in my way. I'm already approaching the turn that will take me out into the armory hallway and I'm barreling along fast toward it, when I hear a hum of voices emanating from a dark stairwell just ahead on the opposite site of the corridor, and I pull up short.

The voices are low and unintelligible. But one is male and the other female, and the male voice is thick and cajoling. From the tone of it, I was about to blunder into a 'lovers' rendezvous,' as Gilles would say, and the thought of interrupting one of Brecelyn's men with a serving wench when I'm all alone in the abandoned corridor gives me pause — particularly if he should happen to be a man the size of Hardy the Hammer. Or worse, old Hardy himself, following up on some of Falko's lessons.

I'm just debating if I can duck past without being seen or if I'm going to have to lose precious time by retracing my steps, when the voices grow louder and the girl lets out a high-pitched giggle. A giggle that's distinctly familiar. Of all things, it's *Tristan*, with the very same maid I caught him with the other day. That he'd get up early this morning to have one last go at her for information about Melissande is the last thing I'd have expected of him, after last night.

I don't mean to eavesdrop. I really don't. But I have even less taste for disrupting Tristan again than I do for interrupting one of Sir Hugo's men. So I hesitate for a moment in indecision, and just as I'm resigning myself to the hassle of circling back up via the west wing again, the girl's shrill voice rises and I hear her clearly — and I can't leave. From what she's saying, it sounds like now at the eleventh hour Tristan's questions are finally going to pay off, and he's about to make a real discovery.

"Was he *angry*? He was furious!" the girl titters. "Snatched it right out of her hand, didn't he?"

A muffled exchange ensues, consisting mostly of noises I don't care to describe. But in it all I make out the following string of teasing exclamations from the girl, given in apparent response to murmured prodding from Tristan:

"How should I know what he thought was in it?" Then, "If you're so curious, why don't you just ask him yourself?," and finally, "Well, he suspected *something*, that's for sure."

Burning with curiosity, I start to creep closer. Then the girl laughs, "I mean, he's big all right! But he's not stupid," and all at once I don't want to hear any more.

I put my head down and dart around the corner, and I keep sprinting down the armory hallway even after I'm in the clear, giddy with relief that no figures were visible in the shadows of the stairwell as I passed; Tristan and the girl must have been further up and around the bend of its spiraling steps than I'd thought.

Then I crash right into Rennie, who's come sauntering around a corner and into the hallway from the opposite direction.

"Whoa, Marek! Look where you're going, why don't you?" he grumbles as I fall over backwards, knocking the pastry he's been eating out of his mouth in the process. It tumbles down the front of his shirt and onto the floor, leaving a splotchy trail of honey in its wake.

"Aw man, just look what you've done to my nice fresh tunic."

From what I can see, the shirt Rennie's got on looks just as rancid and filthy as they usually do; becoming engaged hasn't had the salutary effect on his hygiene that we were all hoping it would. But I don't say so. I just scramble to my feet, treading rather heavily on the fallen pastry in the process, and as we fall into step together, I help him wipe himself off — me dabbing absently at the honey with my sleeve and him scraping it off with his fingers and licking them as he shoves the hastily retrieved bun back into his mouth, dirt and all.

"Oh yeah, before I forget," he slurps, gesturing at the bag over my shoulder. "That Tristan's stuff? Well, if it's not — I just left him, out in the kitchen. He told me to remind you to pack up his things from his room, if you haven't already."

"Who?" I say, surely not hearing him right through all that pastry.

"Your *master*, idiot. Remember him?" he says, slapping me on the back of the head with a sticky hand, hard — and I stumble a few paces forward.

"Hey, steady, Marek! Sorry old man — I didn't realize you'd fallen so hard. You all right?" Rennie asks, and I nod absently, although I'm actually feeling rather dizzy.

If Rennie's just left Tristan out in the kitchen, the voice I heard in the stairwell can't have been his. Somebody *else* has been spending his last hours at the castle seducing the maids for information, too, and I'm too busy wondering which of the boys it can be to respond to Rennie. That is, if the voice I heard belonged to a boy at all.

The one thing I don't bother to wonder is which boy the voices were talking *about*.

I've just started picturing a worrisome scenario of Tristan sitting up at midnight alone in his room last night, hunched over an inkpot and a piece of parchment, spurred on by the burning look he exchanged with Melissande to compose another one of his flowery love letters for her and then slipping it to Pip to deliver for him this morning, when footsteps ring out in the hallway behind us.

It's the maid, crossing the corridor arm-in-arm with one of the cook's assistants back near the spot where I collided with Rennie. They've got their heads together and they're chatting and flirting away so animatedly as they head for the kitchen that I give myself a mental kick. It was only a couple of servants I overheard, gossiping amongst themselves, and after so recently convincing myself that one outrageous theory was nothing but the truth, I should have known better than to go concocting another. I mean, with all the people at the castle, that I should happen to know the ones a pair of servants would be talking about to each other is absurd — almost as unlikely as that I'd actually be acquainted with the owner of a handkerchief lost in Brecelyn's chapel, for instance.

"If you're going to stand around ogling the maids all morning, I'm going on without you," Rennie exclaims, jogging me out of my thoughts.

I give him a slap of my own in response, and we race each other the rest of the way down the long hall.

By the time we reach the armory I've even started laughing a little to myself at my own foolishness, and at my persistent inability to recognize voices accurately. I really am hopeless! Even now, as the voice of the cook's assistant drifts down the corridor behind me, I could swear it sounds entirely different than it did only a minute ago when I heard it back in the stairwell.

I suppose it's just because I can still hear the girl's distinctive laughter, too, that what I'm picturing in the back of my mind we as go through the armory door is a little blue bottle with a cork stopper, disappearing down the front of her dress.

WE FIND THE ARMORY IN AN UPROAR. NOT ONLY HAVE WE LEFT A bigger job for this morning than we bargained for and the squires are all accordingly rushing around frantically, but right in the middle of it all is Falko. He's stuffing his equipment roughly into an oversized bag, grabbing things up indiscriminately and generally making a mess while Pascal flaps around agitatedly behind him.

"What in the world are *you* doing out here, Falko?" I demand. "Where's Pruie?"

"He's gone," Falko replies flatly, and for a horrible moment, I think he means the worst. I guess it is a miracle Pruie's survived so long, after his virulent case of the plague.

"Oh, don't look so stricken, Marek. He's not *dead*," Falko exclaims, seeing my expression.

"Then where is he?"

"*Pascal* here isn't allowing any more pets in barracks," Falko says, jerking his head in Pascal's direction, and I have to say, I rather side with Pascal on that. I can still picture the wet spot left behind by Pruie's plague-riddled rabbit. "And Pruie wouldn't leave here without his chicken. So I took him and Buboes along to Roxanne this morning. She'll keep an eye on him, and he can help look out for her, too."

We all know that Charles' uncle's farm isn't far from here, and Falko's been borrowing Gilles's horse on a regular basis to ride over and visit Roxanne there.

"Between you and me," he says, gesturing toward his temple and using a loud whisper that's probably meant to sound confidential, "I'm not sure Pruie's really *right* anymore, *in the head*," as if we didn't all know that already.

It's probably for the best, but I can't help feeling sad, particularly since we're not to have a chance to say goodbye to the big guy. Just as Falko's blustering,

"Happy as a clam, when I left him," and trying unobtrusively to dab at his eyes with the bottom of his tunic, a thought occurs to me.

"Whatever are you going to do now about a squire, Falko?"

"Yeah, you'll need one — through Firsts, anyway," Armand adds, not very tactfully; with his shoulder, nobody is expecting Falko to need a squire much longer than that.

Falko takes no notice. He gestures to a pile of helmets stacked in a corner and exclaims heartily,

"I'll just use little Faranzi there," and for a moment, I wonder about the state of *Falko's* head. Then there's a small yelp from behind the pile, and I get it.

"You can't mean Frans, surely!" I cry, irritated, and not just because even after all this time he doesn't know the boy's name. I'd rather come to think of Frans as my property. I don't need Falko stealing *my* squire.

"Why not? You've got him trained up a treat. We'll get on famously," Falko insists blithely.

There's another pathetic whine from behind the helmets, and I do sympathize. But I'm afraid there's nothing for it. Poor Frans is stuck, and after a minute or two, I decide it's a good thing. It'll be excellent training for the boy. A real trial by fire. And when eventually Falko is out, I know just what to do with him. If my plans all go well, Pascal will be needing a squire, won't he? And unlike Falko, I'm sure Pascal really will get on famously with

Frans. I can already picture how right they'll look, taking the field together at Journeys.

WITH A FINAL LOOK AROUND THE ARMORY, WE GATHER THE LAST load of equipment into our arms and head out for the wagons as a group. Falko's leading the way, and he's keeping up such a steady stream of his usual blather and our bundles are so unwieldy that none of us are paying much attention to where we're going. When we round a corner quickly only to come face to face with a gaggle of girls, we almost plow right into them.

Melissande's not one of them, of course, nor any of her friends still at the convent, but there are always plenty of other females around Brecelyn's place — servants, and the daughters of Brecelyn's men — and they're always trying to run into the Journeys. This pack must have been waiting nearby, on the lookout for a last chance encounter.

As soon as Falko sees them he skids to a stop, his mouth still open. Then he drops his equipment to the floor with a yelp of his own, and he turns around and bounds off down the hall, looking like he's seen a ghost and muttering a hasty excuse that's completely unintelligible. The girls are all tittering as the rest of us scramble to gather up Falko's gear for him, and pretty soon we're all laughing, too, since it's pretty obvious what's happened. One of these girls must have been Falko's winter indiscretion.

By the time we're approaching the place in front of the castle where our vehicles are lined up and waiting, we've been having so much fun making jokes amongst ourselves at Falko's expense that I've put the morning's strange encounters behind me and I'm feeling much better. So much better, in fact, that I don't stop to think that it's a little hypocritical of me to be so willing to forgive a boy his infidelity that I can even laugh at it — when the boy in question is Falko.

WHEN WE COME OUT INTO BRECELYN'S YARD, WE FIND IT transformed. It's now a madhouse, and the place is swarming with activity. Crews of veterans are riding up and down our line of vehicles, shouting out orders and kicking up great clouds of dust, while men in St. Sebastian's garb mill around, piling their personal belongings into wagons or helping to secure the loads. There are horses and mules everywhere, some already rigged up and others being led into their traces by Brecelyn's men, so I have to dodge around through a sea of hooves to get to our wagon. By the time I'm halfway across the yard, my pulse is ticking along erratically and my nerves are tingling — with excitement, not fear. It's only in the midst of all this chaos that it's really hit me. It's finally happening. I'm going back to St. Sebastian's.

Even better, up ahead I see Tristan and Gilles lounging against the side of our wagon. The other Journeys have already headed out for the guild on horseback, but the boys have decided to slum it and ride back with us in our wagon.

"It's going to be delightful!" Gilles is exclaiming to a dubious Pascal, as I come up beside them. "Why should you squires have all the fun?" he adds, making no move to get out of Pascal's way as he struggles a particularly overstuffed bag of Falko's over the side of the wagon.

Gilles is dressed in an odd get-up this morning, something that looks like it's probably his idea of appropriate attire for a rustic hayride. He could have ripped his shirt right off the back of a peasant bride, but as always it looks fabulous on him — though I'm not sure why he's got what looks like a small reaper's sickle hanging from his belt. I don't ask.

Next to him, Tristan is looking trim and handsome, just like his old self. And when he returns my greeting with one of his charming smiles, I see he's also playing it up this morning. He's plucked a piece of straw from the back of the wagon and he's holding it between his teeth at a rakish angle, but up close, it's all too apparent that his forced cheerfulness is strained. Last night took its toll on him, too, and he looks so drawn and tired I suspect he's probably really chewing on the hay to keep from gritting his teeth.

It doesn't take long for his façade to crack. While we squires have been working around the idle boys to finish arranging everything in the wagon, Tristan's been staring out over my shoulder with increasing irritation, to the place where the horses carrying the other Journeys back to St. Sebastian's can be seen at a distance on the horizon. When he finally he explodes,

"Bloody Bastard!," it's not hard to guess who he's talking about, even though I've been avoiding looking in that direction. I am surprised, though. I've rarely heard him use the boys' favorite expletive before, for obvious reasons. Last night's wretched scene with Melissande must have gotten to him even more than I suspected.

"*Comforting* her!" he sneers. "Why, the brute's been blaming *her* for what happened! Isn't that just like a *man*, to blame the woman?" he adds, as though he weren't one himself.

Next to him, Gilles coughs.

Tristan hasn't noticed; he's too busy grumbling and glaring off after Taran. But the sound brings me to a stop, and I glance over at Gilles. As suspected, Gilles has one of those supercilious looks on his face he gets when he's about to make a pronouncement, and he's begun plucking at his sleeve with that preening motion he uses when he's trying to appear casual. When his mouth opens and his eyebrows go up, I find I'm literally holding my breath.

"Has it not occurred to you, dear boy …" he drawls. Then his eyes come to rest on a line of uneven stitches near his cuff. "Zounds, Pascal!" he exclaims, breaking off. "Are you blind, man? The thread you've used to mend this tear is *entirely* the wrong color!"

"Is it, master?" Pascal replies innocently, but I think he's smirking. It's terribly frustrating, and not only because it's tiresome that two of them are still feuding. I don't know why, but I'm positive Gilles was about to come out and tell us plainly just what it is he thinks he knows about Taran and Melissande.

At just that moment, Master Leon and Brian de Gilford emerge from the interior of the castle, signaling to the veterans stationed at the front of the line. There's a flurry of activity as the call to move out goes up, and with a languid stretch Gilles climbs into the wagon, his intended comment forgotten. As I scramble up into the rocking wagon after him with the rest of the boys, I tell myself it doesn't matter. I don't want to know. Besides, surely Gilles can't really know anything that could adequately explain Taran's outrageous behavior, and anyway, I'm supposed to be forgetting all about him.

One of the mounted veterans makes a last sweep down the line of loaded wagons, and finding everything ready, he raises another cry. Soon our wagon is slowly moving under us. Tristan and Gilles have sprawled themselves out in the prime spots right in the center, leaning their backs against the driver's seat and stretching their long legs out in front of them in the straw. That's left the rest of us nothing to do but wedge ourselves in around the edges, amongst the baggage. Pascal is under such a large pile of bundles (no doubt full of Gilles's clothes) that I can hardly see him, and I have to take both Frans and the old dog Popinjay onto my lap (since of course dogs don't count as pets. Dogs in barracks is a tradition, and there wouldn't be any way to keep them out anyway), but I'm nestled in cozily under Tristan's arm, and I don't mind.

We've only rolled a few yards when Remy appears, carrying a large satchel in his arms and darting between the wagons. He's not been around all morning, and I just assumed he was riding back with Taran. Now he trots up breathlessly alongside our wagon and tosses his bundle over the side with a grin. It lands in my lap next to Frans.

"Can I squeeze in next to *you*, Marek?" he says brightly, grabbing onto the wagon in preparation of swinging himself over the side.

Unexpectedly, Gilles preempts him. "We're all full up here," he drawls dismissively, sprawling himself out wider. Tristan points to the wagon behind us and adds rudely,

"You can ride back there, with the kitchen boys and other riff-raff," and I guess I don't blame him. He's never liked Remy, and after last night he's in no mood to have to put up with Taran's squire. Remy has no choice but to let go and fall back with a frown to wait for the wagon full of servants behind us. It looks to be even more crowded than our own, but it's a merry party. Auguste waves his stick to Remy in greeting from the front of it, and as boisterous hands reach down to pull him up into the wagon, a number of kitchen maids in particular all seem extraordinarily happy to welcome him aboard. The last I see of him, two of them have wrestled him onto their laps between them, and at the helpless expression on his face as they start tussling and fussing over him, I smile. Poor Remy!

Our caravan makes its way in fits and starts across Brecelyn's castle yard, one of many all trying to funnel through the main gate at once. When at last it's our turn and we rumble out under the shadow of the portcullis, Tristan raises his hand back toward the castle in a move that's half a salute and half a rude gesture, and he calls out sarcastically,

"Sir Hugo Brecelyn, your castle, and all your lands! I bid you a *long* farewell!" and we all laugh. And when he adds,

"And if I never see any of you again, it'll be too soon!," I couldn't agree more.

And yet, as the castle begins to recede behind us, I find that a strange feeling is lingering. It's not regret, exactly, and it has nothing to do with Remy — at least, not directly. It's the bag he threw into the wagon. It's much too big to hold his own meager possessions. It must be Taran's.

It's pressing down against my thigh, and there's something small and hard in the bottom of it that's digging into my skin. It feels a lot like one of those wooden figurines he carves, about the size and shape of the little hawk he once made for me, and it's uncomfortable. But that's not really what's bothering me. It's that the bag feels heavy, like the weight of Taran's head pressing down on my lap. And that somewhere shoved down into that bag, I strongly suspect there's something soft and filmy, and sea-foam green. The palms of my hands start itching to rip the bag open and rummage through it, to see. Or to toss the whole thing over the side.

Instead, I shove the bag over as far as I can and tell myself to ignore it, although I can still feel the heaviness of it, even after it's off of my lap. And as the castle slowly fades into the distance, I find myself looking back and scanning the walls, searching for a glimpse of white against the vast expanse of dark stone. When I do spot Brecelyn's gazebo, standing silent sentinel over the empty garden, I watch it for a long time. It grows smaller and smaller, until it's just a speck of white. And then it's gone. I keep staring at the place where it disappeared from view, straining to see it long after I could really hope to make it out anymore. And when I know that I'll never see it again, I don't know what to feel.

Now that I'm headed back to St. Sebastian's with Tristan, I'm leaving it behind forever.

CHAPTER NINE

We're a raucous party on the ride back. Out in the open countryside the morning air is crisp and the smell of the misty fields around us is sweet, and every turn of the wheel is taking us closer to St. Sebastian's. It's a fresh start, and once Brecelyn's walls are out of sight my excitement about returning to the guild takes over again. The boys are all in high spirits. Everybody is laughing and talking, and when now and then somebody breaks into song, we all join in. It's probably a cover for our nervousness, and leaning as I am heavily against Tristan I can feel that he, too, is filled with a restless energy that's more fueled by anticipation about what we'll find back at home than by any lingering regrets.

Gilles is in a particularly effusive mood. It's not long before he launches in on a long and rather gruesome story from his childhood about a bear-baiting gone awry that would be pretty riveting, if I thought any of it were true. As it is, when he gets to the point in his tale where a section of bleachers collapses, sending his elocution instructor tumbling into the bear pit with the dogs, I tune out.

"You've never heard such a colorful string of impeccably pronounced profanities as the one the old boy let rip, when the bear took a big bite out of his buttocks!" Gilles exclaims, but I'm not listening. Tristan's got his arm slung partly along the back of the wagon and partly around my shoulder, and as we've been rolling along my head's come to a rest against his chest. I can feel the contours of his body through the fabric of his shirt, just as I could that terrible day I thought Rennie had died in barracks. It should feel comforting, and it does, in part: I'm already one step closer to being back right where I want to be. It won't be long now.

But it's also an uncomfortable reminder of the little space that's always between us, and it must be the motion of the wagon or the roughness of the tunic Tristan's wearing, or the fact that every now and then out of the corner of my eye I think I catch a glimpse of the other Journeys through the trees on the path ahead — but that little barrier separating us doesn't feel quite as thin to me this morning as it used to. Today it's chafing, and as we've been

105

rumbling along closer and closer to Louvain, it's started to bother me. So I make a decision. If I'm really hoping to find everything miraculously the same at St. Sebastian's as it was last year, I've got to set about falling actively back in love with Tristan myself.

And why not? If I'm going to spend the rest of my life devoted to an unrequited love, well, then it really should be *love*. Besides, I know being hopelessly in love with Tristan last year made me a better squire — at least, I can't be the squire Tristan needs and be in love with anybody *else*.

If anyone had told me just a year ago that *that* would be a problem, I'd have laughed right in his face. But I've tried so hard to suppress my feelings for Tristan for so long that I really have started to think of him as my brother, or at least to feel a little uncomfortable about thinking of him as anything else. It's Tristan I've really been in love with underneath it all, all along, though, I'm sure. So it's just a matter of giving myself permission to indulge in romantic feelings for him. Once I do, all the old feelings will come rushing back, and it should be easy enough. I'll just let myself finally take a good, long look at him, the next time he's in his bath.

That should do the trick.

But for some reason, Tristan's voice floats back to me, saying "*how in the devil do you tell the difference between lust and love, Marek?,*" and I suspect it's not going to be as simple as that. Surely, though, the thought has nothing to do with the fact that to my very great annoyance, Taran's bag is still pressing insistently against my leg.

As chance would have it, as I've been thinking we've come to the place where our wagons are to turn off the main road and into the woods. We're going to St. Sebastian's via the back way, to avoid the trek through town; the paths are bumpier and the road narrower, but it's a shortcut and nobody's entirely sure what our reception will be back in Louvain. I don't mind; we're being tossed around plenty anyway, and a few stray branches to the face is a small price to pay for avoiding town. But at the same place where the track to the guild branches off from Brecelyn's road, another path strikes out in the opposite direction, and I know exactly where it leads. It heads back toward the Vendon Abbey. And toward my old home.

It's funny, but I haven't thought about it for a long time. Maybe it has something to do with reading my father's story, but as the wagon turns under us and I find myself peering intently down that other path disappearing into the woods behind us, I have a sharp and unexpected longing to see the place again, and it brings with it a strange fancy. Tristan's lounging confidently in the center of the wagon, laughing at Gilles's stories, and although it's Gilles who's talking, we're all arrayed around Tristan in a way that leaves no doubt that as always, he's the natural focal point of our group. Tristan is so like a king holding court among his courtiers that for a moment his shirt under my hands becomes a dove-gray tunic, and just like that, I'm headed back to St. Sebastian's with my father, as he was when he was a young man.

I try to shake the feeling off. Tristan is *not* my father. He's *not* my brother. It's thinking like this that's confused me, it's thinking like this that has to stop. But just as when we left the castle, the sensation lingers and I can't banish it with pure will. And I guess, despite myself I don't really want to. It's what I've wanted all along, isn't it? To see Tristan succeed where my father failed. So with a promise to myself that it will be my last indulgence, I snuggle in closer under Tristan's protective arm and I spend the rest of the way through the woods letting myself revel in the feeling of it — that I'm with my father, young and carefree again, and that I'm on my way to the guild with him to help him win the big prize, the one he so well deserved but never got, the one that will make us both immortal. The one that will let us stay together just like this, forever.

The sensation is so sweet, my excitement at returning to St. Sebastian's soars and nothing can mar my contentment — not even the oppressive weight of Taran's bag. Or the insidious little thought it stirs in the back of my mind that if my father really were restored to me as he was then, he surely wouldn't be *exactly* like Tristan. At least, not exclusively.

When I tune into the boys' conversation again, Gilles is still holding forth.

"There's nothing like it, boys, let me tell you," he's exclaiming. "Ah, the feel of her rocking under you, spraying mist on your brow!"

He's moved on from the untimely demise of his servant, I see, and at first I fear he's talking about some overzealous conquest, until Tristan turns to me and says,

"What do you say, kid? Shall we do it, one day, just like we said? Hop a boat to adventure, and sail the high seas? Just imagine it. Sleeping in a hammock below decks, skirmishing with pirates, and romancing beauties in foreign ports!"

"It sounds more like a way to get scurvy and bedbugs, and to spend a lot of time bent over the keel," I say dryly, and Tristan laughs. But I'm serious. It sounds worse to me than the army. If nothing else, I doubt even Tristan could figure out how to find a place for me to change in private on a ship full of men. It's just the boys spouting off, but I tune out again, and go back to my fantasy; I'll not ruin my homecoming by thinking about what's to come if we have to leave the guild, before we're even all the way back.

We've been rolling through familiar woods for a while now, but I've been so lost in my thoughts that it comes as a surprise when Pascal suddenly shoves the bundles on his lap unceremoniously off onto Gilles and struggles to his feet. He brings one hand up to his brow and points out in front of him with the other, and as he raises an excited cry, his legs are straddled so wide to keep his balance in the rocking wagon that he really could be standing on the deck of a ship, eagerly spotting land after a long voyage at sea.

"They're *standing!*" he shouts, pumping his fists in the air. Through the trees ahead the guild walls are just coming into view, and although they look more battered and crumbling than I remember, they are still standing. I raise an excited cry of my own, and in a flash, Pascal's jumped over the side of the wagon. Armand isn't far behind, and soon the two of them are racing down the road, pushing each other and darting between the wagons ahead of us, making it into one of their competitions to be the first boy back to St. Seb's.

I struggle Frans off my lap and dump him over the side of the wagon, and with a shove to Popinjay I clamber out after him. Rennie's right with me, and though we'll never hope to keep up with the fastest squires, we take off down the road after them, with Frans following along behind. Pretty soon Remy catches us up, having leapt from his wagon, too, and we take the last mile to the guild down the dusty L'île-Charleroi road at a dead run, shouting and laughing and moving as fast as we ever have during retrievals, while Gilles and Tristan call out amused encouragements to us from their perch in the wagon. We only pause long enough to catch our breath in the shade of Porte L'île, and as we race along toward the beacon of the guild, whooping and hollering and calling out to the men in the wagons who are all now cheering us on, nothing can dampen my spirits — not even the disturbing wisps of smoke curling up into the sky from inside the guild walls. Or the sight of the postern gate ahead, hanging smashed and broken from its hinges.

Nothing, that is, until we pass through it and I see what's on the other side.

Pascal and Armand have ground to a halt in front of us, and at first I'm so intent on trying to keep from barreling into them that I don't look around me. And when I do, at first I'm confused, like I can't remember where we're supposed to be, or like we've burst into the wrong place. The yard spins dizzyingly, and not only because I'm still catching my balance after coming to a stop so fast. I don't know what I expected. Except that I did expect to recognize the place.

I step forward silently to stand shoulder-to-shoulder with the others, all of us gaping as the bustle of activity in the yard flows around us. Looking out at the scene before me, helpless tears spring up behind my eyes, both at the overwhelming feeling of finally being back inside these longed-for walls again, and in bewilderment at finding everything within them so changed.

I suppose it could be worse. The main guild complex is still intact, more or less. It's mostly built of solid brick and stone, too sturdy for our winter guests to have bothered trying to bring it down entirely, and seeing to its repair must have been the first priority of our advance crews. Even now a veritable army of workmen is crawling over it, hammers in hand. With all the ladders laid up against it, the now patchwork building looks like nothing so much as a cagey old boar, cornered in a glen and bristling with javelins, making one last valiant attempt to shake off its attackers. Or maybe it would be more accurate to say it looks like Rennie squatting on the lavatory floor and submitting reluctantly to a make-over, since the work in progress surely must go beyond what's strictly necessary to restore the place. But every single one of the outbuildings that should be standing in front of us is gone.

There's no trace of the infirmary, the shops, or any of the storerooms. All that's left is an empty field. The vast maze of structures that was once here has been reduced to nothing more than blackened patches of earth; not one wooden structure, one stick of wood, or any piece of flammable material left inside the guild walls survived the onslaught of the villagers. Some of it they wantonly destroyed or pillaged, the rest they consumed as fuel once they'd settled in to squat here and wait out their fate. Our own men have kindled new fires to burn off what's left of the wreckage (and no doubt, to burn off what's left of the pillagers), making it all too easy to imagine what it must have been like on that terrible night when we abandoned the guild into the hands of its destroyers.

The place is anything but abandoned now. Scores of men are hard at work clearing away debris or conferring with carpenters, and the yard is parked so full of carts laden with building materials that the wagons of our caravan have to pull up short outside the walls. As a strange backdrop to the smoking wasteland before us, out on the far field canvas tents and colorful pavilions of the sort we rent out as booths during the trials have been pitched to serve as temporary replacements for the missing buildings, and so many men are swarming around these, too, that I don't know whether it's more like looking out over the carnage of a battlefield or the festivities of a tournament. With all the smoke and noise and commotion, it's a total mess.

"What's this, the squires' social hour?" a passing veteran barks at us as we stand huddled together, gawking at the scene in front of us. "If all the furniture isn't back inside the main hall by time for evening mess, we'll be using your backs as tables!"

I turn to the others, and we all frown. Then we break into grins. It *is* a mess. A bloody mess, and we're probably going to have to clean up most of it. But it's our mess. Our beloved, glorious mess, just as Master Guillaume said. Even if it's in ruins, there's no place any of us would rather be than St. Sebastian's.

We're back.

After that first moment of disorientation, the guild has come back into focus around me. I recognize its familiar bones under its bruised skin, the beloved face of a long-lost friend, and I'm so glad to see it again I don't care what it looks like. I throw my head back, fall on my knees, and stretch my arms out wide. In my best imitation of Tristan's top-of-the-wall voice, or maybe of Master Guillaume's, I cry out fervently,

"St. Sebastian, my love! You'll rise again, if I have to build you back all by myself, brick by brick!" and all the boys laugh. I'm laughing, too, as I leap up and look around for Tristan. But I don't see him anywhere. So I throw myself into Remy's arms instead.

Pretty soon Pascal, Armand, and Rennie pile on, and we wrestle around a bit in a disorderly group hug, sort of a riotous version of one of our huddles out on the field. Frans is hopping around excitedly next to us, too, and I pull him in with us. He's set to squire for Falko this season, so for better or worse, he's one of us now.

◆―――――◆

"COME ON, BOYS. WE'D BETTER GET TO WORK," PASCAL EXCLAIMS, breaking away first. "I don't fancy being somebody's table tonight. And I, for one, have no doubt Gilles would really make me do it."

We decide to unload our archery equipment first and take it straight to the boys' rooms, since surely their wooden Journeymen's cabinets were among the first things to go. Out by the wagons I glance around for Tristan, but he's nowhere to be seen. He and Gilles have mysteriously disappeared, in that way typical of the Journeys whenever there's work to be done. I'd have liked to stage a little ceremonial scene of homecoming with Tristan, too, but I guess it's already business as usual again, and when Remy and I shoulder our bundles and he inadvertently bumps me with his, I'm actually pretty glad that there's no sign of any of the Journeys.

Once we're inside its long corridors, the guild seems more like its old self. There are plenty of signs of violence in here, too, and in the crowded passageways a strange smell is clinging to the woodwork that's all too reminiscent of the days of the plague — an unpleasant combination of vinegar and herbs, the smells of neglect and decay mixed with the scent of recent fumigations. But there are always strange men and strange smells around the guild and it's usually too dark in the hallways to see much anyway, and after Brecelyn's lofty, lonely castle, the familiar tight spaces of the guild are a warm embrace. Although a vague sense that things are somehow different is lingering even in here, in its arteries the old rhythms are still pulsing along and as I fall in with them, I know it won't be long before I feel just the like the boy I was when I left here again.

I'm so busy drinking in all the old sights and sounds that in the press of bodies I almost collide with Pascal when he comes to an abrupt stop outside the barracks. His frown is back, and I can't say I blame him. The air is so foul even I can't really want to breathe it in, and the only way to describe the smell coming from the other side of the door is nasty. Even more ominously, the door is shut tight; the only other time I've seen it closed during the day was when we thought someone was dead inside.

"We can't stop to investigate now, Pascal. Your master isn't the only one who'd love nothing more than an excuse to treat us like furniture," Armand exclaims, prodding him into motion again with his shoulder, and when the phrase *"don't even ask me what we found under the master's desk"* echoes unpleasantly in my mind, I'm glad enough at the reprieve. We'll deal with barracks later.

As might have been expected, we find the Journeys' rooms in pristine condition. The advance crews have them thoroughly scrubbed, and they've all been refurnished. Even the floorboards look new, and the impression of cleanliness and order is increased by the fact that they're empty. Tristan's not here, and neither are the other Journeys. The scent of Gilles's flowery perfume is lingering on the air, but there's no sign of any of the boys.

"The Journeymen?" one of the veterans laughs, when Remy stops him to ask after his master. "They've been marched straight off for wall-mending duty, as part of their *training*. Master Leon says it'll do wonders for developing their shoulders."

Nobody believes Master Leon really cares about the boys' shoulders, of course. It turns out the guild's already engaged every stone mason and wall builder in Louvain, and he's too cheap to pay the hefty fees the local guilds insist on imposing on workmen from outside. Master Guillaume may have intended to spare the Journeys any of the work of recovery, but Master Guillaume isn't here and Master Leon has no compunction about pressing the boys into service.

The boys will hate spending their first day back in drudgery rather than in archery, and I can't say I'm happy about it, either. I'd been counting on spending the day settling back in with Tristan, since I was right. Even in the midst of all the dust and debris and over the incessant sounds of sawing and hammering, as soon as we stepped foot back inside St. Sebastian's the trials suddenly felt closer. Imminent, even. It's high time I started doing *something* serious to get Tristan ready, since it's only now that it's really started to sink in:

Firsts can't be more than two months away.

I still haven't figured out exactly what I'm going to say to Tristan to make him enthusiastic about my half-formed idea for training him, however; I could use some time to think about it, and when I picture Remy's master safely packed off somewhere out on the wall all day, too, I can't be anything but glad of the delay. Wedged in as I am in the narrow corridor amongst the jostling squires, it's starting to dawn on me that it's going to be a lot harder to avoid close encounters with boys again here in the guild's cramped quarters than it was back at Brecelyn's spacious castle — particularly with one of them. And after this morning, I'm in no hurry to have any of *those* again. But the truth is I didn't handle encounters with *any* of them with much grace last year. This year I know I have to do better, and what happens next does little to reassure me.

When we've dodged our way back outside and out to the wagons to get started on our own chore, I see right away that it isn't just going to be tedious, it's going to backbreaking. I had no idea our mess tables were so big or so heavy, since we weren't the ones who loaded them. I can't imagine how the vets managed the job during the chaos of our evacuation, since the solid oak things are massive. Even the benches are too heavy and unwieldy for one of us to carry alone.

After some initial confusion, Frans and Remy grab up one of the long benches between them and disappear back through the wall with it, leaving the rest of us follow with the matching table. It takes all four of us to carry it, and when Armand and Pascal grab up one end, I'm stuck at the other end with Rennie. He's not much stronger than I am, so it's a real struggle for us to keep pace with the stronger boys, particularly once they decide to see which of them can walk the fastest going backwards.

I'm already puffing and sweating like a plow horse by the time we're maneuvering the huge table down the narrow corridor past the masters' offices. Even before we make it to the entrance to the great hall my arms feel stretched out like noodles and what little strength I had is gone. That's when we discover that one leaf of the door is locked and bolted shut and the table is too wide to fit between the closed panel and the doorframe. We're going to have to tilt it up at an awkward angle to fit it through, and down at the other end it's Pascal who lifts his side — Pascal, who's opposite me. I'm going to have to lift my side, too.

Somehow I manage to struggle the table up to shoulder height, but I'll never be able to hold it there. So with a squawk of *"go, go!"* I give it a desperate shove, trying to push it through the doorway as quickly as possible.

I don't make it. Halfway through, it slips from my hands.

With a grating scrape of wood on wood and a crashing shudder that shakes the rafters, the table sticks tight in the doorframe. Our forward momentum just wedges it in tighter.

"Oof, watch it, butterfingers!" Rennie gasps, his stomach colliding with the table.

"Oh, for Pete's sake! What happened back there?" Pascal calls back to us.

"*Marek* here dropped his side," Rennie replies irritably. When he sees me fumbling around next to him, he adds, "and he's too weak to lift it up again. We're stuck."

It's embarrassing enough, even before a trilling voice calls out from somewhere inside the great hall,

"Hang on a sec, Marek! *I'll* save you!"

It's Remy, and in a few moments he's circled around via the vestibule and kitchens to come out into the hallway behind us. Instead of grabbing onto the table next to me as I expect him to, he takes hold of it by first slipping his arms around me, underneath my own. I guess it's just because there isn't much room to maneuver here, but he presses up close behind me and his arms intertwine with mine in a way that feels unexpectedly intimate.

Remy is just being silly, I know; I can't shake him off or seem ungrateful, like a bad sport, and none of the others would understand why having to be helped is so infuriating to me. But my cheeks are flaming, and I feel so much like I did when Remy passed close to me after my disastrous clouts test, on his way out to succeed where I had failed, that I almost expect him to kiss the corner of my mouth. So when his lips do brush my cheek, I'm gritting my teeth just as I was that day, although he's just leaning down to say in a silky voice tinged with amusement,

"Why, isn't it funny? It's just like the story we were talking about at the castle, Marek. About the Trojan horse."

I don't think it's very funny. I'd thought I'd left that damned horse behind.

"You know," he continues, adopting the tone one uses for reciting a quotation: *"Four times the horse stuck fast on the very threshold of Troy —!"*

His hand slides down over my stomach. Before I can thrust it away, he gives the slight swell he finds there a playful squeeze. *"— And four times from its belly there came a resounding clash!* But the Trojans were too blind to take warning."

Unbelievable. He's *flirting* with me. Only Remy would think this was a good moment to attempt to 'woo' me.

"Yeah," Rennie pipes up, nudging me with his elbow as I wrestle Remy's probing hand off me and put it firmly back onto the table. "It's a good thing I'm not as superstitious as *Armand*, or I'd think it was a bad omen! Why, the old hall itself is refusing to let you in, Marek," and he starts cackling.

But I don't see anything funny about that, either. Instead, I feel a pricking down my spine that's only partly due to the way Remy's breath is ruffling the hairs on the back of my neck. The spot I've lurched to a stop is directly below the place on the wall where the plaque marking the entrance to the main hall is prominently displayed. One line engraved there in particular swims accusingly on the periphery of my vision:

No Women Allowed.

"What's the holdup out there, gents?" Pascal demands, as I give the big wooden beast of a table another futile shove, trying to force my way in.

The table lets out another groan, sticking fast and stubbornly barring my way.

"Remy's been spending too much time sitting in on Taran's tutorials, that's what," Rennie crows. "He's started spouting poetry!"

"Rein him in, boys," Pascal calls back. "We've got a dozen more tables just like this one out in the wagons, at least. We'll never unload them all by dinnertime, if Remy's going to compose a sonnet every time Marek wedges one in the doorway."

The boys are enjoying themselves immensely, and they're all laughing as

Remy's muscles tense against me, and with one smooth, easy slide of his arms between mine he lifts the table free. But I'm not even smiling. It's not just that it took Remy embarrassingly little effort to do what I couldn't, and that I'm still trapped between him and the table. Or even that the sign looming over me threateningly now seems to be screaming a warning: *No Girls! No Girls!* No Girls Allowed.

It's also that as I cross the threshold into the great hall within the tight circle of Remy's arms, I'm having an awfully hard time feeling much like a boy at all.

"ST. IRENE'S NIGHTGOWN!" RENNIE EXCLAIMS, DROPPING THE table hard himself when we're only a few steps into the room. The suddenness of it knocks us all off-balance, and when I right myself enough to extricate myself from Remy and look around me, my sentiments match Rennie's exactly.

There's nothing in the room except for us, the table, and the bench Remy and Frans just brought in. Frans is sitting on the bench, staring out in front of him in awe, and wordlessly we all file over and sit down in a line next to him.

The great hall has always been imposing. It's a big room, the biggest in the guild, and compared to the warren of closets and claustrophobic hallways that surrounds it, it's massive. But I've never seen it empty like this. Without one other stick of furniture in it, it's as vast and as lofty as the cathedral of St. Margaret's in the market square, as hollow and resounding as a cavern.

But it's not just empty. It's naked. That's the only word for it. All the tapestries and banners that usually adorn it are gone. The niches that were once crammed full of the coats-of-arms of illustrious members are bare, the bows of past masters that hung along the back wall nowhere to be seen. These things we no doubt snatched down ourselves during our evacuation, but even things that were never intended to be moveable have been violently stripped away. Every one of the elaborate wrought-iron brackets used to hold torches high on the walls to light the room at night has been rent from its mount, leaving ugly holes that gape unmended. Great plumes of soot lick the walls where fires must have been kindled right on the stone floor, and what wood paneling hasn't been ripped from the ceiling above is scorched or partly pried away.

That the ravaged room is so clean just makes it worse. And the fact that there is one thing that escaped the wrath of the villagers. One thing, just as we left it. Ironically, it's the one thing in all the guild that I would have just as soon seen destroyed.

The painting of St. Sebastian.

We're all sitting here in a row, staring at it in disbelief.

"Well, whaddya know?" Armand finally says, his voice echoing around us.

"Why do you suppose they left it?" Pascal asks.

None of us can take our eyes off it. It's always commanded the room, but now with the hall as bare and exposed as the young saint it depicts, it's overpowering.

"I guess they figured they couldn't better Jurian's statement," Rennie says, sounding a little proud, as though he could share some credit with his master for shooting the thing.

I don't say anything, even though I think I know exactly why it's still here. As always, the beautiful boy in the image reminds me sharply of Tristan, and with Jurian's arrow still sticking out of the saint's eye the painting is now a graphic symbol of Taran's treachery. But it's also a vivid reminder of my father's gruesome death. Until I've solved the mystery of my father's murder, I know I'll always have this image hanging over my head.

Nobody else has said anything either, and I can tell that today they find the painting as unnerving as I usually do. Next to me, Remy in particular seems upset by it. He's surely thinking about his own unmistakable resemblance to the boy in the painting, and with so little in the room besides him and it, it is hard to ignore. It's glaring, even, and I shift on the bench, uncomfortably aware both of Remy's proximity and that I'm staring up at what might as well be a naked picture of him. It's not like I don't know from previous experience with him in the lavatory that it's pretty darned accurate.

The hairs on the back of my neck prickle, and it occurs to me to wonder if I haven't been worrying all morning about close encounters ... with the *wrong* boy.

Somehow, I'd managed to forget Remy's pledge to win me over. And that from now on, he's going to be sleeping on a cot only inches away from mine.

Every single night.

"Okay, boys. No more wagon rides for Marek! All that fresh air's gone to his head," Pascal exclaims, when a nervous noise escapes me that probably does sound a little hysterical. But I doubt it's really because of Remy. With that image of a brutal punishment looming over me again, for some reason I've started muttering *"a good bludgeoning, right"* to myself under my breath.

AFTER THE FIASCO OF THAT FIRST TABLE WE DISTRIBUTE ourselves more evenly and we have no further mishaps. They aren't getting any lighter, though, Remy's stationed himself solicitously next to me, and each trip requires passing directly under that plaque again. So I'm plenty glad of it when Brian de Gilford wanders past and appropriates me for a task of his own. He's pilfered a cache of wine from Brecelyn's cellars and he needs help getting it unloaded.

It's a pretty big job, since the casks are huge and de Gilford's stolen a whole wagon full of them. But rolling the big barrels along has got to be easier than hauling tables and I thoughtfully take Frans with me, since he's the only other boy who's been having as much trouble with our original task as I have.

De Gilford's appropriated an empty office on the masters' hallway for use as his own private storeroom, and after a few false starts, by rocking the casks forward on their rims and using the ropes tying down their lids as leverage, Frans and I manage to get the barrels moving in pretty good order. I'm still feeling a little shaky, though, and so far being back at St. Sebastian's is not going quite as I'd imagined it. So as we roll the casks along, I start putting my mind to the problem of how to explain my training idea to Tristan, when the chance arises. If I want to get the day back on track, I've got to be ready with something to say.

The morning wears on and the wagon slowly empties of casks, and all the while I'm thinking furiously away. But I just can't get past the one glaring flaw in my idea to make Gilles our ally, the thing that's been eluding me all along: I've never figured out exactly what it is I think Gilles can actually *do* for us, even if he'd be willing to try (I mean, I know Gilles said he wants the happy ending for his friends. But he wants it for himself, too — and only one boy can win). He's unlikely to be anything but a frustrating trainer. I doubt he could help make Tristan stronger, either, since he comes by his own surprising strength naturally, and even he's never beaten Taran at clouts.

Convincing Tristan to practice with Gilles should be easy enough; he was likely to do that anyway. But convincing him that practicing with Gilles is going to result in him *defeating* Taran? That's another matter entirely. Without that I've got nothing, and what's worse, I'm not sure even I really believe there's anything Tristan could do to pull himself up in the rankings enough to do that. The bitter truth is, unless I can do now what I haven't been able to do in weeks of trying and make something 'more' of the notion, no amount of purple prose is likely to persuade him.

We're just positioning the last of the casks and de Gilford is already in the process of taking inventory of them when a rather desperate thought occurs to me. It's a longshot at best but it's worth a try, and it's so obvious I don't know why I didn't think of it sooner. As it is, it's not until de Gilford straightens up for a moment, stretches, and with an exaggerated inhalation of breath exclaims heartily,

"Ah, smell that, boys? The scent of trials is already in the air!," that he gives me the idea. And the perfect opening.

"You didn't happen to witness any of the trials of that man everyone was talking about so much last year, did you, master? You know, the one who was Master Guillaume's squire. Jan Verbeke."

There's no point in subtlety with de Gilford, so I don't bother to explain why I want to know. I just wait.

"Jan Verbeke's trials?" he replies, licking the quill of his pen thoughtfully and bending over the casks again. "Sure. Hmm. Let me think. Was it his Firsts, or his Seconds? Or both? It was a long time ago. I wasn't there for his *accident* at any rate, if it's more of the grisly details you're after, you naughty boy!"

"I hear he was full of tricks," I continue, not letting myself get sidetracked. Of course, I know for a fact from reading Meliana's journal that he was at my father's First trials, but I can hardly say so, and it isn't really this that matters. "Good tricks. Incredible, even. I overheard some of the veterans talking the other day about a butts trick he did at one of the competitions, and I was wondering if you happened to see it."

"A butts trick of Jan's?" He considers for a minute. Then he shakes his head. "Nope. I'm afraid that doesn't ring any bells. Funny, but now that you mention it, I don't recall ever seeing Jan shoot butts at all."

I wasn't really expecting much; it was a long time ago and I already knew de Gilford was an unreliable source. And the man has always been infuriating. Now I have to bite my lip to keep from crying out in frustration, or from kicking him in the shins. How can he have forgotten *everything* about that day? He must be going senile, or he spent the whole of the competition looking down Meliana's dress. Or else he's just plain lying.

My hand is resting on one of the big casks, and as we've been talking I've been fiddling absently with the rope securing its lid. To hide my annoyance now, I start plucking roughly at the knot in it under my hand. That's when I notice something about the barrels I didn't before that's so curious, it drives my irritation at the man to the back of my mind — temporarily.

It's how he's sealed the things.

Hardened lumps of clay cover the knots in the ropes around all the barrels, and into each one de Gilford's impressed a large symbol, marking the casks as his personal property and making them impossible to open without obviously breaking through the clay. It's a pretty normal way to make sure that stores aren't opened by anyone but the owner, so that's not what catches my attention. It's the symbol in question.

There are some floral motifs around the edges that haven't transferred enough for clarity, but right in the center is a big, bold capital letter *G*.

Seeing me staring at one, de Gilford chuckles. "That's right! I slapped my *own* crest on 'em, back at the castle! Clever, eh, boy?"

I nod slowly, not taking my eyes off the seal.

"Master ..." I finally ask. "Don't you have a title?"

It's probably very rude and he never uses one, so maybe I'm mistaken. But I could have sworn my brother Jules said something about it, the first time I ever saw de Gilford years ago in the market square.

"Count something ... Mons... Mont ...?" I venture, trying to remember.

"*Montevillier!*" he booms, not at all offended. "Fancy you knowing about that," he continues, bemused, as he bustles around counting the casks again. "The Old Prince gave it to me, bless his heart. Now there was a *real* prince, not some mewling boy, or stingy regent like the one we're saddled with. *He* knew how to reward a loyal man. I never use it anymore, though. It's not really my style. You know, too stuffy, and honorary, mostly — just for show. No *land* with it, anyway; certainly nothing *useful*, like *vineyards*. Ha!"

"Your monogram, though," I persist. "Shouldn't it be an *M*, then?"

He laughs. "Good God, boy! Only the most posturing, entitled sort of aristocratic prat would use his *title* for his monogram. The *family* name, that's what's used, like this," he gestures toward the nearest cask. "G, for the house of Gilford. Or for a more personal item, a man might use his given name. But his *title*? Unheard of."

"What's the matter, Marek?" Frans asks me, once de Gilford's dismissed us and we're alone together out in the hall.

"Nothing," I reply, unsure if it's true.

Oh, I'm not trying to picture the buffoonish *de Gilford* wiping the sweat from his brow with a handkerchief after puffing his way through a clandestine tryst out in Brecelyn's chapel, only to lose it in the process. Well, maybe I am — a little. But mostly I'm thinking about the conversation I had with Gilles about monograms, and wondering.

Then I cast off the unworthy suspicion with a shrug. After all, Gilles really is just about the most posturing, entitled aristocrat I know.

Except, of course, for Aristide.

By the time we meet up with the boys again they're just finishing with the mess furniture, and soon we're all whisked away on a whirlwind of menial chores that kept us working like dogs out in the yard for the rest of the day. But as the day wears on with no sign of the Journeys, after failing to get anything useful out of de Gilford I just don't have the heart to keep worrying about my so-called plan. It's never going to be more than it is now, and I'll just have to do what I do best — say whatever comes into my head at the moment and hope the boys can make something more of the scheme than I could.

It's depressing, though. I can't help feeling that my first day back is not turning out at all as I envisioned it, and it's not until much later, in the middle of evening mess, that something unforeseen happens to alter my perception of the day — and to transform my mood entirely.

Although admittedly, it gets off to a rocky start.

And I can't in all honesty say it ends that well, either.

CHAPTER TEN

"All right, boys," Pascal declares, leaning a newly-constructed cot against the wall outside the still-closed barracks door. "If we're not to miss our dinner, we're going to have to prop these out here for now, and haul them inside later. And as for whatever mess is in there," he adds, "Well — we can put up with anything for one night, and get it cleaned up in the morning."

Darkness has already fallen and it's terribly late, and I'm sure Pascal is right. But as I fall into step behind him with the other squires to join the steady stream of men coming in from outside and heading toward the great hall for their supper, I get the distinct impression he's stalling. I can't say I blame him. We're all tired and hungry, and after seeing the state of the rest of the guild, I'm not sure I'm ready to face whatever's waiting for us on the other side of the barracks door yet, either.

We find the hallway outside the main hall already packed with loud, sweaty veterans. There are too many of them to be lodging at the guild; Master Guillaume's summoned men from all over Ardennes to help with the reconstruction, and all the inns and taverns in town are full. Rumor has it there's even a contingent staying in what's left of the Drunken Goat, where in fond memory of their own Journey days some of the veterans have taken it upon themselves to pitch in and help rebuild that place on a more lavish scale, too. But everyone wants to be on hand tonight for the meal that will mark the formal reopening of our guild, and even with all the tables we unloaded earlier I don't see how there's going to be space inside for all of us.

With the noise the raucous men are making on top of all the clattering and banging still coming from somewhere above us, it's bedlam in here. But there's a party atmosphere brewing among the vets that's infectious, and by the time we've maneuvered our way forward through the crowd to position ourselves strategically in front of the big double doors, I've worked myself up into a state of high anticipation; one of the doors is open just a crack, and through the opening the interior of the room is visible — more or less. It's really dark inside, since for obvious reasons the room isn't lit tonight by the usual wall torches. Instead, rows of candles arrayed down the center of the tables provide the only light; it's purely practical, but it adds to the sense of occasion. Even better, platters of food have already been laid out on the tables, ready and waiting — it's going to be a real feast, and for once we squires aren't going to have to serve.

"Looks like we're in for a celebration tonight, boys," Armand exclaims, rubbing his hands together and peering into the room. "Oh, I can already taste that meat! Where in the heck *are* they? I'm starving."

Nobody can go in until the Journeys show up, and with the good smells that are wafting out into the hallway things are already getting plenty rowdy. I've had to put a protective arm around Frans to keep him from getting trampled underfoot when a cheer goes up at the far end of the hall signaling the arrival of the boys.

"What do you want to bet they've been loafing around outside, waiting to make a 'grand entrance'?" Pascal grumbles, bumping into me as the hungry crowd surges around us. "And now we're going to have to listen to *them* complain all evening, although we're the ones who did the real work. I mean, slapping a little mortar on some holes, how hard can *that* have been?"

I'm hardly listening. Tristan does love to make a grand entrance, and I'm eagerly picturing how satisfying it's going to be to stride in through the great double doors next to him, the king and his courtier. It's finally going to be just like old times, the perfect little ritual of homecoming together, at last. But just as the Journeys are shouldering their way forward and I'm catching a glimpse of Tristan's dark head in the crowd, before I can even manage to raise my arm to him in greeting, a fanfare blares from somewhere behind me. The doors to the hall swing open, and I'm swept forward and away from him in the middle of a little knot of squires on a tide of jostling men.

Everyone is trying to push through the doorway at once and we're all squashed together, and in the press of bodies it's too dark to see much of anything. I'm wedged in tight between Pascal and Frans and there's nothing I can do but let myself be swept along. I'm already thoroughly annoyed — even before a horrible scraping sound of heavy boots grating across the wooden threshold rises up from the men shuffling forward around us, and Rennie crows loudly in my ear,

"Un*believ*able! The old hall is warning you off *again*, Marek!" and he starts laughing. The other boys next to me all laugh too — because it is unnervingly just like the sound the table made when I dropped it here earlier. And I *have* suddenly lurched to a dead stop, directly under the doorway's lintel — just as I did then.

But it isn't the Saint who's barring my way.

I'm about to crash right into the man in front of me. And it's only in the instant when I'm already so close to him that the rough fabric of his tunic brushes against my cheek that I realize who it is.

In the flow of the crowd, I've ended up directly behind Taran.

I clench my fists, and with a stifled oath I try to pull back — only there's nowhere to go. I'm still being pushed roughly forward, and I'm being shoved up so close behind him that I'm trapped with my nose basically between his shoulder blades. His shirt is moving against my skin and I can feel the warmth of his muscles moving underneath it, and the sensation brings on a sudden and sharp memory of what it felt like to have my arms around him this morning — right before he pulled that stunt of his at the gazebo. And what it felt like to watch him kiss Melissande, last night. Or maybe it's the faint scent of lemon balm that sets me off, I don't know. But before I can stop myself, I reach up both hands eagerly and I put my palms flat on the small of his back.

And then I shove him, as hard as I can.

I really put my body into it.

And I have to say, it feels just *marvelous*.

For a weak girl it's a pretty impressive push and it catches him unawares, so the results are spectacular.

Taran pitches forward, like a mighty oak toppled in a forest — only not nearly as gracefully. His arms and legs flail out and he goes down with a crash, and all around him angry shouts rise up from men scrambling to get out of his way. As it is, he takes down four of five others with him, and as they all fall in a satisfying heap to the floor, ripples from the disturbance spread across the crowded hall and a number of subsidiary scuffles break out.

By the time Taran's thrust the others off of him to leap up to his feet and swing himself angrily around, I've ducked back out of sight and it's Gilles who's standing directly behind him. Even over all the commotion in the hall, I can hear the brutal thud of Taran's fist connecting with his jaw as I slip unobtrusively past to take my seat for dinner.

Luckily for Taran, Gilles is better able to withstand one of his punches than I was, and just as his fist is landing Brian de Gilford wanders in. He's spent the better part of the afternoon with his head stuck down inside one of his stolen casks of wine, and he's feeling fine. So when he sees Gilles hit the floor, he just bellows gleefully,

"A *fight*, gentlemen! It's a *fight!*" and he starts throwing out random punches of his own. Pretty soon everyone's brawling, and Master Leon lets it go on for quite some time before calling for order. There's nothing a St. Sebastian's man loves better than a good, clean fight, and no doubt Leon rightly assumes that Master Guillaume would think a little bloodshed was as appropriate a way as any to mark the grand reopening of our guild.

I'm still plenty flustered, though, by the time things have settled down and the others are all taking their seats. So much for handling myself gracefully. 'In the moment' it felt great to get some of my pent-up rage at Taran out, and he deserved what he got. But as I look down the table to where Gilles is now making a show of rubbing his jaw, my arms are still shaking and all I feel is out of control and guilty. And when Tristan comes past a few moments later to pluck at my sleeve and say,

"Coming to sit down by me, Marek?," all I can do it shake my head. Needless to say, I'm no longer in the mood to celebrate with the Journeys, and when I'd been eagerly picturing evening mess with Tristan, I'd forgotten about the inevitable presence of Taran.

None of the other squires is eager to join the Journeys at their end of the table, either; with Taran forced to take his meals with the boys again it was bound to be tense, even before he started assaulting them. So the squires all pack in around me, and it doesn't improve my mood that as Pascal whispers gloatingly to Armand,

"Did you see *his majesty* go down? Just like a sack of moldy flour!" Rennie starts up his comments about the great hall objecting to me again.

The jokes are stale and they weren't that funny to begin with but he can't come up with anything else, and when Remy joins in, using it as a pretext for slipping his arm around my waist as though reenacting his earlier grip on the table, it's not long before he's got everyone talking about the Trojan horse again. It's the last thing I'm in the mood to hear about right now.

"It's all about the danger of ignoring *warning omens*, Marek," Rennie cackles, and it's irritating enough.

"What tutorials have *you* been listening to?" Armand shoots back, nudging Pascal meaningfully. "It's about how *two men* in love with the same *girl* can only end in disaster," and it's not much better. When Remy gives me another big squeeze and chimes in huskily with,

"*I* think it's about how even something strong and noble can be brought low by the *deception* of one *weak* and selfish *girl*. Don't let it worry you, though, Marek, that *you're* as weak as any girl. *I'm* keeping my eye on you," it's the last straw.

I guess I didn't really think coming back to St. Sebastian's would miraculously erase everything that happened at Brecelyn's castle, or make it instantly easier for me to keep Taran from getting under my skin. But I did expect my first day back to consist of *something* other than reminders of all the reasons I was convinced last year I'd never make it as a boy through a second one. Now it looks like the most memorable moment of my return isn't going to be anything with Tristan, but a humiliating fumble with the furniture. At least, the boys don't seem inclined to let me forget it.

It's such a stupid thing and I shouldn't let it get to me, and it wouldn't, really, if I didn't know the real reason I've been clinging so hard to the delusion that some scheme I could come up with was going to make all the difference for Tristan this year. It's my oldest fear of all, and the boys' jokes are just stirring it up all over again — that I'm too weak to make a good squire, that without some training technique of my father's to contribute or some new strategy or gimmick or trick, I won't have anything to offer Tristan except for my own presence, out on the field. Given my many 'deficiencies,' I know what that will mean. Far from being the guild's best squire, I'm likely to be its worst. At least, not one that's Black Guard material.

Just when I think things can't get any worse, Gilles gets up and wanders down to our end of the table. I don't *think* anyone noticed that I was really the one who shoved Taran, or that I did it on purpose; it was dark and everyone was getting bumped around. But he must have been standing right next to me to have ended up getting punched for it, and I've been beginning to get the impression that beneath his unflappable demeanor, Gilles can hold a grudge with the best of them. Getting on his bad side now is the last thing I need.

Luckily, it turns out that the Journeys have already divvied up all the wine set out at their end of the table, and Gilles has simply come down to appropriate some of ours. Upon overhearing the boys' conversation, as he bends over the table to help himself to a jug sitting right in front of me, he drawls,

"The Trojan horse, you say? That's easy. And it has nothing to do with *girls*. It's about how brains will always trump pure brawn. It's about how a clever strategy can be decisive in any kind of competition."

"You mean, it's about *cheating*," Pascal snaps.

"If you like," Gilles replies coolly. "I'd have thought at least *you'd* see it, Marek," he adds teasingly. "It's just like I said on our *little outing*, about happy endings. It's about finding another way."

I don't see how burning a city to the ground and killing everyone it in can really be considered a happy ending, but Gilles is leaning over and looking down at me expectantly, and in the dim glow of the candles he looks exactly like he did in Brecelyn's chapel, on the night I lay on the floor at his feet and he offered me his hand. His words have taken me back to that night and I feel much as I did then, tired and discouraged, and the sight of him reaching down over me with his hair loose around his shoulders brings on a sense of déjà vu so sharp I could be back there in the chapel with him.

All the ideas he stirred up in me that night have come crowding forward again, and with them the nagging certainty that there *is* something to it all, if I could just figure it out. My mind goes slack, and disjointed thoughts drift through it, all the things that have been rattling around in the back of my mind for weeks mixing and swirling with the events of the day and the things the boys are saying now.

Wedging the table. Failing clouts. Pushing Taran down. Tristan wanting *me* to train Falko. Deception. Trickery. An unbeatable trick.

"Maybe so," Remy is saying. "But it was terribly risky, don't you think? I mean, the slightest error by any one of them and they'd *all* have been discovered, *inside*. They'd all have paid the price. That's the downside of your precious *teamwork*, Marek, isn't it? What happens to one happens to all."

And that's it, right there. That's when it happens.

Out of the blue, at Remy's words a thought drops into my head, like the missing piece of a puzzle falling into place, the one that makes the underlying picture suddenly make sense. Around it the blurred outlines of my unfocused plan shift and break apart, only to come together again in a new and different image — an image of blinding clarity.

My arms were already halfway raised to shrug off Remy in annoyance. Instead, I throw them around him enthusiastically. With a whoop of pure joy, much to his surprise (and delight, I must say) I give him a great, big kiss, right on the mouth. I don't care what he makes of it, or the other boys, either. Because just like that, I have my 'something more.' I have my brilliant plan.

Okay, it may still not be brilliant, but this time it really is a plan. What's more, with a little luck and a lot of help, it just might work — and it was Remy with all his talk about the bloody Trojan horse who gave it to me.

When I see the livid bruise that's starting to bloom on Gilles's jaw, I'm no longer as worried as I once was about getting him to go along with it, either.

I'M STILL TRYING TO PROCESS MY LUCK WHEN MASTER LEON GETS up from his seat at the head table to address us not much later. Gilles has gone back to his seat, and after my kissing of Remy things at our end of the table have gotten pretty riotous. The boys' jokes can't bother me anymore and I'm joining in with plenty of my own, so it takes us quite a while to settle down and listen even after the formal call for attention goes up.

Unlike Master Guillaume, Master Leon is not one for making speeches. But the master isn't here and the occasion demands something, and so we all listen courteously as Leon drones his way through the expected platitudes of homecoming with a bored expression on his face. Nobody's really paying much attention; the head table's empty except for Leon and de Gilford, who's slumped at the far opposite end of the table with a glazed look on his face, and he's tipped so far back in his chair that we're all waiting for the inevitable moment when the legs give way and he falls over backwards. Down at the Journey end of the table I can hear Aristide and Gilles making a bet about whether it'll happen during Leon's speech, or after. Nobody's really listening, that is, until Master Leon looks up from the notes Master G's obviously left for him, tosses them dismissively onto the table in front of him, and says,

"And so it is up to us to see our glorious guild through its phoenix-like rise from the ashes, and to count ourselves privileged to be a part of this splendid process of growth and transformation, *blah blah blah*. Now let's talk about what's *really* on everyone's mind: the competitions."

All the whispering and shuffling in the hall stops instantly. We're all listening now.

"Let's not mince words, boys," Leon continues, looking pointedly at the Journeys. "This place is a wreck. It's going to take months to get it back into decent shape and everyone, including you lot, are going to be expected to pull your weight. Well, be that as it may. Come hell or high water, we're going to stick to our traditional competition schedule. I have instructions from Master Guillaume to proceed with the selection of the theme for Firsts, whether he has returned from Meuse in time to officiate or not. In case it has slipped your minds in all your lounging around at Brecelyn's manor, the appointed hour for that selection is in exactly two days' time. I shouldn't have to tell you all what this means: from the moment you get up from table, preparing for the competitions should be your first and only priority. So unless you plan on making an even shoddier showing at the next trials than you did at the last, you'd better start doing something to get *yourselves* back into what passes for decent shape. Guillaume is expecting Firsts to be an exhibition of unprecedented proportions. Don't disappoint him."

Master Leon's said his piece and he's already making to sit down again when Aristide gets to his feet.

"Master," he calls out respectfully. "Can you tell us, please, what the standings are at this point? There was never an official announcement of the rankings, after Thirds last year."

"Oh yes, about *that*," Leon grins, and I cringe — and not only because I've never seen Master Leon actually grin before. I didn't know his facial muscles were capable of it. It's even worse than one of Master Guillaume's oily smiles, and it can't bode anything but ill; whatever he's going to say is going to be nasty, and I don't want to hear it. I've been trying not to think about the rankings for months, since Tristan can't be anywhere but at the very bottom, and let's face it: there's no 'something more' brilliant enough to bring him up to first place — from dead last.

My newly raised hopes are about to get dashed, and I'm stealing myself so hard for it, at first I don't realize what the master is saying.

"Thank you, Guyenne, for reminding me," Leon drawls, drumming his fingertips together lightly in front of him as though anticipating saying something that nobody's going to like much, but him. "Master Guillaume is determined that the disarray of our guild not keep us from upholding our ancestral customs, that's true. But in the interest of spicing things up for the spectators and enticing back the crowds, the master *has* decided to make one *slight* departure from the norm." He pauses, and from the look on his face I half expect him to say that we're all going to have to compete in the nude, or blindfolded, or that the boys are going to be shooting at each other.

I don't think any of those things would have surprised me half as much as what he actually does say.

"Last year's rankings?" He laughs. "They no longer matter. For the first time in guild history, we won't be carrying them over. This year we're wiping the slate clean. You're all back to square one, zero, zilch, nada. You'll all be starting out absolutely equal."

It was already quiet, but the stunned silence that meets this pronouncement is positively profound. The only sound in the entire hall is a choking, gurgling noise coming from Remy.

I can't believe it, either. In one fell stroke, the master's cut Taran's advantage right out from under him.

It's unprecedented. It's arbitrary. And it's horribly, horribly unfair. Cruel, even.

It's wonderful.

We squires all start looking around at each other in amazement, and down at the other end of the table, even in the low light I can see the Journeys eyeing each other warily, too, like stray dogs sizing each other up in an alley. They're all trying to figure out whether the announcement benefits them or not, and since Leon never said what the rankings would have been, from the resentful looks on their faces it's clear they've all convinced themselves that they would have been ahead of at least some of the others. But there's no question about which boy benefits from the master's decision the most, and from the way the others' gazes slowly start to settle on him, it's clear everyone is thinking the same thing as I am:

After counting him as good as out, Tristan's back in the game.

I lean forward eagerly, and I look down the table to the place where Tristan is sitting between Falko and Gilles and staring down in front of him with a dazed expression. Slowly a huge, disbelieving grin spreads across his face. He leans over eagerly, too, looking for me, and when his eyes lock on mine, it doesn't matter that I've been away from him all day, or that we missed out on our grand entrance, or that we're not sitting next to each other now. Everyone else in the hall recedes, and I couldn't ask for anything more. It's our perfect moment of homecoming together, right there.

"Well, *I* for one think it's a *grand* idea," Gilles finally declares in a loud voice. "It will simply give me the pleasure of beating you all, all over again. And if I don't mind, why should any of you? Since *I* was surely in first place," and everyone laughs. Nobody bothers to contradict him, and we all know he's not really serious (at least, I don't think he is); he's just trying to diffuse the tension.

And it works — more or less. Because there is one boy who isn't laughing. I haven't been watching him, I swear. But I know he's been sitting sullenly at the far end of the table throughout the meal anyway, beyond the reach of the candlelight, stiff and silent. And I don't look at him now. But I hope he can feel it:

the great big target that the master has just painted, right on the middle of his back.

MASTERS

AFTER THAT, THE EVENING PASSES FOR ME IN A FLOOD OF WINE and laughter. I have plenty to celebrate, and I give myself over to it with abandon. I don't know how Taran knew about the rankings — insider information from his father, or from Brecelyn, or simply because he's always been the master's favorite. But Guillaume must have taken him into his confidence about his plans long ago, before the plague ever hit, even, mustn't he? No wonder he tried so hard to get me to run away, before I could find out about it! When I think of him knowing this all this time and not telling any of the boys, not even his own squire, I don't know whether to find it enraging or hilarious that Master Leon has just publicly announced to the whole room the very thing I've been thinking for weeks I had no way of discovering. Somehow, the timing of it feels perfect, and I confess I don't remember much of the rest of the meal, I'm feeling so elated about it.

Once we've jollied Remy back into a festive mood, we're all having such a good time down at the squires' end of the table, in fact, that nothing happening among the Journeys can dampen our spirits — not even when it becomes increasingly clear that the tensions at their end of the table never really dissipated.

I suppose nobody expected the antipathy between Tristan and Taran to simmer safely away below the surface for long, the way it did last year, and the master's bombshell can only have exacerbated things. But Taran's been keeping to himself and at least he's sober, and I did think they'd make it through at least one meal together. So it's not until after most of the veterans have stumbled their way back to their lodgings in town and the hall is emptying out that I even notice something is brewing. The boys are right in the middle of one of their more fatuous political discussions when the situation starts showing all the tell-tale signs of boiling over.

The evening is winding down, and for a while now down at the Journey end of the table Aristide's been holding forth, grousing drunkenly about the English. I've had little interest in listening in, so it's not until Gilles makes a loud comment during a lull in our own conversation absurd enough to catch my attention that I get drawn in.

"I'll grant you this, Ari," Gilles exclaims boozily, gesturing toward the masters' table. "We've been allied with the English so long, we're even beginning to resemble them! Is it just me, or is it beginning to look a lot like *Camelot* around here?"

Ever since our alliance became official, the boys have been assigned Arthurian romances as part of their tutorials. I can't say it's been very good for them.

"What in the hell are you talking about, Gilles?" Tristan laughs back.

"We're losing masters faster than the round table lost knights!" he says.

"Yeah," Jurian chimes in, pointing at the seats at the head table that have stood empty all evening. "Poor old Master Gheeraert's chair has been vacant for so long, it could be the *siege perilous*."

"The siege *what*? The siege of Calais?" Falko demands, confused. "I thought Calais fell to the English a long time ago," and the boys all laugh at him. I can't help laughing, too, even though I don't know what they're talking about either.

"The 'perilous seat' at the round table, dunderhead," Aristide slurs back. "The place reserved for only the purest of knights. Anyone else who tried to sit there would die."

There's an awkward silence, as we all remember the dramatic way Master Gheeraert rose from that very seat and died right in front of us.

"It *is* odd, now you mention it," Falko says more seriously, ignoring Aristide. "That it's been empty so long, I mean. During the plague, it made sense. But why hasn't a new master been appointed?"

"If they're waiting for a *pure* master, it'll never be filled!" Jurian laughs (and Pascal and I exchange another glance, remembering Gheeraert's secret stash of pornography). "But maybe that's what Guillaume meant when he said to expect some new faces around here. Maybe he's bringing a new master back with him from Meuse. They usually elevate one of the Guardsmen, don't they?"

"Oh mercy, that must explain it, boys!" Tristan cries, amused. "*That's* why old Boring de Gilford's been hanging around here so long. He must be angling to be appointed master! Can you imagine it? De Gilford trying to keep the guild books, a ledger in one hand and a bottle of wine in the other?"

But I'm not laughing anymore. I've had a terrible thought. Surely the highest rank at St. Sebastian's after the three masters in residence is the captain of the Black Guard. Before I can get too worked up about the thought that Lord Mellor might soon be taking up residence among us, though, a deep, somber voice unexpectedly answers. I'm not sure what's so ominous about it, except that Taran usually never joins this kind of conversation. And that he's not said anything else all night.

"If you had ever bothered to learn *any* of the guild rules, DuBois," he says darkly, "you'd know that only a crowned prince can appoint a new master of St. Sebastian's. There can be no new master here until after the prince's coronation."

"Well, isn't it lucky for the rest us that you've nothing better to do with your free time than pore over a pile of musty rulebooks?" Tristan shoots back.

It's really nothing different than the usual sort of cheap shot the two of them often take at each other. But an uneasy silence falls over the table; the air between the boys is crackling with tension, and there's an uncharacteristically sharp edge to Tristan's banter that suggests he's only barely containing genuine anger. So I think that's why Gilles jumps in immediately to suggest a game, and before long he's got all the boys engaged in comparing themselves to famous figures from English lore.

"*I would be King Arthur, of course,*" he proclaims unselfconsciously. "Fair and just, the beloved liege lord of all his knights ... and a delight to all the ladies."

"Oh, *brother,*" Pascal snorts, as Falko demands, "Which one of the knights was the biggest?" and Aristide replies, "Don't you mean, which one was the biggest *idiot?*"

"*You* could be Mordred, Ari," Gilles suggests. "And Jurian here'd be gorgeous Gawain."

"And I would be the king's right arm, naturally," Tristan exclaims with a grin, throwing his arm around Gilles's shoulders. "Lancelot, the truest and most perfect knight, an equal lover and a fighter, and by far the most dashing."

Through all of this, the only sound from Taran has been the dull thud his knife is making as he flicks it into the tabletop next to his plate — a frequent little habit of his when he's annoyed. The sound has been getting progressively louder, though, and at Tristan's pronouncement he can't contain himself. He suddenly lets out an explosive and sarcastic cry of "*Ha!,*" and he flips the knife over in his hand, catching the point of the blade deftly between his thumb and forefinger.

And then he throws the knife across the table, hard and fast.

It lands with a loud twang only a hair's breadth from the inside of Tristan's wrist, neatly pinning his arm to the table through the fabric of his cuff.

Tristan looks down at it for a while.

Then he raises his eyebrows, and says evenly,

"It seems my *dear brother* would beg to differ. If you've got a better suggestion, I'm sure we're all listening."

But I don't think anyone else is listening; we're all staring at the knife, where its handle is still vibrating. It's so quiet at the table now I think I can hear it giving off a gentle hum.

"Quite to the contrary, *brother,*" Taran replies, his deep voice thick with mock courtesy. "For once, I agree with you entirely. Lancelot suits you perfectly. Or how about your namesake, '*Sir*' Tristan? So appropriate. If I remember their tales aright, they were *both* adulterous sleazebags, *too!,*" and in a flash Tristan's on his feet, all pretense at control forgotten.

He's gotten up so fast, the sleeve of his shirt rips and he leaves a piece of his cuff still tacked to the table in front of him. He's so flushed and angry he doesn't seem to notice, and Taran's started raving, his voice rising dangerously into a shout:

"— selfish, self-absorbed scum-sucking snakes-in-the-grass who thought nothing of dragging everyone and everything down into the muck with them —"

"And what name should I find for *you?*" Tristan flings back. "Sir '*Can't-Keep-It-In-His-Pants*'? Or how about '*The Knight of the Dirty Shot*'?" and all at

129

once Taran's on his feet, too, his face even more livid than Tristan's, and the two of them are squaring off and Armand is muttering under his breath,

"*Oh man, here we go again,*" and we all know how this is going to end. The only difference is, this time it looks like it's going to be Taran who hurls himself across the table first. He looks so furious I think he really would have done it, right there in the middle of the great hall — particularly when Tristan next says, "*You know, I think I liked you better when you were drunk,*" if at that moment Master Leon didn't materialize right behind Tristan. We'd all forgotten all about him and he must have been making his way out of the hall for the night, but now he reaches out one big, meaty hand and puts it on Tristan's back, right at the base of his neck.

"I think we've all heard about enough from *you*," Leon says, and he gives a sharp and powerful squeeze.

Tristan's head lolls back, the insult he was about to deliver coming out as a squawk, and he drops roughly back into his seat with a plop.

"And as for *you*," Leon barks across the table, "One brawl per mess is my limit, Mellor. Start another one and I don't care who your father is. I'll shoot you myself," and Taran has no choice but to back down, too. With a curt bow and a clipped "*master*," he stalks away from the table, grabbing up Remy by the scruff of his neck as he storms past and taking with him as he disappears out of the hall.

As we watch them go, Frans whispers to me tremulously,

"Is that what it's like in here *every* night?"

"Pretty much," I concede.

In point of fact, though, the boys usually did manage to control themselves much better than that last year, and I know I should be worried. They're already at each other's throats, and we haven't even been back one whole day.

Instead, I can't help smiling to myself, because as soon as Taran's out of the hall, Falko slaps Tristan on the back and exclaims,

"The Knight of the Dirty Shot!," as though he's only just now getting the joke. "Say, that's *funny!*," and I know Tristan's aptly coined nickname for Taran is going to stick. It serves him right.

It's sweet payback, for dubbing me Woodcock.

As usual, Taran's dramatic departure from the hall seems to signal the end of the evening's festivities, and soon the other boys are all climbing over the benches to take their leave. Falko's still got one arm draped over Tristan's shoulders, and as they stumble past behind me, I try to scramble to my feet to follow them — only to find to my dismay that Master Leon is now standing right behind *me*. He never left the hall, and he's looming over me in an anticipatory fashion that makes me suspect that it wasn't actually the boys' argument that brought him past our table.

Sure enough, before I can get to my feet he's thrusting a piece of parchment roughly under my nose.

"What's this?" I ask, squinting down at the sheet now in my hand.

"It's a *list*, hotshot," he says unhelpfully. I can see that much.

When I just look up at him in confusion, he adds sourly, "Of *crossbow tutorials*, remember? Master Guillaume wants you to start on private sessions tomorrow, one every afternoon. You're to begin at the top of the list, and work your way down."

I peer closer at the column of names scrawled on the paper; there's nary a squire on it. They're all Journeys, except for the last:

Brian de Gilford.

Seeing me staring at the master's name incredulously, Leon reaches over, and he scrolls his finger slowly up the list.

"*Enjoy*," he says sarcastically, and I can hear him laughing all the way out of the hall.

Master Leon really is one cold son of a bitch.

Of course. The second name on the list is Aristide's. And the one right at the top?

It's Taran Mellor.

THE REST OF THE BOYS ARE ALREADY OUT OF THE HALL BY THE time I've tucked the list into my waistband with a grimace and hurried out after them. But when the other squires head off down the hallway toward barracks together, I hang back. Then when the coast is clear, I dart down the Journey corridor to Tristan's room. I can't be anything but glad I ended up spending my first day back with the squires rather than with Tristan, given the result. But there's no way I'm really going to let it go by entirely without getting my minute alone with him.

I give his door a quick rap, and when I let myself in Tristan's sitting on the edge of his cot, fiddling with the rip in his sleeve.

"*There* you are, kid. I was beginning to think you weren't coming," he teases.

"You should know me better than that," I tease back, and when our eyes meet, we both start laughing; we're right back in the moment at table when the master made his announcement, and it feels so good, I keep laughing long after I'm sure just what it is we're really laughing about.

Then I stop as abruptly as I started, when I see what Tristan's really been doing. He hasn't been toying with his cuff at all. He's pressing a small square of white cloth against the inside of his wrist.

"Tristan, you're bleeding! Let me see," I cry.

He obliges, pulling back the cloth as I sit down next to him. There's the faintest of scratches along the inside of his wrist, from which a thin trickle of blood is seeping.

"That damned barbarian grazed me, *on purpose*," he grumbles. "And it stings like the dickens!"

"So he missed. Again," I exclaim. But Tristan just shakes his head.

"Taran doesn't *miss*, Marek," he says, not sounding light anymore. "He just can't resist an opportunity to spill a little of my blood," and I'm not sure what he's trying to tell me. But I don't want to think about Taran now, or about what an incredible shot of his it was to nick Tristan so slightly — or what a lucky one. I'm not sure which would be worse.

So I don't say anything. I just take the cloth from him gently, and I dab the wound for him. As I do, I notice just how dirty and grubby he is. He's not had a change or a wash since working on the wall, and he's looking curiously around at his new furnishings in a way that makes it clear this is the first chance he's had to see them. When he finally says wonderingly,

"Everything's exactly the same, and completely different," I know he's not just talking about the room. It's what I've been thinking myself all day, isn't it? And when after a pause, without looking up from where his hand is still resting on mine in my lap, he says quietly,

"Ready for it all to start up again, squire?," I know what he's really saying, too.

He's telling me he's not, and he sounds more tense and worried than he has all winter. It could be just because he's exhausted, or because of his run-in with Taran, or because the competitions are suddenly a reality again for him, too. But I doubt it. He knows better than anyone what the master's decision means. He's got a real chance again, however slim, and he's scared to death he's not going to be able to make anything of it. Finding himself unexpectedly back in the running has just put the pressure on him again, and I don't have to see the way his eyes are fixed on the thin, red line Taran's cut into his wrist to know what he thinks is going to happen.

It's the opening I've been waiting for all day, and I almost take it. I can feel all my plans for him bubbling up to my lips, ready to spill out in an incoherent jumble. But I can see how tired he is, and strangely enough, now that I know my plan is good, I no longer need to take it. I don't want to waste this moment, when Tristan's not acting and his guard is down, in talking about plans and strategies. There's something much more important I want to say to him, and it's funny. All day, I've wanted everything to be the same here as it was last year. Now I know it can't. Things *are* different. *I'm* different. And I couldn't really want everything to be exactly the same, anyway — because of the one thing that's so beautifully, so wonderfully, so gloriously changed:

Last year, I was sure Tristan would lose. Now I know a way he can win.

So I content myself with asking quietly,

"Tristan, do you trust me? Really trust me?"

"Of course I do. I'd be a fool not to," he replies loyally.

"Then get some sleep. Trust me, tomorrow you're going to need it!"

He grins, and I get up to go and let him rest. Before I do, on impulse I wrap my arms around him, and rest my head down for a moment on the top of his. There is one thing here in this room that can never change, and it's the most important thing of all. So when I hug him tight and whisper against his hair,

"*Welcome home, master,*" I hope he, too, knows what it is I'm really telling him.

I RUN ALL THE WAY BACK TO BARRACKS. AS I GO, I REACH OUT and let my fingers trail lovingly along the wooden paneling of the wall, just as though I were running my hand along a boy's ribs, and for the first time in weeks, maybe months, my heart is light.

When I round the corner, I pull up short, surprised to find the squires all still milling around in the corridor outside barracks, taking their time about gathering up their cots. I'd forgotten all about it, but there's one last task ahead of us before the night is over.

It's time to find out what's on the other side of the barracks door.

"We're all here now. You do the honors, Pascal," Armand says magnanimously. But he sounds apprehensive.

With a determined nod, Pascal lifts the latch, and throws the door open.

My first thought is, *it's not too bad.* There aren't corpses piled up to the rafters or ravening beasts lurking in the corners, and it doesn't actually smell that much worse on the inside than it did through the closed door. It doesn't even really smell that much worse than it did when there were twelve of us living in here and Rennie wasn't bathing, in fact.

My second thought is, *it could be a lot better.* That half of Louvain was camping out in here in our absence is obvious enough. That they weren't bathing or cleaning up after themselves is obvious, too, and from the number of festering wet spots dotting the floor, more than just Pruie's rabbit died in here. The advance crews have done us the favor of carting away the rotting carcasses they must have discovered in here, but they were above stooping to cleaning up for mere squires, and the smell of decay is lingering in the stale air like a bad perfume. The room is crawling with insects and thick with flies, and the sound of scuttling is audible for a long time after Pascal flings open the door.

As suspected, nobody bothered to evacuate *our* furniture from the barracks on the night we fled the guild, and all that's left of it are charred splinters and scattered piles of moldering straw, the wreckage of more squatters' campfires kindled here in our absence. But just as in the great hall, there is one thing that's escaped destruction. One thing, against all odds, exactly as we left it. Behind Pascal we all jerk to a stop, holding our noses and staring across the room at it, as awed by its salvation as we were by that of the painting in the great hall.

It's my cot.

It's standing unmoved from its usual spot waiting for me, the sole survivor in a sea of carnage, and I don't care how ridiculous I look. This time it's no melodramatic impulse, no act for the amusement of the boys; I run straight to it and fling myself down, falling to my knees and burrowing my face into the dank and foul-smelling mattress, not caring who or what's been there in my absence. Ever since I thought the Saint appeared to me in Brecelyn's chapel, I've wondered if it wasn't just a figment of my imagination. And all the other things I've thought were signs, well, I've questioned them, too. But there's no question about this.

So the great hall rejected me. So I'm weak, and ugly. So I'm really a *girl*. I'm a St. Sebastian's squire, one of the few that are left, and barracks is welcoming me back again.

I sink my arms down deep into the mattress and I hug it tight, and when the moldy straw inside it surges up prickling and tickling around me, I could swear the old cot is hugging me back.

Long after I finally throw myself down for sleep, as the other squires drag in their own new cots and settle themselves wearily down, I lie awake, reveling in the soft, familiar sounds of the other boys around me, and in the convergence of events that has provided both the means and the opportunity to open the door for Tristan and me here again. I feel the gentle weight of the medals I always wear around my neck pressing down against my heart: my St. Margaret, and my St. Sebastian. And I think to myself:

The Virgin and the Archer, that's me.

They're the only two roles that have ever suited me, and I've finally gotten a sign I fully understand. It's ironic, but it's the one time I didn't really need a sign to know what this one is telling me: it's been a long and painful process and I wouldn't have said so at the time, but everything that happened this winter was for the best. I'm back where I belong, on the little two-by-six space that defines my proper place in the world, and there's no boy's embrace I'd rather be in than that of my old cot.

I guess.

After almost losing myself in Brecelyn's woods, I've found my way home again.

BATTERED, NOT BROKEN

PART TWO

CHAPTER ELEVEN

When I wake up the next morning, my back is aching from the lumps in my mattress and its moldy straw's given me a rash, and the sounds of banging and clattering have already started up outside again. Heavy footfalls of men moving around on the roof overhead are sending a steady trickle of sawdust falling through a gap in the ceiling onto my head, and in the humid morning air the rancid squalor around us smells even worse than it did last night. But it's so good to be back in with the boys that I hardly notice any of it, and I feel fantastic. Pascal and Armand are already up and dressing by their cots, and next to me Remy's fast asleep. His hair is tousled against a blanket pulled up high across his bare shoulders, and he's got one long arm stretched across the space between our cots as though he fell asleep last night reaching out for me. Now and then his limp hand gives a little twitch, and somewhere across the aisle Rennie's snoring.

It's a typical morning in barracks, and after accepting last night that things have changed, strangely enough today I feel just like my old self again. I've got a clear goal ahead of me, and for the first time in months I know exactly what I have to do and I have the confidence to do it. It's time to get the boys on board for training together, and Master Leon was right: from now on, Firsts has to be my first priority. I can hardly wait to get up and at it.

Before I do, though, just for good measure I rest my elbows on my knees, put my head in my hands, and I mutter to myself,

"Just don't think about him. Just don't think about him." And it works. It really does! Sort of.

Next to me, a very excited Frans is hopping around anxiously. Today is to be his first official day of squiring, and he can hardly contain himself. He's already fully dressed in a trim little costume Pascal scrounged up for him that's only slightly too big, and he's such a nervous ball of energy that as I pull on my boots I'm trying without much success to talk him down. I'm pretty excited about the prospect of getting back on the butts, too, and although I suppose it's only natural, I can't help but be flattered that it's me Frans is looking to most for help today rather than one of the more experienced boys. I'm just promising to keep him close this morning, even though it'll mean having to set up Tristan next to *Falko*, when two large, bare feet land on the floor in front me.

Remy's awake, and his familiar toes with their hairy knuckles are disturbingly close under my nose.

"Morning, Marek!" he chirps. His voice has that unnaturally cheerful note in it that always makes me apprehensive. And that's when I notice that his shins are bare, too.

Bare shoulders. Bare arms. Bare legs. It can only mean one thing.

I was right to worry.

Remy's been sleeping in the nude.

Right on cue, from somewhere above me Remy makes the sort of unmistakable sound that always accompanies a languid stretch, and declares brightly,

"Gilles was right! It does feel absolutely *marvelous*."

Sure enough, when I straighten up carefully, trying not to get *too* much of an eyeful but not shrinking from looking at him either, he's standing there squarely in front of me as bold as brass and as naked as a jaybird, gazing down at me drowsily and gently rubbing his washboard belly.

The expression on his face is all innocence, but he's not fooling me any. I seriously doubt it felt even remotely marvelous. It can't have been anything but cold and scratchy, and I know what he's up to. He's doing it entirely for *my* benefit. I can't believe he thinks such an obvious ploy is going to work.

But it probably will.

"Yeah, Marek. *You* should try it," Rennie laughs over from where he's just waking up, too, as Remy and I contemplate each other for a moment.

"You really should, you know," Remy finally says, his voice full of innuendo. "I'm sure you'd like it, if you tried it," and it doesn't take much to see that he's planning to make a habit of it.

I'm in too good of a mood to let even Remy ratcheting up his advances bother me today, though. And so Frans and I sit side-by-side on my cot and wait for Remy to dress, swinging our legs back and forth and openly watching him. Why not? It's nothing I haven't seen dozens of times, more or less, and he makes a pretty good show of it. Besides, what can it hurt, really? It's just Remy.

By the time the three of us are heading arm-in-arm out of barracks together, though, I'm feeling a little strange about it. So I say,

"*Er*, Remy. About that kiss, last night. You do know I was just playing along with your joke, don't you?"

"Maybe," he replies smugly. "But sooner or later, you're going to have to admit it, Marek. You like me," and there's nothing I can say to that.

I take Frans out with us past the sideboard first, since I have no intention of letting him make the same mistakes I did on my first day.

"Isn't this way quicker, master?" he asks, when we've grabbed up some

MASTERS

breakfast to share with the boys and I turn around, intending to head down the corridor and out via the stables as usual. Frans is gesturing across the empty great hall, toward the door standing open on the opposite side of the room. Remy's gone on ahead, as it's taken us quite a while to fill a fold in Frans's tunic with enough food to satisfy Falko, and Remy's back is just now disappearing through the doorway and into the shadows of the portico beyond.

"You've really got to stop calling me master, Frans. I don't outrank you anymore," I reply. But I'm stalling. My eyes flit up to the painting; since yesterday morning someone's removed the arrow from the saint's eye and done a hasty job of mending the rip in the canvas across its painted face. The tortured figure now looks uncannily like Baylen with his eyepatch, suffering the arrows of plague that killed him, and I can't help it. The damned thing still intimidates me, and I don't want to step into that empty room with it. But Frans is looking up at me expectantly, so I make a decision.

This year, painting or no painting, I'm taking the shortcut.

◄────────►

I GET THE OPPORTUNITY I'VE BEEN WAITING FOR RIGHT AFTER morning practice.

With Master Leon occupied, Master Guillaume away in Meuse, and all our regular trainers dead, we're to be left to the tender mercies of Brian de Gilford for our first drill session back on the butts. Although the man is something of an acquired taste, I'll admit I've become rather fond of him. But he's always unpalatable first thing in the morning, and we all know that today he's sure to be anything but tender. He's been talking for days of nothing but how much he's going to enjoy whipping us all back into shape.

We squires are in high spirits anyway as we prepare the boys' stations. It's too good to be setting up on our old familiar range again to worry about de Gilford, and for me there's an added satisfaction in walking Frans confidently through all the same steps of set-up that Pascal and Auguste helped me struggle through just one year ago. I take it as a compliment, too, when Pascal sets Gilles up next to me but he doesn't interfere, and by the time we've got everything ready and we're sharing our breakfasts in the fresh morning air and waiting for the boys, we're all laughing and joking around; I've started taking exaggerated breaths and exclaiming, "*Smell that, boys? It's the best scent in the world — the whiff of trials in the air!*" in imitation of de Gilford yesterday afternoon, and as Armand quips back, "Don't take too big a breath, Marek, or you're likely to get a whiff of *Rennie*," even Rennie's horsing around, periodically running out onto the butts and throwing himself down to roll around in the dust with increasingly ecstatic exclamations, in imitation of me yesterday morning.

When the Journeys come jostling out through the stable doors together

139

not much later, they're all in high spirits, too — even though it's instantly apparent that Tristan and Taran are starting off their day at about the same point where they left off after evening mess last night. They're both trying so hard to 'accidentally' shoulder each other into the doorframe or knock each other into one of the water barrels that the other boys give them a wide berth, and Remy and I have to hasten over and herd them to their respective places at opposite ends of the line before an open fight can break out between them. With so few Journeys left and squires no longer allowed to shoot at practice, the line is a little too short for comfort, and from the way the two of them keep trying to bump or jab or generally trip each other up all the way out to the field, I fear even the original line of twelve probably wouldn't be enough to keep a safe distance between them.

Once I get Tristan over to our station and some breakfast into him, he's in a fine enough mood, though — to begin with, anyway. Getting him away from the castle's done him a world of good, and he's so cheerful, in fact, that as I put his bow into his hand, I say a bit nervously,

"*Do* promise me you'll pace yourself, won't you Tristan?" and he laughs. He knows I'm not talking about archery. And we both know that pacing himself is the last thing he's likely to do.

It's all downhill from there. Before the boys have had a chance to finish even a single round of warm-up shots, de Gilford comes striding out, full of his usual vim and vigor and in the throes of one of those disgustingly hearty moods that always seem to possess him first thing in the morning, particularly when he's overindulged the previous night. A much less energetic Jurian is right on his heels; he was the only Journey not to come out with the others, and he's cutting it as close to being late now as he can without risking getting another beating. When de Gilford skids dramatically to a stop and throws his arms out wide, he almost whacks Jurian right in the face.

"What's all this?!" the big man bellows, as Jurian ducks around him to slip unobtrusively over to his place. "Pick 'em up, and move 'em down, boys! There'll be no mamby-pamby, fancy-shmancy butts shooting on *my* watch. I'll make *real* men out of you yet," and we have to pack everything up and haul it down, to set up all over again on the only corner of the far field that's been left free of temporary pavilions. He then proceeds to pummel us all morning with the most punishing series of drills we've yet been subjected to at St. Sebastian's, one after the other, hour after hour, in his own specialty: clouts.

It's all poor Frans can do to keep up, and not only because he's new to it and he's so small. Falko's shots are still plenty long and they're all over the place, and when his arrows keep sailing through the tops of the closest tents we have to regroup twice and move the whole line down. Remy's having his own problems, since de Gilford's brought out a bow for himself and he's set up his station next to Taran's, so Remy has to retrieve for the both of them, but the truth is we're all being run ragged. Between retrieving for my own master and helping Frans field Falko's shots, I barely have the time or the energy to pay attention to how the other boys are shooting, or to worry too much about how Tristan's holding up.

Unfortunately, it doesn't require paying any attention at all for it to become increasingly clear to everyone as the practice wears on that there's really only one boy who can keep up with the grueling pace de Gilford's setting, or shoot as far. Taran's little descent into decadence back at the castle apparently didn't hurt him any. It seems only to have refreshed him, and it does nothing to improve anyone's mood that as the morning progresses, de Gilford becomes increasingly effusive in his praise of him. Tristan isn't the only one who's thoroughly demoralized after five solid hours of listening to the man exclaim *"Wow! Another showstopper!"* or *"Bless my stars! Why, you're even better than your old man!"* every time Taran takes a shot, and by the time practice is winding down, there's no escaping a most depressing conclusion:

Taran's *already* much better at clouts even than the master.

So when de Gilford finally dismisses us and Tristan immediately shoves his bow into my hand with a disgusted grimace, and he and Gilles proceed to drag themselves straight into the garden without bothering to stop at the water barrels to splash off, I know I can't wait any longer. I toss Tristan's equipment unceremoniously down in a pile against the archive wall, and I follow them in.

The boys have already sprawled themselves down on some chairs at one of the little tables by the vines when I join them, their legs spread wide and shoulders thrown back in attitudes of utter exhaustion, and Pascal is with them. It's going to mean talking to the boys in front of him, too, but it can't be helped; he's leaning up tiredly against the trunk of a tree a few feet behind Gilles, staring at the back of his master's head with a sour expression. Now and then he tosses a little piece of bark at him, trying surreptitiously to get it to lodge in his hair. I *had* once hoped that Pascal might be of some help to me, but anything he might say now is not going to do me any good, I can tell.

"Clouts!" Tristan groans, reaching up both hands to run them through his hair, as I settle myself on the ground between him and Gilles. "Why did it have to be clouts?"

"I'll grant you, this morning I almost missed sadistic old Baylen. May he rest in peace, of course," Gilles says, with a nod across the garden toward Baylen's grave.

"If I *never* hear the word clouts again, it'll be too soon," Tristan agrees.

I'll never get a better opening than this. So I put a hand on Tristan's knee and jump in with,

"What would you say, master, if I told you you could forget all about them?!," and when he shoots me a look that says he's not in the mood to joke about it, I launch right into an incoherent description of my plan.

"Are you suggesting that *you* train *me*, Marek?" Gilles interrupts, before I've gotten very far.

"Not at all," I reply, overlooking his mildly condescending tone. "I'm suggesting that *you* and *Tristan* train *each other*." Before either of them can interrupt again, I rush on:

"It makes sense, doesn't it? You're each the best respectively, at wands and butts. And so who better to train each of you in the other skill than the boy who's the best?"

"And what about clouts, Marek?" Tristan asks sarcastically. "I suppose Taran will chip in, and train us at those?"

"I *told* you, Tristan. Seriously. We're going to forget all about them."

At this, Tristan gives me a supremely disbelieving look (and I'll admit, I did spend most of last year hounding him to work on his distance), and Gilles just looks bored. He's reached up one hand to massage his shoulder and he's inspecting the fingernails of his other hand in that way he has of suggesting detachment, and I know I'm not making a very good start of it. So I marshal my thoughts, and begin again.

"Look, I know I'm not explaining it very well, but you said it yourself last night, Gilles. A clever strategy is crucial in any competition, and I've got one to propose to the both of you. I've given it a lot of thought. Just hear me out, won't you?"

When I put it like that they can't very well refuse, and neither of them says anything. From their grudgingly indulgent expressions, though, I can tell they're both expecting to be underwhelmed.

"I know it goes against everything I was saying all last year, and I've been guilty of buying into the myth of Taran's invincibility as much as everyone else," I continue nervously, talking mostly to Tristan. "And it's true, nobody's going to beat Taran at clouts."

"If this is supposed to be cheering me up, it's not working," Tristan interjects. I ignore him.

"The thing is, Tristan, if you two work *together*, you won't *have* to beat him! *Nobody* has to beat Taran at clouts. I don't know why I didn't see it sooner, but it was apprentice trials that first started to show me the way. If I'd had to rely on just my disastrous clouts test, I'd have failed them for sure."

The boys shift uncomfortably, and Pascal in particular looks embarrassed; I've never openly admitted failing clouts to anyone but Tristan. My cheeks redden, but I can't let myself get distracted.

"But I *passed*, because I followed that failure with the success of our show, and it was my other talents that pulled me through. It was teamwork that got us *all* through. If you two work as a team, you can pull each other through, too. Gilles," I say, turning to him. "You've *already* beaten Taran in competition, twice! *You're* unbeatable at wands. And Tristan," I add hastily, as I can tell that this line of argument isn't appealing to him much. "*You* won the garland last year. And if you'd been well and sound, and with no distractions, you surely would have beaten Taran, too. *You're* unbeatable at butts. So maybe one of you two would win it all anyway, with no strategy, just through the luck of the draw. But do you really want to risk it, and count on luck? And if the draw goes against you, what then? The problem is, Taran's good at *all* the skills. Really good. Right now, he's at least the *second* best at all of them. And that's a very big problem."

Gilles has stopped looking at his fingernails, and he's now contemplating me through half-closed lids. He and Tristan exchange a glance.

"All right, Marek. We're listening," Tristan says evenly, and I know it's true. I've gotten their attention now.

"This is how I see it, boys," I say, slowing down. It's time to lay it all out and really convince them. "No matter what, Firsts at least is in the bag, for the both of you. There are only six boys left, with two boys to be cut at each competition. There's no point pretending that Falko's shoulder isn't still a wreck. He's got no aim anymore. And Jurian may pretend not to care, but we all know he's just covering for the fact that he's never regained his strength, after suffering from plague. It's too bad for them and I am sorry for their misfortunes. But the reality is they're sure to be the two boys cut at Firsts, no matter what the theme. So if you're really lucky, Firsts will be clouts and you'll both pass easily, and you won't have to worry about facing them later."

I'm actually not entirely sure that Falko couldn't still pass clouts by virtue of his pure strength alone, but there's no point in saying so. If Falko's still in contention, we're dead in the water.

"So Firsts won't be about passing," I continue. "It'll be all about putting yourselves at the top of the rankings, so you'll be in a strong position going into Seconds. That's going to be the crucial competition this year: it's all going to come down to Seconds. And as I said, the problem is that Taran's good at *all* the skills. So far he's never placed anything lower than second in any competition, and that's where you two training together comes in. You've got to help each other become *second best* at your own best skill. That way, whether Seconds is wands or butts, the two of you can place first and second. And if you do, well, with only four boys in Seconds, only two boys can pass. You two will be the ones to move on to Thirds, and you'll freeze Taran out. He'll be gone, before thirds ever happens! So even if thirds *is* clouts, it just won't matter. Taran won't be there. One of the two of you will win."

"I'm not sure that the rankings are going to matter much this year at all, Marek," Gilles says thoughtfully. "We're all too close for there to be much difference between us, and who knows? After Leon's announcement last night, the masters might be planning to do away with rankings this year entirely."

"All the better for us, then!" I reply smugly. "That way, even if Firsts is

143

clouts and Taran wins, he won't be coming into Seconds with an advantage. That'll make it even easier for you two to sweep Seconds outright, and eliminate him."

"And if clouts is *Seconds?*" Tristan demands, reasonably enough, and he's right. It would be the worst-case scenario.

"It wouldn't be ideal," I admit. "And I didn't say it was going to be easy. Luck is going to play a role. But even if we're unlucky and clouts *is* second, well, then Firsts will have to be either wands or butts, and as long as you two have put yourselves at the top of the rankings after Firsts, then *one* of you two is sure to pass along to Thirds with Taran. After all, last year both of you made a better showing at clouts than Aristide, who'll be the only other boy left by then. And if clouts is Seconds, then it *can't* be Thirds. Thirds'll *have* to be either wands or butts, and whichever of you two makes it to Thirds along with Taran will simply beat him then. Don't you see? It's foolproof. No matter *what* the draw, if you train each other to be the top two boys in *both* wands *and* butts, *one* of you will ultimately be the next Guardsman."

I don't have to say which of the two I'd prefer for that to be. Or that at Thirds, teamwork will inevitably have to come to an end.

Both boys are frowning slightly now, thinking through what I've said for themselves, and I'm pretty sure I can tell what each one is thinking. Gilles knows he's got a better shot at beating Tristan in the finals than Taran, and if he has to lose, I think he'd prefer to watch his best friend win. Tristan's just thinking about watching Taran lose.

"Not bad, Marek. Not bad," Gilles drawls, shifting around and re-crossing his legs. "But there is one flaw in your plan. Firsts is fast approaching. That doesn't give us much time. Even if we throw ourselves into this idea of yours with abandon, we could hardly transform each other in time for the competitions."

"Not to mention the fact that neither of us has any clue how to be an effective trainer," Tristan adds. But he's sitting forward now and he's started to jiggle one leg with nervous energy; he's beginning to see the potential of the idea, I can tell.

"That's the beauty of it, boys," I insist eagerly, pressing my advantage. "You're both so good already, you don't *have* to transform each other. All you have to do is figure out how to give each other an edge, to nudge each other past Taran in your respective skills. Surely if you put your minds to it, you can figure out how to do *that*. And Firsts may be coming up soon, but there are months between now and Seconds. That's going to be the big one, the decisive competition this year. There's plenty of time before then for you to give each other a little extra flair. And it's not just about training each other, either, or giving each other a *physical* edge. I can't really explain it; you have to experience it like we did during our show to fully understand the power of it. But I'm talking about giving each other a *mental* edge, on and off the field.

I'm talking about approaching the trials *as a team* and doing everything you can to ensure the success of the other, about using real *teamwork* — even right in the middle of competition."

I pause, looking to Pascal for support. As might have been expected, he just rolls his eyes and says annoyingly,

"Ugh, *teamwork*. Not on *that* dirty word again, are you, Marek?"

Fortunately I don't think the boys hear him, since at the same time Tristan is saying,

"I don't know, Marek. It sounds good. But you're right. Taran's never come in anything less than second. He's the judges' darling. Even working together, I don't see how we're going to ensure that he's kept out of one of the top spots," and I grin.

I've been saving the best for last, the 'something more' that came to me last night. It's time to deliver the *coup de grâce*.

"You're right, Tristan. That's going to be the hard part. But I've got an answer to that, too. Taran's the favorite and the judges *are* going to be inclined to rank him at the top, no matter how he shoots. So we're going to have to make it impossible for them, and there *is* a way. Look at it this way: there's so little to judge between you boys who are left, surely this year the exhibition shots are going to be all-important. A good trick could make all the difference. So that's why you two are going to do an incredible trick, *together*. Tristan, remember how much the audience loved it when I shot down that apple during Seconds last year?" When he nods, I turn to Gilles excitedly, warming to my theme. "Or how the crowd went wild, when Aristide shot an apple off *your* head? Think how much more they're going to love it, when *two Journeys* do a trick together. Each of you is fantastic alone; together, you'll be unstoppable. And this is the key to the whole thing: Remy was right in what he said about teamwork last night: *what happens to one, happens to all*. He meant it as a negative, but it can be a positive, too. Because if you two do an exhibition shot *together*, then the judges will have to judge you *together*. No matter how biased the judges are, Taran won't be able edge one of you out, because you'll have to be ranked together. Whether it's butts or wands, *whichever* of you is already leading the field going into the trick will bring the other up into second place with him."

"*Plan* an exhibition, together?" Pascal says incredulously. "Are you crazy? Master Guillaume isn't going to like it. He won't stand for it."

"Master Guillaume'll love it, if the crowd loves it!" I snap back. "He as good as told me he was counting on me to provide a little spectacle. All I'm doing is giving him what he asked for. Besides, *beforehand*, Master Guillaume isn't going to know anything about it. Neither is anyone else. We're going to sneak it in. It was your comment about using a deceptive strategy that gave me the idea, Gilles."

"Don't you mean *cheating*?" Gilles teases, mimicking Pascal's tone last night, and Pascal pulls a face behind his back.

"If you like," I smile back. "I prefer to think of it this way: we're going to pull a Trojan horse."

"If you're expecting me to leap out of a wooden horse in the middle of trials while DuBois shoots at me, you're going to be sorely disappointed," Gilles says dryly; Tristan just looks bemused, since he wasn't privy to our conversation last night.

"I don't mean *literally*. We're simply going to set up a trick so that it's a shot within a shot — one trick embedded in the other. That way you boys can practice your parts separately, and nobody'll be the wiser. Nobody'll know you're going to do them together. And then during competition, whichever of you is first in the order will start the trick, and the other will jump in and finish it. The second trick will be concealed *inside* the first. It's going to be absolutely fabulous! It's going to be unbeatable."

I've said my piece, and all I can do is wait. Throughout this last Tristan's fallen silent, but his posture has been gradually changing. He's now resting his forearms on his knees, and his head is bent down in concentration. I can tell he's really thinking about it, maybe even trying to decide whether he's willing to open himself up to the vulnerability of letting himself get hopeful again. I can't stand the suspense, so I burst out nervously,

"What do you think, Tristan? Will it work?!"

He lifts his head, and a slow smile spreads across his face. It grows steadily, until it's one of his signature dazzling smiles that's so bright it lights up the whole garden, and when he throws his head back and laughs out loud, I start laughing, too.

"I do believe you've done it again, kid," he says enthusiastically, slapping me on the back and rubbing his hands together in anticipation. "Yes, it's really brilliant. So, what's the trick?"

"Well, I haven't quite worked that part out yet," I admit, and his face falls — until I say hastily, "You're missing the point, Tristan! The details of the trick don't matter. It's not the trick that's unbeatable, it's the *doing* of it as a team. As long as we come up with one that's halfway decent, and as long as you boys do it together, you're both so good it's bound to be fantastic and the plan can't fail. I've got a few ideas, and we'll figure something out," and before long he's enthusiastic again.

It's all going really well, but I can't let myself get too excited yet, since I suspected all along that convincing Tristan wouldn't be the hardest part. He'd do just about anything, including really jumping out of a wooden horse, if he thought it would bring Taran down. It's Gilles I've really been worried about, so I turn to Gilles with a pleading look.

"What do *you* say, Gilles? Will you do it?"

He considers for a moment.

I wait anxiously, hoping against hope that Pascal keeps his mouth shut, and this time I'm not sure what Gilles is thinking. I know he thinks he's capable of winning with no help at all, so all I can do is hope he's smart enough to want to buy himself a little insurance, or a good enough friend to go along with it for Tristan's sake.

Finally, he shrugs.

"Gang up on the old boy, eh?" he chuckles, as though just getting a joke, and he rubs the bruise on his jaw. "Well, why not? Where'd the fun be in making things *too* easy for him?"

I leap to my feet and embrace him warmly. But as Tristan's exclaiming, "That's the spirit, old man!" and I'm raving, "You won't regret it Gilles, I promise you!," he puts up a lazy hand to forestall us.

"We can start training each other right away. That's not a problem. But as for the trick." He gives me a pointed look. "*If* you can come up with something that meets my approval, and *if* you can come up with it in time to allow for sufficient practice, I'm in. Otherwise, I'm afraid I'll have to go ahead with a little trick of my own devising, and all bets will be off. I have to look out for my own interests, after all."

"Why not? It's what you do best," Pascal grumbles under his breath, but I cry out,

"Fair enough!," and the boys get up to reach across the table to shake on it.

When they sit back down again, Tristan's a bundle of excited energy. That one unruly lock of hair of his has fallen across his forehead in the way that always makes him look like an earnest little boy, and he's animatedly talking to himself a mile a minute, throwing out ideas for the trick and dismissing them again. I'm so busy watching him contentedly that it's not until he says,

"I'm sure Marek's right, and Guilly'll love it, *after* the fact. But just in case he might veto a joint trick if he finds out about it in advance, we'd better keep it under wraps. It certainly wouldn't do us any good if *Taran* decided to team up with someone, too," that I notice when Gilles sat down, he positioned himself so that his back is no longer to Pascal. He's now contemplating his squire in silence, with a mighty speculative look on his face.

I don't *think* Pascal would ever be disloyal enough to Gilles to leak our plan, even if he is angry with him.

But he might.

Just as I'm thinking this, Gilles's countenance transforms. His shrewd look is gone, replaced by that mildly banal expression he often wears when he's about to make a pronouncement, and his voice is even fruitier than usual when he drawls,

"Come now, Pascal! Companion of my boyhood, my dear old chum. Isn't it time we make an end to this silly feuding? I've been quite losing my beauty sleep over it. What do you say? Shall we bury the hatchet?"

Pascal shoots him a look that suggests he'd like to bury the hatchet, right in Gilles's back.

"Tsk tsk. You're going to feel mighty foolish, my boy, when you find out

147

what it is I've *really* been doing, lo these many weeks, on your behalf," Gilles says smugly.

"*Master?*" is all Pascal says, rather rudely.

"Uh, oh, boys," Tristan laughs. "Gilles, just what have you gone and done?"

"Patience, Tristan," Gilles sniffs. Then he breaks into a grin, as though he can't contain himself. "Oh, all right. Pascal, my boy — I've decided to let you marry!"

"Come again?" Pascal says uncomprehendingly.

"That's right!" Gilles beams. "I have taken it upon myself to float an offer of marriage on your behalf, to that redheaded girl you're so infatuated with, the one you've been sneaking off at night on *my* horse to visit at St. Genevieve's convent. Don't pretend you don't know what I mean. *There.*" He spreads his arms in a sweeping gesture of magnanimity. "*Now* what do you say?"

But Pascal can't say anything. And he's no longer slouched up against the tree. He's bolt upright, his eyes are wide, and his mouth is hanging open. He keeps opening and closing it, but no sound comes out.

"You can't actually 'tie the knot' until after the competitions, of course," Gilles continues merrily. "After all, I need a squire. But I've made all the necessary inquiries, and I've assured her family that when we leave here you will have a position in my household with a title and an allowance sufficient to make you a more than suitable match for the girl. And I of course will stand the bride price. Just last night I got an answer, so it's official. Congratulations, my boy! You're engaged."

With a strangled cry, an overcome Pascal throws himself at Gilles's feet, all his previous complaints against his master forgotten. He hugs Gilles around the knees, weeping tears of joy and making inarticulate noises, as Gilles pats him on the back and clucks absently, "*there, there.* Breathe, my boy."

This goes on for quite a while, as Tristan and I both barrage Gilles with questions, most of which he sidesteps quite neatly, until at length Pascal gets hold of himself and Gilles waves a hand regally to indicate that Pascal's groveled enough to satisfy him. As a dazed Pascal gets unsteadily to his feet and dusts himself off, still stuttering out a profusion of thanks and apologies, Tristan says,

"You know, Gilles. For a while there, I thought you were going to be tempted to keep her for yourself."

"I *may* have fancied her myself, at first," Gilles concedes coolly. "And it was awfully *naughty* of Pascal to sneak around behind my back and force *me* to borrow Taran's horse to follow him. But I'm nothing if not forgiving, and it just goes to show how much dear Pascal's happiness means to me. Besides, I can't let *my* squire be outdone in barracks by the likes of *Rennie*, can I?"

"The real reason, at last!" Tristan exclaims with amusement, and Pascal slaps his forehead.

"The barracks!" he exclaims. "Oh, I must go and find Armand at once! Is he ever going to be *green* with envy," and he dashes off in two directions at once, at first heading the wrong way out towards the butts, then turning himself around and racing down the portico to disappear with a skid into the great hall. I've never seen Pascal so giddy and flustered. He must really be in love.

"Looks like we've got plenty of plans to celebrate this day, Lejeune!" Tristan exclaims heartily, getting to his feet, too, and looking almost as buoyant as Pascal. Something about his arch tone and the look he exchanges with Gilles makes me a little uneasy, though. So when he says,

"I don't know about you boys, but I'm beginning to look forward to noon mess. I think I'll run along and spruce myself up for it properly. Coming with me, Marek?" I shake my head.

"I'll catch you up, after I put away the equipment," I say.

But as Tristan takes his leave, I make no move to get up. Gilles and I are now seated across from each other, and as we listen to the sound of the boys' footsteps receding, we contemplate each other across the tabletop. When I'm sure we're alone, I say,

"Out with it, Gilles."

"Whatever can you mean?" he replies.

"You're up to something."

He doesn't answer. The corner of his mouth twitches, and he raises his eyebrows slightly, but that's all.

"If that was all a lie, Gilles, you're going to break his heart."

"Me? *Lie?*" he replies indignantly. "My, but you squires are a suspicious bunch. I wouldn't have thought *you* were in a position to question my willingness to do a favor for a friend," and he's right. We both know he's just agreed to do a mighty big one, for my own master. I probably should apologize, but Pascal's a friend, too, and I have a bad feeling about the whole thing.

"What's wrong with her, then?" I demand. "Is she insane? Or does she have a homicidal ex-boyfriend, or a contagious disease? It's got to be something."

We stare at each other for a while, and when I won't back down, he shrugs.

"All right. *Seriously*, I assure you, everything I said was quite true. I have indeed arranged a marriage between Pascal and his beloved at the convent, and there is absolutely nothing wrong with her — that I know of, anyway. Except, of course, for having the rather questionable taste to prefer Pascal to *me*. There. I swear it on my father's life. Satisfied?"

I'm hardly satisfied, since Gilles's father is dead, and if nothing else, I don't know how even with his connections Gilles can have located the parents of a girl we all assumed had no family left. But short of accusing him of blatantly lying to my face there's nothing I can do about it, and I know Gilles well enough to doubt he's actually lying, anyway. He's up to *something*, though. And whatever it is, Pascal is not going to like it.

Gilles is looking at me so sweetly and innocently, and so much like he's genuinely pleased that his scheme gladdened his friend just as mine gladdened Tristan, that I waver. I must have imagined the look Tristan gave him, and really, I can't be anything but grateful to Gilles right now. I shouldn't risk rocking the boat, and after Tristan's gratifying reaction to my plan, I'm too happy to want to. Even so, I'm not sure I'd have dropped it, if Gilles didn't fix me with a knowing look and say,

"I wouldn't start questioning motives too much if *I* were you, Marek. After all, we both know that if your little plan works, it's much more likely to result in my victory than in Tristan's."

"I have no idea what you can be implying," I huff, although I know exactly what he means. He's saying my plan is a dirty shot at Taran, and my face flushes with indignation. And guilt, too — because I can't really deny it. It *is* true that I can't stand the thought of Taran getting everything he wants, while Tristan and I are left with nothing. Or that if Tristan has to lose, I'd much prefer for *anyone* else to win than him. It's only natural I should want Taran to suffer a little, after everything he's done to me, though, isn't it? To see him humiliated, the way he humiliated me. But that's not my main motive, surely. So I mean it when I say,

"Maybe I have more faith in Tristan than you do, Gilles."

"I hope so," he says pompously. It doesn't make me feel easier about any of it when he adds,

"A squire's bond with his master is sacred, Marek. He deserves what he gets, if he lets anyone come between them to break it."

I STASH TRISTAN'S EQUIPMENT AWAY IN ONE OF THE TEMPORARY cabinets that the carpenters busily erected for boys yesterday afternoon, and as I do, I'm already plotting. It's going to be mostly up to the boys to figure out how to train each other effectively, but it's not too early to start putting my mind to my end of the bargain: delivering the trick for them to do together. I'm not that worried about it, since I'm sure I'm right that the trick itself doesn't have to be all that incredible, and there's no point in thinking it through too carefully until after the theme for the competition is announced. But I'm not sure how long Gilles is going to give me after that, and I don't want to hand him a ready excuse to back out of our bargain, if that's what he's intending. I figure I've got about a week. It should be ample time.

My head is already teeming with ideas by the time I round the corner into the Journey corridor, when Tristan surprises me by popping his head out of his doorway. He's changed into his best tunic and trousers, and he wants me to take his discarded dirty clothes along with me to the laundry. He's slicked back his hair, too, and he's looking very dapper indeed. When I say so, he jokes,

"Well, if I'm going to be the next Guardsman, I'd better start looking the part. Oh, and take this, too, will you?"

He pulls off the soiled cloth from around his wrist and hands it to me. The cut is closing nicely, and Tristan doesn't need it anymore.

"Ask Pascal to return it for me, when he's got his head out of the clouds! Gilles lent it to me last night."

Tristan sounds so buoyant, I probably shouldn't say anything. But we're both looking at the thin, red line on his wrist, and I can't stop myself. I say softly,

"You'll promise me now, won't you, what you wouldn't this morning?"

There's a pause.

"You mean, promise I'll stay away from Taran. That I won't try to pay him back."

"Yes." I can't look him in the eye. "No plan in the world will do us any good, if you go and get yourself into trouble."

There's another pause.

"All right, little brother," he finally says. "I promise to steer clear of him. You've come through for me again, and it is a good plan. It'll keep me in long enough, anyway. So I won't do anything to jeopardize it. But if *he* comes after *me*, well, it's like Gilles said. All bets are off."

There's more than one thing about this assurance I don't particularly like, but's going to have to satisfy me.

When I get back to barracks, Pascal's in the middle of telling the boys all about his engagement. He's got the squires lined up in a row on the edge of one of the cots, and he's standing in front of them and retelling the story of how he met the girl who is now his fiancée, ostensibly for Frans's benefit. He's apparently already described how he pulled the girl up onto the guild wall to save her from molesters, and now that he and Gilles are friends again, he's been giving Gilles his due and recounting his master's part in the rescue with equal enthusiasm. When I come in he's just finishing off the story (for obvious reasons omitting the part where Gilles gave the girl the kiss of her life), and he's segueing into praising the girl's charms in terms so extravagant they'd be excessive even of Melissande.

"Isn't it *romantic*, Marek?" Remy sighs, scooting over to make room for me with a little inviting pat on the mattress. "*Another* wedding to look forward to!"

I manage a wan smile, but as I plop down heavily next to him, my arms full of Tristan's dirty laundry, I can't honestly say that there's any upcoming wedding I'm looking forward to, and frankly Remy is the only squire who looks even remotely excited about Pascal's news. Frans is too young and too sensible to care anything about girls, Rennie looks annoyed that Pascal is stealing his thunder, and Armand is openly fuming. This is one of their contests of one-upmanship that Armand can't hope to win, since Aristide would never go out of his way to drum up a bride for his own squire, even if there were any likely candidates about. Pascal knows it, and he's doing everything he can to rub it in. Pascal's only been engaged for about half an hour and he's already getting on everyone's nerves, so when Armand makes some excuse to get up and head out early for noon mess, the others are all eager to follow and I find myself momentarily alone with the beaming bridegroom-to-be.

I'm not entirely sure what motivates me. Maybe something still seems fishy to me and I don't dare probe about it, or I'm just in a suspicious mood, I don't know. But on a whim, instead of handing the cloth on the top of the laundry in my lap to Pascal, I hastily tuck it down into my waistband. Then when Pascal's back is turned, I rummage around in my traveling bag. The embroidered handkerchief I found in Brecelyn's chapel is still there, shoved down into the bottom of it.

"What's this?" Pascal asks, when I go over and hold it out to him.

"Tristan borrowed it from Gilles. I thought you could return it to him for me."

Pascal glances at it with distaste; I'd forgotten how filthy it was, but Gilles was right about one thing. The scent of cheap perfume is no longer lingering on it.

If I was expecting something dramatic, I'm disappointed. Pascal just shrugs, and says,

"Okay, Marek. You might have *washed* it first. But I suppose I can throw it in with Gilles's other things," and he takes the cloth out of my hand, turning away to carry it over and toss it onto a pile of Gilles's washing waiting to be delivered to the kitchens for boiling.

Pascal would never make a mistake about haberdashery, and it can only mean one thing. I feel a thrill of triumph tinged with annoyance; it's all exactly as I suspected at the time. The handkerchief is just Gilles's, and I've caught him out in one of his little practical jokes. He was deliberately lying to me about it that night, just to tease me. There are no traitors, or new plots afoot — no midnight conspirators meeting to plan 'skullduggery' out in Brecelyn's chapel.

Just as I'm working myself up into a satisfying state of indignation about it all, Pascal turns back to me with a frown. He's looking down at the cloth, only now taking a good look at it.

"Uh, wait a minute, Marek. You've made a mistake somewhere. This isn't Gilles's. *Red embroidery!*" He sniffs. "Whoever heard of such a thing? So *gaudy.*" He gives a little shudder that's just like the one Gilles made when I tried to hand the cloth to him. "Gilles would never own anything so tacky."

"But it's got his monogram on it," I insist, just as I did then.

"Gilles doesn't have monogramed handkerchiefs. And anyway, his monogram is a C, for Chartrain."

"Are you sure?" I press, and Pascal fixes me with a withering look. Of course, he knows every piece of Gilles's apparel inside out. "It's just that someone told me only a colossal ass would use his title for his monogram."

"What's your point?" he demands.

Pascal's back to idolizing Gilles again, so I let it drop. I fumble around a bit as though confused and then produce the cloth that Tristan actually gave me to return, and Pascal's mind is too full of thoughts of his fiancée for him to wonder about the origin of the other one. As I stuff it back down into the bottom of my bag, its big, red *G* staring up at me, I'm trying hard not to wonder where it came from either.

CHAPTER TWELVE

Pascal's engagement is the talk of the table at noon mess, and the boys are all much more inclined to be enthusiastic about Pascal's news now that toasting can be involved. At the Journey end of the table Tristan and Gilles are particularly exuberant, but from the way they keep putting their arms around each other's shoulders and pointedly calling each other 'partner,' I think it's more because of our plan than out of joy for Pascal, and I'm in a pretty good mood about it all, too.

After last night I've promised myself not to let fear of Taran keep me from enjoying mess with Tristan, so I'm just about to join them when Taran himself shows up, looking cool and collected and annoyingly not tired by the long morning of clouting at all. Tristan is as good as his word and he behaves himself, but the other Journeys aren't inclined to forgive Taran for his stellar performance at practice yet. Falko and Aristide exchange a glance, and sit down purposely on either side of him. Then they proceed to fall into exaggerated fits of coughing as a cover for choking out *dirty shot* at him under their breath. It doesn't help that for some reason Taran's got a brick from the wall with him, and as soon as Aristide sees it, he joins in by cackling,

"Hey, Mellor! Going to throw *that* at Tristan, too?" and when Taran sneers back,

"Maybe I am," I decide to sit down with the squires again.

After being proven wrong about the handkerchief, I'm feeling more inclined to be happy about Pascal's news myself, and guilty for thinking there could be anything wrong with it. And when Gilles gets up beaming to start off the toasts with a rousing,

"Gentlemen, join me in lifting our cups to my own dearest Pascal, and his lovely lady!," I have the grace to feel quite ashamed of myself. I give myself over to the convivial spirit and there's only one awkward moment, when down at our end of the table I get to my feet to lead the squires in a toast of our own.

"Hear, hear, boys!" I cry out enthusiastically, "Here's to Pascal and ... *er*, what's your fiancée's name, anyway?" and Pascal blushes.

"Oh, for mercy's sake!" Armand exclaims, seeing it. "Don't tell me you're *marrying* the girl, and you don't even know her *name?*"

But it's obvious that he doesn't; in typical fashion, Pascal's fallen in love with the girl knowing even less about her than Tristan did when he decided to fancy himself in love with Melissande. And when Rennie suggests,

"Why don't you just ask Gilles? He must know, to have arranged it all," Pascal's unwilling to admit ignorance in front of the whole table, particularly after Armand jeers,

"Yeah, Gilles probably got the name *right off the girl's own lips.*"

But the moment passes, and when Remy suggests,

"Why not just call her 'Ginger'? You know, for her red hair," we proceed to drink happily to Pascal and his Ginger; the name is so appropriate that the Journeys pick up on it, and soon I hear them toasting to 'Ginger,' too, down at their end of the table.

I'm determined not to get sidetracked or to rest on my laurels, though, so before long I'm only half-listening to the toasts, and I've started thinking about how to make the best use of the rest of my day. Master Leon's announced that the Journeys are to spend one more afternoon working out on the wall, so getting Tristan and Gilles started on practicing together is out ("So much for *'Firsts are our first and only priority'*" Gilles hissed, when he found out about it). So I suggest to the squires that we use the opportunity to start up squires' club again. But the boys remind me we've got our own task to finish, and I'm just resigning myself to a drab and unproductive afternoon of swabbing out the barracks when Remy nudges me, and something crinkles in my waistband.

"What's that, Marek?" he asks.

"It's a *list*," I reply, my throat suddenly dry, and I hold out my cup so he can refill it; I've only just remembered what it is that I'm actually going be doing this afternoon, and I'm definitely going to need another drink.

After mess I make my excuses to the boys back in barracks. My crossbow tutorial with Taran isn't due to start until the third hour, but it's going to take me a while to scrounge up the necessary equipment out in the tents, and even longer to scrounge up the necessary courage. Okay, so maybe I didn't really forget all about it. Maybe it's been lurking in the back of my mind ever since Master Leon showed me the list — crouching there biding its time, like a big hairy monster growing teeth and fangs, and I've just been trying not to think about it. Refusing to think about it.

Well, I refuse to let worrying about it now take up my whole afternoon. I will *not* let Taran get to me again. It can't last long anyway, can it? There's not that much to the repeating bow, which must be what the master wants me to show to the boys. I'll keep it short and sweet, no more than a quick demonstration of the basic mechanics of the thing, and then Taran'll take a few trials shots with it. It'll all be over before it's started, and Taran's not going to want to drag things out, either. We can both be adult and professional about it, I'm sure.

As I pass the entrance to the great hall on my way outside, I hear a faint scuffling coming from the shadows under the sideboard that stands outside it. I'd probably have just assumed it was a rat, if Falko didn't stump up beside me just then, his arms overflowing with the most disgusting and huge pile of filthy tights, and demand crossly,

"Have you seen my blasted squire anywhere, Marek? This backload of washing isn't going to take care of itself."

I tell him quite honestly that I haven't. When he's gone, I stick my hand down to help Frans crawl out of his hiding place, and I invite him to come along outside with me.

We end up wandering around for quite a while before we manage to locate the tent that's being used to house the guild workshop, and it's only when we're actually out among the pavilions that I really begin to get a sense of the scale of the work in progress on the field before me. Everywhere crews are hard at work digging trenches and laying foundations for the reconstruction of the wooden structures that once stood out here, and from the looks of it the new buildings are not only going to be much bigger than the originals, they're all going to be constructed entirely of stone.

From out among the tents I have a different view of the guild hall itself, too, or else I didn't notice before the full extent of the work that's being done on it. All the shutters and doors look like replacements, and some of the windows have even been fitted out with expensive bubbled glass where there was none before, so the place looks both better and worse than it did when we left it, an odd combination of old and new, ravaged and restored. Master Leon may have read them sarcastically, but the master's words about the place rising reborn out the ashes now seem fitting. It rises up behind us battered but not broken, and I feel an odd sense of kinship with the scarred old building. We've both had a tough winter. I know exactly how it feels.

Once we find the shop, the head fletcher Marcel greets us warmly, and I set Frans about the task of searching through the boxes stacked up in the back for one of the repeating bows and enough bolts to use with it. Soon he's poking around among the crates and chatting happily with the workmen, all of whom know him from his work in the shop last year. I leave him to it, and I find myself going over to one of the workbenches. It's standing empty toward the back of the tent, and on it materials for fletching a batch of arrows are already laid out neatly to hand.

I pick up one of the long, thin shafts. It's been beautifully smoothed and shaped, and without thinking I settle myself down at the bench. I look through the materials and choose a cock feather, and once I've positioned it carefully, I begin to attach it deftly in place with a thin silk thread. I'm behind on my fletching and it's been a long time since I replenished Tristan's stock, but there's no time for that now and that's not what brought me over. I'm not sure what it is — the angle of the bench, or the way the light is coming in through a flap in the tent, or the meticulous way the tools are ordered on the workspace, but there's something familiar about it that drew me over, and I know it isn't the destroyed guild shop where I spent so many hours last year that I'm thinking of. I'm thinking of my bench in my father's workshop back at our old home, and as I watch the red thread weave through the tines of the feather in my hand, I could be back there again, finishing a batch of broadheads for my father on the last day of his life.

When Marcel comes up beside me and puts his hand on my shoulder, and says in that reserved way he has,

"Good, Marek. Really good," his voice is deep and male, and I don't look up. I know it isn't my father. But it almost could be, and I have to blink my eyes. It makes me feel strange, too, when I realize how long it's been since I've thought of working with my father like this, or thought about our old life together. I've thought of my father often, of course. Every day. But I've always thought of him as I imagined he would have been, as a young man. I never let myself think of him as I really knew him, and it makes me sad to think that maybe I can think of it now because it doesn't hurt as much anymore, and because I'm starting to forget. I don't want to forget him. I don't want to get over it. But maybe I am. It's been a full year since he died, and I can't stop the healing force of time. As I watch my own hands run lovingly over the wood, though, thinking about the sensitive hands of a strong and silent man who took pride in his craft, I know the timing of it all isn't a coincidence, and time's not the only reason I'm thinking about the kind of man my father really was, right about now.

By the time I've accumulated a small pile of arrows next to me and I know I can't put it off any longer, Marcel tells us where to look to find the things packed up from the armory, and after some digging around, we dredge up one of the sorrier-looking dummies left over from our St. Sebastian's day show. We drag it feet first through the maze of tents and out onto the far butts, and Frans helps me prop it up to use as a target. But when one of the veterans emerges from the stables and looks around, and upon spotting us comes over to say,

"Are you ready out here, squire? I'm on my way to send Mellor in now," Frans scampers back off to barracks with an apologetic look and he leaves me to face Taran by myself, since he's even more afraid of running into Taran than I am.

There's nothing for me to do but stand in the middle of the field, alone except for the dummy, and wait for him. As I do, I go over nervously in my head some of the phrases I've worked out to use to explain the bow as efficiently as possible, and I repeat under my breath *"it can't last long,"* and "*how bad can it be?*" But I don't sound very convincing, and before long I've already picked my fingers into a bloody mess.

When I spot him, he's coming around from behind the embankment of the near butts. He must have been at work on the wall at the one place hidden from view from any vantage point in the yard, and as he comes ambling along across the butts he's in no apparent hurry whatsoever — even after he can surely see that I'm standing here like an idiot in the hot sun surrounded by a pile of equipment waiting for him.

Whatever Master Leon's got the boys doing, he must be working them pretty hard. Taran's covered from head to foot in a fine dusting of white and pinkish-red powder, and it's clinging to his skin and running down his chest and back in little rivulets of sweat. As he approaches he's reaching up one hand to shake more of it out of his hair, and as soon as I catch sight of him all the brave words I've been telling myself are pushed aside, replaced by a million things all racing through my mind at once: how angry I still am at him, and how glad I am that I've set a plan in motion to beat him; how good it felt to push him last night, and how nervous I am to face him now; and most of all, how determined I am not to let him get to me again.

At least, that's what I'm trying to think about. But it's damned hard, when what I'm really thinking is: Gilles was right, in what he said about Taran in the lavatory that day. He really is one magnificent bastard.

I'm not sure when it fully registers that he's bare-chested. For once even he's stripped off his tunic and he's got it flung across one shoulder. That must be what made me think of the lavatory, since I see now why he doesn't make a habit of it to go around shirtless like the other boys: Taran's so big and tall, with no shirt on and his trousers slung low there really is an indecent amount of his naked flesh on display.

He's moving along so slowly that by the time he gets close, I've managed to will my hands to remain still and I've calmed my nerves, and I've gotten myself nicely under control. But just when I open my mouth to deliver one of the pat little statements I've thought up to start things off, Taran walks right past me without a glance. He struts over to a shady place by the stables, tosses his tunic onto the ground, and proceeds to start splashing himself off with water from one of the big barrels standing against the archive wall. I have to admit he probably needs it. But he takes his own sweet time about it, deliberately making an exceptionally thorough job of it. There's nothing I can do but stand there as awkwardly as the dummy next to me, and watch him.

By the time he picks up his tunic and slings it over his shoulder again, he's probably used up an entire barrel's worth of water and he's left me hanging for so long that I'm thoroughly annoyed. A flush of anger has flooded my cheeks, and my irritation just makes me feel even more hot and bothered. When he finally saunters arrogantly over, reaching up both hands to run them through his wet hair in that move that always does incredible things to those incredible arms of his, all I can think is: *how in the hell can he have gotten to me already?!* It's enough to make me want to snatch up the bow, and give him a dirty shot myself. I don't know what irritates me more — the thought that he's purposely flaunting himself to try to fluster me. Or that maybe he isn't, and it's flustering me anyway.

He comes to a deliberate stop about two feet in front of me, and two feet over to one side. So when he straddles his legs wide, folds his arms behind his back, and snaps to attention in a stance that's such an exaggeration of our usual pose of respect that it's a parody of it, he's really in front of the dummy, not me. Then he opens his mouth, and it only takes about two seconds to see that Taran does not intend to be at all adult or professional about the lesson. That he intends to be a colossal jerk about it, in fact.

And I have to admit, it doesn't take me long to lose my cool, either.

Taran's standing stiffly at attention, and staring out in front of him over the dummy's head. Without looking down at me he raises his eyebrows, purses his lips, and says in a voice thick with sarcasm,

"You *required* my presence, *master?*" He drags out the words insultingly.

"It wasn't *my* idea!" I snap back.

"Wasn't it, though?" he asks, and I grit my teeth.

"Not at all," I say primly, running my hands down the fabric of my tunic and taking a breath to gain control of myself again, and then I launch straight into my spiel, determined not to let him get the best of me. I won't let him win this — whatever it is. As I do, he doesn't move or say anything; he just stands there uncomfortably close, but I refuse to give him the satisfaction of being the one to back away.

"Master Guillaume simply asked me to show everyone the basics of the repeating bow. There's not much to it, so it shouldn't take long. The first thing to remember about the bow is, er... well, the first thing, uh ... aren't you going to put your shirt back on?!"

It just slips out.

"Now that you mention it, I don't think I will," he says smoothly, and I blink.

"Unless, of course, it's *bothering* you," he adds. He looks down at me. He drops his tunic casually onto the ground. And steps one step closer.

Damn him! He is doing it on purpose.

"Not at all," I repeat, even more tersely than before. But my voice cracks, and I feel my cheeks redden. It *is* bothering me, and he knows it. And that it isn't just making me mad. He's known for a long time that I find him physically attractive. And that I'm not very good at controlling myself. He's going to milk the situation for all it's worth — and short of really shooting him, there's nothing I can do about it. I can't just walk away.

I regroup, and I try to start over again. But it's hard to concentrate. Taran's wearing his veteran's medal on a string around his neck and it's lying against his chest, beaded with moisture and resting between his impressive pectoral muscles, right at my eye level. Every time he takes a breath and his chest expands, the medal rises and falls, sliding distractingly out of place and then nestling back down into its resting place again. So I drop my eyes, only to be confronted with the sight of a single drop of water trickling down past his navel to wend its way through that soft line of hair below, the one I know from experience feels so good under my hand, and it's even worse. Particularly when I realize I've fallen silent, and that I'm just standing and staring down at it, biting my lip and watching its progress. And he's standing just as silently, watching me.

"Uh, what was I saying?"

"The repeating bow."

"Right."

Somehow I manage to stutter my way through an explanation of the mechanics of the bow by picking it up and holding it up between us, and focusing all my concentration on it. But the thing is heavy; the only one Frans could find out in the shop was one of the ones we expanded to hold extra bolts, and holding it out in front of me is making my arms tremble. Or maybe that's not the only reason I'm shaking, and the more obvious it gets the more flustered and incoherent I become, and Taran accordingly gets more and more amused — which just makes me angrier. It's a vicious cycle and it doesn't help that periodically he interrupts to ask something annoying, like "Is there something wrong with my medal? *No?* Then why do you keep staring at it?" or "Is it just me, or is it exceptionally *hot* out here today?," while making a show of wiping off some magnificent part of his body with his tunic.

At first, I try to counter with a few barbed comments of my own. At one point I exclaim tauntingly,

"So, I suppose being the son of 'Jakob Mellor' and all, you're never going to have to pay a price for any of your *dirty shots*, like starting a brawl in the main hall, or throwing a knife in the middle of evening mess!"

"Oh, *yes.* Yes, I am," is all he says, and he says it so ominously, I don't ask. But I can't resist adding,

"From now on then, maybe you'll know what's good for you, and keep your hands off Tristan!"

"*I* will, if *you* will," he sneers back.

After that, I stick to getting done with the lesson as quickly as possible.

When at last I've said my piece and I'm loading up the long box on top of the bow with the bolts Frans found for me, I take an inward sigh of relief. It's almost over. All that's left is to hand over the bow and let him try it.

"All you do is lift to engage and load, and then pull down swiftly to release, in one smooth motion. Go ahead and give it a go," I say, reaching out the bow to put it into Taran's hands.

He doesn't make a move to take it. With his arms still folded firmly behind his back, he says,

"I don't understand, *master*."

"What do you mean, you don't understand? It's very simple."

"Nonetheless."

I glare at him. He looks innocently back. So I start explaining, all over again. Before I get very far, he interrupts me again.

"I don't understand, *master*," he drawls, and it goes on like this for a ridiculously long time: me explaining the same steps over and over again in different ways, and him interrupting to repeat "I don't understand, *master*," with a smug look on his face.

"Oh, for Saint Peter's sake! It's totally obvious! What's to understand? And *stop* calling me *master!*" I finally explode, not bothering to hide anymore the fact that he's getting under my skin. By this point, it's not just Taran I'm furious at. I've also started feeling plenty angry at Master Guillaume into the bargain. The bow *is* obvious; a child could figure it out. I'd thought the master asking me to train the Journeys was an honor, but maybe what he was really doing was setting me up for humiliation all along. At least that's sure what it feels like now.

"Maybe so," Taran smirks. "But *maybe* you're not as good a trainer as you think you are, and you're just not explaining it very well. Try again," and I know who it is who's really trying to humiliate me. So I shove the bow against Taran's belly so hard and let go of it so fast that he has to take it, and I exclaim hotly,

"If you're so good at training, figure it out yourself! I'm done. The lesson's over."

I've already started to stalk away when he clears his throat, and not making any move to leave or change his stance, he says dispassionately,

"I'd hate to have to go to Master Leon, and tell him that you refused to train me. That you shirked your duty. I'd hate to think what the penalty might be, for that," and I have to turn around fuming and trudge back. I snatch the bow back out of his hand, hissing,

"Ratting out members now? That's a new low, even for you!"

"Just taking a page out of DuBois's book," he hisses back.

"Well, I'm all out of explanations. So what do *you* suggest?"

"There's only one solution," he says evenly. "You're going to have to take me through the motion yourself. You know, the way *I* showed *you* clouts."

"You've got to be kidding me!" I snap, incredulous. He can't be serious. But he is.

"I never kid about archery. So unless you want me to call Master Leon over, I'm going to have to insist."

He fixes me with a look that tells me he's going to drag this out excruciatingly until he's exacted every ounce of malicious pleasure from it he can, and that he's not going to let me go until I do things his way. So there's nothing for it. I have to follow him as he paces off a line thirty yards from the dummy, and when he's positioned himself with the big, loaded bow in front of him, I have to step up behind him.

"I don't suppose you'd consider putting your shirt back on for this," I mutter.

"I wouldn't dream of it," is all he says.

I'm fully expecting him to keep up a steady stream of insinuations and nasty comments as I position myself as carefully as I can behind him, but he restrains himself. And as I try to reach around him to get my own hands over his on the bow, he seems as tense and uncomfortable as I am. I've shuffled around for quite a while, bumping and pressing up against him, by the time he demands tightly,

"What's the holdup back there?"

"I can't reach!" I complain. "You're too big. Your arms are ridiculously long."

"It's your arms that are too short," he retorts. "Or you're not really *trying*," so I have to strain to push myself up closer.

To my horror, I start trembling again as I press my cheek flat against his bare back, and this time I don't have the excuse of holding up the bow, since I still can't reach it. It feels a little like he's trembling, too, but I'm probably just shaking so hard that it's my own motion I feel, and before I can stop myself, I hear myself groan,

"Oh *God*, do you have to smell *so* ..." I was about to say "*good*," but Taran bristles and snaps,

"*I've* been working out on the wall for the past two hours. What's *your* excuse?," and I have a sudden and violent urge to shove him again, as hard as I can. Instead I strain harder, eager to get it over with, but my fingertips still can't stretch far enough even to reach his wrists.

"This isn't going to work," I say flatly, dropping my arms, but for some reason not lifting my cheek off of his back.

There's a pause, and then he says softly,

"Try putting your arms underneath mine."

He doesn't lift his big arms away from his body. So I have to slip mine under his, sliding my hands around his waist, my open palms skimming along the tops of his hips just as though I really were taking him in a slow and intimate embrace. It takes all my will power not to think about the night I stood behind him in his hot little room in just this way, and reached out of my own accord to slide my hands eagerly over him — and I let my hand slide down.

"I still can't reach," I croak. "And if I *try* any harder to get closer behind you, I'm going to end up in front of you."

"All right. Do it," he croaks back, and we switch positions. And it's even worse.

As soon as he steps up behind me and puts his arms around me, we're right back in the windmill — in that reverse embrace that first stirred desire for him in me. Or out on Brecelyn's field, when he guided his hawk down to land on my hand and all at once there was something more there between us. At least, I'd thought there was, and at the memory I'm hot with shame. And when I think how often he must have held Melissande in just this way, of what must have come next between them, my cheeks blaze hotter until my skin could be on fire. But with him pressing up behind me and his arms around me I can't think straight, and such a confusion of emotions has bubbled up in me that I can't sort them all out or think at all beyond the feeling of him warm and close all around me. He must feel how hard I'm shaking now but I can't even worry about that, or about how pleased with himself he must be at my obvious reaction.

For some reason, though, Taran doesn't seem inclined to gloat. He's fallen silent, too, and his ragged breathing is moving me just as my trembling and swaying are moving him, and our bodies have begun to fall into a rhythm just as they did in the windmill that day. It feels so right and natural to be in his arms like this that I've almost forgotten what it is we're actually doing here by the time he rouses himself to take the bow gently out of my hands, and in a voice that's as soft as a whisper against the back of my neck, he says,

"Go on, Marieke," and I put my own hands over his on the bow.

"Just aim, and shoot," I tell him, when I've found my voice. But it's no more than a whisper, too, and I know I sound bitter. "Just imagine that dummy is your worst enemy, and pump the lever for all you're worth."

And he does. Slowly at first, and then faster and faster, the muscles of his arms tensing and releasing as they slide against my arms, and I'm pumping right along with him. I close my eyes, and I let myself lean back hard against him. What does it matter? I've got nothing more to lose, so I fling my head back against his chest, and as I let his motion vibrate through me, I give myself over to it — and God help me, when we reach a fever pitch and I don't think the lever can fly any faster, in my mind I twist around in his arms as he lowers me onto the ground, and I'm joyously finding out what it would be like to experience with him what surely would have happened next that night on the floor of his hot little room, if Remy hadn't interrupted us.

I'm not sure how long we've been standing with the bow lowered and the lever still before I realize he's done, and I come back to earth with a thud. He's shot all his bolts, and he must be waiting for me to say something, since he hasn't released me. He's still got his arms wrapped around me and it must be my imagination, but it feels a lot like he hugs me to him tighter for a moment, and rests his own head heavily down on the top of mine.

I open one eye tentatively, afraid to see what he's done. I'm not strong enough really to aim the repeating bow; it's too heavy and unwieldy. But holding up the massive bow is nothing to Taran. So I'm fully expecting that he's aimed his shots carefully and done some virtuoso grouping of the bolts, to demonstrate just how much he didn't need a tutorial of any kind from me.

Since I told him to picture his worst enemy, he's probably done something like arranging the arrows on the dummy's face in the exact shape of my scars, all except for one — straight through the eye.

And it's true, he *has* arrayed his shots with remarkable precision. They're just not at all in the place I expected them to be. There's nary an arrow in the dummy's eye, or anywhere else on its head. He's put all thirty bolts into the dummy in a perfect circle, low and tight — right in the center of its belly.

It's so disturbing, I lurch forward with a little cry of surprise and dismay, and Taran drops his arms from me with a start, like a man snapping out of a trance.

"So, what do you think? Have I got the hang of it?" he sneers. I feel like someone's poured a bucket of icy water over my head and brought me back to myself with a jolt, too. But the full weight of embarrassment over my flagrant and one-sided reaction to him doesn't fully hit me until he adds,

"Or wasn't my performance enough to *satisfy* you?"

He drops the bow in the dust at my feet and stalks off, leaving me alone on the field with the ravaged dummy. I'm still staring at the arrows bristling horribly from its abdomen and I know I shouldn't do it. But I can't let him leave the field the winner without at least getting in a parting shot, to get a little of my own back.

So I call out tauntingly after him,

"So, what are you going to do now, Taran? Run off and do it, with Melissande?!?"

AS SOON AS TARAN'S OUT OF SIGHT I LEAVE THE EQUIPMENT where it fell and I run off the field, heading for the first place that offers concealment and willing myself not to cry. I make straight for what's left of the stables; it's the only place that doesn't have workmen crawling all over it, and by the time I throw myself down onto the hay in one of the innermost stalls, a steady trickle of tears has started to fall and my chin is quivering with barely contained anger. *How in the hell can I still want a boy I don't even like, one I can't respect?* But it's just lust. It's meaningless, and it's nothing new. It's my whole story with him, isn't it? Responding to a boy I despise, just because he's the only one who knows I'm a girl. I've dealt with it before, and if it weren't so humiliating it would almost be funny: I'm literally *right back* where I was after the windmill. I feel just like I did then, too: furious at Taran, for pulling such a cheap trick. And at myself, for being such an easy target. But I know being manipulated by Taran isn't really why I'm crying.

I can still feel what it was to have his arms warm and close all around me, and I'm finally doing what I've wanted to do all these weeks and haven't let myself, and I'm crying for the loss of him. Or at least, for the boy I once believed him to be, and for the loss of what it was I'd thought he felt for me.

I'm crying, because he broke my heart.

I throw myself down onto the straw, and I have a good, long cry. I really let myself go, and I sob out huge gulping sobs that wrack my body, and I wallow in it. And maybe that's exactly what I've needed all along, to put it behind me.

I'm still sprawled face-down in the hay when Remy finds me less than five minutes later.

Back in barracks, Pascal's apparently managed to round up a crew of reluctant kitchen boys to help put the place in order, and in the resulting hubbub Remy's taken the opportunity to duck out and come looking for me. I'm not sure how he managed to find me so quickly, but Remy always seems to have a sixth sense about this sort of thing, and I suppose it serves me right for picking one of his own master's favorite hiding places to squirrel myself away.

I must look quite wild, because Remy takes one look at me over the top of the stall and with a little cry, he bustles in and plops himself down next to me. Before I can protest or make an embarrassed show of straightening up and pulling myself together, he puts an arm around me and guides my head down onto his shoulder. He strokes the hair out of my eyes while cooing soothing little noises, and he's being so gentle and so solicitous that before long I'm glad he's found me. There's something so sweet and familiar about being nestled up protectively against him like this that again I have the strange sensation I could be back on that disastrous day when my encounter with Taran in the windmill changed everything, and Tristan came to comfort me over it here in the straw.

"What's the matter, Marek?" Remy asks softly, after a while. "Do you have a *secret?*"

When all I do is mumble, he says earnestly,

"You *do*, don't you? I knew it! Won't you trust me, Marek, and tell me what it is? You can trust me. You'd feel better, if you shared it. And, well, *you* know how I feel. There's *nothing* you could tell me that would ever change the way I feel about you."

He's looking at me with big, sad eyes and he looks so concerned, for a split-second I almost do it. The temptation is there, so sharp I can taste it. It would be such a relief finally to unburden myself and to have someone to confide in, and I do trust him. He's my best friend now after Tristan, and of all the boys I think he'd take the news the best of all of them. I'd finally know what the boys would think, if they knew I was a girl. What Tristan might say, if I ever end up having to tell him.

But I know I can't do it. I can't be disloyal again, and it's bad enough that I've already let one boy find out something so serious that I haven't told my own master. So I just shrug, and although I can tell he's not happy about it, after a while he stops pressing.

We sit there together for a while longer, me with my head resting against his chest and him with his head resting down on top of mine, and it's nice. Companionable, and to his credit he doesn't try anything. But when I catch myself thinking that I can feel the contours of his body through the thin fabric of his shirt, I pull away.

I'm confused enough already.

I sit up and wipe my eyes, and when I've composed myself, I do feel better. All my tears are spent, and as Remy helps me to my feet, I make a silent promise to myself that this will be the last time I ever let myself cry over a boy — particularly Remy's master. And I tell myself firmly:

So what if I haven't quite figured out how to keep Taran from getting to me, *yet*? I'm sure I can get a handle on it, eventually — and in the meantime, there is one thing I can do. I can make damned sure I never let Taran see just how much he does affect me, ever again. If rattling me in this fashion is going to be his new ploy for undermining me this year, he's going to have plenty of opportunities and I'm just going to have to find a way to deal with it, because I know it wasn't my imagination. He *was* purposely trying to elicit a response from me, out on the field.

Seducing me, even.

The only thing is, there was just nothing subtle about it.

If *that* was Taran's idea of seduction, I don't see how I can really believe he's ever been the smooth operator de Gilford made him out to be.

CHAPTER THIRTEEN

By the time Remy's helped me store away the dummy in an empty stall and we've made our way together back to barracks, the boys have the place all cleaned up. I'm at my leisure for the rest of the afternoon, and what I really should do is get to work replenishing Tristan's stock, and my own. But I can't face going back out to the shop today, and now that I know where the Journeys are working, I decide to head out to find Tristan. He won't be in any shape to practice, but Master Leon's promised not to keep the boys out too late today and I figure I can go and watch for them a while. It might even be possible to do a little brainstorming about the trick, if Tristan's working alone or if he and Gilles have stationed themselves somewhere together. I'll admit to a certain curiosity, too, to see for myself just what it is that Master Leon has the boys doing.

Before I'm even halfway across the butts, a steady chorus of resounding booms and cracks fills my ears, followed by the sound of men shouting. The commotion is so loud it was surely audible during my tutorial with Taran, and I cringe to think how preoccupied I must have been not to have noticed it earlier. I can't imagine what can be causing such a racket; it's the loudest wall-mending operation I've ever heard.

The noise gets increasingly louder as I make my way around the embankment at the far end of the butts, and when I come out on the other side, I stop in my tracks. I'm still some distance out but the Journeys are all there in front of me, lined up along the guild wall and interspersed among a crowd of older veterans. The men are all in the same state as Taran was in earlier: stripped down to breeches and drenched in sweat, and covered in a fine powdering of brick and mortar dust. But they're not laying bricks, or slapping mortar onto holes in the wall with trowels in their hands. They're swinging sledgehammers. And most of the northwest wall is gone. They're not building the wall back up. They're tearing it down.

"Has everyone gone crazy? What in the world is going on?!" I demand. I don't expect anyone to answer.

To my surprise, a deep voice behind me says,

"We're expanding! Master G's appropriated dozens of properties adjacent to the guild that were abandoned after the plague, and bought out others. That whole section of the wall behind the butts is coming down. Then we're going to rebuild it — about 300 yards further out."

I'm too busy taking in the unexpected scene in front of me to wonder at the unusual friendliness of the man. Or for it to fully register that there's something familiar about his voice, until I ask,

"What's the master going to put back there?!" and he replies,

"He's got big plans, Marek. More barracks, I think, and I'm not sure what else, but I do know one thing. The guild's going to get its own forge, so we'll be self-sufficient. Points, laths, triggers, and cranks — everything you need for a bow or a crossbow, you name it — we can make all our own equipment. I ought to know. I'm going to be in charge of running the place."

I whirl around.

Sure enough, I'm looking up into the smiling face of my favorite former Journey, Charles. I'm so glad to see him back inside the walls that I throw my arms around him with an enthusiastic cry, despite a disturbing thought that flashes through the back of my mind as soon as I get a good look at him: in the short time since I've seen him last, he's already grown into a man.

As it happens, Charles was coming out to watch the work in progress, too. So we make our way over together to the place where Gilles and Tristan are standing, leaning on the upturned handles of their long hammers and wiping the sweat from their brows. The veteran overseeing the work has gotten himself embroiled in a disagreement with one of the brick suppliers and a ragtag group of workers he's brought with him to sort through the rubble for reusable material, and the boys are taking a self-imposed break. Even in all the hubbub it's easy to spot them, although with the dust covering their hair and shoulders the men all look much the same; only one of them is wearing peacock blue silk tights, and I'd recognize the silhouette of the boy next to him as Tristan's anywhere.

As we go, Charles catches me up on all his news.

"I won't be living at the guild, of course. Once we break ground on the smithy, though, I'll be working here every day and I'm to have a special associate member status. That'll mean putting up with you lot again regularly for mess," he says affectionately, and I'm really glad that one of the familiar faces Master Guillaume was talking about has turned out to be Charles's. But as he tells me more about the master's plans, I can't help asking,

"What about the other smiths in town? Won't their guild object?"

"How can they? We won't be taking on outside work. It'll all be in-house. Everything we make will be strictly to supply St. Sebastian's."

I refrain from saying that supplying the guild probably represents more than half the blacksmith orders in town.

"Besides, the biggest forge in the local guild belongs to my own father.

He's certainly not going to object," Charles laughs, and I have to admire Master Guillaume's savvy. Charles is so capable I'm sure he is the best man for the job. But hiring the son of the head of the blacksmiths' guild was also a damned clever move.

When we join the boys, Tristan greets me with a sweeping motion that takes in both his filthy state and the wreckage of the wall behind him, and with a grin he says dramatically,

"Behold your master, Marek, and all his works! Oh hullo, Charles. We're about done out here, but there's still time to get in a swing or two, if you're game. Look at those shoulders! I bet you could take down the walls of Jericho now, all by yourself," and I see from his casual tone that everyone *else* has known since yesterday that Charles was back. In typical fashion, nobody bothered to tell me anything about it.

"Gads if DuBois isn't right," Gilles exclaims, giving Charles an exaggerated look up and down. "Whatever *have* they done to you at that smithy, Charles? No proportion! All arms and no legs. If you get any more top-heavy, you're going to keel right over."

"Speaking of keeling over," Tristan sneers, looking over my shoulder, "I'd gladly knock a few blocks off *his* wall," and I turn to look. I see I was wrong. All the Journeys weren't here.

Taran is just coming into view, trudging around from the opposite end of the embankment, only just now returning from our tutorial. I'm not sure what he can have been doing all this time (gloating, probably) and I don't know why, but as I watch him take his place stiffly next to Jurian about 40 yards down the wall, an image of him hiding out behind the stables with his head resting heavily against its back wall flits through my mind. I see he's put his shirt back on.

"Where in the hell has *he* been?! So he's a shirker, too," Tristan's continuing sourly, glaring at Taran so hard I almost expect the air between them to catch fire. "I can't believe I ever thought there was *anything* honorable about him. Honor!" He spits, then picks up his hammer and smashes it into the wall in a way that suggests he's picturing Taran's head. "He doesn't know the meaning of the word!"

"There was an *incident*, at the castle," Gilles drawls to a bemused Charles, by way of explanation. To Tristan he says soothingly,

"Come, come, man! Surely you're not still up in arms about that kiss. He was stinking drunk. *Stinking!* (Really, Charles, you should have seen it. *Taran*, drunk! It was *most* entertaining). Anyway, *I* for one am inclined to forgive a man his first serious bender."

"And what about *that?*" Tristan demands, gesturing to Gilles's jaw. "Are you going to forgive him for laying you out flat?"

"Goodness, I seem to have missed quite a lot," Charles exclaims, as Gilles reaches up to finger his jaw gingerly, and I miss some of their exchange as I fill Charles in on highlights of Taran's recent activities. Down the wall, the quarrel between the supervising master and the brick supplier is heating up; since the veteran in charge is a burly man named Bernard who's known for his temper, nobody expects it to blow over very soon and the other men have all stopped working, too. A few wander down to watch, while the others mill around starting up conversations of their own or openly eavesdropping on ours. So there's already a group of veterans standing around the boys in a loose circle as Gilles says,

"Hmm. You have a point there. However, I do believe the old boy *may* have had some provocation. I rather suspect he was pushed. By a squire, standing right next to *me*," and I look over at him in alarm.

Fortunately, Gilles isn't looking at me. He's inspecting his fingernails with disapproval (although somehow he's managed to avoid getting nearly as dirty as everyone else), but there's something about the bland expression on his face I don't like, and I've just remembered who *else* was standing right next to me last night. I'd hate to think what it might mean, if Gilles thinks Pascal purposely set him up for a fall.

What's more, Tristan is still glaring down the line toward Taran with a murderous expression. And when he says vehemently,

"Forgive what you like, Gilles. But *I'll* not excuse his crude treatment of her. Nothing can excuse that,"

Gilles clears his throat meaningfully.

He does it in just the way he did yesterday morning, when I'd thought he was about to tell us exactly what it is he thinks he knows about Taran and Melissande — only much more loudly. And this time, Tristan hears it, too.

"If you have something to say, Lejeune, by all means, say it," Tristan says coolly.

"Possibly the *timing* of it all had begun to bother Taran, too," Gilles replies mildly.

Next to me Charles falls silent, and the veterans around the boys all fall silent, too. They all lean in collectively closer, as though they've understood the point of Gilles's comment and they're eager not to miss what Tristan's going to say about it. That it can't be anything good is obvious from the dark expression that's come over Tristan's face. But it's too cryptic for me. So it comes as a shock when Tristan says in a voice so cold and hard I never thought to hear him use anything like it to Gilles,

"Are you saying that *I* was the father of Melissande's baby?"

All the men take an eager step closer.

Charles wisely takes a big step back. I'm taking a hasty step backward, too, and thinking to myself miserably: *so much for the shortest partnership in the history of teamwork.*

Thankfully, Gilles just chuckles.

"Mercy, Tristan! Don't be daft. Of course I'm not. I know you much too well to suspect you of anything like that," and the moment passes.

Tristan's mollified, and when one of the veterans listening in grumbles,

"Nothing doing here after all, men," and with a gesture toward the place where the irate master of works is now overturning one of the stone supplier's wheelbarrows and kicking the spilled contents around the field, he adds, "Let's go see if old Bernard's going to haul off, and hit him with a brick!," the men all move off in search of better entertainment. But I'm still feeling off-balance and Tristan is frowning, as Gilles continues,

"*I'd* never think it. All I'm saying is that *Taran* probably does. Why, you boys said it yourselves, didn't you? That Taran *already* suspected last year that you'd gone too far with his fiancée. I mean really, admit it! Running around Louvain naked with her veil strapped around your middle was not the subtlest of moves. And after that searing look you two were exchanging when he stumbled in that night, can you blame him? Surely that explains his vulgar kiss."

Next to me Charles shifts around uncomfortably, in a way that suggests the idea that Tristan had taken things too far with Melissande had already crossed *his* mind last year, and Tristan himself is uncharacteristically at a loss for words, because it's true. We *did* think it, and it's all so obvious, I can't believe the possibility didn't occur to me before.

I mean, *I* know Taran was the father of the baby, of course. But how could Taran himself be so sure? He'd have no way of knowing that Tristan had no opportunity with Melissande, the way I do. Tristan was with me all the time during our Christmas stay at the castle — except when he was training, or when I was busy with my chores, or with squires' club. Or whenever it was that Tristan snuck off to practice scaling the wall. Or any number of times, really. But that's not the point. It's my own faith in Tristan's character that assures me he'd never have done it, and I doubt Taran has the same faith in him. We all know exactly what Taran thinks of Tristan, in fact; the pointed insults he was hurling at Tristan at mess last night leave no doubt about that, and it all fits. All I have to do is think of Taran's carefully grouped bolts right in the dummy's belly to be absolutely sure that Gilles is right.

"You can't expect me to believe that that brute would publicly claim a baby he thought was *mine*, just to protect a woman's reputation!" Tristan objects indignantly.

"Why not?" Gilles drawls back. "I've always thought there's no end to the amount of absurd nonsense Taran's capable of, in the name of honor and duty. But there's no need to think he did it for her, or for any other noble reason," he adds hastily, seeing Tristan's expression. "He'd have had a selfish motive, too, wouldn't he? He'd want to protect his own reputation, and to avoid more unseemly scandal. Think of the talk! It would have been worse than anything you boys endured back in Meuse. What a laughingstock he'd have been, if he'd had to admit that *you* got to her first! Why, it's positively *Greek*: his fiancée, carrying a bastard son — fathered by his own father's bastard! No offense, dear boy."

As we absorb this horrible statement, Charles and I look nervously at

Tristan to see how he's taking it. He doesn't look mad at Gilles, exactly. But his face is turning a funny shade of green and he's staring down in front of him with a stony look on his face, and I can tell the sordidness of the situation is starting to hit him. It doesn't help that Gilles seems perfectly delighted about it; he's blathering on as though talking to himself, rubbing his hands together gleefully and almost chuckling,

"Can you *imagine* anything worse than finding out you're engaged to a girl who's *already* carrying another man's child — a man who's your virtual *brother* — and knowing there's absolutely nothing you can do about it? How much worse, if you really love the girl! Besides," he adds briskly, bringing himself back to the point,

"You can't convince me Taran's ever even as much as touched her."

Tristan gives him a supremely sarcastic look, and he amends, "Well, not in *private*, anyway."

"Wait a minute," I object, beating Tristan to it as what Gilles is saying fully sinks in. "Aren't you're forgetting something, Gilles? If the baby wasn't *Tristan's*, and it wasn't *Taran's*, then whose baby *was* it!?!" I demand.

But Gilles can't answer that. And when pressed, even Gilles has to admit it's exceedingly unlikely that Melissande was fooling around with yet a *third* boy, back at the castle. Finally he has to concede that the baby must have been Taran's, saying,

"Well, I'll grant you this much. I doubt it was anyone else's."

THE CALL TO RESUME WORK SOON GOES UP, AND AS THE battered and bloodied brick supplier is wheeled off to the infirmary in one of his own wheelbarrows and the veterans all give a cheer for the success of old Bernard's subtle negotiations, the boys have to turn their attention back to the wall. I'm mighty glad the conversation is over, but when Charles wanders off to check on the progress of his smithy, I'm left alone with nothing to do but watch Tristan's angry back and think about Gilles's words. From the way Tristan's swinging his hammer mercilessly against the wall in front of him, I'm pretty sure he's thinking about them, too.

Okay, I'll admit it. What I *should* be doing right now is worrying about what Tristan's thinking. But what I'm really doing is feeling bitterly disappointed at finding out that *this* is what Gilles has been hinting at, all along. I guess I've been secretly hoping that Gilles really did know something about Taran and Melissande that would make the whole thing more bearable. This just makes it worse.

It doesn't help that there is one detail I'm pretty sure Gilles is wrong about, and that's the timing of it all. His comments about Taran's ridiculous sense of honor have dredged up an uncomfortable memory — of Melissande quarreling with Taran in the guild chapel on the day of our squires' exhibition, only to run out in a flood of tears to vomit in the rose garden afterward. And of Taran telling me the very next day that he'd just sacrificed his own happiness for honor's sake. I'd thought at the time that he meant he'd broken off with Melissande, but it's all so obvious now, isn't it? Melissande surely already knew she was pregnant that day, and she was telling him so. For Taran to have reacted to the news as he did, he must have suspected way back then that the baby was Tristan's. Taran's doubts didn't start that drunken night at the castle; he's been tormenting himself with the possibility that the son he lost might really have been Tristan's, all this time.

It takes the men less than an hour to bring down what's left of the wall, and with the day's work done, they're soon all crowding thirstily around a gaggle of kitchen boys who've come out with jugs of ale and tin cups to offer them refreshment. But Tristan doesn't join them. He hardly waits to be dismissed before he throws his hammer down in disgust. Wordlessly he shrugs back into his tunic, dusts himself off, and without a backward glance he strides off around the embankment. Soon he's disappearing across the far field, and I'm hurrying after him.

Now I *am* worrying about what Tristan's thinking, and it can't be good. If his thoughts are anything like my own he's sure to be in a foul mood; I mean, he *did* pursue Melissande shamelessly last year, and if Taran's gotten the wrong idea about it, when I think of how I procured her white rose for him, I know I share a portion of the blame. Tristan's posture as he weaves his way through the crews of workmen and the pavilions in front of me seems to confirm it: I can almost see little eddies of steam rising off of him as he stalks along, and he's moving so fast I can't catch up with him until he's passed all the tents dotting the far field and he's already climbing over the back wall at the place where it separates the guild grounds from the woods beyond.

"Tristan, it's already getting late!" I call, clambering up after him.

"Come on, if you're coming," he calls back. "I've got to get some air."

There isn't any more air to be had on one side of the wall than the other, but I know what he means. Unlike me, Tristan is always more relaxed outside the confines of the guild. So I don't say anything. I just scramble over to follow him, and it's not until he's crossed the open space outside the wall and plunged into the forest beyond that he's forced to slow his pace enough to allow me to come up breathlessly behind him.

He's still moving awfully fast, so it takes all my wind to keep up with him, which is fine by me. I have no idea what to say, and Tristan's not inclined to talk, either. So there's nothing to break the silence that settles between us until we come to a place where we're accustomed to cross over a little stream on a fallen log. Even then, when Tristan reaches back to help me across and for a moment his eyes meet mine over our clasped hands, all he says is,

"I hope you've been giving some serious thought to our trick, Marek. Because whatever it is, it had better be damned good."

After that, Tristan gradually slackens his pace so that eventually I can fall into step beside him. At first, I try to use his comment as an opening to draw him into a discussion of some tentative ideas for the exhibition, since it's all going to be a bit tricky, actually; I mean, neither boy is likely to consent to a stunt that allows the other boy to outshine him. But how can I make the skills required for all the shots absolutely equal and really have it be one trick embedded in another, and not just the same trick done side by side? And if I do come up with something where one trick sets up the other, what a disaster it would be if the first boy missed his shot entirely, leaving none at all for the second! Particularly if that second boy is Tristan. But he won't be drawn in, and when the only thing I can get out of him is a rather sour,

"What about something, with *birds?*," I let it drop; it doesn't take much to guess what's put him in mind of publicly shooting down the things, given how much Taran loves them. I content myself with mulling over the possibilities silently to myself, and by the time we've put some distance between us and St. Sebastian's, Tristan is noticeably calmer. But I'm just beginning to think that coming up with even a mediocre joint trick is going to be something of a challenge.

We've been ambling along for a while now, to all appearances wandering aimlessly and in no hurry to get anywhere in particular. But I know where we're going. I knew it the minute Tristan climbed over the wall, and when we inevitably come out into the meadow in front of the embankment where the old windmill stands, I'm not at all sure how I feel about it. It's our place, and it wouldn't be returning to St. Sebastian's without coming here with Tristan again. But it's also the last place I want to be so soon after my crossbow fiasco with Taran, and the crumbling structure with its broken arms reaching out for me now could almost be a monument to the confused state of my feelings for the both of them.

Once inside, Tristan takes his accustomed seat by the window and I settle myself in my usual spot on the floor. He swings the shutters open to let the late afternoon sun stream in, sending a cloud of dust swirling lazily in the shafts of light between us, and when he turns his head to gaze out of the window, I watch him for a while in silence.

He's perched on the windowsill, his back resting against the place where the open shutter fits into the wall, and he's wearing his usual attire: black trousers and a loose white shirt that's open at the neck. One of his long legs is down, the other in its tall black boot is bent up high on the sill in front of him so he can drape one arm lightly on his knee. By chance his pose is almost identical to the one I first saw him in on the top of the garden wall, and with his head thrown back against the open shutter, his face is in sharp profile against the rich afternoon light. It's a magnificent profile, and I'm struck by it almost with surprise, as though I'd half-forgotten just how beautiful he really is. With the look of brooding melancholy that's settled over his handsome features, even sweaty and dirty he looks every inch the romantic hero, and I wonder how I could have ever thought falling back in love with him would be a chore. I'm halfway there already, just looking at him.

He's got a faraway expression on his face, and I don't think he's looking out at St. Sebastian's in the distance, or into the meadow below. He's seeing much further in his mind, out past the treetops and the fields beyond, all the way back to Brecelyn's castle and down into the little clearing in Brecelyn's woods. I can read his thoughts so vividly I could be there again, Taran's broken arrow clutched in my hand. I can't bring myself to question him about the things Gilles was just saying at the wall, but I've never asked Tristan anything about what happened in Brecelyn's woods that day or how he felt about the revelations of that morning, and I feel so confused about it all now myself that I have to ask him about it.

At first he doesn't respond.

"If I tell you the truth, you'll laugh at me," he finally says, and it's so not what I was expecting, I almost do laugh.

"Go on."

"I guess what I feel most is disappointed, in him."

It takes a full minute for the gender of the pronoun he's used to register with me. And when it does, I almost laugh again, I'd been so certain he was thinking about Melissande. But it isn't funny, and I can't even smile. Not when it's so close to how I feel about Taran myself.

"So you *do* think he tried to kill you, after all," I say, confused. I'd thought he was saying the opposite, last night.

"Yes. No. Oh, I don't know. What does it matter?" he sighs. "I don't care about that."

"I do!" I protest. "And I thought you did, too. At least, you were plenty angry about it, when you first saw his broken arrow."

"I can't explain it, Marek," he says, and he sounds so tired, for a minute I think he's not going to try. "I *was* angry. That wasn't a lie, or pretend. But I don't think it was really real to me. It was all sort of a game, you know? Part of our rivalry, another thing to hate him for. I was even glad of it, if that makes any sense. Proof positive, that self-righteous, holier-than-thou Taran Mellor wasn't any better than the rest of us! That he was *worse*, in fact. I don't know if I ever really believed it, deep down. I was just working myself up into a glorious state over it, getting ready to give one of my best performances, if you know what I mean, Marek — it would have been a thing of beauty, a real tour de force! — when Remy let slip about the baby, and, well ..."

He breaks off, shifting around and lowering his eyes. "Well, to say it was a shock is an understatement. I couldn't be glad of *that*. It wasn't a game anymore. Whatever I may have said about Taran in the past, I never thought he'd do something like it. If he could treat her that way, well, then he's capable of anything. Except, of course, of *missing*," he adds bitterly. "So did he shoot me? I don't know. I guess now I wouldn't put it past him to try to kill me. But Taran doesn't miss, Marek, and Gilles was right. That arrow could have gotten into the woods any number of ways."

"His colors were on it, Tristan," I insist. I don't mention Remy. Something tells me that bringing him up wouldn't be a good idea right now, since Tristan still calls him Taran's little rat.

"That's just it, Marek," Tristan says. "Taran's big, but he's not stupid," and I grimace uncomfortably at the memory of the phrase. Mistaking my reaction for objection, he adds more adamantly,

"Only a fool would shoot another Journey with an arrow marked with his own colors, and Taran's no fool. Besides, the arrow that *did* hit me was *unmarked*."

I've already opened my mouth to argue with him when what he's saying hits me, and I have to clamp it closed again. Tristan's perfectly right. I know better than anyone that the arrow I pulled out of Tristan's side *didn't* have Taran's colors on it, and I don't know why I didn't notice it before. It *is* odd.

"If it were the other way around," Tristan's continuing, "it might make sense. If he'd brought an unmarked arrow along with him to use on me during the *first* hunt, he could have been angry enough when you bumped me out if its way to risk using one of his own on the *second* hunt, when he got an unexpected second chance ..." He breaks off, shaking his head. "But it was the *first* arrow that was marked, not the second — that is, if that broken arrow of his you found really was the one that missed me, and there isn't another unmarked arrow still lying around somewhere out in Brecelyn's woods."

"Well, couldn't it have been the reverse?" I say, trying to piece a theory together to make it fit. I know there has to be some explanation, since Remy as good as admitted to me that he saw Taran take the shot. "Maybe his first shot was pure impulse, in a moment of anger. And then when he found he had a second chance, he had a cooler head and he used an unmarked arrow."

"That he got from where, exactly?" Tristan asks sarcastically.

"There were plenty of archers around who weren't Journeys, Tristan. He could have taken it from the quiver of one of Brecelyn's men easily enough, couldn't he? They weren't shooting, but they were armed," I argue, but I see what Tristan's saying. The simple fact that the first arrow was marked means that Taran didn't bring unmarked arrows with him from St. Sebastian's. Whatever else may be true, Taran's attack on Tristan wasn't premeditated.

"What does it matter, Marek?" Tristan says, cutting me off just as I'm starting to feel unpleasantly muddled. "There's no way now to know what really happened, and in any event he's not stupid enough to try it again. And frankly, I don't care about it anymore. Even if it is true, he's done worse."

I know Tristan doesn't mean to be absurd, and I can see he's genuinely upset. But how anyone could think that Taran fooling around with his own fiancée before his wedding is worse than almost killing his half-brother is beyond me. So before I can stop myself, I hear myself protesting,

"I was shocked too, Tristan, that *Taran* of all people would be ... er ... that the two of them were, *uh* ... well, you know. *Not letting the grass grow*," I stammer, stumbling over the words and trying not to picture it. "Is it really all that surprising, though? I mean, it's actually pretty common. Why, Rennie and his fiancée were, *uh*, 'fraternizing' all the time at the castle, and nobody batted an eye. After all, a marriage contract's as good as permission."

"Are you trying to defend him?!" Tristan snaps.

"No, of course not!" I cry. But maybe I am, and I can't believe I've just quoted *Brian de Gilford* back at him. I must be more upset than I'd realized, that in all of this what Tristan still cares about the most is Melissande. That she was an active participant in it all seems to have slipped his mind.

"You still don't get it, do you, kid?" he says, seeing my baffled expression. "It's not just that all his hype about being so honorable wasn't true, or that *he's* the one who's dragged her name through the mud and exposed her to ridicule. Oh, I know what you're thinking," he adds hastily, and I must look a little accusatory, "and you're right. I *did* set out to win her over, and I *did* try to rub his face in it. And maybe *that* started out as a game, too — at first. But I really love her, Marek. So if I helped precipitate what happened to her, I'll never forgive myself. And how was I to know he'd think so little of her as to really believe the worst of her, or that he'd treat her so cruelly? That's all on *him*, Marek, and I will never forgive him for that."

"Tristan, what *are* you talking about?" He's not making any sense, and he sounds so irrational I've started to get worried. His voice has started taking on a suspiciously dramatic coloring, too, and for a moment the disloyal thought even crosses my mind that this is all some kind of act. Either that, or for once he's actually as overwrought as he often pretends to be.

"You don't think what happened between them was any of *Melissande's* doing, do you?" he demands vehemently. "I should have known it, right from the start! She'd never have willingly compromised her virtue, or her reputation." I stare at him blankly. He stares back. Then he bursts out,

"At least, not when she's still in love — with *me!*"

I struggle to keep any hint of an expression off my face. Needless to say, I don't have quite the same faith in Melissande's virtue that Tristan does. But I guess he didn't hear the tone of her voice when she invited Taran huskily to kiss her that day in the chapel, while he was lying passed out stone cold only a few feet away, and it must be exactly as I feared. That blazing look she gave him back at the castle's gotten him all fired up. So I try to keep a blank look as he continues,

"He set about cold-heartedly to seduce her, Marek, or he threatened her. Or *worse*. We all know how violent he is. It's the only possible explanation. And Gilles was right about *one* thing. He's never cared anything about her, not really. Why, he's hardly ever spoken of her with anything but scorn! And *you* know what a cold fish he is," he sneers, and I blink. My eyebrows shoot up, but I think I get them under control again pretty quickly. "So I know why he did it. It was to punish her, for preferring *me*. And to punish me, too, and to put the rumors to rest. He used her cruelly and made her a laughingstock, Marek, just to prove himself to the boys! And then he *bragged* about it, to everyone in the clearing. Can you imagine what it's like for her, knowing what everyone is saying about her, after what *really* happened? So yeah. I don't care if he tried to kill me. He's worse than a killer. He's a monster. You know it's true. You've seen the way he treats her. *You* saw that vile kiss."

It takes a while for the full ugliness of what Tristan's saying to sink in. When it does, it's worse than anything I ever thought of Taran, even in my first flush of anger at him in the clearing. But it's true. I did see that kiss, and it was rough and cruel. And at the time, it made me sick. What Tristan's implying makes a horrible kind of sense, and there's no reason why I shouldn't believe it. After his behavior at the crossbow lesson, I'd love to believe him capable of anything. But when I try to call up an image of Taran as a brutal ravisher of women, what leaps embarrassingly to mind instead are my own hands groping over him aggressively while he groaned out *"I can't, I can't"* with tears in his eyes, and I can't quite do it.

The thing is, I *do* remember everything about that kiss at the castle. Quite vividly. And not just that Taran was stinking drunk, just as Gilles said. In particular, I remember Melissande's rather enthusiastic response to it. Oh, I have no doubt that Melissande is in love with Tristan. Who wouldn't be? But Tristan of all people should know there's a difference between love and lust, and if he really thinks Melissande's never felt at least one of those things for Taran, he's deluding himself.

Tristan's said his piece and although he's looking out the window again, I know he must be waiting for me to make some kind of answer. But there's nothing safe for me to say. I can't in all honesty agree with him and it would surely be unwise to encourage him anyway, since things between him and Taran are tense enough already. But I can't defend Taran to him again either, and I don't want to. And I certainly can't tell him what I'm really thinking. Not when for some reason what I'm picturing in the back of my mind is that perfect circle of bolts, bristling from the practice dummy's belly.

My head swims, and all of Tristan's accusations and Gilles's and my own swirl around me like the dust motes over my head, and I don't know what to think. Except that I don't want to think about Taran anymore. I'm tired of thinking about him, and I certainly don't want to think about the kiss he gave Melissande at the castle anymore, either. Not when I can still feel him pressing in all around me. And not when something most unpleasant about it has started to dawn on me.

At the time, that drunken kiss of his *did* shock me. A lot.

And the thing is, it just shouldn't have — not if deep down *I'd* ever really been able fully to believe the worst of him.

"You do understand, don't you, Marek? You do see what this means?" Tristan is saying, his voice right in my ear. He must have gotten up and come over to sit down next to me while I was lost in my own thoughts, and I didn't notice.

From his confidential tone I get the impression it's only now that Tristan's getting around to telling me what's really on his mind, the real reason why he wanted to come out here in the first place. So I force myself to concentrate, since what he's saying is plenty disquieting.

"Remember last year, when we sat here together just like this, and I told you I couldn't leave Melissande to Taran?" he says earnestly. "That I'd be letting her in for an awful fate? Well, maybe that was a game then, too. It's no game now. *You* saw the look she gave me. She's looking to *me* to rescue her from him, Marek. I can't be the man I aspire to be if I let her down."

It's exactly the wrong response, but Tristan's caught me off guard. I burst out accusingly,

"My God, Tristan! What are you planning to do?!" I practically shout it.

There's a pause. A short one. But a definite pause, before he says flatly:

"Nothing."

Seeing that I'm about to start questioning him, he adds preemptively,

"I don't have to do anything, do I? According to *you*, *I'm* going to be the next Guardsman, right? That'll make me more than legitimate enough for Brecelyn, and my own dear daddy's 'little darling.' I doubt *Father* cares much which of us he uses to get his hands on Brecelyn's title, and I'm betting Brecelyn'd rather have as his son-in-law the son of Jakob Mellor who's the newest national hero. It'll mean swallowing my pride, but if I can win this thing, I should be able to convince my father to break the engagement contract he made for Taran and arrange to marry Melissande to *me* instead. So as long as you're right and I have a shot at Guards, I won't have to do anything else."

I have to admit Tristan's twisted logic makes some sense, and if anyone could pull off the necessary persuasion, it would be him. But I'm pretty sure this isn't what he was going to say.

He's decided not to confide in me, and it hurts. It's frustrating, too, since I now suspect the stagey tone he's been using hasn't really been for my benefit. He's been trying to convince *himself* of Taran's villainy so he'll feel justified in carrying out some dodgy scheme to win Melissande away from him, and he was looking to me to give him permission to do it.

Late afternoon shadows are already lengthening around us, so I'm not surprised when Tristan soon gets to his feet with a signal that it's time to go. I don't like leaving with things unsettled between us, so when Tristan turns to me as though about to offer to help me to my feet, to clear the air a little I make a joke of it.

"For a minute there, Tristan," I say with a grin, "I almost thought you were going to tell me you were planning to abduct Melissande right from the middle of her wedding, and you wanted me to help you do it!"

There's another horrible pause.

These little pauses have become quite a regular feature of our conversations, but to say that this one is awkward is an understatement. This one is positively *pregnant*, and a mighty strange look comes over Tristan's face, like a toad is about to leap out of his mouth and he's trying to swallow it down. I've never seen an expression like it and I'm not sure what it means. But he looks a little guilty, and I feel myself starting to get alarmed again.

Then he bursts out laughing.

"Don't be absurd, Marek," he exclaims. "It wouldn't be abduction, if the girl were willing. And if I were going to do it, it'd have to be a lot sooner than that."

Honestly, for a moment I just can't tell whether he's teasing me, or not.

Of course, I don't really believe even Tristan would ever attempt anything that crazy. But he's thinking about doing *something*, all right, and whatever he's got in mind, he's clearly not going to tell me. Unless I want him to lie to me, I should just drop it. So I force out a little answering chuckle of my own. It comes out as more of a croak, and when he finally does reach down to pull me to my feet, I can't resist.

This time, as our eyes meet over our clasped hands, I'm the one who says deliberately:

"Tell me you're not really going to do it, Tristan."

"You tell me, Marek," he says back. "Tell me I'm not going to have to."

WE BICKER ABOUT IT ALL THE WAY DOWN THE RICKETY STAIRS. Tristan refuses to be serious; he brushes it off and insists it was just a joke, and maybe it was. So when we emerge from the windmill into the golden light of late afternoon and he pauses to stretch his arms and breathe in the earthy scents of the meadow already fragrant with evening, I decide to believe him.

We stand side-by-side on the threshold while the evening settles around us, looking out over the path leading back to St. Sebastian's and working up our courage to go back. After a while, I sneak out a hand, and I slip it tentatively into his. When he squeezes it firmly back, it doesn't matter that I'm still not sure what Tristan's thinking, or that there were really four of us inside the windmill from the moment we stepped in. It's the two of us against the world again, and a warm feeling steals over me I haven't felt for so long I hardly recognize it. But I know what it is.

Next to me Tristan's been scanning the scene in front of us, and all at once he cries out,

"I don't believe it!" and he bounds excitedly forward into the tall grass.

I wade in after him, and when I catch up with him, he's standing in the middle of the meadow, pointing down with a stunned expression at a single red flower, its papery petals just opening atop a spindly stem. It's in the exact same spot where we came across one unseasonably early bloom here last year.

"A St. Sebastian's poppy, so early!" he exclaims.

This time, neither of us makes a move to pluck it.

"*Once*, that's possible. But *twice*? It's got to mean something, Marek. It's a sign," he says eagerly, looking down at the splash of red between us in a sea of green. "A sign, that what's been lost can return."

This time I'm the one who lets a pause lengthen between us. And when I finally answer,

"Not everything, Tristan" is all I can say.

Dusk is already falling as we cross out of the meadow. It's too dark to see much of anything, but as we step into the woods, I find myself looking back over my shoulder into the glade anyway. I can't hope to see the poppy from this distance, and it's not what I'm looking for. I'm not entirely sure what I'm expecting to see, or hoping will be there.

A stag, maybe. But the meadow is empty.

We don't talk much on the walk back, and neither of us mentions the trick. But I know we're both thinking about it.

So much for it not needing to be anything too incredible.

Tristan may have been teasing me out in the windmill, just as he said. But I got his message, loud and clear. Unless I want him committing to some scheme sure to end in complete disaster, I'd better be coming up with something bloody spectacular.

CHAPTER FOURTEEN

I find out Master Guillaume is back the very next day — in the lavatory.

When I'm awoken at the crack of dawn by the sound of commotion starting up again out in the yard, despite the ungodly hour I roll bleary-eyed out of bed, determined to get up and out while the other squires are all still safely tucked away under their blankets — particularly *Remy*.

After Tristan's alarming comments in the windmill I've promised myself I'll make real progress on coming up with a joint trick for the boys today, and it's occurred to me that the best way to jog loose a few ideas for it is to get my own bow back in my hands. If I'm quick about setting up our station there should be enough time for me to get in a little shooting of my own before the field has to be given over to the Journeys, and I've been itching to do it anyway; the last time I took aim at anything was out in Brecelyn's woods, and shooting at stumps hardly counts as practice.

It's been even longer since I had a proper wash, and after Taran's rude comments about my hygiene yesterday I'm feeling self-consciously grubby. So when nobody much is about on the Journey corridor, I grab up a bucket of water for myself and take it along to the Journey lavatory, since it isn't just eagerness to get out on the butts again that's roused me from my bed so early. I had a bad night of it. Not only did I lie awake late into the night fretting about the trick, among other things — but when I finally managed to fall asleep, it was only to be beset by nightmares. They were pretty transparent anxiety dreams, the kind where a whole forest full of beasts is chasing you and you can't seem to run away — shaggy bears and vicious boars, and gruesome fantasy creatures like the ones Father Abelard sometimes draws in the margins of his illuminations. This morning I still feel like something's breathing down my neck, and I'm eager to wash the feeling away.

Out in the stables, I have to dodge an unusually large number of stable boys wrangling horses and mules into overcrowded stalls, and although it's rather early for veterans to be reporting in for work from their lodgings in town, my brain is still too groggy with sleep for me to make much of it. In

182

my haste I've overfilled my bucket, and keeping it from spilling is taking all my concentration.

All's quiet on the Journey corridor as I stumble back inside, so I'm looking down at the surface of the water as I shoulder open the lavatory door and maneuver the brimming bucket around the corner. My guard is down, since I'm fully expecting the room to be empty.

Boy, am I wrong.

Imagine my surprise, when I look up to find that I'm not alone in the room. And when I see just what it is that's in here with me.

At this hour it's awfully dark in the lavatory, but someone's left a single oil lamp burning. It's sitting on the opposite side of the room, next to one of the basins lined up on a long shelf under the row of polished metal mirrors the boys use for shaving. In its murky light, a huge, misshapen shadow looms up before me out of the gloom.

It's a great, hairy beast, a creature straight out of my nightmares last night, with a hideous hump on its back. It's easily as tall as a man, even hunched over, where it's drinking noisily from the basin in front of it, sloshing around grunting and slobbering out a thick slaver of foam onto its chin. Something's flashing in the lamplight near its mouth, too, like the glint of a razor-sharp tusk, and I'm too stunned by the sight of it to wonder how such a beast could have gotten inside the guild undetected, or even exactly what kind of an animal it is.

My mouth flies open in a silent scream, but no sound comes out. Just as in my dreams I'm too petrified to move, even to run away, and the creature must sense something behind it. It lifts its head to the mirror, and cocks it to one side. With a cold feeling down to my toes, I know it's seen me, too, reflected over its shoulder onto the polished surface in front of it. One huge, round monstrous eye fixes on me, flickering with fire, and I don't know what comes over me. Fear must make me foolish, or maybe the determination I woke up with to dispel my demons drives me, I don't know. But I dump out the water from my bucket straight onto the floor and I charge the thing, waving the bucket wildly over my head.

The creature whirls around.

It shrinks back in alarm.

Its arms flail out, and something clatters from its hand. It clutches its shaggy breast, staggers backward, and just as my bucket comes crashing down painfully on its head, with a crack and a twang and a gurgled cry of,

"*Oh God, oh God! Marek?!*," it collapses onto the lavatory floor in a dead faint.

It's not a beast or a creature, of course.

It's my other favorite former Journey, Jerome.

His chin is slathered with shaving soap, and he's got a traveling cloak of thick rabbit fur on his back. I suppose I really should have recognized the curve of the lute slung across his shoulders underneath it. And that the mess of wire and glass tied firmly around his temples and distorting his features is just the *occhiale* his father procured for him, when he started losing his sight last year. But I didn't know he'd started *wearing* the device, and I certainly wasn't expecting to see him here. From the expression on his face right before I knocked him out, I see nobody ever bothered to write to him in Meuse to tell him I didn't actually die from my wounds at Thirds, either.

"What in the hell happened, Marek?!" he demands, when I've hastened guiltily to revive him. I don't know if he means just now or up on Brecelyn's tower, so I try to explain everything to him at once as I help him to his feet, asking anxiously,

"Oh, Jerome! Is anything broken?"

"Only my *lute*," he says.

Once we've exchanged a much warmer and more proper greeting and I've given him enough of my story to satisfy him, I lean up against the wall as he shakily retrieves his straight razor from the floor. He resumes his shaving and I settle in to watch him, my own intention of washing forgotten in the excitement of finding another friend restored to me in such an unexpected fashion.

"Whatever are *you* doing here Jerome, and how did you get here?" I finally think to ask, once I've gotten my wits about me again. "Do any of the others know you're back?"

"I arrived with Master Guillaume from Meuse this morning," he tells me. "After being on the road for three days, this was my first stop. Well, after the front desk," he says, looking a little sheepish, and he doesn't have to explain. He'd have gone straight to see his former squire Auguste, of course, since despite having shot him at Seconds last year they've remained the best of friends. "The master tracked me down at the University with an offer of employment. With Master Gheeraert dead there's no one to keep the guild books, and apparently the master doesn't think any of you boys can count."

"Guillaume's making you a *master*?" I ask, surprised, and I suppose it's rather rude. But I can't imagine a boy filling a master's position, not even one as mature and as intelligent as Jerome.

"Don't be daft, Marek," he laughs, not at all offended. "I'm to be little more than a glorified clerk. I'll hardly outrank Auguste anymore, probably, and it's only temporary. But the pay's decent, and who knows? If I make myself indispensable there might be an assistant's position in it for me later, after a new master can be appointed."

When Jerome's finished freshening up, I go along with him to deposit his gear in his old Journey room. The boys are all still asleep, so afterward he agrees to come out to the field with me to keep me company and to await the arrival of the others.

There's an even bigger jam in the stables now than when I came through earlier, and when we emerge out onto the field far enough to get a good view back into the yard, it's a sea of men. The commotion I heard earlier wasn't just from workmen; uniformed men are barking out orders to troops still in the process of dismounting, while others lead their horses to tether or get mules and carts unpacked. Everywhere men are milling around trying to stay clear of the carpenters' wagons, and although many are wearing the distinctive garb of St. Sebastian's, there are plenty of the uniforms in the crowd I don't recognize. It's a madhouse, and I can't help exclaiming,

"Just how many men were traveling with you, Jerome? It looks like the master's brought back a veritable army."

"It doesn't just look like an army, Marek," Jerome replies. "It *is* one. If you think that's a lot of men, you should take a look outside the wall. The master's convinced the regent to loan him a whole regiment of the King's Guard, and they're setting up a temporary camp out on the exhibition grounds across the street as we speak."

"The King's Guard? What would Master Guillaume want with them?" I ask.

"Word is Guillaume told the regent he wanted the reinforcements to safeguard the town in case of trouble from the French. But nobody in Meuse knows how rumors of a possible French invasion got started, or believes there's any truth to them. So everybody's saying that what the master *really* wants the troops for is to defend the guild from his own *townspeople*, in case of another outbreak of plague!"

Jerome laughs, but he wasn't here when we were overrun by the local villagers last year, and I don't see anything funny about it. I'm in no hurry to have either the French or their disease come to Louvain again, so instead of replying I silently chalk up another point for the savvy of Master Guillaume.

Jerome helps me set up Tristan's station, and as I warm up and begin to put myself through my paces with my longbow, he fills me in on the details of his trip from Meuse and I tell him all about our plan to have the boys do a joint trick at Firsts. Tristan and Gilles are sure to tell him all about it themselves anyway, and it feels so good to be back shooting on the butts again and to have someone sympathetic to talk to that it doesn't even bother me, much, when the best thing Jerome can come up with is,

"What about something, with *birds*?"

We bandy the idea around a little and Jerome gives me some pretty compliments on my shooting, but he's not really paying much attention. He's too eagerly awaiting the arrival of his friends, and I'll confess I'm waiting for it pretty eagerly, too. It's going to be mighty sweet to be the first one to know something around here for a change.

With the competitions on the forefront of everyone's mind again, the Journeys seem to have a sixth sense about when any of the others are on the move these days. So when eventually the boys do come spilling out of the stables, it's in a close-knit pack, and their reactions to seeing Jerome standing casually on the butts next to me don't disappoint.

Falko's the first one to spot him. He comes stumping excitedly over, chuffing and snorting as happily as a bull discovering a patch of fresh clover as he shoulders me out of his way and wraps Jerome in a suffocating bear hug that lifts him right off the ground. The others are close behind, and it's not long before everyone's crowding around, Journeys and squires, and everyone's asking a babble of questions. It's already quite a scene even before Gilles comes wafting over, waving his arms around in the air and rapturously warbling out a string of fruity exclamations, like *"Lo, doth yon troubadour returneth, in fair countenance resplendent?!"* that are so incomprehensible he must be quoting them from somewhere.

I doubt Jerome has any idea what Gilles is saying either, but the old friends fall affectionately into each other's arms, and even Aristide looks happier to see Jerome than I would have imagined. Everyone is glad to welcome back a friend who's no longer a competitor, and in the excitement of Jerome's return Taran and Tristan even forget all about trying to trip each other; as soon as they catch sight of him, they rush up side by side, almost as though they, too, could be friends.

Not surprisingly, though, to my eyes the best sight of all is the look on Tristan's face, when he's pushed his way to the front of the throng and his two best friends open their arms to him, to pull him into their embrace. It's the look of sheer joy, and I sidle up through the crowd to get a better view of it: the old trio, together again.

The three of them stand there laughing and embracing and slapping each other on the back for a long time, and after a while, sensing me hovering next to him Tristan slips an arm down around my shoulders, too.

"What did I tell you, Marek, about the poppy?!" he says, turning to me for a moment, eyes shining and shaking his head in disbelief. "See? What was lost *has* returned! Mark my words, kid. Things are looking up."

I sincerely doubt it was *Jerome* that Tristan was thinking about out in the meadow yesterday, but I don't say so. Tristan looks happier and more confident than I've seen him in weeks, and even if the poppy wasn't a sign of it, Jerome's return is indeed fortuitous. With Jerome standing between them, all trace of the tension that was lingering between Tristan and Gilles after their conversation at the wall yesterday is gone. If I was worried about the state of their fragile alliance, Jerome is exactly the glue that was needed to ensure it stay firmly cemented.

"That's good for us too, kid," Tristan whispers to me, nodding toward the hubbub of uniformed men beyond out in the yard. "Just look at all those new sources of information, fresh from Meuse!"

"Information? About what?"

"Your *father*, Marek. And politics in the capital, and the plot at Thirds, remember?" he whispers back, sounding amused that I'd forget about his intentions.

I didn't, of course. It's just that I assumed *he'd* forgotten about all that, when we left the castle. Or at least, after he'd decided to believe that Melissande is still in love with him.

This is hardly the place to discuss it, but Tristan's caught me off guard. So I reach up and yank on his sleeve hard enough to make him bend down to me, and I hiss in his ear,

"You can't mean you're still planning to investigate Sir Brecelyn, can you?"

"Why not?"

"Because he's *Melissande*'s father, for one," I hiss back. "And because you promised me you were going to be careful!"

"What's that got to do with it?" he demands blithely. "If she's worth her salt, she'll want to see a traitor brought to justice just as much as the rest of us. Now that Guillaume's back, we can get started right away."

I don't bother reminding him that everyone isn't as ambivalent about their own father as he is about his, and before I can think of another objection the conversation's moved on and Tristan's turned back to Gilles, who is exclaiming,

"Gads, Jerome. I suppose *seeing* is desirable, but must you really go about with that contraption strapped around your head? You look quite ridiculous."

"So much for *'fair countenance resplendent'*," Jerome laughs, as Aristide declares,

"For once, I agree with Lejeune. Come on, Jerome. Do us all a favor and take those blasted things off. Show a little self-respect."

Jerome cocks his head to one side. Then he starts pushing up his sleeves, and for a moment I think he's going to do something entirely out of character, and bop Aristide on the nose. At least, I'm hoping he will.

Instead he gives one of his cheerful grins, and he reaches out his hand to me.

"Marek, your bow, if you don't mind."

I hand it over to him.

"Now five bodkins, if you please. Lined up here, points down."

He gestures beside him and I oblige, sticking the tips of the requested arrows into the ground so that the fletches are near his hand. As I do, the other boys fan out on either side of Jerome, staying well back and spreading out enough so that they can get a good view, since it's clear now what he's going to do. I've got a six-inch square cloth-mark pinned to the backstop 80 yards in front of us, and Jerome is eyeing it carefully. When the arrows are all ready and he's centered himself, he lifts my bow and we all watch him in silence, anxious to see how he's going to do.

Slick as a whistle, he plucks up the first arrow, nocks it, and with a cry of,

"Call the square, Tristan!," he begins to shoot, as Tristan accordingly barks out "Top Left! Lower Right! Top Right! Lower Left!" in rapid succession. At each command, Jerome sends an arrow with remarkable precision straight into the corresponding corner of the cloth-mark. When he's thus crossed the square, he snatches up the last arrow and sends it dead center through the target, neatly cleaving the pin.

"Stuff *that* in your quiver, boys!" he crows, lowering the bow triumphantly as the other boys all whistle. It was some mighty beautiful shooting, and with a gesture at Jerome's *occhiale* Tristan exclaims warmly,

"Point taken, old friend! Looks like we're all might lucky your father didn't get you those in time for the trials last year."

"All of us but *Auguste*, you mean," Aristide sneers, but nobody's listening to him. Everyone's talking at once again, and at the reminder of the trials, it's not long before I hear Falko say,

"Say, that's right, Jerome! *You* must know if the master's brought a new trainer back with him from Meuse for us."

When Jerome can't help breaking into a knowing smirk, soon everyone's crowding around and demanding that Jerome tell us who it is. But Jerome won't give; he refuses to tell us anything about it, saying he doesn't want to ruin the master's surprise. All he'll say is,

"*Wait for it, boys. Wait for it!*," and just when I think Falko's about to forget himself and beat the information out of him, right on cue the stable doors bang open loudly behind us, and we all turn to look.

A man I've never seen before is strutting out onto the field behind us like he owns the place, with a retinue of gaping stable boys following along slavishly in his wake.

Around me the boys have all fallen silent, and we're all gaping, too, as Jerome whispers gleefully "*Surprise!*" under his breath.

I've seen a lot of unbelievable boys, and even more unbelievable men. After all, I've been at St. Sebastian's now for a long time. But of all the characters I've seen, this one takes the cake.

It would be inaccurate to say that the man now strutting towards us is more flamboyant than Gilles. That would be impossible. But in his own way he's just as inconceivable.

To begin with, everything about the man is exaggerated. His tall, lithe frame is even wirier than Aristide's or Gilles's, and every exposed inch of it is covered in a knot of ropey muscles under skin so tanned and thick it could be made of rawhide. It really should make him look like he's had a hard peasant's life toiling in the fields, but for some reason the effect is more like he's been weathered by a life of adventure; maybe it's the impressive array of scars on his arms and torso that suggest *he's* done more than just wear a rapier hung decoratively at his belt. Or maybe it's the cocky glint in his eye, I don't know — or the confident way he carries himself, despite the strange outfit he's wearing.

His long legs are encased in lavender grey tights, which peek out from under loose black pantaloons that cover them like chaps except for a wide triangular patch at the groin. These are tucked into short black boots, and on each forearm he's sporting an elbow-length leather cuff in place of a bracer. He's got no shirt on at all; instead, he's wearing a long, sleeveless black coat open like a vest. Like the rest of his clothing, this unusual garment is dusty and worn, and quite at odds with the most striking item of his apparel: a bright purple sash he's got tied with a jaunty knot around his waist. The long, frayed ends of it hang down almost to the ground along one leg, and although there's nothing overtly feminine about it, it doesn't take much to guess that it must be a lady's favor. Something about the way he's wearing it, as though he's purposely setting it off and putting it on display, reminds me uncomfortably of Melissande's veil.

To top off this unlikely ensemble, down into his sash the man's tucked a long, slender whip of blonde leather. Despite its elegant proportions it looks nastier to me even than the one of Baylen's that's now lying back in barracks in the bottom of my traveling bag, and from his attire I suspect the man, too, is a nasty combination of incongruities; I can't tell if he's supposed to be an acrobat, a street thug, or a vagabond king. It's definitely not regulation, but the man doesn't look like he gives two figs for Master Guillaume's rules. Or for Master Guillaume either, for that matter.

All of this would be enough to make the man unusual. But none of it is what's most remarkable about him. It's that he's even older than Brian de Gilford. He's got to be 60 if he's a day, and the hair on his head is as pure a white as the cloud of hair on his chest, although it's cut in an oddly boyish fashion: shorter on the sides and longer on top, so that a big hank of it flops down rakishly over one eye in a way that makes him look a little like an extreme version of Tristan, gone to seed. That, and the fact that despite his age, I can still feel it from here — the pull of his attraction. Whatever 'it' is, he's still got plenty of it left. When he was younger he must have been as sexy as hell, and there's only one person this can possibly be.

It really is old Poncellet.

Seeing our dumbfounded expressions, he spreads his arms wide and saunters up, flashing us a grin so dazzling I have to put up my hands to shield my eyes from the glare off his teeth.

"That's right, boys! Papa Poncellet is here," he cries. "All the rumors you've heard are true!"

"Well, not *all* of them!" Falko blurts out, staring pointedly at the man's groin. And he's right. There's a bulge in the front of the man's lavender tights so outrageously huge, there can be no doubt about it. Despite the stories de Gilford was circulating about him last year, old Poncellet is still very much a full member.

"That's right, Tubby!" Poncellet laughs again, giving Falko a sharp slap on the gut. "De Gilford's been busy spreading his vitriol, has he? Well, let that be a lesson to you, not to believe everything you hear."

Up close, I'm surprised to find that Poncellet isn't actually much taller than the boys; it was just the force of his personality that made him seem so, like he's got an extra foot or two of arrogance. I notice something else about him I didn't before, too. Along the top of his upper lip, Poncellet's got a little pencil-thin line of clipped white hair.

I've never seen anything like it.

"Ugh, *facial* hair. How *dreadful*," Gilles exclaims in one of his whispered asides, when he sees it.

Unluckily for him, the man's hearing is as remarkable as his appearance.

"Don't knock it 'til you've tried it, Frills," Poncellet shoots back, giving Gilles a dismissive look up and down that says he knows exactly who he is, and he doesn't care. "*Women* love it. It really tickles their ... *fancies!*"

He's rewarded for this by a big roar from Falko (or at least as much of a roar as he can make while trying hard to suck in), while Gilles mutters under his breath between clenched teeth,

"The name is *Gilles*."

Poncellet ignores it all. He puts one hand dramatically on his hip, and as he strokes the little caterpillar of fur on his lip with his other hand, he proceeds to walk up and down in front of us, making a show of looking the boys over and sizing them up with a series of personal observations that are as cutting as they are accurate. By the time he's found a rude appellation for all of the Journeys, I've shrunk back as far as I can to the back of the pack of squires, and not only because I'm afraid to hear what nickname he might find for *me*. Something about the man makes me suspect that unlike Tristan, he might really be able to smell a girl from a mile away.

It's only taken Poncellet about two minutes to insult just about everybody, and a cloud of resentment has started forming over the boys' heads so thick I can almost see it. So I'm just assuming that Poncellet is well on his way to becoming St. Sebastian's most hated trainer without having given a single instruction, when he notices Jerome's arrows sticking out of the butts.

"You do that, Bug Eyes?" he asks Jerome, since Jerome's still got my bow in his hands and none of the other boys have had a chance to arm themselves. "Not bad, for a beginner. What do you say you give an old timer a shot?," and the boys all crowd around again as Jerome obligingly hands the bow over. I'm crowding forward now, too, since we've all remembered Poncellet's *other* reputation; the man isn't just a fabled womanizer. He's also supposed to have once been a legendary shot.

"You there, where do you think you're going?" he barks at me, when I start to trot down to clear Jerome's arrows. "Leave 'em. And keep *those* coming," he adds, nodding at the quiver over my shoulder as he flexes the bow. "Fletch first."

There's a pause, in which I just gape at him. Then he demands, "Whose squire *is* this? Is he addled?," and he snatches the quiver and shoves it into Pascal's hands instead. "Here, *you* look like you have your wits about you.

Feed me fifteen, nice and easy," and I step back dumbly to watch Poncellet shoot, too mesmerized to feel embarrassed.

I'm sure the others all think I didn't understand the order, although it was simple enough, or that I wasn't paying attention. But that's not it at all. I've been struck by sheer amazement, because from the moment Poncellet took my bow into his hands and stretched it, he's transformed before my eyes. He's no longer an oily old geezer in a crazy get-up, but a vibrant young god. Maybe I'm the first of us to feel it, since I'm a *girl*. But as soon as Poncellet begins to shoot, he casts a spell over us all.

I wish I could describe what his shooting is like. It's not just that he's so fast, Pascal can hardly keep up with him. Or that he's accurate. It's that no two shots are the same. I can't even tell exactly what he's doing; he keeps the bow in constant motion, handling it more like a recurve bow than a longbow and pulling back on the bowstring only about halfway. It hardly looks like he releases. He just waves the bow about nonchalantly in a continuous, languid circle, stretching the string back and forth like he's kneading dough or working a loom, and I can't imagine how he's managing to nock. He does it while the bow is moving; while he's already *bending* it, even, and he shoots with equal ease on the upswing as on the down, and as the bow is sweeping dizzyingly from side to side.

When he's shot fifteen arrows, he brings the bow down to rest beside him, and for a while nobody can speak. Pascal keeps extending his arm with another arrow in it out to him and retracting it again like an automaton, while staring like everyone else in disbelief down the field. I think I'd have been impressed enough just by his motion, even if he'd missed the butts entirely. But of course he didn't. Poncellet split every one of Jerome's arrows, straight down the middle.

And then he split his own.

Twice.

I'd never have believed it, if I didn't see it with my own eyes. It's the most incredible shooting I've ever seen in my life.

Before any of us can recover ourselves enough to react, he leans on the bow, strokes his upper lip, and says,

"You know what's the most remarkable thing about it, boys?" He flips the bow into his other hand, and winks.

"Actually, I'm *left*-handed."

He motions Pascal around to his other side, and gestures for him to feed him more arrows.

And then he does it all over again, shooting with his *other* hand.

This time, before each shot, he tosses the arrow, sending it up in a somersault. He gives it two end-over-end turns before he snatches it out of the air, nocks, and shoots in a single fluid motion that looks more like he's popping peanuts into his mouth than wielding a bow with a 90-pound draw.

When he's split more of Tristan's arrows than I care to think about and

191

he's emptied the quiver, he spins neatly around, strikes a pose, and with a toss of his head and a spirited laugh he declares,

"If you boys behave yourselves, one of these days I'll cross the square for you in under five seconds, *alternating* hands!"

After a beat, we all raise our voices in a spontaneous cheer. Poncellet's gone from villain to hero in a minute flat, and even I'm starting to get a warm feeling about him. There's still something about the man I don't like, but as the boys all gather around him eagerly, clamoring for him to do one of his infamous tricks (since nobody now doubts that he really can do them), in the back of my mind a thrilled little voice is repeating,

"I'm in need of an incredible trick, and the master of them all magically appears."

I say a silent prayer of thanks to all my saints, since the timing of Poncellet's arrival at St. Sebastian's just can't be a coincidence. If I can't figure out a way to use it to my advantage I don't deserve the name of squire, and Tristan was surely right. Things are definitely looking up.

For obvious reasons, I'm pretty eager myself to see what kind of tricks old Poncellet can do. So I'm begging and pleading for a trick along with everyone else; that is, everyone but Taran. Predictably, he's the only one of the boys who doesn't seem entirely won over. But that's probably just because he doesn't like the competition. He's used to being the best archer around the place, the one everyone's fawning over at practice. Either that, or he's still mad about earlier, when Poncellet called him 'Pecs.'

At first Poncellet demurs, saying,

"A man doesn't get a reputation for tricks by revealing his secrets." But the boys won't relent, so eventually he gives in.

"If you insist," he says, with a pretty show of reluctance. "Bring me two coins, and I'll show you the one that cost the King of Castile a pretty penny!," and accordingly Aristide sends Armand inside to fetch his purse from his room.

Armand's back in a flash, and when he's fished around in the purse to pull out two bronze pennies, Poncellet declares lazily,

"It'll only work with gold coins."

So Armand roots around some more, and pretty soon he's handing over two big golden guilders.

One of these Poncellet slips down into his sash. The other one he palms, and after taking up a bodkin arrow into his hand with it, he pokes around Tristan's station until he finds a broadhead that's gotten mixed in with the target arrows by mistake. When he then takes up my bow again and orders us all to stand well back, I'm watching eagerly to see what he's going to do.

This time, he plants the two arrows tip downward next to him exactly as I did for Jerome, with the heavy broadhead arrow closest to hand. Then he lifts the coin to the bowstring just as though he were nocking an arrow, and with a swift pull he sends the coin high into the air overhead and only about fifteen yards out in front of us. While the coin is still rising, he grabs up the broadhead and sends it after it. The arrow hits the coin with an audible ping.

It's a good shot but nothing extraordinary, and after his stunning display on the butts I can't help but be a little disappointed. I've seen the boys shoot down coins before, and I was expecting something, well, *more*. Something with flair. But I've forgotten about the bodkin. Poncellet now grabs it up and sends the slender shaft after his broadhead already in the air. Its narrow point strikes, hitting dead center on the wide, flat head that gives the broadhead arrow its name. Incredibly, he's shot *his own arrow* right out of the sky, without breaking a sweat. The whole thing probably took less than three seconds.

"Blessed St. Sebastian! Un*believable!*" Aristide exclaims, as all the other boys let out astounded exclamations of their own and Armand runs out onto the field to retrieve the coin.

"Nope," the man replies smoothly. "The name's *Poncellet*."

"What about the other coin?" Aristide asks, when eventually the commotion caused by Poncellet's impossible trick dies down.

"That one's for me," Poncellet says. "I told you it'd cost a pretty penny," and although Aristide's face turns red, he doesn't have the guts to demand it back.

We're all still standing around in an admiring knot around Poncellet when there's a crash and an oath from the direction of the stables of the kind that usually signals the arrival on the scene of Brian de Gilford. Sure enough, when I turn to look, I see him making his way across the field, rubbing his hands together and gathering himself up to deliver one of his hearty greetings that are always so irritating first thing in the morning.

"What's all this?" he booms, stomping over. "Not set up yet, and standing around like a lollygagging gaggle of gossiping g …?!"

He doesn't get any further than that.

At the sound of de Gilford's voice, Poncellet's little caterpillar of a mustache twitches. He puts out his hand, gesturing to the boys in front of him to stand aside.

The crowd parts.

When de Gilford gets a good look at Poncellet standing revealed in our midst in front of him, leaning on my bow and casually stroking his upper lip, he lurches to a stop. His voice dies out in a strangled gurgle. His eyes bug out. His nose wrinkles, and his lips screw up into a sour frown. And then a look as dark as doomsday descends over his features, and he starts snorting — literally. I almost expect him to start pawing the ground. For some reason, I particularly notice it when he starts clenching and unclenching the fist of one hand.

"*Poncey*," he mutters dangerously.

"Brian."

Poncellet says it quite evenly. But his mustache twitches again.

That the two men have met before is obvious. That there's no love lost between them is obvious too, and as they stand there for a long minute, each man holding his ground and staring at the other as though preparing for a duel, we all stand around watching them, bemused.

At least, de Gilford looks like he's gearing up for fight. From the murderous expression on his face I think he'd like to charge right over and tear Poncellet's head off, and he might have tried it, too, if the man weren't still holding my bow in his hands. For his part, Poncellet actually looks rather amused. It's clear he already knew de Gilford was here at St. Sebastian's, and he's enjoying being a nasty surprise for him. When he finally takes a mincing step toward de Gilford and the two of them then begin slowly circling each other, he's so poised he could be inviting de Gilford to join him in a courtly dance. But I've been around the boys long enough to know when a man is acting, and although he hides it well, Poncellet doesn't like de Gilford being at St. Sebastian's either.

As the masters square off, we've all naturally congregated together on the sidelines to watch. And when Tristan asks Jerome,

"So, what's with *them*?," we all gather in closer to hear his answer.

"They're rivals, from way back," Jerome tells us, as the two men make another slow circle. They're not paying any attention to us, and De Gilford's started to growl slightly.

"I don't know all the details, of course," Jerome continues in a low, gossipy voice. "But the men on the ride back were full of it. It seems old Poncellet's been kicking around for ages. Whenever he's down on his luck he turns up here, and the masters put him to work. Word is something happened between them when de Gilford was a Journey and Poncellet was one of his trainers. Nobody knows the details. But whatever it was, it was bad enough to leave them with a grudge that's lasted for decades."

"Come now, Jerome!" Gilles presses. "You must know more than *that*. At least tell us some of the juicier rumors," but Jerome insists that's all he's heard.

The boys all prod him for a while, but nobody can get anything out of him and I assume with disappointment that that's going to be the end of it, since I'm plenty curious. But Tristan's looking at his old friend speculatively, and when he demands firmly,

"If you *do* know something, Jerome, I think you'd better tell us what it is," Jerome hangs his head, and relents.

"All right, all right. I don't actually *know* anything else, I swear it. But it so happens I'm acquainted with de Gilford's oldest son, slightly. I've seen him around the University."

He licks his lips, and Gilles prompts, "Yes, *yes*. The university. *Go on*," and Jerome finally breaks down and says,

"The thing of it is, de Gilford's son ... well, he looks an awful lot like

Poncellet." He pauses, shooting a nervous glance at Tristan. "*Exactly* like him, actually."

We all digest this information in silence. Jerome's looking uncomfortable, and I don't know how many of the rumors about the boys' present situation with Melissande he's heard. But Jerome does know how sensitive Tristan is about being a bastard himself, and although nobody's taken their eyes off the two men still circling each other warily, none of us has to look at Tristan to know how he's reacting to Jerome's information. I can feel the heat of his angry flush from here, and I'm not even standing next to him. His face must be almost as red as de Gilford's, and after what Gilles was saying yesterday at the wall about Melissande's baby, I suspect there's one face in the crowd redder even than his.

And that's before Jerome adds dismally,

"That's not even the worst of it. I've seen Master de Gilford's younger boys around town, too."

"Let me guess," Jurian says for him. "They look exactly like their brother."

Jerome nods his head in confirmation.

"Every last one of them."

There's another impressive snarl from de Gilford, and Aristide demands exasperatedly,

"What in the world was Master Guillaume thinking then, bringing him here?! It's going to be a bloodbath."

I sincerely hope that Aristide's words aren't prophetic. But standing as I am somewhere between a flushed Tristan and a fuming Taran, as the two trainers square off for a showdown I can't help worrying. Poncellet's arrival here was no coincidence, that's for sure. I'm just no longer entirely sure whether I think it's going to prove to be a blessing for us, or a curse. And I'm wondering about the master's motives, too.

It *is* odd, particularly since Poncellet strikes me as exactly the type that Master Guillaume usually despises. So after a minute I hear myself asking,

"Poncellet. Is that the man's given name, or his surname anyway?"

"What does it matter?" Tristan laughs, valiantly regaining his good humor. "The man's incredible. *Finally*, we're getting a *real* butts man as a trainer, instead of some clot of a clouter," he adds, dismissing poor dead Royce with a wave of his hand. "Besides, once a man is a master here, he only goes by one of them. So take your pick," and it's true.

I don't know why I never thought about it before, but all the masters do go exclusively by one name, usually their given name. I don't know *what* Master Guillaume's surname is, for example.

Or Master Leon's.

For all I know, it could start with a *G*. So could Poncellet's. But when Gilles gives me a playful poke in the ribs and says,

"The kid must want to monogram him a handkerchief!," I stop asking questions.

I'M NOT SURE WHAT MIGHT HAVE ENDED UP HAPPENING, IF AT just that moment Master Leon himself didn't come striding out onto the field. He comes to stop between Poncellet and de Gilford, and with a sour look at both of them, he says sarcastically,
"I see you two are getting reacquainted. *How grand*. Now if you're *quite* finished, I hardly need remind you that despite the chaos around us, *I* run an orderly practice. And that trials are right around the corner. It's true, Master Guillaume expects these boys to be worked within an inch of their lives. But when it's over, nobody had better actually be dead." He gives the two men a pointed look, and then in typical fashion he turns around and stalks back off the field again, calling back over his shoulder, "And somebody, come and tell me when it's over!"

With that, de Gilford and Poncellet have to make an outward show of putting aside their differences and starting the practice. Their bitter antagonism is still palpably there between them, though, so it's with a sinking feeling that I resign myself to the fact that just when Tristan needs serious practice the most, morning drills are destined to be debacles of unprecedented proportions.

Sure enough, the practice starts off as badly as anticipated. While the other boys head over to the cabinets to arm themselves and to fetch their masters' equipment, I'm left fidgeting between the two trainers as they start bickering over where to get set up. Poncellet is a butts man and de Gilford a clouter, and neither of them is willing to run a drill in the other man's best skill. But eventually they settle on wands as a compromise, and when I've accordingly lugged Tristan's station down to the far butts and the practice actually gets underway, a strange thing happens.

Predictably, Poncellet and de Gilford can't agree on anything. They've got opposing ideas on every point of technique. But they're both so eager to belittle each other and to demonstrate the superiority of their own style to the boys that information is pouring furiously out of them. In their competition they argue each point in excruciating detail, with the result that they actually explain the theory behind their advice in a way that none of our previous trainers ever did. When at one point they get in a heated debate about the proper position for optimum draw while standing on either side of Tristan, they take turns whirling him around, repositioning his fingers on the string and then guiding his arm back into his draw so many times that by the end of it, Tristan's been given a whole new array of options to work with. The same thing keeps happening, all down the line: while ideas fly out of the two trainers thick and fast, with Poncellet's suggests finessing those of de

Gilford and vice versa, the boys can pick and choose between the techniques on offer to combine them into a method that works for them. Before long Tristan's experimenting with a mid-distance draw that starts with an arc like de Gilford's and then ends all the way back by the corner of his mouth like Poncellet's, and I'm beginning to see the genius of Master Guillaume in pairing the old rivals together. In the space of a single morning, the boys are getting more instruction than they ever did last year in an entire month of drills.

It's also turned out to be a good thing for us that the masters can't agree to drill anything but wands, since it's the skill Tristan most needs to practice. So if that were the whole story of the practice, I'd have to mark it down as an unexpected but unqualified success.

Unfortunately, neither Poncellet nor de Gilford can confine his digs at the other to archery, and as the morning wears on, the subtext of the men's comments becomes increasingly personal and pointed. Most of the boys would be inclined to prefer Poncellet's insouciance to de Gilford's bluster anyway, but after Poncellet's performance on the butts this morning he's the boys' clear favorite. He's nothing if not a smooth talker, and he's been keeping the boys entertained with a running commentary of boasts, wisecracks, and innuendo that is at first relatively innocuous. Not surprisingly, most of it is sexual in nature, however, and I'm sorry to say even I've been laughing at a lot of it, because the man's pretty clever. After a while, though, his jibes begin to sound suspiciously like thinly veiled attacks on de Gilford's manhood, and even though I'm sure the others all realize it, too, he builds up to it so slowly and he's gotten us all so jollied up that each one still elicits a merry roar of laughter.

For a while, poor de Gilford tries to give as good as he gets. But he's no match for the man's quick wit, and every comeback he makes just sets him up for more abuse. Soon de Gilford's face is bright red again, and to make matters worse, since he's unable to make any headway directly against Poncellet, before long he's lashing out at an easier target: the one person on the field with a reputation for being even more inarticulate than he is.

There's a particularly bad moment, when Poncellet notices me and Pascal sorting out some of the boys' arrows that have gotten mixed up after a long retrieval. With a thrust of his hips that can leave no mistake about his meaning, he crows loudly,

"Now you see why these *babies* are all marked with their Journeys' colors, boys! Just one look at 'em, and you can tell instantly who was *man enough* to *father* each shot. So watch out, squires. Your master won't like it one bit, if he finds out some *other* boys' shafts have been *slipped* into his quiver!"

When Taran accordingly fumbles the arrow he was in the process of nocking, a furious de Gilford barks at him,

"What's the matter, *Dirty Shot?* Can't you 'keep it in' your *bow*, either?"

De Gilford keeps this up for quite a while, harping on Taran with comments designed to liken him to Poncellet, even though it should be obvious that the more accurate comparison lies elsewhere. Sensing blood in the water, Poncellet is soon circling Taran, too, and it's not long before he's become the target of both men's attacks — much to Tristan's delight, I might add. But I don't think I have to explain why the whole situation's started to make me feel rather uneasy.

Eventually, what little wit de Gilford can muster inevitably fails him. But Poncellet is just getting warmed up. So slowly de Gilford falls into a gloomy silence, while Poncellet continues to pound him mercilessly with withering attacks that he no longer bothers to veil at all. By the time practice is finally winding down, I'm not sure who's suffering the most: de Gilford's become so sullen he reminds me of Falko when he sulking around Brecelyn's castle over Roxanne, Remy's fuming, and although at first I think Tristan was thoroughly enjoying watching de Gilford turn on Taran (after having to suffer through his praise of him yesterday morning), by this point even he's started to see the unpleasant resonances between the men's rivalry and his own with Taran.

As for Taran himself, he's not surprisingly turned that impressive shade of purple he always does when he's thoroughly embarrassed. It's a deeper color than usual, too — so much so that from a distance I can already tell just how angry he is, even before he brings the practice to a close on an all-time low.

It's probably about time for the practice to end anyway, when Poncellet strolls up behind Taran just as he's settling into a shot. Suddenly he slaps Taran on the back of the head, hard — and with one of the pelvic thrusts he's been using to punctuate his cruder comments, he cries out enthusiastically,

"Atta boy, *Stud*! I knew it wouldn't take *you* long to get 'er properly '*nock*'-ed up again."

Taran's arrow wobbles out at a crazy angle. He takes a staggering step forward, and even over the laughter that's ringing out around him from some of the cruder boys I can hear him struggling to swallow down an oath. If I thought Tristan had a toad in his throat the other day Taran could now be choking on a goat, and we all lower our bows to watch him — to see if he's going to lose control, and lash out at the master. The man's made a direct reference to his fiancée's recent condition that's so indecent, it's unforgivable. But insubordination to a man of superior rank goes against everything Taran stands for (in *public*, anyway) — and Poncellet seems to know it; he's leaning casually on his bow and watching Taran's straining back with amusement, fingering his wicked little whip in a way that suggests he's hoping Taran will give way and give him an excuse to exercise it on him.

Just when it looks like Taran's going to manage to restrain himself, once he's drawn himself up and turned to face the master in a pose of rigid if not fully respectful attention, Poncellet twitches his caterpillar of a mustache at him.

He purses his lips.

And then he blows him a little kiss in the air.

Much to everyone's surprise, Taran doesn't launch himself at the master. In fact, he doesn't move from the spot. But he does sway dangerously forward. And as he does, his nostrils flare and his eyes roll back — and he clenches his fist so hard that with a splintering crack, he snaps the massive bow in his hand clean in half.

It took immense strength and it's pretty darned intimidating, but old Poncellet just chortles,

"Leave it to 'Pecs' here to do me one better, boys! He's split the *bow*, instead of the arrow! That's a trick not even *I* can do. Looks like we'd better call it a day, before he moves on from busting bows to busting heads, and we bring down the wrath of Master Sourpuss, eh men?," and he heads off the field, still chuckling to himself.

Finding themselves thus unexpectedly dismissed, the boys all scramble to follow him, congratulating Poncellet on his witticisms as they go and pestering him to tell them more about some of his tricks, and Tristan goes with them; while I doubt Poncellet's final jest was much to Tristan's taste, it's effect on Taran can't help but have pleased him and it wasn't enough to put him off of the man, unfortunately.

I hang back. Taran's stalked straight off and disappeared inside the guild with the pieces of his bow still in his hand, and the other squires are already lugging their masters' benches back toward the cabinets, but the field's not empty. Brian de Gilford is standing alone in the middle of the butts, silently stuffing his arrows back into his quiver with an unsteady hand.

He's behaved quite badly himself this morning, but he's always been kind to me and he looks so dejected now, I can't help feeling sorry for him. So I go over and offer to help.

He gives me a gruff greeting as I take the quiver out of his hand and start gathering up the shafts for him, but he doesn't say anything. He just stands there awkwardly, halfheartedly making some of his chuffing noises, so after I while I say,

"You're a fantastic archer, master. One of the very best."

Then I don't know what comes over me. His eyes look suspiciously moist, and I can't help thinking about all his sons, looking exactly like Poncellet. Before I can stop myself, I hear myself saying,

"Master Poncellet's smooth, all right. And he's a dead shot on the butts. But I bet he can't touch you at clouts. Tomorrow morning, why not insist on a clouts drill? Show the boys what you can really do. Surely he can't beat you at that."

Clouts is the last thing Tristan needs to drill right now, and if he knew I was suggesting it, he'd kill me. I'm not even sure why I'm doing it. I mean, I do like de Gilford. I really do. But not that much.

Instantly de Gilford brightens. "You're right, squire!" he declares, and before I know it, he's dragging me with him across the field, over to the place by the cabinets where the Journeys are all still crowded animatedly around Poncellet.

"Listen up, men!" de Gilford announces, shouldering his way into the center of the group and bringing me along with him. "Young Vervloet here's had a smashing idea. He suggests we have ourselves a contest tomorrow. A competition between you and me, Poncey, to settle once and for all just who is the *bigger* man."

"Wait, what? No I didn't!" I squawk, as the boys all start whooping and Poncellet fixes me with a speculative stare.

"Just what does the clever young lad have in mind?" he demands not very pleasantly, when things have settled down and as I'm tugging at Tristan's sleeve and saying frantically,

"I didn't say anything of the kind, Tristan. I swear it!" But Tristan's not listening to me and neither are any of the others. The boys all love a competition, and the idea of a competition between *masters* has gotten them all worked up.

For some reason Poncellet doesn't look much keener about the idea than I am, but if he wants to keep the boys' favor he can't very well decline. So after a little negotiation they fix it up to meet out on the far field tomorrow morning in lieu of practice, where each man will attempt a challenge in the other man's competency, with the Journeys to act as the judges.

I already have a bad feeling about it, even before Gilles says portentously,

"This ought to be interesting, men! A *showdown, between clouts and butts*. Who do you suppose will win?" And even before Poncellet forestalls de Gilford as he's turning away, by coughing significantly. When de Gilford looks at him inquiringly, he says,

"Not so fast. We have yet to discuss terms."

"Saint's rules, of course," de Gilford replies, apparently referring to some convention of contest or fair play.

Poncellet shakes his head.

"I'm talking about *stakes*, Brian. A wager. You don't expect me to compete for free."

"You're not suggesting we bring *money* into it?!" de Gilford protests indignantly.

"Why not? Or don't you have any? What, did the regent cut you off, *Monty?*" he laughs, shortening de Gilford's title into an insult and poking de Gilford in the stomach with his forefinger. "Or didn't the Old Prince remember to include an income with that empty position he gave you?"

De Gilford draws himself up and snaps back, "Name your price, charlatan!," and to his credit, he only flinches a little when Poncellet then rattles off an outrageous sum, since I'm pretty sure Poncellet is right and he doesn't have any money.

"If you win, I agree to pay," he nods. "As long as you agree to a condition of mine. What do you say we make this a *real* wager?" He points at Poncellet's belly. "If *I* win, *you*'ll hand over that sash — permanently! And *publicly*."

He glares at Poncellet. Poncellet glares back, and there's an awkward silence, since it's not hard to guess what's behind the request. The sash must once have belonged to de Gilford's own wife. Understandably, the man just wants it back.

Poncellet wavers, fingering the purple edge of the sash with a frown on his face, and for the first time today I think de Gilford's gotten under his skin. When de Gilford taunts him with *"what's the matter, Poncey? Not so sure you can beat me?"* he reluctantly agrees to the terms, and the deal is set.

"Spit and shake on it, gentlemen!" Gilles trills, thoroughly enjoying himself. He clearly thinks the competition is a simply marvelous idea, and I can tell the boys all agree with him. But as I watch de Gilford head inside, rubbing his hands together in anticipation and his mood completely transformed from what it was only moments ago out on the field, all I can think is how crushed he's going to be when Poncellet inevitably defeats him. And how broke. And how much everyone is going to think it's all my fault.

My big mouth's gotten me into trouble again, and no matter who wins, by this time tomorrow I'm sure to have made another enemy. I feel a little like a traitor, too, since in my heart of hearts, I know I can't really want de Gilford to win. Much as I hate the thought of watching Poncellet humiliate him further, I have to say Poncellet is the superior archer, and Gilles was right: it *is* going to be a classic showdown, butts vs. clouts. So even though the competition really *wasn't* my idea, it should be perfectly obvious why I'm plenty anxious to see what's going to happen. And why there's just no way I can hope that clouts will win.

CHAPTER FIFTEEN

If you've never tried it, prying arrows whose shafts have completely splintered away out of a thick clay embankment isn't very easy, and after Poncellet's virtuoso arrow-splitting display the near butts is bristling with them. The pieces are all marked with my master's colors so the job falls to me, and by the time I've managed to clear them all and get Tristan's equipment put away, the boys have gone inside and the area around the cabinets is empty.

Empty, that is, except for old Poncellet. For some reason he's still hanging around, leaning up casually against the outer archive wall and fiddling with his whip or something.

He's not paying any attention to me, but I'm not happy to find myself virtually alone with him. The man terrifies me, and it's not just his incredible skill or his cruel wit that I find so intimidating. It's his obvious experience.

Poncellet is a man of the world, a ladies' man. Or maybe he's just a *man*, and strangely enough, I feel like I haven't really been around very many of them — at least not at close quarters. I've been living with a bunch of boys and a guild full of celibate, archery-obsessed fanatics. Fooling them about my gender is one thing. Fooling a man like Poncellet is likely to be another kettle of fish entirely, and I've been trying all morning to keep a safe distance from him. I was making a pretty good job of it, too, until de Gilford singled me out. So I put down my head and walk fast, trying to get past him as quickly as possible, not wanting to draw any more of his attention.

He doesn't stir as I go by, although I'm trying so hard to clomp along in a manly fashion that I must look drunk and ridiculous. So I think it's understandable that I freeze and let out a nervous whinny, when just as I think I've made it safely past him, he says,

"Whatever *your* story is, I bet it's mighty interesting."

He hasn't looked up, but his mustache twitches.

I stumble to a stop, twisting my hands together. I don't dare say anything, sure in my nervousness my voice will sound even more girlishly high-pitched than usual.

He glances up. His eyes slowly rake over me from head to toe and then back again, almost as though he could somehow see through my tunic and past my bindings to take in every contour and curve of my body, and his mustache twitches again. I'm beginning to really hate it when he does that. He takes his time about it, and just when I don't think I can stand the scrutiny one second longer and I'm debating throwing myself at his feet, confessing everything, and begging for mercy, he gestures towards my face.

"The *scars*," he says.

"Kicked by a mule," I manage, my head reeling, and unsure whether to let myself feel relieved yet, or not.

"*Marek*, is it?" he drawls, stretching the name out disbelievingly, exactly the way Tristan did when I first gave it to him. "Well, *Marek*. Looks like it was your bad luck to meet up with a mule with dead aim."

For a confused second, I think he's talking about himself, and even when I realize he's not, I'm not entirely sure what he's implying. Whatever it is, it isn't good — but it's an opening, of sorts. So I screw up my courage. I haven't forgotten about the boys' trick, and this might be my only chance to try to get the man's help with it. If by some miracle de Gilford manages to beat him tomorrow, I can kiss his good-will permanently goodbye. So I sidle over as close as I dare, and I try some flattery. That always works with the Journeys.

"Speaking of dead aim, that was an incredible trick you did for us, *master*."

"Of course it was," he says matter-of-factly. "I'm the best shot that's ever been at St. Sebastian's."

I don't doubt it, but I can see flattery is going to get me nowhere. There's nothing I can say to him he hasn't already thought about himself. So I use a direct approach.

"Better, even, than *Jan Verbeke*?"

That gets a reaction out of him. For an unguarded moment he looks startled, and I feel a thrill of victory. He knew my father, I'm sure of it.

"Jan?" he says, giving me a sidelong glance. He doesn't seem as insolent anymore, or as amused. Under his cocky attitude something new has crept into his demeanor, and if I didn't know better, I'd say it was a shadow of respect. And of suspicion.

"Jan was good, I'll grant you," he says at length. "But how in the world do *you* know about him?"

I quickly rattle off a lie in a gruff voice that's actually mostly the truth, about all the rumors that were flying around the guild last year after my father's death. In my excitement, I can hear my voice getting higher and squeakier, but I can't care about that. All at once I can sense that I'm so close to finding out about the trick of my father's Meliana described in her journal that my whole body is tingling.

"And with *your* reputation for tricks, well, it got me thinking. I heard Verbeke did a trick at his butts trials that was impossible to believe. *And* that he cooked it up with the help of a veteran. After seeing you shoot, I figure that veteran must have been you."

Poncellet stares down at me for a long minute, stroking his mustache. I can't tell what he's thinking, but my heart is pounding in my chest, because I can see it in his eyes. He knows exactly what I'm talking about.

Then, horribly, he laughs. My heart plops down into the pit of my stomach with a thud.

"Nice try, kid. Need a trick for Slick, eh? Well, maybe you weren't listening earlier, when I said I don't give my secrets away. Surely *you* can appreciate that."

"But you *do* know the trick, don't you? You saw it, you know what it was! It was *you* who helped him come up with it, wasn't it?" I cry, and I'm sure I sound a little desperate. But I'm too intent on finding out what I can from him while I've got the chance to worry about what he might think about my insistence, or what else he might be implying.

He gives me a long look, and I can almost feel him debating.

"Did I help Jan Verbeke with a butts trick? No," he says at length, sounding amused again. "I'll give you this much, though, son," he adds, before pushing off the wall and walking away. "I *did* see Jan's butts trials. And the trick he did at them, it *did* make one hell of an impression. But for what was most impressive about it, I can guarantee you Jan didn't get any help from me."

As soon as Poncellet is gone, I duck into the garden, my heart racing and feeling shaken, and not only because I always feel the effects of these rash little encounters of mine more after the fact.

I simply can't believe it.

I suppose I should have anticipated it, given the man's personality. But I didn't expect Poncellet to *admit* he'd witnessed my father's trick, and then baldly refuse to tell me about it. And there's absolutely nothing I can do. I can't force him to describe it for me, or even to tell me the truth — because I'm also pretty sure he was lying. I didn't imagine the calculating look he gave me, right before denying helping my father come up with the trick. It was him all right. Or at the very least, he knows who it was. That much is clear.

I wander over and lean my back up against a tree in the middle of the garden, and think. I can't let it get me rattled. There must be some way I can persuade him to tell me about the trick, if I put my mind to it. And in the meantime, I can still use Poncellet's arrival here to my advantage. If he won't help me out directly, I can at least use him to inspire me to come up with some ideas for the boys myself, since he really is most remarkable. So I try to settle myself back into the feeling I had this morning when I was watching him shoot, and I replay some of his spectacular shots in my mind: if only I could combine what's best of Poncellet with *Tristan*, what a heady combination that would be!

I close my eyes, letting myself picture it for a while.

It's been an eventful morning, so I'm not entirely sure if I've actually nodded off for a moment or just fallen into something of a reverie, when I'm brought back to myself by the sound of footsteps ringing out in the portico.

Of all things, it's Taran, coming out into the garden via the door from the main hall. He's still got his broken bow in his hand and he must be circling around to stash the pieces of it back in his cabinet, now that the coast is clear.

Before I can clear my head or straighten up, he catches sight of me. Seeing me staring at him rather dreamily with my head lolling back against the tree, he stops in his tracks and pulls a frown. Then he rolls his shoulders, gives an irritated jerk of his head, and he continues on his way, marching right past me.

As he goes by, he casts me a dirty look and mutters,

"Not *you*, too!" and I flush, since I'm pretty sure I know what he means. I *have* been thinking about Poncellet, and I suppose I probably do look a little starry-eyed. So I snap defensively,

"So what if he's a little, *er*," and then I can't think of an adjective. 'Sleazy' comes to mind, but I can't say that about a master. "Even you've got to admit, he's the best shot that's ever been at St. Sebastian's!"

"Oh *yeah?*" Taran chides back. "He tell you that himself?"

I'm about to deny it, but in point of fact, he did. So I settle for saying,

"Well, I for one believe it!"

"Oh *yeah?*" he says again. For him, it's a pretty snappy comeback, actually — particularly when he follows it up by taking a menacing step towards me and demanding only inches from my face,

"If he's so good, then why isn't he in Guards?!"

With that he stalks off, banging the garden gate behind him. I'm left to head in for mess alone, asking myself as I go why it didn't occur to me earlier to wonder the very same thing.

"THERE ARE ONLY TWO KINDS OF MEN IN THE WORLD, BOYS. BIG, dumb clouters ... and the *rest* of us!" Tristan declares, slinging an arm around my shoulder and practically shouting into my ear as he leans across the big wooden table to be heard over the din in the great hall.

"Spoken like the vain butts man you are, DuBois!" Falko barks back merrily, sloshing down a huge gulp of ale.

The return of Master Guillaume and his retinue has caused quite a stir around the guild, and although the man himself has yet to put in an appearance, the atmosphere in the hall is even more riotous for noon mess today than it was in here last night. The place is packed to capacity, and word is Guillaume's brought back such a large entourage with him that he's busily arranging for cooking fires to be kindled out in the kitchen garden so that the new arrivals can be fed from stewpots set up out of doors. Even with most of the men from Meuse thus taking their meal outside, the gossip they've brought back with them is buzzing through the room and the ale is flowing, nowhere more freely than at the Journey table. Both Jerome and Charles have joined us, and between having them with us again, Poncellet's arrival, and the anticipation of a competition between masters tomorrow, the boys were likely to be excitable anyway. But the timely return of Guillaume has also served to remind us all that the next time we're gathered here on these benches tonight, it will be to hear the master preside over the official announcement of the theme for Firsts, and I'm sure I'm not the only one whose boisterous mood is being fueled partly by tension.

Adding to the exuberance at our table is the fact that Master Guillaume isn't the only one absent from mess today. Taran, too, has failed to appear. After the roasting he suffered from the masters during practice this morning nobody's very surprised he'd take to skulking in his room again, so when I noticed Remy hovering around out in the corridor on my way in and he spouted some lie about Taran being summoned for something by the masters, I didn't call him on it. I just dragged him reluctantly along inside with me (although technically he shouldn't be in the mess hall without his master, and with his master being such a stickler for the rules, it took some doing to convince him), and I took the opportunity to sit down at the Journey end of the table next to Tristan, where at first all the talk was about the bet between Poncellet and de Gilford. Before long, though, the conversation had turned to a phenomenon we've all had occasion to observe before: how much a man's shooting style tends to mirror his personality.

"I'll say one thing, men," Gilles is now proclaiming, inclining his head regally and spreading his hands. "After watching those two bicker all morning, I've never been gladder to be a wands man myself. Elegant, smooth, and supple, like the willow wand itself. Poised under pressure. Versatile. The perfect, all-around man."

"*Hear, hear!*" Pascal burbles, half-rising from his seat to salute his master, his renewed slavish devotion to Gilles already starting to get as tiresome as his former resentment.

"What about Aristide then, Gilles?" Tristan laughs. "*He's* a wands man, too."

"An aberration," Gilles sniffs. "More of a stick in the mud than a wand, I'd say."

"And what about me?" Jurian joins in. "What's my style? You can't pigeonhole me that easily."

"Jurian dear," Gilles replies, "I wouldn't dream of trying."

"Seriously, boys," Tristan grins. "After watching Master Poncellet this morning, tell me you've ever seen anything as glorious as a butts man in top form. Why, he's going to beat the pants off *Boring* de Gilford without even breaking a sweat, and I for one am going to thoroughly enjoy watching him do it!"

I'm not sure why it should bother me, since it's only natural that Tristan would root for Poncellet. They share the same skill, and Tristan's right. Watching him shoot this morning was thrilling. I should take it as a positive sign, that Tristan's starting to get excited about competing again himself. But I'm not feeling very charitable toward Poncellet at the moment and for some reason Tristan's enthusiasm for him makes me nervous, and I can't help feeling sorry that nobody seems inclined to root for poor de Gilford. So before I realize exactly what I'm saying, I'm elbowing Tristan in the ribs and demanding irritably,

"Oh *yeah*? Then answer me this. If he's so good, why isn't he in *Guards*?!"

Regrettably, Poncellet himself is standing right behind me.

He's come strolling into the hall unnoticed while the boys have been arguing, and after casting a grimace over at de Gilford and Master Leon at the masters' table, he's moseyed over to come up to the Journey table right behind Tristan. Even before all my words are out his open palm whacks me squarely on the back, and with a command of "*Push over, there, you! and let me in*" that's outwardly jovial enough, he shoves me rudely out of his way. The man's always rude, though, and from his demeanor I honestly have no idea whether he's heard my comment or not. So I hastily scoot aside as he springs over the bench, landing himself down between Tristan and me with a flourish like a stunt rider jumping into a saddle. Then without missing a beat, he pulls Tristan's plate in front of him and starts eating off of it without any shame, while launching into an animated discussion of himself before anyone else can object or say anything.

Not, of course, that any of the boys look inclined to object. They all seem thrilled that he's deigned to join us. It's much too close for comfort for me, though, and although I suppose I can understand not wanting to join the masters, why a man Poncellet's age would choose to sit with a group of boys I'm sure I don't know — at first. It only takes listening to him for about two seconds for it to make perfect sense, and not just because there doesn't seem to be any other natural place for him in the hall. The man is stuck in Journey mode himself.

Since he's still refusing to tell the boys anything about how he's perfected his style or how he accomplishes his tricks, it's not long before he's launching into the story of his life *after* St. Sebastian's — or to be more accurate, he's telling the boys a lot of rot about his supposed adventures. To hear him talk, he's done everything from campaigning with mercenaries, plundering with pirates, and worst of all, rescuing damsels in distress. He's got a scar to go with every story, too, and although the scars are real enough, there's something about the larger-than-life stories and the exaggerated way he tells them that reminds me of the evasive tall-tales Tristan told me about himself when I first met him. The man knows how to tell a good story, I'll give him that. But I don't like the way the boys are hanging on his every word, and each of the man's exploits is more outrageous than the last. It's doubly annoying that the majority of them involve extolling 'that purest of pleasures, liberating womankind from the tyrannies our oppressive society has placed upon her,' and other euphemisms for adultery. It all sounds uncomfortably like Tristan's Capellanus-inspired definition of 'noble love' last year to me, and so when Poncellet says heartily,

"Personally, I couldn't wait to shake the dust of *this* stultifying place off of me, let me tell you, boys! Why, there's a big, wide world waiting out there," I bite back the retort *"Why'd you come back here, then?"* and I climb out over the bench to make my escape, and I go down to sit with the squires.

Unfortunately, the squires are all listening to the man's stories, too. And as I settle in next to Remy, Poncellet starts in on a particularly vivid tale of infiltrating a seraglio that gives Rennie a bright idea.

"Hey Pascal," he says, leaning across the table. "Whaddya say we get Marek here to lead us on another little convent outing? We could nip out after lights out one night and go pay a visit to Ginger. I'd sure like to get another look at her, now that I know she's your fiancée."

"Yeah, and I bet *Pascal*'d like to get another look at her, too — since he's barely ever seen her, for more than five minutes," Armand agrees sourly.

Predictably, all the squires think it's a fantastic idea, even Remy, who's started trying to grasp my hand excitedly under the table; he didn't get to go along on our first excursion, and he's rather surprisingly turned out to be a terrible romantic.

But Pascal won't hear of sneaking around behind Gilles's back again. So when after a while Poncellet's finished Tristan's dinner and he's wandered off, and accordingly the boys too are getting up from table, over my protestations the other squires prod Pascal into calling out *"Master!"* down the table, to ask Gilles for his permission to arrange an official visit to the girl when an opportunity next presents itself.

Needless to say, going back to the convent school of St. Genevieve is about the last thing I ever want to do, particularly for an official visit. I have no intention of letting the Mother Superior get another good look at me, and

explaining to the boys why I don't want to tag along isn't going to be easy. So I'm just wondering what excuse I can use when the time comes, when Gilles says unexpectedly,
"I'm afraid that's entirely out of the question."
He says it so abruptly, on reflex I demand,
"But *why?*," even though I didn't want to go in the first place.
All the other squires are staring at Gilles, too, and Pascal looks particularly puzzled. So Gilles launches into some long spiel about how he's personally vouched for the match, and he's not willing to risk besmirching the lady's character with any prenuptial visits.
"Everything must be above board, *from now on* anyway," he says sternly. "I'll not give any further opportunity for gossip, as there's likely to be plenty circulating already."
There's nothing Pascal can say to that, since he as good as admitted he'd been sneaking off on Gilles's horse to try to visit Ginger at the convent this winter, and Gilles knows it. So he blushes prettily and proceeds to thank Gilles profusely for his foresight, apparently really believing his master is motivated solely by the desire to safeguard his fiancée's reputation.
The others all accept Gilles's pompous statement at face value, too, and I suppose it is in keeping with Gilles's character. But it didn't escape my notice that Pascal's request caught his 'unflappable' master by surprise. Or that as Gilles was talking, he looked an awful lot like a man thinking his way out of a corner, and I can only think of one explanation for that. For some reason, Gilles doesn't want to let Pascal get a good look at his own fiancée before the wedding.
The timing of it is terrible, since all my plans for Tristan require that he and Gilles get on well together and I shouldn't be sowing the seeds of dissension between them. But that shrewd look of Gilles's is weighing on me, and I haven't forgotten the note of glee in his voice at the wall the other day when he was talking about how horrible it would be for a boy to find out only too late that someone else had already gotten to his fiancée. And so as Tristan and I are heading out of the hall together, when Tristan exclaims,
"That Poncellet! What a shot! And what a character. It's going to be damned refreshing having a man of experience around the place. Somebody who knows something of life outside these narrow walls. Could you *believe* his stories, Marek?"
"Frankly, no," I say dryly; Tristan's looking dreamy-eyed, and it doesn't take much to guess which of Poncellet's stories *he* liked the best. So before Tristan can launch into a recap of the thrill of rescuing a damsel in distress, I interrupt to ask him,
"You don't think there could be anything *wrong* in Pascal's engagement, do you master?"
"Wrong?" he says. "What could be wrong about it?"

He looks genuinely surprised, so I just shrug. It would be the height of foolishness to bring up to Tristan now the unworthy suspicion that's crept into the back of my mind, and the stresses of the day are probably just getting to me. Gilles is a man of honor, and I've simply gotten muddled — from a long morning spent helping Pascal sort out his master's arrows that had gotten slipped into the wrong boy's quiver.

CHAPTER SIXTEEN

That afternoon finds me nervously rolling a freshly smoothed arrow shaft between my fingers out in the shop, while Tristan and Gilles head out to a secluded corner of the far field for their first joint training session — alone.

I'm apprehensive about letting them manage it without me, of course. But I've got Aristide's crossbow tutorial to deal with later, and after Poncellet's arrow-splitting frenzy this morning catching up on Tristan's fletching has turned into something of a crisis. Besides, if our plan is going to work, the boys have to figure out for themselves how to train each other. I've got to leave them to it and not interfere, and I've got my own part in it to worry about: coming up with the trick.

It wouldn't be accurate to say I'm exactly panicking about it, since the theme for Firsts hasn't even been announced yet. But the selection is *tonight* and it is starting to worry me that I've made no real progress on it, and I had a niggling feeling all through mess that maybe I was on the verge of coming up with something out in the garden this morning, before Taran's untimely interruption chased it away. It's the same feeling I had about Gilles back at Brecelyn's castle, like an idea is hovering there somewhere in the back of my mind just out of reach, and if so, it must have been inspired by thinking about Poncellet. So I settle myself in at a workbench, and while my fingers busily wind thread and weave on feathers, in the back of my mind I replay each of Poncellet's shots, trying to imagine how I might recast some of them as part of a joint trick.

What if the boys could learn to nock their arrows on the fly, the way Poncellet did? Then they could toss arrows to each other between shots. That'd be impressive, wouldn't it?

I try picturing it, but even if the boys could manage to do it, they'd probably just look ridiculous — more like jugglers than archers — and none of the other techniques the man used seem like they'd work for the boys much better. By the time the hour for Aristide's lesson is approaching, I have a stack of freshly fletched arrows piled up, but I just can't see how I could make *anything* Poncellet did into something that would really be a trick within a trick. It's probably because the heat in the canvas tent is stifling and sweat is trickling down between my shoulder-blades, but I feel like something's breathing down my neck again. So I knock off a little early and I head inside, telling myself that I still have plenty of time, and hoping to sneak in the wash I didn't get this morning before I have to face Aristide out on the field.

I am vaguely aware that the master's office isn't empty as I pass it — that there's a large group of men crowded inside it, in fact. But I'm too intent on keeping out a sharp eye as I wend my way down the corridor to think much of it; I assume the Journeys are all safely out practicing somewhere at this hour, but I'm in no hurry for another unexpected run-in with Taran. Or Poncellet, for that matter; I'm even less eager to collide bodily with him. So I'm thoroughly startled when the master's voice booms out into the hallway at me,

"*There* you are, Vervloet! Where in the hell have you been?!," just as though he'd summoned me and I've been late in coming. Again.

When I stumble to a stop outside the door and look in, for once the master isn't seated behind his big desk. He's standing behind it, surrounded by a huddle of men I don't recognize and leaning over to consult an assortment of large sheets of parchment spread out in front of him. The men are leaning over the papers, too, and as the master gesticulates down at the one on top and barks out questions, they're all talking over each other trying to answer him. None of them is paying any attention to me and the master is thrusting his finger around here and there at the page so vigorously and he's so engrossed in arguing with the men that I think I must have been mistaken that his shout was meant for me — until he glances up, frowns, and breaks off right in the middle of a colorful expletive to bellow,

"Don't just stand there gaping, for God's sake. Get *in* here, squire!"

And then he proceeds to ignore me again.

I hover in the doorway for a moment, unsure what do to. Then I slowly edge my way into the crowded room. The men are all too focused on their discussion to pay me any mind, so I creep up closer, curious to see what it is they're looking at so intently. When I've ducked under a few elbows and insinuated myself forward enough to see down onto the big chart spread across the master's desk, at first all I can make out is an incomprehensible array of boldly drawn lines and squiggles. But after listening in for a while and following the master's hand as it moves over the diagrams, I figure that this must be a construction plan for the newly acquired area behind the butts, out beyond the wall that the Journeys just finished tearing down.

Before I can get myself oriented enough to make much sense of it, though, Guillaume snaps,

"That's *still* not the right angle for the covered butts, Martin! I told you, it has to be north-north*east*, to catch the morning sun. It's going to be a thing of beauty! The first of its kind. So it's got to be situated just right. And where are the elevations? They were *supposed* to be ready by yesterday," and the plan is whisked aside, as an ascetic man who must be Martin patiently reaches down to pull out another scroll from a canister next to him under the desk.

When he opens it out, I quite forget myself. I lean forward eagerly across the desk to get a better look, and as I do, I let out a little high-pitched noise of appreciation and surprise. Unlike the other plans littering the desk, this is a sketch of a single building shown from all angles and inked in bright colors — a building that's going to be absolutely beautiful, just as the master said.

At my outburst, the master laughs.

"Looks like you've met with a *squire's* approval at least, men!" he chortles, thrusting some of the men aside and stepping around the desk to come up beside me, slapping me on the back so hard that my face almost smashes down onto the drawing. Then with one hand he yanks me back upright, and with the other he begins running the tips of his fingers over the picture lovingly, the way another man might caress a mistress.

"Yes, yes, even I have to agree," he exclaims rapturously. "My architects from Meuse here have outdone themselves, haven't they, Marek? Just look at the lines of it! Four long lanes inside, a high-pitched roof of imported cedar timbers, and wicker backstops at the far end, so two pairs of archers can practice side-by-side in any kind of weather. And this whole exterior wall here will be made of real glass, to let in maximum light."

All the details the master is describing have been meticulously drawn by the architects, and they are all impressive. Only one is commanding all my attention. It's a tinted sketch of the oversized double-doors that are to open midway down the wall of glass. Each of its two wide panels consists of an exquisite stained-glass window like one might find in a cathedral, and on each one a life-sized archer is depicted, holding up his equipment.

And one of them is holding a crossbow.

"How's your Latin coming along?" Guillaume demands, when he sees me staring at the crossbowman. "That master of yours gotten around to teaching you any yet?"

"Not really," I murmur absently, not taking my eyes off the image.

"Pity," he says, pointing to a place where two scrolls are depicted, unfurling just above the archers' heads. The one above the longbowman bears the guild motto, *non me occident sagittae*. The one above the crossbowman is blank.

"You could have made yourself useful, and come up with something suitably sentimental, for that."

The master doesn't seem to expect a response, which is fortunate, since I have no idea what to say. He's already grumbling under his breath, "We're still a few months out from construction, but we're going to have to come up with *something*. Can't just leave it empty," and before I can wonder what he's

213

talking about or what I'm even doing in here, suddenly he straightens up and starts rolling up the plans, reverting to his former brisk tone to demand of the men,

"That the lot, then? All right. I expect to have the rest of the drawings on my desk by first thing tomorrow morning."

Without waiting for an answer from them either, he starts piling the rolled-up plans into my hands. The men all break into a fresh flurry of questions, which he brushes off with a terse *"I can't make any more decisions until I've looked everything over out on site,"* and shoving one last scroll onto the unwieldy pile already in my arms, he strides right out the door without a backward glance.

When I just stand there dumbly, trying to balance the jumble of papers and wondering what I'm supposed to do with them, Guillaume barks back over his shoulder at me as he disappears around the corner,

"Come *on*, Vervloet. You don't think I called you in here for a *squire's* opinion, do you? Do your job, and carry those for me. You don't need to know any Latin for that."

And so I find myself scrambling down the long corridors of the guild after the master, struggling to catch up with him and to prevent the tower of scrolls in my arms from tumbling to the floor. It's harder to keep up with Master Guillaume than it ever was with Baylen, and I feel just as ridiculous trotting along awkwardly about ten paces behind him with a teetering stack of papers overflowing out of my hands. It feels even stranger when we've crossed through the main hall to come out into the garden and the master slows his pace enough to reach back and drag me up next to him. We're still moving uncomfortably fast and my legs have to take two steps for every one of his, but that's not what's so strange about it. It's that I've never walked around the guild side-by-side with the master like this.

Stranger still, just as we reach the end of the garden Master Guillaume drapes his arm around my shoulders, grins down at me, and demands,

"So, *missed* me much, have you, son?"

And I find to my surprise that I have.

As luck would have it, however, at just that moment Master Guillaume is ushering me out of the garden, and something about the way we bang through the little wooden gate brings on a flash of a scene from Meliana's journal — the one where she described pushing out onto the butts in just this fashion, only to find Guillaume waiting ominously on the other side, barring her way. It's probably just the heavy brocade on the master's sleeve, but a funny feeling tickles down the nape of my neck that's like the old adage, *'a goose is walking over my grave.'* It doesn't help that by chance we're passing the very spot where earlier Poncellet and I had our conversation, and something about it occurs to me now that didn't then. Master Guillaume isn't the only one to call me 'son' here this morning. So did Poncellet — right *after* I asked him about my father's trick.

MASTERS

The master hasn't slackened his pace, and as he leads me right out onto the practice range, I must have crossbows on the brain after seeing that beautiful image of one in the drawing back in his office. Somewhere out of the corner of my eye I think I see Aristide out on the far butts, too, and so I clear my throat and say tentatively,

"Uh, master. I'm supposed to be giving Master Aristide a crossbow tutorial, in about five minutes."

"Guyenne? Let him wait," the master laughs, and without breaking stride he hustles me all the way across the butts, around the embankment, and past the line of the downed guild wall. Soon we're coming out on the other side and into the newly acquired area beyond, where men in uniform are already busy tearing down and clearing away the debris of the hovels that once stood out here.

The men are all wearing the distinctive red tunics trimmed in grey that mark them out as members of the King's Guard, and as we weave our way around the crews and through the rubble, I wonder again what possessed Master Guillaume to request to bring a unit of them here. Most St. Seb's men don't have much respect for the King's Guard, since although I suppose they're what passes for a standing army in our country, they're really little more than a policing force in Meuse that's made to do the strong-arm tasks the Black Guardsmen find beneath them. There's something of a traditional rivalry between the two groups, and they're under the direct command of the prince's constable Hieronymous — a man I know for a fact is a personal enemy of the master's.

For his part the master isn't paying attention to any of the men, and it's not until he's steered me to an open place near the center of the field where there's a clear vantage all around that he comes to a stop. He rifles through the pile of parchment in my arms for a moment, and when he finds the scroll with the general construction plan on it, he pulls it out and unrolls it. He studies it for a long time, looking back and forth from the paper to the scene out in front of us and muttering to himself under his breath.

After a while, though, the master's no longer talking to himself. He's talking animatedly to me, pointing out the places where all the new structures are going to go and describing them to me in great detail.

"Over there, see? Where the line of the old wall and the new wall will meet? That's where our tower is going to be. A real fortifiable tower, not something empty, just for show! You'll appreciate *that*. No more leaving the defense of the place to a bunch of squires with wheelbarrows, eh, Marek?" he chuckles. "And a new, bigger armory over there, and an auxiliary barracks for veterans, complete with stables. There'll be no more lodging St. Sebastian's men in seedy taverns in town, either!," and if I didn't know the master had no sense of humor, I'd think he was trying to make a joke. But the master is always serious, and standing next to him and listening as he gestures out in front of us, the feeling I had that day in Brecelyn's office

215

steals over me again, that exhilarating feeling of sharing in the master's vision. I can almost see the structures he's describing rising before me as though summoned up from the ground by the force of his personality, and when I picture what the guild as he's reimagining it is going to be like, it *is* going to be spectacular — like a phoenix rising reborn from the ashes, just as he said.

It's so thrilling, in fact, that at first I hardly notice I actually have no idea what he's talking about again.

"This central area here'll have to be left open for *their* target range, framed on one side by the covered range, and on the other, by *their* barracks. I won't have them out on the Journeymen's butts, ripping it up or getting in my Journeys' way. So that's the question. How much space will they need for a practice field? I've got a whole row of stone storage units planned out here, too, and the Urbain boy's forge, so I'm only willing the spare the minimum. Say 250 by 75 yards, max."

He looks down at me expectantly.

"Well?" he demands, when I don't say anything. "What about it? Think that'll do the job?"

"What job, master? And, er, whose barracks?"

"Our new crossbow contingent's, of course!" he bellows. "For goodness' sake, squire," he adds, seeing my dumbstruck expression. "Weren't you listening to anything I said, back at the castle? I *told* you we'd been missing a bet with crossbows. Just think of it, Marek. Twice the competitions! And twice the *money.*" He shoots me a shrewd look. "It'll be nothing to compare with the Journey trials, of course. An empty bit of frivolity, actually; didn't I tell you I was counting on you, for that? But it's bound to be popular. And if we can parlay it into some additional certifications, all the better."

While I'm still floundering to process what the master's saying, he continues thoughtfully,

"I won't have them interfering with our Journeymen, naturally, or stealing any of their thunder. We are a longbow guild, and I won't sully our reputation. But I've said it before, *desperate times call for desperate measures.* So here's what I'm thinking: half the number of boys, and a little younger than the Journeys — say maybe fourteen, or fifteen? Something like that — to compete on the Saint's day every other year, in conjunction with the Journeys' veteran year. That way it can serve as some extra pomp to set the second year of competitions apart, and as sort of a warm-up event to the boys' trials. We'll have to think of something to *call* them, of course. I won't have them called Journeymen. And we'll need something to do with the winners; we can't send *them* to Guards. But we can worry about the petty details later, as it's too late to get a new competition up and running in time for *this* year, more's the pity. All I really need right now are the dimensions for their practice field, so we can firm up our plans out here. That, and before long, the motto. It's got to be ready before we can commission the glass."

The master looks down at me, his eyebrows raised, and I look up at him, and I blink. Twice. I can't have heard him right. It sounded a lot like the master is saying he's instituting a competition in crossbows at St. Sebastian's. And that the squires' exhibition *I* organized was the inspiration for the idea.

"Well?" he demands again. "Will 75 by 250 be enough?"

"It'll be perfect," I finally manage.

"Excellent," the master exclaims, and he proceeds to roll up the plan and put it back on the top of the stack. He's obviously ready to head back in, but there are a million questions I want to ask him, and before he can turn to stride off again, I have to ask him at least one of them.

"Why *me*, master?"

It's not the one I meant to ask. But despite what the master said back in his office, he *is* asking my advice. I have to know why.

"You really want the truth, *son*?" he says, emphasizing the word and looking down at me with such a penetrating look that I'm sure I know what's coming. My stomach does a slow somersault, like a ship rolling on a wave at sea. There can only be one reason Master Guillaume would ask a squire's opinion. He's finally going to tell me he knows I'm the son of Jan Verbeke.

"Why am I asking *you*, Marek?" he repeats. "To be perfectly honest, you're the only one around here who gives a *damn* about crossbows! And in my experience, to do a thing well a man's got to have a passion for it. An overriding passion. A passion that comes before anything else."

It's not at all what I was expecting to hear, and I don't know whether to be relieved, or not — since I've known from the moment I stepped foot inside St. Sebastian's that the master must either love Jan's son, or want to kill him. And it's not exactly how I'd describe my feelings about crossbows, either. But I decide to take it as a compliment anyway. It's the only one I'm likely to get.

The master stares down at me speculatively for a minute longer. Then he asks abruptly,

"So, have you started up squires' club again?"

"I'm not done giving the crossbow tutorials yet," I remind him, and he frowns.

"Well for God's sake finish them up, squire! Double 'em up, triple 'em, whatever it takes. I'll give you one more day to get them done. Then I want you out training with your club, every afternoon. We'll need some decent candidates trained and ready when the time comes, if we're going to get this new crossbow division underway successfully; impressive boys, for the first competition. Some of the squires who aren't Journey material might just do nicely. What about the St. Juste boy, Gilles's squire? He's a handsome devil."

"I think Pascal intends to try for Journey, master," I tell him, and Guillaume rolls his eyes.

"He'd better learn to *shoot*, then," he says dryly. "Hmm. Well, what about the little Urbain boy, Charles's brother? He'll be about the right age, and he's an attractive little fellow, too." Master Guillaume pauses. He gives me a hard look, right in the eye. He holds my gaze, just long enough for it to start feeling uncomfortable, and as does, he says deliberately,

"*He'd* look the part, anyway," and I know what he's telling me.

He's saying that I don't.

I stand there for a moment, letting exactly what the master's telling me fully sink in:

A competition in my own best skill is coming to St. Sebastian's, and I'm not to compete.

It should make me miserable. It really should. And I do feel that slightly queasy feeling in the pit of my stomach I always feel when I have to think about the way I look. But it's funny. After lying out under the stars in the ruins of our show on that bitter night when Master Guillaume told me I could never be a Journey, I must finally be over the disappointment of not competing myself. From the sound of it, the master is asking *me* to train the others for it, and that actually sounds more exciting to me now, like it's the bigger challenge. Maybe I really am becoming a Baylen.

Or maybe I'm just kidding myself.

"Speaking of squires' club," the master continues, slinging his arm around my shoulders again and adopting such a confidential tone that the queasy feeling lingering in my stomach begins to shade into unease. I haven't forgotten the master's nasty habit of delivering his lowest blows right when he's softened me up to least expect them, and everything about the master's posture suggests he's about to come out with something unpleasant. I suddenly remember that at the time, I'd thought Guillaume hated our St. Sebastian's day show. After all, we hit him in the head with a chunk of wood. He probably hasn't forgiven me for that. Or for starting squires' club without asking his permission. I have a funny feeling that what I'd thought was a compliment might yet turn out to be one of the master's more creative punishments instead.

Sure enough, soon the master is saying gleefully,

"Now that that club of yours is *official*, I've decided it's high time you boys had an official trainer." He gives my shoulders a bone-crushing squeeze. "And not just any trainer! A *master*. A man who excels at training *and* shooting. Why, just between you and me, he may well be the best shot that's ever been at St. Sebastian's."

The master doesn't have to tell me who he's talking about, of course, and my heart sinks.

So that's it. The master's not putting me in charge of anything — far from it. Not only is he going to load me up with menial chores that nobody

MASTERS

else wants under the guise of flattering me about my 'passion' for crossbows, he's also taking squires' club *away* from me. And he's going to stick me with old Poncellet.

As the master's been talking, he's slowly started guiding me back through the crews of men toward the old line of the wall, and I've been letting myself be led ploddingly along, unresisting.

"That's a beautiful sight, too, isn't it kid?" he says with satisfaction, oblivious to my mood and smirking at a group of men piling charred timbers into a wheelbarrow, their red tunics streaked with soot.

"What are they doing here anyway, master?" I grumble.

"Free labor!" he chuckles, and I suppose that could explain it. But from his gloating expression I get the impression he's enjoying forcing them into menial tasks, too — ones that would ordinarily be below their station.

As though reading my mind, with a sidelong glance he gives my shoulders another squeeze and says,

"You've heard the old saying, haven't you Marek? Keep your friends close, and your enemies closer."

I have to wonder which of the two he thinks I am.

The funny thing is, though, that the master's arm is still slung casually around me, and despite everything he's said, as we're walking along today it feels oddly companionable. At least, it no longer feels like a hunk of meat, and I can't help still feeling excited and a little overwhelmed at the thought of a crossbow contingent coming to St. Sebastian's, even if I'm to have little direct part in it. It occurs to me, too, that Master Guillaume never said exactly what it is he *does* want me to do to help him with it, and I get the impression he genuinely expected me to find his news about an official trainer for squires' club thrilling.

So I make a decision. A risky one, but it's like the master said: *desperate times call for desperate measures.*

We've come back around the embankment far enough by now that I can see out onto the far field, to a place where some of the Journeys have set themselves up to practice. I can't see Tristan and Gilles from here, but I know they're out behind the pavilions somewhere, and at the thought of how their practice is probably going, I know I've got to do something to help them. Poncellet isn't going to tell me about my father's trick. But there is one person left who surely knows all about it — who knows all about my father, actually, and I've just never been brave enough to ask. Maybe Master Guillaume *is* a friend, and I'm never going to get a better chance to find out than this.

So I screw up my courage, and I ask him about my father's trick.

I lead up to it gradually, of course. But I'm nervous and I'm not very subtle about it, and before I can get the question out, Guillaume yanks his arm away from me. He comes to an abrupt stop, and twists me around to face him. Even before he opens his mouth, I know I've made a grave mistake.

"Don't think I don't know why you're asking, squire!" he snaps scornfully. "*All* of Jan's tricks were incredible, that's the truth. But you've got another thing coming if you think I'll stand for having any of this lot sullying more of *my* squire's tricks — least of all *your* master. So let me be blunt, so that there can be no misunderstanding. If I catch *anyone* trying to replicate another one of Jan's tricks during the trials, I'll toss him right out of the competition."

He towers over me for a moment in silence, arms crossed, his intimidating form casting me in shadow as he gives me another penetrating stare to make sure I've gotten his message. Then he laughs. But he doesn't sound very amused.

"And next time, get your facts straight before you go asking questions! Jan Verbeke's First trials weren't butts. And as for the trick he did at his butts trials, no boy in his right mind would try to match the performance he gave of it."

With that he turns heel and stalks off, and this time I don't try to keep up with him.

I trudge along a good ten paces behind him, wondering bitterly what the master would know about being in one's right mind, and cursing myself for being so reckless as to blow Tristan's chances of ever using one of my father's tricks again. Now even if I could figure out how to get the information out of Poncellet, I couldn't use it.

I've lost my father's unbeatable trick, for good.

By the time we're coming back around onto the butts again, I feel like I've been jerked around from one extreme to the other by the master this afternoon more than I ever was by Taran. I'm starting to feel mighty sorry I was careless enough to let Meliana's journal out of my possession, too, and not just because the master's made my father's butts trick sound even more impressive than I'd imagined it. I'd thought I'd learned everything the book had to tell me about my father's past, and that all its secrets involved what happened to him at his Third trials. Now I'm beginning to suspect there's some mystery to my father's First trials, too.

Otherwise, I can't see why everyone keeps insisting on lying to me about them.

ARISTIDE IS ALREADY OUTSIDE AND WAITING FOR ME WHEN WE get back to the stables. He's leaning up against the outer archive wall with a sour look on his face, and I can tell he hasn't liked being made to wait by a mere squire. When he sees I'm with the master, though, he doesn't say anything, and as long as Guillaume is still visible in the yard where he's stopped to confer with some of the workmen, he even grudgingly helps me lug the equipment for the tutorial out of the stables and onto the field.

Once we've gotten everything set up and ready, I pick up the repeating bow and I launch straight into one of the pat little speeches I came up with to explain the bow to Taran, wanting to be done with the lesson as quickly as possible and sure Aristide feels the same way. With the big crossbow in my hand, in the back of my mind I'm thinking back over everything the master's just told me, and with the selection ceremony tonight looming, I'm antsy to check in on the boys' progress. So it catches me by surprise when Aristide suddenly interrupts me to sneer,

"I don't understand, *Marek.*"

My head bobs up. He's said it so much like Taran did yesterday, I'm sure Taran's put him up to it.

But it's soon apparent that Aristide really doesn't understand. As it turns out, the bow isn't as intuitive as I'd thought, and I should have guessed that Taran had some experience with crossbows for it to have occurred to him to suggest one for me. So after a few more half-hearted attempts to explain the finer points of the bow's action fail to register much with Aristide, simply to expedite things I instruct him to put his arms around me, just as Taran did.

"You've got to be joking," he says. But when I promise him it'll make the lesson go faster, he reluctantly agrees, and soon I'm walking him through the proper motion using the 'Mellor method,' although of course I don't call it that.

Needless to say, there's nothing sensual about the feeling it gives me to be in a boy's arms, this time. There's a smell clinging to Aristide underneath his expensive perfume that's as sour as his personality, and his sinewy arms digging into mine feel tough and stringy, like I'm being wrestled by the carcass of an over-boiled and over-dressed chicken. So as soon as I've got him doing a motion that's halfway passable, I lower the bow and exclaim heartily,

"*Fantastic,* master. You've really got the hang of it. Give it a try on your own, and we can call it a day."

To my dismay, instead of letting go of me Aristide suddenly squeezes his arms around me tighter, just like Taran did. He bends down until his cheek is almost pressing against mine, just as Taran did, too — except that there's nothing sensual about this, either. The feeling it gives me is pure terror.

"What in the *hell* were you thinking, stealing her *private diary?!*" he hisses, right in my ear.

I see he's finally gotten around to reading Meliana's journal.

"I don't blame you for wanting to read the thing," he continues nastily, tightening his grip as I try to squirm away. "What a sordid story! Poor old Verbeke. He didn't stand a chance, did he? But *bringing* it back here to St. *Sebastian's,* knowing what it said?! Are you a raving lunatic? Didn't you give any thought to what could have happened to the both of us, if the masters had found it on me!?" he demands, just as though I was the one who brought it back here, not him.

I stop squirming. I lick my lips. "Uh, just where is the book now, *master?*"

"Don't *master* me, *Marek*," he snaps back. "And don't go getting any ideas. The book's gone up in smoke. As soon as I realized what it was, I threw it straight into the archive fire. You're damned lucky I had the foresight to deal with it before it could get us both into serious trouble."

I don't know why it should bother me, since I let the journal go a long time ago. But once Aristide's gone and I'm dragging the dummy feet first back to the stables alone, I feel like I've just lost my father, all over again.

It doesn't improve my mood any that I've had to double over at an awkward angle to get a good grip on the dummy, and as I'm struggling along with it moving backwards, my head is bent right over its abdomen. One lone arrow is still sticking out of it right in front of my nose, one I know Aristide didn't put there; *he* missed the thing entirely. It's a broken one of Taran's.

I don't notice that Taran himself is right outside the stables until I'm almost on top of him.

I haven't seen him since this morning and I have no idea how long he's been there, but now he's leaning up against the wall under the archive eaves in about the same spot Aristide was in earlier, his arms hanging heavily at his sides. His head is thrown back, and he's slowly and rhythmically banging the wall behind him with the back of his head.

His eyes are closed and to all appearances he hasn't noticed me approaching, although lugging the dummy along by myself isn't easy, and hunched over puffing and pulling as I am, I've probably been making quite a lot of noise. It must be because I wasn't expecting to see him, and because I suspect he must be brooding over the vile jokes the masters were making this morning at his expense. Or maybe it's because I now see that he's squeezing that same brick the boys were teasing him about the other day at mess so tightly in one hand, his knuckles stand out white against it — as though simply clenching and unclenching his empty fist is no longer enough for him. But he looks so miserable, I can't help it. I feel a little bubble of sympathy for him rising up in my chest.

Then Taran's head jerks up. His eyes fly open, and he fixes me with a malevolent glare.

"Isn't there *any* man's embrace you're not eager to jump into?" he demands sarcastically, and the little bubble goes 'pop." I swallow it down, just like indigestion. "How convenient these little tutorials must be proving to you," he jeers. "Although after this morning, I would have guessed the *next* man's arms I found you in would be Poncellet's!"

"*Ha!*" I shoot back. "And I'd have thought *you* of all people would know there's only *one* boy around here whose embrace a girl would really be eager to jump into! Only one whose arms she wouldn't have to be *forced* into, in fact — and that's Tristan's!"

And then I cringe.

I don't really care that I've just let Taran catch me fraternizing with

Aristide, of all people. Surely I don't care what *he* thinks anymore. But I spoke without thinking again, saying the first thing that came into my mind just to annoy him, when the last thing I should be doing is using Tristan to goad him. And I was just thinking about our crossbow tutorial and his 'Mellor method,' I swear it. But it must have sounded like I was trying to taunt Taran with the same things the masters were this morning, and just as crudely. Even worse, to my own ears it sounded a lot like I've just thrown at him the terrible accusation Tristan made of him out in the windmill — the one that was so bad, I couldn't even pretend to believe it.

It must have sounded the same way to Taran.

He lunges off the wall, a look on his face worse even than the one he wore when being teased mercilessly earlier by Poncellet. Only this time he doesn't bother to restrain himself. In two long strides he charges over and he rips the dummy right out of my hands. I'm fully expecting him to fall on it and tear it to pieces, or maybe toss it over his shoulder like a rag doll and brain me with the brick, when a strange thing happens.

Just as I'm figuring my neck is about to find out what it felt like to be Taran's bow this morning, Taran lurches to a stop. He just stands there, staring down at me over the dummy with a wild look in his eye and breathing heavily, and I stare back, determined for once to hold my ground with him. My gaze is locked on his and with the dummy between us, I can't see his hands; but from the expression on his face, it won't be long before that brick in his fist is nothing but dust, if it isn't already. It probably only lasts for a few seconds, but it feels like a ridiculously long time and the tension is killing me.

Then with a snort that's partly a sigh, Taran shoulders the dummy.

Wordlessly, he rolls his eyes.

And then he turns around and stalks off, carrying it off silently back into the stables for me.

I stand there watching him go even after he's disappeared from sight, thinking to myself:

"Now what in the heck was *that*?!"

I'M NOT AT ALL SURE WHAT JUST HAPPENED. SO I DO MY BEST TO shrug it off, assuming it was some new ploy of Taran's to rattle me, and I hurry straight out to find Tristan and Gilles. I've been rattled enough all afternoon just worrying about how their first practice session together must be going, and I've been waiting too long for a chance to find out to waste any more time letting Taran make *me* feel guilty, if that's what he intended.

I've been mighty apprehensive about how the boys have been getting on, so it's with considerable relief that when I come out around behind the temporary pavilions far enough to spot them in the distance, I see that

Jerome is with them. He's perched on the edge of Gilles's bench and he's got his hastily patched-up lute on his knee, and from the looks of it he's been using it to keep the boys jollied up enough to keep them in line. At least they don't look to be quarreling, as I half expected they would be, and it *does* look like they've been practicing. They've got a wand set up about 200 yards out that's bristling with arrows, and as I draw nearer, I can make out Gilles lifting his bow in preparation of taking a shot. He's wearing his freshly laundered peacock-blue tights, and as usual when the trainers aren't around, he's stripped off his tunic. His hair is flowing loose around his shoulders and as he flexes to stretch his bow, his lithe, muscular body does look as strong and as graceful as a willow tree swaying gently in a summer's breeze.

When I get close enough to hear what he's saying and to read Tristan's body language, however, I see that Gilles is proving to be every bit as irritating a trainer as I feared he would be.

Tristan's leaning against his bow in an attitude of barely contained annoyance, and now that I'm closer I notice that all the arrows in the wand in front of them have white bands on them. Gilles hasn't let Tristan take a single shot.

It's apparent, too, that I'm coming in on the middle of a long lecture when Gilles barely pauses what he's saying long enough to greet me.

"It's not one of your glory shots, old man. You can't force it, or pluck at the string like you were plucking a chicken. You're not trying to 'wow' the crowd. You're *seducing* it, with a *caress*. It's got to linger. That's what's wrong with all you butts men, and clouters, too. No follow-through. You're all ping and pizzazz. Muscle, with no finesse. Oh, hullo there Marek. Now Jerome, do be a good fellow and play something for me. A dulcet strain, to give us the proper mood," and as Jerome accordingly strums a lilting chord, Gilles sighs as though he really were seducing a lover, and he pulls back in a languid move that's as beautiful as it is smooth. When he releases, it sends a sinuous ripple through the muscles of his chest like the surface of a pond responding to the toss of a pebble, and he sends his shot sailing up in a shimmering arc that's so high and light his arrow seems to hover for a moment, levitating in mid-air, before it descends swiftly and gracefully to stick dead center in the wand.

As Tristan and I are trudging back inside not much later, somewhere behind us I hear Gilles saying clearly,

"I fear he just doesn't have the *personality* for it, Jerome," and I don't bother asking Tristan how it went. I'm sure Tristan's heard him, too, and besides, he's too busy muttering under his breath,

"If he says *'be the wand'* one more time, I swear I'm going to kill him."

"Have patience, master," I tell him brightly. "Today was only the first day, and it was bound to be a little rocky. It's sure to get better. And tomorrow, it'll be *your* turn," although the thought doesn't actually make me feel much better.

It doesn't do much for Tristan, either.

We don't say anything the rest of the way inside. But when we reach the Journey corridor and Tristan opens the door of his room, before closing it behind him again he turns to me long enough to say,

"You know, Marek. There is one flaw in that brilliant plan of yours."

"What's that, master?" I ask nervously.

"As I see it, there's only one way that *Gilles* is going to fail to win Guards. And that's if Taran beats him."

MESS IS TO BE A FORMAL AFFAIR FOR THE SELECTION CEREMONY tonight, and so once I've made myself as presentable as I can alone in Tristan's room (considering I never did get that wash), I join Tristan and the others milling around out in the Journey corridor to assure myself Tristan's cloak is firmly attached at his shoulders, and to get that one wayward lock of his lying back properly, for the moment, anyway.

It's easier to smooth a boy's hair than it is his nerves, however, and Tristan's plenty jittery. I may have convinced him he's sure to pass Firsts no matter what the theme, but we both know it's the subsequent trials that are going to be the real challenge. And that there's actually more than one flaw in my plan. If Firsts is butts, for example, it'll be a disaster. Tristan's best skill will be as good as wasted.

"You're not worried about the selection, are you Tristan?" I ask him, once I'm satisfied with his appearance.

"Why should I be, when I have a plan in place to cover every eventuality?" he replies, and I suppose it should reassure me. It would make me feel a whole lot better, though, if I could be sure I knew which plan he was talking about.

For my part I've been worrying about the selection all day, since waking from nightmares last night. So by the time the big double doors are thrown open and we're all filing into the overcrowded great hall, I feel like one of those beasts from my dreams could be breathing down my neck again (although it's probably actually just Remy, getting characteristically too close as he tries to whisper something excitedly into my ear), and I'm not the only boy who's on edge.

After his absence Master Guillaume is more formidable than ever presiding over the head table in his full regalia, and tonight the masters' table is full. Masters Leon and Poncellet are in ceremonial dress as well (although I notice Poncellet is still sporting his purple sash underneath his cloak), and even Brian de Gilford looks surprisingly sober, though it's probably not in honor of the selection tonight. He's trying to keep in shape for his big competition with Poncellet in the morning.

Between the capacity crowd, the solemnity of the masters, and the seriousness of what's riding on the announcement they're to make after supper, it's enough to make me glad to have the excuse of squires' solidarity to sit down at the opposite end of the table from Tristan, where I can hide my obvious nervousness from him. The selection of the theme for Firsts isn't the only ceremony set for tonight; Frans is to be sworn in as Falko's squire, and with so many unfamiliar veterans packed into the hall and his own brother Charles in attendance, the poor boy's been justifiably petrified about it. But his induction comes off with hardly a hitch, and there's only one tense moment. When Master Guillaume asks Falko formally who it is he's presenting, he hesitates, and I'm afraid he's going to forget the lad's name again. As it turns out, Falko's just swallowing down a bite of meat he'd snagged from the sideboard on his way to the front of the room, and it's not long before a relieved and official Frans is plopping down next to me and we're all welcoming him properly into our midst by giving him a thoroughly hard time.

As soon as the platters are cleared away, however, and the masters start sending around the port as a signal that the time for the selection is fast approaching, I go down and slip in next to Tristan. His hand feels cold and clammy as I take hold of it under the table, and I can see beads of sweat forming on his upper lip.

Not that the other boys look any different. We all know the order of the themes is going to make all the difference this year, and everyone's head is on the block. So when Master Guillaume finally calls for the urn with the lots in it to be brought forward, I put my head down, close my eyes, and I do something I never thought I'd do. I start chanting *"clouts, clouts. Please, let it be clouts!"* fervently under my breath. All down the benches, I think the other boys are doing the same thing: praying for once that tonight the masters will pick their own *worst* skill.

That is, all but Taran. I doubt *he* cares what the theme for Firsts is. I open one eye to sneak a look down the table at him when I hear Master Leon stepping forward to swirl the tiles around in the urn. He's drumming the fingertips of one hand on the tabletop with a scowl on his face (the masters having confiscated his knife), but whatever he's thinking, it's not about the trials. And except for Gilles. He's been lounging next to Tristan all evening, looking as unruffled and as silky as the fur on a sleek cat's back in a way that would be enough to get on anyone's nerves. It's certainly been getting on *Tristan's*. And so when Master Leon finally pulls out a token and hands it to the master and soon Guillaume is booming out,

"Gentlemen, it's *wands!*," even though it wasn't the result I was hoping for, after this afternoon I can't be too disappointed that the boy whose best skill we'll be getting safely out of the way at Firsts is Gilles.

I only have time to say, "That's good for us, isn't it master?" and for Tristan to reply,

"Better than *butts*, anyway," before Master Guillaume is calling for attention.

"Journeymen," he says seriously. "I shouldn't have to tell you that I expect your exhibition shots to be extraordinary this year. This will be our first competition since the, er, *unfortunate incident*," and when he pauses, Gilles interjects, "I suppose by that he means the *plague*," before the master continues: "It therefore falls to you to win the people over to us again. So for your individual exhibitions, think big! The sky's the limit. It's such a pity that wands is such a *static* skill. We need action. Excitement! Movement. So find a way to work a little motion in. Oh, and gentlemen," he adds sternly, "There had better actually be a *wand* in it."

"How in the world are we supposed to put a wand in motion?" Falko complains, once the master's sat down. "Isn't it by definition a piece of wood sticking up out of the ground?"

"I suppose you could throw one at the target, like a javelin," Jurian jests. "Although I rather think the master meant for *you* to be in motion, not the wand."

"Putting a wand in motion won't be a problem for *M. le Marquis* here. He can just strap one to Pascal's back and have him run around the field as a moving target," Aristide says snidely, motioning at Gilles and having apparently forgotten that he, too, planned an exhibition involving shooting at his own squire for Seconds last year. I cast Pascal a nervous look, afraid he's going to leap up and offer to do it. In his present mood I wouldn't put it past him, and needless to say, if Gilles and Tristan really are going to do a trick together, I'm not eager for it to require using squires as marks.

As though reminded of it by the subject of shooting at squires, all of a sudden Jerome asks brightly,

"Say, Marek. You never did tell me this morning exactly what happened to you at Thirds, up on that tower," and before I can answer, Tristan is clearing his throat.

He does it in that stagey way of his that would make me nervous anyway. But even from the opposite end of the table it didn't escape my notice that in his nervousness earlier Tristan was tossing back ale at an alarming rate all through dinner. He can usually pack away an impressive quantity of the stuff without being the worse for it, but he can't drink like a fish the way Jurian can, and ever since the relief of learning that wands is to be the first theme he's been chatting away a mile a minute in a fashion that usually means he's getting tipsy. The last thing we need on Master Guillaume's first night back is for Tristan to climb up and give one of his drunken performances from on top of the table.

"That's just it, isn't it Jerome?" he slurs, waving his arm in a blousy motion across the table. "We never did find out the whole story, did we?" He stabs his finger in the air in what I suppose he thinks is the direction of the boys opposite him. "Not *you*. Or you. Or — why, *none* of us *really* knows what happened, do we?"

And just like that, he's launching into his theories about Sir Brecelyn and the plot at Thirds again, and rallying all the boys to commit to helping him investigate.

"You can't tell me any of you actually *believe* the man who shot Marek was working for anyone other than Brecelyn, can you? Don't we owe it to a squire who'd risk his life for his master to find out what really happened? If it turns out there was no plot, then where's the harm in it? It'll just be a game. But if Sir Hugo was plotting against our country with someone here at the guild, well, I shouldn't have to say more." He pauses dramatically, then says soberly (well, as soberly as a drunk boy can), "We won't all be here together for much longer, boys, and it's going to take all of us working together to figure this thing out. If each one of us takes on different people and asks only one or two discrete questions of each, it should be perfectly safe. Nobody'll catch on or be the wiser. Then we can pool our information in the evenings, at mess. It's now or never, men," he ends rousingly, sweeping unsteadily to his feet and raising his tankard. "What do you say? Are you true-blooded Ardennese, or a lily-livered bunch of traitors?"

All the boys give him a cheer; they're all a bit drunk, too, and Tristan always gives a good speech when he's in his cups. But I know they're all thinking it is a game, just as Tristan said— nothing more serious than Gilles casting the boys as knights of Camelot the other night, and I bet they wouldn't be so willing to go along with it if some of the tension stirred up by the thought of Firsts weren't still hanging over the table. Tristan's proposal is a welcome diversion, and even I have to admit that the way Tristan's described it, it does sound safe. He's just talking about asking a few simple questions. It's nothing he hasn't done before, and how much trouble can that really cause him, anyway?

Soon the boys are eagerly fixing up a plan amongst themselves. Tristan declares mysteriously that he's going to follow up on some leads of his own, while Falko and Jurian as the most convivial amongst us offer to befriend some of the soldiers camping out on the exposition grounds.

"Ugh," Gilles exclaims, when he hears it. "You boys can slum it across the street if you like, but *I'll* have nothing to do with them. And can somebody please tell me what we're doing with a *King*'s Guard anyway? After all, our country is ruled by a *prince*," but nobody's listening to him, and eventually he and Aristide have agreed to take on the aristocratic element among the veterans. Charles is to tackle the crews working out in the new area, and Jerome will take what opportunities present themselves to poke around while working on the guild books. Before long, the only one who hasn't volunteered to help is predictably Taran.

To my surprise, though, he hasn't objected, either; after all, he's usually scornful of this sort of thing and he's engaged to marry Brecelyn's daughter.

And he hates Tristan. He'd be likely to object to anything Tristan proposed, just because of that.

Instead, he's still sitting stone silent at the far end of the table. And when I sneak another glance down at him, he's staring down at the tabletop in front of him with a look on his face that suggests he's torn between two options, both of which he finds equally distasteful.

I know he doesn't like Brecelyn, and there's something about the set of his profile that reminds me of how I once thought he was trying to break off his engagement with Melissande because of his suspicions of her father. Looking at him now, I can almost hear him debating with himself with the same edge in his voice as it had that day in his room at the castle, when he said to me *"Brecelyn is going to be my father-in-law, and there's nothing I can do about it. Absolutely nothing."* But that was all an illusion at best, wasn't it? And at worst, it was a lie. In point of fact, Taran tried to scare me off from investigating Brecelyn all winter, so I'm not sure why he's keeping quiet now. Unless of course he's hoping that it really will end up getting Tristan into trouble.

As it is, he doesn't say anything until Pascal chimes in with a suggestion that he and Armand try to ingratiate themselves with the new additions to the kitchen staff or some of the soldiers' grooms and retainers, and the other squires all start clamoring for a part in the game. With the topic thus dwindling, Jerome pipes up again, and over the babble of squires' voices, he demands,

"Seriously, though, boys. What *did* happen to Marek? Isn't anybody ever going to tell me how he survived that shot at point-blank range?," and to my consternation, Charles calls down the table,

"Come on, Taran! Tell us. *You* must know."

When Aristide adds,

"Yeah, we never did get *your* side of the story. I bet it's mighty *interesting*," Taran rises abruptly to his feet.

"No squires," he says, and he says it so forcefully that nobody questions his right to decide the matter. Without saying another word or meeting anyone's eye, Taran steps over the bench and hurries out of the hall, moving awfully fast, as Aristide's amused voice pursues him, calling out *"Don't think you'll get off that easily, Mellor! We'll get the whole story out of you yet, one of these days,"* and I'm so glad the unwelcome topic's been averted, it's not until later that I realize what Taran's blunt statement must have meant:

Whatever his motives, Taran's exclusion of the squires from Tristan's scheme surely signaled his own intention to be included in it.

I help support Tristan as he staggers back to his room not much later. But once I've gotten him through his door with difficulty and I'm trying to prop him up against the wall long enough to get his cloak unfastened, he springs upright and extricates himself neatly from my grasp, exclaiming,

"Heavens, Marek. I'm not really drunk."

"Then why were you pretending to be?" I ask, not really sure, as I watch him unclasp the garment himself quite deftly. He flings it down onto the bed, and then throws himself exhaustedly down on top of it.

"You don't think the others would have gone along with me if they'd thought I was sober, do you?" he says.

And then he proceeds promptly to pass out.

I close the door softly behind him to leave him to sleep it off, and I make my way back to barracks, ready to crash down on my own cot, too — only when I round the corner into our hallway, I find Gilles lounging up casually outside the barracks door.

I don't have to ask to know what he's doing there. He's waiting for me. I've been half expecting it, from the moment I heard Master Guillaume's announcement.

Sure enough, when I come to a stop in front of him, without looking up from where he's arranging the lace of one cuff, he raises his eyebrows and says mildly,

"So, come up with anything for the trick yet, Marek?"

"I've got a few ideas I'm working on," I reply warily. "Something, with *birds*."

I suspected it was coming, but it annoys me anyway. I have no intention of making it easier for him to weasel out of our bargain, although I suppose it's only natural for him to want to make the most of his own best skill. He's already got a fabulous wands trick all worked out for himself, I'm sure.

"That's splendid, Marek. Truly splendid," Gilles drawls. "I'm on pins and needles to hear all the details. But I'm afraid it's going to have to be *tomorrow*, dear boy. I'm sure you understand." He spreads his arms out in the helpless move of a man succumbing reluctantly to the dictates of fate. "Under the circumstances, I simply can't wait any longer than, say, mess tomorrow night."

As soon as he's gone, I slump back wearily against the wall, and I let my head fall heavily back against the boards behind me. I close my eyes, and on a whim, I start rhythmically banging against the wall with the back of my head.

It feels surprisingly good, and after a while I get a grip on myself. Tristan was right. It's now or never and if I'm really going to help him, I've got to stop looking to my father or to anybody else to do my job for me. *I'm Tristan's squire*, and I'm just going to have to buckle down and come up with a trick, all by myself.

It's got to be possible, right? And I suppose it could be worse.

After all, Gilles did give me one more day.

CHAPTER SEVENTEEN

The next morning finds me standing out on the butts under a dark cloud of resentment. It's going to be a glorious day and the morning fog's already lifting, and I'm right in the midst of an ecstatic group of Journeys and squires. We're all gathered here to witness the competition between the masters in lieu of regular morning practice, and the air is sweet and cool and the boys are in a splendid mood — all except for me. I'm all too aware that no matter who wins I'm going to be the loser, since whichever man is beaten is sure to blame me for supposedly coming up with the idea. If that weren't enough, between being stuck here all morning and then having to finish up the crossbow tutorials all afternoon, I'm going to have precious little time to put my mind to the boys' trick. Gilles has only given me until tonight to come up with one, and maybe the trick doesn't have to be all that spectacular. But as Master Guillaume might say, it does have to be *something*. It can't really be something with birds.

De Gilford is the first of the two masters to come out, and as always he's ridiculously cheerful first thing in the morning. Today he's positively bursting with high spirits, and he's so inflated I can't bear to imagine what he'll be like when Poncellet lets the air out of him. He'll be just as limp and soggy as one of the bladders of porridge we exploded during our show, and I'm not looking forward to the guilt I'm going to feel when I see it.

As though reading my mind, Tristan rubs his hands together in anticipation and says to me,

"These insufferable clouters! It's time someone took one of them down a peg or two."

"Don't you think there's any chance he can win?" I ask, feeling sorry for the man.

"Not without taking a *dirty shot*," Tristan says, and I don't ask again.

By the time Poncellet comes strolling out of the stables, everyone else is out and we've all been waiting for quite a while. He moseys over with his usual cocky air and he's got the purple sash that surely once belonged to de

Gilford's wife tied around him at a particularly rakish angle, but I get the impression he's actually in a foul mood this morning, and I wonder why. I'd have thought he'd be looking forward to humiliating de Gilford further, and true to form he starts straight in on needling the man mercilessly as soon as he steps onto the field. But he's in such an irritable mood that today de Gilford isn't his only target. He's letting his barbs fly where they may, and he gets off a particularly nasty one just as the competition is getting underway. When Gilles looks around officiously and declares,

"Are we ready to start, then?," and not seeing Taran anywhere, de Gilford asks,

"What about the Mellor boy?," Poncellet shoots back: "Which *one*?"

The comment seems destined to set the tone for the whole affair.

With the Journeys to serve as the judges of the competition Gilles has naturally appointed himself master of ceremonies, and he's got a long scroll in his hands that he's been consulting which I assume contains the 'Saint's Rules' de Gilford mentioned the other day. So once Rennie's chimed in sarcastically, "He must have been summoned by the master for something, *again,*" and Remy's tremulously confirmed that Taran's not coming, Gilles gives the parchment one last look-over, rolls it up, and clears his throat for silence.

"All right, men. As far as I can see, the 'Saint's Rules' call for a straightforward matching of skill against skill, with no tricks, stunts, or frills." There's a pause, as Gilles has to quell some snickering that breaks out amongst the squires at the word 'frills,' since this was one of Poncellet's nicknames for him yesterday. "From what it says here," he continues sternly, waving the scroll in the air, "we begin on butts, with a two-inch cloth-mark affixed to a target at 80 paces. Then we move the mark back by increments as you men alternate taking shots, until one of you misses. Then we proceed to clouts, and do roughly the same thing. It's a simple matter of seeing which man can match the most of the other's shots in his opponent's best skill. That seems clear enough. Armand, Pascal, you boys fix the mark and station yourselves down by the target, where you'll be ready move it back. Mind you use a small enough pin; there should be a quarter inch one in the bottom of my cabinet somewhere. Masters, you may each choose a squire from the boys at hand to help you manage your equipment."

A big hand clasps me on the shoulder. "I'll give that honor to this saucy little lad here," de Gilford booms, and with a gulp I have to muster a "thank you, master."

"Perfect," Poncellet drawls. "And I'll take Slick." He throws his arm around Tristan's shoulder and the two of them give a merry laugh, as though Poncellet's already scored a point by taking a Journey as a squire.

I can't say I'm very happy about it, and not only because it seems to put Tristan and me in opposite camps. But as it turns out, squiring for the masters doesn't really amount to much, and once the target is set and it's time for the shooting to start, I forget my qualms as curiosity to see the men perform takes over. It's going to be a pure test of skill between two of the best, and now that it's actually happening, I'm pretty interested to see how it's all going to come out.

As anticipated, Poncellet's performance on butts is flawless. Even without being allowed to do any of his fancy draws or trick shots, he's a revelation to watch. And needless to say, he sticks every shot right into the pin, even though it's a ridiculously tough mark. There's no way de Gilford can hope to match him for long, but since all he has to do is hit somewhere on the cloth-mark he stays in longer than I would have thought, and he ends up doing a pretty credible job of it. I'd forgotten that the man was a Journey once, and he had to have been good enough at all of the skills in his day to win two years' worth of competitions. He even cleaves the pin with his first shot, nestling his arrow in close against Poncellet's, and he stays in the white through 90 and 100 yards. But a two-inch target is awfully small, and at 110 yards de Gilford's arrow goes wide, bringing the butts portion of the competition to a swift conclusion in just the manner that anyone could have predicted.

He's matched Poncellet through only three shots, and so as I gather up de Gilford's heavier bows and stock his quiver with longer, thicker clouting arrows, I know the end is coming soon. With Poncellet's accuracy and the size of clout targets, there's no way he can fail to last through more than three shots with de Gilford. When I shoulder the quiver and look up at de Gilford, though, he's rocking forward on his toes with a satisfied expression on his face, and when he sees me looking up at him morosely, he winks.

"It won't be long now," he chuffs, and I can't understand it. I mean, I didn't think de Gilford was a genius, but you'd have to be a complete nincompoop not to see the direction that this competition is going. Not wanting to see any more of de Gilford's misplaced confidence, I hurry my pace, and as we're all heading out to the clout field I trot up alongside Tristan, who's walking along next to Poncellet.

Poncellet's got the same sour expression on his face he's had all morning, and as I join them Tristan is echoing de Gilford's sentiment, saying encouragingly to Poncellet,

"It won't be long now, master! De Gilford's all right. He did better on butts than I was expecting, but you made short work of him. And he may be a fine clouter, but he's hardly the best."

Poncellet just purses his lips, and when he responds, it's not to Tristan. He looks pointedly around past him, and to me he says,

"So, you wanted to know why I'm not in Guards, did you, squire? I'll tell you why. I had the bad luck of the draw to end up in Thirds against a clouter. And I've got no distance."

In the event, Poncellet is, of course, exaggerating.

But not that much.

It isn't that he can't get his arrows to go down the field. He can, with some effort. It's that to muster the strength to do it he has to sacrifice much of his accuracy. It's hard to believe a man who's such a phenomenon on butts could be such a disastrous clouter, although I suppose it would be fairer to say that as a clouter, he's just ordinary. After his extraordinary skill at butts, though, it *seems* like a disaster, and one thing is clear: de Gilford's known it all along, and he's been counting on it.

"This test is just like the first, men," Gilles informs us, when we've regrouped down on the clout field and a big, white circular clouter's mark six feet in diameter has been spread out on the ground at a place 325 yards from the line. "Only this time, since the skill is clouts, the increments will be larger."

De Gilford's accuracy at clouts is nothing to match Poncellet's on butts, but he can make the distance with no effort. His first shot sails down the field to stick into the white with room to spare, and then it's Poncellet's turn.

The man's strong, I have no doubt. Much stronger than I am, anyway. But as I watch him bend the massive clouter's bow for his first answering shot, I'm reminded a bit of myself at my own clouts test, struggling against the bow rather than working with it, and although his arrow lands on target, it's dangerously close to the edge. All his precision is gone, and a cold feeling stirs in the pit of my stomach that's partly the memory of how I felt at my own test, and partly a feeling of foreboding. I've been feeling depressed, thinking the beleaguered and maligned de Gilford was going to lose. Now I'm beginning to think that something worse is going to happen, and he's going to win.

The boys have all been expecting Poncellet to win easily, too — to wipe up the field with de Gilford. So after the first round of clouts an uncomfortable hush falls over the group, and for once Poncellet himself is all out of rude jokes. They finish the test in silence, and nobody is terribly surprised when Poncellet narrowly makes the shots at 350 and 375 yards, but at 400 he strains too hard to get the necessary distance and his arrow lands wide of the mark, much to de Gilford's delight.

"Remarkable, men!" Gilles says, rallying first of the boys. "You each made exactly three of the other's shots. It looks like we have ourselves a tie. Let's see what the Saint has to say about that."

"I should win," de Gilford exclaims indignantly, as Gilles makes a show of consulting the scroll in his hands. "I could have kept on going and going. I can hit that mark out to 450 yards, at least."

"That doesn't tell us anything, does it?" Gilles replies mildly. "Master Poncellet surely could have kept going on butts, too. What we need is a tie-breaker. Hmm. I don't see anything here about that; it must not happen very often. Surely an obvious solution is at hand, though, isn't it? We'll simply do the wands challenge, and whoever wins that wins the whole thing. Now, where are the rules for wands?!"

He searches around on the sheet while Poncellet and de Gilford contemplate each other warily, and the rest of the boys shift around or start whispering; I think I can hear Jurian and Falko hastily renegotiating the terms of a bet. I cast a nervous glance over at Tristan; after witnessing Poncellet's first graceless clouts shot, he hasn't said a thing.

"Here it is!" Gilles declares finally. "We start with a two-and-a-half-inch wide willow wand, set at 275 yards. Not at all an easy mark, gentlemen. I should know, being a wands man myself."

There's a slight delay in the proceedings as Rennie and Remy are sent out over the wall and into the woods to cut the necessary wand, and when they've got it set up, it does look like an awfully hard target. The wand's so narrow it's no more than a string from here, and I'm pretty sure there's no way de Gilford will have the accuracy to hit it. But it also looks an awfully long way away, and I'm not sure Poncellet can make the shot either.

He's got to have a better chance at it than de Gilford, though, and to increase his odds, as the boys have been pacing out the distance Poncellet's begun trying not very subtly to rattle de Gilford by starting up his crude comments again. I'd thought his jabs were cruel before, but the things he's saying now are downright vicious. Even the boys seem surprised by the lewdness and the directness of some of his insinuations, and before the wand's even been fixed in place de Gilford's already out of comebacks and he's quivering with rage. It's enough to make me suspect Poncellet of trying to bait the man into making a physical attack on him that would break up the competition, and just when I think de Gilford's not going to be able to contain himself any longer and he's about to give Poncellet his wish, the boys signal that everything's ready and Gilles instructs Poncellet to take the first shot.

A hush falls over the crowd as Poncellet takes his bow from Tristan. But he doesn't bend it immediately. Instead, he fishes around under his sash to pull something out, and then he makes a show of attaching it at a point about midway on his bowstring. I don't get a very good look at it, but looks a lot like a knot made from a lock of a blonde woman's hair.

"What's that?" de Gilford demands, suspecting a trick.

"That, my dear Monty, is what's known as the kisser." He thrusts the bow under de Gilford's nose, letting him get a good look at it. From the apoplectic expression that crosses de Gilford's face, it's not hard to guess what color his wife's hair must be. Before he can object, Poncellet jerks the bow back and up into the ready position. He pauses there a moment, looking down the field to the target with an air of fierce concentration.

Then he slowly draws the bow. As he does, he cocks his head far to one side and brings the bowstring deliberately all the way back, until the charm he's affixed onto it is pressed up hard against the corner of his mouth. He holds it there long enough to lift his forefinger from the bowstring and stroke his mustache, while giving the little braid a great big smooch. And then with a loud smack of his lips and a twang of the string, he lets the arrow fly. The effect is just as though he's sending his shot on its way powered by the exaggerated kiss, and from his posture as he watches the arrow in its flight, I half expect him to shout out *"come on and do it for me, baby!"* the way Falko did at Thirds last year.

We're all watching with him as his shot sails down the field, to hit the wand about three inches up from the ground.

As soon as he sees it and the boys signal back confirmation from down the field, Poncellet lets out a whoop and leaps three feet straight into the air. All the boys crowd around to congratulate him, and it's such a beautiful shot even I can't resist giving him a boisterous cheer.

"That's the nail in your coffin, Brian!" he crows, and he runs out a few yards onto the field and proceeds to strut like a rooster in what I suppose is meant to be a victory dance. "That's right, Monty! I *nailed* 'er. I nailed her good, right under your nose, *again!*" he taunts, grabbing the ends of the sash in both hands and pumping his fists in the air with them, all the while gyrating and grinding in de Gilford's general direction in a way that would make anyone see red.

As chance would have it, while Poncellet was taking his shot de Gilford had dropped to one knee, to say a little prayer that Poncellet would miss. Now when he sees Poncellet waving the ends of the sash at him and calling out mockingly, "and what are *you* going to do about it? Nothing!," without rising to his feet de Gilford reaches over and snatches his bow angrily out of my hand. With a sputter and a gurgle he nocks an arrow and shoots at the wand, aiming virtually right through Poncellet to do so and without giving the other man a chance to get out of his way.

De Gilford's arrow whizzes past Poncellet so close, the feathers of its fletching ruffle his hair.

As it goes by, Poncellet bends backward, and he turns his head as though in slow motion to follow the arrow in its path with wide eyes, watching in amazement along with the rest of us as de Gilford's arrow spirals down the field and strikes the wand only a few inches above his own.

It was an incredible blind shot, and I didn't think de Gilford had it in him. None of the others did, either; they're all staring at de Gilford in astonishment, but nobody looks more surprised than the man himself. He jumps to his feet with a look of sheer incredulity on his face that's matched only by the one on old Poncellet's. Now it's de Gilford's turn to strut, and he's earned it. So we all suffer through some of his moves that I have to say make him look more like a gassy turkey than a preening rooster. But when Gilles trills,

"Fabulous! It looks like we have ourselves a real competition here, men. Squires, move the wand down to the 300 mark," and both men get a good look at the new target, neither of them is inclined to gloat any longer and the expressions on both of their faces turn grim. A two-and-a-half inch target at 300 yards is a virtually impossible shot — the ultimate combination of distance and accuracy, and both men know that even with more crazy luck, they can't hope to hit it.

Poncellet misses his shot, and so does de Gilford. And when after consulting the rules Gilles orders the wand to be moved down another 15 yards for the next round, de Gilford momentarily grabs the scroll out of Gilles's hands.

"It can't say to do that," he exclaims, frowning down at the parchment. But it does, and Gilles replies coolly,

"If you are sure you cannot make the shot, *master*, feel free to concede. The first man to forfeit his turn is the loser."

We all know neither man is going to be willing to do that. But with Poncellet lacking the distance to hit the wand and de Gilford lacking the precision, there's also no chance now that either of them can win. We're going to be stuck here all day, and there's nothing I can do but watch in frustrated silence as precious time ticks away, while the masters send arrow after arrow vainly down the field until the wand's receded so far into the distance that it must be somewhere past the 400-yard mark.

The shot's gone from virtually impossible to impossible and there isn't much of the clout field left, so eventually Remy and Rennie leave the wand where it is and wander back down the field to rejoin us, having tired of waiting by the wand for someone to hit it.

"Why don't they just give up?" Rennie complains, when Gilles asks him what they're doing back at the line. "They're never going to hit it. Nobody could make that shot."

"Nobody, except for *Taran*," Remy replies smugly. He's just being loyal to his master and I shouldn't let it bother me, but I can tell Tristan's heard him. So I'm about to make a scathing retort, when it occurs to me horribly that Remy's right. The combination of skills required is an awful lot like what it took for Taran's incredible through-the-visor shot at Thirds last year.

The only difference is, the shot Taran made was actually harder.

To make matters worse, soon the masters have fallen to quarreling more bitterly than ever, and Poncellet's taunts have become so merciless there can be no question but that he's trying to goad de Gilford into violence. Even if it wouldn't win him the competition, with the threat of an outright defeat now gone, Poncellet's good humor has been restored and his wit is as keen as ever, and he's enjoying getting back to something at which he can easily beat his rival. He's no longer concerned with trying to hit the wand; he's concentrating all his energy on creative verbal shafts aimed directly de Gilford, and he's being so amusing about it that it's not long before he's got all the boys in hysterics and on his side again. For his part, de Gilford's no better equipped to compete with the man's quick tongue today than he was yesterday, and now that his own chance for victory is gone, he's lost the will to try. He's getting trounced, and he looks so crestfallen I've started to feel every bit as guilty and miserable about inadvertently putting him through the ordeal as I thought I would.

I'm not sure why, too, since Taran isn't here. But his absence all morning has been marked, and now that Remy's brought him up his presence seems to be hanging over the competition, and it's not just because by this point we're probably all wishing he'd come stalking out, hit the mark, and put the competition out of its misery. Inevitably most of Poncellet's gibes involve questioning the legitimacy of de Gilford's progeny and taunting him about his wife's infidelity, and they're so unpleasantly similar to the ones both men were directing at Taran yesterday that I can't stop thinking about how Taran would be reacting to the awful jokes, if he could hear them. And so when the men are on their fourth try at the now distant wand and Poncellet sneers:

"How many misses is that for you, Monty? *Four?* How appropriate! One miss for each of your *sons*," I find I'm really hoping de Gilford will lose control and clobber Poncellet, and not only because it would surely bring an end to the competition. It would serve Poncellet right to have to pay for that sharp tongue of his, and ever since he refused to tell me about my father's trick I've rather wanted to punch the man myself.

"What do you say, Brian? I'll wager there have never before been so many blanks shot in a single day — at least, not since your wedding night!" Poncellet continues, and it's such a low blow that nobody's much surprised when it's one too many for de Gilford. As Poncellet lines up to take his own shot, de Gilford picks up a rock and throws it at him. It hits Poncellet squarely on the back of his head.

It wasn't a very big rock and it can't really have hurt that much. But Poncellet is not amused. He lets out a snarl, and in a flash the two men are squaring off, de Gilford rolling up one sleeve although he's still got his big bow in one hand, and Poncellet brandishing the arrow he was about to nock and shaking the point of it menacingly at him. The boys all crowd forward eagerly to egg the men on for the fight that's long been coming, and I'm not sure what might have happened or how the competition would have come to an end, if at just that moment Master Guillaume didn't come storming out of the stables and onto the field.

At the appearance of the master everyone freezes guiltily in place. Even the old masters hastily attempt to straighten up as Guillaume strides angrily over, gives Rennie a shove out of his way, and situates himself squarely between the two men.

He crosses his arms and looks from Poncellet to de Gilford. He looks back at Poncellet. He looks down the field.

Then without a word, he grabs the bow out of de Gilford's hands, snatches the arrow from Poncellet, and nocks it.

Then he shoots the wand himself.

"*I* win. You both lose," he says dispassionately, not bothering to look around at the ring of our stunned faces. "And I expect the both of you in my office within the next five minutes!"

With that he turns heel and stalks off again, taking de Gilford's bow with him.

When Poncellet tries to slip around past Gilles to beat a hasty retreat in the master's wake, de Gilford calls out after him.

"Hey, not so fast, *Poncey*! Aren't you forgetting something?"

When Poncellet just raises his eyebrows at him, de Gilford says,

"The *sash*." He puts out his hand. "You heard the master. You *lost*. We both did. So hand it over."

"Fair is fair," Poncellet concedes; with all the boys looking on, there's not much else he can do. But the look on his face is sheer hatred when he purrs back,

"I'll tell you what. *I'll* hand over the sash, when *you* give me my *money*."

"Well, that was something, wasn't it?" Tristan exclaims not much later, as he watches me gather up both masters' equipment, and I have to agree. It *was* something — I'm just not sure what.

I'd never seen Master Guillaume shoot before, and it was damned impressive. And I have to admit that he brought the competition to a close in a way that was probably better than I had any right to expect. But Tristan's rubbing the back of his neck with a troubled expression, and I'm not sure exactly what he's made of the whole thing. I've been left with an unsettled feeling too, like there was a message for me in it all somewhere — a message that when I figure it out, I'm not going to like. What Poncellet told us himself is bad enough, and I can feel the implications of his words hanging in the air between us as we head together off the field:

Not even the best butts shooter I've ever seen can beat out a clouter, if the draw goes against him.

When I've gotten de Gilford's equipment arranged neatly back in its cabinet and I push the door closed, I find Gilles lounging up against the garden wall right on the other side. There's no good reason for him to be still out here, so I'm not surprised when he drawls,

"So, did the masters' competition give you any inspiration?"

He's pestering me about the trick again, of course. And when all I can do is mumble, he flashes me a smile that's probably supposed to be rueful, but that actually looks like a pretty good imitation of one of Poncellet's more blinding ones instead.

"I, for one, found it *most* illuminating," he says. With that, he stuffs the scroll with the Saint's Rules down into his waistband and gives it a satisfied little pat, and when he then links his arm through Tristan's, I'm left with nothing to do but follow them inside, worrying.

It doesn't take much to see what *Gilles* thinks the masters' competition had to tell him. And that it surely wasn't anything about the inevitability of a butts man losing out to a clouter, but this:

A man who's good at wands can beat them *both*.

I'm beginning to think maybe pinning all our hopes on a strategy that also benefits Gilles wasn't such a good idea.

CHAPTER EIGHTEEN

After wasting all morning on the masters' competition, I'm determined to get through the rest of my crossbow tutorials as quickly as possible. So I take Master Guillaume's advice and double them up, starting with Jurian and Falko. I find them out on the butts with their squires right after noon mess, more intent on arguing about how to resolve the side bet they made on the masters this morning than on practicing, and when Jurian shows about as little interest in trying the repeating bow as he has in shooting his longbow these days, it suits me fine.

That leaves only Falko, who can't wait to get his big, hot hands on it. With a cry of *"out of my way, Marek! I was born to shoot this baby!,"* he snatches it away from me before I've barely had a chance to start on my instruction, and when he proceeds to strafe the dummy from head to foot and back again I can only agree with him. The repeating bow's motion doesn't require any rotation of his shoulder and Falko's aim with it is disturbingly good, so there's some delay as he insists we squires retrieve the bolts so he can do it all over again. But once he's shot both of the dummy's arms clean off, it's not too hard to take the bow back and declare the tutorial over. And when he then announces his intention of spending the rest of the afternoon chumming it up with the soldiers across the street and Jurian decides to go with him, that suits me fine, too. It frees up Frans to help me drag the dummy out to the place beyond the pavilions where Tristan and Gilles are practicing, since I figure I might as well take the last lesson to them. It'll save me some time, and the dummy will just have to go back into storage in the nearby armory again afterwards anyway.

Once Frans and I have lugged the dummy out past the last row of tents far enough to get a view out to the place where the boys are practicing, I can see right away that the concept of teamwork is continuing to prove a challenge for them. Today they're alone; Jerome's finally been put to work on the guild books and Pascal's nowhere to be seen, Gilles having sent him off on some errand or other to his tailor. Or maybe Gilles just figures that today

241

he's in no need of a squire, since even though Firsts is wands they're shooting butts, and now it's Tristan's turn to be annoying.

This time all the arrows in the target are his, and today it's Tristan who's stripped off his tunic. As Frans and I make our way over and begin propping up the dummy nearby for their lesson, he's busy doing every flashy shot he can come up with as payback for Gilles's wands display yesterday afternoon. He's shooting behind his back, under one leg, over his head, all in rapid-fire succession and accompanied by a running commentary. Seeing him, I have to say I agree wholeheartedly with his sentiment that there's nothing more glorious than a butts man when he's on top form — particularly when that man is Tristan. He's shooting better than he has for weeks, and so as I thank Frans and send him on his way, I chalk up a mark next to my own savvy in having the boys work together. Tristan may not be learning anything about shooting wands, but he's starting to get back into the proper spirit of competition.

"Don't knock giving it some *bang*, my friend!" he's declaring cockily when I come up next to him, as he zings another fabulous shot straight into the target. "You can seduce 'em subtly all you want, but when *I* 'wow' a crowd, it stays wowed! One look at the face of any girl in the audience is enough to prove it. Isn't that right, Marek?"

Before I can figure out to respond safely to that, Gilles preempts me by getting lazily to his feet.

"If you can *get over* yourself for a moment, old boy," he drawls, "I think you'd see your squire is waiting to teach us how to deal with *stumps*."

Tristan lowers his bow, and he turns to me with a grin. He and Gilles look at each other. They look at the weapon in my hands.

And then they both bust out laughing.

I wasn't foolish enough to mention the master's plans for introducing a crossbow competition at St. Sebastian's to anyone, of course. I knew the boys would all be as disdainful of it as the master himself seems to be. But nothing stays secret at the guild for long, and at noon mess the hall was full of it. And when one nosey veteran wandered past our table to inform everyone with a laugh that *I'd* been assigned the job of coming up with an official name and motto for the competitors, all the wisecracks the boys were making about it were naturally aimed at me. So when Gilles now starts up some of the same jokes and Tristan joins in, I suppose I should be glad that they're finally using some *teamwork*, since it's all very good-natured. But it's annoying anyway, particularly since I suspect that what Gilles is really doing is trying to derail the tutorial so as to waste as much of the time I've got left this afternoon as possible.

"If the master doesn't want them called Journeymen, then what about Journey*lads?*" he suggests, "Or better yet, 'Crossytots!,'" much to Tristan's amusement, who puts in,

"We could just call them Tillers and Cranks. And for that one without a cranequin," he points at the bow in my hands, *"Repeat Offenders!"*

It goes on like this the whole time I try to give them their lesson.

To my surprise, though, once I've finally stammered through the interruptions and managed to say my piece, when I try to hand Gilles the bow for his turn with it, instead of prolonging things he says dismissively,

"No offense intended, dear boy, and I'm sure it's all very ingenious. But you can't really expect *me* to shoot it. It's terribly loud, and so *vulgar*. Not at all my style. So I'll take a pass if it's all the same to you, and nobody need be the wiser," and I assume I must have been mistaken.

To my even greater surprise, when I try to hand Tristan the bow for his turn with it, to continue some joke he's been making he steps behind me and puts his hands over mine on the bow instead, and he urges me playfully to instruct him using the 'Mellor' method, although of course he doesn't call it that, either.

As soon as Tristan's arms are around me and I feel his cheek press down against my cheek, I tense. It's not because of the feeling of Tristan's bare skin next to mine. Well, maybe that *is* part of it. But it's also a reminder that so far, I've been too big of a coward to do anything to make good on my promise to let myself fall headlong back into lust with him.

This is the very thing I was longing for all last year, isn't it? To have an innocent excuse to be held intimately in Tristan's arms like this. If I'm really going to do it, now's my chance. Tristan's not slowed his banter with Gilles and it's just more of our usual horseplay to him, but I'll never get a better opportunity than this. All the old feelings are still there, I know it — the sweet longing and the sharp desire, the breathless infatuation fueled by that ideal image of him as he appeared to me on the garden wall. They're always there, just below the surface. How easy it would be to tear away the flimsy barrier holding them all in and let them come flooding forward! All I have to do is close my eyes, and block out Gilles's drawling voice, Tristan's jokes, the dummy, the crossbow, the field — everything but Tristan, and how it good feels finally to be held warm and close by him.

But I can't do it.

"I don't suppose you could, uh, *stop talking* for a moment, could you, *master?*" I say a little shortly; he's babbling away right in my ear.

"No, I don't think I could!" he quips back, and he and Gilles bust up again. But it's not really because the boys aren't making it very easy.

Maybe it's because my tutorial with Taran is too fresh and I can still hear his jeers when he caught me with Aristide, or it's simply because so much time has passed. Or maybe I am just a coward. But trying to be a girl with Tristan now feels like a lie.

So I give up and I give myself over to Tristan's antics instead, and as always when we're together we end up having a good time of it. I can't help feeling unsettled by the lesson, though, and like I'm letting my opportunities pass me by — particularly when as it wears on, I begin to suspect that I was right. Gilles is being pretty subtle about it, but he *is* trying to drag things out.

Every time I think I'm about to manage to bring the session to an end in good order, he makes some new jest or silly suggestion to set Tristan off again. When once or twice I catch him eyeing Tristan critically as he handles the heavy bow, I'm pretty sure I know what he's doing. He's not just squandering all my free time this afternoon. He's trying to gauge exactly how much stronger he is than Tristan, and from his satisfied expression, I gather the answer is 'plenty'; keeping that information to himself must be the real reason he didn't want to take a turn with the repeating bow in front of me.

By the time the lesson's finally over and Gilles has wandered off inside, the sun is low in the sky and I must be looking defeated. Tristan's offered to help me take the dummy back to the armory, and when he asks me if I'm ready and I don't respond, he puts a hand under my chin and tilts my face up to his. Seeing my sullen expression, he teases,

"Hey, what's the matter, Marek? Is it a *secret?*" and he looks and sounds so much like a parody of Remy I almost laugh. Only it isn't funny. I guess there is something it's time for me to say.

"I'm afraid you're not going to like it, Tristan," I tell him, and he frowns, surprised by my seriousness. So I add hastily, "I didn't mean to lie, or to deceive you. Not really. And I think I only just figured it out, today."

"Go on."

"What I told you about clouts. It's not true. We can't forget about them. In fact, I think we'd better start practicing them again, right away. Somewhere where it can be *our* little secret. Otherwise, if clouts is Seconds, I don't think you're going to be able to beat him."

"Somewhere, like out by the old windmill?" he says archly, not sounding at all surprised, and I'm sure he knows that for once I'm not talking about Taran. He, too, must have seen the smug look on Gilles's face.

"That's not all, master," I say dismally, and I tell him about Gilles's deadline for the trick.

"If you really can't come up with something in time for Firsts, maybe we can hold off, and do our first joint trick together at Seconds. That's the big one after all, isn't it?" he says, even though we both know that *might* have worked, if Firsts were clouts. But after witnessing the masters' competition this morning, letting Gilles do an incredible wands trick without us now is out of the question. It's like Master Guillaume said: keep your friends close, and your enemies closer — and I'm no longer entirely sure which of the two Gilles is.

"Want me to stay out with you then, so we can work up something, together? There's still a little of the afternoon left," he offers, and I almost throw myself straight into his arms again. But this is one task I've got to do myself, and I'm just about to tell him so — when I hear a chuffing sound behind us.

It's Brian de Gilford, puffing his way around the pavilions and over to join us.

"*There* you are, you rascal!" he exclaims. "I've been looking all over the guild for you. Imagine! Setting up for my crossbow lesson, way out here."

Of all the rotten, miserable luck!

I'd forgotten all about it, but de Gilford's name was scrawled at the bottom of my list.

When Tristan tries valiantly to object, de Gilford booms at him dismissively,

"Run along there, DuBois, run along! You've had your turn. Now let us get to it," and there's nothing I can do but watch as Tristan shrugs back into his tunic, and with an apologetic look back over his shoulder at me he heads reluctantly inside. My last hope of coming up with a trick in time flies away with him, leaving me alone on the field with the dummy. And de Gilford.

AT FIRST, I'M SO FURIOUS AT FINDING MYSELF TRAPPED INTO wasting more of my day on folderol of de Gilford's — the last of it I've got left — that my arms are shaking and I can hardly concentrate.

After a while, though, I swallow down my resentment and resign myself to the reality that I'm going to fail to meet Gilles's deadline. The truth of it is I've had days to come up with a joint trick, and it's not really de Gilford's fault I haven't been able to do it. I'm just going to have to pitch something lame to Gilles about shooting a latch off a cage of larks or tying some poor dove to the top of a wand, and hope that Tristan can talk it up enough to get Gilles to go along with it.

De Gilford's such an eager pupil, and unlike the rest of the boys he seems to have a healthy respect for crossbows. At least he's the only one around the guild who appears to be as genuinely excited about the master's plan to bring a crossbow contingent to St. Sebastian's as I am. So once I've calmed myself enough to start in on his lesson, eventually he wins me over. Particularly when I ask curiously,

"So, *master*. Why do you suppose Master Guillaume put you down for this tutorial anyway?" and he snorts back,

"Hell, son! Guilly had nothing to do with it. I added my name to your list *myself*."

There's no doubt the man is impressively learned, too, when it comes to anything having to do with arms or defense, and once we've really gotten going, he's so full of astute questions I can hardly keep up with him.

"What's the maximum rate you can get out of this thing, Marek? And how many defenders, *erm*, I mean *attackers*, do you think one man could take out with it before he was shot himself, if he had the element of surprise on his side?" he asks enthusiastically.

"It doesn't have much range or power. But with a little luck and a lot of practice, a strong man like yourself could probably take on at least five or six," I reply, considering, and my answer seems to please him so much that we debate it animatedly for a while. He's obviously as interested in the bow's strategic potential as he is in simply shooting the thing, and after all the jokes I've endured about crossbows lately and my repeating bow in particular, it's gratifying enough that we end up having a pleasant enough little session.

Once he gets around to taking some shots of his own, however, a change comes over him. Or maybe I just begin to notice that underneath his good humor, he actually seems rather depressed. After he makes a particularly great shot that hits the dummy right through the side of its head, he lowers the bow and stares down the field morosely at his own bolt for a while, and I get the impression he's thinking back to his competition with Poncellet. I'm not sure if he's thinking about his failure to make the most of his one chance to outdo the man or about the cruel jokes Poncellet was making at his expense, but both would be plenty upsetting. All my sympathy for him from this morning returns, and so I really mean it when I say,

"You're mighty good with a crossbow, master. And you were mighty good with a longbow this morning, too. All the boys were really impressed. Why, that blind shot you took at the wand — it was unbelievable! Although it *was* rather risky," I chuckle. "Why, if you'd missed, you might have even hit Master Poncellet."

To my surprise, he hangs his head.

"Don't kid yourself, son," he grumbles. "I *did* miss. I wasn't aiming at the wand. I was trying to kill him."

There's a moment of deep silence as I absorb this horrible statement. The dummy creaks on its post and a tent flaps in the breeze somewhere, but they could be miles away.

After a while, de Gilford glances up at me sheepishly, and seeing my shocked expression, he blusters,

"I'm sorry I did it *now*, of course. Mostly. And I *am* glad I didn't actually hit him. He just made me so damned mad, Marek! *You* know he was purposely baiting me. Even then, I wouldn't have done it. I can take a joke as well as the next man. But everything he was saying, well …" he drops his eyes, and hangs his head again. "It was nothing but the truth."

I think back to some of Poncellet's more vicious jabs this morning and his cocky attitude, and I know what de Gilford's confession must be costing him. His face is as red as it was then and he looks so wretched and defeated, I feel furious at Poncellet myself. Before I know exactly what I'm saying, I burst out vehemently,

"I don't blame you one bit, master! Nobody would. Why, if I were you, I'd have done it myself!"

As soon as the words are out I realize what I've done, and I wish I could catch them back.

I can't believe it. A man's just told me he took a *dirty shot* at his smooth-talking rival out of jealousy over a woman, and I excused him.

More than excused him.

I told him I'd have done the exact same thing.

Surely I didn't really mean it, though, did I? It's just one of those things you say, and what happened between the boys — it was entirely different. At least that's what I tell myself, and luckily for me before I have too much time to dwell on it de Gilford's talking again.

"Serves me right, I suppose. I was a fool to try to compete with him in the first place," he's mumbling to himself. "What was I thinking? I mean, he shot his *own arrow* right out of the sky. Who does that? I should have known. A man who can shoot an arrow out of the sky is unbeatable."

"Uh, what was that you just said, master?"

My throat's gone dry, and there's a strange humming in my ears. I'm back in the garden daydreaming, with my head against a tree and picturing Poncellet.

"I should have known better than to compete with him."

"Not that. The *other* thing."

"Shooting an arrow out of the sky. It's an unbeatable trick."

"Master!" I cry, slapping my forehead with both hands. "You really *are* a genius!"

Then without a word of explanation, with an ecstatic little jump and a click of my heels, I turn right around and run off as fast as I can go, leaving the repeating bow in his hands and the dummy where it is out on the field.

I FIND THE JOURNEY CORRIDOR IN A STATE OF EXCITED CHAOS to match my mood. My thoughts are racing and my nerves are tingling; thanks to Brian de Gilford I've finally come up with an idea for the boys' trick, just in the nick of time. What's more, it really is a trick within a trick, and one that's going to be fantastic. More than fantastic. It's going to be unbelievable, and I can already picture Master Guillaume's face when he sees it. There's only one tiny little problem with it, really:

Probably nobody but Poncellet could actually do it.

I'm determined to find Tristan and Gilles before it's time for mess, but to do so I've got to dodge my way through a disorderly line of men in uniform that's snaking its way down the Journey corridor and disappearing around the corner up ahead. Apparently de Gilford's enlisted some of the kitchen boys to help him sell off the wine he stole from Brecelyn's cellars to pay off his debt to Poncellet, and half the Kingsmen are packed into the hallways, purses in hand. Not only are the men waiting to make a purchase getting unruly, but those who've already acquired a cask are literally barreling down the corridor in the opposite direction, rolling the huge kegs along in front of them on their way out to take them back to their camp.

Tristan and Gilles are right in the middle of the commotion, leaning up against the wall outside Gilles's room where they can call out to the men going past, and where they can watch Pascal as he attempts to wrangle two of the massive barrels he's acquired for Gilles into his master's room all by himself. I put my head down and weave down the hall, leaping over a runaway cask and shouldering its owner out of my way; when I reach the boys I hustle them hurriedly inside Gilles's room, casks and all, and I shut the door behind us.

"Goodness, Marek! What's so important that we've got to hear about it all jammed in together like a bucket of sardines?" Gilles demands. We're crammed into the narrow space of his room so tightly that the lace of his shirt is tickling my nose and I'm treading on Tristan's foot, and Pascal's had to climb up on top of one of the casks. But I'm too worked up to let any of it bother me.

"Gilles," I demand, with no preamble. "That shot the masters missed this morning — a two-and-a-half-inch wand, at 300 yards. Could *you* have made it?"

"But of course," he says, sounding offended I'd bother to ask.

"And do you think you could teach *Tristan* to make that same shot?" I continue, not letting his tone sidetrack me.

"Possibly. If he'd really *commit* to it," he sniffs. "But I'm afraid a mere shot at a wand, however distant, is not going to satisfy the master, Marek," he adds dismissively.

"I could *definitely* make it, with a little *decent* training," Tristan puts in from somewhere behind me. "And it would be good, Marek. But Gilles is right. It wouldn't be enough for a trick."

"No," I concede. "But with two of the judges knowing *for a fact* that they couldn't have made the shot themselves, it's a good start. And that's all it would be, a start."

I let them all dangle for a beat, while Tristan extricates his boot from under my foot and Pascal cocks his head to one side at me from his perch atop the barrel, until Gilles clears his throat.

"Well?" he finally demands.

"*Well*," I repeat, "Think how spectacular it's going to be, when *one* of you steps up to take an exhibition shot at the wand, a wand the masters *missed*, mind you — and while his arrow is still in mid flight, the *other* one of you runs up from the sidelines, and shoots the arrow right out of the sky! And then proceeds to shoot the wand himself. And for the grand finale, before the audience knows what's hit them, you two switch roles and do it all over again, for the second boy's trick."

Outside, a barrel rumbles past. Inside, all I can hear is the boys' breathing. I know they're all picturing it — picturing just how incredible it would be. And just how incredibly risky, particularly for the boy doing the initial jumping in.

When finally Tristan throws back his head and starts laughing and Pascal lets out an appreciative whistle, Gilles shifts around in a way that makes me think he's about to object. So before he or anyone else can say anything, I add,

"It would be the talk of the competition! Although I suppose I do understand, Gilles, if *you* think you can't do it. If you're not up for the risk. I mean, I know *Tristan* can surely master it with a little effort, being a butts man. But nobody can expect a *wands* man like yourself to match for precision the techniques of Master Poncellet."

My words have the desired effect. I can feel Gilles debating, and I'm pretty glad I'm too close to him to see his expression. For once I think I've outmaneuvered him, and when Tristan says,

"It'd be sweet all right, kid, if we could really pull it off! Oh, can't you just picture the look on his *face?*," although I know it's not Master Guillaume *he*'s thinking about, even Gilles has to admit the master would be duly impressed.

I've done my part and delivered an unbeatable trick, and just like the masters this morning neither boy is willing to be the first to concede that he might not be up to the task. There's not much they can do but agree to give it a try, and so once the corridor has cleared and we're all heading out together for evening mess, I'm justifiably feeling pretty satisfied with myself.

◄━━━━━━━━━►

I'M FEELING SO PLEASED AT HAVING JUST SQUEAKED PAST Gilles's deadline that I don't even mind when as soon as we've settled ourselves on the mess benches, Poncellet comes over to join us again. Failing to beat de Gilford hasn't put much of a dent in his ego — or had any adverse effect on the boys' enthusiasm for him, unfortunately. Just like yesterday at noon, he pushes his way in next to Tristan. And just like then, he doesn't so much join the conversation as take it over, by launching into a colorful monologue all about himself.

The only difference is, tonight Taran is with us.

He's sitting down at the far end of the table as usual and he's interacting with the group as little as he has at every other meal. But he has every reason to despise Poncellet, and for some reason just knowing that he's here and that he's listening in makes the man's stories seem even more unsavory to me. So when at one point Poncellet slings his arm around Tristan's shoulder and proclaims,

"You know something? I like you, Slick! In fact, you remind me a lot of myself, when I was a young man," I wince.

Involuntarily my eyes flit down the table. Sure enough, Taran's head has popped up and he's looking down the table, too — right at Tristan and Poncellet. For once, I have no trouble at all reading his expression. It says *he* thinks Tristan's exactly like old Poncellet already, right now.

Then his eyes dart to me, and he catches me staring at him. Even though it's only for an instant, when his eyes lock on mine it's long enough for me to read this look of his, too.

It says he thinks he's caught *me* thinking the exact same thing.

I look angrily away, and I clench my fists in fury under the table. I *wasn't* thinking it, I swear it! And even if I was, a little, it wasn't in the way he thinks. So maybe some of the qualities that make Tristan so appealing now won't age well. Tristan *is* glorious, and I'll never let him become a caricature of himself. How easy it is for the likes of Taran to judge! If *he* should find himself out of St. Sebastian's, he'd still have prestige and position as his father's heir to back up that arrogant attitude of his. And Gilles — *he's* the Marquis de Chartrain. They don't need Guards to have a heroic role to play, but it won't be so easy for Tristan. Just like it can't have been that easy for old Poncellet.

I'm jolted out of my thoughts by the sound of a purse fat with coins plunking down heavily on the table in front of me.

Brian de Gilford's come up behind us. He's gotten Poncellet his money, and he wants the sash.

"There's your pound of coins!" he announces triumphantly. "It's time for my pound of *flesh*," and he gestures down at the man's middle.

I can't say I like the sound of that, but as Poncellet gets slowly to his feet all the other boys look wildly enthusiastic. We're all curious about the bet, of course, and I have to admit de Gilford's made it all rather mysterious.

Once he's weighed the purse in his hands, Poncellet nods resignedly and he begins to unknot the sash, although he's taking his time about it.

"Remember our terms, *Poncey*," de Gilford adds gloatingly, when Poncellet's finally gotten the fabric untied and he's pulling it reluctantly from around his waist. "Make sure you show the boys just what you've got *under* that sash."

"What do you think, Marek?" Tristan whispers in my ear, amused. "Sounds like we're about to get a little first-hand knowledge of the state of old Poncellet's *member*ship," and I sincerely hope he's wrong. Although I was thinking the same thing myself.

Once Poncellet's gotten the sash unwound and he's pulling it off from around himself, mercifully there doesn't seem to be much to see, much to the boys' disappointment. Poncellet's tights cover him up to his waist, and I suppose they are a little frayed and dingy. But that can't be what de Gilford's been so excited about revealing. The show isn't over yet.

Poncellet's still holding the sash bunched up in his hands in front of him, and he seems awfully loath to let the thing go. To my surprise, before he finally gives it over to de Gilford he lifts it lightly to his lips, and for a moment he burrows his face in it, as though drinking in its fragrance one last time. He doesn't do it in his typical showy way, though, and there's something about it that's so out of keeping with the man's usual posturing that I find it oddly moving.

For his part, de Gilford doesn't seem particularly interested in the sash itself.

He grabs it out of Poncellet's hands and demands impatiently, "the *waistband*, Poncey. You know the deal," and with a shrug Poncellet accordingly reaches down and takes hold of the top of his tights with both hands, right in the middle.

Then he begins to ease them down. All the boys lean in eagerly again, and for a horrible moment I'm sure we really are about to get an eyeful of a pound of Poncellet's flesh. Or worse, maybe no flesh at all.

But what actually meets our eyes as the man slowly bares his belly is something I couldn't have anticipated.

Right below Poncellet's navel, on the tender swell of the abdomen where there should be only a soft line of hair, instead he's got an angry, puckered welt two inches long burned deeply into his flesh. It's a Journeyman's brand, exactly like the ones the boys burn into each other's arms after the trials, a welt in the shape of an arrow.

And it's pointing straight down.

As soon as they see it, the boys all break into uproarious peals of laughter.

"There it is, boys! The best thing I ever did," de Gilford crows. "Gave it to him right in the tent at my own Third trials, as soon as I won Guards and outranked him!"

Given Poncellet's reputation as a ladies' man, I suppose it is pretty funny, since I don't think I have to explain what it looks like the arrow is pointing down *at*.

I'm not laughing, though. Instead, a horrific scene is rising up in my mind: de Gilford, wrestling a struggling Poncellet to the floor and holding him down, a smoking branding iron hot in his hand; a mighty thrust, a bloodcurdling scream; and then the smell of hair frying and skin sizzling, as the white-hot rod sears into that most delicate of flesh. To have made a welt that deep, de Gilford must have really ground it in and held it there for a long time. Getting that brand must have been as excruciating as it was humiliating, and I had thought the source of the men's feud was obvious. Now I'm not so sure. At least, I can see now why Poncellet's not been able to forget about it. All these years, he's been carrying a permanent reminder burned onto his belly of a blow that was definitely below the belt.

Poncellet lets the boys all get a good look, and when the hint of a flush starts creeping up his neck, I think de Gilford's finally gotten the best of him. Then he starts laughing.

"I have to admit it, Brian," he says, his voice as cocky as ever. "I really should have thanked you for this little gift a long time ago. It's saved me a lot of unnecessary talk, over the years." And when he winks, the boys all give him a cheer. But as I've said, I can tell from experience when a man is acting.

Curiously enough, though, I think he really doesn't give a damn about the scar. It's losing the sash he cares most about.

The boys are all still laughing about it when Falko wanders into the hall, uncharacteristically late for dinner. He's lingered across the street over a drinking game with some of the soldiers and he's just now coming in with his squire for his supper. Seeing Poncellet with his pants around his hips, he stumps over and demands,

"What's up, gents? Or down, as the case may be," and before anyone can think how to answer him, Masters Guillaume and Leon enter the hall. Upon catching sight of both Poncellet and de Gilford over apparently causing disorder amongst the Journeys again, instead of taking his place at the head table the master comes powering straight over, with Master Leon following closely on his heels.

For some reason, Leon is carrying two large wooden boards in his hands, each one fitted out with a long loop of twine.

"If you're so eager to strip, gentlemen," Guillaume barks, giving Poncellet's lowered britches a disparaging look, "Then by all means, strip! For all I care, you can do your penance for this morning's fiasco just as well in the all-together. In fact, I insist on it."

He gestures to Leon, who steps forward to shove the boards into Poncellet's and de Gilford's hands. Each one has the word *pécheur* or 'sinner' painted on it in big red letters.

We all watch as the two men are hustled to the front of the hall and made to strip off every last stitch of their clothing, and to hang the placards around their necks. Guillaume then orders them to assume a stance of attention at either end of the masters' table, buck naked, while taking turns crying out at the top of their lungs for the duration of the meal the following refrain:

"*I have sinned against my guild and my Saint, and I have disgraced the name of master!*"

It's one of Master Guillaume's more ingenious punishments and I find it quite disturbing, for a lot of reasons — not the least of which being that I sincerely hope the master never takes it into his head to want to punish *me* this way. Needless to say, there's a heck of a lot more than a pound of Poncellet's flesh on display now, and let's just say it finally puts all the rumors about the man to rest. Although I'm trying awfully hard not to look, even from here it's all too apparent that the outrageous bulge in the man's tights was entirely natural.

The boys, of course, are loving it. So the first half of the meal is taken up with them all trying to outdo each other with whispered comments, since the situation is providing plenty of material. And I have to admit that at first it is actually pretty entertaining. But what with all the shouting it makes it awfully hard to have much of a conversation during dinner, and after a while the men's voices get so hoarse and it's so cold in the room that I start to feel quite sorry for them, although for once I have to say I find the master's perverse punishment rather fitting.

It doesn't take long for the men's cries to start grating on the master's nerves, too, even though the form of their torture was all his idea. So when after wolfing down his meal Guillaume departs from the hall without touching his port, at first I think the men are going to get an early reprieve. But Master Leon is in no hurry to leave. He puts up his feet, tops off his wine, and shows every sign of settling in. He's made no secret of the fact that he finds both men odious, and he knows they can't stop as long as he's still at table. He's going to enjoy dragging out their discomfort as long as possible, and from the looks of it most of the veterans feel the same way. The penitents are in for a long night of it, or at least that's what I'm assuming, when almost as soon as Master Guillaume is gone Poncellet takes the evening in an unforeseen direction.

Emboldened by the master's absence, when it's his turn, instead of chanting out his line Poncellet looks down pointedly at himself. Then he looks up and pointedly over at de Gilford. Or I should say, he looks *down* at him. His eyes come to rest derisively on a point significantly below the bottom of de Gilford's placard, where de Gilford's shriveled manhood his dangling limply on full display. Without lifting his eyes Poncellet raises one eyebrow, and with a twitch of his mustache he calls across the table at him,

"Well, I'll say this much for old Guilly's punishment! It certainly explains *a lot.*"

There's a roar of laughter from the veterans, and an equally loud roar from de Gilford. All the men in the hall come to their feet as he then rips the placard from around his neck, charges around the table with it, and launches himself at Poncellet, just as Poncellet is saying,

"Really, that sign of yours shouldn't read *'pécheur.'* What it really should say is *pe—,"* and I miss what it is he says in the ensuing commotion. Or maybe he never gets the whole word out, because de Gilford's placard has come crashing down brutally on his head, and before I know it the two of them are rolling on the floor in front of the masters' table, beating the pants off each other (well, they would be if they were wearing any pants) while everyone in the hall scrambles to gather in a circle around them.

That is, everyone but Master Leon. He hasn't moved, and it's pretty obvious he has no intention of stopping the fight. Quite to the contrary, the expression on his face says he thinks watching the two of them tear each other to pieces is a perfectly delightful way to end the evening, and he continues to sip his port while the men proceed to kick the tar out of each other virtually at his feet. It's not a sight I'm too eager to see, but this is one fight the boys have been robbed of too many times to want to miss it now, and I'm carried along with them when they all rise up from the benches and surge forward to get a closer view of it.

I suppose this should be funny, too, since they're still stark naked and they're both pretty old. And at first while they're just getting started it is sort of entertaining, in an appalling sort of way. There's so much sagging flesh and flaccid muscle and grizzled body hair in surprising places all jumbling up together as the men grapple that I'm not sure whether it looks more like something from Master Gheeraert's secret stash of pornography or two geriatric pachyderms battling it out over a watering hole. But I've never seen two fully grown men fight in deadly earnest before, and despite their age both of them are plenty strong. This is no friendly tussle, and it's no joke, either. The men genuinely hate each other and I don't doubt they really are trying to kill each other. As the fight proceeds each blow is more vicious than the last, and before long they're both doing serious damage; I can hear organs rupturing and bones breaking, and after a bloody tooth skitters across the floor to stop at my feet, it doesn't take more than seeing de Gilford's massive fist land with a sickening crunch against what was once Poncellet's nose for me to feel thoroughly nauseated.

Poncellet's tough, and he knows plenty of dirty tricks. But de Gilford's got a good ten years on him and at least forty pounds, so the result is inevitable. Once de Gilford gets the drop on him and proceeds to sit straddled on his chest, it's all over for Poncellet. Even though his opponent is down and open gashes on his forehead are flowing freely, de Gilford continues to pummel him mercilessly with both fists until both men are slick with each other's blood. It's pooling on the floor beneath them and poor Poncellet's face is a juicy pulp; I'm no longer in the mood to watch Poncellet get trounced, and I can't look anymore. Even the boys have been shocked into silence by the extreme violence of it. Tristan in particular is as rigid as a board next to me, and I hide my head against his shoulder and whisper hoarsely,

"*Do* something, can't you, Tristan?"

But there's nothing he can do. With Master Leon content to let it continue it just keeps on going, until Poncellet is surely senseless and de Gilford himself is swaying with exhaustion. Even the veterans have fallen into an uncomfortable silence, broken only by de Gilford's grunts and the thuds of his fists, and an occasional disapproving murmur from the crowd.

It's not until de Gilford reaches down, grabs Poncellet's upper lip, and growls, "*And while I'm at it, I think I'll rip this damned mustache right off your face!*"

that Master Leon seems to think *he's* had enough. He gets lazily to his feet and gestures to some of the veterans, who surge forward to pull de Gilford away. The last I see of the masters that night is de Gilford being supported out of the hall on the shoulders of two veterans, while four others drag Poncellet feet first off to the kitchens, whether to get him some serious first aid or to prepare his body for burial, I honestly couldn't say.

As they go, Master Leon looks over calmly at the boys, and says,

"Let that be a reminder to you, men. Sooner or later, *St. Sebastian's punishes its own,*" just as though he'd anticipated from the beginning that the men's penance would end in this way, and maybe he did.

"And for heaven's sake," he adds, stepping around the blood, "somebody send out the kitchen boys, to clean up this mess."

As we all file out of the hall after him, shaken, Falko rubs his hands together and exclaims enthusiastically:

"I'll give 'em this. Those old boys sure know how to put on a good show! Say, I wonder who's going to run tomorrow's practice?"

Nobody answers.

All the other boys are looking so subdued as to be downright somber. But I think Tristan and Taran look particularly grim, and much as I hated witnessing the nauseating spectacle tonight, I have to wonder if the masters didn't inadvertently do me a favor. Their fight was so ugly and degrading, and let's face it, so reminiscent of some of the boys' own confrontations, I have to assume it's quite put the both of them off resorting to violence to settle their own differences — for the time being, anyway.

At least, I'm pretty sure *Tristan* will think twice before baiting Taran again, since I know he hates the sight of blood — most of all his own. Particularly after Falko slaps him on the back and exclaims happily,

"Care to have another discussion about pitting a butts man against a clouter *now*, old man?"

CHAPTER NINETEEN

When I leave Tristan at his door I can tell the events of the day are weighing on him, and they're weighing on me, too, although not necessarily for all the same reasons. So maybe that's why before I turn to go, I blurt out,

"Tristan, you're nothing like old Poncellet!"

He gives me a sarcastic look, and I amend, "I mean, you *are* a fantastic butts shooter. One of the very best." I refrain from mentioning any other possible similarities. "But that's not all you are. You proved at Thirds that you can go the distance. And you're not just a great archer. You're a great man, and a greater friend. What's happened to Poncellet —," and I'm not sure what all I mean, but I know it's more than just the fight tonight. "That's not going to happen to you, I promise."

"You're right, Marek. It's not," he says darkly, and as always when I don't know exactly what he means, it worries me a little. Then he grins. "And do you know why? Because I have something he didn't have. An ace in the hole. A secret weapon."

"What's that, master?" I ask nervously, afraid he's going to tell me again that he's got a plan — some dodgy plan he's been cooking up since the castle that's he's not felt he could confide in me.

"You of course, little brother," he replies instead.

We say our goodnights, and I head away down the corridor, feeling warm at Tristan's praise — and a little apprehensive. I hate to think what's going to happen to Tristan's faith in me tomorrow, when he actually tries to do the trick I've come up with for him.

When I round the corner into the hallway ahead, to my consternation I find an elegantly dressed boy leaning up against the wall outside the barracks door and waiting for me again, fiddling with his cuff. Only this time the boy isn't lounging there imperiously; his expression is almost shy.

It isn't Gilles, it's Pascal.

I can't imagine what he can want to talk to me about at this hour and after what's just happened, particularly since it must be something he doesn't want the other squires to overhear. So I'm taken aback when after we've exchanged a wary greeting and I look at him inquiringly, he asks,

"So, are the rumors that were circulating at noon mess today about crossbows true?"

"Of course not," I sniff. "I mean sure, anybody can shoot a crossbow. But it takes real skill to be good. They're not just for little boys and old men. Or *girls*," I say defensively, thinking back to some of the Journeys' more annoying jokes, hardly noticing that it's Taran's phrase that's popped into my mind to use to defend them.

"Not *that*, Marek. I mean about squires' club starting up officially again, tomorrow afternoon."

"Oh, right." I tell him that it is true, as far as I know (while trying not to picture our new official trainer being dragged feet first out of the great hall), and he licks his lips, and says,

"I was just wondering if you were still willing to train me seriously, for Journeys." He looks over his shoulder, drops his voice, and continues bashfully,

"I've got to look to the future, Marek, and I really want to make Ginger proud of me. I don't want this to be just an arranged marriage, something that's foisted onto her," he admits, and it doesn't take much to see that the masters' rivalry has disturbed him. "I want her to *want* to marry me."

"Pascal, any girl in her right mind would be thrilled to marry you," I reply, meaning it. "Why, if I were a girl, I'd be thrilled to be marrying you myself."

"Not if you were hoping to marry Gilles instead," he says, and there's nothing I can say to that. I mean, Pascal is great and all. But on top of everything else, Gilles has got to be one of the richest men in all of Ardennes.

I think for a minute. Tristan's confidence in me is still weighing on me, and I've got to look to the future, too. So at length I say,

"Of course I'll train you, Pascal. But only if *you'll* train *me* seriously, in exchange."

"Me? Train you? At what?"

By this time Armand's come wandering out to see what we're talking about so intently, and he's leaning up against the doorframe listening. I don't really care if he hears, so I say,

"To be a better squire."

"You're already a great squire, Marek," Pascal protests, as Armand murmurs in agreement. "One of the best. You can fletch your own arrows, and you're a great coach. And what you did for Tristan on the tower. None of us can top that."

"All of that, it's *off* the field," I wave dismissively. "I want to get faster and stronger. To cut a better figure when I'm actually *on* the field. I want you to help me get better at the actual work of retrieving,

257

the stuff that might be of some real help to Tristan during competition."

Why not? If I'm going to be a professional squire, I want to be a good one, and I'm actually not at all sure what being a squire in Meuse is going to entail. After watching two grown men brawl in earnest, the thought's beginning to worry me, a little.

"I don't know, Marek. I'm not sure I'd know how. I've never really thought about it before. But if you're game, I'm willing to give it a try."

And so we strike a bargain and we shake on it, and I assume that's that. When afterwards we head into barracks and Armand follows me all the way back to my cot, however, I'm pretty sure I know the reason.

"So, I suppose now you're willing to let me to train you for Journeys, too?" I say, a little sarcastically, flopping down on my back on my bed. I should have known he wouldn't want to let Pascal outdo him at anything else, since he still hasn't forgiven Pascal for trumping him with his engagement.

"If you're offering, Marek, sure," he says, sitting down on the edge of the cot next to me. "But that's not what I wanted to talk to you about."

Then he drops his voice, just like Pascal did earlier, and says confidentially,

"It's this marriage of Pascal's, Marek. Do you think there could be anything *wrong* in it?"

It's the last thing I was expecting, and it startles me to hear him say aloud exactly what I've been thinking to myself. I imagine he must be a little pleased at the prospect, though, so I say shortly,

"I'll not indulge in idle speculation, just to give you more ammunition to needle him. And besides, what wrong in it could there be?"

"I don't know," he says thoughtfully, and he sounds genuinely worried. "And I suppose I deserved that. I *have* been jealous. But Pascal is my best friend. If this is all some game of Gilles's, Marek, I'm afraid it's going to unhinge him. At least, I don't know *what* he'll do. We've all just seen the proof that a man who feels he's been crossed in love is capable of almost anything — and justifiably so, I reckon." He drops his eyes to his hands. "I know I'd do just about anything for love. Wouldn't you, Marek?"

"I should hope not!" I sniff.

But coming from a girl sitting on a flea-ridden cot in the middle of a boys' barracks in an archers' guild, it's not very convincing.

WHEN I THROW MYSELF DOWN ON MY COT NOT MUCH LATER, despite my exhaustion sleep won't come. It's not nightmares that are keeping me awake tonight, or Armand's concerns, or even any of my own —

not really. Every time I try to close my eyes, what I see behind my eyelids is a massive fist slamming into a charming face.

With the masters' competition decidedly over, I know what I should be doing is counting myself lucky to have come out of it all so well. While I can't be anything but horrified by its conclusion, it's provided me with a trick that's sure to be spectacular, and I'm pretty sure I can count on Tristan and Taran to behave themselves for a while, too; I doubt either of them wants to end up standing naked next to the other in front of the mess hall with a placard around his neck. But there was also plenty to disturb, and the effects of it are going to be hard to dispel. The one ugly, glaring fact of it at least is sure to linger:

It's *de Gilford* who ended up in Guards, not Poncellet. And failing that prize, for all his incredible skill Poncellet's come to nothing.

It's a sobering vision of Tristan's possible future, and I can't let it happen. But Poncellet doesn't just worry me for Tristan. He reminds me of myself, since it doesn't take much to guess what happened to him: his glory days at St. Sebastian's took him so far beyond the expectations of his former self that when he found himself out, he no longer belonged anywhere else.

Maybe it's just because it's the first chance I have to dwell on it, too, or because my uncertainty tonight that I've been reading the dynamic between the masters correctly is making me question my assumptions about a lot of things. But losing Meliana's journal for a second time is hitting me harder now than it did then. It's bad enough knowing *Aristide* read more of my father's past than I could. But something in his comments about the little book has given me the uncomfortable feeling that there's more to my father's story with Melissande's mother than I suspected, and it's made me curious to know exactly what happened between them. But mostly, after having such an unsavory parody of the boys' rivalry paraded in front of us all so blatantly by the masters, now I *am* starting to feel mighty curious to know what really happened between Taran and Melissande. And between Melissande, and Tristan.

I lie in an uneasy half-slumber long after the barracks has fallen silent, forcing myself to think back over everything I read in Meliana's journal, and over other things I've been trying for so long to forget. As I do, visions of lovers' triangles I can hardly tell from one another anymore swirl around together in a confusion in my head: my father, Sir Brecelyn, and Lady Meliana; Melissande and the boys; even Gilles, Pascal, and his Ginger — until for all their differences they begin to merge into each other, and blend into the rivalry between de Gilford and Poncellet. But for all my poring back over everything that happened this winter at the guild and at the castle, it's not until much later that night that I finally figure out what the masters' competition had to tell me.

And I was right.

I don't like it.

It must be well after midnight and I'm finally drifting off into uneasy sleep, when I hear the soft padding of bare feet on the barracks floor behind me. A hand gives my shoulder a gentle shake. Of all things, it's Remy. He's chosen tonight of all nights to make his move.

"Can I crawl in again with you, Marek? It's cold tonight, and I'm freezing."

"Then why don't you put your clothes back on?" I tell him groggily.

"I can't. I kicked over my water jug, and they're all wet."

I'm pretty sure he's lying, but I'm too listless to argue with him. So I scoot over and I let him in. I make him get in front of me, though, where I can keep away from his roving arms and legs and other sundry appendages, since I know from experience that Remy can be something of an octopus when he wants to be. I'm in no mood to spend the whole night fending off his advances, if that's what he's got in mind.

Once he's settled in, the cot is so small and we're wedged onto it so closely together that I can feel him shivering. He's shaking so hard the whole frame is vibrating, and I think I can hear his teeth chattering. He really is freezing, so I pull the blanket up around him higher and I wrap my arms around him. His skin is cold and clammy, and instinctively I snuggle up closer. The poor boy's been trying so hard to get my attention he's probably going to catch his death of it, and it's actually terribly sweet. But if he thought crawling in naked with me was going to be seductive, he's going to be sorely disappointed.

Remy's body feels surprisingly big on the bed and I can't deny it's impressively muscled. But tonight he feels more like a little boy in need of comfort than a lover. He's had a rough few days of it; he always takes his master's misfortunes hard, and with all the ribbing Taran's been suffering lately he really does need some comfort. So when he half-turns on the cot to put his arms around me, I let him, since let's face it. I'm feeling rather cold and lonely myself.

We hold each other close, sharing our warmth and our breath mingling, our heads nestled together, and it's nice. It is comforting. But after a while I just feel colder, and even more depressed — because I know exactly what this is. It's just as his master once described it: a little easy physical comfort, when you can't have the one you really want. And because at the memory of that phrase, I guess I *do* know exactly what it is I can really believe now of Taran.

I knew it the moment I heard de Gilford's awful confession. I just haven't let myself think about it.

Even worse, it's probably what I've really believed of him all along, deep down.

Tristan's no Poncellet, that's true. And Taran's not a de Gilford, either. But after watching the masters' rivalry play out, I can't convince myself any longer that he's a cold-blooded killer. His dirty shot at Tristan wasn't part of some calculated master-plot to drive us from St. Sebastian's. It was the act of a jealous, hot-blooded boy, just as Falko said, and even without witnessing Poncellet's merciless taunting of de Gilford, it should have been obvious enough from the beginning what really led Taran to lash out at Tristan. And to reach out for a little easy physical comfort from me, too, to soothe his wounded vanity.

After all, Armand pretty much said it all, didn't he?

A man's capable of doing almost anything, for love.

A vision of Melissande in all her beauty swims before my eyes, and even in the dark I feel my hand sneak up protectively to the scars on my face. I know I'd love nothing better than to blame Melissande for everything that's happened and for the boys' bitter enmity, since it's pretty obvious she's been fooling around at least to some degree with the both of them. But I guess I can't really blame her for that, and when I hear Tristan's scornful voice in my head, saying *"Isn't that just like a man, to blame the woman?,"* as a girl I know I should know better than to fall into that trap. It's not Melissande's fault she's caught between Tristan and Taran, and much as I've resented the fact of her, I don't really want to despise her. She's my own flesh and blood, the only thing of my father's out there that's left to me, and I don't want to hate her the way the boys hate each other. There's only one thing I've ever really blamed her for anyway, even if it is unfair:

It's not her fault there's no such a thing as a boy who prefers a defiant look to a lovely face.

My eyes are wide open, stinging in the dark. But they're dry, and I'm not crying. I promised myself I'd never do that again, and I have some self-respect.

"*P-l-ease*, Marek. *Won't* you give in?"

It's Remy, whispering tremulously in my ear.

For a confused moment I fear he's getting frisky, and the remark is some sort of proposition. But he must have read my mood, and he's just pressing me to confide in him again.

"If it's something about your scars, you can show *me* what you're concealing, can't you?" he says, sliding a hand down as though asking permission to slip it up under my tunic. "You'd feel *so* much better if you did. Or don't you trust me?"

His voice is even more urgent and insistent than it was out in the stables, and I can tell he's genuinely distressed. In my fragile state his concern for me is so affecting and he's being so tender and persuasive, I can feel my resistance wavering, even though it would be a disaster to tell him anything. Remy's too guileless to keep a secret, even his own, and anyway what's weighing on me now is the last thing I could ever tell him. So I roll over, and I turn my back on him instead.

I don't mean it as a rejection but maybe it is, and Remy seems to take it that way.

"Don't *bother* telling me your secret, Marek," he says sullenly. "I know it already. You're still in love with him, aren't you?"

I know he's thinking of the night I told him I was desperately in love with Tristan, and that it's Tristan I'm thinking of right now. So it's only a half-lie when I reply,

"You're right, Remy. And that's my problem, right there. I am still in love with him."

WHEN I WAKE UP THE NEXT MORNING, I'VE BEEN HAVING A disturbing dream. All night long there's been a naked boy luxuriating in bed with me, and I'm not supposed to be having any of *those* kinds of dreams again. But what's most disturbing about it is that it's actually quite delicious. So I lie with my eyes closed for a while, trying only half-heartedly to dispel it and feeling surprisingly invigorated. It's amazing what a sound night's sleep can do, and it's a testament to how refreshed I am this morning that it can't ruin my mood entirely when I open one eye, only to find that my dream was entirely real. Only the boy in bed with me was *Remy*. And he's still here. We're all tangled up together and he's fast asleep, drooling on my shoulder. I simply fold up his limbs and scoot him over gently, and I sit up with a satisfied stretch.

The masters' competition is behind me, my crossbow tutorials are finished, and an idea for the joint trick is finally in place. All I've got to worry about now is helping the boys perfect it, and today I'm to have my own chance to start getting into shape for the trials, both with squires' club (a much more pleasant prospect now that Poncellet's out of commission), and with Pascal and Armand, as we've arranged. So I swing my legs over the side of the cot, ready to start on what's sure to be a productive day.

Before I do, just for good measure I put my head down in my hands for a moment and I mutter to myself under my breath,

"Just don't think about him. Just don't think about him." And it works. It really does.

No, seriously.

Today it really does, and I know why.

After settling things in my own mind last night, I no longer have to be confused about Taran. It gives me a surge of confidence, too, to know I've finally owned up to the truth about him.

So maybe Taran's not a villain. And maybe I *have* been feeling awfully sorry for him. Just because I can understand his actions doesn't mean I have to excuse them, does it? And he *has* been behaving badly; even if he's not really a cold-blooded killer or a calculating seducer, it's not as though I've been completely misjudging him, just to soothe my own wounded vanity. At the very least, there's no question he's not the honorable boy he pretends to be. Whatever his motives were, he *did* shoot Tristan. There's no getting around that. Remy saw him. He blatantly lied about breaking off his engagement, too, at least by omission. And then cheated on his pregnant fiancée.

With *me.*

There's no getting around that, either.

I pull on my boots, and I tuck the blanket up around Remy and I leave him there. Then I head out to gather up some breakfast for Tristan, secure in the knowledge that admission is surely the first step in a cure, like for an addiction or a disease. Now that I've acknowledged the true nature of my affliction, I'll just sweat Taran out of my system for a while, like a bad case of the plague, and my long preoccupation with him will be over. My infatuation will crumble away naturally, brick by brick, since it's founded on nothing. All I have to do is avoid him. It should be easy enough.

While I'm still at the sideboard, Remy catches up with me.

"*Good* morning, Marek," he drawls drowsily in my ear. His clothes seem suspiciously dry this morning but I don't mention it, since he's remarkably chipper considering the mood he was in last night. When I ask him about it, he chirps,

"It's amazing what a really *sound* night's sleep can accomplish. And last night, I finally got exactly the one I needed."

It's just what I've been thinking myself, so I don't know why it should bother me. Except that as Remy says it, he slips his arm around my waist.

He's just reaching past me for an apple, but there's something about the familiar feeling of it that brings on a flash of my dream last night, a part of it I've only just remembered. It's so vivid that for a wild moment I even think it must have really happened:

A hand, fumbling inside my tunic.

Sliding under my bindings.

Feeling around between my breasts.

But it wasn't some new iteration of my old dream of the windmill where there were three of us in one embrace, with Remy now thrown into the mix (at least, I certainly hope it wasn't!).

Because it was my *own* hand.

And what I was doing was slipping a little blue bottle down the front of my dress.

I can't imagine what could have made me dream of *that*; it must have been because I was thinking back to all the things that troubled me at the castle this winter when I drifted off last night. But letting Remy crawl in with me can't have helped. It's time I put a stop to it and I tell him so, as gently as I can. Unless I want to be as selfish as Taran, I can't keep stirring up false hopes in a boy who is a friend.

"Okay, Marek. If that's what you *really* want," he says, taking a juicy bite of his apple and giving me a look that's way too steamy for first thing in the morning. "I doubt I'll be needing to do it again any time soon myself." When I give him a questioning look, all he says is,

"Mark my words, Marek. This morning, things are looking up!"

I don't know why, but it always makes me nervous when anyone says this other than myself.

As I link arms with Remy and we head out to the field together, though, I know he's right. Things *are* looking up. I've rounded a corner, and from here to Firsts it's sure to be smooth sailing. My days will now fall into a predictable pattern, and one that'll be refreshingly monotonous: drills in the morning and squires' club in the afternoon, followed by a quick check in on how the boys are coming on their joint trick. I'm feeling more confident about that, too, this morning: Tristan has faith in me, and I've got to have faith in him. With a little work, I'm sure he can figure it out.

THE KNIGHT OF THE DIRTY SHOT

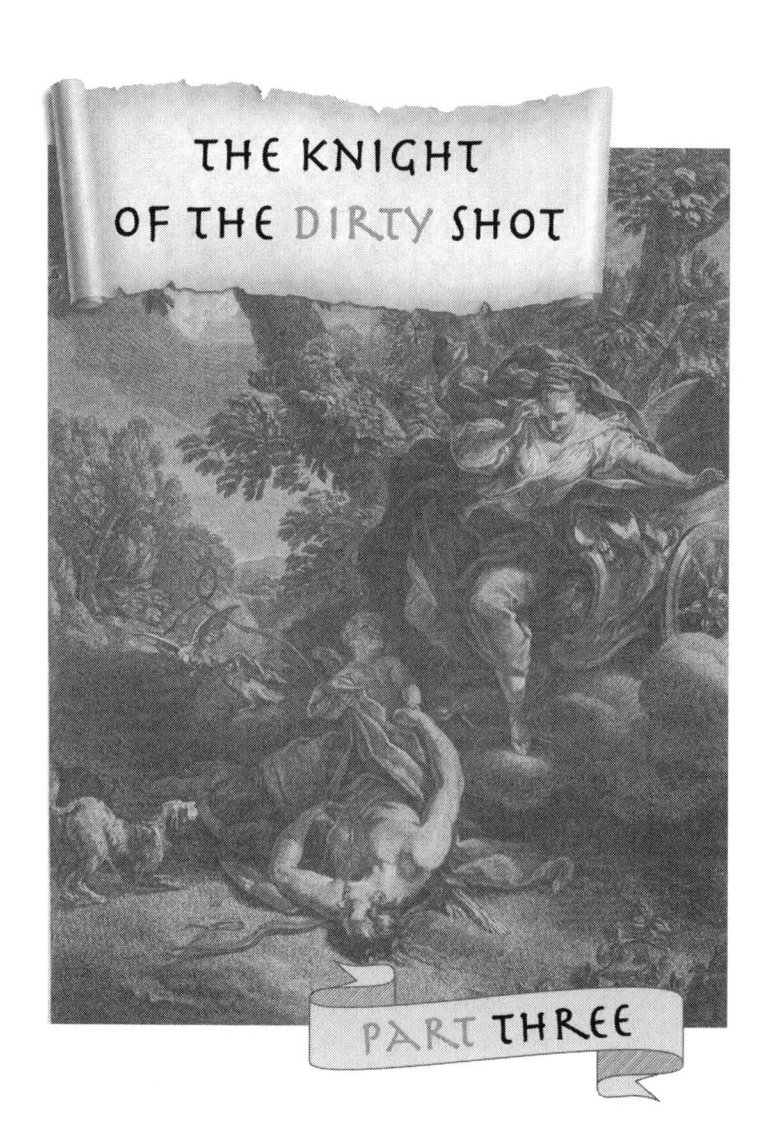

PART THREE

CHAPTER TWENTY

The few short weeks leading up to Firsts turn out to be anything but monotonous. Instead, they're punctuated by a series of nasty surprises that are as unexpected as they are unpleasant. In all fairness, I probably should have been able to see some of them coming. But the nastiest one of them all is something I could have never predicted.

The first surprise comes that very morning.

Once we get out to the field, Remy and I naturally move to set up our masters' stations at opposite ends of the line and we lose track of each other. And when the Journeys come out, I'm so busy with Tristan that I'm hardly tempted to cast any looks down the line in his direction. I was right: the guild is small, but with my own tasks to occupy me and with a little effort, from now on I bet I'll barely even have to notice Remy's master at all. So it's not long before Tristan and I have breakfasted together, and Master Leon appears to commence the morning's drills.

"Gentlemen, I will be leading the first half of practice myself this morning," he announces sourly once we've all lined up at attention, "your erstwhile trainers finding themselves indisposed this morning. One of them, I'm sorry to say, could not be roused at all. The other will be joining us eventually, after a thorough bandaging-up in the kitchen."

None of this is much of a surprise. The master usually avoids leading drills himself, but after the vicious fight between our trainers last night none of us was expecting anything different, and when Rennie whispers to Jurian,

"You don't suppose Poncellet is *dead*, do you?," it's what we're all thinking.

"Nah. At least, I don't *think* so. But it's going to be a long time before he's tickling anybody's fancy, I'll wager," Jurian replies, and it's what we're all thinking, too.

Master Leon has no intention of running our practice on his own, of course, and so it's not long before one of the veterans is coming over from the direction of the cabinets to join him. It's a man I don't recognize at first, although there's something familiar about him. He's big and burly, and when

Leon introduces him as Master Bernard, I remember him. He's the man we all watched beat up the brick supplier out at the wall the other day.

"Great," Tristan mutters to me, under his breath. "Wouldn't you know it? Another great big behemoth of a clouter." But he's grinning, and we exchange a look that says he's not forgotten our conversation about clouts yesterday. I can't say I'm very optimistic about the possibility of cultivating the likes of Bernard to our advantage, but having a clouter leading drills will keep Tristan working on the skill without us having to sneak around too much to do it. So I'm grinning, too, and practice goes smoothly, until about a half an hour in.

We're set up next to Gilles, and since Firsts is wands, we've started out drilling on that. Today Gilles is behaving himself; he doesn't seem to be trying to get under Tristan's skin and he's been shooting well, but he's not doing anything flashy. When Pascal and I are getting back to the line after our fourth or fifth retrieval, though, we find Tristan engrossed in watching Gilles attach something to his bowstring, just the way Poncellet did during his competition with de Gilford.

"What's that, master?" Pascal asks, when we're close enough to get a good look at it.

"That, Pascal," Gilles replies, "is what's known as the kisser. I thought I'd give it a try myself," and I don't have to look to know what it is.

It's a little knot made of red hair, just like the lock Gilles supposedly brought back to Pascal from Ginger, on the night Gilles gave her a daring ride to the convent of St. Genevieve. It's the exact same shade, too — a shade I'd thought at the time was suspiciously like the color of Gilles's own hair.

I shoot Gilles a quick look, wondering just what he's playing at. But his expression is all innocence, and as the call for the next round goes up and a dubious Pascal asks,

"Do you think it's going to be of any help?," Gilles raises his bow, pulls the string back to press the little knot against the corner of his mouth, and as he releases with an exaggerated smack that's louder even than the one Poncellet gave to his, he exclaims,

"I do believe it's going to be hugely gratifying."

And that's when it happens.

Behind us there's a crash and an oath, and a slam of the stable doors in just the way that usually signals the arrival of Brian de Gilford. And when I turn to look, I do see a man making his way forward to join us who shows every sign of having been in a brutal fight last night. There's still a hint of a swagger in his gait but he's moving gingerly, as though each step is painful, and he's got so many lumps and cuts that at first I don't recognize him. That's not what's surprising, since he's got a big cloth bandage wrapped around his head and some sort of splint holding his nose in place, and the rest of his face is a discolored mess of swollen bumps and bruises. But he's the wrong size and shape for de Gilford. And right in the middle of the misshapen mass that should be his face, there's a little pencil-thin mustache.

It isn't de Gilford, it's Poncellet.

I should have realized it sooner, since he's wearing the same dusty old sleeveless long coat he wears every day.

All the boys lower their bows and stare at him as he saunters up, swings down his bow with only the slightest of grimaces, and strikes a fair if a bit creaky imitation of one of his jocular poses with one hand on his hip.

"Not who you were expecting?" he says saucily, out of the working corner of his mouth. "Let me tell you something, Journeymen! To have lived as long as I have, and to have slept with as many *women*, you've got to have a certain resilience. '*I Bounce Back*,' that's my motto," and he winks. At least I think he does, although he does have the good sense not to try to punctuate the comment with one of his usual gyrations.

"Believe me, boys," he says. "In my day, I've been beaten by better men than Brian de Gilford."

Then he lifts his bow, and although I can tell it's costing him something he steps forward and proceeds to run the practice with Bernard so Master Leon can take his leave. He shoots all morning with no sign at all that having his eyes half swollen shut is much of an impediment to his accuracy, and it takes us all much longer to settle into the session than it does him, since at first we're all watching him in disbelief — until finally Rennie pipes up again, this time to ask his master,

"So, do you suppose *de Gilford*'s dead?"

Nobody really thinks so, of course. But at this point I'd probably believe anything.

I suppose I should be relieved to find that the men came out of their fight last night better than I'd expected, and I am, and as surprises go, this one's more irritating than nasty. But after thinking I was going to be spared having him at squires' club, it's something of a blow to *me* to find I'm back to being stuck with old Poncellet.

After practice is over, when I'm heading back inside through the garden after stashing away Tristan's equipment, I find that Poncellet is there. I'd have thought after making it through the drills he'd have gone straight back inside to collapse. Instead he's got his slender blonde whip in his hands, and as I come through the gate he's cracking it quite expertly.

He's set one of the little garden chairs out about four yards in front of him, and as I stop to watch he gives a sharp flick of his wrist, and the whip lashes out. The tip of it wraps tightly around the chair's leg, and with another quick jerk Poncellet pulls the chair over to him, and he sits down on it. It's a mighty neat trick, and when he sees me watching him, he says,

"It's a rough world out there, son. So take my advice. When a man's smaller than the others, he's got to have a way other than a longbow to defend himself. Outside St. Sebastian's you can't go around shooting people, unfortunately. If I'd have had this with me last night, I can assure you things would have ended quite differently."

"Is it hard to do?" I ask curiously.

"It's not easy. But if a man's got good aim with a bow, he can be good with a whip, too. Like anything else, all it takes is practice."

While we've been talking, Tristan's come circling back out through the portico. He's wearing a clean tunic and he's got his hair slicked back, and he's already looking refreshed. He pulls up a chair, sprawls himself down, and when he proceeds to lie smoothly,

"Say, *master*. Do you know who else I hear was good with a whip? That man, Jan Verbeke," I make my excuses and I hurry inside without asking anything else.

THE NEXT SURPRISE COMES LATER THAT SAME AFTERNOON, AND I'm sorry to say this one is much bigger. And this time, it is entirely nasty.

"So what am I aiming for, the *head,* or the *shaft?*" Tristan demands plaintively.

Tristan, Gilles, Pascal, and I are all standing in a huddle out in the pasture beyond the pavilions, staring down at a single wand we've set up what seems ridiculously far away. It's make-or-break time for the boys' trick, and now that the time has come for them actually to try it, I'm predictably feeling nervous about it again. We all know it's not going to be easy. In fact, it's going to mean figuring out how to replicate two virtually impossible feats: the long shot of Guillaume's that won the masters' competition, and Poncellet's unbelievable arrow-downing trick.

We've gotten as far as deciding to start out with Gilles making the shot at the wand and Tristan being the boy who jumps in, since it's logical enough. Now we're stuck again.

"What do *you* say about it, Marek? Heads or tails?" Tristan asks me again. He doesn't say it rudely. He's just asking my opinion, as usual. But today I have no advice to give him. Even though the trick was my idea I have no idea how to do it, either, and it *is* a problem. Poncellet downed his own arrow by hitting it on its head, but he made a point of using a broad-headed arrow. The tips of the bodkin shafts the boys use during competitions are a heck of a lot slimmer, and I'm not even sure that a direct hit to one would drop the arrow entirely. It's one of the many things I didn't bother to think through, and I don't like the feeling: if the trick's going to be successful, Tristan's going to have to figure out how to do it without any more help from me.

I've had my doubts, too, about how seriously Gilles is going to commit to trying it. Firsts may well be in the bag for us, even without it. But if Gilles proves an unreliable ally, Firsts is likely to be as far as Tristan gets, and more is at stake than just this trick's viability. By the end of the afternoon something even more important should be clear: whether or not we can really count on any help at all from Gilles.

Luckily, today Gilles is all compliance. He seems as genuinely enthusiastic about attempting the outrageous stunt as Tristan is, and as Pascal and I lugged out the boys' equipment and set it up, both boys were busy bandying about suggestions for how to approach it and imagining how satisfying pulling off such a daring exhibition together is going to be. The boys really are the best of friends, and I remind myself of it — and that for all their differences, they share some crucial qualities: they're both natural show-offs, and risk-takers. Usually these are things that worry me about Tristan, but today I have to think they'll work to our advantage. Gilles, at least, I know from experience has no problem making a spectacle of himself. As long as the trick proves doable, I'm pretty sure he's 'in.'

"All right then," Tristan says briskly, when no answer to his query is forthcoming. "Let's proceed by trial and error, shall we? If it's really to look as though I'm jumping in on Gilles's exhibition, and if my arrow is to have any chance of catching up to his, I'd better take my shot at an angle, from somewhere midway down the field. Marek and I'll go down and estimate a likely spot to start from. Once I'm on my mark, Lejeune, you float one up nice and easy, in that way of yours — really hang it up there. And then when your arrow hits the top of its arc, I'll aim straight for those big white bands of yours. They'll make a prominent target."

It sounds reasonable enough, so Tristan and I leave Gilles and Pascal on the line, and we head downfield to try it. As we go, Tristan's musing eagerly,

"If we're going to give this thing a little flair, Marek, it can't be just a standing shot from the sidelines. A trick this good deserves a proper send-up, and besides, we want to be sure the spectators in the stands can understand exactly what's happening. So I think I'll dash a ways out onto the field before I shoot, and then drop down dramatically onto one knee. That way we can be sure I've got everyone's full attention, and that all eyes in the crowd are firmly on me. What do you say?"

I'm awfully glad Gilles is too far away to hear him. But it does sound good, so I encourage him to try it. I might as well. He's going to do it anyway.

When we gauge we're at the right jumping-in point on the field, while Gilles limbers up Tristan takes a few dry runs at it: he paces back a few yards and then he sprints past me, scanning the sky and nocking as he goes, not taking his eyes from the place where an imagined arrow of Gilles's would be. Then at about 15 yards out in front of me he drops down abruptly into an exaggerated crouch, and at the same time he swoops his bow up into position with a great upswing that does look terribly dramatic. If he really does it at the trials with the crimson lining of his cape fluttering out behind him, there's no question where all eyes in the crowd will be. But I'm not imagining how good it's going to look when he makes that shot in front of a stunned audience at Firsts. I'm thinking how it will look, if he runs right out into the middle of another boy's exhibition like that during the competitions — and misses.

When Tristan's satisfied with his approach and Gilles signals back that he, too, is ready, the boys try it in earnest. Before I know it, one of Gilles's arrows is sailing high overhead, and with a grin and a shout of *"here goes nothing, kid!,"* Tristan dashes forward onto the field again. The whole thing looks even more thrilling now that Tristan caps the performance by actually loosing an arrow, and I'll give him this: when it comes to style, Poncellet's got nothing on him. But he misses Gilles's arrow by a mile.

He misses the next one, too. And the next. And so it goes, for about half an hour.

By the time Gilles is on his eighth quiver-full of arrows and the time for squires' club is fast approaching, I'm more than ready to have an excuse to leave. Tristan's not yet hit even one of Gilles's arrows, of course, but that's not the reason. I never expected him to perfect the trick so easily, and I've actually been immensely encouraged by Tristan's progress on it. After each one of his failures he's regrouped, and adjusted the distance and trajectory of his own shot accordingly. Slowly but surely, he's been edging closer to striking Gilles's arrows. If he continues narrowing in on them at the rate he's going, and if Gilles can keep his own shots consistent, I don't see any reason why Tristan won't soon be nailing every one of them, every single time.

Shooting an arrow out of the sky must not be as hard as I'd thought.

But there's been nothing for me to do but stand here watching, and fidgeting. I'm itching to do something constructive, and watching the boys preparing something that's so sure to be extraordinary has only whetted my appetite for honing my own skills. I've been looking forward to squires' club all day, and I know Pascal feels the same way; we're both determined to cut a better figure on the field this year for different reasons, and so when the appointed hour arrives we're quick to make our excuses to our masters. With a promise to return once our own practice is over, Pascal and I head out for the butts together, and as we go, I'm feeling so generally encouraged, and so happy to be starting up our old club again, that I even decide to be more optimistic about the prospect of old Poncellet as our trainer. Maybe it *will* be fantastic, after all. At the very least, I can take it as an opportunity to learn everything I can from him.

WHEN WE COME OUT AROUND THE STABLES, WE FIND MOST OF the other squires already gathered at the Journey cabinets waiting for us. They're a lively group this afternoon, and from the looks of it they've all decided to be positive about the prospect of training with Poncellet, too.

Except, of course, as I now suddenly remember, that none of them knows anything about it.

As soon as Armand catches sight of us, he comes bustling straight over, looking all very serious and eager. For some of the boys, squires' club is mostly an excuse to get out of an afternoon's retrieval, but Armand apparently hasn't forgotten my promise in barracks last night to train him for Journeys. Now he's all business, and while I'm rooting around in the back of Tristan's cabinet for a bow small enough to lend to Frans (Falko not having thought yet to arm him), he pulls Pascal aside. Soon the two of them are discussing animatedly just how they intend to proceed with our inaugural session of the season, and I can see it's all going to be rather awkward.

The club was originally all my idea (and let's admit it, I'm the best trainer of the bunch), but I've always been careful not to be too proprietary about it — except when there's any blame to be had. We've always run it as a group venture, and as the most senior squires, the boys have quite naturally assumed they'll be the ones in charge today. Now it's occurring to me rather belatedly that I never got around to mentioning the fact of Poncellet to any of them.

After last night, I just assumed I wouldn't have to. But if Poncellet could show up for morning drills, he's sure to be turning up at any moment. If I want the resumption of our club to go smoothly the boys are going to need some warning, since they're likely to find the thought of dealing directly with the man as daunting as I do. But it's sure to strike the boys as peculiar that I'm the only one who knew about the master's plans. And even stranger that I didn't see fit to say a word about it.

I'm still wondering how I can casually broach the subject when the garden gate bangs open. It's Remy, the only one of the squires who wasn't already here. He's looking awfully sullen, and after his good spirits this morning it's disconcerting enough. But a few paces behind him is Taran. What in the world is *he* doing here?

His expression is even sourer than his squire's, and to my chagrin, instead of continuing on his way out across the field, he proceeds to stand stiffly a few feet behind Remy as he arms himself. From the way he's looking pointedly off over Remy's shoulder and refusing to say anything, if I didn't know better, I'd even think the two of them have been quarreling. I can't imagine why he's hanging around here and not off practicing insatiably somewhere. But I suppose he's being overprotective as usual. He must be checking up on us and making sure we're not going to do anything else to get ourselves into trouble, and it's made Remy angry; and anyway, when he finds out about old Poncellet he's sure to turn tail and flee. So I ignore him, and I remind myself I don't care *what* he's doing. I'm not going to think about him at all today.

"I propose we concentrate on wands," Pascal is saying importantly, when

I've focused my attention back on him. "That's what's on everyone's minds. And that way we can try out for ourselves the things the trainers have been telling our own masters," he adds, although we all know that's not the real reason Pascal wants to work on wands; he's picturing himself sweeping back in a motion even more elegant than one of Gilles's and impressing the hell out of Ginger. But before he can get any further and before I've thought of what I'm going to say to introduce him, right on cue Poncellet comes strolling out through the stable doors.

"Uh, Pascal," I interrupt, putting up a tentative hand to hail Poncellet over. "I don't think the plan for today is going to be up to us," and when all eyes turn inquiringly to me, I shift around to turn my back on the place a few yards away where Taran is unaccountably still lingering. Then I launch quickly into some of what Master Guillaume told me — although I may embellish it, a little. I end with:

"The master's been *so* impressed by the progress we've made all on our own, he's seen fit to do us the honor of giving us an official trainer! And not just *any* trainer. One of the *masters*. He said it himself, an extraordinary man, and one who excels at shooting *and* at training."

Out of the corner of my eye, I'm pretty sure I see Taran startle. I guess *he's* figured out who it is. But I don't think the others have yet taken in what I'm saying, despite the fact that from the other direction Poncellet is now moseying over.

He's not got his bow with him, and from the bored expression on what's left of his face I can see he isn't going to take training a bunch of squires very seriously. Instead he's got his whip coiled around one shoulder, and I sincerely hope he's not planning to take Master Guillaume's instructions literally and whip us into shape. I've started to get a bad feeling about the whole thing, and so I step aside dramatically as though revealing Poncellet to the boys with a flourish. As I do, I wave my arms in his general direction, exclaiming rather over-enthusiastically,

"And it's going to be *Master Poncellet!*"

Nobody says anything.

Somewhere behind me I hear a satisfying sort of choking sound. But to my annoyance Taran doesn't slink away like I thought he would. He just shifts around some more, and I can almost feel him refolding his arms and settling back into one of his bland, superior expressions.

The expression on everyone else's face is close to pure terror. Frans in particular sidles a few steps over so that he's standing completely out of Poncellet's view behind me, and I'm pretty sure the others have all started imagining with horror the nicknames the man's sure to find for them. It's not something I care to dwell on, either.

"What's up, *Journeylads?*" Poncellet says, surveying us with amusement.

"We're ready and eager, master, for our first lesson!" I chirp, mustering all the enthusiasm I can.

"Are you, now?" he drawls. When all he does is twitch his mustache, I add encouragingly,

"*You* know, squires' club. It's time to start our practice."

"What's that to me?" he laughs dismissively, and I see he's not going to make this easy, or pleasant. But he also looks like he has no idea what I'm talking about.

"You're to be our new trainer. *Uh*, didn't Master Guillaume tell you?"

"Must have slipped his mind."

But we both know Master Guillaume never forgets anything. Something's wrong. And horribly, I probably already have an inkling of what it is.

"If *you're* not our new official trainer, who is?!" I hear myself demanding anyway, just as there's a meaningful cough behind me. To me, it sounds rather sarcastic.

I don't turn around. I don't have to.

Sure enough, all the boys' eyes have shifted from Poncellet to a point off over my right shoulder. Soon I hear Taran's voice behind me, saying derisively:

"*Who's* your new official trainer, squires? Not Poncellet. *I* am. Master Leon insisted. It's my *reward*, for starting a brawl during evening mess."

"*You?!?* It can't be *you!*" I cry, whirling around and flinging the words at him rudely. "Master Guillaume said he was giving us one of his very best! He said he was giving us a *master*."

"I'm still a *master*, to *you*," Taran snaps back, just as rudely. "One crossbow lesson notwithstanding."

"But the master *also* said —!" I start indignantly. And then I can't finish. I've only just remembered exactly what else the master *did* say about the man he was giving us as a trainer, and there's no way I'm going to repeat it.

I'm being inexcusably insolent to a man who outranks me, and it's probably going to end up getting me in trouble. But I'm too upset to stand down, and instead I take a few challenging steps toward him. My mouth is already opening again when Taran takes an angry step forward of his own, and he hisses down furiously at me,

"Step *back*, damn it, squire! And if I'm going to have to *look* at that *face* of yours all afternoon, *keep it the hell out of my way*."

There's nothing for it but to force myself to step back into ranks, and hold my tongue.

But it's not easy, and I'm gritting my teeth. And not just because I feel like I've just been slapped. Or because our new *trainer* has turned out to be yet another bully who's going to let power go to his head. After all my resolve of this morning, what bitter irony it is to find I'm to be stuck not with Poncellet as I'd imagined, but with *Taran*. And since I'm the one who pushed him, I have nobody to blame for it but myself.

It's so frustrating that I don't even realize what a spectacle I've been making, trying to square off with Taran like some absurd parody of the masters last night, until Poncellet laughs,

"Well, boys! I think I'll leave you to *enjoy* your training, before old Pecs here starts busting bows again. Enjoy babysitting, Mellor! Looks like you'll have your hands full. Want me to whip this one back into line for you before I go?"

"Believe me, *master*," Taran replies, his jaw clenched. "When this one needs a beating, I'm going to enjoy giving it to him myself."

"I bet you will," he chortles, and with that Poncellet wanders off, still laughing.

Needless to say, I find nothing even remotely amusing about the situation.

As might have been expected, the other squires all look thrilled by this turn of events. Not only has scrutiny by Poncellet been avoided, but they're wildly enthusiastic about the prospect of being trained personally by Taran. Around me, they've started nudging each other excitedly.

For his part, Taran simply refolds his arms across his chest. And then he proceeds to stand there impassively. When after a while it seems clear he's not going to make any move to get things started, the boys begin shifting around and casting glances at each other, wondering what's going to happen.

"*Look* at him," I grumble under my breath, to the boy next to me. "He's not going to make any effort to teach us anything. Why, instead of being flattered by the assignment, he looks like he resents it!" Regrettably, the boy next to me is Remy.

"Of course he resents it, Marek," he answers back bitterly. "If he's stuck out here coaching us, when is he supposed to do his own practicing?"

I suppose I should feel chastised, since Remy's right. Instead, at his words I begin to see a silver lining to the whole thing.

"Uh, what should we do first, *master*?" Pascal finally ventures, when Taran still shows no sign of getting the practice going. To my immense irritation, Taran replies coolly,

"Don't look at me. *I* have no intention of running this."

When the boys all just stare back at him, he adds,

"I consider myself here in entirely an advisory capacity. We all know it's not *my* baby," and then he falters for a moment. It's a truly unfortunate turn of phrase, the sort of thing only Taran could blunder into saying, and at the grimace that flashes across his face, next to me Frans sidles over again — this time so that I'm between him and Taran. But soon Taran's continuing even more sarcastically,

"What I mean to say is, it's *Vervloet's* club. As far as I'm concerned, he's in charge. In fact, I *insist*. I'm quite curious to see just how he does run things, seeing as he's got a reputation for being such an impressive trainer."

The boys all turn to look at me, their expressions ranging from disappointed to resentful. And as soon as I see it, I know instantly what

Taran's doing. Un*believ*able! Oh, I knew he wouldn't lift a finger for the good of the club, but I didn't expect him to sabotage it, and I know what he's up to. He's not just trying to get out of doing a job he finds distasteful and beneath him. Under the guise of not interfering, he's trying to turn all the boys against me. And it's working. They might not have minded being trained by another squire when we were alone. But with one of our own masters looking on, taking orders from me would be like admitting I outrank them, and I can tell Pascal and Armand in particular don't like it (even though they were practically begging me to coach them last night). Remy likes it even less.

If I let Taran spoil the camaraderie of the group we've got nothing, and he must know it. It's an awfully dirty trick; I can't believe last night I was ready to excuse him everything, and maybe he's not a villain. But he is just as insufferable as ever, and he's always had in it for squires' club. So if I don't want him to kill it off now, I know what I have to do.

But it's damned hard.

I take a big step forward, before I can lose my nerve or Taran can bark me back again. And as I turn to address the boys, I'm clenching and unclenching one fist.

"I think I owe you boys the truth of it," I begin.

"*That* would be a change," Taran interjects, but he doesn't try to stop me. So I continue bravely:

"An explanation, for why I was the only one the master told of his plans. And why I'm the one he asked to *help* Master *Taran* here train you. And it's not because squires' club was my idea or because I have any special claim to it, or anything to do with what I'm like as a trainer. It's because the master thinks *you* all have real potential. He wants truly impressive boys for the guild's first crossbow competitors, and he thinks some of you may have what it takes. So he wants *me* to concentrate on helping *you* boys get ready for it, since I'm not to be in contention myself."

None of this is what's hard, of course. It's all nothing but the truth, and I've been taking a page from Baylen's book and saving it back for the right moment. But it's not going to be enough, and I know how the boys are going to react.

Sure enough, before I'm even finished Pascal is demanding a little accusingly,

"If it's crossbowmen he wants, Marek, surely you're the best amongst us," and I shake my head. I clench my fist tighter, to keep a tell-tale hand from creeping up to my face.

"The master's let me know in no uncertain terms that I'm not competition material. That I don't make the cut, physically."

"Crossbows don't require that much strength," Armand objects, and I can tell they don't get it. Of course they don't, being all so handsome themselves.

My face is burning hot, and the disfiguring welts across my nose must be standing out whiter than ever. I'm going have to say it.

"It's not because I'm too weak," I say, so softly even I can barely hear it. "It's because I'm too ugly."

Horribly, I hear my voice crack.

It's one thing to have to say out loud to all the boys that you're an ugly boy. It's another thing entirely to have to admit you're an ugly boy in front of the one boy who knows you're really a *girl*. Particularly when you've just admitted to yourself that you're still in love with him. And when he's in love with the most beautiful girl you've ever seen in your life.

Instantly all the shuffling in front of me stops. For a moment there's a complete and awkward silence from the ring of boys around me, and I can tell they're all embarrassed for me. But the silence emanating from the place behind me where I know Taran is standing is particularly deafening.

Or maybe it just seems that way, since I know I'm not the only one who's thinking right now about the vicious remark he just made about having to look at the scars on my face.

Just when I think I'm not going to be able to stand my ground any longer or avoid the humiliation of tears and flight, Rennie comes to my rescue.

"Well, that lets me out, too, then!" he cackles, and the tension is broken. And when Pascal chimes in, declaring,

"If anyone can get us in, Marek, it's you," soon the boys are rallying around me and we're a team again.

My admission was worth it, since it's swept away any resentment the boys might have been feeling, and it's not long before the others have forgotten all about the master's cruel judgment of me in their excitement over his confidence in them. But I can't forget about my own words so easily, and they cast a pall over the beginning of the session for me. I'm pretty sure Taran hasn't forgotten about them, either, since he alone must know what the words really cost me. At any rate he's stopped making sarcastic comments, and as we finally get down to starting on the practice he's unusually quiet, even for him. At first I even get the impression there's something he wants to say to me, but he can't or won't bring himself to say it.

Whatever his reasons, Taran is as good as his word and as I organize the boys to begin shooting, he seems content not to interfere. He hangs back to watch at a detached distance, and the boys are all now being so supportive that after a while I can almost forget about his scrutiny. Remy in particular is being awfully sweet, trying in his usual bumbling fashion to make things up to me by burbling out, "Marek's features are actually remarkably delicate, aren't they, Pascal? As pretty as a girl's," and "Have you ever noticed just how unusually *dainty* Marek's hands are compared to ours, Armand?" and a whole string of other things that are hardly helping. But he can't know why his clumsy compliments are less uplifting than unnerving, and all the boys are trying so hard to cheer me that I resolve not to let Taran's presence spoil something that means so much to me.

I struck a bargain with Pascal and I mean to keep it, and I'm not about to let worrying what Taran will think about it stop me. So once I've gotten the boys marshaled and ready, I announce that today we're going to take things nice and easy, and that we'll work out the winter's kinks by having each boy drill on whatever he wants individually. I've made sure to station Pascal and Armand together at one end of the line-up, and for a while as they warm up I make my way back and forth behind all the boys, making small corrections and suggestions in the way our regular trainers usually do. Then after a while I plant myself firmly behind Pascal, and I turn all my attention to him and Armand.

I don't feel too bad about it; Remy doesn't need my help if he wants to make Journey, since he practices with Taran every day. And Rennie's right; I doubt the master would find him competition material either. I do feel a little guilty, though, when I glance over at one point and I see that Taran's roused himself, apparently having noticed that I've left half the boys to their own devices. He's started going back and forth behind them himself, making comments in a voice too low for me to overhear, and I notice him zeroing in on Frans. I'd forgotten about the boy and he's petrified of Taran, who now seems bent on terrorizing him, since he's shoving his own massive bow into the poor boy's trembling hands. *Of all the typical arrogance!* Frans can barely lift a crossbow, and Taran's going to teach him to shoot by starting him out on clouts.

There's nothing I can do about it now, so I promise myself to make it up to the lad later by giving him a proper lesson, and I turn my attention back to the task at hand. Figuring out how to transform Pascal into Journey material is going to take some doing, and I'll confess I don't really know how I'm going to set about it. Armand is an even more daunting prospect.

I concentrate on Pascal first, and for a while I just watch him shoot, really studying him. He's improved since I met him, of course; squires' club last year helped, as did practicing for our show. But his aim is unreliable, and worse, he's got no flair to speak of. Watching him shoot is about as exciting as watching him fold up a stack of Gilles's laundry.

"You're not a butts shooter, that much is clear. So that's the first question. What *is* your style? Which skill suits you best? It's got to flow from your personality," I declare, thinking it through aloud, just as Armand comes strolling back from a retrieval.

"So, what style have you got to fit a dogged, meticulous perfectionist?" he quips, but he's right. It's a real problem, and frankly I fear Pascal just doesn't have the right attitude to match any of the skills. He's probably much too level-headed and modest to be a Journey at all. So I continue thoughtfully,

"You're certainly not a clouter, either. So maybe we'd better try wands.

Only somehow, in a little different way than your master," but I don't feel very confident about it. Surely wands isn't just the lack of the personality for something else, and Pascal couldn't be more different from Gilles. I can't see Pascal 'being the wand,' for example. "Maybe we can tweak out something, some shade to your personality you didn't know you had," I add, even though the idea of tweaking Pascal makes me nervous. I like him fine, just the way he is.

Before I can get any further, there's a snort behind me. I know Taran's come up unnoticed, even before I hear him exclaiming incredulously,

"Is *this* what you call training? I've never heard anything so patently ridiculous in all my life. *Don't* tell me. You can only have gotten such an absurd idea from your master. You really do believe everything he tells you without question, don't you?"

I know I shouldn't do it. But I've had just about all I can take of Taran this afternoon, and so I find myself whirling around and preparing to take him on again. But the comeback I was about to make dies on my lips when I look up at him, and I see something that takes me by surprise, although I'm not sure why it should. I've been so angry at Taran for so long, it never occurred to me that he might be just as angry with me. But he is. That much is clear from the expression on his face.

"Going to poke me with that?" he demands, looking down at the arrow I didn't notice I had clutched in my fist. "Or call me more insulting names? There may be a few you have yet to use on me," and I know he's not just talking about my reaction to finding him in charge. He's talking about the wretched morning I found his arrow, and I know what I'd *like* to say. But I've been insubordinate enough in front of the others already, and anyway before I can think how to respond he leans down so close our noses are almost touching and snarls, *"Don't you think I find everything about this situation just as intolerable as you do?,"* and then he turns his back on me dismissively.

"What kind of shooting do you *want* to do, Pascal?" he inquires coolly, as though I were no longer standing there. "Don't choose wands just because Gilles does it. Do what you love, and you'll make a success of it. Don't do it at all, if it's just to compete with someone else. You'll never out-Gilles Gilles," and it's all rather rich, coming from him. It's pretty cruel, too, and just what I'd expect from him — until he adds, "By the same token, Gilles is no Pascal. So if this girl of yours would really prefer a prattling, prancing peacock to a man of quiet integrity such as yourself, you're better off forgetting all about her," and Pascal blushes. He doesn't take offense at Taran's comments about his master either, since we all know Taran's not really talking about Gilles.

I should just drop it. But Taran's not just insulting *my* master. He's insulting me in front of the others and undermining the authority I've just sacrificed my last shred of dignity to win. So I demand,

"Are you really going to tell me that a man's basic nature and his

MASTERS

personality have nothing to do with it? Or that *you're* not such a great clouter, because you're so big? Because you're such a big, dumb *brute?!*"

Behind me I hear Pascal groan, and Armand whispers back to him, "*Oh man,* what was Master Guillaume thinking, putting the two of *them* together? It's going to be a bloodbath."

Taran doesn't visibly rise to my bait. He just turns and looks pointedly back down at me as though to suggest I'm beneath his notice.

"I'm not saying body type doesn't play a role," he replies evenly, though I can tell he's still plenty mad. "But if I'm a *brute,* that's entirely incidental. Leave it to DuBois to think there's some sort of magical shortcut to hard work. Do you want to know why I'm a good clouter? Why I'm so big, as you say? Because *my father* put a clouter's bow in my hand when I was five years old, and I've spent every single day since then breaking myself with it, that's why!" he snaps. "It's work and sweat and practice that make a man's style, that forge his personality. It's doing the same moves over and over until they become second nature that makes a man a specific kind of shooter. Nobody's born that way, and if your master is miserable at clouts, it's not because he's too *charming* for it. It's because he refuses to practice." He points at Pascal and Armand. "Take these two here. As alike as peas in a pod. They could be brothers — in body type *and* in personality. In three months I could make either one of them a butts shooter, the other one a clouter." He pauses, looking them both up and down closely for a moment. "Pascal, you're now a butts man. Armand, you're a clouter. There. Personality has nothing to do with it."

Taran seems to be announcing that he's going to train the boys for Journey himself, and I know I should be pleased. Pascal and Armand both look thrilled and a little overwhelmed, and I think they're also pretty pleased with the identities Taran's assigned to them. Still I can't help feeling that he's doing it at my expense, to slight me, and I can't let it go. So I fling back at him recklessly,

"If you're so sure personality has nothing to do with it, then why is *Tristan* so much better at butts than you are?!"

Taran glares down at me for a minute, and the look on his face tells me I've finally gone too far.

"Why is Tristan better at butts than I am?" he repeats carefully, his voice so cold and steely I know I've just created another problem for myself. "That's easy. He's *not.*"

Boy, do I wish I could learn to keep my big mouth shut.

◄──────►

AFTER THAT, TARAN LEAVES US ALONE FOR THE REST OF THE afternoon. Now and then he wanders down our way as though to check on us, but it's purely *pro forma* and he doesn't say anything. For all his talk

281

about training Pascal and Armand he's obviously going to leave their instruction entirely to me today, so I do my best to forget about him and to put them both through their paces myself. I know plenty about training a boy for butts, so I start Pascal on some exercises I remember my father having my brother Jules do when he was just starting out, and although I really don't know what to do for Armand I make something up, and I have to admit it. I'd never have thought of it myself, but it's probably a smart thing to train them in different skills, if only to keep them from their habitual rivalry.

When I think I've given them a pretty good first day's work-out and I've gotten them both exhausted, I remind them of their end of the bargain and we turn to working on some squiring pointers for me instead.

It doesn't take long to see that neither of them has given it any thought.

"Remind me just what you have in mind, Marek," Pascal says, leaning on his bow and wiping the sweat from his brow. "You want to get faster on retrieval, is that it? Hmm. Armand, any thoughts?"

"He could grow longer legs."

"Aren't there some exercises I could do, Pascal?" I ask. "To build up muscles, or something? How did you get so fast?"

"I was just born that way, I guess," he says, sounding just like his master. Then he gets a thoughtful look on his face, as though his own words have given him an idea. "Maybe if you want to improve on nature, the only way is to practice. To practice retrieval, I mean."

"*Really* helpful, Pascal," Armand mutters sarcastically. "Retrieval is about the only thing we do practice regularly around here."

"No, it's not, Armand," Pascal insists. "Think about it. We retrieve, sure. But we don't push ourselves. Mostly we stand around watching our masters, and then we trot down the field. We don't act like we're in the middle of competition, and really push ourselves. At least I know I don't. If Marek wants to get faster, he's got to push himself for a quick start and a fast sprint, every time. Until running faster is second nature." When Armand and I both give him a dubious look, he adds, "It's worth a try, anyway."

Nobody has any better ideas, and so I do give it a try. I feel pretty foolish, trying different starting stances and then sprinting at breakneck speed a few yards down the field, over and over again. It's darned exhausting, too, and I can feel curious eyes on me from down the field. Rennie, Frans, and Remy must think I've gone crazy. And I don't even want to know what our *new official trainer* is making of it. But the very fact that it is tiring me out so much makes me think Pascal was right. Maybe the key to improving as a squire is a little targeted practice.

It's already getting late when Taran calls an end to things, and by that point I've practiced getting quickly away from the line so often and pushed myself to run so fast that I'm feeling light-headed, and my legs are about ready to give out. I don't know if any of it is really helping, but I'm already feeling more confident and it's only been one day. So as we're heading in I thank both boys heartily, saying to Pascal in particular,

"It was an inspired idea, my friend! And what's more, I think it might actually work."

"Of course it will! And thank you, too, Marek. But I'm not the one you should be thanking. It wasn't really my idea. It was Taran's."

I see no reason to dignify such an annoying comment with a response.

I take my time arranging my bow and arrows back into Tristan's cabinet. Even after the others have all gone in I hang back, fiddling with my equipment but not really seeing it. I listen for a while to their receding voices echoing down the portico, and when I'm sure everyone else is gone I close up the cabinet carefully. Then I turn around, and lean back heavily against the rough wood of the cabinet door. And then I start banging it rhythmically with the back of my head.

It's not Pascal's statement that's bothering me, exactly. My cheeks are flushed with sweaty heat that's prickling everywhere, but it's not because I've thoroughly exhausted myself that my heart is racing, pounding as hard now as it has been ever since I first saw Taran coming out this morning through the garden gate. I've been holding myself in all through practice. Now that it's over, I can't keep myself in check, or keep Master Guillaume's voice from replaying over and over inside my head.

I want you out practicing with your club, every afternoon.

Every afternoon.

How in the hell am I supposed to forget about Taran, if I'm to be thrown in with him every single day?

Even that, though, I could find a way to handle, if it would mean giving Tristan an advantage. I tell myself I'll gladly put up with *anything,* if it really will buy Tristan some time. Besides, there's no question that the master was right, and Taran is a good trainer. If I'm to be stuck not with Poncellet but with Taran, I might as well still try to turn the situation to my advantage, and resolve to learn everything I can from *him* instead.

I give my head one last bang against the cabinet, harder than the others.

Every afternoon.

That's bad enough.

But it's not the only statement of the master's that I can't stop hearing, or the one that's gotten me the most upset. It's what *else* Master Guillaume said about the man he was giving us as a trainer — the thing I almost flung at Taran in disbelief, only managing to swallow it down a moment before it was too late.

I've been choking on it all afternoon, and now I've got to go and check on Tristan's progress with it hanging over me, just as though it were inscribed on a big black banner, unfurling above my head:

"He may well be the best shot that's ever been at St. Sebastian's."

CHAPTER TWENTY-ONE

When I step out onto the far field, I'm met with a glorious sight. It's the very thing I need to lift my flagging spirits.

I've been making my way out to join the boys through the maze of temporary structures, and just as I'm approaching the last line of pavilions, an arrow of dazzling white comes sailing overhead, soaring high above the tent tops in front of me like a graceful bird in flight. It's one of Gilles's arrows, of course, and I bend my head back to watch it make its lazy way across the sky. I still have my eye on that arrow as I emerge out onto the open pasture, and as I do, a sudden blur of red streaks past the periphery of my vision: Tristan's arrow, barreling straight for Gilles's, the red arrow after the white.

I stop in my tracks, waiting for the inevitable collision. It's like watching a red-tailed hawk swooping in for the kill on an unsuspecting dove, and Tristan's arrow is moving so fast and with such deadly accuracy that with a catch of my breath I know it's going to hit, even when it's still several yards out. I stand rooted to the spot, watching Tristan's arrow close the distance as though in slow motion, while time hangs suspended; and when that crimson shaft of his does strike dead center between Gilles's bands of white, it's with a resounding clash that shakes the heavens, and the clouds part to illuminate both arrows in a brilliant beam of light. They plunge headlong in a drunken free-fall to the ground, and as they spiral down together angels sing, women faint, and wild cheers ring out from an astounded crowd.

Well, maybe not. But it *is* miraculous, and I do hear cheering. It's the boys, shouting out excitedly across the field to each other; Pascal's gotten out before me and he's standing back at the line by Gilles, where the two of them are now jumping around and slapping each other vigorously, and raising their hands in salute toward the place mid-field where Tristan is calling back to them just as triumphantly.

I'm shouting, too, and running straight for Tristan. When he catches sight of me he starts running towards me, but I don't slow down. I must barrel into him about as hard as his arrow just struck Gilles's, and we both go tumbling backward laughing in an exuberant jumble onto the grass.

"I had my doubts, kid, I'll admit it," Tristan exclaims when I've rolled off him and he's had a chance to catch his breath. "But you were right! The trick is bloody fantastic."

"Let Master Guillaume nock *that* in his tiller and crank it!" I agree enthusiastically, thinking gleefully to myself, *so who's the best shot at St. Sebastian's, now?*

By the time we've managed to recover, down the field Gilles and Pascal have already started packing up in preparation of going in. The days are getting longer and it must still be quite a while until evening mess, but the boys have been at it for hours and I don't blame them for wanting a chance to rest. Now that I have my wits about me enough to notice the state of the field around me, however, I see that although the wand we've set up as a target for Gilles is riddled with arrows, there are plenty of others with both boys' colors on them strewn about. So as Tristan helps me to my feet, I say,

"Oh, Tristan! Call out and stop them, will you? I'd really love to see the trick again. Just how many of the shots did you make today, anyway? From all of Gilles's arrows in the grass, it must have been dozens of them."

"*Er*, actually, that one was the first, Marek," he replies casually.

"But all those arrows ..."

I look back down the field at the cluster of white arrows lying in a disorderly ring around the base of the wand.

And then horribly, I get it. Tristan didn't shoot them down. He missed every single other shot, all afternoon. And for all his boasting, Gilles missed his own shot at the wand regularly, too.

At my worried expression, Tristan slings his arm consolingly around my shoulders.

"Look on the bright side, Marek! Now we know it can be done, little brother," he declares confidently. "So don't worry. It's a great trick, and I'll get it. Eventually."

I can see he really means it, and I do believe him. And he's right, the trick looked more than great. I'm not ready to give up on it. If Tristan's going to sway the master from his opinions, we can't afford to play it safe. But Firsts is in *three weeks*, and we don't have 'eventually.' If Tristan's going to risk it all by attempting the trick in public, it's going to need a serious adjustment.

———◄————►———

I THINK THAT'S WHY I DECIDE TO GO ALONG WITH TRISTAN TO the mill pond not much later, when once we've made our own way back inside we find an excursion out for a bathe in the making.

It's the first really hot day of the season, and between our long club practice and the Journeys' own increased preparations for the trials, all the boys have worked up a serious sweat. The lure of the first bathe of the spring has even attracted the attention of some of the veterans, and it's to be a large party. Everybody's rank and grimy, and after missing out on washing so often lately I'm in as much need of a chance to splash off in some cool, shady water as any of the men. But the thought of such a big group of men intent on frolicking in the all-together would ordinarily make me nervous, so I only make up my mind to tag along when I find out that one of them is to be old Poncellet. I still feel like he owes me something, and if anyone knows how to tweak a trick, it's him.

On the way out through the woods, I walk along with Tristan. We've brought our lightest bows with us, and as we go we take turns calling out some lazy marks for each other along the path. We're not really practicing; we're just winding down and enjoying each other's company, and Tristan hits every mark I set for him. His mood always affects his shooting, and he's still riding high from downing Gilles's arrow and rightly feeling mighty proud of himself. But he wasn't out beyond the wall with me that day to hear the master gushing over Taran. So all the while I'm thinking, too, about how to convince Poncellet to divulge some of his secrets, and it's not going to be easy.

Once we come out into the glade that surrounds the millpond, I wander off at a discrete distance as I always do when it's time for the Journeys to undress. Soon the little pond is full of thrashing bodies, and at first I content myself with sitting under a shady tree a ways up the bank to watch the bathers, not wanting to risk getting wet. Poncellet's made no move to bathe, either; he's settled himself alone even further up the slope, and he's still fully dressed. Ordinarily I'd be glad the old reprobate is keeping his pants on for once, since I've already seen about as much as I care to of his pounds of flesh. But he's sitting so apart from the others and with such an aloof air about him that wandering over to join him seems an awfully daunting and conspicuous proposition, and I fear my idea that the outing will somehow provide an opening to talk to him is not going to pan out. He's already bluntly refused to help me and laughed about it into the bargain; anything I might say now if I intrude on his meditations is likely to get an even worse reception. So I simply sit and watch the bathers until most of the men have had their fill of splashing and they're getting out to lounge around and dry off in the grass. Then I roll up the cuffs of my trousers, and I take my own chance to wade about in the shallows near the place where the squires have started up a game.

I won't try to describe what it's like to feel the cool mud ooze between my toes and to trickle a little water down the back of my neck. But after being so hot and bothered all afternoon, it's heaven, and the boys are having such a good time around me that I have to be glad I came along, even if I'm not to get anything out of it from Poncellet. It's just what I needed to relax and to let everything go for a moment, and forget. But as so often happens relaxation makes me careless, and I'm enjoying being on the fringe of the boys' fun so much that I don't have the sense to move away when their game begins to get too rowdy — not even when Falko barges over, bringing Jurian with him.

They've found themselves without any company, since none of the other Journeys are still in the water. Aristide's not come along on the outing; he'd already ridden off somewhere before we even left the guild. And Taran's not here either, no doubt for his usual reasons. But Tristan and Gilles have abandoned them, too, and made an unusually short bathe of it. They're already out on the opposite bank sunning themselves amidst a group of veterans, and although there's nothing particularly strange about it, I've noticed Tristan getting up and moving to a better spot suspiciously often. I'm pretty sure I know what he's doing — particularly since every time I glance over, he's engaging a different man in what looks like awfully earnest conversation for a lazy afternoon. Gilles looks like he's taking a nap.

As soon as Falko's waded over, with a gleeful cry of *'chicken!'* he grabs up Frans and hoists him onto his shoulders. Jurian follows suit with Rennie, and soon they've engaged their squires in trying to be the first to topple the other from his perch atop his master. It's quite entertaining, as the teams are pretty evenly matched, and it's not long before Armand's struggled Pascal up onto his shoulders, too, having taken to his new identity as a clouter and not wanting to be left out. Remy's the only squire in the water without a partner, but even he's participating, by darting around between the others and harassing whichever team looks to be getting the upper hand. It's just when it's getting really exciting that I make a grave miscalculation, and I let myself get sucked into the game.

I've been rooting hard for Frans, and so when Falko delivers a most unsportsmanlike but effective knee to Jurian's groin that makes him stumble and double over, without thinking I slosh up closer, waving my arms around and yelling at Frans to grab Rennie's hair with both hands. Just as I'm urging him to pull Rennie straight off over backwards, Remy grabs up one of the boys' tunics that's been lying discarded at the water's edge. He fills a big fold of it to the brim with water, and then he flings it at Falko. Or at least he tries to. Only he loses his grip, and it slips from his hand.

About two buckets' worth of water come crashing down over me, right across my head and chest.

Instantly I'm soaked to the skin, like a rat that's just crawled out of a sewer.

At that very moment, Rennie sticks his toe in Frans's eye. Both of them go tumbling into the water, leaving Armand and Pascal the victors and the game over. But I'm pretty sure the piercing wail I let out when Remy's wall of water hits me would have ended things anyway.

"Oh mercy, Marek! I'm so sorry!" Remy cries, dropping the tunic and rushing over, and as the other boys in the water sort themselves out they, too, come crowding around. Across the pond, some of the veterans look over; seeing nothing more serious that a wet squire they soon settle back in again, and I put up a hand in a hasty motion to Tristan, to get him to sit himself back down. It's the smallest motion I can get away with, however, because I don't dare lift my arms away from my body. Instead I'm huddled over, holding my forearms across the slight swells of my chest, wondering desperately what I'm going to do now.

Seeing my panicked expression, Remy asks worriedly,

"Hey, are you all right?"

Then he sees something else.

The lumpy outlines of my bindings, standing out clearly under my drenched tunic. There's no way I can hope to hide them, and before I can think what to do, Remy's exclaiming loudly,

"What in the world have you got on under there, Marek?!"

All the boys crowd in a few steps closer, and I know they're all curious.

Think, Marek. Think.

But I can't think of anything, and I know they're not going to drop it. They've been too kind to pry, but they've all been dying to know what I've got under my tunic for a long, long time, and I don't blame them. I know I'd be mighty curious about what could be so bad that I'd resort to begging Taran to take me down from Brecelyn's tower just to keep Tristan from finding it out.

It's the thought of the tower that saves me.

"Oh, this old bandage?" I reply, as casually as I can, hugging myself closer and blowing the wet hair off my face. "It's just something I put on when my old wound is bothering me. You know, from the tower. With the change of season it's been aching, and it feels much better when it's tightly bound."

A look of consternation flashes across Remy's features, and I feel a little guilty. I know he's blaming himself for my soaking and that my lie's upset him, and I *am* sorry to make him start worrying about me again. But it can't be helped, and soon Falko's chuffing,

"You're lucky it's such a scorcher then, Marek, or you'd have had to strip right out of those wet togs, or catch your death! As it is, no harm done — no thanks to *butterfingers* here," he pauses to cuff Remy on the side of the head. "A little sun's all you need. Best thing for you, for drying out, *and* healing. Why, just look at old Poncellet." He nods up the hill behind me, where the man is still sitting alone in the one sunny spot on this side of the pond. He's unwrapped the bandages from his head and he's got his face tilted upward, as though sunning his own wounds and giving them some air. I could almost kiss Falko for his big brass lungs, when he next bellows loudly enough to be heard by half of Louvain,

"Best go and grab yourself a sunny patch right next to him, and you'll be feeling better in a jiffy! Scoot, squire! Master Falko's orders."

The battered old master basking alone in the sun still makes one of the least inviting images I've ever seen, but Falko's right. I've got to dry out as quickly as possible and away from the others, and even more than that: Falko's given me my opportunity, and I have to grab it. So with a grateful grin I turn to trot dripping up the hill. Before I go, Remy's looking so downcast I pause long enough to say,

"It was an accident, Remy. Don't worry about it. It's okay."

"It just didn't go at all as I expected," he says glumly.

"I know," I commiserate, as Falko strong-arms him into another round of their game.

It's probably the worst possible moment for me to be seeking out the company of a man with Poncellet's reputation. My wet clothes are clinging to me like a second skin, and it's not just the curves of my chest I've got to worry about. My drenched tunic's sticking to my hips, too, and to the swell of my belly, and I haven't got enough arms to cover everything. But at least I think the contours of my arms and shoulders really do look like those of a fit young boy now, and anyway Poncellet's eyes are closed. And as I near him, I can see the full extent of the damage to his face. De Gilford really did a number on him, and with all his bruises out in the open he doesn't seem quite as intimidating as usual. So I walk right up and plop myself down heavily next to him.

He doesn't move, even though I know he's heard me come over. So I pull up my knees and I cross my arms around them in front of me, and plucking up my courage I say by way of greeting,

"Thinking back to some good old times here, master?"

It's only after I've said it that I remember the rather sordid story Sir Brecelyn told us about Poncellet and all seven of the miller's daughters, and it's not at all the conversation I meant to start. But it works, since Poncellet just laughs.

"Don't believe everything you hear, squire," he drawls. "Half the rumors about me aren't true. I ought to know. I made up most of them myself."

"What about the one where you balance a cup of wine on an arrow, and shoot it without spilling a drop?" I shoot back.

It's not a very smooth opening, and at first he doesn't say anything. But I don't have another, so I just sit looking out at the boys still splashing in the water, waiting.

"I'll say this for you," he replies at length, without opening his eyes or tilting his head from where it's angled up to catch the sun. "You don't look like much, but you don't give up, do you, squire? I told you already. I don't help anyone. I only look out for myself."

"I don't believe that."

I'm not sure what makes me say it, but as soon as it's out I find I mean it. My conviction must sound in my voice, because after another minute he says,

"So you think you know me, is that it, squire? Got old Poncellet all figured out?," and he does open his eyes. But he doesn't look at me.

We're both now staring across the pond, to the place where Tristan is sitting with the other veterans. He's right in the middle of some story, gesticulating wildly and talking animatedly enough that now and then the lilting accents of his voice float across the pond to us, followed by the sound of the men laughing.

"I think I know the kind of man you once were," I say softly. "I think you used to help people. At least, I think you helped Jan Verbeke."

I sneak a look at him out of the corner of my eye. From this close his face looks painfully raw and swollen, and it's hard to read any expression there. But he's not laughing anymore, and now I think I do know what to say to sway him. So I press,

"*Look* at him, master. You know he's good. Really good. But so are all the others. And unlike them, he doesn't have anything but charm to fall back on. Don't let him lose his chance. Don't let the de Gilfords of his year beat him."

This time he's silent for so long that I start to feel uncomfortable, and I shrug around in my tunic, trying to keep it as it's slowly drying from becoming even more plastered against my back and chest. Just when I think it's not going to work and that he's going to refuse me, I sneak another look at him. And I think I've got him, when I see the shadow of one of his cocky grins spreading across his face.

"So you want to know how to do the wine-balancing trick?" he laughs. "That one's easy. Before you try it, just make sure everyone else watching you is dead drunk!"

He's teasing me, and after thinking that he was going to relent and say something helpful it's terribly frustrating. But when a grunt of irritation escapes me, he says sharply,

"You've got to learn to listen when someone's giving you some real advice, son. The key to an impossible trick is selling it. It's not about making an impossible shot possible. It's about convincing your audience that a *possible* shot is an *impossible* one. And it's about having a little insurance. Take the trick I did for you boys. Not an easy shot, I'll grant you. But hardly an impossible one."

"You shot your own arrow!" I protest, thinking of Tristan's arrows littering the far field this afternoon. The trick seemed plenty impossible to me.

"Did you ever stop to think *why* you thought that shot was so impressive? It was because I told you it was! I never did that trick for the King of Castile. I've never been to Castile. I've never set foot outside of Ardennes."

"But shooting down a *flying* arrow," I insist, and he turns to me. And raises an eyebrow.

"It wasn't flying when I shot it, was it? It was *falling*. Actually, the shot at the coin was probably harder."

At my expression, he starts laughing again.

"It's not so easy to tell where a coin's going to go. But that big, fat old broadhead? Its tip is bigger than any coin. And once it hits the coin, it drops like a rock — nice and easy. I know exactly where it's going to be, every single time."

"So," I say slowly, after what he's saying has had a chance to sink in. "*Could* you shoot down an arrow, in free flight?"

"Might do. Might not. It's unpredictable."

I don't like the sound of that.

"Anyone can miss," he says simply.

I like the sound of that even less.

"Even *me*. Even a shot a man's done a hundred times," he continues, warming to his theme. "So when it really counts, you've got to have a back-up. Something to distract from a miss, if the need arises. That's where insurance comes in."

"What was your insurance, then, for the trick you did for us? You only had two arrows ready," I ask, still unsure if this is all some joke of his.

"I didn't need any insurance for *that* trick, son. If I'd have missed for you boys, it wouldn't have mattered. But I'd never have been fool enough to try it in a competition."

I like the sound of that least of all.

By this time all the boys are out of the water, and across the pond men have started shrugging back into their clothes. Most of the squires have gone over to join their masters on the far bank, but Remy is now making his way up the slope towards us and Jurian is with him. They've got their breeches back on and their tunics slung over their shoulders in preparation of heading back to St. Sebastian's, and Poncellet takes it as his cue to leave. He gets to his feet and shakes off his long coat. Then before he goes, he gazes down at me, this time looking me right in the eye. And this time, there's no question but that he looks amused.

"Let me know when you want to start up those whip lessons," he drawls. When I give him another incredulous look, he quips, "Don't think I didn't know what you were thinking. With that mouth of yours, you're going to need one."

He's already moving off when the boys reach me, but as Remy plunks himself down next to me and Jurian leans up against the trunk of a nearby tree, he turns around long enough to call back,

"Without it, in Meuse you'll never stand a chance!"

"What was that all about, Marek?" Remy asks once Poncellet's out of earshot, the reference to Meuse evidently having caught his attention, and I'm not sure what to tell him. I'm not sure what's just happened, myself.

But I think I know. At least, I think I know what got the man to open up to me, and it wasn't really being softened up by de Gilford, or sympathy for Tristan.

It was the name Jan Verbeke.

"Marek's probably been trying to get something out of him for a trick for Tristan," Jurian says shrewdly. So I ignore him, and to Remy I say,

"Actually, he was just telling me that *anyone* can miss."

I don't think I intend it as dig at Taran. But maybe I do; understandably, I'm still feeling rather uncharitable about him.

Remy, at least, seems to take it that way. He starts frowning, as Jurian scoffs:

"Don't waste your time on Poncellet, Marek. He's never going to tell you anything. If you want to know the key to doing a trick that'll please the masters, *I* can tell you. It's simple, and it's no secret. It's the same way you please a lover." He pauses meaningfully, looking from me to Remy and then back at me again. "Just give 'em what they want."

With that Jurian makes his departure, leaving Remy and me sitting side-by-side alone together in a silence that's amiable, but a little awkward.

I'm not entirely sure what Remy's thinking, and I don't ask. From the way he keeps plucking at my sleeve to see how it's drying, he still feels guilty about my soaking. And after my snide comment about his master, I suspect he's also worrying over my altercation with Taran this afternoon at squires' club; in fact, I can almost feel him sitting there calculating how best to bring Taran up to me again. But he doesn't say anything, and we just sit staring out over the pond front of us, each lost in his own thoughts.

Now that it's devoid of thrashing men to churn up its waters, the millpond is remarkably still and quiet. It should be peaceful looking out at the water, since only the slightest of breezes is ruffling its surface and setting the reeds at its edge gently to swaying. But to me those reeds look a lot like wands, waving to get my attention and mocking me. So what I'm sitting here thinking about most is the problem of how to go about salvaging the boys' exhibition.

The last thing I want is for the boys to go out in front of the crowds at Firsts and really try to do the impossible, since if Poncellet is right I've set them up for failure. But if I'm going to suggest we change the trick somehow, I've got to think it through while Poncellet's comments are still fresh in my memory, and even more, while the *trick itself* is still fresh; unless I want Tristan to think I've lost confidence in him, any proposal for a tweak to the trick has to come now, when Tristan's just done the stunt successfully. After he tries it again tomorrow and misses, it'll be too late.

But *how?* The master's comments were singularly unhelpful. *Insurance.* I'm not even sure I really understand what that means. How can I hope to build a little insurance into a trick that Poncellet himself, the master of outrageous stunts, said he'd never risk trying? And Jurian's comment isn't much better. *Give 'em what they want.* Master Guillaume wants *motion.* How'm I supposed to give him that? Falko was right. It's ludicrous, another impossibility.

From where I'm sitting, the waterwheel of the defunct old mill is directly across from me, and as I've been sitting here, I've been idly staring at it without really seeing it. Now it, too, seems to be mocking me. It's stuck, just like I am, rocking slowly back and forth as though in a rut, trying to make one of its old revolutions but unable to get any further around than a few feet. A slow current from the sluggish stream that feeds the pond keeps pushing it forward, until inevitably it catches. Then in a gentle rhythm it creaks back into its old position again.

Into the *same* predictable position, every single time.

"So the master wants a wand *in motion*, does he? Well, by God, he's going to get it!" I exclaim excitedly, as an idea occurs to me.

Regrettably I say it out loud, and Remy cocks his head. He looks sharply back and forth from me to the waterwheel speculatively.

"What's that, Marek? Something about my master?" he asks anxiously. But he's not fooling me.

He didn't mishear me. He's just trying to use my outburst as a way to start up the conversation he's been sitting here plotting, and as much as I don't want to have to hear him make apologies for Taran, at least I'm not going to have to explain what my words really meant.

Sure enough, he shifts around so that he's facing me, and with big cow eyes he says earnestly,

"You mustn't mind too much about what Taran said at squires' club, Marek. He didn't mean to say it, I'm sure. He'd never say anything so cruel about your poor face on purpose! It must have just slipped out. You know how much stress he's been under. And you can't really blame him for *thinking* it. He's worked so hard to achieve perfection in himself, it's only natural imperfections in others would offend him."

"It's fine, Remy," I lie. "No big deal. Let's just drop it." But as always when defending his master, Remy's on a roll. Dropping it is the last thing he's going to do, I can tell.

"And he doesn't *really* despise you, underneath it all," he continues brightly. "Why, I think he even respects you, a little, Marek. No, really!" and it's all terribly unconvincing. He's a horrible liar. "He made you that funny little bird, didn't he, after you took those lashes in barracks? So comical. I'm sure that's how he *really* sees you."

Just when I think he can't possibly say anything that would make me feel worse, he says more seriously,

"Besides, it's only natural that he'd hate you a little, too, isn't it? The way *your* master hates *me*. After all, you are Tristan's squire. He's put Taran through hell, you know. All winter, he's been suffering *so*. So whatever Taran feels about you, it's nothing personal. And I know he shouldn't have taken it out on you. But he was just venting, Marek. So believe me, *whatever's* happened between the two of you, there was just *nothing personal* about it."

It shouldn't bother me, since I know it's true. It's exactly what I was thinking myself last night, isn't it? But hearing Remy put it so baldly feels like a sucker punch to the gut. Before I can stop myself I'm back in the Journey corridor, in a stifling, airless little room. Taran's throwing me against the wall and ripping at my tunic, and my hands are grabbing at him everywhere, tangling in his glorious hair while his mouth comes down hard and hot on the side of my neck.

Nothing personal, indeed.

When all of a sudden a huge hand reaches down and grabs me by the back of my tunic, I'm not going to describe the embarrassing sound I make.

It isn't Taran, of course. And the hand isn't really all that huge. It's Tristan, come along to fetch me. I was too caught up in listening to Remy to notice him come over, or that now all the boys are heading in.

"All dried out, kid? Ready to go back?" he asks, and I don't think I have to explain how glad I am that he's rescuing me from more of Remy's consolations.

At the arrival of my master Remy's scrambled to his feet, and Armand and Pascal are already leading him away into the woods with the other squires when I reply to Tristan,

"I think I'll stay on to sun a bit alone, if you don't mind, master," and I give him a grateful smile. When he sees it, he bends down and asks in my ear teasingly,

"Find out something useful, did you?" and I nod.

"You?" I ask back, and he winks confidentially.

"I daresay I'm getting close to the truth of it all already," he declares breezily, and I have better sense than to believe him. But I'm glad his buoyant mood is lasting, and it doesn't bother me. So once I've promised him solemnly not linger or to do anything foolish, I watch him disappear into the woods after the others affectionately.

CHAPTER TWENTY-TWO

I have no intention of staying outside the wall by myself for long. I just need a chance to get out of the cloth I use as a binding so it can dry out a little, since I don't relish the idea of being stuck in one that's sopping wet for the rest of the evening. So once the sound of the boys progressing through the woods has receded, I quickly strip off my tunic and my binding, and I wring them both out thoroughly. When I've gotten out the worst of the water, I spread the binding on a warm rock to dry in the sun. The tunic I slip back into immediately; it can dry out on my body, in case one of the boys comes circling back around for something. I've already been caught nude by this pond once, and I'm not about to make *that* mistake again.

It's only about fifteen minutes later when I bind the cloth back in place and I set out myself for St. Sebastian's. I could probably afford to stay out a little longer, as evening mess must still be a good hour away and the cloth is still uncomfortably damp. But it's livable, and by now the other boys will have all returned to the guild, and I have no desire to linger. Nothing good ever happens to me when I'm outside the wall all by myself.

As I make my way back through the woods, I should be feeling rather pleased with the way the afternoon's turned out. With Poncellet's guidance, the old waterwheel has given me an idea for the boys' exhibition that I'm pretty sure I can sell to Tristan as an improvement — as long as I word it carefully. I'd feel a lot happier about it, though, if I didn't suspect I might have inadvertently given Remy an inspiration for a trick, too, with my outburst. Or if I'd really been able to brush off the things he was saying about Taran's scathing words to me at squires' club as easily as I pretended — and lying stretched out alone in the very place where Taran once chanced to spy upon me naked was about the last thing I needed to help me keep from thinking about him. So as I'm trudging along, what I'm really doing is trying not to let Taran's taunt about my scars upset me, and to block out the words of Master Guillaume that have started repeating in a dismal loop again inside my head. Only this time, the statement of his that's bothering me most really is the *first* thing he said.

Every afternoon.
Indefinitely.
My nerves are already shot, and it's only been one day.

As I plod along, I've started taking a frustrated whack or two at bushes that line the path, and after a while, I find I've plunged unnoticed off the beaten track and into the forest. I'm not lost; I'm just following along parallel to our usual route but about twenty yards away. Forcing my way through the underbrush with its thorns and brambles fits my mood, so I just keep going — tripping over roots and swatting low-hanging branches miserably out of my way. And as chance would have it, before long I emerge out into an open place in the forest that I've never come across before.

Instantly, I regret the impulse not to regain the path.

It's a little clearing uncannily like the one in Brecelyn's woods, complete with a stunted tree just like the one I once used for midnight target practice standing on the far side opposite.

I stumble to a stop. It's a revolting coincidence, and I can't believe it. After thinking this morning that I was on my way to leaving Taran behind, I've found myself *right back* in the clearing with him.

I bend over, and I brace my palms against my knees. I tell myself to breathe. But three big gulps of air later, I don't feel any better.

Every afternoon.
With Taran.
It's more than I can bear.

I look up across the clearing, eyeing that damned stump disfavourably. *Just venting*, huh? Well, maybe a little venting of my own is exactly what I need.

Why not? It worked once before, and there's nobody about anywhere.

I swing down my bow, and I nock an arrow. And just as I did that midnight in Brecelyn's woods to exorcise myself of Taran, I focus all my anger and all my frustration on the gnarled tree before me. I'm not planning to shoot; it'll just ruin a perfectly good arrow of Tristan's, and with Poncellet's penchant for arrow-splitting I've got precious few to spare. But going through the motions will feel good. And so I bend my bow and sight along my arrow, and as I do I summon all my conviction, and I call out loudly to the stump in my most accusing voice,

"*Ha!* Do you think I don't see you lurking there? Do you think I don't know who you *really* are? You're a liar, and a bully. You're the coward who took a dirty shot at Tristan, and I should hate you for it! Well, let's see how *you* like it. Let's see how *your* face looks, when I've put this arrow through it! Then maybe I can finally be rid of you. Then maybe I won't have to be stuck here still *in lov...*"

Crackle.

A loud rustling comes from among the bushes on the far side of the clearing. A large animal is fast approaching, and I think I *was* vaguely aware that something was moving through the woods in my direction, I was just too caught up in what I was doing to pay it any mind. Now the sound is too close to ignore. I was already in the process of lowering my bow and slackening the string, but at the unexpected noise, I startle. And as I turn sharply toward the direction of the sound, my bow is still bent, a little.

My pulse leaps, my fingers twitch — and my hand slips off the bowstring. The arrow flies out of my bow.

It doesn't hit the stump, of course. Far from it. Instead, it wobbles across the clearing and disappears into the woods beyond.

But it does hit *something*.

That much is clear, from the thud and crash of underbrush and bloodcurdling scream that immediately follow. My first thought is terrible — that I've accidentally killed a stag, or some other noble forest creature.

It's much, much worse.

Because to my horror, moments later Taran comes staggering into the clearing, with my arrow sticking out of the side of his neck.

"*For the love of God*, are you kidding me?!?" he bellows. "You *shot* me? Are you completely insane?!"

He takes three big, weaving strides towards me. Then he lurches sideways, and falls back heavily against the trunk of a nearby tree — and proceeds to slide slowly down it into a slump at its base.

Instantly I drop my bow and quiver. With a little cry I rush over, and I throw myself down onto my knees beside him. I start fussing around him, trying to see the damage and burbling out, "*Oh God, oh God, Oh God Taran!*" while he fends me off with one big hand.

He's got his other hand clenched tightly around the shaft of the arrow at the point of entry, and to my immense relief from up close I see that it isn't really sticking out of his neck.

It's actually further down, near the base of his throat. It looks to have stuck fast in his collarbone, and I've never been so glad that I'm not the strongest of archers, or that my bow was only slightly bent.

"Oh, thank Goodness!" I exclaim, when I see it. "It doesn't really look *too* bad." But blood is already seeping out steadily between his fingers, and the color is slowly draining from his face.

"Let me *see* it, damn it, you big ox!" I cry exasperatedly, since he's still holding me off at a distance; his eyes are closed, and he's alternately swearing and muttering,

"You *shot* me?" in disbelief under his breath.

"It was an accident!" I exclaim indignantly. "I didn't even know you were there."

His eyes pop open.

"I *heard* you," he says.

A brief and terribly awkward silence ensues, and I stop struggling with him, since I'm not getting anywhere anyway. There's nothing I can say. I certainly can't tell him what I was really doing. Or what it was that I was just about to say.

"Well, *you* shot *Tristan*, didn't you? So I guess that makes us even," I finally huff. But when a wince flashes across his features, I exclaim,

"Oh, what does any of *that* matter now?!" and I'm already scrambling frantically to my feet to run back to St. Sebastian's, when his free hand shoots out and grabs me.

"Where do you think *you're* going? Planning to leave me here to rot? How convenient."

"Of course not! You're hurt, and you're bleeding. I'm going back to the guild for help."

"And get *me* kicked out of the guild in the process? I don't think so," he says, and absurdly we start struggling again, only now he's pulling me towards him, and I'm the one who's trying to pull away.

"Surely Guillaume wouldn't kick *you* out, for anything. Not his 'new official trainer.' Certainly not for *that*," I protest, nodding at the arrow. "Why, it's no more than a scratch."

Even as I say it, though, I'm not so sure; by now there's an awful lot of blood running down his fist, and even though I doubt my feeble arrow can have penetrated far with that big bone of his to stop it, I have no idea how bad his wound really is. Or *what* the master is capable of doing.

"I'd be a fool to risk it," Taran grumbles, apparently thinking the same things. "Not when I'm sure to win it all, no matter *what* my condition," and he sounds awfully arrogant, for a man with a bloody arrow sticking out of him. "I could beat that master of *yours* anyway, with *both* hands tied behind my back."

It must be the stress of the situation, but for a moment I actually pause, and try to picture it.

The claim is patently ridiculous, and he's being ridiculously stubborn in that infuriating way of his. So I'm already trying to tug free again and opening my mouth to argue with him, when he says,

"Besides, I'd like to see you explain it to the masters, when they see one of DuBois's arrows sticking out of my chest."

Instantly, I close my mouth. I stop struggling. And I let the full and terrible weight of what I've done settle over me.

It's bad enough that I've shot a man. That I've *shot* Taran. But he's right. Tristan's colors are on the arrow. It's sticking out of Taran like the last nail in Tristan's coffin, and I can't believe what an utter and complete careless fool I've been.

What in the world am I going to do now?

"Don't think I don't know what you're thinking," he growls, seeing my expression. "That I'm going to march right back to Master Guillaume myself and show him this arrow, and use it to finally rid myself of *him*. Of the *both* of you, and good riddance! Well, by God, I'd like to," and when he has to pause to grimace at the effort of speaking so furiously, without meaning to I grab up his hand and I squeeze it comfortingly. He squeezes back, and I don't think either of us really notices that he's still holding my hand tightly, as he continues vehemently:

"But it's not worth getting kicked out myself. And whatever *you* may think to the contrary, I have no intention of letting DuBois slink away from here that easily. Not before I've had the pleasure of giving him a public trouncing! I've been training every day since I was five years old to beat him, with all Ardennes as witness. I'm going to revel in his humiliation, and in proving once and for all to, uh, *er*, to *the girl I love*, which one of us really is the better man. It's going to be the best day of my life, and it's going to take more than a *dirty shot* to take it away from me."

"Too bad you didn't feel that way in Brecelyn's woods," I mutter, as I reach up to brush back a lock of hair that's fallen forward across his eyes.

"Obviously, you have no idea *how* I felt in Brecelyn's woods."

He says it so pointedly, he must be mocking me. All at once, I remember exactly how *I* felt in the clearing with him that day. And at our *crossbow* tutorial. And afterwards in the stables. And last night in barracks, and at squires' club, and by the pond. And all day every day, really. I'm suddenly aware that one of my hands is still clutching his and that the other is unaccountably lingering on his forehead, and I snatch them both hastily away.

"Well, Tristan didn't shoot you," I say baldly. "*I* did. *Accidentally*. And actually, it's starting to look pretty bad. So I'm just going to run back to the guild now, fetch the masters, and explain to everybody exactly what happened. I won't have anybody else paying for my mistakes. I'll just tell the truth, that my hand slipped on the bowstring, and that I'm entirely to blame."

"What good'll *that* do?!" he says sharply, lurching forward and gripping my arm again, more tightly than before. From his expression, he must now really be in a lot of pain. "Do you think it'd make any difference to the master? DuBois would still be out. And you'd be strung up into the bargain. I daresay it's all very touching, just how eager you are to sacrifice yourself for him again. But I told you, I'm not going to let anyone deprive me of the chance to beat him, fair and square. So you're not going anywhere. And now if you don't mind, perhaps we could hold off any further debate on the subject until later. Because right now, I think I'm going to pass out."

His head lolls back, his eyes slide shut, and his grip on my arm slackens. But I don't get up and run for help, and not just because I know he's surely right about the consequences, for Tristan, and for myself. A sheen of sweat has appeared on Taran's forehead and he's getting paler by the second, and he's taking on the same waxy look that Tristan had the day I tended his wound in Brecelyn's chapel. So instead I throw myself at Taran, and I start trying to shake him awake. And when he shows no sign of responding, I

299

wrap my arms around him and I press my cheek to his, and with a rising sense of panic I start raving,

"Oh no you don't! Don't you dare leave me, you great, big bastard! What will I do, if you leave me? If you up and pass out on me now, Taran, I swear I really will kill you!" and it's so much like a bizarre parody of my scene with Tristan that I could almost start laughing.

Only it isn't funny.

If anything happens to Taran, I don't know what I'll do.

Then before I know what I'm doing, my lips are seeking his, and just as I did that day with Tristan, I start kissing Taran fervently.

I only stop when I realize rather belatedly that he's started kissing me back.

I pull away anxiously, and his eyes flutter open.

"Where am I? What's going on?" he demands groggily.

"We're in the woods outside St. Sebastian's, and I've just *shot* you," I say rather shortly; from the dreamy look in his eye, he's obviously been imagining he was 'not letting grass grow,' with Melissande.

"We were just deciding that I shouldn't go for help, for *Tristan's* sake, remember?"

"Ugh. Right. *Swell*," he grunts. But when he doesn't say anything else, I ask worriedly,

"What *are* we going to do, Taran?"

"That's easy. You helped DuBois. Now you can help *me*. The arrow's got to come out."

"Surely you don't expect me to push that arrow all the way out through your shoulder?!" I cry, thoroughly alarmed again. Forcing an arrow through Tristan's body almost killed me; I can't imagine having to do it to Taran. If nothing else, there's a heck of a lot more body to him. An arrow could get lost in there.

Luckily, he just snorts,

"Don't be ridiculous."

Before I can feel too relieved about it, though, he adds,

"It can't be *pushed* through. In case you hadn't noticed, it's lodged in my clavicle. It's going to have to be dug out, with *this*."

He fumbles around at his waist with his free hand, until he finds the little knife he uses for whittling where it's dangling from his waistband on a piece of twine.

"I see the masters gave it back," is all I can think to say, as he shoves it roughly into my hand.

"Just in time, apparently."

When he sees me staring at it in revulsion and hesitating to take it, he says disparagingly,

"For a would-be assassin, you're awfully squeamish. Don't be such a baby! I'm just asking you to cut away my tunic. I can't do it with one hand.

Get it off, and tear it into strips. I'm going to need something to sop up the blood, and to use as bandages once the arrow's out. And *quickly*, if you don't mind. I can't keep holding up this arrow. My hand is getting a cramp."

I know what he's really saying is that the pain is excruciating, and that he can't take it much longer. And he's right. We've wasted too much time already, and dealing with the injury can't wait. So with trembling fingers I untie the knife, and I set to work on the task at hand.

It's not too hard to slice through fabric, so it doesn't take me long to cut away the tunic from the front of him. The way he's positioned, though, it's a little tricky to get at him, and to do a careful job I have to inch up so close I might as well be sitting in his lap. He must be as aware as I am of how intimate it is, since I'm essentially slowly undressing him. But it can't be helped, and I try not to think about how my breath must feel warming up his skin, or how his bare chest looks with a ribbon of blood trickling down it. Or the distracting way he breathes harder and a shudder shivers through him, when once or twice my hand slips and I nick him. But he doesn't say anything, and I think I make a swift and credible job of it, considering — that is, until to cut away the tunic from his back, I have to pull him forward onto me.

He tries to brace himself, but even so he slumps against me heavily. His arm falls limply forward around me, and his cheek that comes to rest against mine is so cold and slack it's like another gruesome parody — this time, of our last embrace around the crossbow, and I start to feel afraid for him again. It wouldn't be so bad, if he weren't now moaning softly, and if the sculpted muscles of his back as I free them from the tunic didn't look every bit as beautiful to me as they did the night I tended him in front of Brecelyn's fire, slathering lemon balm over him lovingly. Even then, though, I think I would have held myself together. But as I'm removing the last of his shirt, when I pull back the fabric gingerly from his freshly-wounded shoulder, to my dismay what I find staring up at me from underneath it are the marks of the old wound he sustained that night during the fire, when a burning beam fell on him painfully. And then I can't help it. Tears start to well up in my eyes.

I'll be damned if I let them fall, though. So with a yank I rip the shredded tunic away and I plop him back up against the tree, more roughly than I intend.

"Ow! *God damn it*," he swears. Then from under half-closed lids, he fixes me with a hard stare.

"So, what are you waiting for? This arrow isn't going to jump out of me by itself."

"You said you just needed me to cut away your tunic!" I protest, even though I knew it was coming. There's no way a man could cut an arrow out of his own chest.

"Well, I lied," he says bluntly. "But *that* shouldn't surprise you. I'm 'a liar *and* a bully,' remember? So what's it going to be? You've got the knife. You can either stick it in my heart and finish the job you started. Or you can pry out the arrow. It's your choice," and I can see I'm really going to have to do it.

Taran has squeezed his eyes shut, thrown back his head, and he's now thrusting out his chest as though to bare his wound to the blade in a pose so melodramatic he could have borrowed it from Tristan. He looks just like a martyr, preparing for the executioner's blow.

I'm looking wildly around the clearing.

There's nobody. No one is going to come. It is all up to me. But my hands are now shaking so hard and I'm so genuinely frightened, I don't think I can do it.

"*Well?*" Taran demands, opening one eye. "And what in the world are you doing?" he adds rudely, when he sees me sitting here blinking at him furiously.

"If you must know, I'm trying not to *cry*," I snap back tremulously. Then much more softly,

"What if I really hurt you, Taran?"

"You've *already* shot me," he replies. But when my lower lip starts to tremble, he exclaims,

"Oh, for pity's sake! *Gimme*," and with a lurch, he lunges forward and snatches back the knife.

Then he plunges it straight into his own shoulder, and he starts digging around in the wound with it nauseatingly.

He can't see what he's doing, and he's using his left hand. So it's not long before he's made a bloody mess of it. He's gouging away so vigorously and churning the knife's tip around in his pulpy flesh so deeply, I almost think he's being as savage as he can about it just to spite me. But from the way his eyes are glazing over and he's hardly showing any signs of pain, he must also be in shock.

I'm in shock a little, too. At least, I'm too shocked to try to stop him. And even once I come to my senses enough to try to wrest the knife from him, he just keeps hacking around blindly and grunting, "*I can get it by myself, thank you very much. Unlike* some *people,*" while keeping me off with his elbow.

Just when I think I'm going to be sick and that he's going to do himself a serious injury, with a wrench and a scrape of bone and a snarl from Taran, the arrow tip pops free.

After that Taran's spent, and when he falls back exhausted, he lets me take over. Once I've gently pried the knife out of his hand, I make quick work of it to finish ripping up the tunic, and to clean the wound with it.

I was right, and the arrow didn't penetrate far. The wound itself does seem pretty superficial, though all Taran's jabbing at it hasn't helped it any; it's all jagged edges, and it's now bleeding freely. It takes every shred of the tunic to stanch the blood and to get him bandaged up, and from the little chips of bone I pick out of the wound and the stiff way he flinches every time

I wrap the strips around his shoulder, I begin to wonder if the impact of the arrow didn't give him a fracture.

When I suggest it to him, though, Taran just scoffs, "It'd take a stronger archer than you are to break anything in *me*," so I drop it. But I bind him a little tighter, just in case.

Then I sit back to inspect my handiwork, and I'm pleased to see that with the arrow out and his shoulder firmly bound, Taran's already looking much, much better. So I lean in to tuck in one last loose end of the bandage, and as I do I declare in relief, as much for my own sake as for his,

"You're going to be fine, Taran. Just fine." Needless to say, by this time I've started to feel rather bad about the whole thing.

"Of course I'm fine," he says smugly, sounding exactly like his old self again. "It's no more than a scratch, as you said," and I look up at him sharply.

Then I squint at him suspiciously.

He *does* look perfectly fine, and all at once I remember that he's as strong as an ox. And that my bow was only slightly bent.

When he raises his eyebrows and gives me a disingenuously innocent smile, I get it.

Of all the lowdown, dirty tricks! He's been *pretending* this whole time, milking the situation and trying to make me feel guilty.

Sure enough, he now bends down and whispers gleefully in my ear,

"*Oh, Taran! Don't leave me. What will I do if you leave me, Taran? Oh, Taran! Oh, oh!*"

For a second, I seriously consider shooting him again.

Before I can think of something suitably nasty to say to him, just as he's taking another big intake of breath to gather enough hot air to start mimicking me again, instead he coughs, and he flinches. And I feel uncertain. I honestly can't tell if Taran's really fine, or if for some reason he just wants me to think he is.

I settle for asking,

"So, now what? Do you need help getting to your feet?"

"If I *were* going to get up now, I could do it by myself, obviously," he declares. "But right now, what I'm going to do is watch you gather up those rags and bury them, before some animal can get to them," he says, nodding at the blood-soaked scraps of tunic that we used to do his initial clean-up, and making a show of settling in and acting like the only reason he's not going to help me isn't because he's too weak, but because he's enjoying bossing me around. "And then I'm going to sit right here and kick back, and wait for you to come back from St. Sebastian's with a fresh shirt for me."

"You can't mean to try to hide the fact that you've been hurt entirely, can you? You said it yourself, it's only a scratch. You can't really think the master would eliminate you because of it, surely," I protest, wishing again that I had any clue just how serious his injury really is.

"Be that as it may, I have no intention whatsoever of letting anyone at St. Sebastian's find out I've been shot, by a squire. *Tristan's* squire, at that! I'd never hear the end of it. I'd be the laughingstock of the guild. Even more than I am already," and I can't argue with that.

So I do as he bids and I dig a hole, and I throw in all the pieces of his tunic that were too soiled to use to bind him. But when I try to pick up the bloody arrow to toss it in with the rest of the scraps, he grabs it up himself.

"Not so fast. This, I think, I'd better keep for myself. Consider it a souvenir. Or better yet, a little *insurance*. Just in case you get any bright ideas about letting it slip to the master that I'm wounded, now that the proof that *your* master is responsible for it is no longer sticking out of me."

"But he's *not* responsible. *I* shot you. By *accident*. And whatever you might believe about that, surely you can't think I'd knowingly rat out a member?!," but he just twirls the arrow between his fingers at me accusingly.

"Maybe you would and maybe you wouldn't, but we both know *your master* would do it in a heartbeat."

"That's not fair! He never would," I cry. But in point of fact, the first time I met Tristan he was threatening to do just that. I'm actually not entirely sure, and Taran smirks knowingly when he sees it. And I'll admit it. At that moment, the idea of sweeping away Tristan's stiffest competition by ratting out Taran to the master myself is pretty hard to resist.

So I insist hotly, "*He* wants to beat *you* fair and square, too! We *both* do," before Taran can read my thoughts again.

"Only we both know he can't do that, don't we?" he says smugly. "So best not put temptation in *anybody*'s way. So let's get this straight, once and for all. You're not going to say anything about my 'accident,' to anyone, least of all your master. It's going to be another one of our little secrets. And just in case you're tempted to tell or to do something noble to help him, like confess to the crime yourself, remember: if I show this arrow to Guillaume and I put the blame on DuBois, the master will surely believe me. So you're going to do your damnedest to help me conceal my injury, from *everyone*. Have I made myself clear, *Woodcock?*"

I grit my teeth, and reply tersely, "Perfectly."

I'd be a villain to do anything else. Even if it was an accident, I did shoot him.

By the time I've gotten the rags buried it's getting really late, and if I'm going to fetch a clean tunic for Taran from his room in time to make it back afterwards for evening mess, I'm going to have to be quick; Taran might be able to get away with missing meals without having to answer for it, but I don't have that luxury. Only by now I'm so confused about what Taran's condition really is that I feel mighty reluctant to leave him propped against a tree alone in the woods. So before I go, I kneel down briefly next to him.

"Promise you won't wander off," I admonish. "In fact, don't move a muscle until I get back!" and for good measure, I scoot his bow and quiver over closer to him. I don't know exactly what I think he's going to be able to do with them, and the thought troubles me, a little. But I don't have time to stop and think about it now, and anyway when he sees me frowning, Taran snaps,

"I can still shoot just fine, if *that's* what you're thinking. Much better than *you*, anyway," and he grabs my arm, gripping it most painfully.

"Remember, don't let anyone see you," he orders me. "The fewer questions asked, the better. And for God's sake, Marieke, don't tell anyone the truth about what's happened. Do you understand me? Don't tell *anyone*," and from the pointed way he says it, I'm pretty sure he's thinking specifically of someone and he's reluctant to name him. For once, I doubt he's talking mostly about my master. Even Taran knows Remy can't keep a secret for the life of him.

With that I scramble to my feet, and I dart off into the woods, heading back to St. Sebastian's as fast as my legs will carry me. The last thing I see when I cast one last worried glance back over my shoulder is Taran lying wounded in a clearing, with the bloody, broken arrow of Tristan's that I've just shot into him clutched in his fist.

I can hardly believe that only a few short weeks ago, it was a sight I thought I'd dearly love to see.

CHAPTER TWENTY-THREE

All the way back through the woods and over the wall, I'm flying. I'm concentrating so hard on getting back quickly that my mind's a blank, or if I'm thinking anything, it's this:

There had better be no more surprises in store for me today, because really, I think I've had quite enough of them for one day already.

As I dodge my way between the temporary pavilions, I'm still moving fast. Once I get closer to the main buildings, when I start to see some familiar faces among the men moving around in the yard, I slow my pace. I've spotted Falko and Jurian lounging around by the water barrels outside the stables, looking like they've got nothing better to do until evening mess than give a hapless squire a hard time, and I've got to be careful; I've taken Taran's warnings to heart, and I can't afford to waste precious time getting waylaid by any of the boys.

With the Journeys outside the stables, I'm going to have to zip across to the far side of the yard and enter the guild hall proper via the masters' hallway, and it's risky. It'll be bad enough if I run into Tristan and he tries to send me on some errand; it's one thing to keep a secret or two from my master, but I'll be damned if I'm going to start lying to him directly, for *Taran's* sake. But if one of the masters should spot me and give me a direct order, it'll be a disaster. Not even I could lie my way out of obeying.

There's nothing for it, so I put my head down, and with a glance all around I scurry across the yard and make straight for the side door of the guild; the whole way my are nerves jangling and I'm alternately muttering to myself under my breath, *"how in the heck could I have been so careless as to get myself into this mess?"* and *"if he'd just have gone for a bathe with the others like a normal boy, none of this would have happened!"*

Once I'm inside the guild building proper, I trot warily along, moving as quickly as I dare without risking attracting undue attention (particularly when I have to slip past the open barracks door) and all the while I have my ears open and I'm on my guard for any sign of the boys.

That must be why it catches my attention so clearly, when a quiet, determined voice comes floating out into the hallway to me from behind one of the closed doors. That, and the fact that right as I'm passing, the voice is saying,

"It can't come off before Firsts, that much is certain. But we've got to be ready to spring into action when the time comes. The hitch of it is, it can't happen here at St. Sebastian's."

It's so much like the ominous words I overheard in the masters' corridor last year about the plot at Thirds that despite my hurry, I grind to a halt. Then I take an involuntary step closer, all thought of Taran and his tunic momentarily forgotten, as the voice continues,

"It's got to be done at the castle. I see no way around that. But finding a suitable opportunity to provide the necessary cover for an undertaking as audacious as this is going to be virtually impossible. And if we're not careful, it won't be just our own fellow Guildsmen we have to watch out for. We're likely to bring half the King's Guard down on us."

"My dear fellow! *You* worry about the logistics. Leave access and opportunity to *me*," a second voice replies silkily, and I don't wait to hear anything more.

The voices are coming closer, and the sound of boots creaking on the floorboards right on the other side of the door brings me to my senses. I don't duck into the shadow of an open doorway to lie in wait for the men as they come out so I can discover who they are, and not just because I'm in a desperate hurry. This time, I don't assume I've just overheard a pack of traitors, or that what the men were talking about was some new plot against our prince. Because for once, I'm absolutely sure I have recognized some voices accurately.

I'm already in the *Journey* hallway, and the room whose door I'm standing next to belongs to Gilles. One of the voices was unmistakably his.

And the other voice was Tristan's.

Whatever they were talking about, right now I don't really want to know.

Any minute Gilles will be opening his door, and I can't let the boys find me here. So I turn around and I run back along the corridors the same way I came, feeling mighty frustrated, for a variety of reasons. Under the circumstances, though, I guess I can't feel too indignant about this unpleasant confirmation that my master has been keeping a few secrets of his own, from me.

I stop to catch my breath again out behind one of the temporary tents, and I regroup. So, waltzing straight into Taran's room in the middle of the afternoon was not a good idea. There's no telling who might be behind the doors of any of the Journey rooms. For all I know, Remy's in Taran's room right now, sitting cross-legged on his cot and waiting for him. It wouldn't do me any good to get caught sneaking out of Taran's room with my arms full of his clothing, either. If nothing else, I'd surely end up getting branded as a

307

thief again. I'm going to have to get a tunic for Taran from somewhere else. But *where*?

It's probably not really that hard of a problem, but after the afternoon I've been having, I think it's understandable that I'm not at my best. So when I see the hulking Master Bernard out past the butts torturing some workmen, I seriously consider running over and asking him to lend me the shirt right off his back, or begging one from some other bulky passing veteran. I'm just stepping out from around the side of the tent to go out and do it, in fact, when as I'm looking around for a likely candidate, luckily I see something much better instead.

A familiar little head is now peeking out around the other side of the tent. Someone else has been concealing himself out here, too, and he's now peering out towards the stables with an anxious expression. It's Frans, no doubt hiding from Falko, and I've never been so glad to see him. Or that his master wears a very large size in shirts.

"*Psst!* Frans! Over here," I whisper, beckoning the boy over urgently. It's true that Taran told me not to mention what happened to anyone. But fortunately for me, Frans does anything I ask of him without question.

Sure enough, seconds later Frans is scampering off toward the guild hall, skirting around in a wide loop to avoid his master by the stables, and I'm leaning back against the canvas of the tent and indulging in a moment's relief while Frans nips inside to fetch me a tunic of Falko's.

It's not long before I'm craning my neck around the side of the tent again, scanning the yard impatiently for any sign of Frans returning. With nothing to do myself now but wait I'm getting antsy, and I've started to imagine all sorts of things: back in the woods Taran could be slowly bleeding out, or a pack of wolves could be attacking him. Soon I'm picking furiously at my fingers, and irrationally enough, just the fact that I feel so worried about Taran is starting to make me annoyed at him.

As it happens, from where I'm standing I can only get a partial view back to the guild entrance. But I do have a clear view of a place out behind the kitchens that's notorious as a trysting place. The bolder of the kitchen staff use it all the time, and it was a favorite amongst the Journeys, too, before the master's dire warnings against dalliances with the maids. It's the very spot, in fact, where I chanced to see Tristan earlier this fall with his hand quite far up a kitchen maid's skirt, though at the time he tried to deny it. But Tristan's not the only boy who's used it, for the very reason that it isn't visible from most places in the yard.

Except, it would seem, from this one.

There's a couple there now, and from my particular vantage they're so exposed and their activity is so flagrant that it can't help catching my attention. One of the boys has a kitchen maid backed up against the wall in just the way Tristan did that day, but that's not what most catches my eye. It's that even from a distance and from the back, I recognize him. Of all things, it *is* Tristan. He's bracing himself against the wall with one arm over the girl's head, and from the looks of it he's leaning against her heavily and nuzzling the side of her neck.

I could have sworn I just heard him back in the Journey hallway! How in the world did he get out there so quickly? And I don't even want to know how he's gotten so far with the girl so fast.

Even for Tristan, it's impossible. Unless he really has perfected the art of being in two places at once, the voice I heard just minutes ago wasn't his. I wouldn't have thought I could mistake a voice I know and love so well, though; at least, surely not even I could mistake *Gilles's*. And I guess that explains it: I simply assumed a boy Gilles would be talking to was Tristan, and now I can't help feeling a little indignant that while I've been busy shooting Taran, *this* is what Tristan's been doing.

It's the strangest thing, too, but I even feel a little twinge of indignation at him, for Melissande's sake. I mean, I'm sure Tristan just sees it as more of his investigations. But I think she really loves him, and after all, she is my sister.

Before I can feel too irritated with him, the couple breaks apart. And when the boy turns around and with a satisfied stretch starts to mosey in my direction, to my surprise I see that it isn't Tristan. It's Remy, and I've been wrong about the whole thing.

I suppose I've made *that* mistake before. But it's still embarrassing, and I have the grace to feel ashamed of myself for thinking so badly of Tristan, and for leaping to such a swift conclusion about what the couple was doing, just because I thought the boy was him. There must be some innocent explanation, since Remy's never shown the slightest interest in girls; in fact, he's never done anything but run when any of the maids have shown an interest in him. But I can't really think of any, and I'm puzzling over it so intently that I only realize too late that if I have a clear view of Remy, then he must have a clear view of *me*.

He's spotted me and he's now trotting over, not looking the least bit self-conscious even though it must be obvious that I've been watching him. I can't pretend I haven't seen him, either, from the friendly way he's now hailing me. There's nothing for me to do but wait for him to come over, trying not to hear Taran's sarcastic voice inside my head, chastising me.

"Why, whatever are you doing way out here, Marek?" Remy asks me brightly, adjusting his tunic a little.

"Oh, I'm, *er*, just waiting here, for Frans," I trill. "And here he is!" just as Frans comes beetling up from the other direction, carrying one of Falko's big tunics balled up in his arms.

"What are you guys doing *out here*, though?" Remy persists, eyeing the wad of clothing curiously, and I look wildly around. We must be only a few yards away from the temporary tent that's now being used to house the fletchers and bowyers, so I say,

309

"We're on our way to the shop. Yes, that's it! And we're taking these, uh, *old rags* out to Marcel, to use for oiling bows and things."

I cringe a bit as I say it, since from the looks of it the tunic that Frans has pilfered from his master is one of Falko's very best. So before Remy can make further inquiry, I preempt him.

"What were *you* doing, Remy, out behind the kitchens?"

"Me?" he replies sweetly. "Why, I was just helping out one of the girls. The kitchen fires can be *so* sooty! She had a bit of grit in her eye, Marek. I'm sure *you* know just how irritating that can be."

It's not a very good lie. I ought to know; I've used it myself, on him. And from Remy's tone, I don't think he expects me to believe it. But I don't press him about it. The last thing I want to do is prolong our conversation, and it *did* look an awful lot like he was kissing that girl, most vigorously. So I know what Remy's telling me. My rejection of him this morning hurt him more than he let on, and if he was taking a page out of his master's book, I drove him to it. I can hardly blame him for seeking a little physical comfort when he couldn't have the one he really wanted. Not when the one he really wanted was *me*.

"Headed to the shop, you say?" he drawls. "I might as well tag along, and then we can all go in for supper together," and I've got a bigger problem than being responsible for Remy's degeneracy. I'd thought the lie about the shop was a pretty good one, but instead it's only served to trap me. There'll be no subtle way to shake Remy now, since I can't flat out refuse to let him come along. And if I know Remy, no matter what I say he's going to stick to me.

Evening is falling and the temperature is dropping, and the tunic I need is in Frans's hands right in front of me. All my nerves are screaming just to grab it and run off into the woods with it, but of course I can't. If I let Remy follow me, Taran'll kill me. I can't go along to the shop with Remy and hand over Falko's tunic as a rag, either. So the three of us just stand there, looking around at each other expectantly. It goes on so long it starts to be absurd, and just when I think I'm going to have to relent, tell Remy everything and damn the consequences, seeing my wild-eyed expression Frans pipes up hastily,

"Actually, I've just remembered. Taran's looking for you, Remy. The last I saw him he was out in the garden, and he looked pretty mad," and Remy has no choice but to hasten off with a frown in search of his master.

Frans and I stand side by side watching him go just long enough to be sure he's really leaving, and I'm not sure what Frans is thinking. But as we prepare to part ways, what I'm thinking is this: when Remy does eventually find his master, I hope he doesn't notice that what he's got on is the rag of Falko's that Frans is now putting into my hands.

"You know something, Frans?" I say, once Remy's out of sight and I'm taking the garment from him gratefully. "You're shaping up to be an excellent squire."

"I'm learning from the best, *master!*" he replies, as he scampers away.

I gather up the tunic tightly in my arms, turn around, and I set out for the woods at a dead run.

I only make it about fifteen feet, before an authoritative voice hails me.

"Hu-*llo* there, Marek!" it calls.

And I ignore it. I just keep running.

Or at least I try to. But the owner of the voice soon steps out of a tent directly in front of me. It's Marcel, the head fletcher; I was right that the workshop tent is close by, and my route has led me right past it. Marcel must have seen me coming through one of its open flaps.

"Fancy chancing upon you out here at this hour. What perfect timing! Whoa, hold up there a second, squire," he exclaims, and I'm forced to grind to a halt again. I can't very well refuse him; even if I wanted to, he's blocking my way.

"I've got a favor to ask of you, actually, Marek."

"You got it!" I croak automatically. "Whatever it is, can we hash it all out later, though? As it happens, I'm in a terrible hurry."

"Of course, of course! So here's the situation," he replies obliviously. "What with the expansion, the master's bringing in a big batch of new fletchers. I could use some help getting them up to speed on the routine here at St. Sebastian's."

"Whatever you need, no problem!" I repeat, trying to dart past and ready to agree to anything, just to get away. Only the tents are awfully close together and I can't get around him in the narrow space.

"Plus, there's one who's a bit of a special case. No experience at all! But his father was a friend of the master's. Poor boy, seems his father died in the plague."

"Sure, sure, *splendid.* Glad to help. It's a plan!" I rave, feeling a rush of relief as I manage to duck past him — when just as I'm almost away, he slaps me on the back, getting a grip on my tunic in the process.

"As it happens, the lad's here now!" he exclaims. "Mess'll be starting any minute, but there should just be time. Why not take a second to meet him?"

I don't care what Marcel makes of it. The empty field beyond is beckoning and I can't let myself get stuck again — not if Marcel's right about the time. So I bolt. With a strangled cry that's half an apology and half a whinny of hysteria, I twist out of Marcel's grip and without a word of explanation I gallop off at breakneck speed, heading straight for the back guild wall. I don't look back but I can imagine what Marcel's expression must be, since the last thing I hear is his bewildered voice calling after me,

"Goodness, son! If you didn't want to meet him now, all you had to do was say so."

I DASH BACK ACROSS THE FAR FIELD, HOPING HARD THAT Marcel was wrong about the lateness of the hour, and wondering what I can say to Tristan if he was right, and I end up getting back for mess hopelessly late. I've got a funny feeling, too, that I wasn't listening closely enough to the things the head fletcher was saying. Now I'm not at all sure *what* I've just promised him.

It's sure to be some thankless chore I didn't need, but it's not until I'm scrambling over the crumbling back wall, in my haste bumping and scraping my knees against its rough, loose bricks, that the obvious hits me:

Unless a cut on his shoulder has somehow mysteriously left Taran unable to walk, there's no reason he couldn't have simply waited for his tunic right outside the guild. That he's making me go all the way back out into the middle of the woods again when curfew is almost upon us must be his way of getting some not-so-subtle revenge on me for the whole incident.

Maybe I don't think badly enough of him anymore to believe he'd blackmail me into any serious harm. But I bet he's going to revel in forcing me into more petty tasks and in generally jerking me around — particularly if it puts me at odds with my master. He's *already* doing it, in fact, and it's frustrating; almost as frustrating as his uncanny ability to keep making me feel guilty, when he's the one who's really been behaving badly all winter.

I mean, *I* shot him entirely by accident. *He* shot Tristan on purpose.

Soon I've remembered all the reasons I was pretending to shoot Taran this afternoon in the first place, and by the time I'm over the wall I'm cursing Taran *and* his tunic. As I race my way back through the woods, I'm craning my neck and squinting up through the trees, worriedly trying to get a glimpse of the sun to gauge the time, while along with the pounding of my footsteps I'm repeating the refrain *"it's fine, it's fine. It's all going to be fine,"* and trying to shake off the feeling that I could be running frantically through Brecelyn's woods again, in the *wrong* direction. But before long, despite myself what I'm really chanting is *"he's fine, he's fine. He's going to be just fine,"* and soon I've forgotten all about Tristan, the time, and my promise to Marcel. Or if a little beat of uncertainty is still drumming somewhere in the back of my brain about it, all trace of it is wiped away when I burst back into the clearing, only to find Taran lying dead under the tree.

He's slumped down all the way onto the ground, and as soon as I see him, I rush over and I throw myself down onto him bodily. Fumbling Falko's wadded-up tunic out of my way I lift his head into my lap, and as I wrap my arms around him, I gulp in a huge gasp of air in preparation of letting out an ear-splitting wail — just as Taran lets out a terrific snore. He's not dead, he's simply succumbed to exhaustion and he's sound asleep. So I jostle him roughly awake instead, feeling ridiculously relieved.

That is, until I notice that the bandages around his chest are wet and sticky with blood. He's already bled through the strips of his tunic we used as bandages; I should have known the butcher's job he did on himself would bleed profusely.

"How could you *fall asleep*, Taran?" I demand, as Taran slowly comes awake and I help him shift himself back up into a sitting position against the trunk of the tree. "You could have been eaten by a bear, or something! And you've let these bindings all get soaked," I scold, as though he could have done anything to stop it. "Now what are we supposed to do? You'll surely bleed through onto this tunic of Falko's before you're halfway back to St. Sebastian's. How are we going to hide that? I can't give this back to Frans covered in blood."

"Perhaps if you hadn't left me waiting out here for so long with nothing but a knife to entertain me, I wouldn't have been tempted to sleep. Just what do you suggest I should have done while you were gone? Communed with nature? Composed a sonnet?"

"You could have whittled your fiancée another unicorn," I suggest dryly. "Or written her a love letter. Apparently you don't even need any paper to do that."

"As it happens," he says back, "I have been composing a little something for her, while I wait. Would you like to hear it?," and before I can stop him, he clears his throat and recites,

"*Roses are red, violets are blue. Your lover's squire shot me, and left me to die in the woods.*"

I don't bother to point out that it doesn't rhyme.

"I don't suppose it occurred to *you* to bring back more binding material with you," he says smartly, once he's done with his poem and as I'm trying to reposition the soiled rags over his wound without much success.

"As it happens, I had a devil of a time getting just this."

I sit back, and look at the rearranged bandages with disfavor. "Well, we're just going to have to hope that holds long enough for you to sneak back into your room and find something else. That is, unless you've got a handy length of fabric squirreled away on you somewhere."

To my immense surprise, a guilty look flits across his features.

"You *do!* Well, why in the heck didn't you say so sooner? Where is it?"

Silence.

Somewhere in the woods, a bird chirps.

"In my quiver," he finally grumbles. But he doesn't meet my eyes, and either his color is returning or I'd swear he's blushing.

I can't imagine what he could possibly be carrying around in his quiver that would be at all useful — although I suppose he does take good care of his equipment, and he could have a cloth to wrap a bow or something. So I shift around to reach his quiver and I stick my hand in, curious as to what he could have in there that's gotten him so embarrassed.

As soon as I shove my hand down into the bottom of it and my fingers feel something soft and filmy, I figure it out. I don't have to pull it out to know it's going to be sea-foam green.

"Her *veil?!*" I cry, snatching it out and holding it up in front of him accusingly, and shaking it under his nose a little. "What in the world were you going to do with this, alone at the *millpond*? No, wait. I don't want to know."

I never bothered asking Taran what *he* was doing out in the woods, since it was obvious enough: he must have waited until he saw the boys returning from the pond, before heading out for his own chance to bathe. It was just my bad luck (and his) that he took the same circuitous route that I did in order to avoid meeting any stragglers along the path.

"Or do you carry it with you now everywhere? How touching."

I've said it as tauntingly as I can, but by now Taran's gotten over his embarrassment about being caught with the garment, and he just says,

"And in the event, fortuitous."

"Wait a minute. You can't be suggesting that I tie *this* around you?"

"Why not? It worked for DuBois," he replies, and I don't know why. But I don't like the comparison. Or the thought of Melissande's token strapped around him. Surely, though, that's not why I say,

"If it gets blood on it, it'll ruin it."

"Fine. Then give me *your* binding, and *you* put this on instead," and I like it even less. But a stain of blood is already showing through the bandage on his shoulder, time is wasting, and we've got to use something. So when he says, "Actually, the dampness of that binding of yours will probably do my wound some good, and make the bandaging tighter. Say, just how did you get so wet?" I relent.

When I start wriggling around and pulling my arms inside my tunic, however, and preparing to undress, instead of averting his gaze like a gentleman he makes a show of stretching out, putting his arm on his uninjured side up behind his head, and settling in with the air of a man preparing to enjoy himself thoroughly. And when I snap,

"Aren't you going to close your eyes at least?" he gives me a fair imitation of one of Jurian's leers.

"Why should I? You didn't mind letting me watch you strip it off the *last* time, and I'm having a rough day. You owe me a little entertainment," so with a snort, I turn my back on him.

He's right that there's no point in false modesty, though, and time is passing. So instead of darting off into the woods to change, I simply I shrug out of my tunic and I undo my bindings right there in the middle of the clearing.

My back is turned and he can't really see anything anyway. But the whole time I can feel his eyes on me, and there's something intimate about this, too, although I'm not sure what it is. Nobody's ever watched me getting dressed before, and for a moment when my binding is off and

I've not yet strapped the veil on in its stead, I feel awfully small and vulnerable.

I pause like that for a moment, somehow not wanting to put on the veil, and when Taran sees me hesitating, he asks,

"What is it? What's the matter?" and a crowd of things rush into my mind that I want to say to him. But I can't say any of them, and as I run my hand over the soft fabric, instead I hear myself mutter under my breath:

"So you *do* appreciate a lovely face, to want to set it off, with this."

Thankfully, Taran doesn't hear it. At least he doesn't say anything, and soon for better or worse I've gotten the veil fastened in place and my tunic back on, and we're both silent as I make quick work of it to add my damp binding to the wrappings around his shoulder and chest. Taran's awfully tense, though, and I suppose it could just be discomfort. But I get the impression he's debating something with himself, and as I'm tucking under the last edge of the binding and I'm patting it down to make sure it's all securely in place, with a frustrated jerk of his head suddenly he lurches forward to grasp my shoulder, and in a rough voice he says:

"Was this all about what I said at squires' club, Marieke?! Is *that* it? If it is, damn it all, you've got to understand —"

And I cut him off. I'm in no mood to hear any more of the same excuses I've already heard from Remy. Not from him. Not with his veil strapped around my chest.

I think I could stand anything, except to have to hear him mention to me directly the scars on my face.

"It was an *accident*," I insist. "If you must know, I was pretending that stump over there was you. *That's* what I was yelling at. That's what I was *aiming* at."

"Well, you missed it by a mile," he says shortly, and it's annoying. But not nearly as annoying as what he says next.

"All right, Marieke. If you say so. *I* believe you."

The way he says it, it sounds a lot more like an accusation than forgiveness.

Once I've helped Taran into Falko's tunic, he insists on getting to his feet by himself. He makes a pretty easy job of it, although the expression on his face as he does it is quite grim. I can't tell if it's because he's in pain, though, or if he's simply recovered enough to start feeling rather angry at me about the whole mess. And as he's grabbing up his bow and quiver, he demands in a tone so thick with resentment that not even his habitual sarcasm can mask it,

"So, is that something you do often, then? Run around the woods shooting at things and shouting abuse at them, and pretending that they're me?"

"No, not *often*," I snap back. "Only occasionally."

With a loud *humph*, he shoulders the quiver, and he starts to stride off out of the clearing with no apparent difficulty, rolling his uninjured shoulder as though to suggest that he's shrugging off the unpleasant episode and that he has no more to say to me. I'm just about to hasten after him, when I see it.

He's left the bloody arrow lying under the tree.

"Well, are you coming or not?" he demands, turning back for a moment. When he sees me staring down at the arrow, he says nastily,

"I don't really need that, do I? You'll keep my secret, won't you, *Marek*?" and from the way he emphasizes the name, I know what he means.

He's reminding me that he's never told anyone *my* secret, and he's right. He doesn't need Tristan's arrow to have a hold over me. It's funny, but somehow, I'd managed to forget all about that. Now it makes me feel a little strange to realize that he's had leverage against me all this time, and he's never used it.

Well, whatever kept him from abusing his power before, now that he thinks I've purposely shot him he can't help but feel quite differently. Making me fetch him a tunic all the way out here was surely only the beginning.

As though reading my thoughts again, Taran sneers,

"I won't be needing any more help from *you*," and with another irritated jerk of his head he proceeds to stalk off into the woods without a backward glance.

I'm pretty sure he's wrong. I know better than anyone the difficulty of concealment, and with a sinking feeling I know if Taran does need help, I'm going to have to give it to him, for one simple reason:

If Tristan's to have any hope of winning us the glorious future together that I've envisioned, I can't let it be built on a dirty shot, from *me*.

And so I hasten back through the woods to St. Sebastian's, trotting along behind Taran's stiff back at a discrete distance and wondering nervously just what this turn of events is going to end up meaning for me. I try to tell myself it won't mean being disloyal to Tristan, and that right now, a squire who's willing to help Taran is exactly the one Tristan needs. But Taran's sure to try to turn the situation to his advantage somehow, and only one thing's certain: sooner or later there's going to be a price to pay, and I can't let Tristan be the one who pays it.

It wouldn't be so bad, though, if I weren't absolutely sure that for reasons of his own, Taran's still trying to deceive me about the extent of his injury. Only for the life of me, I can't tell whether it's because his wound is more serious than he's been letting on — or *less*.

CHAPTER TWENTY-FOUR

Taran doesn't look back or speak to me again all the way back to St. Sebastian's, and once we round the corner into the Journey hallway he disappears into his room and slams the door. He's got to change before supper but he doesn't ask for my help, and I don't offer any. Instead I hasten straight on inside in search of the others, and mercifully I find them all still gathered outside the great hall waiting for the mess doors to open. I've cut it extremely close, but I'm not late; in the anxiety of the moment all the things this afternoon that seemed to be taking forever must have in reality been the work of minutes.

I spot Tristan right away, where he's lounging in the center of a group of Journeys. He's leaning back against the wall and chatting away with Gilles and Jerome, and it can't be more than an hour since last I saw him. He looks exactly as he did then, too: charming, handsome, and carefree — his usual old self. But to me it feels like a lot more time has passed, and as he greets me casually, between my shooting of Taran, his plotting with Gilles, and the present location of Melissande's veil, I can't help but feel that the secrets between us are starting to pile up.

"There you are, Marek! You weren't out in the woods this whole time, were you?" Tristan scolds, when he sees I'm still in my damp tunic. "What *can* you have been doing? You promised me you wouldn't linger."

I don't bother to tell him that I also said I wouldn't do anything foolish, and I didn't keep that promise either.

"Why, the lad must have been out shooting himself more *stumps*," Gilles drawls, and thankfully just then the mess hall doors swing open, and my recent whereabouts are forgotten in the ensuing stampede.

I load up a plate for Tristan from the sideboard, and it's such a relief to have the stressful afternoon behind me and to lose myself in routine that it's not until I'm settling in a little later with my own plate next to Tristan that I notice we're one short at table. Remy's nowhere to be seen. That's when I notice Taran's still not shown up, either.

I cast a glance back toward the open doorway with a frown; it's not like

Taran to be late, and even wounded it really shouldn't be taking him this long to put on a fresh shirt. Sure enough, Remy is there, hovering right outside the room and peering off down the hallway anxiously, as though on the lookout for the approach of his master. I'm still watching Remy when Poncellet saunters past him on his own way in for supper, so when Poncellet pauses for a moment to talk to him, I see it — and the reluctant way Remy ducks his head. Soon Remy's disappearing from sight and Poncellet is strolling past behind us whistling, and I can't resist. I lean back on the bench to inquire of him casually,

"Something wrong with Mellor, *master?*"

"You squires must have run him ragged!" Poncellet stops to chuckle. "He's all in. Popped his head out of his door just now as I was passing, to 'respectfully request' me to send his squire on to the kitchens. The poor lad'll be taking his meal in there with the servants, since his master told me in no uncertain terms that he's going to 'forego his own dinner,' and that he *'doesn't want to be disturbed for anything'.*"

Poncellet's captured Taran's imperious tone to perfection, and he's seen nothing amiss with him. And frankly, it wouldn't be the first time he's skipped the supposedly mandatory meal on what was essentially a whim. So I simply assume Taran's wisely decided to rest up for the night away from the prying eyes of his squire and I don't think any more of it, and anyway, seeing Poncellet has reminded me of something. So I nudge Tristan, and when the others aren't listening, I tell him in a low voice that I need to talk to him right after supper on a matter of the utmost urgency.

"Say, you really *did* get something out of the old man this afternoon, didn't you, Marek?" Tristan whispers to me admiringly, when before he moseys off Poncellet reaches down and cuffs the back of my head, almost affectionately. "I don't know what it is about you, kid," he grins, shaking his head. "I've never seen a boy who had such a talent for managing the masters."

I suspect it's the simple fact that I'm not really a boy at all, but for obvious reasons I don't say so to him.

It's been a long day and we're all tired, so it's not surprising that most of the talk over dinner consists of the boys trying to outdo each other in complaining, none louder than Jerome. He's usually the easiest-going of the group, but now that he's been put to work he had to miss out on our trip to the millpond, and spending the afternoon in a sweltering office elbow-deep in stacks of dusty guild ledgers has left him unusually disgruntled. As the meal gets underway, while Charles is grumbling,

"Try building a forge from scratch under the hot sun all day," Jerome is grousing loudly,

"Seriously, boys. If I'd known what I was getting myself into, I'd never have taken this job. What a mess! Even through my *occhiale* old Master Gheeraert's scribbling is harder to decipher than a chicken's scratching, and I swear half his sums don't add up. From the looks of it, he spent more time in doodling in the margins of the books than in balancing them. Why, his entries are in such disarray you'd almost think the guild's been *losing* money, rather than making it! The old boy must have been going senile. Either that or he was skimming off the top, and covering for it by feigning incompetency," he declares, and I wonder what they'd all say if *I* chimed in and described my afternoon to them. Nobody could be having a worse day than I am. Well, except maybe for Taran. But I don't want to think about him, though I'm not really paying much attention to the boys' babble, either — not even when Tristan rather alarmingly suggests that Jerome smuggle one of the guild ledgers into mess some evening, so all the boys can get a good look at it. Instead, I'm trying to focus on what I should have been doing all afternoon, and I'm thinking through how to present the idea that came to me out by the millpond to Tristan, diplomatically.

I'm not paying any attention to the conversation at table, that is, until right as Tristan's saying,

"Just slip it into your lute case or something, Jerome," Poncellet wanders back past behind us.

He's ostensibly on his way to snag another jug of wine from the masters' sideboard, but there are kitchen boys to wait on him and he doesn't need to serve himself. So when he pauses right behind Tristan with an exaggerated air of having just remembered something, I'm pretty sure whatever he's about to come out with now is the real reason he's back here again. Sure enough, soon he's striking one of his jocular poses designed to attract all eyes to him.

"Say *Slick*," he exclaims, when he's sure he's gotten everyone's full attention. "It must have slipped my mind earlier, but Mellor had a message he wanted me to give to *you*, too. He seemed most anxious that I get the wording of it correct. Now, what *did* he say, exactly?," and he looks up at the ceiling and purses his lips, pretending to think about it for a minute, although I'm sure he remembers it well enough — just as I'm sure he purposely held off delivering Taran's message so he could give it a bigger build-up, when he delivers the punchline:

"Ah, yes! He told me to be sure to tell you that this afternoon, it was *your* squire who was a *bloody* pain in his *neck!*"

The whole table erupts in laughter, and Tristan in particular finds the fact that I've managed to irritate Taran enough to make him lose his usual composure uproariously funny. But I'm not laughing, and I can't even appreciate the irony of it when Tristan slaps me on the back and declares appreciatively,

"Ha, Marek! You must have really gotten under his skin."

"Yeah, you had to see it to believe it," Rennie calls down to Tristan, as Poncellet moseys off and leaves the boys to appreciate his delivery. "Stupidest thing *I've* ever seen, but gutsy, I'll give him that. Why, he got right up in Taran's face and *challenged* him, didn't he, boys? Then insulted him to boot, right in the middle of a formal line-up! Belittled his shooting *and* his training. And in front of a *master*."

"For a moment, I even feared Taran was going to let Master Poncellet thrash him for insubordination," Pascal agrees. "In the end of course he didn't, and instead he stepped in and put a stop to it."

"Hey Marek, that makes *two* whippings Mellor's saved you from now, doesn't it?" Rennie pipes in again, and the boys all laugh even harder. But a cold feeling is stirring in the pit of my stomach, and it's only partly because the way the squires are describing what happened at squires' club is not at all as I remember it. They all think Poncellet's pronouncement was just more of the boys' usual antagonism. But I knew instantly what Taran was really saying.

His wound's come open again, and badly. And he can't do anything about it, all by himself.

Since squires can't leave mess before their masters, until the boys decide to get up from table, I can't do anything about it, either.

Around me, the boys have started up their chatter again. I'm picturing Taran sitting on his cot, with a growing stain of blood seeping through Falko's tunic.

How in the heck can he have come undone, already?

I was fully expecting Taran to need my help again, eventually. But I didn't think it would be *tonight*, and I had thought I'd bound him up quite tightly. Now in my mind's eye I see him tangled in strips of soiled linen, impatiently trying to redo his bandages for himself but finding it impossible, and tearing his wound open again in the process. Then I picture Remy or one of the others opening his door to check on him, and I've never been sorrier that the Journey rooms have no locks.

Well, almost never.

And I'll admit it. I have one moment of pure, unadulterated panic.

Then I get it.

The wound really *didn't* look that bad. Taran must *already* be taking advantage of the opportunity to harass me.

I suspected as much, didn't I? Now I picture Taran on his cot again, this time sprawled out with one big arm behind his head, perfectly fine and waiting with a self-satisfied smirk on his face to taunt me when I burst into his room frantically. It's such a convincing image I can almost hear his smug voice mocking me, *"I'm a liar* and *a bully, remember?"* But the devil of it is, I *do* feel frantic, and every time I glance up across the table to see Falko chewing open-mouthed, I feel a little queasy. He's rooting around greedily in a slab of pulpy meat with the tip of his knife, and I can't help staring at the juicy pool of blood that's forming in the bottom of his plate rather desperately. As long as there's any chance Taran really is in trouble, I can't ignore his plea.

After that the rest of mess is a blur, and I'm not sure what I'm thinking.

Except that I'm not thinking about convincing Tristan to tweak his trick anymore. So when at last Tristan pushes back on the bench and rises to his feet much sooner after finishing his own meal than expected, I don't question it, even though he's usually one of the boys most likely to linger after supper. I'm on my feet like a shot next to him, my legs shaking beneath me and an excuse for why I'm about to bolt off on my own as soon as we're out the door already on my lips.

Before I can get any of my words out, Tristan leans forward dramatically and puts his hands flat on the table. It's a move I recognize, a deliberate imitation of the master, and to my dismay I know what it means: Tristan's not leaving. He's gearing up to address the boys, and when he proceeds to clear his throat and demand in his best top-of-the-wall voice,

"Jerome's already made his report, boys. Who's next?," there's nothing for me to do but plop back down onto the bench. Tonight of all nights, Tristan's decided to follow up on his proposal of having the boys all share the results of their supposed investigations into the plot at Thirds last year. I doubt it was Jerome's grousing about the guild books that prompted him, though; I'm paying the wages of my own sins again, since Tristan's surely chosen tonight to reintroduce the topic precisely because Taran's not here.

None of the boys has anything even vaguely useful to report, of course. I doubt any of them even remembered about Tristan's plan, until now. But they all love nothing better than to hear themselves talk, and I know it's going to be interminable waiting through their recitations, even before we all suffer through a long-winded story of Falko's about a drinking game with some of the Kingsmen that nearly ended in a riot. *"Next time, those no-brain, no-talents will think twice before claiming their captain Hieronymous has more clout with the regent than Master Guillaume, I can tell you that!"* he barks happily, and when Jurian confirms, *"Some of them'll be lucky to think* once, *after the way DeBruyn here pounded 'em into the ground!,"* the boys all give Falko a cheer. Ordinarily I'd probably be enjoying it, but tonight's it's just excruciating, a ridiculous waste of time, and Tristan in particular seems bent on dragging it out. He's making a show of taking it all very seriously and nodding along thoughtfully as the boys are talking, even interrupting now and then to ask a question or two about things as trivial as gossip from Gilles's tailor.

To make matters worse, by the time even the most loquacious of them are running out of increasingly silly things to say and I'm assuming it's finally coming to an end, Jurian demands,

"What about *you*, DuBois? Don't tell me you fished all afternoon out by the millpond and didn't catch anything."

I'd forgotten about Tristan's turn, and he's usually the biggest attention-hog of the bunch. To have introduced the topic so deliberately, he's sure to have a long oration of his own all planned out. The other boys assume so, too; they start shifting around as though preparing to settle in and be thoroughly entertained, and I'm shifting around, too — restlessly.

Instead of launching into a performance of his own, however, to everyone's surprise Tristan clamps his mouth shut. And from the way he gives Jurian the evil eye, it's apparent that the question's annoyed him.

"*I* can tell you, Jurian, if Tristan's unwilling," Gilles drawls, when it's clear that Tristan doesn't intend to answer; apparently Gilles wasn't as asleep this afternoon by the pond as I'd thought. "Don't pout, DuBois! Full disclosure. That was *your* idea, remember? Now where was I? Oh yes. According to some of the older veterans, St. Sebastian's isn't the only place Master Poncellet's made a habit of it to turn up when he's down on his luck. Rumor has it he's also been known to scrounge up work at Brecelyn's castle, over the years."

Nobody has to ask what kind of work. There's really only one kind for which a man with Poncellet's particular talents is suited or for which a man like Sir Brecelyn would hire him, and that's dirty work.

"Who's to say *when* that was, Gilles?" Tristan shoots back; he admires Poncellet, and from his frown I can tell he doesn't want to think such an extraordinary butts man could be a villain. "For all we know, he hasn't worked for Brecelyn for years. Where was he this winter, for example? *Not* at the castle. And if Poncellet'd been involved in the events at Thirds, surely he'd have been the one taking the shots into the stands from the tower, not a huntsman like Beaufort," Tristan says, and Gilles has to concede the point. "Besides, the men also said Poncellet had a major falling out with Brecelyn. That could well have happened ages ago."

"A falling out, over some nasty business," Gilles interjects pointedly.

"He must have found out one of Brecelyn's big buddies these days is *Brian de Gilford!*" Aristide quips. "Talk about nasty business."

"Nah, Ari. We're talking about *Poncellet* here," Falko chortles back. "Whaddya wanna bet old Poncey was fooling around with *Brecelyn's* wife, too?! Everybody says she was a real looker," and as the boys' discussion degenerates into jokes, under the table I start poking Tristan, trying to get his attention.

During the boys' exchange, my eyes have involuntarily flitted up over Falko's head and past him to the massive painting of St. Sebastian. The precise placement of the arrows depicted in it rending the giant body overhead has never bothered me more or made me more desperate to get out from under its shadow — since one of the arrows now looks to me to be lodged painfully in the Saint's bloody clavicle. That's bad enough. But I don't really need to see it sticking out of the base of the Saint's throat to be reminded of the one piece of business of Sir Brecelyn's which was to me by far his nastiest, or for which he could well have needed the help of a henchman who was a remarkable shot. And after this afternoon, I guess I don't want to think Poncellet a villain, either. At least, I'd rather believe he helped my father devise an impossible trick than that he helped Sir Brecelyn kill him. So when Aristide sneers,

"Lady Brecelyn's been dead for years, Falko," and Falko replies, "Well, then Poncey must have been fooling around with the man's *daughter!*," having apparently forgotten for a moment that Brecelyn's daughter is *Melissande*, I can only be glad of the big oaf's blunder. Tristan's enthusiasm for the topic was already waning and Falko's comment is sure to kill it entirely, and it's finally going to give me my chance to drag Tristan away.

At least that's what I'm thinking, before Armand calls out to Gilles from down the table.

While the Journeys were busy making their reports, having found themselves excluded from Tristan's conversation the squires started up a one of their own, and for a while now they've been arguing rather loudly about what to do with a free night, should Master Guillaume declare one before Firsts as he did last year. At Falko's mention of fooling around with wives, inevitably some of them started in on Pascal again, urging him to ask Gilles to allow a visit to the convent, and Pascal's been resisting. He's been blushing prettily and stammering out effusive praise for his master's courtesy, and it's finally all become too much for Armand. I'm not sure if it's jealousy or suspicion that's brought Armand to his feet, but he's now demanding in an accusatory tone that suggests being dubbed a clouter by Taran is already starting to go to his head,

"Come *on*, master! How long are you going to make the poor boy wait? Pascal is dying to see Ginger. We all are, aren't we, boys? Surely with *your* connections, you could arrange for a formal visit to St. Genevieve's. If we *all* go along and there are plenty of chaperones on both sides, with you as our sponsor no one could find anything improper in it. Quite to the contrary! Why, surely courtesy demands it."

Soon all the squires and the Journeys, too, are lending their voices to Armand's plea.

Throughout this little speech, Gilles has been sitting serenely and contemplating Armand coolly with a placid expression on his face. But I'm sitting right next to him, and under the table he's tapping his toe against the floor in irritation. I ought to know; I'm tapping mine right along with him. *Taran's fine, Taran's fine.* I know it.

Still, it's agonizing.

"My, but your squire is an impertinent one, Ari," Gilles finally exclaims, once the boys have quieted down to hear his response and everyone has turned to look at him expectantly. "You must not have beaten him sufficiently as a child. I suppose it's too late to remedy that *now*, more's the pity. And the *darling* boy is perfectly right. *Ordinarily*, there'd be no harm in arranging a little appropriately chaperoned meeting. But as should be equally obvious, I must therefore have a truly excellent reason for refusing to do any such thing. I feel quite insulted that anyone could think otherwise." He blinks and looks imperiously around the table. "Yes, of course, I have a *most* compelling reason."

Then he proceeds to pluck at his sleeve, and he doesn't say anything else.

After a full minute of complete silence passes, it's clear that Gilles has no intention of telling us what this 'compelling' reason is. Not the real one, anyway. But by this point Armand's lost his nerve, and he's sunk back down into his seat uncertainly. So for a moment I think Gilles is going to get away with it and I'm going to get away — until Falko booms,

"Give *over*, dammit, Lejeune!" and he punctuates his request by bringing one of his big fists down on the table.

"Oh, very well then, if you insist," Gilles sniffs. "I had rather intended it to be a surprise, but I suppose that's all ruined ...?"

Falko brings his fist down on the table again to confirm that it is. So Gilles composes his features and makes a show of arranging himself as though in preparation of telling a complicated tale, but from the sour look on Armand's face I doubt I'm the only one who suspects that beneath Gilles's supremely tranquil exterior his mind is hard at work, busily trying to think up something to say. I've never wanted to scream at him more *"just get on with it!,"* and it's all I can do to keep from reaching out and giving him a shake. Just when I think I'm not going to be able to restrain myself, all at once the corner of Gilles's mouth curves up, and the only way I can describe the expression that comes over his face is to say that if he had a mustache, it would be twitching.

"Be that as it may, gentlemen," he begins officiously, reclining his head in a move that would look at home on a prince making a concession. "The situation is this: Pascal is of course officially engaged, that's true. And as you all know, all the necessary papers for a *binding* contract have *already* been signed on his behalf, by *me*," he declares, although it's news to me. It looks like it's news to Pascal, too. "But our groom-to-be has yet to have an opportunity to make a proposal to his lady. A mere formality, to be sure, but one so dear to the ladies! For them, we must endeavor to make it an occasion. To this end, Master Guillaume has agreed to an inspired idea of mine, to have Pascal plight his troth to his Ginger as part of the festivities at Firsts. *Right in the middle* of the competition! It's to be the highlight of the staged entertainment between the individual tests. The master's only condition was that it be known the lovers have had *no* opportunity *whatsoever* to declare themselves to each other beforehand, to add to the anticipation. Posters advertising the fact will soon be going up all over town, and I've already got some of my boys hard at work building something for it."

Gilles pauses to look around the table with satisfaction, and when nobody can do anything but blink, he takes it as encouragement to elaborate.

"A flowery bower, in which to woo your lady!" he exclaims rapturously, putting his hands up in front of him as though making a frame. "Picture it thus: a sort of gazebo, on wheels. We'll roll you right out onto the middle of the field in it, as a culmination to the exhibitions! Framed by fragrant blossoms, on bended knee, there you'll proclaim your love in phrases so moving, women will whisper them on their deathbeds, poets will plagiarize them, and Marek here'll embroider them onto a handkerchief! You'll outdo us all, dear boy. Why, I daresay you'll even outdo DuBois and his garland! It will be your moment made immortal, the height of romance. It's going to be fabulous! And so deliciously *public*."

With that, Gilles folds his hands in front of him and he sits back contentedly, looking for all the world like a hen who's just laid a big, fat egg. Then after a beat or two, he calls down the table to Pascal,

"Now, my boy, what do you have to say to *that*?"

But Pascal can't say anything. It's exactly like the scene in the garden all over again, when Gilles first told him he'd engaged him to Ginger, only I doubt this time it's joy that's making Pascal speechless. The poor boy's petrified, and I can think of only one boy who'd find the idea of making a public spectacle of his betrothal more mortifying, really. During Gilles's speech Pascal's been slowly rising unsteadily to his feet, and now he's as white as a sheet. So it's not too surprising that the only response he can give is to let out a little moan and proceed to fall forward across the table, face down in his dinner. He's out like a light, and I begin to fear seriously for his career as a Journey. He really doesn't have the personality for it.

In the meantime, Gilles has risen to his feet. As the squires fish Pascal out of his stew, without resuming his seat Gilles gives a curt bow, and before anyone can question him further he exclaims preemptively,

"And now, gentlemen, if you will excuse me. I find I have a pressing matter of my own to attend to," and he hurries out of the hall, hot on the heels of Master Guillaume who has just gone past behind us on his own way out after dinner.

"Where do you suppose *he's* going in such a hurry?" I ask Tristan, as I, too, scramble to my feet.

"I rather imagine he's got a hasty proposal of his own to make, to the master," Tristan laughs. "That, and he's got to put in a rush order for an awful lot of wood."

If circumstances were different, I'm sure I'd be demanding that Tristan explain himself, and that he tell me just what it is he thinks Gilles is up to. As it is, in Gilles's hurried departure I've seen the opportunity for my own. So instead I tug on Tristan's sleeve, and when I implore him, "Can't we go now, too, master?," mercifully he obliges me.

I've never been so glad to get away from table, and as I follow Tristan back to the Journey corridor to deposit him in his room for the night, I have to force myself not to tread on his heels to hurry him along or to shove him roughly through his door once we've reached it. The hallway is empty and if I'm quick about it, once Tristan's door is safely shut, I should be able to dart into Taran's room without being seen. I'm poised to do it, too, when instead of closing his door behind him, Tristan takes hold of my sleeve and he pulls me into his room with him.

325

"Okay, kid, you've waited long enough, I reckon," he says indulgently. "You've been as jumpy as a jackrabbit all through dinner! Relax. I'm all yours now. So, what did you want to tell me that was so important?"

I swallow twice, hard, my mouth suddenly dry. How could I have forgotten about telling Tristan that I needed to talk to him tonight? That I *do* desperately need to talk to him, in fact? But it's true. Ever since I heard Taran's summons, I haven't spared a moment's thought for him.

Tristan's looking at me expectantly, and in the distance I can hear the sounds of some of the other boys approaching. My window of opportunity for getting to Taran undetected is closing. So is my best chance to convince Tristan to adjust the disastrously risky trick.

I hesitate, for a minute torn between two ways.

But only for a minute.

By chance, in my nervousness I look down to where Tristan's hand is still resting on my sleeve, and I see it: the thin red line Taran cut along the inside of his wrist.

I have no idea if Taran is simply toying with me, or not. And Tristan is my master and my best friend. I made him a vow and I intend to keep it, and I can't let anything to do with Taran distract me from it again — not even the fact that I've shot him.

But I just can't let Taran languish, either.

"It can wait until tomorrow, master," I tell Tristan, swallowing hard again. "Promise me we'll have that talk, first thing in the morning?" And then I practically shove him through his door and pull it hastily shut behind him.

I know what I have to do, and it's not going to be pretty.

ONCE I'M OUT TRISTAN'S DOOR AND I'VE CLOSED IT FIRMLY behind me, I set out at a dead run down the corridor — heading *away* from Taran's room. The hallway isn't empty; Falko's arguing with Aristide about something outside his door, and that's not the only reason. All day I've been letting the situation with Taran derail me. Mess has been just like the fiasco of fetching Taran's tunic all over again, with me skulking around distracted and lying to my master, and even thinking badly of him. It's time for it to stop, and there's only one way I can think of to resolve things properly.

I cut through the now-empty great hall and out to Tristan's cabinet, to get the things I need. On my way back inside, for good measure I snag a full jug of wine that's been left unattended on one of the veterans' tables, and I bring it along with me. Taran's going to need it, and as I head determinedly back to the Journey hallway, I take a stiff swig from it myself. I'm going to need it even more.

Falko and Aristide are gone by the time I get back to the Journey hallway, but the corridor isn't empty. Jurian's letting himself into his own room a little ahead of me, and when he sees me barreling determinedly down the hallway wiping my mouth with the back of my hand and a bottle of wine clutched in my fist, he stops, and leans against his door curiously. But he doesn't say anything. He just watches me with one eyebrow raised as I charge past his room. And right past Tristan's. And as I let myself in through Taran's door. I hate to think what he must be assuming, and maybe Tristan was right that he's no angel. But after everything that happened last year between him and Baylen, I don't think Jurian will rat on me.

I don't bother knocking. I simply open Taran's door a crack and I slip through it, steeling myself to see what's inside waiting for me. I'm half-expecting to find Taran lounging on his cot smirking and ready to bait me, and I'll confess. I've been looking forward to it, too, a little, as I've got a few choice comebacks all worked up that I'm eager to deliver. But I'm also half-prepared to find that with his typical arrogance Taran's assumed he could make a better job of binding himself up than I did, only to find *after* he'd removed his bandages that his shoulder was too sore for him to redo them again properly.

The one sight I'm not at all prepared for is the one I actually do see.

At first, admittedly I don't see much of anything. Taran's oil lamp's gone out and he hasn't bothered to relight it. The only light is coming from a single candle guttering on the bedside table, and its dim, flickering flame can't reach far into the deep shadows across Taran's bed; where the torso and legs of a reclining boy should be I can't make out anything but the folds of a disheveled blanket, and there's such an unnatural stillness in the dark, stuffy little room that at first I think Taran's not here. The only hint that the room must actually be occupied is the warmth in the air, and the unmistakable metallic scent of blood.

As my eyes begin to adjust, I realize why at first I didn't see him. Taran's not lying on his cot. He's sitting upright at one end of it, slumped with his back resting against the wall in the place where the head of the bed fits into the corner of the room. His head is twisted to one side at an uncomfortable angle and in the strange light of the muted candle he looks as ghostly pale as the wall behind him, but that's not what most catches my attention. It's that what I'd thought was a blanket is Falko's shirt, blood-drenched and discarded, and that the bindings that are still on him aren't just bloody, they're in tatters. And it's that what I'd thought were deep shadows across Taran's chest are thick smears of blood.

His arms are lying limp at his sides, palms face-up. They're wet with blood, too, as though he's recently been pressing both hands against his wounds to try to stanch them, and he's only just given up. More blood is caked in his hair; at some point he must have run his hands through it in frustration in that signature move of his, and what I can see of his injured shoulder peeking out from under the wreckage of his bandages looks like a

327

half-chewed chunk of Falko's dinner. Fresh rivulets of blood are running from it down his chest and pooling in the hollow around his navel, and he's making no move to stop them — though his trousers are pushed down to the limit of decency, as though at some point he tried to keep them clear of the blood. Now the waistband is all soaked, too, and more blood is smeared across his hips and belly. I doubt he would look worse if he's been gored by a boar, or trampled under the wheel of a wagon.

I take one look at him and I recoil, stifling a scream.

Then I compose myself, feeling awfully glad of my foresight in bringing the items in my hand with me from Tristan's cabinet.

"So, you came," Taran says listlessly, as I grab up the candle. "Took you long enough."

"*You* try getting away from the boys at table," I retort, sitting down gingerly on the cot next to him. But I hate how snide and defensive I sound, and my hand is already shaking as I hold up the candle and pull the tattered fabric back from his shoulder.

Then I get a good look at the wound underneath.

"My God, Taran! How in the heck did *this* happen?!"

"If I remember it correctly ..." he begins, and I cut him off.

"What I *mean* is, how in the heck can it have gotten *worse*, rather than better?! I know I bound you up really well. Why on earth did you go and try to redo it? And how you've managed to rip yourself open so much further in the process, I'm sure I don't know. Why, it's enough to make me think you purposely tore off your bandages and gouged around in there some more, just so I'd have to come and tend to you, all over again."

It's an awfully cheap shot, and I can't really think it; not even Taran is barbaric enough to take a knife to himself and give himself a thorough bloodletting, just to mess with me (although I suppose I did something similar for Tristan. But that was totally different, surely). It should be obvious to him it's just my nerves talking, but the comment must make Taran pretty angry anyway; even in the low light, I can see his cheeks flushing furiously.

"If you think I *like* the idea of having you sneaking in here every night to wash me and change me, you're crazy," he growls, his face now such a funny shade he really could be blushing. "But until I'm healed, the alternative is discovery. So if I can stand it, so can you. And now unless you want to get caught out of barracks after curfew or you have some third alternative to offer, I suggest you get started. You've got a big job ahead of you. There's a sponge on the table, and water in my splash basin."

For a moment it occurs to me to wonder exactly when he can have brought these items into his room from the lavatory. But he's become so antisocial since our return from the castle I guess he's simply taken to doing all his washing up in here.

"You've managed to get blood on you, just about everywhere," I say, not making a move to pick up the sponge.

"Yes," he says, rather smugly. "Yes, I have."

I peer at him a little more closely. He *is* covered in blood. That wasn't an illusion. But now I see it's actually spread around only rather thinly. I can only imagine what he's been doing to get that way; it must have taken some serious effort.

"*Well?* What are you waiting for?" he demands, when I don't make any move toward the water basin and I start rummaging around in the little bag I've brought with me instead.

"There's no point cleaning you up, until *after*," I reply darkly, fishing around in my squire's kit a little longer. Then I pull something out, and I hold it up triumphantly.

As soon as Taran sees it, he startles.

"What's *that?!*" he demands, even though he must know what it is: a great big darning needle, the kind we squires use for making the boys' targets and for doing their mending.

"An alternative," I say, already pulling out some silk and starting to thread it through the eye of the needle. "Believe me, I'm not going to enjoy this any more than you are," I declare, adding in the tone he used to say the same thing to me, "But if *I* can stand it, so can you."

"Funny," he jeers, still eyeing the needle, "I was under the impression you quite enjoyed shoving sharp objects into me." Then, with alarm: "Hey, wait a minute, you can't be serious! If you think I'm going to let you sew me up like a cloth-mark, you really *are* crazy!," and finally: "Oh, Ow, *Ow*, God Damn it!" as I thrust aside what's left of his bindings and with no more ado I stab the needle straight into him.

After that first jab, Taran grabs my wrist, and just like out in the clearing this afternoon we're at an impasse for a moment. But the big needle is already sticking into him and he might as well let me pull it through, although he only gradually relaxes his grip reluctantly when I say more seriously,

"Look, Taran. Maybe this wound isn't all that deep, and maybe it isn't going to kill you. But it is bleeding profusely. Even if it weren't for the issue of discovery, we both know it can't stay open like this. Tristan only healed properly after the barber sewed him up. And maybe what you really need is a trip to one yourself. But Louvain's only barber died of plague and right now I'm all you've got, and I'll not let you risk infection. So I'm going to do what I should have done back in the clearing and fix this mess I created, properly and permanently. There's nothing you can do to stop me, so don't bother trying. Because if you do, I'm going to go and fetch Master Guillaume myself!"

I don't think it's this brave little speech that persuades him, though. By this point my already unsteady hands have started shaking violently, and it must be obvious I wasn't lying when I said I wasn't going to enjoy the task — that I'm thoroughly dreading it, actually. So all he does is give a curt nod, and as I accordingly bite my lip and bend in closer to pull through the needle, he grabs up the jug of wine I brought with me and with a wild eye he guzzles down a huge, impressive gulp, in a move he must have perfected during his dissolute days at Brecelyn's castle.

"I thought you gave up drinking," I say, more to distract myself from what I'm about to do than anything else.

"I *did*. But there's no way I'm doing this sober. I've *seen* the cloth-marks you make for DuBois, remember," he hisses back, and I resist the urge to make another snide remark about his fiancée and her dainty unicorn embroidering. Instead I snatch up the jug myself, and I take a big swig from it.

"Yeah, well, there's no way I'm doing this sober, either."

I'd like to say that the process of sewing Taran closed isn't really all that bad. But that would be a lie. It's every bit as awful as I feared it would be.

No single jab of the needle can compare with shoving an entire arrow shaft out through Tristan's side, of course. But each thrust is a little mini version of the same thing, and closing Taran up once and for all is going to require dozens of them. The initial, sickening stab for each stitch isn't even the worst thing. It's digging the tip of the needle around afterwards in flesh that's already raw and sore to get it angled correctly to shove it back out again. And it's the feeling of skin pulling up and ripping as the long length of thread comes tearing through behind the needle, juddering and sticking. On top of everything else it's almost impossible to see what I'm doing in the near-dark and through all the blood, or to be sure I'm accurately matching up all the jagged edges and loose flaps of skin.

The first two or three stitches are the hardest. After that, we tacitly work out a system. Taran holds his breath as I shove in the needle. Then while I poke and prod around in the wound, my head bent in so close under his in the dim light that I know he must feel each of my own nervous breaths against his skin, he takes a swig from the wine he's got clutched in one hand. He takes another sloppy draught or two while I pull the string taut, then with his other hand he daubs away the blood from the new stitch with a rag made from a cloth-mark I've brought with me: *push in, swig, root, root, swig, pull out, swab* — soon we fall into a rhythm, and after that first jab Taran doesn't cry out again.

Long before we're done, Taran's finished off the wine. From the way he keeps going through the motion of raising the jug to his lips anyway even after all the dregs of it are gone, though, I can tell the pain must be excruciating, or at least something about my close, fumbling handling of him is pushing him to the brink of his endurance. But Taran's determined to be all stoic and manly about it. In fact, he's trying so hard to pretend that having a needle the size of a pitchfork shoved in and out of him repeatedly is hardly bothering him that it would be sort of endearing, actually, if it weren't such utter hogwash. And if the whole thing weren't such a lurid reminder of what he did to Tristan that it's hard to feel entirely sorry for him. Still, there's something about the diffident way he's determined to suffer it all in silence for my benefit that it can't help reminding me a little of the ridiculously noble boy I once thought him to be.

Maybe that's why, when at last I've put the final stitch in place and I'm confident my patchwork job of it will hold him, I find myself saying as I'm tying off the string,

"Taran, I've been thinking. The day of the hunt, in Brecelyn's woods. Maybe *your* hand slipped on the bowstring, too. Or you tripped over a root, or something."

All he does is stiffen.

"*Well?*" I demand, when he doesn't say a thing.

"Well *what?*" he demands back, sounding awfully strained, even for a boy who's just had over thirty stitches rather inexpertly sewn into him.

"*Did* you shoot Tristan by accident?" I ask it very quietly.

"No," he says flatly.

It's a straight answer, and I can tell my question's angered him (although really, I don't see why it should. It seems to me I've just made an awfully generous suggestion). But it's true. He looks livid — angrier about it, even, than about my shooting him. So I don't know why I press him.

"*Uh,* are you sure?"

He fixes me with a withering stare.

"Emphatically."

After that, there can be nothing left for us to say to each other. Our little cooperation around the needle is over, and we're both sullen and silent as I dig around in his cedar chest to pull out two tunics: one to shred for a new, lighter bandage, and another with a pair of matching trousers to dress him in. It's a set of an usual color and I don't recall ever having seen him wear it, but I think it will look rather good on him. And we're both silent, mostly, while I make short work of it to clean him up so I can help him into fresh clothes again.

There's no point pretending, though, that it isn't pretty awkward, or that we aren't both terribly strained. It's nothing I didn't do this afternoon out in the clearing, more or less. But here alone in his dark little room the necessary motions of washing him feel different, and I'm sure we're both thinking back to the past — to his shooting of Tristan, and to other things. So to ease the tension, once or twice we have a terse little exchange. "You'd better not be enjoying this!" I tell him at one point, even though I'm pretty sure the muffled grunts he's making are more from discomfort than from pleasure. "And why not?" he growls back, just as baitingly. "I'm not to have any *other* chances of being sponged off by a girl any time soon, apparently." Then for the rest of the time I'm wiping him down he proceeds to make a

331

whole string of exaggerated and highly inappropriate noises, just to spite me. But I don't think I have to explain why we both fall silent when the time comes for me to help him change his clothes — particularly his trousers — and neither of us says anything else until he's fully dressed again.

Once I've straightened up his tunic to my satisfaction and I've gently wiped the last traces of blood from his hair, he lies back and from under half-closed lids he watches me as I wring out the sponge and pour the bloody water from his splash basin into his chamber pot.

"Empty this out in the garden somewhere in the morning, when nobody's looking," I tell him, nodding at the brimming vessel. Then I gather up all the clothes and scraps of bandage that are too bloody to salvage, and I stuff them down into the bottom of his quiver.

"You can take these soiled rags out in this and shove them down into the ashes of one of the rubbish fires, out behind the kitchens." It's a trick I've had reason to use myself for disposing of inconvenient rags, occasionally.

"What about Falko's best tunic?" he inquires, a little sarcastically.

"Leave it balled up under your cot. If I can, I'll find a chance to nip in tomorrow and take it out to the woods to wash it in the stream. And as for yourself, keep still as much as you can tonight, and you'll be right enough by morning, I'll wager. As long as you don't try to lift your arm above your shoulder, until the stitches have a chance to set overnight," I add, although I've noticed he hasn't tried to do it; he's made a point of it barely to move the arm on his injured side at all, in fact. So on impulse I lean in, to do up the front of his freshly-donned tunic for him.

It's the kind with a deep V-neck that laces up the front, and Taran has to turn his chin and stretch it up out of my way so I can bend in close enough to do up the criss-crossing ties properly. It takes me a while to sort them out and to arrange his collar, and I'm not sure what it is about it. But in a day of finding myself in strangely intimate moments with Taran, this one feels the most intimate of all of them.

I'm sure Taran feels it, too, even before he jeers softly at me,

"One of these days, *Marieke*, you're going to make someone a nice little *wife*."

But this time snide remarks can't dispel the tension. This one only makes it worse, actually, since Taran's right. It *is* the sort of thing only a wife should do — or a fiancée. And as I give Taran's collar one last careful straighten, with my arms up around his neck I can't help imagining how many times Melissande must have done this very thing for him — *after*. And wondering how different he must be when he's with *her*, this way. From the brooding look on his face I can tell Taran must be thinking about Melissande, too — and picturing her slender hands resting lightly like this on a collar, of *Tristan's*.

Before long I'm done, and I have no more excuse to keep fiddling with his clothing. But when I sit back a little to inspect my work we're still sitting awfully close, and the air is heavy with unspoken words between us.

"I'm not going to say it," he finally grumbles, and I know he means 'thank you.' "Why should I? You didn't do it for me."

"Yeah, well, *I'm* not going to say it, either!" I declare. Even though I *am* sorry, terribly.

After that, I should get up and go. We're done, and now there really can be nothing left to say. But I can't seem to make myself leave, and as we sit there a moment longer with our heads bent down towards each other and our knees almost touching, I find there is one last thing I can't leave without saying. This is sure to be my only chance, since I've just ensured I'll never need to be alone with him this way again. So I ask quietly,

"Why did you really do it, Taran?"

I'm not entirely sure what I mean — if I'm asking him why he shot Tristan, or why he didn't tell the master that *I* shot *him*. But of course, there's been something else in the room with us from the moment I stepped in: that thing that happened between us, the last time we were alone at night in here like this. So maybe that's what I'm really talking about, and Taran, at least, must take it that way.

"*Why'd you ask me to?!*" he shoots back. And that ends the conversation, as surely he intends.

With that I get up, and I gather up the last strips of the shredded tunic to take them along with me.

I'm almost out the door, when Taran calls me back.

"This changes nothing, Marieke. You do understand that, don't you? Nothing," he says, and I suppose he means I've not injured him enough to keep him from winning. Or that he's still angry with me for shooting him, even though I've risked punishment to sew him up again. Probably both. But it seems important to him and I'm tired, so I just nod as though I understand.

"You tried to tell me we'd always be enemies, and I wouldn't listen," I agree. "But you were right. Nothing can ever really change between us, can it?"

"Not from my side," he confirms heavily.

I'm already out the door and my hand is on the handle, when in afterthought I take a half-step back into the room.

"*Er*, Taran. Just how much of what I was saying this afternoon did you hear, anyway?"

"All of it," he replies tersely.

"*All* of it?" I echo, my voice sounding awfully small.

"Every last word," he declares, and I blanch. I can feel all the blood drain from my face in less time than it took for me to empty his splash basin of water — since horribly, it's only now that I remember exactly what was the last word on my lips at the very moment Taran burst into the clearing and

333

interrupted me: I was right in the middle of shouting at the top of my lungs that I was desperately in love with him.

Seeing my mortification, Taran adds smugly,

"Cheer up! You won't have to be stuck here *in Louvain* with me much longer. When *I* win guards, *I'll* be on my way to Meuse, and *you* and your *master* will be out. And if either of you thinks you're going to stop me, you're both going to need much better aim."

From the expression on his face as I close the door behind me, I'm sure he has no idea why I find this last taunt of his so blissfully funny.

It's long past curfew, and I know I've got to get back to barracks as quickly as I can. But I have one last stop to make tonight: in the Journey lavatory, where I hastily strip off Melissande's veil and replace it with the pieces of shredded tunic I've brought away with me from Taran's room. All my troubles surely began last year when I let myself start wearing the blasted thing, and it's funny. What once felt so good against my skin now feels rough and painful, although I guess it makes sense. I'd never have admitted it at the time, but the last time I put it on, I must have already opened the door to the hope that somehow Taran could be in love with me. Now it's a hideous weight digging into the top of my belly, and I can't wait to get it off me. But that's not the only reason. It's symbolic. I'm Tristan's squire, and I can't go around wearing Taran's favor again.

I leave the veil outside Taran's door, where he'll find it in the morning. Then I make my way down the dark, empty hallway, and as I go, a dozen different thoughts are troubling me. Chief amongst them is this one: what a powerful and terrible thing jealousy can be.

The thing is, I was plenty mad at Taran this afternoon, that's for sure. But I don't *think* I suspected all along that he would be making his own way through the woods to the millpond eventually. I don't *think* that when my hand was on the bowstring, I already knew the noises in the bushes were coming from him.

No, I really *don't* think I shot Taran on purpose.

It's outrageous. Unimaginable. Unthinkable.

But ... maybe I did.

CHAPTER TWENTY-FIVE

The next morning, I head straight for the Journey hallway. As soon as I'm outside Taran's room I can tell he's already up, since I can hear him moving around within. I don't knock on his door or slip inside to check on him. I know he's come through the night just fine, don't I? I made sure of that last night, and Melissande's veil is gone. That's all I really wanted to see. So I circle back to the sideboard to gather up some breakfast for myself and for Tristan, heaving a sigh of relief.

Taran's surely on the mend, and I've done all I can for him (his beloved's garment is no doubt providing him more comfort this morning than *I* could, anyway). Even better, all my midnight fears and fancies have melted away with the shadows, and I'm embarrassed now by how silly they seem.

Of *course* I didn't shoot Taran on purpose! I'd never have done it, and I really *didn't* know he was there. But if I'm the last person Taran's likely to be feeling charitable about this morning, I can't in all fairness say I blame him, and I'd be a fool to count the episode safely behind me. Taran's threatening dismissal of me last night left no doubt about that, and the reality is that by now he's had all night to think about how to turn my folly to his advantage. Knowing Taran, his payback is going to be as clever as it is creative, and all I can do is wait and see what he's going to come up with. In the meantime, I've got other things to worry about.

My first order of business today has got to be convincing Tristan to adopt a safer version of the joint trick. I've decided to spring the idea on him while we're sharing our breakfast together, out on the field. It'll be harder for him to argue with me with the other boys within earshot, and it's got to be done first thing — since once I've won my master over to the revisions, *he's* going to need to figure out how *he's* going to convince *Gilles*. That's going to require Tristan's powers of persuasion, and although I rather immodestly think the solution I've come up with for tweaking the exhibition is damned impressive, I'm apprehensive.

If Gilles has been wanting to back out of sharing a trick ever since the announcement of wands as the first skill, suggesting any changes now could provide him with exactly the kind of excuse he's been looking for; in fact, proposing a substitution now could prove riskier than simply going ahead with the outrageous stunt as it is. After Poncellet's comments on the subject, though, there's no way we can afford to do that — and letting Gilles outshine Tristan at Firsts is starting to feel almost as dangerous as letting him be outdone by Taran.

We've simply got to get Gilles's compliance, and that will be all up to Tristan. All I can do is fortify him for the task, and so I make a critical survey of the sorry offerings on display on the sideboard. When I've stuffed the heartiest-looking pastries down into the fold of my tunic, as I'm trotting back with them down the corridor past the great hall, through its open door I catch sight of Brian de Gilford. He's sitting huddled at one of the long tables, his fist predictably wrapped around a bottle of wine.

It's the first I've seen of him since his big fight with Poncellet, and I suppose he does look a little lumpier than usual; there are yellowing, purplish stains of once-livid bruises still lurid on his skin, and a tooth or two missing from his sheepish grin. But otherwise he doesn't look too much the worse for his run-in with his old rival, and when he raises a hand in a rather embarrassed gesture of greeting upon seeing me hovering in the doorway, I can guess that his failure to put in an appearance around the guild lately has been due more to shame than to any serious injury. He looks so morose, in fact, that I can't bring myself to ignore his summons. So I go in and join him.

As soon as I sit down, he tells me he's planning to leave for Meuse that very day.

"I guess I know when I'm not wanted," he mumbles, and I'm surprised. For all his faults, I hadn't thought he'd be the kind to turn tail and run away.

"*That's* not the reason," he grumbles, apparently reading disapproval in my expression. "As it happens, I've been summoned to the capital on a bit of business."

From the way he says it, I almost expect him to add, "*nasty* business," and I can tell he's not very happy about leaving. So I tell him,

"*I'll* miss you, master," and I mean it. As I've said, I've grown rather inexplicably fond of him.

"Bless you for that, boy," he replies mistily, releasing his grip on the wine long enough to pat my hand absently. He must already be quite drunk, since he's being awfully maudlin for first thing in the morning.

"Can I leave something here with you then, son, for safe keeping?" he says unexpectedly. Then before I can protest, he's reaching down under the table for something that's been lying in his lap, and he's shoving it into my hands. I have to say, I receive it most reluctantly.

It's his wife's purple sash.

I stare down at it in dismay for a while. De Gilford's looking at it, too — with disfavor, and I guess I can understand why he wouldn't want to take it home to Meuse with him. It's pretty clear he's never really wanted it, actually. He just didn't want Poncellet to have it.

"You're a bright lad, Marek. You'll know what to do with it. Hold onto it for me, until I come back to claim it."

"You *will* be back for it, won't you master?" I exclaim, a little nervously. I'm not sure what makes me say it, except that he's staring down at the garment in a way that suggests he'd just as soon never see it again.

All he does is pat my hand again, and say,

"God willing."

We sit there for a moment longer in silence, while de Gilford finishes off his wine in one long, mournful draught. Then he nudges me, and smiles conspiratorially.

"I'll be taking a little something of *yours* with *me*, too, son, to remember you by," he slurs confidentially, and he looks around cautiously, even though we're alone in the hall and it's otherwise empty.

Then he gestures down exaggeratedly. When I lean over across him and peer down on the far side of him, I see one of my bigger repeating crossbows and a quiver full of bolts to fit it sitting on the bench next to him.

"Don't tell the master!" he chortles, elbowing me again jovially.

A cohort of men soon appears in the doorway leading into the front vestibule to escort de Gilford on his way. And so we rise to say our goodbyes, and as I take my leave of him, the big man surprises me by wrapping me in a huge, impulsive hug. I'd never have sought it, but I'll confess. Right now, the little show of affection is exactly what I need, and it leaves me feeling a little maudlin myself. So before I make my own way out to the field with Tristan's breakfast (now rather squished), I take de Gilford's purple sash back to barracks. De Gilford's trusted me with it, so I look around for a safe place to stash it; it would make a pretty good binding, but I don't think I have to explain why the last thing I'd ever do with it is to strap it around me. There aren't many options, as I can't leave it out in the open on my bedside table, next to my little wooden mouse. So I end up adding it to the odds and ends I've accumulated in the bottom of my old traveling bag.

I shove it down deep, underneath Baylen's whip and the scrap of a love letter Jurian once wrote for him, next to the slippers I wore at the convent when I was pretending to be a girl named Marieke. As I do, it gives me a funny feeling. I'd thought I'd managed to avoid acquiring another man's token *last* night, and I can't help thinking it's a bad omen. Not only do women's garments keep finding their way to me, it's only just struck me:

The owners of most of the things that have ended up in the bottom of this bag are now dead.

I'D BE LYING, THOUGH, IF I SAID I WASN'T KEEPING A SHARP EYE out for Taran later, once I've joined the other squires out on the butts to wait for my master to emerge for morning drills. I'm pretty sure he's fine but I want to see it for myself, and I'm anxious to see if any sign of his injury will be apparent to the others. Most of all, I'm plenty curious to see if his shooting's been affected. And I'll admit it. When I think of ruining that incredible skill of his, I can't want *that*. But would it really be too bad of me to hope that it could be temporarily impaired, a little?

It's while we're all huddled around Pascal and commiserating with him that Taran makes his appearance. As it turns out, I wasn't the only squire lying awake late into the night last night and fretting; Pascal couldn't sleep a wink for worrying over his upcoming proposal to Ginger. This morning he's still feeling awfully glum about it, and we're right in the middle of trying to cheer him when I catch sight of Taran out of the corner of my eye, making his way slowly out of the stables.

He wisely hasn't tried to change out of the clothes I dressed him in last night, and to a discerning eye I suppose he does look a little tired, understandably. Otherwise he's much the same as ever, and to my relief none of the other boys seems to notice anything unusual about him. At least no one remarks immediately upon his appearance, and when he does soon come into our discussion, it's for an entirely different reason.

"You boys just don't get it," Pascal is complaining sorrowfully. "I've got to make a *speech*. In front of all of Ardennes! And it's got to be good. You heard Gilles. He's expecting it to be, well, *poetry*."

"Just keep it short and sweet," Armand is advising him, when Rennie looks over and spots Taran under the archive eaves, going through his morning ritual of sprinkling water over his hands from one of the rain barrels.

"And if you need any help with *that*," he chuckles wickedly, "Why not ask Taran? He's got a way *without* words," and all the boys laugh.

I suppose it is pretty funny, and I've not been above taking an easy shot at Taran for his disastrously blank note to Melissande during Tristan's poetry contest recently myself. But the last thing I feel like doing this morning is laughing at Taran, and as it happens Tristan and Jurian are now making their own way out from the stables. So when I notice them coming towards us, I say,

"Actually, that's an excellent idea, Pascal. A little help is probably exactly what you need."

Pascal shoots me a sarcastic look. "I want her to *like* me, Marek."

"Not from Taran," I snort. "From *Tristan*," just as Tristan himself comes up to join us. "You'll help Pascal compose a proper proposal, won't you, master? One that will win her over completely," I ask him, and when I've explained what I have in mind, Tristan agrees readily.

"Sure," he drawls. "But why get my assistance, when there's a *real* expert

338

closer to hand?," and for a minute I think he's going to make a joke about Taran, too. Instead, he slings an arm around my shoulders and gives me a playful little jostle.

"We all saw what just two lines of *this* boy's prose can do, back at the castle, didn't we, boys? Imagine the effect of a whole speech!" he exclaims, and I can tell he's teasing me. But I can't make heads or tails of his jest, and before I can question him about it, Pascal is shaking his head and declaring that this is one thing he's going to have to do for himself.

"If I don't, it won't mean anything. I don't want my wife cherishing someone else's words for the rest of her life," he declares, and with that I think we're all sorry we brought up the poetry contest.

I'm sure Pascal is right, but it gives me an uneasy feeling. Any attempt of Pascal's to pen a speech romantic enough to make his fiancée forget her daring rescue by Gilles is sure to be painful. I hate to say it, but probably even a couplet by Falko would be better.

The uneasy feeling in my chest turns into a flutter, when Jurian looks off over my shoulder and demands abruptly,

"What in the world is wrong with your master this morning, Remy?"

"What? Nothing. Why?" Remy warbles, following Jurian's gaze to where it's resting speculatively on Taran, who's now reaching up both arms gingerly to run his wet hands through his hair.

"It looks like he's wearing a bandage, under his clothing," Jurian replies.

Leave it to Jurian to be looking closely at the boys' bodies under their tunics! Particularly one as magnificent as Taran's. But he's right. A corner of white cloth is sticking out from under the gray of Taran's tunic right at the base of his neck, where despite my careful lacing job of it last night, Taran's shirt has started to come open.

Remy sees it, too. His little mouth falls open in confusion, and his cheeks start to redden. He always hates it when he doesn't know what's going on with his own master, and from the look of concern and alarm on his face and the equally amused one on Jurian's, I can tell it's not going to blow over. So I rack my brain, and when I think of something, as I look down as though idly inspecting my fingernails in a move borrowed from Gilles, I declare as casually as I can,

"Why, it's obvious, isn't it boys? With the change in the weather, Taran's old wound must be bothering him, too. You know, the one he got during Brecelyn's fire, when that burning roof fell in on him. It *was* that shoulder, wasn't it? In fact, I'm sure of it. Come to think of it, it was *Taran* who suggested to *me* that I wrap up my own shoulder yesterday."

"Really?" Remy says, sounding skeptical, naturally. Taran never talks to me, except to abuse me. "When?" he demands.

And he's got me.

"Er, *hmm*. I can't quite recall. Was it before mess, or after ...?" I begin. But I'm a terrible liar, and when I try to conjure up a mental image of some plausible time I could have been chatting away casually with Taran about our old wounds, what comes to me instead are sharp flashes of the scenes I really did have with him yesterday:

That heart-stopping first sight of him, staggering into the clearing with the blood from my arrow dripping down his hand; Taran's cheek cold and slack against my own, while I cut away his tunic for him; the split-second when I burst back into the clearing and the world stood still, because I genuinely thought he was dead.

Maybe it's because the shock of it all and the danger are now past, or because it's always easier to feel sympathy for Taran when he's not actually right there and I'm not having to deal with him. But now the horrible images come out of nowhere, and for the first time since it all happened, I feel the full weight of it.

My mind goes slack, and I feel my own cheeks starting to redden; what can I possibly say? *"I think it was right before I shot Taran. Or perhaps it was a little later, after I sewed him up back in his hot little room, and I was running a wet sponge over his naked chest?"* All of a sudden I can't seem to think about anything else, and when accordingly I falter, it's Frans who finishes for me.

"I remember it, Marek! It was during squires' club, wasn't it? When Master Taran was chiding you for how stiffly you were shooting," he offers, and I could kiss the little lad for coming to my rescue again. I even manage a chuckle, when Rennie chortles,

"Too bad it's not so easy to cure a chronic *pain in the neck!*"

The chuckle catches in my throat, when next to me Jurian leans down, and in that silky voice of his, he whispers into my ear,

"I suppose *that* must explain all the moaning I heard coming from Taran's room last night, mustn't it, *Marek?*"

I take that as my cue to hustle Tristan away.

———◆———

As soon as I've gotten Tristan alone in front of his cabinet, I hand him over his breakfast, and I remind him that he promised to hear me out about something important this morning. Then while his mouth is full of pastry, I stumble straight into an incoherent description of the idea for tweaking the boys' trick that came to me out by the millpond, cursing myself for not having thought out more carefully ahead of time exactly how I should phrase it, and hating it, too, that the reason I'm making such a bad job of it now is that out of the corner of my eye, I'm still watching Taran. He *seems* fine, but there's something about him this morning that's off, different, only I can't quite put my finger on what it is. Strangely, I don't think it has anything to do with me wounding him.

Tristan listens to my garbled speech in silence. When I'm done, he crosses his arms and says mildly,

"So, let me get this straight. You want to scrap the trick, and replace it with a completely different one."

"Of course not, Tristan! That's not what I'm saying," I protest, even though actually, it sort of is.

I try a different approach. "What we have now, master, it's a good shot. A *great* one. But that's all it is — a single shot, not a trick. You said so yourself, a shot this good needs a proper send-up, and that's all I'm suggesting. Just a bigger production, to really showcase the talents of both of you boys. And the thing is, Poncellet told me that the key to pleasing the master is to give him what he wants." Actually it was Jurian who told me this, but I doubt another Journey's opinion would sway him. "Guillaume wants a *wand* in motion, and if we make the adjustments I'm suggesting, we're going to be able to give it to him."

"And with a set-up as extravagant as the one you're suggesting, who needs the original shot itself, eh? Am I right?" Tristan says shrewdly.

"Well, yes. But don't you see? If the shot's ready in time for Firsts, great. Fine. But if it needs a little more work, this way we can save it for Seconds. That's the big one, and maybe we should save our biggest trick for that anyway." Tristan purses his lips, so I continue hastily, "We don't have to decide now, Tristan. That's the beauty of it! We just keep practicing as we've been doing, adding in the new set-up, and we can wait even down to the last minute to decide if we're going to put the arrow-downing shot in. Either way, we'll have a trick that's sure to be smashing, and the best part of it is, I'm sure you boys can *already* do all the things I'm proposing, easily. They'll just *look* impossible. And that's the key to a great trick, too, or so Master Poncellet tells me."

Tristan pretends to consider it for a while, and he's not smiling. He's not exactly frowning, though, either, and from his expression I suspect that as the excitement of actually hitting Gilles's arrow yesterday afternoon has begun to fade, the reality of all his misses has been setting in. My proposal will allow him to back out of the impossible shot without losing face, and even if he's still determined to try it, he's got no reason to object to dressing it up a little. So I don't wait for him to answer. I grab up his equipment, and with an air of finality, I cry,

"So, that's all settled then! You'll be able to convince Gilles, won't you, Tristan?"

"I could convince anyone of anything," he confirms, and for once I'm glad it's nothing but the truth. "Besides," he says, rolling his eyes. "It's got a lot more wands. Gilles is going to love it."

I'M NOT THE ONLY ONE WHO'S WATCHING TARAN CLOSELY NOT much later, when almost as soon as Tristan and I have joined the boys on the line, he makes a show of sending Remy straight back to his cabinet to fetch an entirely different set of equipment for him. Soon his squire is trotting back past behind me with a bow in his hands so small and light I didn't think Taran even owned one like it, and all the boys stop what they're doing to watch him openly.

The boys rarely vary their routines, so whenever one of them does something new it's bound to get noticed. When that boy is Taran it's practically an event, and I don't think I've ever seen him shoot with anything so flimsy. What's more, while Remy was busy locating the unaccustomed items in the bowels of Taran's cabinet, Taran himself picked up his bench and moved it at least twenty paces closer to the embankment. His station is now standing only about 60 yards from the target — a distance that would be minimal, even for a squire. The whole setup looks more suited to someone like Frans than to a powerhouse of a clouter.

After his show of toughness last night, I was fully expecting Taran to make a point of being all macho this morning, and I was pretty sure he was going to refuse to take it at all easy today. So I'm just glad to see that I was wrong, and that he's being sensible. But when he makes no move whatsoever actually to bend the bow that Remy's brought him, and instead he takes his own sweet time about inspecting it carefully in excruciating detail, I begin to get apprehensive — particularly when he next does the same thing to every single arrow in his quiver, scrutinizing each one from tip to fletch and then back to tip again.

With his shoulder safely stitched up and bound, there's no reason I can think of why Taran shouldn't take a few nice, easy shots at his target, particularly ones from such close range. There's no reason at all, that is, unless moving his shoulder even minimally really is painful for him — unless the suspicion that came to me out in the clearing when I was first binding him was correct, that beneath his messy but superficial flesh wound, his collarbone was damaged by my arrow — bruised, or fractured. Maybe even broken.

Once the idea gets into my head, I can't get it out. The more I watch Taran fiddling with his bracer or adjusting the angle of his bench *yet again*, the more convinced I become that he must really be hurting, and that he's determined to hide the fact by doing as little as possible this morning. By the time Poncellet comes out to start the practice and Taran's yet to do so much as lift his bow into position, I've started to get really worried about him.

With de Gilford already on his way to Meuse and Master Bernard's particular brand of violence apparently required elsewhere, Poncellet has come out to lead our practice alone. He takes the field with his usual swagger, but as soon as he sees Taran set up to shoot at such ridiculously close range, he makes a show of pulling up short.

He looks around with an exaggerated air of surprise. Then he exclaims gleefully,

"Well, I'll be! *Pecs Mellor*, shooting butts — and *voluntarily*! Will wonders never cease?," and when he then proceeds to proclaim that butts is going to be the order of the day in Taran's honor, I know Poncellet means it to needle him. I can't help feeling with annoyance that instead, he's playing right into Taran's hands.

"What in the world do you suppose *he's* up to?" Tristan grumbles, nodding down at Taran as Poncellet heads off to arm himself from the cabinets.

"I wish I knew, master," I reply, with feeling. But we've got our own affairs to worry about, and so as I string Tristan's bow and he begins his customary stretches, before long we've turned our attention to the problem of how to win Gilles over to our new idea for the trick. Since Gilles himself has yet to put in an appearance, we draw Pascal into our discussion, too, rightly assuming that he's probably worried enough about his own master's part in the exhibition to be willing to help us promote a judicious revision of it.

"A picture's worth a thousand words, Marek," Tristan declares, when I ask him how he plans to put the idea over to Gilles. "Or in this case, a demonstration. That is, as long as it's staged properly."

Once Tristan's explained to us what he's got in mind, it's not long before Pascal and I have fixed it up between us to start preparing the materials necessary to set up a small-scale version of the redesigned trick out on the far field as soon as practice is over. It's going to mean trips both into the woods and out to the shop (and a rather embarrassing apology for my recent behavior on my part to Marcel), but if we set to work in good order, we should be able to have everything organized and ready not long after noon mess. By the time Gilles finally emerges lazily from the stables, for some reason dressed in nothing more than his peacock-blue tights, his St. Sebastian's medal on its golden chain, and his big, jeweled ring, everything's all arranged and I'm feeling pretty good about things.

But I'm still watching Taran.

I'm still watching Taran, too, as Gilles glides unselfconsciously into place next to Pascal, despite the fact that he's late. And despite his unorthodox state of *undress*, since he's essentially half naked. But Poncellet's not one to be a stickler for the rules, or for proper attire, either; Gilles must have known he'd be running drills alone this morning and anticipated his reaction, since sure enough, if anything Poncellet is giving Gilles a look that suggests he's finally starting to approve of him. At any rate, all he says is,

"Couldn't remember whose bed you left your boots under last night, Lejeune?," since in addition to being shirtless, Gilles is indeed barefoot.

"Just trying out something new, master," Gilles replies, wiggling his long, elegant toes at him. "I've heard it gives you better grip, if you ground your shots through the soles of your feet. But only if you have long, strong, flexible appendages."

"Far be it from me to keep a man from flexing his appendages!" Poncellet shoots back with a laugh, and after that everyone is too caught up in stripping off their own boots and joining Gilles in his antics to be curious any longer about Taran's.

Everyone, that is, but me.

Or at least, I'm *trying* to watch Taran. But as the practice gets off to a proper start (or rather, an improper one), with Taran at the extreme opposite end of the line-up there are too many boys between us for me to get more than a glimpse of him, and I don't think it's my imagination that he's purposely staying out of my line of vision. He's had to start shooting, of course, and from what I can tell he's having no trouble hitting the target. If he were, someone would surely comment on it. But Poncellet never bothered to move the line back to a reasonable distance. Not only is the motion necessary for Taran to send an arrow 60 yards minimal, but I can't ever seem to catch sight of him in the actual act of *doing* it; in fact, whenever I manage to steal a glance down the line, Taran doesn't seem to be doing much of anything.

By the time the practice is winding down and the boys have started packing up to go in, I've seen my fill of Falko's big shoulders, Jurian's long arms (and Aristide's equally long nose), and Gilles's 'flexible appendages,' but virtually nothing at all of Taran. So I'm not sure why I should be so convinced that he's spent the entirety of it dawdling, fiddling with his equipment, and generally wasting time in exactly the same way that Tristan did when he was wounded. But I am. And I'm not just worried any longer. I'm panicked, and I'm feeling horribly guilty, not to mention mighty sorry for some of my earlier sentiments. I mean, wishing a little stiffness on Taran is one thing. But if it turns out I've sent him the way of Falko, there isn't a word to describe how wretched I'll feel.

At some point during the practice, most of the other boys took off their boots in imitation of Gilles. Nobody's bothered to put them back on, and so once practice is officially over and Poncellet has wandered back inside, the first order of business for us squires is to gather up and sort out all the boys' boots for them. I manage to get Tristan back into his in good order. But as Armand tosses his master one of his boots and he fails to catch it, when it hits Falko in the small of the back instead, before long a full-scale boot fight breaks out around the boys' cabinets, and soon Tristan's tugging off his boots again and hurrying over to join in.

I'm not so eager to be hit by a hard, sweaty chunk of leather. I already know what it feels like to be struck by the toe of one of Aristide's boots, but that's not the only reason I hang back and hover by the safety of the water barrels, in the shadow of the overhanging eaves. Taran's still lingering out on the field, and now there's nobody and nothing in the way between us. So I'm watching him covertly, on the off chance that he's going to shoot again.

At least I think I'm being surreptitious about it, but Taran must see me.

He looks back over his shoulder, right at me. Then he puts the flimsy bow down deliberately on his bench, and he calls out pointedly to his squire to bring him his clouter's bow. Then the whole time Remy is dodging his way through flying boots to fetch it, Taran stands there with his arms folded across his chest, holding my gaze and staring imperiously at me.

As soon as he's got the big bow in his hands, Taran shouts over to the boys,

"Somebody, call a mark for me! And make it a hard one," and his voice booms out across the field so loudly that it interrupts the boys' game, and they all start making suggestions at once, with varying degrees of seriousness.

"What about one of Gilles's flexible appendages?!" Jurian calls out, while Falko counters,

"Nah. Shooting boys through the top of the foot is *DuBois's* specialty. Put one through the back of a King's man, Taran, and at noon mess the drinks'll be on me!," and soon the others join in, pointing out ridiculously distant tent posts or bricks in the crumbling back wall, until Taran snorts,

"I said, give me a *real* challenge."

So Aristide says snidely,

"Put it in the millpond then, Mellor! Unless even your *arrows* are too shy to bathe publicly."

To everyone's surprise, Taran takes the outrageous suggestion seriously. With a clipped *"so be it,"* he nocks a big, fat clouting arrow into his massive bow, and with no further ado and with no apparent difficulty, he rocks back in a motion broader and even more sweeping than any I've ever seen. Then with infinite ease, he sends the arrow sailing up, high over St. Sebastian's.

The arrow flies past the embankment, easily. It flies over the roofs of all the temporary tents, and out over the horse pasture, even.

It sails past all the outrageous marks the boys set for him in jest, and past the end of the far field.

And then it goes right out over the back guild wall, and into the woods beyond.

If I hadn't seen it myself, I wouldn't have thought even a bow the size of Taran's capable of sending an arrow such a distance.

"By Golly!" Falko exclaims appreciatively, "you've outdone even *yourself*, old man! What do you wanna bet that one really *did* reach the millpond? Wow, I sure hope there weren't any girls bathing there today."

When in response Aristide then hits Falko in the back of the head with his other boot, the boys resume their game and everyone forgets about Taran again.

Except, of course, for me.

Even if I wanted to, Taran doesn't let me. He thrusts his bow back into his squire's hands, and while Remy is busy scampering dutifully back to the cabinets with it, he comes striding off the field, heading straight for me. I'm not blocking his way but he makes a point of pushing roughly past me anyway, or rather of pushing *through* me, since as he passes he slams one of his big arms against me so hard I'm almost sent tumbling into one of water barrels.

"Now there's *another* arrow with my colors on it, lying out in the woods somewhere. Go find *that*," he hisses, not bothering to look down as he shoulders me out of his way.

There's nothing for me to do but try to catch my balance, fuming. *What a sneaky, rotten trick!* Why, he's been *toying* with me, all morning — purposely drawing me in, stirring up my concern and feeding my fears — or maybe my hopes; I'm not entirely sure which of the two he thinks I've been feeling — when the whole time he was never affected in the slightest by the little wound I gave him. His motion looked just the same as ever; if anything, it was *better*, and I should have known it. He really does have the constitution of an ox. I bet those stitches last night didn't really hurt him any, either.

All these thoughts flash through my mind in an instant, and it *was* a nasty trick. But I can't help it. Even as I'm clutching the side the water barrel to keep from falling in, all I really feel is terribly relieved.

And yet, as I'm muttering to myself and watching his back disappearing into the stables, I don't know what it is. Maybe it's the thought of those stitches, and how he didn't make a sound as I plied the needle into him. Or maybe it's something about the stiff way he's stretching his neck to one side that strikes me as awkward and a little unnatural. But it makes me replay the sweeping motion of his I just witnessed in the back of my mind carefully, and as I do, I begin to wonder if there wasn't something slightly off about it.

It's true that I saw no visible sign of strain as Taran was shooting, and I can't quite put my finger on what it is. But I've watched Taran shoot so often, I could picture him shooting in my sleep. Even the unbelievable distance of it now seems to me suspicious; it reminds me of Poncellet, straining so hard to get power that his aim was ruined, and I wonder if it was a coincidence that Taran chose to send his arrow out over the wall and not at a mark that we could see. The more I think about it, the more *everything* about the deliberate way Taran set up that one shot to ensure he had my full attention starts to seem fishy, and there's only one logical conclusion to be drawn from it: that seemingly effortless long shot of Taran's was anything but effortless, and it must have taken everything in him to make it look that way. It was a performance, just like one of Tristan's, designed to mislead me.

That's the logical conclusion, all right, and after the way he's just slammed into me, it's all too easy to believe. Instead, I have an irrational, gut feeling that it's exactly what Taran *wants* me to think. Tristan was right, a demonstration *is* worth a thousand words, and maybe it's just wishful thinking. But I can't help feeling that Taran's was a double-bluff, and now I'm absolutely certain that for reasons I cannot fathom, what Taran's really been trying to do ever since he staggered into the clearing with my arrow sticking out of his shoulder is convince me that I hurt him *more* than I really did.

"SUBLIME! DIVINE! TRULY INSPIRED, AND INGENIOUS," GILLES IS gushing rapturously, in a voice that manages to sound both wildly ecstatic and a little bored, actually. Then he adds flatly,

"Regrettably, it'll never work."

"What do you mean, it won't work?!" I demand, thrusting out my chest so belligerently that Tristan has to put his hands on my shoulders and guide me gently out of Gilles's way.

We're standing in the middle of the far field, and it's taken Pascal and me over two solid hours to prepare a mock-up of the boys' trick as I've reimagined it out here where our set-up can be shielded from prying eyes by the colorful rows of temporary pavilions.

The necessary odds and ends of wood and twine we scrounged up from the shop in the hour right before noon mess. Then after a jaunt out into the woods in search of willow saplings pliable enough for our purposes (and after a short detour therein by me to the stream to wash out Falko's tunic, hastily snatched up from Taran's room), it's taken us the hour and a half since our noonday meal to get everything cut to size, shaped, and pounded into place. After a few minor setbacks and one near-disaster, we've finally gotten everything arranged and ready.

Before us on the field now stands a row of eight wands, firmly planted into the ground starting at about 80 yards distant, the one behind the other and at 15-yard intervals. Each wand is a little taller than the one in front of it, but it's hard to tell this at the moment, since the tops of the wands have all been pulled down to one side as far as they'd go without breaking and then attached with twine to adjacent shorter stakes. Now the wands are all bent right in the middle at an approximately 90-degree angle and tethered fast to hold them in that curved position, just as though they really were reeds swaying in a stiff breeze.

If I do say so myself, it looks quite impressive: the wands seem to be curtseying politely, but with a tension in them that engages the eye and creates the appearance that the wands are poised and ready for action. If that weren't enough to create a sense of anticipation, to the farthest wand we've added one last feature: another wand, a little shorter than the others and squarer in section, is standing free and upright but balanced precariously on top of the bent wand below it, near the tethered end of it where it's bent over so far as to be virtually horizontal.

Needless to say, it's been quite a chore to get everything prepared and in precisely the right position. I've been glad of the activity, actually, since it's left me little energy to think about Taran, let alone to worry about him. It's been an awful lot of work, though, and stressful, too, and I'm pretty proud of our achievement. So I think it's understandable that I'd find Gilles's easy dismissal of it all plenty irritating.

But it isn't at all unexpected. In fact, it's precisely the response we were hoping to elicit.

It's all part of the plan Tristan spelled out for us before Gilles turned up for practice this morning, and so far, it's been working perfectly. So while Tristan makes a show of putting me out of Gilles's way, he gives my shoulders a gentle warning squeeze; I'm overplaying my part, and it's time I bowed out and left the rest to him.

"Come now, men," Tristan says mildly as I step aside, just like an actor leaving the stage. "Let's not quarrel. If our friend has misgivings, Marek, let's hear him out, and see if we can't disabuse him of them. Why don't you try walking him through it all again?"

Gilles waves off this suggestion. "I assure you, I comprehend it perfectly well. It's all quite simple, really, isn't it? You're to run up from the side, Tristan, and shoot at those ropes. Then as the wands pop upright, I shoot them."

"As they pop up *to a predictable position*, every single time," I can't help interjecting. "And if you time it correctly, you'll get 'em while they're *still in motion!*" I add, stepping forward a little in my enthusiasm until a stern look from Tristan quells me, and I step back again.

"Quite," Gilles agrees. "That part's all right. I can certainly hit them. It's DuBois's shots at those tethering ropes that are the problem, Marek."

"Surely you're not meaning to imply that I'd miss them," Tristan says smoothly, and I'm impressed. He gives his blandly bantering tone just the right hint of underlying indignation.

"A length of twine's an awfully slender mark, old man. But no. Since you can run up as close to them as you like, you'd probably manage to hit them. I'm not doubting your precision. It's that the twine won't break, even if you do. An arrowhead's not a knife, you know — particularly not the rounded points we use in competition. Even with a direct hit, one that's absolutely dead center, the point'll just slide off, or bounce away. With a broadhead with a sharp enough edge, *maybe* — though it'd be one hell of a shot, from any distance. But slicing a string with a bodkin arrow? It's just not possible — something you boys would know, if you'd bothered to try it. Why, I'd wager not even Guillaume Tell could do it."

"Did you say 'wager'?" Tristan grins, and Pascal has to elbow me to get me to stifle a snicker.

"Not even you can beat the laws of nature, my friend," Gilles says, shaking his head.

"It might be fun to try," Tristan replies cockily, stretching out his hand toward his friend in a gesture that's half a challenge, half an invitation. "I'm game, if you are. Besides, the boys have gone to considerable effort. We owe it to Marek to give it a go, at least," he says. And so the boys shake hands on it, and just as Tristan predicted, soon they've agreed to a bet on the following terms: if Gilles is right and the trick proves impossible, I'm to take on all of Gilles's fletching for a month in penance ("*It's only fair, Marek,*" Tristan tells me, "*After all, this trick was all your idea,*" but I don't mind. It's all part of his act, although admittedly, it's convincing precisely because it's the kind of thing Tristan would say anyway). But if Tristan can free even one of the wands with a single shot, Gilles will agree to adopt the new version of the trick.

Gilles is so confident of the outcome of the wager that while Tristan shoulders his bow and heads down the sidelines with it, instead of preparing to take any shots himself he launches straight into an officious instruction to me on his preferred type of fletching for every situation. Even after Tristan's darted forward with a cry of "*hey, ho, Marek!*" to take a shot at the first tethering twine, Gilles still hasn't bothered to lift his bow. Instead he's lounging languidly against it, but I don't mind this either. I settle in, too, and while Tristan proceeds to crouch down a good 20 yards from the first post and to swing his bow into position, I prepare to savor Gilles's reaction. I want to have a good view of his expression, when he sees what's about to happen — what I know *for a fact* is going to happen, inevitably.

Because of course, we *did* try it. And the way we've got it rigged, there's no way Tristan can fail to make every single one of his shots, easily.

Sure enough, virtually as soon as Tristan releases, with a *zing!* of the bowstring and a *ping!* of the post, the twine flies free, and at the same moment, with an audible and satisfying *whoosh*, the first wand in the row accordingly springs rapidly up into an upright position.

It's not often that anything surprises Gilles. Or at least if it does, he rarely allows himself to show it. The most I've managed to get out of him in the past is a slight lifting of his brows, accompanied by one of those fruity exclamations of his. So his reaction now is terribly gratifying.

He, too, springs upright, almost as though Tristan's shot has also released him from the restraint of some invisible tether, and for a while all he can do is gape at the slender willow now oscillating gently in front of him. His shock is so palpable, he almost seems to be vibrating right along with it.

It takes Gilles so long to pull himself together that Tristan's already moved down the line and he's shooting at the fourth post in the series by the time Gilles has recovered himself enough to snatch up his own bow and start aiming at the wands as Tristan frees them. And almost as satisfying as that first look of disbelief on Gilles's face is the fact that it's all exactly as I anticipated; as the boys proceed to complete the trick together, with all the motion on the field the trick really does look simply dazzling.

Even better, it's taken Gilles virtually no time at all to get onto the timing of it. He can already make his own shots at the moving wands, and it's just

349

what old Poncellet ordered: the perfect combination of a trick that *looks* impossible (Gilles's own reaction leaves no doubt about *that*), but one which is in fact relatively easy — given the boys' skills, anyway.

When Tristan reaches the last wand in the line, Gilles doesn't have to be told what to do, even though we've not yet explained the final element of the set-up to him. As soon as Tristan shoots the twine free and the bent wand springs up, sending the loose wand balanced on top of it tumbling high into the air, no explanation is necessary. Both boys take aim at it instinctively, and when it's at the top of its arc and its entire length is outlined sharply against the pale blue sky, they release their arrows simultaneously, striking it in mid-air with a satisfying *patter-patter* as their arrows hit in nearly perfect synchrony.

The wand twirls gracefully down to the ground with a swirl of red and white that would be absolutely beautiful, if the effect of it didn't remind me a little unpleasantly of a barber's pole.

"Now *that's* a wand in motion!" Gilles crows, trotting down the field to slap Tristan on the back enthusiastically. "By God if you aren't a marvel, DuBois! And I'll admit it. It's about the best trick I've ever seen. But be careful," he laughs. "Do *that* at Firsts, and you'll be burned at the stake for a magician! There *is* some trick to it, I take it?" he adds shrewdly, luckily sounding appreciative rather than annoyed about it.

"Don't congratulate me," Tristan says, nodding in affirmation. "It was all Marek's idea. What do you say, kid? Shall we let him in on the secret?"

I feel ridiculously proud when Tristan then steps aside, and lets me be the one to lead Gilles over to the nearest post to show him how the trick was managed, even though from up close the mechanism of it is readily apparent and there isn't much need to explain. I walk him through it anyway, showing him the large, round hole approximately 2 inches in diameter that Pascal and I cut neatly through the tethering post, not far below the top of it. Then I gesture down to something lying in the grass a few feet away: an equally large, round dowel cut to fit loosely into it.

"See here?" I say, retrieving the dowel and sliding it back into the hole in the post. "Tristan didn't *cut* the twine. He just released it. The twine *was* tied to the top the *wand*, but it wasn't actually tied to the *post*. It was simply looped around the protruding end of this dowel. *That's* what he was aiming at — and from 20 paces, for a butts man like Tristan a dowel with a 2-inch diameter is a nice, big target. When he struck the dowel dead center, his shot not only drove the dowel out through the hole in the post, it caused the dowel to slide out through the twine, too. The arrow itself rebounded just enough to stick in the stake inside the dowel hole, but only *after* sending the dowel right through the loop of twine and out the other end, neatly freeing it."

"What's *really* clever about it," Pascal puts in proudly, "is that when the little dowel is in position, it sticks out from the post only very slightly. It's hardly visible, even from a short distance."

Gilles slides the dowel in and out of the hole in the post a few times for himself, and then he goes over and inspects the length of twine still attached to the top of the nearby wand. One end of the twine is tied firmly to the end of the wand via a small hole drilled neatly through the top of it, just as I said. But dangling at the other end is a little slip-knotted loop, like a miniature noose or a tiny lasso.

"Remarkable!" he declares. "Yes, it's just as *I* said — devilishly ingenious. Marek, you've outdone yourself," and I allow myself a moment to bask in his praise. But I can't take all the credit, so before long I have to confess. Originally, I *had* thought Tristan's shots would cut the twine. When we tried it and we realized it wasn't going to work, Pascal helped me devise the mechanism with the dowels, and I tell him so.

"Didn't *I* tell you, Marek?" Gilles exclaims, after we've all indulged in another hearty round of congratulations. "It just goes to prove what I've been saying all along. With a little effort, *anything* is possible," and in his inimitable way he manages to take credit for the whole thing.

"Admit it, Gilles! Marek's really surprised you," Tristan laughs.

"Enjoy it, dear boy," Gilles concedes indulgently, nodding his head in my direction, "as it's not likely to happen again."

"So, just to be clear. You *do* agree to do the trick this way in the competitions, don't you, old man?" Tristan asks, just to ensure that there are no hard feelings, since we essentially set Gilles up and Tristan doesn't intend to hold his friend to a wager that wasn't strictly speaking fair. But Gilles seems genuinely delighted with the trick, and when he exclaims,

"I'm nothing if not a man of my word. And anyway, you made your point. The trick's fabulous," it's all going so well that I don't even mind it, much, when Tristan next says,

"If you thought it looked good like *that*, wait 'til we've got 15 or 20 wands in play! And of course, we won't just be shooting that last wand together. We'll be shooting down each other's arrows first instead," particularly since I notice that he gives Gilles a sidelong glance as he says it. And then he adds casually,

"Unless, that is, we think the trick's good enough now without it, and we decide to save the arrow-downing element for Seconds, when we'll really need it."

Gilles lets this pass without comment, and I notice he's not commented, either, on the fact that as we've set up the trick, none of the wands themselves are at a particularly taxing distance. We seem to have tacitly done away with the long shot of Master Guillaume's that won the masters' competition, too, and even if Tristan does still intend to try to shoot down an arrow of Gilles's as a grand finale to the extravagant trick, it's precisely in this final element that I've taken Poncellet's *other* piece of advice to heart.

Having that last wand tossed up into the sky isn't just going to give the master the motion he wants, it's my insurance: there'll be so many things flying through the air at the end of the boys' exhibition, hopefully nobody will notice it much if Tristan aims for Gilles's arrow, and he misses.

Both of the boys are scheduled for tutorials this afternoon, so we only have time to reset the field and run through the whole thing from start to finish one more time. I don't mind, since even that first run-through went beautifully, and the boys have the basics of the trick down already. All it needs now is a little polish, so I don't even mind that we'll only have used the set-up that it took us hours to fix twice before Pascal and I have to take it all down and pack it up again. I can't help feeling that after my devastatingly bad day yesterday I've managed to rally and to stay focused, and it's paid off. I've gotten back on track and at long last we've agreed upon a doable trick, and I'm so glad about it there are only two tiny things that are still bothering me at all, really.

The first is that Tristan hasn't actually gotten any better at wands. Having the boys train each other to be second best at their own best skill was the original crux of my plan, and as far as I can see they've made no real progress on figuring out how they're going to do it.

When I try to ask Tristan about it as we're packing up, though, he assures me that he and Gilles have in fact been working on something. But he won't tell me what it is.

"Trust me, and have patience, little brother. A man's style isn't a trick, simply to be learned," he declares evasively. And when I try to press him about it, Gilles pipes in with,

"*True* style can't be taught at all. You've got to be born with it. A man's got to wear it, like a second skin," and soon the two of them have wandered on ahead, deep in one of their frivolous discussions about how a man's shooting style flows from his personality.

I can see that they're both too keyed up about the trick to take me seriously, so I drop it and I decide not to worry about it. I do trust Tristan, and it's not as though he's a slouch at the skill. He's sure to pass Firsts against Jurian and Falko, and that's the most important thing. And anyway, right now the *second* little thing that's worrying me is a much more immediate problem:

It's time for squires' club again.

CHAPTER TWENTY-SIX

Pascal and I stash away the materials for the boys' trick in the back of a nearby tent, since it won't do us any good for anyone to get too close a look at the components of the trick before the competition. Then we make our way together back across the yard, and as we go, Pascal asks me,

"Do you suppose anybody will notice the dowels flying out of the postholes, Marek, or lying around on the field?"

I'm in the process of replying assuredly,

"Gilles didn't notice them, did he? And he was right on the field. And even if someone should notice bits of wood flying about, they'll simply assume Tristan's nicked one of the posts, won't they?," when just as we come around the stables and into view of the butts, we're met with an unpleasant sight.

A motley assortment of kitchen boys and other sundry servants is busily at work on a large construction project, right in front of the stables. I don't have to hear Pascal's sharp intake of breath to know what it must be that they're building, either — and surprisingly fast. Even if I couldn't already guess, from its shape I'd recognize it anywhere: a gazebo, and one that's virtually an exact replica of the one that stands in Sir Brecelyn's garden. The only difference is that this one is mounted on wheels, one set under each corner, and it is as yet unpainted. It doesn't take a genius to guess that eventually, it's going to end up being white.

"Uh, Pascal," I say warily, when I see him blanch. "Won't you reconsider getting Tristan to help you with your proposal? Because really, I can't help thinking that you're being set up for failure."

But Pascal won't hear of it. He's determined to rise to the occasion, and he'll brook no criticism of his master, either, even though it can't have escaped his notice that Gilles has chosen to reproduce the very location where he must think Pascal got his first kiss from Lady Sibilla during Thirds last year. It was actually *Armand* who got that kiss, but Gilles can't know that, since he wasn't there. All kinds of outlandish rumors were circulating about the encounter (most of them started by Pascal himself, I must say) and it's anybody's guess what report of it all Gilles heard. Since Pascal's avid courtship of the lady started soon thereafter, Gilles surely believes (and rightly so) that the whole gazebo incident was what sparked the affair, and I'm pretty sure Gilles hasn't forgotten about it. Or forgiven it, either. It can't be a coincidence, and at the very least Gilles must know it's sure to make Pascal uncomfortable to propose to one girl in a setting so designed to recall a fraught encounter with another one.

Luckily for Pascal, who's now turning a funny shade of green, at just this moment the burly Master Bernard emerges from the stables. Upon spying the makeshift carpenters at their task, he stomps forward, shaking his fists and bellowing at them,

"Hey you, whip fodder! You can't be doing *that* there," and in fear they hastily gather up their tools and materials, and in a flurry of activity they wheel the offending item off into the yard and out of our view, to set up their operation elsewhere. As the big, creaking wooden thing rolls ominously past us, though, still carrying a few of the smaller kitchen boys along inside it, I can't help worrying just what other surprises Gilles might have planned. The whole thing is beginning to show all the earmarks of being a stage set for a little subtle revenge, and if so, I fear I'm going to be partly to blame. At least, I'm really starting to regret having given Gilles the idea of pulling a Trojan horse.

It's right at that moment that we see it.

The gazebo was blocking our view out onto the butts. Now that the boys have removed it, rolling it away past us rattling and swaying and kicking up a great big cloud of dust, as the dust settles behind it and we get an unobstructed view out onto our practice range, the effect is as though a crew of stagehands has just moved aside one prop, to reveal a dramatic new scene already unfolding beyond it — a spectacle, really. Or the culminating act of a tragedy.

"Oh, dear," is all Pascal can say, as side-by-side we're drawn over to get a better view of it.

It's Taran, practicing on the near butts.

There's nothing particularly unusual about that, of course. With Firsts coming up it's only natural that Taran would be practicing during his spare time, and in the few seconds before I get a really good look at exactly what he's doing, I have another sharp pang of conscience; not only did I injure him, but I'm also responsible for significantly curtailing his opportunities to practice, by getting him assigned to overseeing our club.

It *is* unusual, though, that Taran's still shooting butts, and as Poncellet said, *voluntarily*. And that he hasn't moved his bench back from the short distance we were shooting from this morning.

It's unusual, too, that a large group of men is gathered around watching him. Taran's usually too private a person to stand for an audience, let alone encourage one. But now an assortment of veterans, Kingsmen, and other workmen from the reconstruction project are standing in a loose semi-circle behind Taran to observe him, and although they're standing back at a discrete distance and talking in hushed tones animatedly amongst themselves, Taran's clearly done nothing to discourage them.

What's really unusual, though, isn't so much *what* Taran's doing. It's *how* he's doing it.

He's shooting butts, all right. That much is clear. Only he's not using a motion I've ever seen. It's not just that I've never seen Taran use it before. I've never seen *anyone* use anything like it. It's nothing like the sweeping, arcing motions that characterize all the shooting done here at St. Sebastian's. This is something new, something completely different.

I wish I could say it was good. I really do.

But that would be a lie. It isn't just *good*. It's unbelievable, and it's now apparent that all the rattling and banging going on out here wasn't coming just from the gazebo construction. It was coming from him.

"So much for 'a man can't simply teach himself a new style,'" Pascal says sourly, and I don't bother to answer.

I'm too busy just staring.

It's not easy to see exactly what Taran's doing, because whatever it is, he's doing it astonishingly quickly. The motion is so quick and fast, and at the same time so simple and so minimal, I doubt I could convey the full effect of it in words, even if I were sure I really understood what he's doing. It almost looks like he's directly inverting his clouts motion, if such a thing is conceivable.

The first thing that strikes me is that Taran is standing squarely facing the target, instead of sideways to it the way the boys usually shoot. With his legs slightly straddled and his chest out there's something aggressive about the stance, as though he's confronting the target head-on and challenging it. And when he releases, he's holding his bow in a horizontal position, perfectly parallel to the ground at about mid-chest level. I've seen men shoot on the horizontal before, of course. But never in a competition. It's only suited for shooting at extreme close-range and at times when accuracy isn't an issue, since it's too hard to sight along a bow in that position; at the height Taran's holding his bow, sighting at all is impossible. The shots he's taking must be pure instinct.

It would be remarkable enough that Taran's mastered shooting on the horizontal to the degree that he could use it for the precision of butts shooting. But of course that's not all he's doing, and what allows for the most innovative thing about the new motion of his is a novel piece of equipment he's sporting on his bow arm, something that must be his own creation.

It's essentially just a long, cuff-like bracer made of thick leather. But this one is made of two separate pieces and it covers most of his arm, from his wrist to a point about midway up his bicep. And although the inner surface of it is smoothed to protect his forearm from the recoil of the bowstring, just like a normal bracer, its upper surface has been modified to hold a flight of arrows in a most ingenious fashion.

A long series of deep ridges are carved into the stiff leather, parallel to each other but perpendicular to the length of his arm, each one of just the right size and shape for an arrow shaft to fit down snugly into it and essentially snap into place. It's nothing that would work for anything but target shooting, since if Taran swung his bow arm around freely, the long arrows attached to it would swing around, too, and dangerously. But standing stationary as he is with his bow arm out in front of him, he's got what looks like fifteen or twenty arrows fitted down into the slots of the bracer. They're neatly lined up with the fletched ends slightly staggered and ready to hand, and it's easy to see what's allowing him to achieve the speed of his shots. He doesn't need a squire to pass him his arrows, or have to waste time bending over to pluck them up out of the ground.

"How's he loading?" Pascal asks me, giving me a nudge but not taking his eyes off Taran. "It looks like he's reaching *through* his bow, between the string and the limbs."

"He *is*."

And it's true, because as closely as I can reconstruct it, what Taran's doing is this:

He starts square to the target, with his bow arm extended out in front of him and his elbow slightly bent, so that at the beginning of his motion his bow is almost perfectly at the vertical. But he's rotated his wrist just enough to slant the tip of his bow slightly down across his line of vision, so that the fletches of the arrows he's wearing on his bow arm are all slanting slightly, too, and pointing in towards him. All he has to do to get them easily is reach right through his bow, just as Pascal said. This he does in a swift, circular motion, and he doesn't snatch up the arrows the way archers usually do. Instead, as his hand sweeps past his chest, his palm is open and facing him, and he lets his splayed fingers slide along either side of one of the arrow shafts, so that the motion of his hand lifts the arrow free. Without pausing or closing his fist, in one continuous motion he then brings his still-open hand circling back toward the bow with the arrow now neatly trapped between his middle fingers, and as he guides the nock of the arrow back onto the bowstring, his fingers are already starting to curl in preparation of pulling back the string. It's all one small, smooth motion that reminds me a little of the way Turk backloaded his bow during the equestrian exhibition, and it's essentially the same thing: a unique way to load a bow with incredible efficiency.

It's not just the speed with which Taran's loading his bow or even the speed of the shots themselves that's impressive, however. It's also the amount of sheer, raw power he's getting behind his shots, and for this, one last step is crucial. As Taran's guiding the arrow onto the string, he's *already* starting to bend his bow. And as he does, with a sudden twist of his wrist at the same time he flips his bow down, hard, so that it's perfectly parallel to the ground and level with it. While the bow is still rotating, with both hands simultaneously he gives a swift, hard pull on the bowstring and a push on the bow grip, forcing them in opposite directions, so that the whole thing — the nock, the twist, the push and pull, and his release — are all one lightning-fast, coordinated motion that's more like a wrenching spasm, or the springing of a tightly coiled spring.

Or maybe it's more like a sucker punch, straight to the gut. At least, that's how each shot feels to me, and Taran's arrows are flying out so hard and fast that the impact of each one is like the crack of a whip, or the blast of a cannon.

"It's almost like he's shooting a crossbow more than a longbow, isn't it Marek?" Pascal marvels. "Why, I doubt a man could pump even one of your repeating bows any faster than he's loading and releasing," and I don't bother to argue with him. It *is* a lot like watching a man shoot a repeating bow, and the only big difference I can see is one that I'm in no mood to point out to Pascal: shots from *my* repeating bow tend to fly all over the place. Without being able to sight along his shots, Taran may not be splitting his own arrows the way Poncellet did. But he is neatly crossing the square, most expertly.

It only takes Taran a matter of seconds to shoot all the arrows on his bracer, and when he's done with one round, while the men in front of us all applaud and whistle, he merely sticks out his arm and allows Remy to reload the bracer for him. Then he starts up again (*twist, pull, boom! twist, pull, boom!, twist boom, twist boom, twist boom bang BOOM!*), and when he's on about his sixth arrow, Pascal says dispiritedly,

"Well, *that* ought to be enough bang, even for Tristan. Even with arms like *his*, though, I can't see how he's managing it. I mean, where in the heck is all that bang coming from?!" and I know what he means. It does look like all the power behind Taran's shots is coming entirely from his arms, but I know that's deceptive. I can sense it building from his legs, coiling up through his belly and into his torso, so that even though his movement is so contained, he's putting his whole body into it — that is, with one significant exception. The motion ends with those incredible arms of his.

He's not using his shoulders for this move at all, I see.

"I have to say, though, the boys were right about one thing. You know, about a man's style fitting his personality. There's no doubt about it. *That* move is all Taran,*" Pascal is rambling, and as Taran pauses to reload again, I can't contain myself. I burst out,

"When in the blue blazes did *Taran* get so good at butts?!?"

"What are you talking about, Marek?" Pascal replies, startled out of his reverie by my vehemence and sounding surprised. "Taran's always been incredible at them, one of the very best."

I shoot him a sarcastic look, but Pascal just looks puzzled.

"Seriously, Marek. Oh, I know he doesn't particularly like to shoot butts, as he vastly prefers clouts. But this is *Taran* we're talking about. Of course he's a great butts shooter. All he lacked was a little flair."

"It looks like he found some," I say wryly.

"I wonder what can have inspired him?" Pascal muses. "I mean, Firsts is wands, not butts," and there's nothing I can say.

Again I have the uneasy sensation that I know what I *should* be thinking, what Taran surely wants me to think: that he's still covering for the fact that I've injured him, and he's come up with this move that doesn't involve rotating his shoulder as an excuse for why he's been avoiding shooting clouts all day.

But I know it isn't true.

He didn't just come up with this motion since this morning, or that contraption he's got strapped onto his arm. *This* is what Taran was doing all yesterday afternoon, while the rest of us were at the millpond — after *I* was foolish enough to taunt him that Tristan is better at butts than he is.

I must still have a bewildered expression on my face, because Pascal is now giving me a disbelieving look.

"Taran's always been dead accurate, Marek. What did you expect? That a man who can put an arrow through the eye-slit in a visor at 500 yards would lack precision at close range? Or haven't you ever watched Taran shooting butts before?" he says, a little sarcastically.

I'm just about to make an equally sarcastic comeback, when it occurs to me that Pascal is right. I never really *have* watched Taran closely when he's shooting butts — for the simple reason that he rarely does it unless forced to during drills, or during the competitions. During practices he's always at the far end of the line where I can't really see him, and I wasn't watching him at all during the boys' butts trials last year. It was the very first competition, and my mind was elsewhere. Now I remember that he came in *second* in that competition, although there were eleven other boys shooting — including Tristan — and I feel a little ill.

"Oh yeah?" I demand anyway, still not wanting to believe it. "If Taran's always been so terrific at butts, and if he's so much better than everybody else at *all* of the skills, then last year, why didn't he sweep the competitions?"

Instead of taking offense at my tone, Pascal just looks even more puzzled.

"What are you talking about, Marek? He did."

"What?!?" I explode, my voice ringing out and mingling indignantly with the chorus of booms and blasts still thundering from Taran's bow. "You can't try to tell me that Taran *won* all the trials last year, Pascal! I was *there*."

"But he did," Pascal insists, frowning. "Well, except for Seconds, naturally. Nobody beats *my* master outright at wands. He and Gilles tied that one."

This is *not* at all as I remember it.

Gilles won Seconds, didn't he? And Taran came in second (annoyingly enough). At least, that's what I'd thought Master Guillaume said. But Pascal is perfectly serious, and he seems so sure, I waver. Maybe they *did* tie and the master simply *announced* Taran's name second, and I didn't notice — since all that really mattered to me that night was that Tristan had passed.

"Well, what about Firsts, then?" I counter. "That was butts, and Gilles won that competition outright, surely."

This, at least, I'm absolutely certain of, although the glaring fact that Taran placed second in that competition, too, is really starting to bother me.

"Well, sure," Pascal says, unruffled. "But we all know what happened *there*," he says. And then infuriatingly, he starts to chuckle, a little bitterly. My brain is starting to feel like it's rattling around inside my head along with the beat of Taran's shots, so I pull Pascal back by the sleeve a little ways away from all the noise, where I can get his serious attention (although unfortunately, not so far back that we aren't still watching *Taran*), and I demand,

"And the *garland*?"

There's no way Pascal can try to tell me Tristan didn't win *that*.

"There you go," he declares. "You've just explained it yourself," and all I can do is give him an uncomprehending stare.

"The *garland*," Pascal repeats meaningfully.

When he sees with surprise that I really don't know what he's talking about, he sighs. "Taran didn't *want* to win it, Marek."

When all I can do is keep staring unblinkingly, he continues,

"He was ahead of Gilles in the overall competition, going into that final round at Firsts. He was sure to pass the trials easily, and to end up highly ranked. That was all that mattered to him. So Taran didn't try to better Gilles's shot during the garland portion of the competition."

"Are you saying Taran *let* Gilles beat him?"

"Of course he did. Everybody knows that," he says, as though he really can't believe I didn't already know something so obvious.

"But *Tristan* won the garland," I protest. "You can't convince me Taran would ever let *Tristan* beat him, even when it didn't really matter," and Pascal concedes,

"Yeah, that bit must have come as quite a shock! But we all thought Gilles's upshot for the garland was unbeatable. It was Taran's bad luck that Tristan came along *after* his own turn was already over, and split Gilles's arrow. I bet that'll be the last time he underestimates Tristan!" he laughs. Then he turns sober, as a thought strikes him. "Say, *that* must be why he's worked up this new butts motion. To make sure Tristan can't outdo him at *anything*, this year."

I absorb these unpleasant statements for a moment, trying to wrap my mind around them.

"Why wouldn't Taran want to win the garland, though, Pascal?" I finally ask, feeling thrown by Pascal's air of certainty on the matter. "His own fiancée was handing it out. It doesn't make any sense."

"It makes perfect sense to *me*, Marek," Pascal says, giving me a baleful look. "*Think* about it. Getting down on one knee in front of the whole country, to be crowned by his own fiancée? Having his private affairs and personal feelings turned into a public spectacle, a *travesty*, for the crowd to gawk at? Can you imagine Taran subjecting himself, subjecting his future *wife*, to that kind of scrutiny willingly? Only one thing could have mortified him more, really: having to make the actual *proposal* publicly."

Pascal's obviously thinking more of himself than of Taran, and projecting his own situation back onto him. But I have to admit that what he's saying is plausible. After all, when Gilles first announced his plan for Pascal's proposal to Ginger, I thought something similar myself. So I'm not at all sure whether I can believe Pascal's version of last year's events, or not. But it hardly matters. All it takes is one look at Taran blasting another barrage of precision shots straight into the target for a most unpalatable truth to become increasingly clear:

Last year, Taran wasn't trying his hardest.

He didn't have to.

And everyone else knew it, but me.

Seeing my expression and rightly guessing that he's depressed me, Pascal says hurriedly,

"Taran's new motion *is* impressive, I'll grant you. Incredible, even. But Tristan's still the best butts shooter I've ever seen, old Poncellet excepted. So just like nobody beats Gilles outright at wands, nobody beats Tristan outright at butts, either. You *do* still believe Tristan can beat him at butts, don't you, Marek?"

"Of course he can," I sniff, and I mean it. Taran's new motion packs a punch, all right, and it has a certain something that's sure to make the judges sit up and take notice (I try not to let Aristide's awful word *virility* creep in), but Tristan's beautiful motion is exquisite and it just can't be beaten, in my opinion. But freezing Taran out of one of the top spots at the butts trials is going to be even more of a challenge than I anticipated, and if Pascal's right about what happened last year, we've got a bigger problem — because if Seconds *is* butts, for my plan to work Tristan isn't the only boy who has to be able to beat him.

"You know, Pascal," I say worriedly. "I really hope the boys were telling us the truth, that they've got a plan in the works to train each other in their respective skills."

From the equally worried look that crosses Pascal's face, I know I don't have to explain to him what I mean.

We stand there for a little while longer, watching Taran rattle out another round or two in silence. Now I *am* watching Taran shoots butts closely, and as I do, I'm trying hard not to hear Master Guillaume's gushing voice in the back of my mind, or to notice too much how Taran's new motion shows off the power and grace of his big, elegant body to advantage.

Taran's never been bulky, despite his impressive size, and watching him in motion now I can see that he's gotten leaner after the starvation days of the plague, and it suits him. Or maybe he just seems that way because he's shooting butts, not clouts, I don't know. But it's funny. Although I'm sure I've never seen anything like the move he's doing now before, the longer I watch him the more I begin to feel like there's something familiar about the sight of him.

The feeling is so strong it's almost like a memory, as though somehow I've seen someone shooting butts just like this, somewhere before.

As soon as I think it, the gushing words repeating in my brain slowly transform, until they aren't Master G's any longer. They're snatches of lines from Meliana's notebook:

"*Everything about him was in perfect proportion. He was a long, clean line.*"

Even worse:

"*He was incredible. He could do anything.*"

It's only now, with the phrases Lady Brecelyn used to describe my own father echoing in my head, that the most unsettling thing about the entire episode hits me — the thing that's been bothering me about Taran all day since the moment he walked out of the stables this morning. It lands like a blow, as hard as any arrow sent by that confounded new motion of his.

It's been so obvious, I should have seen it a long time ago. But I didn't notice it before, I swear.

It's the color of the tunic and the matching trousers Taran's wearing.

He's a long, clean line, all in dove gray. And *I'm* the one who thought it would look right to dress him that way.

I already wasn't looking forward to squires' club today. Now I'm positively dreading it.

BY THE TIME PASCAL AND I TRUDGE OVER TO ARM OURSELVES for our club practice, the little nervous beat that's been ticking away behind my ribs all day in anticipation of having to deal with Taran at squires' club has climbed up into my throat. Even without the fear of whatever petty tyrannies he's got in store for me, when I think of spending the entirety of the afternoon in close quarters with him after witnessing that new motion of his, I don't know *what* I'm feeling. Except that whatever it is, it isn't sorry for him anymore.

At least, not exclusively.

Not while he's still wearing that blasted dove-gray tunic I put him in.

The sight of Remy trotting over to join us at the boys' cabinets does little to steady me, since it doesn't take much to guess what he's eager to talk about. Taran's finally stopped shooting and the crowd around him's dispersed, and while his master is over splashing off at the water barrels Remy's come over to switch out his equipment.

"What did you think of Taran's new butts motion, Marek?" he chirps excitedly, as predicted. "Isn't it amazing? And guess what?! He told me it was all inspired by *your* crossbow tutorial! Isn't that *flattering*?"

All I do is grunt, but it's not enough to dampen Remy's enthusiasm.

"And he looks *so* magnificent doing it, don't you think?" he gushes. "Although I must say, I don't care much for that color of tunic on him."

This, at least, is something with which I can heartily agree.

It doesn't get much better once the rest of the boys have gathered, and Taran comes over to get the practice officially underway.

Taran's even more acerbic than usual, especially to me, and he alternates between ignoring me pointedly and picking on me mercilessly. It's all small stuff — assigning me the worst drudge tasks or making me do all the demonstrations and then picking apart my technique. And I'll admit it. I'm doing my best to irritate him, too, and trying subtly to undermine him, but it's a strange dynamic.

I've never really thought there was much danger that Master Guillaume would eject Taran from the trials, but Taran's not one for idle threats. If *anyone* finds out he's been wounded, he's sure to put the blame on Tristan, just as he said. And frankly, it wouldn't be much less embarrassing for *me* if the whole story came out. I can't imagine the scene, if I had to try to explain what really happened to Taran to the master — or to Tristan. Even if I didn't get punished for it (and I surely *would*), I'd never live it down. So I'm also hovering around Taran protectively, in case I need to cover for him again, the way I did this morning.

Taran's shoulder must be at least a little sore, and even if he's been faking some of the pain it's true that he's got to be careful not to make any broad movements that might rip open his stitches. So before long I'm fussing and clucking around him so protectively that I'm probably smothering him almost as much as Remy usually does, and I'll confess. In part, I *am* doing it to be ready to jump in and cover for him. But after all of yesterday's close encounters with him, being around him now amongst the others and trying to act as though nothing unusual has happened between us feels strange, and his cold indifference today actually hurts more than any of the barbs he's periodically tossing my way. So I know I'm also just trying to get any reaction out of him, and I can tell it's getting on his nerves, even though he's doing much the same thing: whenever he thinks the others can't overhear him, he makes a show of grunting or grimacing, anything to convince me that his shoulder really is killing him.

It all comes to a head in an exchange we have around one of the moveable wicker backstops, about halfway through the session.

Taran's sent me downfield to lug the bulky thing closer to the line for Frans to use as a target, and it's just plain too big and heavy for me. Usually two boys work together to move them, with one boy pushing forward from each side, and even then I struggle with the task. All by myself, even by getting around behind it and putting my shoulder to it, I've been making only minimal progress. I must look like David trying to scoot along Goliath, but all the other boys are busy shooting. So after letting me sweat it out for a while, Taran comes down to do it himself.

"You're really enjoying this, aren't you?" I hiss at him, feeling humiliated.

"What do you mean?" he says blandly. "I thought you could do it," and for a second, I almost believe him. Then he adds,

"I *thought* shoving big things from behind was one of your specialties."

I get his implication immediately. But before I can gather my wits enough to respond, he gestures to me to stand aside, and with a roll of his eyes he wraps his big arms around the backstop. Then instead of pushing it along the way we usually do, he lifts it clear up off the ground.

As he does, though, he makes a point of jerking his head to one side in an exaggerated version of the move he did this morning on his way into the stables, after that huge clouts shot of his. It's a sort of protective gesture that's surely supposed to suggest a wince, and even though I know he's just doing it to make me feel guiltier, it's working.

I guess it's been building for a while. But instinctively I put a hand on his arm to restrain him, and with a whispered sort of cry, I exclaim,

"You mustn't strain yourself! Let me help you," and when he tries to shake me off, I don't know what comes over me.

I clutch at his arm with both hands, and hanging onto it, I implore him,

"You *must* let me help you, you must! Oh, Taran, *p-p-please*," and to my horror, I start stuttering. But I can't seem to stop. Not even when without intending it, I'm not talking about the backstop anymore.

"*Please* let me, Taran! Let me tell you, just this once, how wretched about it all I feel! I can't bear for you to think I might have done it on purpose, that I could have ever really wished you an injury. Whatever you've done, you didn't deserve to be *shot* for it. And if you really *are* seriously hurt, why ...!"

"Don't flatter yourself," he says shortly, plopping the backstop back down onto the ground and reaching up to run one hand agitatedly through his hair. "And *stop* making a scene."

He casts a quick glance back at the boys, but nobody's stopped shooting; they all assume we're simply bickering again. Then he stands there looking down at me for a long minute with that unreadable expression of his.

"Oh, I give up!" he finally says. "I confess already. Enough of this, Marieke."

"Enough of what? Confess? What do you mean?"

"Did you really think *you* could hit *me*, even by accident? I picked up that wayward arrow of yours and I shoved it into my shoulder *myself*, to teach you a lesson."

"A *lesson!?*" I cry, dropping his arm indignantly. "What lesson could *that* possibly teach me?" I demand. "To scour the woods for lurkers before shooting?"

"Yes, there's that," he replies caustically. "And something more important. Something *you* of all people should have known already. *Things aren't always what they seem.*"

With that he stalks off, and I suppose I should be terribly angry with him. And for a moment, I am. I'm furious, even.

Then all I feel is worse, and even more guilty.

Because I know Taran is lying.

My little speech must have gotten to him, and in his own crude way, he's taken pity on me. Maybe he's simply tired of dealing with me, or else it was my gender that affected him, and the wretched manner of my plea reminded him that although I may be *'not much of one,'* I really am a girl, and as such I require his chivalry. But it couldn't be more obvious to me that Taran said what he did, simply to relieve me.

Taran's left the backstop where it fell, so poor Frans is stuck shooting at a target that's a little sideways, and much too distant for him. Even if I could move it by myself, I wouldn't try. I've forgotten all about it, too, and as I slowly make my own way back to the line a few paces behind Taran, not feeling very relieved, my mind is busy with other things.

With that old phrase of Gilles's ringing in my ears, I've just realized something, and I don't know what to make of it.

All day, I've been waiting for something that's not going to happen.

With that wayward shot of mine, I delivered a perfect piece of leverage against me right into Taran's hands, for a *second* time. And just like last year, he's never going to use it.

Somehow, that doesn't make me feel as relieved as it should, either.

AFTER THAT, TARAN'S MORE SUBDUED FOR THE REST OF THE session and he stops picking on me. I'm more subdued, too, and although I keep my distance, I start trying to assist him more genuinely. Taran must sense the change, or else it's the sincerity of my outburst that's affected him, because slowly he starts to let me — albeit at first only grudgingly. But as the practice progresses, it becomes increasingly clear that he *does* need me to cover for his soreness and restricted motion, and it's in both our best interests to ensure that none of the boys somehow discover his stitches. And so after a while, a funny thing happens. Instead of fighting each other, we start cooperating.

Circumstances have thrown us together, and it's not just hiding Taran's injury that we both want to achieve. Once we've stopped trying to antagonize each other, it doesn't take me long to see that Taran wasn't kidding about training the squires for Journeys, and that he's taking the job seriously. If we're really going to do it, we're going to have to work together. And so slowly over the course of the afternoon, we come to a sort of tacit arrangement: for the few hours of squires' club at least, we'll put our differences aside, and act professionally. We're still plenty antagonistic about it, in our usual way. But as we settle into an uneasy alliance, gradually our accustomed bickering really is all about archery.

It's not much of a surprise that as we begin trying to negotiate running the session together in earnest, we find we have different opinions on just about everything, and on every point of technique. I have to say, though, that once we take the personal element out of the equation, arguing with Taran actually proves rather entertaining. It's more fun than quarreling with my own master, anyway, since we're much more evenly matched; I mean, *I* can never win an argument with Tristan, either. I'll admit it, too, that Taran's the better trainer. He's by far the superior archer and he's full of information, and he's got all sorts of interesting ideas. So it's particularly gratifying when I'm able to impress him with a point or two from the 'Verbeke technique,' and as strange as it seems, by the end of practice I'm surprised to find that I'm a little sorry it's over, and I've even begun to see the genius of Master Guillaume in putting the two of *us* together.

Over the next few days, I'm nervous whenever the hour for squires' club approaches, as though I'm still waiting for 'the other boot to drop,' so to speak. But Taran was apparently serious in what he said out at the backstop, about putting the incident in the clearing behind us; at least, he seems determined to try to run our practices amicably.

I know it can't last; there's too much pent-up anger and resentment on both sides, and all the tensions are still there between us, simmering away below the surface. But I do my best to ignore them, and Taran does too, and for now, it's as though we've agreed to put all our personal feelings in a box, and to shelve them for another day. And so after a while I begin to relax, and I'm not entirely sure just when it is that I stop dreading squires' club, and I start to look forward to it instead.

But I do know the exact moment when it becomes the highlight of my day.

It's about four or five days later, near the end of one of our club sessions. We've spent the majority of the practice divided up into two groups as usual (having found that 'amicable cooperation' is much easier when Taran and I don't have to interact with each other directly), with half the boys working on crossbows with me while the others work on longbows with Taran. We've been running the boys ragged, and I've probably been pushing my group a little too hard in my eagerness to prove that I can run a practice that's just as rigorous as one of Taran's. The boys are exhausted, so when Pascal comes panting back to the line after a retrieval, as he's putting his bolts back into his leg quiver, he says to me,

"What do you say we call it a day on shooting, Marek, and work on something else? It's been a while since *you* had a chance to work on your squiring skills, hasn't it?"

I'm pretty sure what Pascal really means is that he's tired of having me bark at him to run faster, and he'd be happy to return the favor. But the fact is that I haven't been doing any of my sprinting drills lately, and whatever benefit I was getting from them is already starting to diminish. So Pascal's suggesting is pretty tempting, and I waver. The truth is that I've been purposely avoiding my own private drills these past few days, unsure how Taran would react to them, since they're pretty obviously designed specifically to assist *Tristan*, and not wanting to upset the fragile truce we've managed to establish between us.

"I don't know, Pascal," I reply, casting a quick glance over at Taran. Pascal must sense the source of my hesitation, because before I can get any further, he interrupts to say,

"The thing is, I've had an idea. An idea, for the *club*. More of a *proposal*, really," and when he winces a little at his own word choice, it doesn't take much to guess what's inspired him. When Pascal clears his throat and resumes earnestly, the other boys just straggling back to the line gather around to catch their breath and listen in.

"I've been thinking, boys. What if we *all* work on our squiring skills, *together*? You know, use some of Marek's teamwork, to make us look collectively better during the competitions."

"Ugh, *Teamwork*," Rennie interrupts jokingly. "Not you, too, Pascal!" But Pascal is entirely serious.

"The retrievals for wands are going to be awfully long, Rennie," he retorts. "We're going to be spread out all over the field, and it isn't going to make those of us who are faster look any better, if the slower boys like, uh, er, *Frans*, are lagging behind. We'll just look ridiculous, like a bunch of ragtag boys, running around the field like chickens with their heads cut off. But if we practice retrieving in unison, like a well-oiled machine, why, we can show the crowd that squiring is *in itself* a skill, and one to take pride in."

"Maybe you're right," Rennie concedes, thinking about it. "Practiced, polished, professional — that's us. Squires' Squad! Hey, maybe it'd be sort of like our show."

"It'll be *just* like it," Pascal insists eagerly, and by this point the boys from Taran's group have started to wander over curiously; Taran's given them a break, and he, too, is now standing off at a little distance, just far enough to give the appearance of keeping apart. But not far enough that he can't listen in.

"We wowed the crowd," Pascal continues, slinging his arm around Armand, who's just come over from Taran's group to stand next to him. "We can do it again, if we commit to working together. Maybe we can even figure out a way to work a bit of a performance of our own into it. Oh, what do you say, boys? Marek, what about *you*? What do *you* think?"

"Oh, Pascal!" I gush, a little wistfully. I can't help it. "I absolutely *love* it."

And I do. I know the 'slower boy' Pascal is really talking about is *me*, but the idea doesn't appeal to me just because I would surely be one of the boys most to benefit from it. I can picture us now, streaming down the field in front of the grandstands in perfect unison, just as Pascal said, and I can almost hear a murmur of appreciative voices rising from the crowd: *the Journeys were impressive, of course. But did you see those squires? They really stole the show!* and I know without a shadow of a doubt that this is what I've been wanting, ever since that terrible night when Master Guillaume told me I could never be a Journey. I've gotten faster, but I'll never stand out during the competitions. Not with boys like Pascal and Armand on the field. Not alone. If I want to be remembered at St. Sebastian's as one of the best of the squires, it's got to be as part of a team, and Pascal's just handed me a way. But I also know what Taran's going to think of the idea, and the last thing I want to do now is antagonize him.

"It *does* sound sweet, Pascal. I don't know, though," I repeat sadly, reeling myself in. "Practicing as a team? Master Guillaume might not like it," but he's not really the one I'm thinking about. I'm looking over nervously at Taran, since as we've been speaking, he's been slowly edging over and now he's standing so close to our group as to be right on its periphery. His arms are crossed over his chest, and he's frowning. So I add hastily,

"Besides, it's not up to me." I nod in Taran's direction. "It's up to our new official trainer."

I say it without any trace of sarcasm. I really do.

"What do you say, master?" Pascal asks him, but it's only *pro forma*. Pascal's head is hanging, and he already sounds deflated. Taran was the one who warned us against working together last year, and Pascal knows as well as I do what Taran's going to say.

Imagine Pascal's surprise, then, and mine, too, when after another minute or two of frowning, Taran asks seriously,

"You boys all want to do this?," and when we all nod vigorously, he shrugs, and declares,

"Let's do it, then."

"Are you *sure*, master?!" Remy titters nervously. "Won't Master Guillaume object?"

"I don't see why he should," Taran says shortly. "He asked for more spectacle, and this'll give it to him. It'll be advertisement for his new crossbow contingent, too, if we can work something with them in. I'll talk to him about the possibility, right after practice."

"And if the master does object to us retrieving as a team, I guess that's that, and no harm done," Armand puts in reasonably.

367

Taran just looks at him blankly.

"I see no reason to mention that part to him," he says.

All the boys stare back at him, trying not to look thoroughly taken aback — myself included — and nobody dares to say a thing. Then when Remy makes a tentative little noise that sounds like he's about to object again, Taran adds bitterly,

"The master saw fit to put *me* in charge of this club. So it seem to me that what *I* do with it is entirely up to *me*."

It doesn't take much to see that what's motivating Taran is the desire to get a little not-so-subtle revenge of his own on Master Guillaume for sticking him with our club, more than any genuine wish to oblige us. But he's also saying pretty firmly that if there's any fallout to be suffered for it, he's going to be the one to take it, and we can't help but feel a little like he's siding with us over the master. Even though Taran's surely too careful and rule-abiding to get himself into any real trouble, just the appearance that a Journey of his stature would be willing to stick his neck out to champion us gives us a renewed sense of camaraderie, and one that's been sorely lacking since the night of our show.

For my part, I don't even mind that Taran's apparently changed his tune and he's now claiming complete control over the club (after previously having pretended that he was merely here to serve as *my* observer). I'm too excited about the idea, and it's hard to avoid the conclusion that this is also in part Taran's way of conceding that he was wrong to discourage me from making our apprentice trials into a performance. It even occurs to me to wonder if a desire to keep the tentative peace between us might not have played a little into his decision.

We spend the rest of that afternoon developing a variety of routines for retrievals, then drilling the elements of them at a pace we can all master while Taran oversees and critiques us. When we realize we'll need someone other than Taran to call out our cadence during the competitions, we unanimously elect Pascal to the post. Pascal really is the best of the squires, and even if he weren't our natural leader, we'd have given him the job anyway. We all know the idea stemmed from his desire to make a good showing in front of his Ginger, and a certain sympathy with poor Pascal's plight must have also played a part in motivating Taran to go along with the scheme. We all suggest everything we can think of to beef up Pascal's role in the proceedings, in the hopes that on the day it'll give him the necessary confidence to see him through the stress of having to propose publicly.

And so Taran and I continue to work awkwardly but cooperatively together side by side every afternoon for the rest of that week, spending half of our club sessions on shooting and half on putting our newly dubbed 'squires' squad' through its paces, and by the end of it we've worked up a number of routines flexible enough to be adapted on the fly to fit almost any situation we might encounter during the trials. It's still strained whenever I have to interact with Taran directly (particularly since he makes a habit of it to wear that damned dove-gray tunic to virtually every practice, even though I don't recall ever having seen him wear it previously). But after thinking my afternoons were going to be pure torture, it's exhilarating to find instead that everything I loved most about squires' club has been miraculously restored to me, and that thanks to our 'gentleman's agreement,' squires' club is now a place where I can forget everything else and lose myself in the pure love of archery. And it should be comforting, too, to find that Taran was right: I've put wounding him successfully behind me, and nothing really has changed.

Except, of course, that I know it isn't true.

Something *is* different, and if I dared to lift the lid and peek into that mental strongbox of mine, I know what I would find.

Despite all my good intentions, I'm already feeling awfully confused about Taran again.

CHAPTER TWENTY-SEVEN

Over the week that follows, my days really do begin to fall into the comfortable pattern I predicted they would on the fateful morning of Taran's shooting. And with that disaster now behind me, I've got plenty to be feeling good about. I'm on hiatus from my feuding with Taran, squires' club is going smoothly, and best of all, the matter of the boys' joint trick is settled and it's all coming together beautifully. As I predicted, it's taken the boys no time at all to master it, and if I do say so myself, it looks terrific. It's sure to deliver a big surprise, and so I can't say I'm too sorry when it becomes increasingly clear that the boys have come to a tacit agreement of their own — to ditch the arrow-downing element entirely. I'm a little disappointed to see it go, of course, since it really was a brilliant idea and would have been fantastic. But in the end, it had one insurmountable, fatal flaw: it really *was* impossible. I'm just glad that Tristan realized it in time, and that I was able to come up with something in its stead good enough to keep Gilles committed to our bargain.

I don't know why it is, then, that instead of being contented, I have an uneasy feeling that trouble is coming. It could simply be the weather; there's something oppressive in the atmosphere these days, like a storm is brewing. But I feel apprehensive, and on edge. Maybe it's just what de Gilford said, and it's the whiff of trials is in the air; Firsts is fast approaching, and I should be nervous. But for the first time we're an entire week out from the competitions and I know we're fully ready for them, and that there's just no way that Tristan can fail.

What's more, for once I'm not anxious about my own part in it; thanks to our group preparations in squires' club, I'm actively looking forward to performing at Firsts this year. I've never felt this confident going into one of the trials, for myself *and* for Tristan, so I don't think that's it, unless without my usual last-minute frenzy of preparations to occupy me I've been left feeling restless. So maybe I'm already looking ahead to Seconds, and worrying. But I have that unpleasant feeling that so often accompanies advance readiness that there's *something* I should be worrying about, and I've forgotten what it is. I think, though, it could simply be that I've learned my lesson, since every time I start to get complacent and think that things are going to get better, they usually just end up getting worse instead.

I'd be lying if I said I wasn't also a little worried that being so ready for the competition so early isn't good for Tristan, and that it might affect his competitive edge. He's always his best under pressure, and I can't help but notice he's getting complacent, too, and lazy. Lately, he's even started looking a little unkept. I put it down to the fact that there are no girls here for him to impress — particularly *one* of them, since despite his efforts to hide it, it doesn't take much to see that Melissande is on his mind more than ever these days. Even so, somehow he just doesn't quite seem himself, and I worry that it's indicative of a worrisome trend in his mood in general of late. I'm not sure what it is exactly, since it's not as though he and Gilles have stopped practicing. He puts himself dutifully enough through his paces. But it doesn't look to me like he's pushing himself, and often when Pascal and I look for our masters after squires' club is over, we find that they've already packed up and that they're holed up in Gilles's room instead of out on the field. Even worse, whenever we're together Tristan seems content to lounge around, draped on the furniture or with his booted legs up on a chair, drawling idly about things that seem to me to be a bunch of nonsense.

I think that's why, when we're sitting together out at one of the little tables in the garden together on a muggy afternoon in the middle of that next week, when Armand pops out to see if Tristan's ready for his usual Wednesday afternoon trim and Tristan waves him off for a second time in as many weeks, I can't help chiding him.

"You're starting to look awfully shaggy, Tristan."

"Really?" he says, pretending to look pleased. "How perfect!"

I know this uncooperative mood, so I really should drop it. But he's getting on my nerves, and he's not given me a straight answer anyway about why we're sitting around here swatting flies and not out practicing. It doesn't help that from somewhere out past the stables is coming a steady drumming that sounds a lot like hammering. Whether it's Taran blasting out a round or two out on the butts with that new contraption of his or the kitchen boys finishing off the replica of Brecelyn's gazebo, I don't know; I find both prospects equally irritating.

"And maybe you *are* ready for Firsts already," I continue, trying not to sound as annoyed as I feel. "But, you know, Falko's still got his distance. And who knows *how* Jurian's shooting these days, he does so little of it. You want to place higher than Aristide, too, don't you? Wasn't that the plan, for you and Gilles at least to *try* to take the top two spots? Well, you're never going to outrank Ari, let alone Taran, if you don't improve at wands. Time is running out, and it's not too soon to start worrying about Seconds, either! *Taran's* already working on those, *that's* for sure. You promised me that you and Gilles were going to do *something*, at least!"

"I told you we were working on something, Marek," he replies, unruffled. "And we *are*. In fact, I'm working on it right now, as we speak," he says. And then, infuriatingly, he proceeds to tip back in his chair, sprawl out, and stretch out his long legs to rest them with ankles crossed up on the table in front of him.

"Well? Aren't you going to share this strategy with your squire, Tristan?"

"But of course! Eventually."

"And just *when* might that be?" I demand sarcastically.

All he does is reach up to feel the back of his head, and say cryptically,

"A day or two more should do it, I reckon," and I can't get anything more out of him. When I ask exasperatedly,

"Is all this secrecy really necessary, *master*?" he just beams at me and trills,

"Absolutely."

It's probably a bad idea to press him about it, since of course I'm fully aware that he and Gilles *have* been working on something together — or plotting it, rather. But the alarming plan I overheard them discussing in Gilles's room was surely more about Melissande than about archery, and the last thing I want to do is encourage him in it. I suspect his indolent mood all stems from brooding over her as it is, and the simple truth of it probably is that he and Gilles haven't yet been able to come up with any solution to the problem of how to train each other. Still, I can't help prodding him, one last time.

"Won't you give me at least *some* hint as to what you're planning?" I wheedle, and all he says is,

"Believe me, Marek. You'll know it, when you see it."

IT'S NOT UNTIL THE AFTERNOON OF THE FOLLOWING FRIDAY that I realize I should have been listening more closely to what Tristan was saying, and I find out to my chagrin just exactly what it is that's really been going on with him. When I do, I never would have thought I could be so sorry to learn that Tristan's been telling me nothing but the truth.

It's not long after noon mess that storm clouds start to gather, quite literally. Then before Pascal and I have barely finished setting up the field for the boys' afternoon practice, the heavens open up in earnest, to unleash a torrential downpour that drives us indoors again. It's one of those violent, early summer squalls so typical of the season, and it's just too wet for anyone to stay out on the field. Although I am sorry it's going to mean cancelling squires' club, I can't help but hope that the rain will dispel some of the humidity, and with it some of Tristan's lethargy.

Like most of the other Journeys, Tristan takes the opportunity to retire to his room for some welcome sleep, and I find myself at loose ends. I don't have much desire to slosh my muddy way out to the shop tent in the driving rain, and the barracks is empty. So it's not long before I'm wandering into the great hall to look for the other squires, where I suspect most of them have gathered to spend an idle hour in gossiping and gaming.

Upon finding the place packed to capacity, I decide first to skirt around the edges of the unruly mob that's taken refuge in here from the weather and pop out into the front vestibule for a while to visit with my old friend Auguste. I rarely get to spend any time with him anymore, since he's always on duty at the front desk.

"Hullo, Marek," he says sullenly, as soon as he spots me slipping in through the big double doors. It's not the greeting I was expecting, but I don't take it amiss. It only takes one look at his puffy eyes and watery nose to see that something's wrong, and it doesn't take him long to come out with it.

"My girlfriend's *dumped* me, Marek," he tells me, hanging his head, and I'm surprised. Auguste's been courting one of the younger kitchen maids for months now, and I'd thought everything was going really well.

"What happened, Auguste?" I ask him, just to be polite, since girl troubles isn't a topic that much interests me.

"She's going with *Remy* now," he mumbles, and I shift around uncomfortably, since I can guess what's happened. The girl Remy was using to try to make me jealous out behind the kitchens must have been Auguste's girlfriend, and I can't help but feel a little responsible for his distress.

"Cheer up, Auguste," I tell him. "I have a funny feeling it's not going to last."

"Well of course it's not," he sniffs unexpectedly. "Remy's affairs never do. Why, he's already worked his way through half the kitchen staff! But he's just so damned good-looking, Marek, and he knows it. How could I hope to compete with such a smooth operator, a subtle seducer like *him?* I couldn't. Not even if I did have two legs."

For a moment I'm thoroughly taken aback. But I guess I have reason to know as well as anyone that a jilted lover is eager to believe anything that will allow him to save face. So I try not to crack a smile at Auguste's characterization of Remy; I mean, I can well understand why Auguste would find it comforting to think his girl wasn't the only one to have succumbed to the boy's undeniable charms.

"Oh, uh, sorry Marek," he says contritely, misinterpreting my expression. "I forgot. Everybody in barracks knows you're sweet on him yourself, and that you've been pursuing him relentlessly."

"Actually, it's the other way around," I correct him wryly, but he just shrugs, "Suit yourself."

I don't bother arguing with him about it, and when he next says rather gleefully,

"Just wait 'til she finds out Remy makes all his girls *do* things for him.

Unusual things," I make my excuses, and with a few more murmured consolations, I beat a hasty retreat.

I duck back into the great hall, smiling to myself a little as I go, trying to picture Remy as the 'subtle seducer' Auguste painted him, or as some sort of deviant. It really is too funny. My smile wavers a little, though, when I remember Remy's surprisingly accomplished kissing technique.

Then it disappears entirely.

I've just remembered that under uncomfortably similar circumstances, I tried to convince myself that the same phrases fit Remy's *master*, and I feel ashamed of myself for laughing at Auguste.

Back in the great hall, I find most of the other squires gathered around the Journey table, taking turns sending one boy out to duck under the portico to check if the weather shows any sign of breaking, while the rest stand around watching Charles and Jerome play a game of draughts. It's a little hard to tell what's going on at first, however, since it's something of a madhouse in here.

The storm has put a stop to all work outdoors, both out in the yard and in the newly acquired area, and it's coming down hard enough outside now that most of the workmen have given the day up for lost and gone home. In an unusual display of consideration, Master Leon's even sent the Kingsmen back to their camp on the exhibition grounds. But a big, rowdy crowd of veterans intent on waiting it out long enough to get a free evening meal has congregated in here instead of going back to their lodgings in town, and they're occupying all of the other tables. To all appearances they've settled in to spend the afternoon picking fights and drinking themselves into a stupor until time for evening mess, and to add to the chaos the rain's driven all the guild dogs indoors, too, and even some of the chickens. The din in the reverberating room is terrible enough (and all the howling and barking isn't just coming from the *dogs*, either), but between the heavy scent of the rain, the sickly-sweet odors of sloshed ale and sweaty men, and the pungent aromas of wet dog and wet feathers, the smell in here is almost enough to rival the stench of the plague.

Charles has been driven indoors from work on his forge, too, and although I can see no real reason why the weather is any excuse for Jerome to be shirking, I don't bother asking him what he's doing out of the archives. From the intent way the boys are crowded around to watch the game he and Charles are engaged in it must be a pretty close match, and I've no doubt there's serious money riding on the outcome. So I pick my way around the crowded tables and I dodge through the livestock over to join them, and I circle around to take up a position behind Charles in a sort of tacit solidarity with him, even though I don't have anything to wager.

The boys are seated on opposite sides of the Journey table, with the gaming board spread out in front of them. Pascal and Remy have evidently both put down sizable sums on Jerome, since they're standing behind him and yelling a babble of contradictory suggested moves into his ear. Rennie's the only boy who's risked money on Charles, but since it's his turn to stand outside and watch the weather, he's entrusted Frans (who is of course rooting for his own brother) to keep an eye on his investment for him.

I suppose it all starts not long after Frans has scooted over to let me squeeze in next to him, when across from me Remy looks up to greet me. Just as he's casting me a smile that's so shy and sweet it almost makes me laugh out loud at the thought of Auguste's recent description of him, something past me must catch his attention, since soon he's looking off over my shoulder. Then nudging Pascal, he says,

"You were looking for Armand. Well, *there* he is. I wonder where he's been? Huh. What he's doing, lurking there in the doorway? Why doesn't he come in?," and I glance back over my shoulder.

Sure enough, Armand's hovering out in the shadows of the corridor beyond the double doors of the hall, peeking his head furtively around the doorpost and peering into the room nervously. He looks a little guilty, and when Pascal puts up a hand to beckon him over impatiently, instead of heeding his friend's gesture he ducks his head back into the shadows and disappears. But I don't think much of it, assuming he must owe Pascal money or something similar, and anyway at just that moment Charles takes one of Jerome's men, and before long we're all fully absorbed in the game again. A few tense moves later, I'm just in the process of crowing rather loudly,

"Ha! That's *another* one for our side, boys! You're going to have to king him, Jerome," when I hear the sound of boots ringing out on the wooden floor close behind me. Someone's come tromping into the hall through the big double doors to join us, but I'm too busy taunting the boys across the table from me to turn around and see who it is.

Indeed, I'm too busy gloating at first to notice that the boys across from me have all stopped talking entirely. Or that they're all now looking past me with their eyes wide and their mouths hanging open, or even that Jerome has frozen in place, and that he's now sitting as stiff as a board and holding out his gaming piece in mid-air in front of him. In fact, I only notice the astonishment on all the other boys' faces when I'm startled by a voice I almost recognize exclaiming loudly right in my ear,

"What's up, boys? Say, kid, who's winning?"

The words and the phrasing are Tristan's, of course. And the voice does sound uncannily like his. There's something about the timbre of it and the careful way he's pronouncing each word that are a little off, though. But it's only when a hand reaches out to ruffle my hair affectionately that it fully registers with me just how stunned the boys around me seem. They're all staring at a point just past my right shoulder with expressions of exaggerated disbelief on their faces. But Pascal looks by far the worst. In fact, he looks just like a thunder-blasted tree.

I twist around, to look up into the face of a boy who is Tristan, and not Tristan.

He's dressed just like Tristan, in a casual white linen shirt open at the throat, and plain black boots and trousers. In fact, the clothes *are* Tristan's. He's got Tristan's lazy grin on his face, too, the one that could charm the birds right out of the trees. And he's got Tristan's exact hairstyle, complete with one wayward lock falling in a wave across his forehead, although perhaps his hair is just a shade longer than usual. He's even got a tiny sliver of one eyebrow missing.

And just like with Tristan, too, the effect of all of it together is devastatingly handsome, and I'm now staring up into the face of one of the most devilishly attractive boys I've ever seen.

But his hair isn't black.

It's red.

It isn't Tristan. It's *Gilles*.

Pascal's hands fly up to his throat, and while the rest of us are still trying to assimilate what we're seeing, he lets out a shriek:

"*Master*!! What have you done to your *hair*?!?"

With that, he proceeds to keel straight over backwards. We're all still too surprised to do anything but let him fall, and although I can't say I blame him, he's passed out again.

This year, it seems to be becoming quite a habit, with *him*.

While the rest of us are all still too stunned to react, Gilles bustles around solicitously to crouch down next to Pascal and to lift up his head, and after a beat we all crowd around to help him try to revive his squire.

"Hey, kid! Easy there," he exclaims, patting Pascal bracingly on the cheek just as Rennie comes trotting back inside. "It's just *hair*. It'll grow back," he laughs, and I have to say, I never thought I'd hear a sentiment like it from Gilles.

"Hey, who won the game, Tristan?!" Rennie demands, shouldering his way forward through our little group and apparently not noticing that the boy in Tristan's clothes isn't him. "And what in the devil happened to *him*?" he adds, when he catches sight of Pascal. "Say, just what is going on?!"

Nobody answers him. The other boys all look at a loss, and the only other boy who could probably explain it is out cold. I'm still reeling too much from the effect of Gilles's transformation to try to explain it either, but I think I could, if I were so inclined.

Because Tristan was right.

I *did* know it, as soon as I saw it.

Gilles has adopted Tristan's personality, like a second skin.

So I really *should* see it coming — the obvious corollary.

There's no excuse for it, really, except to say that my mind must still be numbed by shock. But I swear it takes me completely by surprise, when while we're all still huddled around and bent over Pascal in a babble of confusion and trying to revive him, an impeccably accented voice somewhere over my head behind me drawls,

"*Gads*, lads! Whatever *can* have come over our dear Pascal?"

And it's my turn to freeze.

This time, it's not just the boys at our own table who suddenly stop what they're doing. In an instant the whole room falls silent, and all the raucous babble that was emanating from the men's tables around us recedes, like a wave being sucked back out to sea. Even the dogs fall silent, as everyone and everything in the room — men, boys, dogs, and chickens — all stop and stare in open-mouthed amazement, their attention riveted on the new arrival in the hall, the owner of the voice who is now standing directly behind me.

One lone dog lifts its head, and lets out a long, heartfelt howl.

Or maybe it's a wolf whistle.

Then it tucks its tail between its legs, and pads quickly out of the hall and out under the portico.

Nobody else in the room moves a muscle.

I know what's coming, of course. So I really should be prepared. But when I twist around with trepidation to look up at what I know must be Tristan, what I feel can only be described as gobsmacked instead.

I *know* the apparition before me must be Tristan. It can't be anybody else. But looking at him I can't seem to wrap my mind around it, and it isn't just the outrageous outfit he's wearing.

Although admittedly, that is *some* of it.

To start with, he's wearing Gilles's peacock-blue tights. That alone would probably be enough to make a roomful of men stop and stare, since if I thought they looked good on Gilles, it's only because I'd never seen them on my own master. Even if Tristan were just wearing plain black tights it would be something, since as a rule he never wears them, and he's got about the best legs of any boy I've ever seen (not to mention a few other mighty shapely features). But he's also wearing thigh-high polished leather boots of the same matching color. They too must belong to Gilles, as must the rest of the ensemble: a fitted, long-sleeved jerkin of luxurious rubbed leather, also of a startling peacock blue and embellished with so much brocade and embroidery that the fixtures alone must have cost a fortune. This he's wearing over the requisite ruffled silk shirt of a most unusual color. Its rich, dusky bronze hue is the exact shade of the accents on a peacock's feathers, and with all that vibrant color and soft, clingy silk shifting in response to his slightest movement, in the candlelight his whole body seems to be shimmering so much that he could be hovering in mid-air. He looks so radiant and unreal that for a moment I think he really is an apparition, and I find that I'm holding my breath, waiting for the inevitable moment when he'll disappear with a 'pop,' or be assumed straight up into heaven. And that's only the beginning.

Slung around his shoulders is a mid-length cape, covered entirely on its exterior surface with real peacock feathers. The interior of the gossamer fabric is lined with deep blue silk, but the plumes of countless hapless birds have been woven into the fabric on the outside so that they look like they're cascading down his back, and into a little cap of peacock-blue felt perched atop his head one more long, crowning feather is stuck at a jaunty angle. I almost expect him at any moment to spread his cape out like a tail behind him and strut about the room bobbing his head, just as though he really were an exotic bird. But the one thing that strikes me most about him is what he's got *under* the cap.

He's scraped together all of his hair and pulled it back to fasten it at the nape of his neck in a blue silk ribbon, and I see that Tristan was right: he does have just enough of it now to wear it in the shortest of ponytails.

To top it all off, his ruffled shirt is open at the throat just enough to reveal Gilles's St. Sebastian's medal on its golden chain resting flat against lightly tanned pectorals, and on his finger winks Gilles's big, jeweled ring. At his waist, he's sporting the *pièce de résistance*:

Gilles's rapier, thrust through a belt of more woven peacock feathers.

Across the table from me, Jerome is the first to break the silence.

"Wouldn't you know there was more to *that* outfit?!" he laughs, his loss at draughts forgotten as he snatches up his lute to pluck out an appropriately lively tune. Tristan accordingly spreads his arms, inclines his head regally, and makes a stately turn.

He really should look utterly ridiculous. It's one of Gilles's most preposterous outfits, one even its rightful owner would have some trouble pulling off. And as the initial shock of it begins to recede, he probably does look a little absurd. But if so, I really can't see it. He obviously *has* been practicing, because he's got Gilles's aristocratic, condescending bearing down pat. It's all there: the posture, the expression, and most of all, that air grace and of unimpeachable nobility that allows Gilles to wear anything with dignity, the overpowering confidence that elevates even the most outrageous of ensembles into a showcase designed to set him off to advantage as the stunning centerpiece of the display, a priceless work of art. On Tristan the effect is taken to another level entirely, since even without any trappings he really is astonishingly gorgeous, and the sumptuous colors and rich fabrics simply serve to bring out that extreme beauty that's always been his. At the same time, there's something about the flagrant show of wealth and power inherent in the luxurious clothing that emphasizes his masculinity, particularly since Tristan is bigger and more muscled than Gilles, and the clothes are clinging to every contour of him. For all his frills and finery, there's even something a little dark and dangerous about the effect of it.

Whatever 'it' is, Tristan's always had it, in spades. But looking at him now, the best way I can describe him is to say that *this* is what it must have been like, to gaze upon a younger, sexier-than-hell Poncellet.

Tristan completes his slow revolution, and when does proceed to spread out his cape behind him like the fanning of a peacock's tail, strike a pose, and declare to me with glee:

"Whatever *do* you say, dear boy!? Isn't it all too simply *marvelous?*," I'm pretty proud of myself that unlike Pascal, I don't pass out.

I am feeling a little woozy, however, and by this time Gilles has managed to prod Pascal back into semi-consciousness. He's starting to sit up and come around on the floor behind me, so all I say is,

"Move over, Pascal! I'm coming down," and I shove him over, and I stretch out next to him on the ground.

Pascal takes one look at Tristan, and he passes out again.

I don't think I ever fully faint; I simply close my eyes to rest them from all the spectacle for a moment. But we must make quite a sight: Gilles-*cum*-Tristan and Tristan-*cum*-Gilles in all his dazzling array, kneeling by their recumbent squires — both of whom are stretched out on the floor as pale as corpses awaiting burial, and to all appearances both out like lights.

I'm the first to revive, having never really passed out, and by this time there's such a big crowd of men all circled around laughing and pressing in curiously that I hasten to sit up, and I busily start helping the boys with Pascal, who's proving rather harder to bring around. After another well-aimed slap by Gilles eventually Pascal's eyes flutter open, and he looks around dazedly while Rennie, Remy, and Frans work from behind to get him propped up into a sitting position again.

Tristan, Gilles, and I are all three leaning in close in front of him and peering down at him anxiously.

He looks at me. He looks at Tristan. Then he looks at Gilles, and back at Tristan again. Then he puts his head in his hands, and the first thing he says is,

"Oh, I'm so *confused!*"

The second thing is:

"Somebody, warn Armand! Because when I find him, I'm going to kill him."

"Come on, good buddy," Gilles says, lifting an unresisting Pascal to his feet. "Let's go and get you a stiff drink."

Tristan and I accompany Gilles and his squire back to his room, ostensibly to help Gilles usher Pascal along, but mostly so that the four of us can have a chance to talk in private. I've got plenty on my mind to say, so as soon as Tristan closes the door behind us, while Gilles is pouring out a bracing cup of wine from one of the barrels of de Gilford's pilfered stash that's still clogging up his room and while he's offering it to Pascal to steady his nerves, I burst out,

"*This* is your plan to *train* each other?! Dressing in each other's clothes? Are you *serious?* In what world is *that* a training strategy?!?"

"It's not *to train* each other, silly!" Tristan trills. Or at least he tries to. He hasn't quite gotten the hang of it, and it comes out more of a gurgle. "It's to give each other a little of the proper *style*," he declares, clearing his throat and rescuing the cap which is starting to slip sideways off his head. "You know, to give us a mental edge, just as you said."

"We're not just 'dressing in each other's clothes,' kid," Gilles puts in. "We've adopted each other's personas, *internally*."

"But, you cut your *hair!*" Pascal moans again, and while Gilles hurriedly feeds him another big gulp of wine, Tristan exclaims,

"There, there, son. Think of the results! Why, it can't fail to work like a charm. In fact, it's going to be absolutely, positively *fabulous*."

Needless to say, I have my doubts. But there'd be no point in voicing them, and so when not much later Rennie comes running down the hallway, banging on doors and announcing that the rain has finally let up, we all agree to head out to the far field, Tristan as Gilles and Gilles as Tristan, to sneak in one run-through of the boys' joint trick. I'm mighty curious to see what's going to happen, and not just to see if the boy's unusual experiment is going to have any effect — because this time, the boys are going to try the trick *switching* roles: Tristan, now being the 'wands' man (if not actually 'being the wand'), is to shoot at the moving wands, while Gilles does the butts shots from the sidelines to free them.

True to Gilles's spirit, Tristan takes his own sweet time limbering up. Then before he lifts his bow, he makes a show of putting aside Gilles's rapier, and he proceeds to strip off his belt, his leather jerkin, *and* his ruffled tunic, piling each item ceremoniously into my hands, and then he even orders me to assist him in pulling the long boots right off his feet (*"All this mud! It's so damaging to leather,"* he exclaims, though I doubt that's the real reason). He's going to shoot in nothing but the peacock-blue tights the way Gilles did this morning, and as he bends his bow with Gilles's St. Sebastian's medal on its golden chain glinting against the smoothness of his chest, and as his sweeping motion sets all the beautiful muscles beneath it to rippling, it occurs to me that there might be some advantages to the boys' plan, after all. At the very least, at this moment falling headlong back into lust with Tristan seems a lot less like a chore than an inevitability.

To my utter amazement (and great delight), the boys do the trick flawlessly. Not only do both boys make all of their shots, but Gilles even manages to give his the proper swagger suited to butts shots, and a hint of the old Verbeke flair.

And as for Tristan?

He's never looked so relaxed or so elegant, and he's shooting wands better than ever.

It's the most unlikely thing, but the boys' ridiculous scheme seems actually to have worked. I have no idea if it's really the clothes (or lack thereof, as the case may be) that's made the difference, or the fact that after that first run-through of the trick, Gilles exclaims, "now that you're in the proper frame of mind for it, my friend, it's time to teach you the infamous

Lejeune upswing," and he sets about giving Tristan the kind of practical pointers on technique that I'd been hoping he would, for the first time since they started working together. But I can't argue with success. If they can keep it up, it's going to mean that *both* boys can use a version of the joint trick for their exhibition; they'll simply reverse roles, depending on whose exhibition it is. I can picture it all now, and it's going to be sheer perfection. So if acting like each other is what's going to give them the confidence to pull it off, I can have no complaints.

Still, as we're walking back inside later side-by-side, Tristan's still wearing nothing but the peacock-blue tights, and it's distracting, to say the least; I mean, they call them 'tights' for a reason. So I ask him a little uncomfortably,

"So, how long do you think it will be, before you're, *er*, 'back to your old self,' master?"

"I see no reason why I should want to remain a wands man after Firsts are over, Marek," he sniffs in reply, and I heave a sigh of relief. Firsts are less than a week away. If it'll mean acing the competition, surely for *that* long, I can take anything.

I have a feeling, though, that the next six days are going to be awfully long indeed.

Chapter Twenty-Eight

It's not until the next day that I begin to find out just how long six days can be.

Before I'm even up and off my cot in the morning, Pascal comes down and shoves a pile of neatly folded clothes into my hands.

"Gilles's orders," he says sullenly. Then he adds unnecessarily, "They're for *Tristan*," since I can see well enough that what I've now got in my hands is Gilles's red-and-white motley outfit, complete with boots and ostrich-plumed hat.

Then when I've hurried up and gotten myself ready and I take the garments down to Tristan's room, I find him still abed. He doesn't answer at my knock, and when I accordingly open the door and go in, I have to prod his shoulder to wake him, since he's still fast asleep.

"Run along, there's a good lad! Run along. A chap needs his beauty rest, if he's to look as fresh as a rose," he mumbles dismissively, rolling over and pulling his blanket up higher around his neck, as though preparing to go straight back to sleep.

Maybe it's the sight of his longish hair splayed across his pillow, still tied back loosely in its ponytail, I don't know. But it's all already starting to grate on me; the day hasn't even started, and Tristan's already referring to himself in the third person. By noon he'll probably have moved on to the royal 'we.' So I reach over, and I pull the blanket roughly right off of his majesty.

Instantly, I'm sorry.

With a strangled cry of *"gah!,"* I try to gather up the blanket to drop it back down over him in a hurry, but he's already rolling over to face me and giving a huge, languid stretch.

The blanket slips from my fingers.

Silently, it puddles on the floor.

How could I have forgotten something so basic?

Gilles always sleeps in the nude.

"Mercy, Marek! What a way to rouse a man from his slumbers!" Tristan exclaims, in no apparent hurry whatsoever to get covered up.

Instead, he proceeds to get up and strut around the room, stretching and flexing the way Gilles usually does in the lavatory, while I steady myself with one hand against the wall.

"Why, I do declare! Good old Lejeune was *per*fectly right," he purrs, stopping for a moment to tilt my chin up toward his face with one hand, while languorously rubbing his washboard belly with the other, just the same way Remy did. "It *does* feel simply *marvelous!*"

It doesn't get any better, when I have to help him into the tights.

It takes a ridiculously long time to get Tristan all decked out in Gilles's outfit, and it doesn't help that it's at least one whole size too small for him (or that I have to pause periodically, to steady my hands and compose myself). It's not just the wedging of him into the skin-tight portions of it that are stressful, either, and there are some intricate bits I'm not entirely sure I ever get right. But I buckle and tie and fasten him in to the best of my ability, tucking under whatever I can't figure out, and by the time I've doused him with an excessive amount of Gilles's most expensive perfume (at his insistence) and I've finally gotten Tristan dressed to his satisfaction, I have a renewed respect for Pascal.

My day has only just started, and I'm already feeling worn out.

I manage to get through the rest of that day and most of the next without significant incident, but it's wearing. There are the endless jokes, of course, and the comments from the others — when Poncellet comes out to lead morning drills that first day, for example, he stops dead in his tracks. He takes an exaggerated look at the boys. Then rubbing his hands together with an expression on his face like he's just hit the jackpot, he exclaims,

"Well bless my soul, if it isn't Gistan, and Trills! I wonder which is which?" And that's only the beginning.

I also find that before long I'm having to fight my way through a growing crowd of hangers-on, sycophants, and admirers just to attend my master. Kitchen boys, stable hands, and sundry other staff all take to following him around obsequiously, and even some of the veterans, all seemingly so blinded by his elegant attire and his enhanced charisma that they've failed to remember that underneath his expensive clothes he doesn't really have any money.

Unfortunately, none of them actually offers to give me any assistance, since I soon find out that taking care of a Gilles is a lot more work than taking care of a Tristan. It's not only dealing with all the clothes, either, that's so tiring, although of course the clothes are *a lot* of it: there's washing them, mending them, sorting them, airing them, choosing them, plumping them, polishing them, folding them — the list is endless — and of course, most of all, there's getting Tristan in and out of them. It seems like I've barely stuffed him into one complicated outfit, when before I can get started on some other chore I turn around and there he is again, wanting to change it. But it's not *just* the clothes.

It's also the relentless nudity.

I've never thought Tristan was particularly modest, but in the past he's always been natural and unassuming when changing. Now he can't seem to wait to jump out of his clothes and parade around the room, almost making me trap him in a corner with his tights or his tunic to get him to put something back on again. And then there's the *bathing*. He's started demanding hot baths after every practice, the way Gilles usually does, and between having to heat all the water and carry it by myself (Gilles's serving boys apparently not having come along with the deal) and then having to wash him to his newly exacting specifications, the whole experience has left me mentally and physically exhausted. As long as he's imitating Gilles, he's sure to require at least one full bath every single day, and I don't know how much longer I'm going to be able to take it — because all of a sudden, I'm feeling awfully shy around him again.

It's the strangest sensation. He's so achingly familiar, and at the same he's now someone brand new, a different boy entirely. And maybe it's just because *this* boy doesn't seem much like my big brother, but I can't help feeling the attraction of him keenly again. It's almost like I'm meeting Tristan for the first time all over again, or like I've been thrown back into those early days at the guild with him, before I was used to being around him so intimately, and before I knew him so well that I couldn't see him as anything but my family, and my friend. And that's the hardest thing of all, right there. I know his slightly aloof and superior manner is all part of his act. But I miss my best friend.

There is one person who doesn't say a thing about the boys switching personalities. He doesn't need to; everyone can guess what *he* thinks about it. Still, at squires' club when we're standing next to each other, stiffly discussing bow grips or the like, I can feel Taran almost busting to make some snide remark. But we've got an unspoken agreement and he holds his tongue, and he never mentions Tristan's transformation, to me anyway. Since none of the others dares mention Tristan around Taran at all, ironically enough squires' club soon becomes a sort of haven, the one place I can escape from the teasing comments and the sheer work of it all for a few hours every afternoon, and just relax. Even the grueling workouts Taran plans for us are a heck of a lot easier than managing my master's newly acquired wardrobe, and I can forget all about brocade and buttons — and bellybuttons, and soft lines of hair — well, at least I can try. Just one short week ago, I never would have believed it. But training alongside Taran at squires' club now seems like the most normal part of my day.

All these things I might have anticipated, if I'd had a chance to sit down and think about the logical consequences of the boys' switch. But there is one unexpected result of Tristan's transformation that I never would have guessed. His assumption of the easy arrogance of nobility gives him an overweening confidence, and as a result he throws himself into his not-so-subtle investigations of Sir Brecelyn and the shooting at Thirds with more vigor and directness than I've seen yet. He was never particularly timid about it, but the adoption of Gilles's personality now makes him more reckless than ever, and from the way he's acting he seems to think that donning Gilles's clothes comes with an aristocratic exemption from consequence.

We can hardly make it the length of a corridor these days without Tristan waylaying some new man and demanding that he answer his questions. But I don't think too much about it, beyond the fact that his manner is a little worrying, since his questions are actually rather boring. They're mostly gossip about the regent's latest hunting party or the minutiae of the wool trade, or even a rehash of last year's uprising in Liege, of all things — matters too dull to make anyone suspicious of anything other than that Tristan has a strange idea of what aristocrats like to talk about, and to me they don't make much sense. So I only really start to get alarmed when I figure out that his trappings of privilege have made Tristan so bold as to intend to confront the masters themselves.

His first attempt is on old Poncellet that first morning, right after morning drills. Needless to say, he doesn't get much of anything out of him, and at the time, I don't recognize it for what it is: only his first step.

And Master Leon is next.

It's almost time for evening mess only a few days after his transformation when it happens. I've finally gotten Tristan successfully into another complicated outfit, and I'm following along in the wake of his fragrance as he sweeps down the corridor in front of me, moping my brow and thinking to myself, *only four days to go, only four more days,* when I realize we've already passed the great hall. I'd assumed we were on our way to wait outside the double doors until mealtime like usual. I suppose it is a little early, though, and Tristan's striding along so purposefully I don't say anything, even when we pass the barracks. And then the masters' offices. When we round the corner onto a narrow hallway I've never dared enter, however, I have to ask him nervously,

"Uh, master. Just where are we going? You know, I don't think we're allowed in here," since all that lies beyond this point are the masters' own private quarters.

The only response I get is a dismissive wave over his shoulder from a wrist dripping with emerald-colored tassels, and to my chagrin in another moment he's stopping in front of an open doorway, where Master Leon is visible beyond, seated within.

Leon's sprawled on an old, ratty over-stuffed chair next to a roaring fire, drinking a nasty-looking dark ale from a dirty mug and perspiring, with his untucked shirt hanging open and a large book open on his lap. Strangely, it looks a little like one of the guild ledgers, though I'm probably mistaken, and when he looks up and sees us intruding on his privacy (Tristan having draped himself against the doorframe and given a presumptuous little cough), for a moment he looks so sour I think he's going to spray the room with the liquid he's just in the process of sucking into his mouth.

"*Good Lord*," he exclaims instead, swallowing hard, like he has a foul taste in his mouth. "What can you possibly want, Lejeu— I mean, DuBois?" he demands. But even Master Leon must be dazzled by Tristan's borrowed elegance a little, since when Tristan sniffs, and then plucking at the lace on his cuff he replies casually,

"Just a word, *master*," instead of depositing his boot in Tristan's rear and kicking us down the hallway as I expect he will, all Leon does is say,

"It had better be a *quick* one, before the glare off that ridiculous shirt you're wearing permanently damages my eyes."

"A little light reading, *master?*" Tristan drawls back, unperturbed, inclining his head toward the book on Leon's lap, and the master accordingly makes a show of closing the book firmly, and slipping it onto the floor beneath his chair. Then he folds his hands across his lap.

"What do you want, DuBois?"

"I was wondering if there was any further word about that perfectly hideous affair last year, the murder of Jan Verbeke. I seem to recall you saying something about ongoing investigations, and I wanted to know if his killers had ever been found."

Whatever Master Leon was expecting (if anything), it wasn't this. For once his usual sour expression disappears, and in rapid succession his face registers first surprise, then suspicion. As it gradually settles into a look of calculating speculation, I'm glad I'm back in the shadows, where no one can see what I know must be there plainly on my face for anyone to read: pure fear.

"I'll take that as a '*no*'," Tristan is continuing, the inane tone of his voice taking the edge off his impertinence (slightly). "*What* a pity. But you know, I've had a thought. It's true, isn't it, that he was here, at the guild, shortly before he died? That was un*usual*, wasn't it? After all, I've heard that Verbeke hadn't set foot inside St. Sebastian's for years. That's a mighty suggestive coincidence, don't you think?"

"What's your point, Tristan?" Leon demands, and it's bizarre. I've rarely heard Leon use any of the boys' first names before; I didn't think he'd ever bothered to learn them. But the result isn't very reassuring. It's sort of chilling, actually, particularly since Leon's lip is curling, and I think he might even be trying to smile.

"Since you ask," Tristan obliges, plucking at a tassel and apparently not concerned by the master's tone in the least, "Do you suppose there could be a connection? I'm just speculating here, naturally. But perhaps when Verbeke was here, he overheard something he shouldn't have. Or even more likely, somebody *induced* him to come here in the first place— perhaps by calling in a favor, like asking him to help out with a rush order of broadheads, or some other product not usually made by fletchers here at the guild? Yes, that's it, surely. Verbeke was *lured* here, in order to make him an offer. An offer he refused, to his peril. After all, he was a legendary shot. And a loyal friend."

"Is there a question in there somewhere?" Leon asks, almost sounding amused.

"Not really. *You* were a great friend of Verbeke's, as I understand. So I was simply floating a theory, and wondering if you had any thoughts on it."

Leon takes another sip of his beer, swishing it around in his mouth a moment as though savoring it. Then he meets Tristan's eyes over the rim of the cup.

"You want to know what *I* think? I think if you go around spouting that theory, you're going to end up getting that newly-elegant neck of yours stretched, until it really is as long as Gilles's."

It's not until we're all the way back in front of the barracks and I'm right in the middle of chastising Tristan for his foolhardiness that the force of his words to Leon fully hit me.

"Are you crazy, Tristan?!" I'm demanding, as soon as I'm sure we're far enough away that the master can't hear us, and when all Tristan does is give me one of Gilles's innocent looks and raise his eyebrows at me, I explode recklessly,

"You basically just accused Master Leon of killing my father!"

"Of course I didn't, Marek. Don't be so dramatic," he scoffs. "That's not what I was implying at all," he says, and it's only then that I realize just what he *was* implying.

"Tristan," I say shakily, feeling suddenly ill. "Are you saying that my father was lured here to join the men in their plotting, and that he was killed for refusing? Are you saying that the original plan was to have *my father* shoot the prince for them?"

There's a moment of awkward silence, in which I really wish that the Tristan standing in the hallway with me was the one into whose arms I could throw myself with abandon, to burrow my face comfortably against his chest.

"I think you have to admit that it's possible, isn't it?" he finally says gently. "But it's just a theory, and anyway, that wasn't *quite* what I meant."

I don't ask him to elaborate. I don't want to think about it, or about a fact that's been obvious from the beginning: it was to indulge my own desire to see St. Sebastian's that my father accepted the summons that killed him. I want to think about Tristan getting his neck stretched even less. So I simply implore him,

"Please, Tristan. *Please* tell me you're not planning to question Master Guillaume like that! *Promise* me you won't question anybody else."

"For you, dear Marek," Tristan replies sweetly, "I'd promise anything. And anyway, *that* one's easy. Because you see, I've no need to ask anyone anything. I've already got it all figured out."

If I was hoping that Tristan was bluffing, I'm soon to be seriously disappointed, since it's not much later that very night when Tristan decides the time has come for him to unveil his grand theory to all the boys at evening mess.

I've spent the meal sitting down amongst the squires, trying to take my mind off the things Tristan's just suggested about my father by engaging the boys in a lively recap of this afternoon's squires' club session. Although we've only been training seriously as a squad for about a week, our retrieving routines are already coming together nicely. The boys are also all pretty pleased with the training they've been getting on their individual skills, so it hasn't been too difficult to keep them talking enthusiastically. The only boy not participating is Pascal. He's refused to speak to Armand throughout the entire meal (having taken to referring to him as *'that insufferable clouter'*), and in addition to feuding with his best friend, it doesn't take much to see that Pascal's finding it as hard to adjust to the new incarnation of his master as I am.

For one thing, whenever Gilles happens to glance down the table and catch his squire eyeing him with disapproval, he lifts his cup, flashes him a cocky grin, and calls down the table to him with a wink,

"Yo, there buddy! *Bottoms up,*" or some other earthy colloquialism that Pascal's likely to find equally appalling.

For another, with Gilles no longer bathing regularly there's been no left-over water for Pascal, and he's so fastidious that it's been driving him crazy to be dirty. Throughout the meal he's been shifting around in his tunic, itching and scratching and imagining he's getting a rash. The boys have all been teasing him about it by pretending that he's starting to stink, and now and then Rennie leans over to pick an imaginary louse out of his hair. I can't imagine Pascal ever really smelling anything other than fresh and clean (and I have to say, it's a little hard for me to sympathize; it's only with great forbearance that I've resisted the urge to tell him *'welcome to my world'*), but it's getting on his nerves, and on top of everything else, Firsts are almost upon us and he hasn't managed to compose even a single line of his proposal to Ginger.

"Come on, Pascal! Be reasonable," Armand is pleading as the meal winds down, and as up at the head table the masters are polishing off the last drops of their post-supper port. "What was I supposed to do? Gilles *asked* me to cut it. I couldn't very well refuse him."

"I think he looks really good this way," Remy says brightly, while Rennie puts in unhelpfully,

"I'm telling you, Armand old buddy, you should have *been* there to see Pascal's *face*! Why, he was so dazed when he first came to, he mistook *Marek* here for a kitchen maid!" Luckily before Remy can jump in to elaborate, Pascal just shakes his head and says,

"You boys don't understand. It's going to take *months* to grow back," and I feel for him. I've only got to make it for a few more days; the thought of being stuck with a Gistan for months is daunting indeed (or is it *Trills*?). "And that's not the only thing," Pascal moans. "Firsts is in *four days*, and I'm desperate. I have no idea *what* to say to Ginger, and now I couldn't ask Tristan for help, even if I wanted to — because, you know, he's not Tristan anymore. Now he's *Gilles*."

Nobody has a response to that, since I'm sure we'd all dread to hear a proposal penned by Pascal's master. At the very least, it wouldn't be something Pascal could possibly deliver.

To my surprise, Pascal turns imploringly to me.

"Marek, will *you* help me?" he says. "Tristan says you're good with words; you must be, if you're the one who really wrote that note to Melissande for him, as he says you did. And we all know you've got a way with girls. You know how to talk to them. What do *you* think I should say to Ginger?," and he's looking at me so hopefully, I don't have the heart to tell him that Tristan was just teasing me. So I take his request seriously.

I think about it for a minute. As I do, my gaze drifts down to the Journey end of the table, and it lingers there a minute.

"If I were you, Pascal," I tell him sincerely, "what I'd say is this: *I've loved you from the moment I first saw you, on the guild wall.*"

The boys think it's pretty good. So soon we're all pitching ideas to help Pascal work it up into the opening for a proposal that'll be short and sweet, just as Armand suggested. We've got the outlines of something roughed out and we're just putting the finishing touches on it when the masters finally call it a night. They file out of the hall behind us and as soon as they're gone, down at the Journey end of the table Tristan proclaims loudly enough to command the attention of the whole table,

"All right, Jerome! The proverbial cost is clear. Whip it out!," and to everyone's astonishment, Jerome proceeds to pull a large guild ledger surreptitiously out of the lute case he's got sitting on the bench next to him.

Jerome hastily opens up the big book, and as he and Tristan bend protectively over it, Tristan makes a sweeping gesture and announces,

"Huddle up, gentlemen! Huddle up. It's time to put my cards on the table."

"Oh, great! I love a good card trick," Falko exclaims, rubbing his hands together in anticipation, and Tristan gives him one of Gilles's quelling looks.

"You're going to lose Jerome his job, Tristan," Jurian says with a low whistle, eyeing the ledger, while Aristide demands,

"Seriously, what's this all about, DuBois?" But they both get up to move around and huddle over the book, just as Tristan ordered. Soon we're all crowded around and looking down over the boys' shoulders, shielding the ledger from the prying eyes of curious veterans at the nearby tables — all the squires, and all of the Journeys. Even Taran.

"Nonsense!" Tristan trills musically, having by now gotten the hang of it. "And what I meant, Falko *dear*," he explains sternly, "is that the time has come for me to let the rest of you boys in on what *really* happened at Thirds, seeing as I've finally succeeded in getting to the bottom of things."

"*Man*, this oughta be good!" Gilles hoots, and as Pascal cringes, somewhere behind me there's a derisive snort.

When Tristan sees that this rude noise clearly coming from Taran accurately sums up the reaction of most of the boys to his announcement, he sniffs.

"As you'll soon see, I've got a theory that explains everything: the shot from the tower, Sir Brecelyn's motive, even my own wounding at the hunt! It's all been coming together for a while now. All I needed was confirmation, and *there* it is," he declares triumphantly, thrusting a finger down onto the musty page in front of him. Unfortunately for him, the move is ruined a little by the fact that whatever he was pointing at is now obscured by a cascade of tassels.

"Why don't you spare us the theatrics, and just get on with it," an icy voice demands. But now that he's Gilles, Tristan's not as inclined as usual to pick a fight with Taran. So he simply inclines his head, and obliges.

"Where is Marek? *There* you are. Come over by me, there's a good lad. Make room for him, men!" he commands, as I scoot obediently onto the bench next to him. "Because you see, our Marek here was right about everything, all along! Well, *virtually* everything. The shooting at Thirds last year *was* a plot against the crown, and it *was* masterminded by Sir Brecelyn. And my wounding at the hunt — that *was* practice for it, too, just as he originally suggested."

All the boys start talking over each other at once with objections. But Gilles's voice is the loudest, although it takes me a moment to recognize it as his. I'm still not quite used to his slightly strange take on the kind of things Tristan might say.

"Sorry to deflate you, old man. But haven't you forgotten something? The prince wasn't in the royal box when Brecelyn's man Beaufort started shooting down into the crowd. I'm afraid *that* rather shoots *your* theory straight to hell, and right back again."

Tristan turns to his friend, looking completely unruffled (well, as unruffled as a boy can look who's wearing the frilliest shirt I've ever seen).

"Ah, but you see, that's the key to everything! The prince *wasn't* in the royal box, precisely because the *prince* wasn't the target! It's the *regent* they've meant to assassinate, all along."

He pauses to look around the table with apparent self-satisfaction, in that way typical of Gilles.

"As soon as I realized that, everything else fell into place," he continues smugly. "Why kill the prince, anyway? He's just a boy. The regent has the real power now, and everyone knows he's a force to be reckoned with. *And* at the time, he was on the brink of making an unpopular alliance with England."

Tristan has to pause for a moment to let the boys voice the expected grumbles about the English, but before they can derail his momentum, he silences their grousing by talking loudly over them again.

"An *alliance* that would allow Ardennese weavers to import English wool cheaply, without taxes or tariffs," he says pointedly. "And as we all know, most of Brecelyn's lands are pasture lands, and virtually all his riches come from his flocks. The last thing he wanted was cheap but superior English wool flooding the market, and he was right to worry; we've all seen what's happened to him, and the plague's just made it worse. Brecelyn and his associates must have thought they could stop the alliance by getting the regent out of the way. And besides, a young, inexperienced boy would be easy to manipulate. Even without the threat of the English alliance, there are surely plenty of reasons why ambitious men would be eager to have a leader in place that they thought they could control to their advantage."

"That's all perfectly plausible, of course, DuBois," Aristide interrupts condescendingly, "but it doesn't *prove* anything."

Tristan ignores him. "The way I figure it is this," he continues smoothly. "The original plan must have been to shoot the regent during a hunt organized in his honor, while he was staying at Brecelyn's for the competitions. It's no secret the regent's an avid sportsman; the opportunity to hunt on Brecelyn's land is probably what induced him to agree to bring the court to Louvain for the trials in the first place. That's why Brecelyn's huntsman Beaufort was such a key player. He was in charge of staging the kill to make it look like an accident, and our hunt at Brecelyn's was surely practice for it. Oh, I thought at the time it was a strange coincidence that *both* of those deer ended up in that same clearing! And that *both* of them came straight past *me*. But it was no coincidence. Beaufort knew just how to herd the deer and lead them on, and he was using our hunt to see if he really could induce an animal to pass a specific, pre-selected spot, every time. *He* must have been the one who shot at me. Then when it appeared that Beaufort managed to miss me *both* times, despite the perfect set-up, the original plan had to be scrapped, no doubt on the assumption that there were too many obstacles in the way for Beaufort to make the shot — you know, trees and shrubs, and things," and when Gilles interrupts to put in archly, "And *stumps*," Tristan just turns to him and exclaims,

"*Exactly!* And if I'm right, I rather imagine our plotters *had* been originally counting on having a better marksman for the job. When that fell through, and then when Beaufort apparently failed them in the forest, they came up with a new idea. Hence the shot from the tower, where the target could be pinned down and there would be nothing in the way to obscure the shot of an inferior archer. Nothing, that is, except for *me*."

"I don't know, Tristan," Gilles protests, considering it all thoughtfully. "The regent as the target, that makes sense. And I don't like Brecelyn any more than you do. But I can't believe an aristocrat would commit treason solely for money. A proud and arrogant man like him would have at least convinced himself that he was acting in his country's best interest, that his venal motives were in fact patriotic."

"Fine, Gilles," Tristan says shortly, getting so caught up in making his point that he forgets for a moment to play his new role appropriately. "Maybe Brecelyn told himself that France would be a safer ally for Ardennes, and that plotting with his contacts among the French nobility to ensure a French alliance once the regent was out of the way was an act of loyalty to our country. Maybe he even believes it, who cares?"

As Tristan and Gilles have been talking, around the table the atmosphere has been subtly changing; Tristan sounds so confident and he's such a persuasive speaker, around me I can feel the boys' disbelieving indulgence starting to fade into tentative conviction. Even Falko sounds uncharacteristically serious when he asks,

"Is that where Brecelyn's money has been coming from then, Tristan? Bribes and backing from French aristocrats?," and Tristan shakes his head.

"No, I don't think so. At least, not all of it," he says, rolling up his sleeve carefully to point down at the ledger again. "And this is what proves it. Look for yourselves."

We all lean in closer again, and over Tristan's arm I see that he's pointing at a crudely shaped spiral drawn near a column of numbers. As I watch, Tristan runs his finger down the page, drawing our attention to a number of similar symbols sprinkled down the margins.

"See these marks? These are what Jerome took for squiggles, or doodles."

"Looks like the old boy was trying to illuminate the borders, almost like a manuscript," Aristide remarks, and I put in excitedly,

"It *does*! Why, those could even be poor attempts at battling snails!"

I've seen Father Abelard embellish the edges of pages with little figures of snails dressed in armor and tilting with knights dozens of times; when I asked him why, he just shrugged and said, *"All monks draw them, Marek. I have no idea how the tradition started. But they're easy, and fun to draw,"* and I never thought to press him about it.

"Quite," Tristan says, unimpressed. "But in fact, these spirals are neither snails, nor idle doodles. They're marks next to unexplained amounts of money, missing from the accounts. Money that surely went to fund Sir Hugo Brecelyn. Yes, boys — these ledgers prove it, without a shadow of a doubt: the money to back Brecelyn's scheme was coming from *us*. It was coming from St. Sebastian's."

"Are you suggesting doddering old Master Gheeraert was part of the plot?!" Jurian scoffs.

"I don't see why it isn't possible," Tristan replies. "And that *could* explain it. Much more likely, though, is that Gheeraert put these purposefully cryptic marks here for himself, because he was suspicious. Maybe he even figured it out. Surely I don't need to remind you all of how he got up from table right in the middle of this very room during mess this winter and *died*, without having shown any visible signs of plague."

"Are you saying old Gheery was *poisoned*?!" Falko barks, for once getting Tristan's insinuations before anyone else, and the boys all have to shush him.

"Oh, I don't know. Maybe. Why else hire an inexperienced, callow boy to take over a master's job, unless there was something to hide? But that's not important," Tristan says, waving off the untimely demise of Master Gheeraert with an impatient hand, and an indignant Jerome, too, for that matter. "The point is, Marek was surely right about this, too: Brecelyn had accomplices *right here* in our own guild. Top men. Important men. *They* were giving Brecelyn the funds to host us all along, and providing him with henchmen. And they provided him with opportunity, too, by bending the rules for him so he could hold Thirds at his estate. Probably some of the Guardsmen were even in on it, and don't tell me you can't all think of plenty of motives for *that*. Why, we've all heard de Gilford puffing about how many privileges he used to have before the regent took over. It's not just Sir Brecelyn who'd have been likely to think he'd have a better chance of grabbing some power and influence for himself with a young new prince than with the cagey, controlling regent — influence for himself, influence for the Guards, and influence, for St. Sebastian's."

Tristan pauses and looks around the table expectantly, looking to see if anyone's going to object again.

I think we'd all like to, but there's nothing anyone can say. It's the last thing I was expecting, but Tristan's theory is actually pretty convincing. So he sits back, folds the ledger closed, and laying a hand on it solemnly, he says in conclusion,

"And this is really the crux of things, men: why do you think Brecelyn has been hosting us at his estate so often? Nobody can really think it's because he's desperate for his future son-in-law's witty conversation." He slips the insult in with admirable dexterity, but the mood at the table is by now so somber that nobody laughs, and he's not waited for a reaction anyway. "It's the perfect excuse for him and his henchmen from St. Sebastian's to plot without raising any suspicions. And you all know what *that* must mean. The *whole time* we were at Sir Hugo's this winter, not only we were eating at our own guild's expense — no wonder there's been no guild money for us yet! — but somewhere in shadowy corners or in dark back rooms, villainous men were busy secretly plotting how they're going to try to do away with our regent, *again*."

"Or in lonely chapels," Gilles says seriously, meeting my eyes across the table with a look that says the time has come for us to make a confession.

This isn't the moment I would have chosen, but I know Gilles is right. It's time for me to come clean to my master about some of my midnight skulking back at the castle. The meal is technically over and the masters are already gone, so I beg Tristan's leave to absent myself briefly from table, and I dart back to barracks. When I return, I've got the handkerchief I found out in Brecelyn's chapel tucked down into the band at my waist. Then I make short work of it to tell the boys an abridged version of the events that transpired on the night I went out for midnight target practice to Brecelyn's clearing, and about everything that ensued thereafter, after Gilles found me there.

"I didn't mention it earlier, Tristan," I tell him ashamedly, when I'm finished. "I didn't want you to worry, and, well, I didn't think it mattered. We just assumed it was a pair of *l-l-*lovers we'd interrupted in the chapel," and to my horror, I trip over that awful word again. Somewhere behind me I hear a sort of strangled wheeze, and for a moment, I freeze — even though it turns out the sound is just coming from Aristide, of all people. Needless to say, publicly confessing that I've been keeping something so foolish and so embarrassing from Tristan is bad enough. Knowing that Taran is listening in makes it excruciating. I hate having him hear just how many secrets I've been keeping from my master, and I'm sure the point of my midnight stump-shooting excursion to the clearing isn't lost on him — not after my recent disastrous reenactment of it. And I'm pretty sure he knows, too, that one of the lovers I'd assumed was trysting out in the chapel that night was him.

There's nothing I can do about it, though, so I swallow and continue bravely,

"And as for the handkerchief. Well, I thought Gilles was just teasing me, and that it was his," I say, and as I do, I bring out the handkerchief and I spread it out face up on top of the ledger.

It's big, bold, blood-red *G* stares up at us all from the center of the table.

For a solid minute, nobody says a thing.

Nobody has to. The handkerchief says it all.

I'm not sure if Tristan's really fully convinced the boys of his theory, or not. But at the very least they're wavering, and anyway there's always been only one logical man to suspect of being Brecelyn's accomplice inside St. Sebastian's, even though it still makes no sense to me. Now with that handkerchief with his initial emblazoned on it out in the open for all to see, I've got to accept it:

the man who betrayed his country, his friend and my father was of course Master G.

Falko is the first of us to break the silence.

"Criminy!" he croaks, just as behind him comes the sound of two big hands clapping slowly and loudly together, in that deliberate way that's surely meant to imply extreme sarcasm.

"*Bravo*," Taran drawls emphatically, drawing out the word as all the boys turn around to look at him. He's been notably silent throughout Tristan's recitation, and everyone's obviously eager to hear what he's going to say about it. Tristan himself looks delighted.

"All very neat, and tidy," Taran exclaims derisively. "Yet it seems to me we've heard things like this from you before that have all turned out to be a hot swill of hogwash, haven't we? What's next? Claiming that *I'm* the one who was originally slated to be the shooter?"

"Yeah! Who better for it than the *Knight of the Dirty shot*, am I right?" Falko chortles, looking relieved and clearly thinking it's all a joke again. "Either that, or old Poncellet!"

"Not at all," Tristan replies coolly, to Taran. Then he pointedly ignores him, and addresses the rest of his reply to Falko:

"And I don't see why it isn't possible to think that you might be right. Poncellet is a remarkable shot, after all. But it's *my* idea that the man who refused the role of assassin last year was Jan Verbeke. So unless I miss my guess, the reason Poncellet is here now is to ensure the success of the *next* attempt."

Tristan sounds so certain that Falko frowns, and it sounds so plausible that I can't help gazing up at Tristan in admiration, even though I didn't want him to investigate in the first place, and for a moment, even Taran seems taken aback.

Not to be stymied, Taran soon rallies. From the annoyed glare he gives us when he sees Gilles's smug, superior look on Tristan's face and the openly fawning expression on mine as I gaze up adoringly at my master, I can tell he has no intention of letting Tristan win another argument with him — particularly not now that he's Gistan.

"Oh, yeah?" he demands. "Well, too bad there's one huge, glaring flaw in your theory, *brother*. Or did you really forget?" He pauses for one long beat, and as he does, he rolls his eyes at me and thrusts his open palm out in front of Tristan's face.

Then he snarls,

"*I'm* the one who shot you!"

As he says it, he slaps his hand down on the tabletop in front of Tristan so hard that the ledger jumps and all the boys recoil, looking almost as stunned as I feel.

I mean, we all knew he did it. But he's never admitted it so openly before, let alone claimed credit for it. I feel a little ill at hearing him say it out loud — and even more, at knowing that I've been making excuses for it for him, for a long time now.

"And as for that handkerchief," Taran says, regaining his composure and giving it a dismissive flip with his fingers. "*Marek* here's as gullible as a *baby*," he jeers, shooting me another derisive look. "*He'd* believe anything. But I'm surprised at the rest of you. Gilles is having you on, boys, and laughing up his sleeve! This surely *is* his. It looks exactly like something he'd own to me."

With just two blows, Taran's shot Tristan's theory full of holes. He's so forceful about it and so blunt that he can't help sounding like the cold voice of reason, particularly since he's finally owned up to his crime, and the outlandish get-up Tristan's wearing isn't helping. Before long Taran's got the boys convinced that Tristan's words are as fanciful as his outfit, and that the whole thing is just another one of the boys' antics.

All of them, that is, except for Gilles, who's now giving Taran a look that for once fully captures one of Tristan's, since he clearly doesn't appreciate the implication that he's been lying.

Tristan's theory is already cracking, then, when Taran delivers a final blow that kills it off entirely.

"So, let's pretend for a moment that all this rot you're spewing is true, DuBois, and our regent really is in danger. Tell me this: what are *you* going to do about it?!"

For once, Taran's succeeding in saying something to which Tristan can find no answer. All he can do is sit there simmering with rage, absolutely still — well, still except for all the little tassels on his shirt, which are now gently quivering — because there's only one thing Tristan could possibly do, if he really thought his theory were true, and Taran knows it. And that's write to their father, Jakob Mellor, the Captain of the Black Guard.

And we all know that that's the one thing Tristan will never do.

Tristan does his best to laugh it off for the rest of the evening, in the spirit of Gilles. Even after Taran's made one of his typically abrupt departures, Tristan lingers at table, bantering casually with the others and to all appearances fully enjoying his evening, even though it's got to be obvious to him that Taran's succeeded in convincing the boys to dismiss his grand theory out of hand, and that now none of them believes him.

As soon as we're alone back in his room, however, Tristan plops heavily onto the edge of his cot and swears,

"Damn it all, Marek!" in a way that suggests he's forgotten for the moment that he's supposed to be as imperturbable as Gilles.

Then he throws the handkerchief onto the floor, and he kicks it into the corner of the room with such violence that I fear he's going to throw off Gilles's personality entirely, and head straight into Taran's.

As I sit down gingerly next to him, he puts his head in his hands and sighs dispiritedly,

"That blasted thing *does* look a lot like one of Gilles's! I ought to know. I've been carrying around enough of them lately. Even so, I swear he'd never have gotten the best of me if I'd really been *myself* tonight, Marek."

I cluck out some soothing noises, and he looks so downhearted, I reach up instinctively to smooth back that one unruly lock of hair of his. Then I remember that it's not there; it's still safely pulled back into his stubby ponytail. So I drop my hand awkwardly back into my lap, and instead I say consolingly,

"It's a good theory, master. Some of it is probably true, anyway."

"*All* of it, Marek. In*du*bitably," he counters, drawing himself up and rallying for a moment. Then his shoulders slump again.

"Oh, what does it matter? Taran was right about *one* thing. There's nothing *I* can do about it. Nothing at all, and I might as well forget all about the whole damned thing."

I can't bear to see him looking so defeated, and I can't help feeling guilty that I've been so unhelpful and so discouraging all along about his investigations. I desperately wish there was something I could do or say to cheer him. But there's nothing; even if I could be sure that Tristan was right, I'm powerless. That's been the crux of the problem all along, hasn't it? So I settle for taking his hand in mine, and saying gently,

"You don't have to save a prince, Tristan. Or a regent, or even a king. Not to be a hero to me. And don't forget, you've got other plans. *Big* plans. Glorious, even," and once the words are out, I regret them, since I'm not entirely sure *what* all the plans are that he's been preparing. But Tristan knows I'm talking about the competitions, even before I remind him,

"Four days, master — that's it. Stay focused, and it'll be just *four more days* until you beat him, at the thing that really matters."

"You're right, little brother," he says affectionately, flashing me the hint of one of his old, easy grins. "We *do* still have a plan. A brilliant one. The *best*, and I have you to thank for it. How good it's going to feel, *finally* to outdo that devil! And I promise you this. When *I* win Guards, I *will* thank you properly, Marek, for everything, I swear it — since *then* my situation will be entirely different," and although I get his rather dangerous implication, I have to be contented — because when he reaches down and ruffles my hair, for a moment he's my Tristan again.

After that I make short work of it generally to loosen and unfasten him, and to disentangle the mass of velvet and ribbons that he's ensconced himself in. Then I leave him to his beauty sleep, using the approach of curfew as an excuse to depart before having to help him remove everything.

Before I go, Tristan gestures toward the corner of the room.

"Take *that* thing with you, won't you, Marek?" he says, pointing at the handkerchief. "I don't ever want to see it again." And so I retrieve it, and when I'm at the door with it, I pause long enough to ask him worriedly,

"About your theory, Tristan. Do you really believe it?"

"Every last word of it," he declares, plucking at a tassel dangling from his sleeve. But he's back to being Gilles again, and I don't know whether or not I can take him seriously.

As I make my way back to barracks, I shove the handkerchief hastily down into my waistband, feeling a little afraid of it. Or at least, afraid of having it *on* me, and I can't wait to stuff it safely back down into the bottom of my traveling bag.

To be honest, I don't really know what to make of Tristan's theory any longer, and maybe the fancy embroidered rag really is just Gilles's. But even if it is, with that big, red G emblazoned on it, it's an unwelcome reminder of the one piece of Tristan's theory that I can't pretend any longer to think is anything but the truth.

CHAPTER TWENTY-NINE

After that night, Tristan doesn't mention his theory again. It isn't like him to give up on a project so easily, but after Taran practically dared him to send word of his suspicions to their father, it's painfully clear that this time there really is nothing else Tristan can do. He'd never admit it, but Taran's forceful confession must have shaken Tristan's confidence in his own theory, too, at least a little; I know Tristan well enough to be sure he'd find a way to do *something*, if he really believed in the imminent danger to our regent implicitly. So I do my best to forget about it myself, and once the handkerchief is safely back in the bottom of my traveling bag, with the trials coming up fast it isn't too hard.

The oppressive presence of the handkerchief aside, those last few days leading up to Firsts might not have been so bad, if it weren't soon apparent that the public collapse of his theory at the hands of Taran has left Tristan in need of distraction. I should have known staying focused wouldn't be Tristan's forte; it's never been his way of handling the stress of waiting for the trials, and Taran's cold admission last night must have affected him more than he let on.

The first hint I get of it is early the next morning, when the boys are hanging around eating the last of some hard boiled eggs I've brought out with me for my breakfast and waiting for me and Pascal to finish readying their equipment. Tristan is leaning up against Gilles's cabinet and idly inspecting his fingernails while Gilles fiddles with his hair, when I overhear Tristan say to him,

"What do you say, old man? This is all working such a treat, shall we take it to the next level?"

Soon they've got their heads together, and they're whispering in that conspiratorial way of theirs. I can't hear more than a snatch of the conversation, something that sounds suspiciously like Tristan declaring, "What we really need is to *do* something typical of the other. And not just anything! Something *big*, a grand gesture," and in typical fashion when any dodgy undertaking is afoot, Gilles doesn't require much convincing. It's not hard to guess they're cooking up something to trot out the next time we're all at table, and that whatever it is, it's sure to involve antagonizing Taran. It always does anyway, but after he got the best of them both last night, they're no doubt out for blood, and I shudder to think what 'the next level' could possibly entail.

Before they can plot too long, the arrival of Poncellet puts a necessary end to their whispering. The old master's appeared in the stable doorway to call the boys to drills, and at the sight of him striking one of his more flamboyant poses, I can't help being reminded of some of the things the boys have recently been saying about him.

We're all three now looking over at Poncellet, as is everyone else on the field. The man has that effect, and without taking my eyes off him, in a quiet voice I ask,

"Do you really think he's a hired assassin, Tristan?"

"*I* think he'd do just about anything, for money," Gilles replies easily.

"A man down on his luck usually will," Tristan agrees. "But I didn't say Poncellet was in on the plot, Marek. Only that he was surely brought here for the purpose. If Poncellet were already an assassin-for-hire, he'd be a damned good one. He'd be filthy rich. So I'm hoping that when the time comes and he's propositioned, he'll refuse — just as your father did."

Gilles just snorts, and I have to say, although Poncellet has grown on me lately, I have to agree with Gilles that Tristan's confidence in his character is probably misplaced. I sneak a look up at Gilles, and I give him a secret smile of solidarity. He gives me a quick wink back, and flashes me a grin — one of Tristan's charming, lazy grins. And I don't know why I never noticed it before — just how amazingly attractive Gilles really is.

Maybe it's the haircut. Or it's Tristan's clothes. Or it's Tristan's familiar smile, playing on his lips. But without really meaning to, I reach up a hand to him. I can't resist pulling down that one wayward lock of his thick, auburn hair, and arranging it for him rakishly across his forehead. I just have a feeling he'd look good that way.

"Whaddya say, kid?" he laughs, flashing me another dazzling smile bright enough to make even old Poncellet cringe. "Am I a proper butts man now? Do I look the part? Do I look as good as *Tristan*?" he teases, and to my dismay, when I gush back, "Oh, rat*her*!" I feel myself blushing.

It's just a momentary lapse, I swear. I mean, really; the last few days have been disorienting, but I am *not* going to start lusting after Gilles. So to cover for my blunder, I put my hand on the little place where Gilles has somehow acquired a missing sliver of his eyebrow identical to Tristan's, as though that's what made me reach up to Gilles's face in the first place. It's in the exact place where Tristan was nicked by falling debris in the fire this winter, and the boys must have shaved it off there purposely. I finger it a moment, amused, and I ask them both,

"And how did you manage *this*, masters? Did Armand cut that off, too?"

"Nah," Tristan scoffs, slinging an arm around my shoulders, "*I* did it for him, with my trusty rapier!" and we all three laugh.

For some reason, though, as we prepare to take the field arm-in-arm to line up for practice, my hand is still fiddling with Gilles's eyebrow. It's a bit awkward when Gilles has to take my hand in his, and gently remove it from him. But not as much as when I turn around to see that Taran is now leaning against his cabinet not ten feet away, watching me. His big arms are folded across his chest and there's a frown of disgust on his features. I know how touchy he is about Tristan's scar; I guess he doesn't like it any better, when it's on Gilles's face.

I'm on edge for the rest of the day, even though noon mess comes and goes without any hint of scheming from the boys, and at squires' club that afternoon, the strain beneath our façade of cooperation is even more pronounced than usual. I can tell Taran thinks I was flaunting Gilles's scar at him on purpose, and I have to admit, maybe I *did* reach up to Gilles's face this morning, hoping it would annoy him.

The thing is, it's awfully hard to pretend I've got nothing against a boy who's just bragged publicly about shooting my best friend. And it's not just the *fact* of his dirty shot that's bothering me. It's that Taran's finally admitted to it right when I can't confront him about it without putting squires' squad at risk — not to mention looking like a terrible hypocrite. From the smug, challenging expression Taran's got on his face every time I catch his eye, I can tell he's plenty pleased with himself for the timing of the thing, and it doesn't help that his insistence on wearing that blasted dove-gray tunic every day is starting to get to me. By now he's figured out the mere sight of it irritates me, and although he can't know it reminds me of my father, it's hard to escape the conclusion that he's purposely trying to remind me of the circumstances under which I dressed him in it, as a way of getting under my skin without seeming to be the one to break the accord between us.

And guess what? It's working.

It's for a variety of reasons, then, that I'm fidgety that night when I take my seat between Tristan and Gilles at the Journey end of the table. But I keep my hands to myself and off the boys' scars, and I studiously ignore Taran (although I see he hasn't bothered to change out of the tunic for dinner), and most of our supper passes without incident. By the time the meal is winding down, I've even managed to convince myself I must have been mistaken that the boys were plotting something.

Or at least, I assume they've simply decided to content themselves with the *other* entertainment on offer, since not long after we were all seated, Master Bernard appeared at the head of the table to announce in front of all and sundry that the master has tasked *me* with composing an official motto for the new crossbow contingent. I've got three days to come up with something, and in *Latin*. So ever since, the boys have been teasing me mercilessly under the guise of being helpful about it, while the squires alternate between joining in on the attack and coming to my defense.

"What's Latin for *I'm too weak to shoot a real bow?*" Jurian's now musing, as the meal winds down and the boys are on their last cups of wine. "Or maybe, *Boys, Girls, and Old Men.*"

"How about *'Don't Cross me!'*?" Pascal suggests loyally, and I rather like the ring of it. But the Journeys are in no mood to be serious, and none of them will help me translate it.

"Just what are these crossbow winners of yours going to *do* anyway, Marek?" Falko asks me, and at least he sounds interested. So I admit to him a little shyly,

"I've had an idea about that, actually. I thought maybe they could stay on here at St. Sebastian's as a sort of honor guard for the Journeys, and as a defensive force for the guild. You know, they could stand watch up in that new tower the master is building, and we could call them the 'Saint's Guard,' or something."

I'm fully expecting the boys to start mocking me, since of course they've all been listening in. Instead an appreciative murmur goes up, and when Tristan exclaims,

"Capital idea, my boy! Simply capital," even Aristide agrees,

"That *is* clever, Marek. Not bad. No, not bad," and I can't help preening, since it's rare to get anything but a backhanded compliment from any of the Journeys. Aristide's certainly never complimented me on anything at all, although I'm sure the smile on his lips isn't really directed at me. He's picturing the pleasure of going around town surrounded by an entourage of impressive boys armed with crossbows and commanding them to roust the awed rabble out of his way.

"I thought that was what squires were for," Jurian laughs. "So, how about *this* for a motto? *Squires with delusions of grandeur,*" and my smile turns into a frown.

It's not because of Jurian's comments. I'm used to them. It's because as he says it, a look passes between Tristan and Gilles over my head, and I feel a pinprick of apprehension.

I know that look, and when Tristan next plucks at his sleeve with the exact preening motion Gilles usually executes before coming out with a pronouncement, the hairs literally bristle on the back of my neck.

To my surprise, it's not Tristan who then opens his mouth and proceeds to set about goading Taran, as I'm expecting.

It's Gilles.

I should have seen it coming, I suppose, since the boys have switched personalities.

Sure enough, Gilles is soon declaring,

"So, Taran. You're mighty quiet down there, at *your* little end of the table. What about it, *buddy?* Whaddya say?," and Pascal flinches again at Gilles's bizarre diction. "*You* must have a thought on the matter," he continues, chewing his words the way Falko usually works his way through a gristly piece of steak. "Getting Marek a crossbow was all *your* idea. So what do *you* think the motto for Marek's crossbowmen should be?"

Taran doesn't respond, which isn't surprising, since Gilles is clearly trying to provoke him. But he does get abruptly to his feet, and from the dirty look he shoots Gilles I just assume he's going to refuse to answer and take his leave with some rude remark, or another threat of violence.

Instead, he rattles off something in Latin that makes the others all shut up instantly.

It's not like the boys to be silenced so easily, and I'm almost afraid to know what Taran can possibly have said that was so bad as to have ruined the boys' fun entirely. After the chilly atmosphere this afternoon at squires' practice, I guess I'm not really all that surprised, and anyway our little truce has never extended beyond the confines of the club. But whatever Taran said, it must have been pretty insulting to me.

Taran gives a curt little bow, obviously intending his line as a parting shot. Before he can climb over the bench and make one of his typically hasty departures, however, Master Leon looks over from the head table and bellows at him,

"*Siddown*, Mellor! Dinner isn't over yet, goddamn it!" and Taran has no choice but to sit back down again.

During this interlude, I take the opportunity to whisper to Tristan,

"Uh, *master*. What did Taran say?"

Tristan doesn't answer. He's too busy glaring at Taran through slitted lids, and I'm surprised to see he also looks a little flushed, as though Taran's managed to embarrass him.

It's Jurian who answers.

"Sagittam prendam *pro te*, Marek."

"Yes, but what does it *mean*?" I repeat, and when he translates for me, I don't know what to think.

Apparently, what Taran's just said is,

"*I'll* take the arrow *for* you."

Taran's taken the wind out of the boys' sails, and maybe that was all he intended — although given his usual deadpan delivery, I can't tell whether the barb was also a veiled threat, or something of a compliment.

Whatever his intention, after this reminder of my sacrifice for Tristan on the tower the boys lose their taste for teasing me, and I'm mostly just glad that that's going to be the end of it.

I must be a little shaken by the comment, though, or at least distracted by it, not to realize sooner that the boys have no intention of letting Taran have the last word or get the best of them. Not for a second night in a row, certainly. They waited patiently for this opening, and having found themselves stymied in it, they simply sit back and wait for another.

They don't have to wait long, since Jerome soon hands them one on a silver platter.

Jerome's been silent and thoughtful throughout the whole crossbow-motto discussion, and now that nobody else seems inclined to say anything, he bursts out with the air of a boy who can contain himself no longer,

"Ok, boys! That is *it*. Will somebody *finally* tell me how Marek survived on that tower? I mean, he *did* take an arrow for Tristan, didn't he?"

"Yes," Gilles agrees slowly, and a great big grin spreads across his features, as over my head Tristan shoots him another pointed look. "Yes, he did."

"Yes, *Taran*, since *you* bring it up," Tristan purrs, and it doesn't take a genius to know that something more is coming, since I can feel them both stirring around excitedly on the bench.

"Now's the perfect opportunity," Gilles continues, picking up on Tristan's cue without missing a beat. "Why don't *you* give us *your* side of the story?" he declares, and again Taran gets abruptly to his feet.

He gets up so fast, it puts the whole bench on his side of the table out of balance and Falko almost falls off it over backwards. Only there's nowhere for him to go. There's no escape, since as soon as Master Leon sees him back out of his seat, he barks across the room at him,

"I said SIT DOWN, Mellor! And I meant it. It'll be the lash, if I see you pop up over there again," and I almost feel sorry for Taran. I can't really begrudge Tristan his payback, if it will help restore his confidence and good humor. But if the devilish smile now curling up the corner of Gilles's lip is anything to go by, Taran's really in for it this time, and the truth of the matter is that a little needling and a few empty threats aside, lately I've actually been getting along rather well with him. It seems cruel that the one time Taran's managed to make a comeback clever enough to stop Tristan in his tracks, all he ended up doing was playing right into the boys' hands.

"Well, well, boys! Looks like our man Taran here isn't going to answer," Gilles exclaims, sounding just like Tristan when he begins one of these things. "That's our boy, much too modest to brag! So I'll tell you what, Jerome," Gilles says, slapping his friend heartily on the back. "*I'll* tell you the whole story *for* him, just as though *I* were *him*! I'm sure I could do a better job of it than he would, anyway," and the boys all give him a cheer.

Predictably, they all think it's a marvelous idea.

Gilles has a captive audience — literally, since Master Leon's not letting anybody get up from table. So he makes the most of it. Around me the boys all settle in, preparing to enjoy Gilles's version of Tristan's purple prose, and as Gilles makes a show of clearing his throat and rubbing his Adam's apple as though limbering it up, Taran looks studiously off over the boys' shoulders and settles into one of his bored, impassive expressions. He's not fooling anyone, though. Gilles hasn't even started, and the base of his neck is already starting to turn red. But there's nothing he can do. He's as trapped here as the rest of us, and he's just going to have to tough it out.

"*Hem, hem, hem! Mi, mi, mi,*" Gilles gargles, giving his arms a stretch and flexing his fingers, since Tristan always acts out the most dramatic moments of his recitations and Gilles clearly intends to follow suit. Then he thrusts his hands out suddenly into the air in front of him, as though at the same time demanding silence and already starting to set the scene:

"What'll I call this tale, boys?" he cries. "'The Ballad of Taran and Marek,' or —"

"Just get on with it!" Taran gurgles in a strangled voice, his face looking awfully flushed already.

"As you wish," Gilles nods. "*The Ballad of Taran and Marek* it is!"

Gilles clears his voice one last time. Then before he begins to speak, he takes a moment to compose his features. Somehow by puffing himself up and throwing back his shoulders, furrowing his brow and clenching his teeth to jut out his chin, he manages to capture the look of Taran. Or rather, a pretty convincing caricature of him.

It's even more remarkable when he begins to speak. What comes out of his mouth is Taran's voice, delivered with Tristan's intonation and mannerisms. Gilles intends to tell the whole story as though he really were Tristan *imitating* Taran, and poking fun at him.

"All right, Jerome," he grumbles, and with only three words he's already set everyone at the table to laughing. Well, almost everyone. There are three of us who are as silent as the grave, since Remy doesn't look like he's prepared to enjoy this story much, either.

I'll admit I'm torn. I can't help being terribly curious. From Gilles's title alone, though, I'm beginning to realize I'm surely about to suffer some serious collateral damage.

"There I was, up on Brecelyn's tower," Gilles booms. "*I'd* just saved the day, by shooting Beaufort. It was *my* shot that killed him, see? *I* didn't just nick him on the wrist, like *some* people," he rolls his eyes at Tristan, and a laugh goes up from the boys. "And when I turned around, what did I see? That poor chap who's got the rotten luck of being *DuBois's* squire had gone and sacrificed himself, to save that lily-livered bastard of a master of his! (*no offense, Tristan*).*"

Tristan nods condescendingly, flashing Gilles a conspiratorial grin, and Gilles is off again:

"*I* could see the boy wasn't dying. *I'm* not an idiot. *I* didn't waste precious time, blubbering and blabbering. The kid was hurt, and badly. He needed attention, quick. So I played along. He wanted *me* to be the one to bury him. He didn't want anyone to see the scars he's got underneath his tunic — anyone but *me*. Who cares what a big, dumb brute like me thinks, am I right?" Gilles crows, and I shrink down on the bench. Next to me, Tristan is prodding me with his elbow and somewhere Rennie is giggling, and I don't dare look down the table. Remy's accusing face across from me is bad enough.

But Gilles is just warming up.

"Everybody knows we're supposed to be enemies, though I've got nothing against the little guy, personally. He's a damned sight braver than his own master, and he took lashes for *my* squire. Hell, he took *an arrow* for a member! That makes him okay by me. *I* can respect that, and really, I can think of only one other man at St. Sebastian's who'd do something so goddamned noble — and that's *me!*"

At this, Gilles rises halfway out of his seat while thrusting his thumb vigorously against his own chest, and there's such an uproar at the table that Master Leon half-rises from his seat, too, to glare over at us.

Through all of this Taran's been sitting stone still, looking off over Aristide's shoulder across from him with absolutely no expression on his face. But when out of the corner of my eye I see him dart a quick, sharp glance at Leon, one of his eyelids is twitching and I'm pretty sure I know what he's thinking. Masters Guillaume and Poncellet have both already departed, and Taran's watching Master Leon like a hawk; he's waiting for the instant Leon leaves the room, so he, too, can make one of his typical hasty retreats.

Unfortunately for Taran, Master Leon shows no sign whatsoever of departing. He seems to have a talent for sensing for when his presence is prolonging someone's agony. He's leisurely refilling his glass with port from a half-full bottle Master Guillaume has left up on the head table, as Gilles closes his eyes and puts a hand dramatically to his forehead as though summoning his muse, only to resume *sotto voce*:

"As soon as the poor lad's eyes slid closed, I snatched him out of his useless master's grip. No vain questions or restraining hands could delay me; I dashed straight down the tower steps with him, taking them three — no, *four!* — at a time in my hurry, but hey — I'm not just a man of action. I'm also *sensitive*."

Here there's such a loud, inadvertent snort from Falko that the wine he was in the process of swallowing comes out through his nose, but it doesn't stop Gilles.

"That's right, men, I'm deeply *sensitive*, as only a big, shy guy like me can be," Gilles elaborates, pausing a moment to nod in an aside to Falko, "You know what I mean, DeBruyn," and Falko, typically missing Gilles's irony, preens a little bashfully, looking inordinately pleased.

I can't say the same for Taran, as Gilles resumes:

"So all the while I raced along, my head was bent, to murmur in his little ear the tenderest of encouragements! For I knew there was no time to lose, as soon as I felt his pitiful, cold cheek — pressed roughly against my chiseled pecs!" And with that, Taran gives up all pretense at toughing it out. He drops his head straight down onto the table in front of him with a hollow thud, and he leaves it there for the rest Gilles's recitation. It's probably an attempt to hide the fact that he's turning that deep shade of purple he always does when he's thoroughly embarrassed, but it doesn't really help, since we can all see the back of his neck. It's now so red and hot, it's almost sizzling. I bet it could fry an egg.

"I had to get to the Vendon Abbey, and quickly! There was not one moment to spare," Gilles is now saying, speeding up as though he's just getting to the good part. "The lad had friends there who would help him. There was no time for getting to the stables. So what do you think *I* did? I pulled a passing man right off his horse, punching him in the gut in the process! Then I leapt astride the steed myself, and off I rode with my bundle cradled in my manly arms, right out through the middle of the competition crowds! And what a wild ride it was, boys. We hurtled along at breakneck speed, scattering spectators and busting through concessions; I think we even dragged a pastry tent along behind us for more than fifty feet! Did I stop, for the cries of the vendors? For the shouts of Brecelyn's watchmen, or at the Black Guardsmen's threats? *I did not.* Did I stop, for the bellowed orders of the master himself?! Not at all, men! With a flip of my jet-black cape that said *'Master Guillaume, we'll meet again in hell!,'* I rode off like a madman without a word of explanation, out through the inky night —" and here Charles interrupts to laugh,

"It was *daylight!,*" but it doesn't slow Gilles down. "On through the *inky night* we rode," he repeats loudly, talking over Charles, "thundering through campfires and overturning campsites, then out across the open country, through dense forests and fields," and it's almost as though Taran is inadvertently providing sound effects for the tale, since he's started banging his forehead dully against the tabletop, and the repeated *thwack* of his head sounds a little like hoofbeats.

"Was it easy, men, to ride at top speed with both arms wrapped around my little charge, and only one hand on the reins? To absorb every jolt and jar with the magnificent muscles of my mighty thighs and buttocks, to cushion the ride for him? *No,* it was not. But what cared I, for cruelly lashing branches? For the threat of falling headlong, and breaking my own neck? I had a boy to save, and I am nothing if not selfless, and stupefyingly brave!"

At this, Taran's head pops up as all the boys hoot with laughter, and I think Gilles is awfully lucky that Taran has been barred from bringing his knife with him to mess, or it would by now be lodged up to the hilt in Gilles's chest. But Taran's not glaring at Gilles. He's looking keenly over at the head table, and finding Master Leon still ensconced there, with a growl he drops his head back down onto the table again.

"What happened next, Gille—er, 'Taran'?" Jerome prompts, and there's a sharp bark from Taran, muffled a bit by the tabletop, of "Don't *encourage* him, for God's sake Jerome," prompting Remy to titter nervously, "*Ha, ha,* such good fun! But isn't that *enough,* boys?"

"Oh, but we *must* hear what happened at Vendon!" Tristan exclaims in answer. "That's the part of the tale I'm *most* eager to hear," and I have a bad feeling I know what he means. It's the part that will give Gilles the most scope for his imagination, since none of the boys were there to witness it. The only saving grace is that at least whatever is coming can't be the truth, since Gilles doesn't actually know what happened there either.

"And what a scene it was, men!" Gilles obliges, "when at last we arrived at the abbey. And I'll confess, by then I was in a frenzy of fear. Blood was everywhere, and the plucky little fellow was now so cold and still. He wasn't going to make it — not without some serious heroics. So what do you suppose I did? I rode that horse *right up the abbey steps* (no lesser man could have done it, surely!), and crashing through its massive doors, I charged it *straight* into the cloisters — right into the middle of midday prayers!"

While Gilles pauses to take a breath and Charles interjects again with a laugh, "What happened to the inky *night*?," Jerome takes the opportunity to lean over and whisper down the table to me with amusement,

"Is *any* of this true, Marek?"

"I don't know. I was out cold," I manage to tell him. Needless to say, I'm beginning to wonder the same thing.

It's not that I think Gilles's story is accurate, of course; even if it were his goal to make it so, he wasn't there. But it gives me an uncomfortable feeling to realize that I've never really wondered about it, or tried myself to picture it. Even if it didn't happen at all as Gilles is describing it, getting me to the abbey so quickly all by himself must have been quite an ordeal.

The feeling only gets worse, when Gilles next says primly,

"Modesty prevents me from mentioning the outrageous sum of money I had to lay out to bribe the old Prior, to induce him to let the monks attend to the boy. But let's just say, there's no way Marek here could ever hope to repay it. Or *his master*, either, for that matter, if it ever occurred to them to ask about it. Which it hasn't, by the way."

Up to this point, Gilles's narrative has been plenty embarrassing, and of course I can't help it if I've been feeling a certain sympathy for Taran, who's clearly finding it all excruciating. I have to admit, though, that it's also been rather funny, since Gilles is doing a pretty wicked send-up of him. I can't find anything amusing at all about this comment, however, since from Tristan's momentarily sour expression I have an awful feeling that this, at least, might really be true.

It doesn't get any better from there.

"Back at the castle," Gilles is now saying pompously, "I knew celebrations would be in full swing. A feast was being laid out in my honor in Brecelyn's hall, where I was to be lauded by my father, my fiancée, and even, my prince! But I missed it all, and the chance to bask in the glory of my incredible win. Why, I never even got my second arrow brand, my badge of veteran status! Even *that* was denied me, by my famously overblown sense of duty — and to a boy who *hates* me, almost as much as *I* hate *him*! So in a moment of weakness (yes, even I can have them!) But I've only ever had the one), it occurred to me: *if I hurry, if I ride back and explain, I can still make it; I can experience some of it.* Yet how could I leave that poor frail boy alone, his fate uncertain? No, I had to stay, until I was sure he was out of danger. Honor demanded it!" Here Gilles sweeps his hand up over his heart, and much to Tristan's delight, he rises up as though in a salute, to exclaim with a wink,

"My name is *Mellor*. And we all know just what high moral standards *that* means!"

There's a brief interlude, in which Master Leon now barks at Gilles. As Gilles settles himself down again gracefully, Falko and Aristide take turns slapping Taran on the back and jostling his shoulders playfully, and I think I hear Falko say to him, *"come on, man. It's funny!"* before Gilles's voice turns mock-sober, and all the boys pretend seriousness, too, as they all lean in to listen again.

"I insisted I be present for the whole procedure," Gilles declares somberly, dabbing away a few nonexistent tears. "I refused to leave the room. Why, it was *I* who undressed the boy, *I* who bathed him, and *I* who gently cleansed the wound for him. Yes, I saw it *all*," he drawls meaningfully, to my dismay looking down at me and stretching out the word in a way that for a moment makes me the center of attention. "But have no fear, little squire! Your secret is safe with *me*. I'll never reveal it, or ask for thanks, or ever even tell of everything I did to save you, because, well, as I think I've mentioned, that's just the kind of great guy I am."

Now it's my turn to be jostled about playfully, while Rennie has the gall to call out to me, *"come on, Marek, it's funny!"* just as Falko did to Taran.

"And now, my friend," Gilles exclaims, turning back to Jerome, "I come to the most wrenching part of my tale. And I'm not ashamed to reveal it: beneath my rock-hard exterior, a tender heart beats within this rippled, savage chest! (Or should it be *'savagely rippled?'* or *'rippledly savage?'* What do you think, Tristan? Oh, no matter)," and Tristan merely waves him on again. "For when I saw this poor, scarred, wretched little thing, stretched out all but lifeless on his cot, why, a big, fat tear rolled down my rugged cheek, and pooled in my cleft chin! He looked so small and fragile, so like a bird with a broken wing, that I clenched a fist, and shaking it at the heavens, I raged (and in rhyme, no less!), *'Where are you now, Sebastian? Here lies a lad who gave his all, a boy most worthy of his guild; If ever there was a time to prove true to your motto, do it now, and let him live!'* What can I say, men? The old boy must have heard me, because as you all know, it was *his St. Sebastian's medal* that stopped that arrow," and Jerome interjects *"Ah!,"* since this is exactly what he *didn't* know. "But, alas, the wound was still plenty deep. It didn't take a monk to see that delirium was setting in. So I sat there by his cot the entire time the monks were working on him. And with his little hands clutched tight in my great big ones, I brushed the hair back from his fevered brow the only way I

409

could — *with my own tender lips!* All the while I wept and moaned, and murmured more gentle exhortations, softly in his ear."

As if on cue, there's another involuntary groan from Taran, and I think that this must finally be it. It's Gilles's grand finale, and there can't be any more to the story. But the boys are loving it. So instead, Tristan elbows Gilles encouragingly, and soon he's adding gleefully,

"Even once he was out of danger, I didn't end my bedside vigil. Why, I sat there until daybreak. I was gone *all night*."

When Gilles pauses for effect, Jurian calls down the table,

"What do *you* say, Marek? To hear Gilles tell it, you'd almost think you and Taran were *lovers*."

At this the boys' laughter turns uproarious, and out of the corner of my eye I'm pretty sure I see Taran's head pop up again. This time I know he's not looking at Master Leon, and I don't dare meet his eye. I'm too busy sliding down further in my seat and glaring at Jurian. If he meant the comment to have the effect I think he did, it was a malicious, double-edged barb that was particularly cruel, even for him.

Sure enough, he's giving me one of his most knowing looks, tinged with triumph. Yet for one unguarded moment, I think I see a hint of something else there that's the last thing I'm expecting.

Jealousy. Then his eyes slide from mine to Taran, and I get it, instantly.

Jurian's in love with Taran, too. *Of course he is!* And unless I miss my guess, he has been, for a very long time.

The look is gone from Jurian's face so quickly I could have imaged it, but I doubt it. It explains everything: that kiss of his in the garden, to make 'someone' jealous — all his talk of having his eye on someone, and Taran is his type, exactly. Besides, it's as simple as this, really: *who wouldn't be?*

Mercifully nobody else has any reason to think Jurian might have meant his remark seriously, so the moment passes. And when Jerome calls down the table,

"Hey, Taran! Why don't you tell us where you *really* were? On a bender at the tavern?," soon everyone has forgotten all about me.

"Nah, that was *Tristan*, remember?" Falko reminds him, and much to everybody's amusement, Aristide says,

"He must have snuck off straight from the abbey, to pay a visit to his light-fingered whore!"

I don't find it very funny, and not just for the obvious reasons. I've just remembered something Father Abelard said to me, about Taran sitting by my cot, and Taran had to be *somewhere*. From the boys' reactions to Gilles's story, it's obvious he really was gone all night.

"And what do you suppose my thanks was the next morning, for all my diligent care?" Gilles is now demanding. "*Six lashes* on the back of my legs from the master for my trouble, right at morning drills! I guess staying out all night without permission was too much even for *me* to get away with. I didn't let *that* stop me from riding back that very afternoon, though, did I? And every day thereafter, for the rest of that week. How could anyone suggest I'd do otherwise?! I never shirk my duty, and *I'm* made of the toughest stuff there is."

"Did you really ride after taking lashes, Taran?" Jerome calls incredulously over to Taran, and when Taran's only response is to dart his head up for another swift glance at the master's table, Jerome looks around the table for confirmation, demanding,

"*Did* he?"

"Every single day," Aristide drawls. "Although I doubt it was to go to the abbey, if you know what I mean. Not with that gorgeous fiancée of his waiting for him at the castle, eager for a little *gardening*," and when he and the other boys (with the notable exception of Tristan) make *ooh*ing and *ahh*ing noises, Jerome chuckles,

"Why, you're insatiable, Mellor! A beast!," while Falko says appreciatively,

"But what a way to celebrate a win!," and all at once I'm no longer finding this all merely embarrassing and confusing. Now I, too, am finding it excruciating.

Luckily, at just this moment Master Leon gets to his feet. Taran's not put his head back down on the table since the last time he raised it, and now he's watching Master Leon's slow progress across the room intently. Every muscle in his body is tensed, wound as tightly as a crossbow's cranequin. He's clearly preparing to bolt the moment the master's out of sight, and I'm watching Master Leon, too, silently willing him to walk a little faster; now Gilles *really* must have come to the end of his narrative (I mean, what more could there possibly be? Finding out Taran had to slay a dragon on the way to the abbey? Or maybe that he ravaged a convent full of nuns on his way back and forth every afternoon to check on me?), but by now I'm as desperate for it all to be over as Taran clearly is.

When at last Master Leon disappears out the door and Taran is accordingly already pressing his palms down on the tabletop in anticipation of pushing himself up quickly to his feet, I heave a sigh of relief. And that might have finally been the end of it, if at just that moment Tristan didn't cock his head to one side, and inquire,

"So, Gilles. Just what do you think it was that our boy Taran here was murmuring so tenderly in Marek's ear?"

"That's easy, my friend!" Gilles coos back happily. "Why, unless I miss my guess, it was something *a lot like this*:

'*Don't fly away, little hawk! Come back to me. Please don't leave me. Don't ever lea...*'"

And that is as far as Gilles gets.

There's a resounding roar from Taran — followed quickly by a reverberating crash, as the boy who was poised for flight instead springs up

411

furiously to his feet. With one huge, wrenching jerk of those incredible arms of his he brings the solid oak Journey table right up with him, overturning the massive thing entirely. Before it even hits the ground, while the Journeys and squires all around me are shouting out startled cries of their own and rocking back wildly on the benches to get out of the falling table's way, Taran's already hurdling over it, as agile as a cat — a mighty *big* one, and it happens so fast that he's nothing but a blur as he goes past me, pouncing on Gilles with all the zeal of a ravenous lion on an unsuspecting wildebeest, or on a long-necked giraffe. His onslaught knocks Gilles clean over backwards off the bench, and in a flash the two of them are rolling on the floor beyond, with Taran's big hands wrapped tight around Gilles's aristocratic neck.

Instantly all the boys scramble up and fan out around them in a wide semi-circle, too wary of Taran's temper to try to interfere directly, since it's obvious that Gilles has finally managed to send him over the edge. So everyone's trying to encourage Gilles instead; as Falko demands, "What's with him, anyway? I thought that story was pretty flattering," Tristan exhorts, "Come on, Gilles! You're scrappy. *You* can take him," and the others are all joining in, even though it has to be obvious to everyone that in fact, he can't.

That is, all but Jerome, who's busily stowing his lute under our teetering but still-upright bench for safe-keeping, and muttering, "I'll be damned if I'm going to lose *another* one."

And all but me.

I'm still sitting frozen in place on the bench, staring out over the up-ended table in front of me and all but oblivious to the carnage no doubt unfolding behind me, my eyes unseeing and the words of Gilles's punchline buzzing in my ears.

Not just any words. The *very words* that whispered through my dream of the hawk last year. And Gilles has just repeated them, in Taran's exact tone and intonation — *verbatim*.

Or close enough, at least.

I'm aware of the sound of the boys scraping and grunting on the floor behind me, and of the catcalls of the spectators, but it isn't really registering. My mind's gone numb, and there's a squeezing in my chest. For a moment I feel like I can't get a breath, and I could be back up there on the tower, with an arrow sticking out of my chest.

I'm not sure how long I sit there in the trance Gilles's words have put me in, unseeing and unmoving, but it feels like a very long time — an hour, a day; maybe a week.

I only snap out of it when Pascal cries out in sheer panic right in my ear, "Oh, somebody, *do* something! I think they're really going to kill each other!"

I turn around, and I see that for once it's no exaggeration. Taran's sitting straddled on Gilles's chest, his eyes rolled back into his head and too far gone even for his usual angry alliteration; he's sputtering pure gibberish, and pounding the hard guild floor mercilessly with the back of Gilles's head.

I shudder to think what might have happened, if at that moment Poncellet didn't happen to wander in. He'd absentmindedly left his whip coiled around the back of his chair up at the head table, and he's come back to retrieve it. Although he clearly sees the boys (I mean, it's impossible to miss them, since by now all the veterans in the room have crowded around to egg the boys on, too, and the whole room is in an uproar), at first he simply saunters past, paying no attention to the boys' wrangling and taking his own sweet time about fetching his neglected item. He seems in no hurry as he makes his way back past the fray, either, and for a horrible moment, I think he's going to leave Taran to smash Gilles's head in. But just as Poncellet is making to side-step around the two-man brawl in full swing in front of him, in their writhing the boys roll directly across his path. And as they do, by chance Taran lets go of Gilles's neck long enough to reach down one big hand toward Gilles's partially shaved eyebrow, raving,

"And while I'm at it, I think I really will rip this right off your face!"

At the familiar phrase, Poncellet stops.

He purses his lips, as though remembering his own recent fight with de Gilford. And then he unfurls his whip.

With a flick of the wrist, he gives it an ear-splitting crack, only inches above Taran's head.

The sound is deafening, and it has an immediate effect. Taran's hands fly off of Gilles, his expression as changed and as sobered as if the whip had actually connected. He looks just like a sleepwalker who's been brutally shaken awake, and as his grip relaxes Gilles scrambles up and shimmies out from under him, rubbing the back of his head and giving his neck a deliberate sideways stretch.

"What's all this?" Poncellet demands, when both boys are back on their feet.

"Nothing, master," Gilles replies smoothly, although his voice is raspy, and he's gingerly fingering bruises that are already showing on the delicate skin at the base of his neck. "I chalk it up to a sudden fit of madness. You know how unstable these clouters can be," and the master laughs.

"All right, boys. No harm, no foul. Shake hands on it, and there's an end to it. But don't let it happen again. Not unless you want to find yourselves sporting placards, if you know what I mean."

Gilles gives a shudder to suggest that standing naked in front of the room while everyone compares him with *Taran* is enough to deter him from just about anything. Then he flashes one of Tristan's lazy smiles and sticks out his hand sportingly.

"It was all just a bit of good, clean fun. No hard feelings," he says to his erstwhile assailant.

Taran just stares at it stonily.

"It won't happen again," he says stiffly. "But as for shaking hands, I'd rather take the punishment," and with that he turns heel and stalks out of the hall without another word to anyone.

Poncellet, Gilles, and Tristan watch him go with amusement, standing shoulder to shoulder, and I can tell that the old master is stifling a grin. As soon as Taran's gone, Tristan looks at the others and exclaims happily,

"These clouters! So full of theatrics," and shaking his head, Poncellet agrees, "Real drama queens."

Poncellet then coils his whip around his shoulder and makes his exit, whistling to himself, and while the rest of us get to work righting the Journey table, Tristan slings an arm around Gilles's shoulder.

"Excellent job, my friend! Yes, truly excellent," he says, with satisfaction. "Why, I doubt I could have done it better myself."

"Thanks, old man," Gilles says back, still rubbing his head. "If it's all the same to you, though, I think I'll leave these little performances to you in future. I admit it! Being a butts man is harder than I thought."

I think it's only then that I really get the point of the whole thing.

It *was* a performance, and exactly like one of Tristan's. In fact, it was exactly like the first one of his I ever witnessed, when he climbed up on a table at the Drunken Goat to hurl himself at Taran.

I'm just not entirely sure whether it was Gilles or Taran who ended up giving the most impressive imitation of him.

"Is Gilles going to be all right, master?" I ask Tristan worriedly not much later. I mean, Gilles is tougher than he looks, but a head is a head, and while the boys were scuffling on the ground, I thought I heard something crack.

"He'll be fine, Marek. It probably knocked some sense into him!" Tristan says, ignoring the fact that I'm tugging rather hard on his sleeve. The boys have managed to get the Journey table back on its feet, and unbelievably, some of them are sitting back down at it and I'm not eager for Tristan to be one of them.

"But tomorrow morning, his head is going to feel like a watermelon," he adds, speaking from experience.

"Mine already does, master," I say truthfully, giving his sleeve another tug. "Come on. It's late, and I want to go to bed."

"Leave?" he says innocently. "Whatever can you be thinking? We can't *leave*. I haven't had *my* turn yet."

"Oh, *no*," I protest automatically, my head pounding and a prickly sensation starting up again along my skin. "No, no, *no*, Tristan!," even though I really have no idea what Tristan means. Except, of course, that he clearly intends to do *something*, and I have a feeling that if I were in any shape to do so, I could make some astute guesses as to the kind of thing it's likely to be. And so I say something I never thought I'd hear myself say.

"You're *already* good enough at wands, master! You don't need to do anything else."

But Tristan's not having any of it, and the only saving grace is that Taran's gone, so whatever Tristan's planning to do as his own attempt to take things to the next level and 'out-Gilles' Gilles, at least it can't involve getting into a fight of his own with him.

I should have guessed, though, that Tristan's plan wouldn't involve antagonizing Taran, since Gilles usually gets along well enough with him.

It's only marginally better, however.

It's Aristide.

Tristan wastes no time getting started; Aristide's giving Armand a few last orders for the evening in preparation of leaving, and Gilles is turning a worrisome shade of green. He really should be in bed already, but there's no way he's going to miss what's coming — whatever it is.

Before I know it, Tristan's sauntered over to strike a pose a foot or two right behind Aristide. He clears his throat. Then when Aristide turns towards him impatiently, he proceeds to make a show of stripping off one of the long silk gloves he's wearing, and I give myself a mental kick.

I should have known there was a reason he insisted on keeping the ostentatious things on throughout the entire meal.

He pauses to admire his manicure, holding the glove in one hand.

And then he slaps Aristide right across the face with it.

"Hey! What in the hell was that?!" Aristide bellows.

"A gentleman's challenge, obviously," Tristan replies condescendingly. "Shall we say rapiers, at fifteen paces?"

Fortunately, Armand has always been right about Aristide's basic sanity — at least, he's too sane to fall for this. He just laughs, and refuses.

"A gentleman! You?" he snorts. "I've got better things to do, than to run you through."

"A wager, then," Tristan counters, and when Falko and Jurian crowd forward eagerly hoping to get in on the action, to my dismay Aristide wavers. Like most rich men, he can't resist a chance to make more money.

"What's the bet?" he says warily.

"I'll put up this ring," Tristan says easily, twisting Gilles's big gem on his finger, and although I think I see Gilles startle, he doesn't object or say anything, "against the fact that you're too chicken to go up to the front of the room right now, and sit in the perilous seat."

"That's it?" Aristide scoffs, nodding up at the head table. "Just sit in that empty chair?"

"The *cursed* seat that Master Gheeraert *died* in," Tristan corrects him. "The one at the *masters'* table."

"The masters aren't even here."

"Not at present," Tristan concedes.

For a moment, I think Aristide is simply going to go up and take a seat, and that will be the end of it. But Tristan's cool and collected manner is grating on Aristide's nerves, in the same way that Gilles's unnerving poise always affects him. I can sense him debating, trying to figure out what Tristan's thinking, what more there might be in it that he doesn't see. It doesn't help that Falko and Jurian have started to chant in creepy voices, "*Ooh, beware the curse of the infamous siege perilous!,*" even though Falko as much as admitted the first time it came up that he'd never heard of it. And I have to say, even without believing in curses (and after all, this isn't the real thing. It really is just an empty chair), it sounds like a plenty dangerous idea to me. I mean, having your head pounded against the floor by a boy the size of a gorilla, that's one thing. But sitting in a master's seat? That's sure to get a man into real trouble.

I can tell Aristide's thinking something similar, and I can't help feeling a little sorry for him. Poor Aristide! It's perfectly reasonable not to want to do it, but he's going to look an awful coward to refuse now, after the way he just scoffed at the idea.

I must not be the only boy who's started to worry about how this is going to play out, since next to me Frans has started making small noises, Pascal is fussily trying to herd a gently swaying Gilles toward the door, and Armand even steps forward to put a restraining hand on Aristide's arm and implore him sincerely,

"*Don't* do it, master!"

I'm not sure if it's this uncharacteristic show of concern for him from his squire that sways him, but Aristide caves, and he shakes his head.

To save face, he says,

"I've got plenty of rings, DuBois. You'll not trick me with borrowed trinkets into making a fool of myself," and I feel a rush of relief. Even without worrying how this new stunt might end I've been eager to get away, so for that one moment, I fully approve of Aristide — until he goes and adds,

"Besides, you know as well as I do that *you'd* never do it, either."

"That's where you're wrong, my friend!" Tristan declares happily, and my heart sinks. "And *I* don't need to be dared into it. I'll do it, just for the sheer hell of it!"

Before I can stop him, Tristan strides right up to the front of the room and around behind the masters' table. As all the boys still in the room begin to stomp the floor rhythmically and chant his name, he makes a show of slowly pulling back the so-dubbed *siege perilous.* Then he flops himself down onto it as bold as brass, much to the amusement of the few veterans still boozing it up at the adjacent tables.

It's already bad enough. But the laughter of the men eggs him on, and as I watch helplessly, Tristan folds his hands behind his head and gives his back a big, arching stretch.

Then he spots the half-full bottle of the master's port. Much to the men's delight, with a comic double-take he reaches over and pours himself a great big shot of it. With it filled to the brim, he lifts the tankard and calls over to Aristide,

"From now on, you can call *me* Master G! G for *Galahad*, that is," and he downs the whole thing in one draught, right from the master's own cup.

"Master 'Lack-a-head' is more likely," Armand mutters to me under his breath, crossing himself furiously, while Jurian calls up to Tristan,

"Watch out, boys! Better fetch some buckets, Marek. Any minute your master is going to burst into flames, just like rash Sir Brumant of the legend! The knight who dared what shouldn't have been dared and was burned to a crisp!" But I'm too busy picking my fingers to a bloody pulp to answer him, since I fear he's right. Not that Tristan'll suffer anything out of the boys' Arthurian romances, of course. But there are too many witnesses for some word of Tristan's antics to escape reaching the master's ears, and when it does, I have no idea what Guillaume might do to him. I have a feeling, though, that whatever it is, spontaneous combustion would probably be preferable.

Just as the phrase *St. Sebastian's punishes its own* flits through my mind, I feel someone tugging on the hem of my tunic.

"Not *now*," I say dismissively, brushing the hand away and reaching up to wave my arms around frantically in the air, trying to beckon to Tristan that he's had his fun, and it's time for him to come away from the master's table.

The tugging comes again, this time more insistently.

It's Frans, his eyes as wide and round as clout targets, and when I look down at him and he gestures back toward the doorway behind me, he couldn't look more petrified than if he really were seeing the flaming ghost of poor Sir Brumant materializing out in the hallway.

It's no ghost, of course.

It's something far worse.

Master Guillaume, silhouetted against the pitch-black of the corridor. He's standing stock still and staring up past the boys' backs to the place where Tristan is posturing and posing in the chair and encouraging the men to laugh right along with him, and the look on the master's face can only be described as pure malice.

Everyone else is so riveted on Tristan that nobody seems to notice the master, and in a blink of an eye, he's gone. He's left without saying a word to anyone, and it's strange enough that I even wonder if maybe he wasn't a ghost after all, or an apparition — a trick of the shadows, conjured up by my own worried imagination. But I can't be sure, and for some reason that furtive, uncertain glimpse of him and the silent way he disappeared again leave me more scared than if he'd stormed in and confronted Tristan.

Once Tristan's satisfied that he's milked his performance for all it's worth and he's come back to receive his congratulations from Gilles (and to lord it over Aristide, naturally), when I try to tell him about it, he brushes off my worry.

"I didn't see him, Marek," he says dismissively. "And anyway, what's he going to do, to a boy of *my* rank and position?" he demands, having apparently forgotten himself that he's not actually nobility. "Besides, all I did was sit in a chair. The master's not going to damage a valuable commodity over a trifle," he adds, and I see he really means that's he's a Journey.

It's true that the master needs all the boys to make the trials a success. Guillaume's made a point of telling us how important it is that this year's trials be impressive, and whatever the master might think of Tristan personally, he's a proven crowd-pleaser. At least he's just proven once again that no one knows better how to work an audience. So I try to convince myself that Tristan's right. Even if that shadow out in the hallway really was the master and he did witness Tristan's caricature of him, he's apparently chosen to ignore it, and to pretend that he didn't see anything.

As we all finally make our way out of the great hall together to head off for bed, however, Tristan slings an arm around Gilles's shoulder, and asks him,

"So, my friend, what did you think of *that*? If I do say so myself, I think it went astonishingly well."

"Indeed," Gilles agrees. "But, you know, old buddy. As diverting as it was, I'm not sure it was really *quite* like something *I'd* do."

"Why not?" Tristan demands, offended.

"Because, my friend," Gilles replies, "*I* am essentially sane."

And with that, I start to worry, all over again.

The thing is, maybe Guillaume wasn't really there, and all I saw was a shadow. But I've seen a look just like the one I thought I saw on the master's face tonight before, and I recognized it.

It was the look of a man who knows how to bide his time.

And unfortunately, 'sane' is not at all how I'd describe it.

IT'S BEEN AN EXHAUSTING EVENING FOR EVERYONE, AND FOR once Pascal breaks curfew to linger in Gilles's room, out of concern for his master. It must be well after midnight when he finally returns and when over the other boys' gentle snoring I hear him settling himself down wearily for sleep. But even after all sound of Pascal shifting around in the darkened barracks fades away and I know that he, too, must have succumbed to slumber, I'm still wide awake on my own cot.

At least, that's where my body is.

In my mind's eye I never really left the great hall. I'm back there now, sitting immobile on the mess bench and my mind racing, thinking to myself obsessively:

It was such an obvious metaphor, one anyone might have come up with.

All the boys know Taran likes hawks. Loves them, really. And it's no secret that he once made a little wooden hawk figurine for me. So it's not that I think Gilles's choice of words tonight meant anything. I'll not go down *that* road again, and I'm certainly not going to be foolish enough to think that Gilles could have somehow overheard them on the tower, since Taran never really said them, did he? They were nothing more than my own fantasy, born of wishful thinking and delirium, and the feeling of Taran's arms around me. That Gilles should somehow have hit upon them tonight in his recitation was just the cruelest of coincidences. But it hurt to hear the very words I cherished once in secret proclaimed aloud as entertainment, and although by now the shock of it has started to wear off, it still stings, terribly.

How deluded I was! Even now I can still feel the agony of it, sitting there and listening to all the boys laughing at the absurdity of the idea that Taran could have ever said such things to me.

It wouldn't be so bad, if mocked and humiliated was all I was feeling. But I can't forget *any* of Gilles's story, and all his words keep rattling around inside of me until my poor brain feels like it's been battered as much as Gilles's. It was all a joke, a farce, and Gilles was being purposefully outrageous — I know that. And yet, in the broadest strokes imaginable, *some* of what he said must have really happened.

Taran *did* take me from the tower. He did somehow get me to the abbey. And it can't have been easy. Whenever I've thought about that fateful hour, it's always been to think of my own heroics, or of Tristan's. So about one thing at least, Gilles was absolutely right: I've never spared a moment to think of *Taran's*, or to try to imagine what that day must have been like for him. It never occurred to me that he might have missed out on his own celebrations, or spent all his money, or gotten punished for staying out all night.

More than any of these details, though, one simple thing is hitting me harder than any other, and that's the basic fact of it:

Taran could have let me die that day, and easily. No one would have questioned it. But he didn't.

Instead, to his cost, he saved my life.

Whatever else he's done, that day Taran was *my* hero. And I've never really acknowledged it, even to myself. I've certainly never thanked him. Instead, all I've done since is abuse him.

That, and shoot him in the neck.

The worst part is, I don't even know why Taran went to such lengths to save me. At the time, I attributed all sorts of low and selfish motives to him. And maybe some of those really were his reasons. But Gilles's over-the-top characterization of him has affected me, and I'm starting to have a terrible suspicion that the real answer might well be Gilles's:

'that's just the kind of great guy he is.'

I stare blindly up toward the darkness of the lofty barracks ceiling, more confused about Taran than I've ever been. How can I reconcile the noble portrait Gilles inadvertently painted of him, with the vindictive boy I know *for a fact* tried to kill my best friend? The one who's taunted and insulted me, and who punched me in the face — the brute who spent the evening pounding mercilessly on the floor of the great hall with the back of Gilles's head? I don't know how to do it, and it always comes back to this: even if Taran did save *me*, purposely harming Tristan is something I shouldn't — I mean I *can't* — forgive.

And yet, as I try to force myself to sleep, I can't stop picturing scenes from Gilles's story, and trying to imagine what they might have been like in reality; and as I finally drift into troubled sleep, the fringe of my blanket is brushing against my cheek, as soft and as warm as the feather of a hawk's wing.

FAILING, BUT *WITH STYLE*

PART FOUR

CHAPTER THIRTY

It was bound to happen sooner or later anyway, but it's surely because of Gilles's recitation that it's the very next day when the tensions simmering away below the surface at squires' club finally come bubbling to the surface.

It all starts as early as that next morning, when Tristan and I are breakfasting out on the butts and waiting for drills along with the other boys. I've stuffed the fold of my tunic full of hard-boiled eggs, having rediscovered my love of them after a brief period of estrangement during the plague, and I'm sharing my haul with Tristan. Neither Taran nor Gilles has yet to appear, so we're making rather a nice meal of it, although predictably there are quite a few jests going around about last night that are not at all to my taste. But the sour taste in the back of my mouth isn't because of Rennie's attempts to mimic some of Gilles's choicest phrases from his recitation or Falko's puffing out of more innuendos about Taran ardently sneaking out for trysts all winter, or even the fact that I think one of the eggs was spoiled and the only bread on offer this morning was riddled with weevils. I woke up knowing there's something I've got to say today. And that Taran isn't going to make it at all easy.

I like it even less that Falko's taken Tristan up on his suggestion from last night and started calling him Sir Galahad; Jurian's shortened it to 'Sir Gads,' and although I can't deny it's sort of appropriate, I don't like the boys encouraging my master to joke about something that seemed to me so reckless. So I'm already feeling apprehensive when Pascal suddenly comes busting out through the stables, waving his arms around in the air agitatedly and shouting for Tristan, and my first thought is that Master Guillaume must be hot on his heels.

Pascal barrels over, only skidding to a stop when he's almost on top of us. When he bends over to catch his breath, as Tristan puts a hand on his shoulder and asks him what the matter is, all he can do is gasp,

"It's *Gilles!*"

"He's not *dead*, is he?" Frans squeaks.

"Not exactly," Pascal wheezes cryptically. Then he turns heel and runs straight back towards the Journey hallway without wasting time in explaining, and we all hasten to follow him. Pascal is so uncharacteristically flustered, I'm not sure what I fear — that we'll find Gilles hemorrhaging uncontrollably, or maybe that his head really will be the size of a watermelon.

Once we've all crowded into Gilles's doorway, however, with the Journeys in front and us squires behind, from what I can see around Falko's broad back and by peeking under Tristan's arm, Gilles looks perfectly fine. He's got a ring of nasty bruises around his neck and his eyebrow's rather swollen, true. But he's sitting up on the edge of his cot, bare-chested and wearing Tristan's breeches, and running a hand up through his shortened hair that's now tousled rather fetchingly.

"Really, Pascal. You had us going!" Tristan's starting to say admonishingly, "Why in the world …?" when Gilles looks up and catches sight of us. Then he cocks his head to one side and fixes us with a curious and slightly vacant stare.

"*Wait* for it, master," Pascal whispers tensely to Tristan out of the corner of his mouth, just as Gilles exclaims,

"Well, howdy there, folks! Say, what is this place? Some kind of cult? Or am I in prison again?" Then he gets a good look at Tristan. "Who's *that* clown?" he demands, jabbing his thumb in his direction. "Get a load of him! Hey Fancypants, what's with the crazy get-up?" he laughs.

"He seems to think he's some sort of swineherd this morning, named van Smoot!" Pascal whispers worriedly again. "What can we *do*, Tristan?"

But Tristan doesn't know what to do. None of us has ever seen anything like it, and as we stand there debating it for a moment in hushed voices while Gilles continues to look warily around the room, just when Armand is saying,

"Why do anything, Pascal? Convince him he's *your* servant. Let's see how *he* likes waiting on *you* hand and foot for a change," Falko steps forward.

"Let me handle this, boys," he chuffs, pulling up his waistband like a man ready to get down to business. "It's only temporary. I've seen it before, and I can deal with it."

Seeing as Falko's had more than his fair share of experience with taking a beating, foolishly we let him. We all step aside and make room for him, not thinking through the wisdom of leaving Gilles's sanity in the hands of the one of us who's taken the most blows to the head.

With no further ado, Falko shoulders past Pascal, sticks his hand out to Gilles, and booms,

"*Smout*, is it? Well, put it there, buddy! Glad to know you. *I'm* Falko," and then instead of shaking the hand that Gilles proffers in response, he hauls off and slaps Gilles so hard across the face that he keels over sideways, out cold on his cot.

"That ought to do it," Falko says brightly, brushing his hands together with a motion that says a good job's been finished. "Just leave him, and he'll be right as rain when he wakes up. Back to his old self," he claims, and we've got no choice but to believe him. As we leave a dubious Pascal hovering over his master to make our way out for morning drills, I can hear Pascal muttering to himself questioningly,

"Yes, but *which* old self will that be?"

Against all odds, it turns out that Falko was perfectly right. By noon mess Gilles is back to what passes these days for normal, and when we stop by his room to check on him, he even declares that he's feeling well enough to join us in the hall for lunch. Although Gilles rather conveniently claims to have no recollection of his temporary lapse of memory, preferring instead to wave it off as a figment of the boys' imagination (and probably luckily for Taran, he seems to be a little hazy, too, on the finer details of what happened last night), it doesn't take much once mess has started to see that after this morning's encounter with Gilles's alter ego, the pleasures of being anyone other than themselves are starting to wear thin for both of the boys.

"The hardest thing about being a butts man isn't the *shooting*," Gilles is propounding, almost as soon as we're all seated. "It's the hideous clothes! And the limited vocabulary. And all this dashing about, grinning. It's so exhausting! Why, my cheek is so sore, I must be getting a cramp."

"Hey Gilles, *I* thought the hardest thing about being Tristan was *Taran's* fist!" Falko calls down to him, even though he's actually the one who's just slapped him, and all the boys at the table laugh, since Taran isn't one of them. He's sitting by himself at the end of one of the veterans' tables on the far side of the room (Master Leon having decided it was safest for the time being to sequester him), and all through the meal, I can't help it; instead of keeping my mind on the desultory conversation the boys are having, I keep flitting my gaze over to where Taran's sitting silently and eating, not taking his eyes from his plate or making any attempt to converse with his squire who's sitting sullenly next to him, while thinking to myself:

Nope, it's not going to be easy.

"Do you think it's wise for Gilles to be up and about again so soon after last night's beating, master?" I ask Tristan in an aside during a lull in the boys' conversation, mostly to distract myself from the things about last night that are really bothering me.

"A fellow's got to be able to take a few punches, if he's going to make it in a man's world," Tristan answers back blithely, and I can't say I care much for this reassurance. When I pull a face, he remarks,

"Goodness, Marek! Things won't be so tame in Meuse in the Guardsmen's quarters, I can assure you. Or in their squires' barracks, either.

I can see we're going to have to do something to toughen you up, before we get there," and I like it even less. I love being a boy among boys so much, it never occurred to me that I might not feel the same about being a man among men.

"Not to fear, Marek," Gilles offers, since as usual he's been eavesdropping on our conversation shamelessly. "St. Sebastian's men are nothing if not gentlemen. We may play hard, but we always know when to put our differences to rest."

With this pompous (and demonstrably untrue) statement, Gilles rises to his feet. He gives a general nod and bow to the boys at our table. Then he strides purposefully across the room. When he stops in front of the table at which Taran is now seated, Taran, too, rises precipitously to his feet, a look suspiciously close to alarm on his face. I'm feeling apprehensive, too, and poor, beleaguered Pascal burrows his face in Rennie's shoulder, so he won't have to watch whatever it is that Gilles is going to do next.

But all Gilles does it strike a pose that looks suspiciously like his old, aristocratic self. And in a voice much like his old, fruity voice, too, he says loudly,

"Come, come, my man! Let's put last night behind us and be friends again." He makes a sweeping gesture back towards the Journey table, and then he sticks out his hand toward Taran, exhorting him with a flourish,

"Show the boys that *today* you can take a joke, and shake my hand!"

Seeing last night's combatants now with their arms slung amicably around each other's shoulders, the masters make no objection when Gilles leads a placated Taran back over to our table, with Remy skittering along behind. Gilles has smoothed things over, and to all appearances the boys have put last night's fight admirably behind them. But there's still something raw and on edge about Taran as he rejoins us that makes the boys wary of him, and the atmosphere at table for the rest of the meal is rather intense. For once even Falko seems to be aware of it; he keeps his mouth shut, and nobody else is foolhardy enough to try to tease Taran about any details of Gilles's recitation. Perhaps that's partly because today, Taran's got that brick from the wall with him again. He's brought it with him to have something to fidget with at table in lieu of his knife, but when he plops it down next to his plate hard enough to raise a little cloud of pink dust, it's not hard to imagine that the mere mention of a hawk or a tower would have him busting heads again, in the manner of Master Bernard.

For my part, I keep my head down, and the closest anyone comes to bringing up the subject of last night is when Pascal leans over and complains to me in a hushed voice,

"Why in the heck do you suppose he forgave Gilles so easily, if he's still obviously so mad?"

I don't bother to answer, even though I think I know the answer. I bet Taran didn't mind shaking hands with Gilles so much now that Gilles is acting more like *Gilles*, and less like Tristan, since from the way Taran spends the rest of the meal glaring down at my master, it's clear enough it's really him that Taran blames for last night's performance, though he's not the one who gave it — no doubt rightly assuming that the whole idea was his.

AFTER MESS, INSTEAD OF HEADING IN TO LIE DOWN AND DIGEST a little Tristan wanders out into the garden, where he flops down in a very unGilles-like sprawl at the base of a tree.

"It's funny, Marek," Tristan remarks, as I plop myself down next to him. "You know, for a minute there last night, I didn't think Mellor was going to crack. He was taking it surprisingly well, right down to the end. And actually, I thought a lot of Gilles's earlier jabs were worse — or better, as the case may be. I wonder what it was about that last comment of Gilles's that put him over the edge?"

"I'd rather not speculate," I reply truthfully.

"I guess we'll never know," he says lightly, and as I settle in next to him, he sighs. "I can tell you one thing," he adds, in a voice suspiciously like his own. "I'm getting awfully tired of letting Gilles have all the fun! And really, just talking like him is such a *chore*. It's giving me a terrible headache."

"Does that mean you're ready to go back to being your old self now, master?" I ask him, and he flashes me a grin that's all Tristan.

"I think I'll keep the expensive clothes, though," he winks, "until after Firsts, at least!" and as he extends an arm invitingly for me to crawl in, I laugh back,

"You do look awfully good in them."

They feel good, too, and Gilles's rosy pink shirt is so soft and filmy on Tristan's skin, as I snuggle up to him the little barrier that's always between us feels paper-thin again.

"Do you want to know what the worst part of being a wands man is, Marek?" he says confidentially.

"The tights?" I suggest.

"They are dashed constricting! But no. It's this: I've missed my little brother, and my best friend," he says, and just like that, we're back in perfect sympathy.

After a long, lazy moment of satisfaction in which I hug him tighter, he murmurs,

"You know, I hate it when there's *anything* between us, Marek," and I know he doesn't mean Gilles's shirt, or even Gilles's aloof and superior personality. He's talking about the handkerchief. And he's right. The time has come to clear the air, a little. So I tell him contritely,

"I'm really sorry, Tristan, for not telling you about it sooner. I just didn't want to upset you, over something I thought was a triviality. I thought I was doing the right thing."

"And so you were, as it turns out," Tristan agrees, his voice taking on a bitter edge, and I can tell he's still upset that the theory he'd been building for weeks has all come to nothing. "A triviality! That's the perfect word for it. Oh, don't worry, Marek," he says, his tone softening when he sees he's worrying me. "I forgive you, for keeping it from me. Don't you know, I'd forgive you anything?"

Tristan's looking down at me, and I'm looking up at him. Although his tone is light and he's said it almost teasingly, in that moment, I really believe him.

It's so good to have him back, if only temporarily, and he's forgiven me so easily, all at once I can't stand for there to be any more secrets between us. At least, none except the usual ones, and it's been so hard keeping all my troubles to myself since we returned to the guild that I desperately wish I could come clean and tell him everything that's happened between me and Taran. But I know that wouldn't just be foolish. It would be disastrous.

"Seriously though, Tristan," I say, just to change the subject. "Don't you think you and Gilles were a little too cruel last night, with that recitation?"

"I suppose, kid," he concedes, sensing from my tone that what I'm really saying isn't that Gilles's poem was cruel to Taran. I'm saying it was also cruel to *me*. "And if you were embarrassed into the bargain, that wasn't my intention. The devil of it is, he *did* take you down from the tower! And for that I've got to be eternally grateful," he says, and I can see certain aspects of Gilles's recitation last night must have also bothered him, more than he let on. "But I'll be damned if I ever tell him that. And with everything else he's done, how am I supposed to stomach that holier-than-thou attitude of his!? Why, sometimes it's all I can do to keep from taking a dirty shot at him myself, right into the middle of that great big back of his."

"Or his *neck*," I agree grimly.

"I see you know what I mean."

After a minute or two of companionable silence, he starts chuckling.

"What a sight *that* would be, eh, kid?" he exclaims, now almost hooting with laughter. "I can just picture him, staggering through the forest like a great, big wounded beast — with one of *my* arrows sticking out of him, that *you'd* shot into him! What perfect payback, and no less than he deserves! Why, it'd be priceless."

"I doubt it would actually be very funny, in reality," I try to tell him, but Tristan's not listening. He's too busy crowing,

"And after dubbing *you* Woodcock! Imagine the boys finding out *he* was the easy target, and *you* were the one who ended up shooting *him!*" he chortles, and it occurs to me that conjuring up the image for him even indirectly was probably not wise — particularly not if Tristan really *is* going to go back to acting like his old self again.

"Oh, well. Sweet as it would be, it's a good thing neither of us would ever *really* be idiotic enough to shoot at him. He's such a pompous ass, why, even over the barest of scratches," he pauses, looking down bitterly at the faint red line still visible on the inside of his wrist, "*he'*d be sure to march straight to the master, and get us both kicked out of here. Or worse," he declares, and all I can do is mumble,

"Actually, I'm not so sure he'd do anything," and I miss some of Tristan's response, distracted by Gilles's voice cutting into my thoughts, murmuring, *I'll never reveal your secret, or ask for thanks, or ever even tell of everything I did to save you*, and I have to force myself to tune in again.

"Yeah, publicly picking on squires or ratting to the masters, anything that might sully his precious reputation, that's not his style, is it? But he'd do *something*, all right! Something nasty. It doesn't take much to see the old boy's getting more violent by the minute. At the very least, he'd hold it over your head and enjoy tormenting you with it."

I know for a fact that Taran's not going to do *that*, either. But I don't bother arguing with him. I'm too busy wondering again why Taran didn't react in the way Tristan's imagining, and trying hard to ignore Gilles's voice, which is now whispering *because that's just the kind of great guy he is*.

"Besides, when *I* beat him, I want him to know it. It's got to be fair and square. I wouldn't have it any other way."

"I *knew* you'd feel that way, master," I exclaim, relieved that the conversation's moving in a different direction and relaxing back against him. "You really *are* the most noble boy in the world. You'd have to be, to understand so easily why a squire might keep a secret, if he thought it was in his master's best interest," I add, thinking to myself about more than just the handkerchief.

"Not even the best of friends tell each other everything," he replies, and I don't have to explain why I'm awfully glad he feels that way.

But he also looks a little sheepish. So I ask,

"Is there something *you* need to tell *me*, master?"

"No," he says evasively, and for a moment, I stiffen. I've never mentioned overhearing him in Gilles's room while I was fetching a tunic for Taran, either. But Tristan senses my reaction, and he must have some idea of what I'm thinking, because he adds,

"Not yet. But I promise you, Marek. I'm working up to it."

We decide to forgo practice and to stay in the garden together until time for squires' club; Tristan has a tutorial later anyway, and right after mess, Gilles went back to bed. It's a wonderfully warm and drowsy way to spend the afternoon, and the garden is full of sweet, earthy smells. We don't talk at all, or we talk about nothing, and it's so good to be like this again with Tristan that I don't even mind it, much, when sensing that I don't want to joke any longer about shooting Taran, inevitably Tristan turns to savoring highlights from last night's triumph over him instead. The subject of the tower doesn't seem to bother me quite so much now that I'm curled up close next to Tristan, and as he's been talking, I've gradually crept up so far into his lap that by chance we've ended up in a position uncannily like the one we were in together on Brecelyn's wall that day. I don't remember doing it, but at some point I must have slid my hand up inside his tunic, and now I'm lying contentedly across him with my hand on his heart and my head resting against his shoulder, up under his chin.

Tristan must be thinking back to the tower, too, because after a while, he says softly,

"I've been thinking, kid. Taran may have said it to insult me. But maybe his motto for your crossbowmen is the right one, and I'm sorry I've been teasing you so much about them. You know, I'm awfully proud of you, for everything, don't you?"

I look up at him adoringly, my heart full of all the things I felt for him that day, when I thought I was saying my last goodbye to him. Without removing my hand from where it's resting against his breast, I stretch my lips up to press them lightly to his cheek, and breathlessly, I say,

"I'd do it again in a heartbeat, *master*."

"Well, well, well! How touching!" a sarcastic voice purrs, not far away.

It's Jurian, sounding positively gleeful, and Rennie's with him.

It's later than I thought; Jurian must already be escorting his squire out to squires' club, since they've obviously just come cutting across from under the portico and out into the garden while I was too caught up with Tristan to notice them. Now they're standing only feet away, looming over us so close they're blocking out all the sun from the garden and looking down at us with amused expressions on their faces.

I startle in surprise when I see them, just as though they'd caught me at something — even though for once, my fraternal kiss of Tristan was entirely innocent.

My guilty reaction just spurs Jurian on.

"How de*light*ful!" he exclaims, slinging his arm around Rennie's shoulder. "Inspired by last night's story to do a little reenactment of your own tender moment, up on the tower? *Smashing* idea. Don't let us get in your way. Come on, Rennie," he says silkily, pulling on his smirking squire's sleeve, his voice as always full of innuendo,

"Let's *'give 'em what they want'* — a little *privacy*!"

With that he heads out through the wooden gate, laughing and dragging Rennie along with him.

I can't say I'm relieved when they're gone, however. Because as soon as they move away, they leave standing revealed behind them the *other* boy who was on his way out to the cabinets right behind them, one I only now realize is there.

He's standing directly behind the spot just vacated by Jurian, as cold as stone and as still as a statue.

From his expression, it's clear that he, too, must have witnessed our 'tender little scene.'

Of course, it's Taran.

With my luck, who else would it be?

Slowly, I remove my hand from inside Tristan's shirt, trying not to cringe.

Taran doesn't move a muscle. He just stands there in the middle of the garden, staring at us. Or at least I assume he does, since I can't bring myself to look at him.

"And just what do *you* think *you're* looking at?" Tristan demands baitingly after a while, hugging me closer and to my horror almost bouncing me on his knee. "Or haven't you ever seen a man whose squire genuinely *loves* him?"

"It's a little much for the middle of the afternoon, even for *you*, isn't it, Vervloet?" Taran answers back from between clenched teeth, and even with my eyes lowered I can tell he's giving one of the irritated little sideway stretches of his head that usually means he's thoroughly exasperated with me. He sounds reasonably calm, though, considering how he usually reacts when he thinks he's caught me using some supposedly innocent excuse to put my hands all over Tristan. So I think a miracle is going to happen, and Taran's going to leave it. He'll simply walk away, and that'll be the end of it.

Then Tristan gives him one of his most dazzling smiles.

He looks Taran right in the eye.

And then he says:

"Better watch out, Taran! I wouldn't stick your *neck* out too far if I were you. As it happens, Marek and I were just talking about the pleasure of shooting one of my arrows straight into it."

"WHAT?" TRISTAN DEMANDS INNOCENTLY, ONCE TARAN'S stalked off fuming (having first kicked over one of the wooden tables that stands under the vines, and all of its accompanying chairs), and as I glare up accusingly at him. "It was nothing but the truth."

That's hardly the point. But there's no point in saying so to Tristan, or in getting angry with him. He has no idea what he's just done, and he's right. We *were* just talking about shooting Taran in the neck, and it's my own fault for being so careless as to give Tristan a mental picture of it. So I content myself with demanding of him querulously,

"Must you make a point of it to antagonize people? *Powerful* people?"

Taran. Masters Guillaume and Leon. Aristide. The list is endless. And I have to admit it. I *do* feel angry with him. "Firsts is in *three days*, and for the first time we've got a real shot at winning them! Can't you just keep your head down, and stay out of trouble?"

"I suppose I could. But where'd the fun be in that? And you must admit,

I've got a talent for it! Besides, *I'm* not the one who's really been going around taking dirty shots at Journeys," he says, and he's got a point. I probably should just be glad he doesn't know that Taran is no longer the only boy who fits that description.

I scowl at him anyway.

"Now Marek," he says more seriously, when he sees my expression. "You've been trying to handle Taran all by yourself, and I admire you for it. But anyone can see that he's started harassing you again, and he's getting awfully brazen about it! I've just let him know in no uncertain terms that if he picks on *you*, he'll have to deal with *me*. That'll give him pause, trust me. Oh, don't try to thank me," he says magnanimously, "as I can see you're overcome with emotion."

"I wasn't going to," I assure him. But as crazy as it seems, I can tell Tristan really thinks he's just done me a favor.

I must look pretty pale, since Tristan now gives me a few reassuring pats on the shoulder. "Don't worry," he assures me, mistaking my bleak expression for fear of repercussions from Taran. "*I'll* take care of him, if he tries to threaten you again."

I don't bother to tell him that *that's* hardly the point, either.

I'm not sure I can explain it, even to myself. But I feel almost as miserable about the fact that Taran must surely think I've broken my promise to him not to tell anyone about his wound as I did about keeping it a secret from Tristan in the first place.

"Besides, Taran's not going to do anything. After Gilles's performance last night, the last thing he's going to want now is to make another scene, so close to trials," Tristan is now saying contentedly, and I don't bother telling him I'm not so sure about *that* anymore.

At the very least, he'd really have to be the greatest guy in the world not to be absolutely furious with me.

Once Tristan's gone inside for his tutorial and I can't put off reporting for squires' practice any longer myself, the short trudge out from the garden and over to the cabinets feels like one of the longest walks of my life. This must be what it feels like on the way to the gallows or up to put your head on the executioner's block, and if I was already feeling nervous about facing Taran after hearing Gilles's story last night, now I almost feel like either one of those destinations might actually be preferable to attending squires' club with him.

So much for the half-formed plan I woke up with this morning, to find some way to say *thank you* to Taran today for saving me on the tower.

For obvious reasons, that's not going to happen now, either.

WHEN I FIRST ARRIVE AT THE CABINETS, TARAN'S KEEPING himself occupied at a distance, setting up targets and fiddling around at the embankment, so that's all right. From the way he's kicking the stuffing out of one of the wicker backstops under the guise of reshaping it, though, I can tell what's he's really doing is trying to blow off steam. It looks like he's got enough of it built up to set the entire North Sea to boiling. I doubt there's enough straw in all of Louvain for him to vent it on, and my own nerves are paper thin. I'm to have no opportunity to explain myself, and even if I could, Taran probably wouldn't like the truth much better than what he's surely thinking.

It hardly helps that as afraid as the boys are of teasing Taran, they have no compunction whatsoever about using Gilles's recitation last night to torment me. As we're opening our Journeys' cabinets to get out our weapons, Rennie wastes no time in making cracks about 'manly arms' as he reaches past me, and now and then Armand leans in to coo like a bird into my ear. They're careful not to say anything when they think Taran might overhear them, but I'm sure he's well aware of what they're doing. It can't be improving his mood, and I'm dreading the moment practice starts in earnest.

"It's just a *joke* to them, Marek," Remy says, sidling over to commiserate with me. He's the only boy who's noticed how agitated I seem, and it doesn't take him long to say all the wrong things in his bumbling efforts to comfort me. "You know the boys don't think any of it *really* happened that way. They all know Gilles was just being, er, uh, *Gilles,*" he says, and although it's not entirely clear *who* Gilles was being last night, I know what he means.

"*I* didn't think it was very funny," Frans pipes up loyally, prompting Pascal to put in,

"Your own master didn't seem to think it was very funny, either, Remy," his tone suggesting that he hasn't forgiven Taran for pounding his master's head on the floor last night. But it's just the boys' usual banter, so I'm surprised when instead of laughing it off, Remy stiffens, although I guess I shouldn't be. Of all the boys, he's by far the touchiest.

"It was *wrong* of the boys to tease him about riding back that night *to the castle,*" he squawks, turning on Pascal and his voice shrill. "And calling him insatiable! He *loves* her. After what happened, it was *wrong* of *your* master to tease him about staying out all night. Can you blame him for being mad at Gilles for making a *game* of reminding him of it? The baby *died.*"

Instantly all the teasing stops. With a mumbled word or two of apology, the boys hang their heads and turn back to readying their equipment, looking duly chastised.

Remy, too, bends his head down over his quiver, and he pretends to busy himself with stocking it. But his hands are shaking and his cheeks are quivering, and he isn't fooling anyone. He's said more than he intended, and I feel for him. I have the same problem a lot myself, and from the way Remy keeps darting me mournful little sidelong glances, I can tell his own outburst has upset him.

My nerves were already raw, even before the unexpected reminder of Melissande's baby and its untimely fate. So in my sympathy for Remy, it takes me longer than it should to realize what it is that he's actually just let slip.

It's probably a full minute before it clicks, like the tumblers of a lock sliding slowly into place — *clink, clink, clink!*

And then at last, I finally get it. I finally see the *timing* of the thing.

It was on *that very night* that Melissande's baby was conceived.

Or at least, on one of the afternoons immediately thereafter.

No wonder Taran was always in such a hurry to leave the abbey, every time he came there to visit me! He was eager to get on to a much more pleasant afternoon's occupation, and the bitter truth is this: while I was lying on the brink of death and dreaming delirious dreams of him, Taran was back at Brecelyn's castle, busily impregnating his fiancée.

And as Taran's squire, Remy's known it all along. That much is patently obvious.

Out on the butts, Taran's already rearranged the field about five times. We're all armed and ready, waiting for him, and eventually there can be no more stalling. He changes up the field one last time, as far as I can see putting it all back the way it was to begin with, and he leaves it. Then he makes his way over to join us, walking as slowly and as deliberately as though he, too, were headed to the gallows. Or maybe he's more like the executioner.

Taran's never particularly jovial when he takes up a stance in front of us to get our club sessions underway. Today the expression on his face is so set and hard he could have carved it there himself with that little knife of his, and when he takes his time folding his arms behind his back and looking each boy in line coldly over in turn, it's not long before the boys have picked up on the icy atmosphere. I can feel them shuffling around uneasily, wondering what's going on. They probably just assume that in typical fashion we're going to be the ones to pay the price for the Journeys' feuding, and that after Gilles's repeated jabs last night about Taran being so sensitive, today he's determined to spend all morning demonstrating just what a tough guy he really is. I can almost hear them thinking we're all in for it now.

I know better. Even though I'm the only boy Taran's studiously avoided giving the once-over, from the way one muscle in his jaw is twitching as his gaze passes resolutely over my head, I'm pretty sure the only boy who's really in for it is me.

Besides, I'd have to be the village idiot not to know Taran's madder than a baited bear at me.

And I have to say, right now I'm not very happy with him either.

I know I'm right, when after letting us all sweat it out for a while, without deigning to look at me, Taran commands,

"*Vervloet*, would you *mind* joining me up here, *please?*" and from the tone of his voice I think I'm mighty lucky he isn't armed. Otherwise, I'd surely be sporting a perfect circle of bolts, low and tight, right in the middle of my abdomen.

I comply with a gulp, and if I thought the walk out to the cabinets was bad, it's nothing to the few paces over to take my place next to Taran. My legs feel like sludge, and it seems to be so far and to take me so long that with each step I feel like he's actually getting further away.

I'd wouldn't be so bad, if it weren't so public. I desperately wish there was some way I could talk to him in private, some way I could tell him what really happened in the garden. But even if it weren't for all the boys, what could I say that would both be true and not sound awful anyway? It makes no sense that I should feel so much like I've betrayed him. But I do. And I bet Taran feels the same way.

I have no idea what he's going to do about it, either, but one thing is abundantly clear: the time of our 'gentleman's agreement' is over. There can be no more running the club together amicably.

By the time I've forced myself over and up into the semblance of a St. Sebastian's salute as close beside Taran as I dare, the anticipation is killing me and my stomach is churning, and all I can think is, *whatever's coming, let's please just hurry and get it over with*, and I feel miserable. My *'thank you'* to Taran is in shambles, and after what Remy's just said I'm not even sure any longer that I want to give one to him.

On top of everything else, I've ruined squires' club for myself, again.

I'm not sure what I'm steeling myself for — more insults, maybe — or even another punch in the face. But when I clear my throat and manage to croak out,

"Ready, master!" all Taran does is begin to review our plan for the lesson.

He addresses his stilted comments to a place above my right ear, and from the way he won't unclench his teeth while he's talking his mood is every bit as foul as I knew it would be. But as unbelievable as it seems, to all appearances he's determined to pretend the scene out in the garden never happened. He's going to stick to our tacit agreement even if it kills him, and I guess Tristan was right. He must not want to make another scene in front of the boys (particularly not one involving *me*), and he'll be damned if he lets them think he can't take a joke. Either that, or he's become as invested in training the boys as I am, and he doesn't want to be the one to break our newfound squires' solidarity.

Whatever his reasons, I have to be glad of them. So I do my best to play along, and pretend nothing's bothering me.

But it isn't easy.

That storage box of tensions between us isn't now just full to the brink.

It's busting at the seams, and I can tell the boys are finding our barely contained hostility and clipped politeness to each other more disconcerting than our usual open arguing.

It's become our habit to start out our sessions by letting the boys go through some warm-up exercises on their own, while Taran and I stand back together to observe them and to compare notes. It would look odd if we diverged from the pattern now, although today it's awkward in the extreme.

Needless to say, we don't compare any notes. I'm sure I wouldn't like any observations Taran might be inclined to make right now, and he clearly intends to go through the rest of the lesson without speaking to me again. So I'll be damned if I'm the one who breaks the silence between us. We just stand there a few feet apart, not looking at each other, watching the boys wordlessly. After a while, though, I get the impression Taran isn't really watching the boys. He's just standing there fuming.

The longer it goes on, the angrier he seems, and I'll confess. The fact that he's not going to do anything but seethe and ignore me is somehow worse than the confrontation I was expecting. It's not just because Taran's clearly standing there blaming me for something I didn't do and he's giving me no chance to defend myself, or even because of what Remy's just let slip about the wretched timing of his prenuptial visits. There are a dozen things I'm busting to say and I don't dare say any of them, and what's worse, I can't stop thinking about snatches of Gilles's extemporaneous poetry, since everything around me is conspiring to remind me of it: bows, arrows, the boys shooting — and of course, just Taran's proximity. I'm sure *he's* thinking about it, too — and about what *really* happened. He's the only one who knows what that actually is, and I'm dying to ask him about it. I'm not sure what's stronger — my curiosity, his rage, or our mutual indignation — but before long the tension is as thick as the wool on an unshorn sheep, and I'm suffocating it in.

And so I give in.

As chance would have it, I'm standing on Taran's left side. He's wearing a short-sleeved tunic, and to allow more room for his bulging biceps he's cut a perpendicular slit a ways up each sleeve. One of the tantalizing little gaps is right at my eye level, when I sneak a sidelong glance at him. So I start craning my neck, trying to sneak a peek up under the flap to see if he's got an arrow brand under there, or not.

Frustratingly, I can't see anything, and even when he moves slightly now and then to twitch off a fly, the flap doesn't open enough to confirm or refute Gilles's assertion that he missed out on his rite of passage to veteran's status. So when curiosity finally gets the best of me, without thinking I reach out and I flip up the flap myself.

"What in the HELL do you think you're doing?!" Taran demands, slapping away my hand like he's swatting at an insect, and I can't think of anything to do but confess that I'm trying to see if he ever got his veteran's brand.

"*Satisfied?*" he growls, pulling up the sleeve for a moment to give me a good look, before yanking it back down again.

"Not really," I admit, since all that's there is rock-hard muscle, and smooth, tanned skin.

It's not a very auspicious opening, but the ice has been broken. So while he's still shifting around in his tunic and settling back into a disgruntled pose looking out down the field, I turn to him, and words start pouring out of me.

"It wasn't *at all* how it looked, Taran! If you'll let me explain, I think you'll find it was actually all rather —"

"It *looked* like you were telling DuBois that you shot me, and the two of you were sitting under a tree and laughing about it," he snaps bluntly, and I can't answer.

Technically, that sort of *is* what we were doing. And there's no way I'm going to say the first thing that pops into my head to say to defend myself, either. Not when it's *"things aren't always what they seem."*

"I thought as much," Taran sneers nastily, when all I can do is look up at him with wide eyes and try to swallow down that wretched phrase of Gilles's.

I'm sure I do look quite guilty.

Everything about the situation is impossible, and Taran's now giving me a look that's so cold and accusing, I can't help it.

"And what if I *did* tell him?!" I fling at him, angry that he could think me capable of such casual cruelty. *After the way I came to him to sew him up so carefully, how can he possibly believe I took wounding him so lightly?!* "I don't know why I'm bothering to try to explain myself, or apologizing! I've done nothing wrong. Not really. All I did was not give in to *your* threats! And besides, Tristan is my *master*. If I want to be a good squire, I can't go around keeping secrets from him!"

"Telling him everything now, are you?" he shoots back, and I see I've made a bad start of it.

The comment is singularly annoying, but it pulls me up short. It's a reminder that Taran's never told *my* secret, and I know it *did* look bad this morning. Taran's got plenty of reasons to be angry with me and I was *supposed* to be apologizing, and somewhere in the back of my mind an unsettling thought is vaguely registering:

I've just confessed to something I didn't do, simply because I was hurt that Taran could think me guilty of it.

So I hold in my irritation, and I regroup. And with as much composure as I can muster, I say primly,

"Be that as it may, whether you want to believe me or not, the fact of the matter is that I *didn't* actually tell Tristan anything. I can't help how it looked. And as for shooting you in the first place, it was an *accident*. But for that, I am truly sorry."

Before my words are even out, Taran turns on me, his eyes flashing and looking at me as though I were a gadfly whose constant goading has finally driven him to the brink of insanity.

"You know what *your* problem is?!?" he snarls, abandoning all pretense at paying any attention to the boys practicing and taking a menacing step forward. "You're always sorry — for the *wrong* things!"

When all I can do is look confused, he crosses his arms across his chest, and looks down at me.

"You think I'm angry that you told your master about our little '*accident*'?" he scoffs. "Why should I be?" and for a boy who's not angry, he's giving a pretty good imitation of it. "I *knew* you'd tell him."

"You *what?*" It's so unfair, it's infuriating!

"You took an arrow for him," he replies simply, and there's nothing I can say to that.

I'm getting nowhere, and I can see I was a fool to think explaining things to him was going lead to anything but more bickering. But my blood is up, and I'm now determined to say my piece, even if it kills me.

"About that day, on the tower. And taking me to Vendon. I've been thinking about it a lot since yesterday, and I've realized that I've never really said —"

"Oh, for God's sake! *Are you kidding me?!*" he bellows, in just the way he did right after I shot him and looking about as unhinged.

"I'm *trying* to thank you."

"Well, your timing *STINKS!*" he hisses.

"Oh yeah? Don't even get me started on *yours*," I mutter back under my breath, but I don't think he hears me; he's too busy saying, "It's even worse than your aim." So I push on valiantly, even though I know I'm making a mess of it.

"Seriously, Taran. I'm being most sincere. I was up all night thinking about what Gilles said, and I feel quite miserable! You really must let me thank you, once and for all, and properly."

"Don't mention it."

"I don't know why I never thought about it before. It can't have been at all easy ..."

"*No*," he says darkly, cutting me off again. "*Really*. I mean it. *Don't* mention it."

He leans over until his face is only inches from mine, and to drive home his point he repeats himself slowly, punctuating each word by giving me a sharp, menacing poke on the chest:

"*Do. Not. Mention* it. To *me. Ever. Again!*"

After that, it becomes increasingly impossible to maintain the façade that 'we're all friends here.' Soon more cracks begin to appear, although at first they're relatively minor, and the boys even seem a little relieved. They probably assume we're just settling back into our usual antagonistic banter, unaware as they are of the undercurrents that are flowing together under the surface, gathering speed.

It's particularly bad during the first half of the session, and the unpleasantness begins almost as soon as we divide up into groups to drill the boys on crossbows. Taran's taken his own squire, plus Armand and Frans, the boys who are the worst at the skill. Pascal and Rennie are working with me, and since Rennie's turned out to be a pretty good crossbowman, I've left him to do some shooting on his own while I work with Pascal to correct a few deficiencies.

He keeps pulling up at the last second, and as a result all his shots go too high. It's a problem I know well: his arm gets too tired from holding the heavy crossbow out in front of him to fight the recoil. I'm taking the bow out of Pascal's hands to demonstrate when Taran comes wandering down to see what's happening at our end, and he stops behind me just as I'm saying,

"You should try bracing the butt end of the tiller against your body, Pascal, to steady it. That way your shoulder can help support the weight, and keep your arms from over-tiring."

"That's the worst piece of advice I've ever heard," Taran says flatly behind me. Then he snatches the bow out of my hands without so much as an 'if you please,' and he says to Pascal,

"Hold it like *this*," and he lifts the bow up into position with one big hand, holding onto the tiller near the front of it in such a way that none of the bow touches anywhere on the rest of his arm or body.

"You've got to lift the bow free if you want your shot to be steady, or it'll pick up every movement and vibration from your body. Not to mention giving you a nasty bruise. If you really want to be good, you've got to shoot the crossbow as though it were a longbow, in this at least: move *through* your shot, and shoot instinctively. You want the bow to swing free, right up to the split-second when you find your mark," he gives the bow a casual swing, "Then *boom!*" he barks, pulling the trigger lever while the bow is indeed still moving into his shot. I don't think I have to say that the bolt hits the target, dead center.

It's a disgusting display of easy, casual power, and to my way of thinking, a mighty cheap shot. In one blow Taran's shamed me as a trainer at my own best skill and highlighted my physical weakness. To add insult to injury, he caps it off with the comment,

"Rely on a crutch, Pascal, and you'll need it all your life."

"That's easy for you to say," I answer back testily, hating that he's got me on the defensive. "We can't all be clouters. *Some* of us will never have the *brute* strength for it."

"You'll never have the strength to hold the crossbow free, if you don't try it," he rejoins, in a tone that's just as prickly. "Have you considered the possibility that you're not strong enough, because like your *master*, you never work at it? We all know you *can* do it, when you want to. If you have *incentive* enough," and before I can protest, he raises his eyebrows, and says smugly,

"We all saw that shot of yours last year at Seconds. The one that kept your *master* from certain elimination."

I'd love to make a witty comeback. Something that would really put Taran to shame. The devil of it is, he's right — on both counts.

I did shoot down an apple at Seconds last year as the culmination of Tristan's exhibition. And I did do it without thinking, instinctively.

I stand for a moment with my mouth slack (having already opened it to make a smart retort), and I think myself back into the moment. And when I picture it, I see myself swing the bow up with one hand, the whole time moving freely through my shot.

All I can do is shut my mouth, cross my arms, and watch with annoyance as Taran proceeds to ignore me and take Pascal through the mechanics of it.

More unpleasantness follows soon thereafter, although maybe it's really just a continuation of the same thing. When the boys tire of crossbows, we don't bother switching groups, since Armand and Remy as clouters will stick with Taran, and Pascal and Rennie are to work on butts with me. When I try to usher Frans over to join us, however, Taran barks him back with a curt,

"Frans stays with me."

"That's ridiculous," I object. "Frans is too slight of frame ever to be a clouter," and when we start to argue about it, Frans pipes up timidly,

"It's okay, Marek. I *want* to work on clouts," and I assume he's just trying to smooth things over loyally. But he sounds surprisingly sincere, and when I give him a questioning look, he says enthusiastically, if a little nervously,

"Master Taran's explained it to me, Marek, and it makes a lot of sense. My master is a clouter, and a good squire should know everything about his master's technique. When we've finished going over the basics, he's going to walk me through the special clouting method he and de Gilford came up with for Falko, so I can help him perfect it."

I think the thing that irritates me most about it is the fact that it does make a lot of sense. That, and that as soon as Frans says his piece, Taran adds,

"Maybe he'll never be as strong as Falko. Few boys will. And maybe he'll never be strong at all. Who knows? He's still a kid. But anyone can get *stronger*. Even *you*. In fact, that's a mighty good idea!," and he takes the clouter's bow out of Remy's hands and shoves it into mine. "Let Pascal and Rennie drill on their own for a while."

"You want me to stay here, and practice clouts?!" I demand incredulously.

"That was the idea, yes," he says dispassionately.

"What's the point of that?" I say, handing the bow back to a worried-looking Remy. "I'm never going to be anything but lousy at the skill, and you know it! In fact, you're the one who told me so last year."

"I don't recall saying anything of the sort," Taran replies, irritatingly not losing his cool. In fact, the more flustered I get, the calmer it seems to make him, and I can tell he's looking forward to the chance to humiliate me.

"Are you going to try to deny telling me I was sure to fail my clouts test?" I demand sarcastically, loudly enough for all the boys to hear and hoping it'll shame him. But it doesn't seem to bother him. He simply replies matter-of-factly,

"That's not quite what I said, but no. I don't deny it. Why should I? I knew you'd fail, and you did."

"So I suppose now you're going to say that if I'd just practiced harder, I could have passed them," I shoot back, not really caring that I'm starting to make a scene.

"No," is all he says, and I don't know why it makes me feel even worse that he's conceded so easily that I could have never passed clouts, even though I guess this is the answer I was trying to get him to give.

"Then I put it to you again," I cry, trying to rally. "What's the point?"

"Who cares about the test?" he says dismissively. "And maybe you never will be very good. But you could get *better*. *That's* the point."

"*I'll* tell you what the *point* is," I snap back, feeling dangerously close to tears. All the boys have gathered around, looking a little confused about why I'm taking the simple suggestion to drill some clouts so badly, and I'm not sure I know myself. Maybe I'm still mad at him about the past, or because he's so mad at me and I can't do anything about it, or maybe I'm upset that he'd use my failure at clouts to try to get back at me. But I think in some small way I've also wanted all this time to tell him about what happened on the night of our show, to make him understand how much losing the hope of Journeys hurt me.

"The *point* is *this*: after my clouts test, Master Guillaume told me right to my face, '*you'll* never be a Journey. Not while *I'm* master here.' Those were his exact words, I believe."

I should have known I wouldn't get any sympathy. Not from Taran. Not today. I can't really have been expecting any, and I have no idea what response I thought I was going to get. Maybe none. But I'm not the only one who's thoroughly taken aback by the one he actually gives.

"To hell with Master Guillaume," Taran snorts, sounding for a moment an awful lot like Gilles's imitation of him.

All the boys take a surprised step backwards, glancing around nervously to see if any veterans are close enough to have overheard him, and out of the corner of my eye I think I see Armand surreptitiously crossing himself.

"And to hell with Journeys, too!" Taran continues, just as vehemently, addressing all the boys but of course talking mostly to me. "Is that the only reason to practice, if you think you're going to *win*? What happened to *shooting for the pure love of it?*"

It's a low blow, throwing our club motto back at me. Taran's made me look a fool, and I should just stop while I'm behind, but he's made so light of a failure that meant so much to me I can't stop myself.

"Don't tell me *you* don't want to win! Are you going to try to stand there and tell us all that *you* haven't admitted wanting to win Guards so badly that you'd do just about *anything?*"

I'm as good as saying that the reason he shot Tristan was to take him out of the competition, and everybody knows it. It's as cheap a shot as any of Taran's, particularly since it's an accusation even I no longer believe, and as soon as it's out, I regret it. This is hardly the *'thank you'* to him that I woke up this morning planning to deliver, and instead of explaining myself I just keep digging myself in deeper.

It's too late now to do anything but brazen it out. So I glare up at him accusingly as he answers back coldly,

"That's entirely different. Of course I want to win. I've spent every day of my life working for it like a dog, single-mindedly. What's more, I *am* going to win. Make no mistake about *that.* Everyone expects it. If I don't, I won't just *lose.* I'll be thoroughly humiliated."

I never thought of it that way before, but it's true, and before I can think of what to say he's already shoving the clouter's bow back into my hands, saying,

"So I think one afternoon of clouting isn't going to hurt *you* any. Who knows? Maybe it'll even do you some good. Here's your first lesson: clouters know how to keep their *big mouths shut."*

There's nothing for me to do but take the bow and step back to the line with it and try to stifle my irritation as Taran begins running through some clouting basics for us dispassionately.

It wouldn't be so bad, though, if even in my anger I couldn't see that it probably is going to do me some good.

⸺◆⸺

AFTER THAT, WE STICK TO SHOOTING. TARAN KEEPS US DRILLING on clouts for the rest of the afternoon — over three solid hours of it, just to spite me — and if I thought it was chilly at practice yesterday, today it's positively glacial. Once Taran's fallen back into the rhythm of instructing his own favorite skill, though, it doesn't take him long to get caught up in it. And I have to admit that some of the things he's showing us are pretty interesting. Remy's bow is really too big for me and he needs it for himself, so I excuse myself and of my own volition I go and get a smaller clouter's bow from Tristan' cabinet. Soon I'm throwing myself into the practice with as much gusto as I can muster, and after a while I think we're both relieved at having something to focus on other than each other. As the afternoon wears on and Taran drags us systematically through a meticulous breakdown of the clouting motion, grudgingly I even have to hand it to him. He sticks it out and keeps himself in check for the rest of the practice in a way I wouldn't have thought he had in him, and maybe it's just because the practice is so physically exhausting that it requires all my energy — but as so often happens at these sessions, once we've been pretending to get along for long enough, it gradually starts to shade into the truth.

By the time practice is winding down, it's gotten hard to tell the difference between genuine cooperation and the semblance of it, and when Taran finally heeds the boys' grumbling and calls an end to the practice, we've been drilling so long and we're all so worn out that I think Taran and I have even both temporarily forgotten that our feigned cooperation is a sham. At least we're both so engrossed in a spirited disagreement over a particular point of method that we leave the others to put away our bows and we head inside together, still caught up in an animated debate about it.

I hardly notice as we traverse the stables and enter the corridor near the archives, side by side and heads together, arguing away. There's a roaring fire burning in the archive fireplace, despite the relative warmth of the day. It's always cold and damp inside the guild building proper and a fire is such an attractive thing, although we're both already overheated from the long workout, without pausing our discussion we naturally drift inside, gravitating towards it.

"It's the same thing I've been saying all afternoon, if you'd only listen," Taran is repeating, as we settle ourselves onto some stools conveniently arrayed in front of the blazing fire. "You're letting *this* part bend," and he takes my hand in his, turns it over, and runs his finger lightly along the inside of my wrist, to demonstrate.

"*Glurg*," I think I say, and Taran looks up, without letting go of my hand. Our eyes meet.

And just then, behind us Gilles pops his head in.

"So the repair crews have finally gotten the old archive chimney up and running, I see! After the number our winter guests did on it, I was beginning to think they'd never get it drawing properly. You boys enjoying the first fire in here in months?" he trills. "Ah, I always say — there's nothing like a nice, *intimate* chat about archery in front of a cozy fire!"

And then he winks, and he's gone again.

I don't know if it's the wink, or Gilles's comment, or if after last night it's simply enough that the one who makes it is Gilles. But in a flash all the tensions that were building during practice are back, and then some. Judging from the expression that springs to Taran's features, if he's got a box of suppressed emotions stashed away on an internal shelf somewhere, it's not just bursting at the seams. It's exploding.

He drops my wrist so fast, you'd think I'd just poured molten lead over it. We're too close to the fire, and it doesn't help at all that we're both hot and sweaty, and our faces are horribly flushed. Or that we've drawn so close to each other, our faces are practically touching. It clearly embarrasses Taran as much as it's embarrassing me, since Gilles's adjective was accurate: we have been sitting here talking, *intimately*.

"You just couldn't keep your *big* mouth *shut*, could you?!" he snarls, leaping angrily to his feet, and not so much running one hand through his hair as tearing at it, while I, too, scramble to my feet.

"*Ha!*" I crow back, all at once feeling more than ready finally to have it out with him. I'm all stirred up, and at the sight of his hand up tangling in his own hair, I have a sudden mental picture of it groping through a cascade of long, blonde curls, and my anger flares. It seems the perfect time to vent my rage at him about the *timing* of the thing — to vent my rage at him, for everything. "I *knew* you were mad about it! Why can't you admit it?"

"Just had to tell your master and his fancy friends all about it, didn't you, so you could have a laugh at me?!" he's growling, hardly hearing me and looking a lot like a great, big cat again. Only instead of pouncing on his prey he's more like stalking it, from the way he's started slowly closing in on me.

"I told you, it wasn't like that! I *didn't* tell Tristan I shot you. He doesn't know anything about it, so he can't have said anything to Gilles," I protest, hoping it's the truth, and despite myself I'm backing up in retreating steps in concert with his advancing ones. But my chin is up and my chest is out, and I'm doing a decent job of holding my ground against him.

"Not about *that*, you little idiot!" he snaps, taking one more big step towards me and looming in over me. "About what happened, *at the abbey!*"

I'm too distracted by hitting the wall behind me at first to see what he means.

"Hey!" I grunt, putting my hands up on his chest, and giving him a little shove — partly because despite the fact that he's already backed me up against the wall he just keeps coming, and partly because he's being so unreasonable.

"How dare you try to blame Gilles's story last night on *me*!" I shoot back. "*I* didn't like it any better than you did, and I didn't know anything about it! And as for what happened at Vendon, how could *I* have told Gilles anything? I was out cold, and *I* know nothing about *that*, either — because *you* refuse to tell me!" But by now it's obvious Taran isn't listening. He's too busy leaning into me and muttering gibberish to himself. I can't make out much of what he's saying, but from the unnaturally high voice he's using and the few snatches of his sarcastic phrases that are intelligible, like 'I never really bothered to think about *you*, at all. Not until *Gilles* mentioned it,' I can tell he's trying to mimic me, and he's making me sound terribly ungrateful.

It really is stiflingly hot in the room, and we're way too close to the fire. And to each other. I don't know what's driving up the temperature more — the roaring flames, or Taran's body heat. His face is flushed and there are beads of sweat on his temples, and with his eyes rolling back in his head he looks like he could be delirious, if not downright insane. I'm not at all sure what the expression on his face is, though, since it's now too close to my own for me to see it properly, but he's shaking with emotion, and it doesn't take a genius to tell he's angrier with me than he's ever been.

I'm feeling rather hot myself. If not actually feverish, then at least a little dizzy. I feel like I've been stuck right into the fire and my clothes are itching me to distraction; I want to tear at the neck of my tunic or somehow loosen my binding, or claw right through them — or maybe right through *him*. All my anger and frustration with him all these months have come boiling up to the surface, and irrationally it makes me angrier still that what he's insinuating about me being ungrateful is correct. I can't think straight, but it also sounds like he's saying that some part of what Gilles said happened at the abbey must have been accurate. And if so, I bet I can guess. It must have been the part about Taran being the one to undress me and to wash me, and the thought isn't helping. Not with him so close, and my hands flat against his chest.

"Why, I ought to! ... Oh God, what I am going to do about you? ... Tell me, just what in the hell am I supposed to do ...?" he's raving. So I snap,

"I've already said I'm sorry!," even though I haven't really. "What more do you want me to say?!"

"*Why* did you have to be the most pigheaded, obstinate, obtuse little thing I've ever met?!" is all he says, his eyes roving over my face as he braces himself heavily against the wall with one big arm over my head.

"Yeah, well, *you're* every bit as self-righteous, pompous, and opinionated as Gilles painted you, and just as proud of yourself! In fact, his story wasn't just funny, it was damned accurate!" and when all he does is lean in closer, nostrils flaring, I burst out hotly,

"And if you're not angry that I shot you or that I told Tristan about it, then why in the heck *are* you so mad?! Why, you must *really* be angry, because it *did* all happen that night exactly as Gilles said!"

I'm not at all sure what it is I think I've just accused Taran of, actually — stupendous heroism, maybe, or superhuman strength. It makes no sense, and I don't see why it should put Taran over the edge.

But it does.

"*Is there NO way to shut up that MOUTH of yours?!?*" he hisses, and maybe it's because as he says it, his eyes are on my mouth. Before I can stop myself, I hear myself fling tauntingly back,

"Why don't you kiss me? I know you're thinking about it. Isn't that how you punish girls, by kissing them?," pretty shamelessly hoping to provoke him into doing it.

It's what I've been thinking about the whole time we've been fighting, of course, from the moment he ran his finger down my wrist. It's what I was thinking about when I bound up his wound in the clearing. And it's what I wanted, the night I sewed him up again. It's what I've wanted all along, really, isn't it, since the day of our crossbow tutorial? Maybe even from the first moment we met. And now every inch of me is aching for it, and the little space between our lips is prickling with heat. I'm not sure either at what point during our heated exchange my hands that were holding him off began slowly sliding up his torso instead. All I know is that one is now groping at him and the other is up around his neck, and as soon as my words are out, the room itself and everything in it seems to me to be holding its breath.

"Believe me, Marieke," he finally says roughly. "If I kiss you now, it won't be to punish you. It'll be to punish myself!"

But then his arms are tight around me, and he *does* kiss me.

At least, his lips come down toward mine and mine stretch up eagerly to his, and everything in me is opening up for his kiss. My mind's gone blank, and we're both so caught up in it we seem to have forgotten that we're supposed to be fighting, and that we're standing out in the open, in the middle of the archives, in the middle of the afternoon, and I've forgotten everything but him.

And then at last his mouth meets mine, and I can taste his kiss — or rather, the promise of it. Because at that very instant, before his lips can do more than lightly graze my own, and as I'm letting out an involuntary sound from somewhere deep within my throat that's something between a choke and a gurgle and a moan, all of a sudden a loud voice behind me booms right in my ear:

"HEY, WHAT IN THE *HELL* DO YOU THINK YOU'RE *DOING* THERE, MELLOR?!?"

Taran's arms drop from around me instantly.

He leaps backward with alacrity.

I only have time to catch a glimpse of the look of sheer calamity on his face as we break apart before a pair of huge arms grab me and I'm pulled roughly backward, and I can't believe it.

What incredible fools we've been! We let our feuding get the best of us, and now we've been caught red-handed, flagrantly letting off steam in broad daylight, right in the middle of the guild.

Panic rises in my chest and I make another strangled choking sound, this time not from desire but because I really feel like I can't breathe. I hardly care what punishment is coming from the masters, although knowing Master Guillaume, it's going be something interesting. All I can think is how the boys will surely soon know all about it — Gilles and Pascal, Jurian, Aristide — and *Remy.*

And most of all, Tristan.

From the ashen look on Taran's face, I know he's thinking the same thing; he only kissed me because I goaded him into it, but I doubt that will mean much to Melissande, if she finds out Taran's been spending his time at St. Sebastian's 'fraternizing.'

All this flashes through my mind in one instant of pure terror, as two big, hairy arms wrap around me. Now they're pulling me backwards, slamming my back against a massive torso so hard I really can't breathe. In an instant I'm being squeezed so tight around the middle that I can't process anything at all any longer, except for one thing:

The voice now bellowing in my ear — I *recognize* it.

It's *Falko's*.

And what he's saying is this:

"Good God, Taran! *That's* no way to deal with a boy who's choking. Good thing *I* came along when I did. *This* is how you get something out that's stuck in a man's throat, old man!"

And then he gives me one massive jolt of a squeeze with the meaty ham hocks that pass for his forearms that must crack about four of my ribs.

The pain is searing and my head swims, and I'm pretty sure I do cough up something — my tongue, maybe, or a chunk of my lungs.

As I sputter and cough in the aftermath of Falko's assistance, and as Falko accordingly loosens his grip to whack my back encouragingly, Taran is still staggering backwards. He only stops when the back of his legs hit one of the chairs we pulled up in front of the fire and he plops down onto it heavily. He puts a hand on his forehead, his expression dazed and incredulous, a vivid mixture of relief and disbelief.

"There!" Falko says with satisfaction. "Whaddya say, Marek? That get it all out of your system?"

Somehow I manage to tell him most sincerely that it did.

"I'm awfully grateful *you* came by when you did," I also manage to tell him, since Gilles is just now coming back past the open door in the opposite direction, and seeing us all within, he pops his head in again.

"Goodness! Aren't you boys getting awfully *warm* in there?" he exclaims merrily. "Ah well, I suppose it is mighty hard to resist the first archive fire of the season!"

With that he wanders inside, rubbing his hands together as though preparing to join us, just as Taran gets up abruptly. He gives the bottom of his tunic a few jerks, smooths his unruly hair, and with one roll of his eyes in my direction as if to say it's been an escape much too close for him, he stalks out, his face blazing with embarrassment and sneering at Gilles.

I'm right behind him. When I'm at the door, Falko calls out jovially,

"Say, Marek! Just what were you choking on, anyway?," and without bothering to turn around, I mutter back,

"Just my *dignity*."

I hasten after Taran down the Journey hallway, but I'm not following him. My legs are as weak as water and I still feel like my chest is in a vice, and maybe Falko hasn't really jolted Taran entirely out of my system. But he has cleared my head enough for the point of Gilles's teasing comments finally to sink in.

The archive fireplace was *damaged* on the night our guild was overrun by villagers, and there have been no fires in the room all spring. None whatsoever.

Aristide was lying to me.

When somewhere in front of me Taran disappears inside his room and he slams the door, I don't slow down. I stumble straight on to Aristide's door, where I don't bother knocking.

I swing the door open angrily, and I go right in.

CHAPTER THIRTY-ONE

I'm lucky, and Aristide's room is empty. I guess I know I'm being foolishly reckless, yet again, and I should waste no time in looking for the diary. But I'm still flying on emotions that are bouncing between extremes, and although I *am* relieved that the boy who just caught me in Taran's arms was the habitually clueless Falko, 'relieved' doesn't really cover how I'm feeling. As soon as I close the door behind me, I sink down onto Aristide's cot before my wobbling legs can give out under me.

I bend my head down over my knees, to try to catch my breath and to keep my senses from swimming, and I grasp the bedframe with both hands, to stop them from trembling. But even though I grip the rough wood so hard I can feel the prickling of splinters, I can't stop my palms from itching with the sensation that they're still sliding over Taran. My lips feel bruised and swollen, even though Taran's lips barely touched them, and although I promised myself I'd never cry over a boy again, my eyes are brimming with tears of frustration.

I *have* been doing better about controlling myself this year. I *have*.

Just not around Taran.

At the sound of footsteps passing by out in the hallway, I pull myself together. I get up, and dry my eyes. I will away the sensation that every inch of my body is still crying out for Taran's. Then I get down to business.

I throw back the covers of Aristide's cot with arms that are still shaking, and I feel around under the mattress. I search down inside a quiver he's got leaning against the wall, and under his bedside table. And when I don't find anything, I ransack his cedar chest, rifling through his expensive clothes indiscriminately.

I find what I'm looking for at the very bottom of the chest. Aristide could be back any minute, and I can't wait. I open Meliana's notebook right then and there and I shuffle through it, too afraid that something or someone will stop me to look for a safer place to read it.

I'm tired of being jerked around by boys, lied to and confused by them.

So once I find my place in the little book's pages and I begin to read, I know I should be being more cautious. Instead, all I can think is,
there had better be some answers in here for me today, because right now, I really need some.

With my ribs still aching from Falko's bear hug and my lips aching even more, there's one thing in particular that can't wait one second longer. It's time to find out once and for all what kind of boy my father was — and if that gorgeous fiancée of Taran's really is my sister.

I promise myself that come hell or high water I won't put Meliana's journal down again until I've gotten my answer.

It's taken months of concerted effort, but my plans are all progressing nicely. Getting the Brecelyn boy to fall for me was easy. Child's play, no challenge at all. But I knew right away I'd have no trouble with him. I think the surprise of finding that I supposedly preferred him to his idolized Jan was almost as much a lure for him as my own charms. Be that as it may, I got him to propose in less than a week, and he even agreed to keep our engagement a secret until after the competitions, 'to avoid any hint of favoritism from falling on Father,' I said. Of course, the real reason is that I can't risk having Jan find out about it, until I'm really certain of him. Yes, getting Hugo right where I want him has been more than easy. But Jan Verbeke — that's been another matter.

He came around, eventually, of course. I knew he would. He's a boy, after all. And there aren't any other girls around here to catch his eye, even if he weren't too focused on his training to notice them, are there? Even so, it's been harder work than I bargained for. Exhausting. If it were anyone else, I wouldn't bother. I'd have given it up as a bad business and moved on a long time ago. But Jan ... he's not like the others. I can't give him up. He's like a fever in my blood, boiling under my skin, and I know I'd do just about anything to keep the tenuous grip on him I've fought so hard to win. I've never had so much trouble with a boy before. Maybe that's why I want him so much.

Juggling both Jan and Hugo has been tricky, although the logistics of it are really the least of my worries. It wouldn't do to have that idiot Jakob Mellor spouting off about Hugo to Jan, or vice versa, so I've also had to make sure nobody else can figure out what I'm up to. I've managed it all quite cleverly, if I do say so myself, and Mother's been a big help. She's naturally eager for a connection with the Brecelyns, too, but she doesn't begrudge me my pleasures. So she's wheedled the boys' tutorial schedules out of Father for me. After that, it's been easy. Now I only show up at the guild when I know one of the two of them is safely occupied in the archives, and since Guilly's taken to keeping a close watch on me, I've restricted my operations to the garden. That's fine by me. I've no desire to watch the boys train, and now that the boys know where to find me, I have no need of going out onto the butts to hunt for them. I let them come to me.

So far, I don't think anyone's the wiser. None of them has figured out the timing of my visits. It's meant having to flirt with all the boys to hide my preference, and it does get tedious, flattering that washout Royce, or suffering through Mellor's idea of courtship. I don't mind it when I'm just babysitting Hugo. But on days when he's safely out of my way, it's pure torture waiting for the others to disperse so I can be alone with Jan.

Jan. Jan. It must be obvious to all of them that he's the one I really want, no matter how I try to hide it. I can hardly keep my hands off him. He's like an addiction; I'm never satisfied. I just want more of him. Maybe it's because I know I shouldn't want him, or because I'm never quite sure where I stand with him. Oh, he finally came out and asked me himself for a token to carry with him into Seconds. That's when I knew I was starting to get my way. He won again, easily, of course — even though the competition was his worst skill, supposedly. But I couldn't see it. To me, Jan was like a god on the field. Now he's so far out in front of the others none of them can touch him, not even that lout Mellor in second place. But he's no threat to Jan. It is a foregone conclusion, whatever Jan might say about there being no such thing: Jan Verbeke will be the next Guardsman, and when he wins, who knows? Maybe I'll even consider marrying him. No, seriously! I just might do it. He's gotten to me that much.

If I'm going to pull it off, I've got to be smart, I've got to keep my wits about me. Lately I seem to be always on the verge of taking a wrong step. Jan's gotten moody around me, I can tell. I suppose it could be the competitions weighing on his mind, and I know it sounds crazy. But I've started to get the feeling that maybe he's beginning to get bored with me. It's probably all in my imagination, but the thought that he might be slipping through my fingers has made me quite anxious. I can't lose him. So I've decided to take a bold step. It's risky, since I usually don't let boys go too far too early; you have to keep the lure of sex dangling over their heads to hold them. That's what's always worked for me. And Jan's one of those upright, honorable boys. I'm always having to pretend to be loath to let him take liberties. But I've got to do something. So I'm going to lure Jan into making a serious move today. I'm sure I can do it, and once he's tasted the fruit, as they say, well, then he'll be hooked. I'll have him, right where I want him.

I've arranged to meet him in the garden this afternoon, while Hugo's in a training session. It was a little hard to convince him at first, since Jan usually practices all afternoon, staying out on the field long after all the other boys have gone in. He's such a perfectionist. Whenever I complain to him about it, pouting about how little time he spends with me or wheedling something like, 'You don't need more practice now, Jan! You're sure to win,' he just laughs back, saying 'It's not just about the competitions, Meli. I don't just want to win. I want to get keep getting better. Archery's a passion with me, and I want to be the best I can be. For that, you have to have discipline.' But eventually he agreed to quit early today, and in case things do go my way, I've taken precautions — a tiny sip from the little bottle of tonic my mother keeps in her case of medicines. Not too much, of course! It tastes awful, and too much could make me seriously ill. And after all, it's a sin. So I was sure to take just enough to prevent any inconvenient consequences.

...How can everything have gone so bloody wrong, when it all started out so well?!

I hardly know whether to count what happened in the chapel today as a triumph or a disaster. I got what I was after in the end, though, didn't I? In a way, and at least it's made me more determined than ever to see my plans through to fruition.

I arrived early for my meeting with Jan this afternoon, to bait my trap. The garden was empty, so I arranged myself prettily under a tree in the shade to wait for him. I made an alluring picture, with my skirts spread out artfully around me, one I knew he'd never be able to resist. I was sure I could maneuver him into kissing me without too much trouble. We'd see where things went, from there.

It wasn't long before I heard boys approaching from the direction of the butts. As soon as they come through the gate, banging it hard on its hinges and laughing and joking as they all tried to fit through the narrow opening at once, they came crowding around; they've learned to look for me there, and I usually reward them all with some mild flirtation. Today it didn't take me long to chase the others away with a few well-chosen comments, so I could have Jan to myself. I saw the amused looks they exchanged and the way they slapped Jan on the back before they wandered off into the guild hall, and I suppose I wasn't being as subtle as usual, but I couldn't wait. Not anymore.

Jan settled himself against the trunk of the tree I was under, leaning against it and looking down. Not at me, though, I noticed. He was fiddling with one of those infernal carvings he's always working on, a little animal or bird, or the like.

"Put that away, Jan!" I pouted, looking up at him prettily from under my lashes. "Why, anyone would think you'd rather handle that bit of cold, hard wood, than me. I'm anything but cold. Or haven't you noticed? ...Oh!"

As I was talking, little bits of debris had started floating down onto me from the tree. I'd been brushing aside the leaves and twigs and trying to ignore them, but when a large stick fell into my hair, I lost my composure. Maybe sitting under the tree wasn't such a good idea. Annoyingly, Jan laughed.

When an even larger twig fell, grazing my forehead, I let out another cry of dismay. Instead of making solicitous noises, though, Jan grinned up into the tree. So I followed his gaze upward. To my immense annoyance, there was a dirty little boy crouched on a branch high over my head. At first, I assumed it must be one of the kitchen boys. Then I saw it was wearing a dress. Of all things! It was a girl. Well, not much of one, but unmistakably a girl — a girl with a snub nose and dressed like a child, in an apron and clunky lace-up boots, though she can't really be that much younger than I am. Disgraceful.

"Watch it, wretch!" I hissed, while Jan called up to the girl in an amused voice,

"What are you doing up there, little bird? Building a nest in milady's golden hair?"

"It should be good for something, other than just covering that vapid head!" the little beast sniffed. And infuriatingly, Jan chuckled again.

"Filthy urchin!" I muttered. "Climbing trees, for pity's sake!" Then I called up to her warningly,

"You'd better watch out, or I'll set my father on you! We'll see how sharp that rude tongue of yours is, after he's given you a proper licking!"

"Easy now, Meli!" Jan protested, putting up his hands, but still grinning up into the tree. "It's just the groom's daughter. She means no harm. She climbs up there to watch the shooting, don't you, little bird?"

"That's where you should be, Verbeke. Practicing!" the girl called down archly. "Do you think Mellor's hanging around in the garden, drooling over blondes? He's out

shooting. If you don't watch out, you'll go as soft as she is," she punctuated this last with a rude gesture in my direction, "and Mellor'll catch you for sure!"

"Of all the nerve! How dare you!" I exploded, struggling to my feet. But before I could work myself up into an indignant reply, Jan cut me off with a gesture of truce, waving his hands in front of my face apologetically and acting like he was trying to keep from bursting into laughter again.

"Duly noted, little one," he said, still talking up to the girl and essentially ignoring me. "Now I think it's time to fly away, little bird, before the cat catches you in her claws. Here," he added, tossing the figurine in his hand up over my head. "Go find a safer place to make a nest, for this."

"Can I really keep it?" the girl asked wonderingly, making a neat catch and marveling at her luck. When Jan nodded in the affirmative, she scrambled off happily, hoarding the little wooden thing like a treasure. Pathetic.

You can bet I was plenty annoyed, and not just because my carefully arranged tableau had been ruined. I didn't really care about a wretched bit of whittling, of course. But I rather imagined Jan was about to give it to me. It was that whole silly scene with that ridiculous girl that rattled me, I confess. It threw me off. And so I made a mistake.

"What an ugly, dirty girl! Disgusting. I can't see why you encourage her, Jan," I said, settling my skirts again and rearranging my face into a simpering smile; the girl was gone, and I was prepared to pick up where we'd left off again. But Jan frowned. I shouldn't have forgotten that boys don't like it when girls are catty.

"She's just a child, Meli," he said admonishingly, "and she likes the archery. She's up there every morning, watching us boys practice. I've got to say, she's got a good eye. She's even given me a pointer or two." He shook his head, smiling to himself as though remembering it.

"A child, my foot!" I said, annoyed. "She's a girl, Jan. She's not watching you boys practice. She's just watching you. It's not archery she loves, trust me. It's you!"

"Really?" he said, sounding much more interested than he should, and looking off in the direction the girl had gone with a speculative look on his face.

By that time I'd gotten to my feet and brushed myself off, and I leaned back against the tree only inches away from Jan. I took his face between my hands, and turned it firmly to face mine. I'd had enough of the interruption, and it was time to get things back on track. So I gave him my most smoldering look, and purred,

"Are we going to spend all afternoon talking about children, and archery?"

"And what would you rather talk about, my lady?" he replied teasingly.

"We needn't talk at all. You might kiss me, you know," I said, letting one hand slide up his torso and then up around his neck, and he laughed. But he obliged me, and he leaned in to kiss me lightly on my lips.

Jan's kissed me before, of course. Just not very often. And at the feel of his lips on mine and his body under my hand, I forgot caution and I pulled him toward me harder, opening my mouth hungrily, trying to drink him in. Instead of responding eagerly as I was expecting, Jan pulled back in surprise at my open desire for him. It was so frustrating, I made another mistake.

A big one.

"Come into the chapel with me, Jan," I urged, my eyes shining. To my disgust, I sounded pleading. "Nobody'll be there, at this hour. We can be together, and nobody'll know."

"I think I'm a lot safer out here, Meli," he said lightly, making a joke of it. Then when he saw I was serious, he replied seriously, too:

"We both know what will happen if we go in there, Meliana. I'm only human. But it's up to the man to control himself, and not to give in to urges. Think of the consequences! It's not the right time. After we're married ..."

"Married?! You can't really expect me to marry you!?"

Through all of this I'd been trying to guide him toward the chapel door, and he'd been putting up his best gentle resistance, so it took me a minute to realize what I'd done. But Jan was being so ridiculously prim and upright, and his refusal to play along was so annoying, that before I could think what I was saying, I'd just blurted it out with scorn.

Jan went rigid, like I'd slapped him in the face. He came to a complete stop and stood there staring down at me as though he'd been turned to stone. Instantly, I tried to backpedal.

"Now Jan, don't look at me that way!" I pleaded, my voice cajoling, flirty. "You know I'd love nothing better than for us to marry. But a girl's got to think of her future, you understand that. Besides, my father would never agree to the match, surely you see that. He'd never let me marry a man with no prospects."

"No prospects?" Jan repeated, his expression not changing, and I could see I'd put a foot wrong again. His voice was so soft it was barely audible as he added,

"Is that really what you think of me?"

I started shaking my head vigorously and trying to explain, when he cut through my protestations with a tone in his voice I'd never heard from him. I didn't recognize it, but I knew enough to be afraid of it.

"Isn't a Guardsman good enough for you? Or are you the only one in Louvain who doesn't have faith that I can win?"

"Jan, I didn't mean ..."

"And what if I don't? I'll have my guild money, and I've been thinking," he continued, now sounding like there was something he cared about that he wanted to explain, that he wanted me to understand. "Maybe I'll follow my master's example, and stay on here near the guild somewhere, even if I do win. As a trainer, I could keep honing my own skills, and perfecting my method. Maybe pass it on to other boys. I wasn't kidding when I said I was a country boy, and I know myself. I know what would suit me, better than a life in Meuse. We could have a little cottage on the edge of town, where I can have a workshop out back. I like working with my hands. I'm good at it. It would be a good life and a good place to raise a family, just like my own childhood. The city's no place for kids. And we'd be together. That's what really matters, isn't it?"

As he was talking, I'd begun shaking my head harder and harder, almost frantically. What in the hell was he saying? I was sure it was a test of some kind, but I couldn't figure it out. I still don't know what he wanted me to say. Surely he couldn't really expect me to agree to that.

"Don't tease me, Jan!" I cried, trying to put my arms around his neck again. "Oh, I know you have a right to be angry, but can't you see I'm serious? Can't you see how much I want to marry you? But it's impossible!"

"And why is that, Meli?" he said coldly, putting up his hands to grasp my wrists firmly and to pull them from his neck. He was still holding them tightly out in front of him, almost painfully, as he asked,

"Would it really be so bad, to be a fletcher's wife?"

"I can't marry you," I cried out, groping for an answer. I never anticipated having such a conversation, and I'm not quick on my feet. That's why I always plan everything out. I had to say something, though, and quickly. So I said the first thing that came to mind. It was just my dumb luck that it was the truth:

"I can't marry you, because ... well, if you must know, I'm already engaged to Hugo Brecelyn, that's why!"

Damn it all! Even now I feel furious with myself when I think about it. How could I have let that slip out? It was more than a big mistake. It was fatal. I saw it right away.

If I'd thought Jan was rigid and unresponsive before, it was nothing to the expression that came over him then. Everything in him closed down, his face shuttered tight.

"Just when were you planning to tell me about this — before, or after we went together into the chapel?" he said hollowly.

"I know I should have told you, Jan! I just didn't know how!" I sputtered, as he looked down at me with a look so cold, he could have been made of ice. "I was afraid you'd react this way, that you wouldn't understand. But I can make you understand, can't I? You'll listen to reason, won't you Jan?"

Tears that were entirely real started streaming down my face. I wasn't acting anymore, but I might as well have been talking to a block of wood, one of his little carvings.

"You must believe me! You know you're the only one I want. And I tried to get out of it, I did! If you could have seen me, how I threatened, cajoled, why, I even starved myself," I continued, clutching at him and spouting any lie I could think of. "Father wouldn't budge. Not this time. It's too good a match. Surely you must see that."

When he didn't respond and I couldn't read his expression, I thought maybe I was getting through to him.

"Oh listen, do! I've been thinking. It doesn't have to be so bad. This can be good for us, actually. It is an advantageous match. There will be money. Lots of it." I started talking faster, warming to my theme. "As Hugo's wife, think of the connections I'll have. I can use them, to help you. I can get you a post, at his manor house. Something easy, with good pay. We'll be together and that's all that matters, just like you said, isn't it? Hugo need never know anything about us ..."

"Are you suggesting," he interrupted incredulously, "that I be your kept lover, after you're married to my friend?!?"

"It won't be like that," I protested. Why did he have make it sound so ugly? But before I could say anything else, he'd dropped my hands and he was turning away.

"No, it won't be like that," he said firmly, his back already to me. He was going to walk off, and leave me flat.

So I grabbed at him desperately. I couldn't let him go. If we parted like that it would be a disaster, and I knew what I had to do. There was only one way.

"Please, Jan, stay," I begged. "Stay and talk to me! We can work this out, I know we can. I can make you understand, make you see reason. Come with me into the chapel, just for a moment, where we can talk privately. Just talk," I promised softly, lowering my eyes and sounding conciliatory. But I let a hint of my old, flirty tone creep in, just enough for us both to know what I really had in mind, what was surely going happen, the moment I was alone with him, and before he could react, I put one hand flat on his chest and I slid the other back up around his neck.

I could tell he was going to try to resist. But even knowing how wrong it was, that I was engaged to another — as angry as he was, and maybe even hating me, a little — I knew he couldn't do it, not with my arms warm and close around him and the heat of our argument prickling between us. So for good measure, I pressed myself up shockingly close against him. And when his eyes flashed in response, I knew I had him.

"What in the *devil???* Marek?!?"

I didn't hear his footsteps in the corridor.

I didn't hear the door opening.

And I definitely didn't hear Aristide come in. But when I'm startled out of my intense concentration on the diary by an irate voice and I look up, sure enough, there he is, silhouetted in the doorway. Saying that he doesn't look happy to see me in his room is an understatement.

Then he sees what I've got in my hands.

Aristide's face convulses with rage, and when he lets out a roar and makes a lunge for me. So I do the only thing I can. Quick as a wink I duck under his outstretched arm and I dart out into the hallway, still clutching the diary. I don't know what I'm thinking, but I can't let go of it. I can't lose it. Not again.

Soon I'm barreling down the Journey hallway with Aristide hot on my heels, and I don't know where I think I'm going, either. All I know is I'm awfully glad I've been practicing my sprinting at squires' club all week.

We're still running full tilt when we hit the corner. And as we skid around it, as improbable as it seems, I'm still desperately trying to read. The little book is bobbling around in my hand and its pages are flipping, but I've got my head bent over it as I go skittering into the hallway outside the great hall, with Aristide gaining on me.

He probably would have already caught me, if he weren't wasting his breath on yelling at me,

"Why you no-good, stinking guttersnipe! You really *are* a thief!"

And that's when I crash right into a wall. Not a brick wall. This one is

MASTERS

more of a monolith. Because as it happens, right as I'm making the turn, a group of boys is coming around the corner in the opposite direction — and one of them is Falko.

I bounce painfully off Falko's chest, for the second time in less than twenty minutes.

He's now coming from the direction of barracks, and Rennie and Frans are with him. They, too, skid to a stop beside a surprised (but unmoved) Falko as we collide, and at just the same moment Aristide grabs me by the scruff of my tunic, yanking me backwards. I feel Meliana's diary slipping through my fingers.

As it does, I make one last-ditch attempt to finish reading the first line of another entry, the one to which the little book has fallen open while I've been running with it. The one which reads:

What a fool I've been! A careless, stupid fool. Of all things, I've gone and gotten myself pregnant. And it's all Jan's fault."

It's an answer, all right.

A definitive one, and as the little book falls to the ground, I'm glad enough now that it's no longer in my hand.

The book wafts to the floor with another flutter of its pages. It lies there for a moment, face up between me and the other boys, and now splayed open to the page with the sketch of Meliana on it.

We all stare down at it for a moment, before Frans bends down and picks it up.

"Tell that runt of yours to hand it over, *Marek*," Aristide sneers, still holding me by the back of my shirt and giving me a bone-rattling shake.

I give Frans a reluctant nod, and with an apologetic frown he starts to hand the book over to Aristide, when Falko suddenly exclaims,

"Hey, you can't talk to *my* squire that way! And say, isn't that book Marek's?!"

He peers at it a little more closely.

"It is! That's *Marek's* porn, the stuff he was hiding back at Brecelyn's castle in the suit of armor. Give it back to him!"

"You *knew*?" I cry stupidly, gaping up at the big guy with astonishment. Needless to say, it comes as quite a surprise to find that Falko can be more perceptive than I've previously given him credit, not to mention discrete. But Falko just sniffs,

"A St. Seb's man knows how to keep another man's secret," and I can't argue with him, although I can't say I appreciate it much when he adds,

"We *clouters* know how to keep our big mouths shut, Marek!"

I don't have the energy to spare to wonder at it or to be too embarrassed by his assumptions about my reading habits, or even by what a fool I must have looked to him at the castle, thinking I was hiding the little book from him. Given the scene he just witnessed in the archives, though, I do rather have to hope his flashes of insight are few and far between.

"As it happens, it's *mine*," Aristide snaps, cutting in on our absurd little exchange impatiently and putting out his hand for the book. When all Falko does is frown, he adds nastily,

"It's my word against a squire's. Of course, we *could* go along to Master Guillaume's office, and see whom *he* believes. We could, that is, if both you and Tristan have any use for squires who've had both their hands cut off for stealing."

With that, the game is up. There's nothing for it but to relinquish the diary back into Aristide's hands.

"I've got a good mind to turn you in to the master," Aristide says to me as soon as he's got the book back, but he's just saving face in front of Falko. He's even less eager for Master Guillaume to see the notebook than I am, as is clear from the fact that he's already striding off, tucking Meliana's journal safely into the sleeve of his tunic, and calling back over his shoulder,

"Don't bother looking for this again, Marek. This time, I'll put it where not even a light-fingered thief like you could ever find it," while Falko slings his arm consolingly around my shoulder.

"Don't take it so hard, squire!" he says, when he sees the expression on my face. "The world is full of porn. In fact, if you'd care to accompany me to the market square this afternoon with a little change in your pocket ..." he offers, and I have to say, I don't feel very consoled.

My head is reeling, and Rennie, who was too much of a coward to do anything but hide behind Falko while Aristide was here, has started elbowing me and asking me if I pocketed the book out of Master Gheeraert's secret stash, and soon the boys are all teasing me playfully about being a thief. But I don't play along. I just put my head down, shrug off Falko's arm, and I head outside without looking behind me.

I march straight on down the long hallway.

I march past barracks, and down the masters' hallway.

Then I let myself out and I go around past the kitchen gardens, out to the place where I chanced to observe Remy with Auguste's girlfriend, the place behind the stables that can't be seen from any vantage point anywhere in the yard. I slump against the wall where I know nobody can see me, and I rest my head back against its rough wood.

And then I let the tears I've been holding back ever since I was wrenched from Taran's arms fall in earnest.

So it's true.

It's true!

It's all true, every awful suspicion I ever had of my father, all of it.

It shouldn't hurt so much to get certain confirmation of what I knew already, but it does. It's one thing to suspect an ugly truth, and another thing entirely to see it written out in black and white on a page in front of you.

My father *did* father a bastard, and on the fiancée of a fellow Journey. And for whatever happened to him thereafter, I know he was himself partly to blame — for turning Hugo Brecelyn into an enemy from a friend.

I stay out behind the stables for a long time, staring up at the sky unseeingly. But there's something that's upsetting me much more than the foolish notion that the perfect image I had of my father is tainted. From the sound of it, my father *was* a noble boy. He was just young and hot-blooded, and he made a mistake. God knows, I've made plenty of those myself.

It's that I've been judging him so harshly in my mind for so long, simply for being human. For making the *very same mistake* I can't seem to stop making myself.

And it's that I miss him, more than ever.

I'd been thinking I was getting over him, but that was foolish. I know now that will never happen.

How I wish he were here with me, right now! I wish at least that I had *someone* I could talk to. I even almost wish that Melissande were here, so I could tell her that we're sisters. How sweet it would be to have a confidant, someone to share the secrets I can never tell to Tristan, even when he isn't being *Gilles*. I have a feeling she better than anyone would understand.

Because there *was* one thing in the journal about which I was entirely in error.

In it, I'd thought my father sounded a little like Taran.

He didn't.

He sounded *a lot* like him.

I wipe my nose with my sleeve, and I lean back again heavily against the boards of the wooden wall behind me. And I give it one good bang with the back of my head, hard — just for the hell of it. I squeeze my eyes shut, and I run my tongue over my upper lip to wipe away the feeling that's still lingering there that my lips are just about to press against Taran's.

And then I mutter to myself determinedly,

"Just don't think about him. Just don't think about him."

And it works. It works! It really d ...

Oh, who am I kidding?!

It's not working at all.

On the periphery of my vision, a blur of something big and white catches my eye. It's the gazebo Gilles commissioned, standing silent sentinel in a corner of the yard. The kitchen boys must have rolled it out here to tuck it safely out of the way until the competitions, and it looks essentially finished. At least nobody's working on it, and I can see it's acquired the coat of paint I predicted. Looking at it now, I could be back in Brecelyn's empty garden on the day we left the castle, and I don't know why. On a whim, I go over, and I plop myself down heavily on the gazebo's rough wooden step.

I might as well. I guess I never really left it.

CHAPTER THIRTY-TWO

I'm still sitting on the gazebo steps with my head in my hands over two hours later.

I'm in no mood to go back to the Journey hallway, or to the archives, or out onto the butts — anywhere I could run into Taran. I've been sitting here all afternoon, chastising myself for letting him get me so unraveled so close to the trials, and trying to tell myself it's just the natural result of being trapped here at close quarters with him. That it's only for a few more months, at most, one way or other. That maybe it's even some sort of test, sent by Saint Sebastian.

A few short months, that's all.

If I can't control myself that long, I don't deserve to be a Guardsman's squire.

I'm no mood to go to barracks either, just to be met with more jokes about being a thief. So when Marcel spots me on his way across the yard and he stops to ask me to go out to the workshop tent with him, I agree.

"Ah, Marek! This is well met indeed," Marcel exclaims, putting out a hand and helping me to my feet. "As it happens, that chap I was telling you about the other day is here now. You know, the new boy with no experience. That is, if you'd care to come out and meet him," he adds, rather tentatively, and I can't blame him after the way I bolted the last time he suggested it.

When I don't shy away or run off raving, he continues,

"And if you're game, I thought you could start right in working with him tomorrow morning. You know, to get him started, before the competitions." He doesn't say, "before there's a chance you and your master are out, and it's too late," but I bet that's what he's thinking.

I've already promised and I'm going to have to do it sometime, and I figure it'll provide a welcome diversion. So I tell Marcel that for once, the timing of it sounds perfect.

As we fall into step side by side, I see Marcel must be coming directly from a meeting with Master Guillaume. He's come into the yard from the side door that leads out from the corridor near the masters' offices, and under one arm he's got a jumble of scrolls of the kind that usually contain orders from the master. Under the other he's carrying a rectangular wooden lidded box, and as we walk along, whatever's inside it is periodically giving out a gentle, tinkling rattle.

"A little blue bottle, in a wooden case," I mumble, the sound having jogged loose an unpleasant memory.

"What's that?" Marcel asks. Then he laughs. "Oh, *this!*" he says, and he shifts around the things in his arms enough to open the lid of the box for me. Inside is an assortment of copper implements, awls and punches of the kind used for tooling leather, complete with a little matching hammer.

"A gift, from the master," Marcel exclaims warmly, and I murmur appreciative noises, since the set really is lovely.

"Master Guillaume can be extraordinarily generous," he beams. "What he's doing for this local boy goes to prove it. Although it is something of a headache, for me."

"About that," I say, as we weave our way past an open construction pit and between the pavilions out to the far field. "Remind me. Just what do you want me to do, exactly?"

Marcel fills me in, no doubt repeating the story precisely as he's already told it to me, while I nod along thoughtfully, doing my best this time to pay more attention than I did the last and to shut out the other thoughts still rattling around in my head. Only it's not long before I'm not really listening again, because I've started to have a funny feeling. Something about it all seems strangely familiar.

I suppose it should, since Marcel's already told me all about it. Only now I remember vaguely that there was something that troubled me the first time he told me about this charity case of the master's, and the same nebulous feeling of unease I had then has started to steal over me. But it could simply be because at the time, Taran was lying wounded under a tree.

"You see how it is," Marcel is saying when we reach the workshop tent, and while he holds open the tent flap for me. "He's got no fletching background whatsoever, and I have to say, he seems pretty unpromising. But his father was a friend of a friend of the master, so we've got to do our best to accommodate him."

It takes a moment or two for my eyes to adjust to the dim interior of the tent, so in contrast with the bright afternoon light. At first all I can make out are the shapes of the workbenches and the featureless outlines of men seated behind them, bent over their work. But as Marcel ducks inside behind me, form slowly resolves itself from shadow and across the tent, I see that there is a large boy standing with his back to me, his shoulders slightly stooped to allow him to peer down and observe one of the fletchers working a nock into the shaft of a freshly sanded arrow.

"Just do your best with him, won't you, Marek?" Marcel says to me softly, sounding apologetic and putting a hand on my back to guide me over to him. "I can't help but feel sorry for him, with his father dying of plague and all."

From behind, the boy looks awfully big and clumsy to be a fletcher, but I don't say so. And if there's something a little familiar about the look of him, too, that's hardly surprising. All these local boys look the same to me, and I don't actually know any of them personally. So all I really notice is that he's surprisingly large, more of a man than a boy, and although his frame's not athletic like the Journeys', his body is so hulking, I can't help but be reminded of a great big ox that's come lumbering in from a field.

Then Marcel taps the boy on the shoulder, and he turns around.

He looks down at me.

I look up at him.

And then the whole tent sways.

Or maybe I do, or he does, or else we're all swaying together, and my heart takes a crazy leap in my chest. For one moment of pure dread, I really wish it were that day again, when Taran was lying out in the clearing and I was running to him, away from this tent — and that I had just kept running, and never come back again. Or maybe that Taran had shot *me*, instead. At least, right now I'd rather be lying wounded and bleeding out somewhere under a tree — or even facing down Taran in the archives, or wrestling over the notebook with Aristide — or anywhere, really.

Anywhere, but here.

Because there *is* one boy in Louvain that I know. Just one. Now he's standing right in front of me, and I'm staring up into the astonished face of my former fiancé-to-be.

Somehow, I'd managed to forget all about him.

The casual greeting I was about to make comes out as a gurgle, as Marcel exclaims happily,

"Luc, this is Marek. Marek, meet Luc. Luc Fournier."

My hand was already extended out stiffly in greeting, and I leave it there. But the rest of my body recoils in amazement, and my expression must be an impressive grimace of shock and fear.

From the look of wide-eyed shock on Luc's face, too, I'm sure he's recognized me.

Then I blink my eyes, and the stunned look on Luc's face is gone.

It's slid right off his face, as quickly as it appeared. So I force myself to swallow down my fear. Maybe what I thought I saw in Luc's eyes was just my own panic, reflected back at me, since the expression on his face as I calm myself is actually one of mildly inquisitive politeness, and he's simply gazing down at me rather shyly. He looks as harmless as a fly.

Still, I can't help it. I turn around and I dart straight out of the tent. From the fleeting glimpse I get of Marcel as I push past him in a mad dash to the door flap, I'm sure he thinks I'll soon be halfway across the far field.

I'm not running off again, though. I just have to get outside, before I'm violently sick.

I only just make it. As soon as I hit the outside air my stomach heaves, and I only manage to stumble a few steps down along the side of the tent before I have to brace myself with one hand against its canvas wall to vomit.

Is it conceivable that Luc didn't recognize me, as easily as I recognized him?

It's not until my stomach is empty and I've had a chance to breathe that a possibility occurs to me.

Luc only saw me once, and a long time ago. To say I've changed a lot since then is an understatement. My hair, my face, my clothes and body, not to mention my mannerisms and demeanor — they must all be quite different, and I feel a little startled myself, thinking about it. Besides, if Luc Fournier was startled at the sight of me just now and he then tried to hide it, that would hardly be surprising. It's how most people react, the first time they get a good look at the scars on my face.

I'll just have to hope I'm right, and brazen it out. So I spit, and I compose myself. And then I go back inside with as much dignity as I can muster, although it isn't easy. Both Marcel and Luc are exactly as I left them, and from the stiff way Marcel is standing it's obvious that he wasn't at all sure I was going to come back inside again. It's also obvious that he and everyone else in the tent have been standing around silently listening to the sound of me outside retching.

All I can do is mumble apologetically, "must have been something I ate."

Nobody says anything, and Luc is still shuffling about awkwardly and staring down at his feet. So I wipe one hand down my trouser leg to steady myself, and I stretch it out to give Luc a belated welcoming shake.

After my dramatic reaction to meeting him, he understandably hesitates to take it. So I say with a little nervous chuckle,

"Don't worry. I won't bite you."

Before the phrase is past my lips, I regret it. I think I even snap my teeth at Luc a little, trying to catch my words back.

By God Almighty and all His Saints, and by my St. Sebastian! What in the world made me say that? It's the *exact same thing* I said to Luc Fournier the first time I met him. In the stress of the moment, thinking back to that day must have brought it out.

I dart a sidelong glance up at Luc through the thick haze of sawdust swirling around in the murky tent, afraid to see his reaction.

But to all appearances, Luc hasn't reacted. He's still looking down at his own feet with an open and a slightly dull-witted expression, with nothing about his demeanor to suggest that the comment registered with him at all, or even that he's thinking anything. He seems quite sweet, if a little simple-minded — even more so than I'd thought when first we met.

So I have no idea what to make of it, when at last he does take my hand to give it a timid shake. And still not daring to meet my eyes, softly he says,

"Good. Then I won't have to bite you back."

After that, somehow I manage to stand with a crooked smile plastered on my face while Marcel coaxes us into exchanging a few more pleasantries. Before long we've fixed it up between the three of us to meet back here first thing the next morning so I can give Luc his first lesson. I must look pretty pale, though, because throughout the discussion Marcel keeps darting me concerned little looks. Soon he's guiding Luc gently back to his observation post by other fletchers, and he's sending me on my way with an order to lie down in barracks until time for mess. Then when I'm halfway out the door, he calls me back for a moment with a frown, and I'm afraid he's going to ask me for some kind of explanation.

Instead, he puts a hand on my shoulder.

"A word of advice, Marek," he exclaims sternly. "Tonight at dinner, don't eat so many hard boiled eggs."

I give him a wan smile, even though I don't think he meant it as a joke. I'm too busy worrying about the joke *Luc* just made to reassure Marcel, and hoping fervently that it's the only one the big, slow boy knows. Otherwise, I am in big, big trouble — because unless I'm greatly mistaken, Luc's quip in response to *my* joke was the exact same one he made, one year ago.

I trudge back to barracks, feeling like there's still sawdust swirling around inside my head and my boots are made of lead. I hardly notice passing any of the colorful pavilions, or the noisy construction crews still busily at work around them. And when I cross out into the yard and I pass the replica of the white gazebo, I vaguely remember that not so long ago I was sitting there, upset about something.

But I can't remember what it was.

Compared with the arrival at the guild of Luc Fournier, everything else now seems to me to be trivial.

I'M JITTERY ALL THE REST OF THAT AFTERNOON AND EVENING. I can't sit still at mess, where I barely eat a bite or say a word to anyone. Taran's nowhere to be seen and Aristide's at the far end of the table, but I hardly notice. All around me the boys are abuzz with speculation about the upcoming tests; while the Journeys talk over each other trying to guess what the others are going to do for their exhibitions, the squires are just as noisily helping Pascal put the finishing touches on his proposal speech. It's just the stuff I usually love, and ordinarily I'd be eagerly joining in.

Tonight I can't concentrate on any of it. I'm jiggling my leg so hard that my knee keeps banging the underside of the table, and now I *really* wish there were someone I could confide in. But Tristan is back in full Gilles mode and he doesn't seem to notice, and anyway, what could I possibly say to him? *I think the new fletcher's apprentice knows I'm a girl, because, you see, at this time last year, I was about to be engaged to him?* Tristan may have said he'd forgive me anything, but this would surely be too much, even for him.

I don't sleep much that night, either. I'm too busy wondering if the fleeting expression I thought I saw on Luc's face was real or imagined, and whether that joking comeback of his was some kind of coded warning. I tell myself that Luc barely dared to look at me directly, even back when we first met. He probably couldn't have recognized me again that very day, let alone a whole year later, and St. Sebastian's has to be the last place he would ever be expecting me. It must have been an unconscious trick of his memory, dredged up in response to the half-remembered comment of my own. But after such a brief encounter I can't be certain of anything, and by the time I've convinced myself one way, only to change my mind back again at least a hundred times, I'm eager for the dawn to come. Anything has to be better than this uncertainty.

It's easy enough to get up earlier than usual the next morning, since I never really went to sleep. And when I swing my legs over the side of my cot, they're still jittery. But after hours of thinking it all through, I've managed to calm myself. If Luc intended to go to the masters, he would have done so immediately. By now a whole afternoon and evening have passed, and anyway, Luc is a nice boy, the son of my father's friend. Even if he did recognize me, maybe he's just waiting to talk to me in private, so I can explain. He's lost a father, too, so I think he'll understand.

I dress hastily, and I waste no time in making my way out to the shop through the cool morning air. There's no point in delaying the inevitable. My hands are steady, when I raise them to my lips to blow against the chill, although it's more mechanical than necessary on a spring morning like this — a tick that betrays my nervousness. And they're only shaking slightly as I cross the yard, though that may not be entirely because of Luc. My route takes me past the rolling gazebo, and I haven't really forgotten everything else that's happened to me recently.

When I enter the workshop tent, Luc's already there. He's sitting huddled awkwardly at one of the workbenches in the back, eyeing the tools laid out in front of him with a look bordering on alarm. Then he glances up. And he lets out an audible sigh, as soon as he spots me coming through the open flap. An unmistakable look of recognition *does* light up his broad, open face. But it's the kind of look a man lost in a foreign city might give to a friendly stranger who's materialized to guide him safely through the perils of the place, and I see nothing more there than the shy recognition of an acquaintanceship that goes back only as far as yesterday. He looks uncomfortable and out of place — both like he can barely contain his relief that I've arrived to take him in hand, and nervous about getting a lesson, even from a squire.

Nobody's *that* good an actor. And he *is* a nice boy, just as I remember him. Finding no threat in him gives me such a welcome feeling of release, I end up almost enjoying a task I would have surely otherwise resented.

I never quite relax, however. And I can't say why. There's just some undercurrent there between us, something that feels off. Maybe it's my own sense of guilt or the simple fact that it's not so easy to throw off a long night's worth of anxiety and suspicion, and I'd be lying if I said I wasn't still keyed-up and jittery from that almost-kiss of Taran's. But throughout our whole lesson I still feel nervous and tense, like something more is coming, and I can't seem to shake a little lingering kernel of unease.

I spend most of that first session with Luc explaining the tools and going over the basics with him. Then I leave him to the task of sanding down a big stack of arrow shafts for the rest of the day. They've actually already been shaped and they don't really need much more smoothing, but it seems safe, since it hasn't taken me long to see that Luc Fournier may be a nice boy, but he's never going to make anything but a wretched fletcher. His big, calloused hands are just as clumsy as I suspected they would be, and although he listens to my explanations attentively, I'm not sure how much of what I'm saying is getting through to him. He's strong, though, so I'm sure I can find a way to make him into a useful addition to Marcel's team, and with Master Guillaume sponsoring him, his position is secure. So I tell him,

"Just concentrate on that today, and we'll work up to the rest," and I head off for morning line-up, feeling a strange combination of relieved but on edge.

All during drills, after my night of terrors I'm giddy with light-headedness fueled by a lack of sleep. With the trials fast approaching, the boys are restless, too, and Rennie's wasted no time in telling everyone about my run-in with Aristide. All the squires are accordingly teasing me every chance they get, jokingly calling me a thief. But I think what's really unnerving me more than anything is that I can feel Taran's eyes on me all morning, even from down the field.

From the frown on his face, I bet he's trying to figure out what happened between me and Aristide yesterday, and even more, why I look so wound up and rattled. When I imagine telling him it's the thought of my fiancé, now safely ensconced out in the shop and inexpertly sanding down arrow shafts, I even start laughing. I don't care if I'm upsetting him or if his curiosity is piqued, or even that I must seem a little hysterical. I know Taran was almost as shaken up by our debacle in the archives as I was, and that's what he's thinking about — and for once, it looks like *he's* the one who's feeling guilty about it.

Just as practice is winding down, Master Leon makes an announcement that confirms this assumption: our squires' club practices are to be suspended until after the trials, Taran himself having requested it, on the pretext that our squad is ready and that he needs what precious time is left to practice with his own squire. With Firsts so close, it's only a day's reprieve. But it will mean Taran and I won't have to face each other again until after the competitions, by which point so much else will have happened, our little dust-up in the archives will be old business.

It's a most welcome turn of events, one that can't help leaving me feeling that I've spent a long night worrying over nothing. And maybe that's why it doesn't occur to me sooner that Luc Fournier could still pose a serious threat, even if he never recognizes me.

◂––––––▸

THAT AFTERNOON WE RUN THROUGH THE BOYS' TRICK SIX TIMES, before deciding to knock off early. The boys have polished the exhibition to a shine, and if I do say so myself, it really is ingenious. In its scaled-back form, the shots involved may not quite look impossible. But they do look plenty difficult. Pascal and I have even worked up a little routine to use for setting it all up efficiently, and to make it into something of a performance of our own. It's just a bit of coordinated dashing about, tossing the wands and posts to each other theatrically, but I think that's looking polished, too, and I know we're as ready as we're ever going to be.

Still, once Tristan's ambled back to the line after his last successful turn at shooting the posts for Gilles, I can't help asking him a little nervously,

"Is it enough, master?"

"Not enough? Don't be silly! Why, it's quite the opposite."

"Is it *too much*, then?!" I cry.

"What a worrier you are, Marek! Too much, of *me*? There's no such thing." He sniffs, then he grins cockily, switching back smoothly into his butts personality.

"Unless of course, what you mean is *too much* over-practicing."

Tristan's just being lazy, the way he always is right before the competitions, and the boys have been switching personas back and forth all afternoon for the trick so often that it's starting to get dizzying. But everything is going so well that it would be foolhardy for the boys to risk straining themselves two days before a test they're so sure ace, and as crazy as it seems, what Tristan probably does need most now is more time lounging around with his feet up, in the manner of Gilles.

As soon as our practice breaks up, Pascal announces that he's off to find a secluded spot to practice his proposal, having refused to set foot inside the fateful gazebo in advance of the big day on the pretext that it's bad luck. I suspect he simply doesn't have the stomach for it, and I can't say I blame him. In my experience, nothing good ever happens in gazebos. He needs all the practice he can get, so I offer to clean up the field and to take the materials for our exhibition back out to the shop tent for safekeeping by myself, intending to stay on and do some fletching. I figure I can kill two birds with one stone, since I've been feeling a little guilty about leaving Luc out there alone with nothing to do for hours but sand wood.

Once I've pulled up the stakes from the field and I've gathered up all the little dowels and strings, I straighten up to see to my surprise that Tristan is approaching with the wands in an unwieldy bundle under his arm. When I try to take them from him with a word of thanks, he announces his intention of coming along with me.

"I'd be glad of the company, of course, master," I tell him. "Maybe you should rest up, though, and save your strength. Besides, you can't fletch."

"I have no intention of fletching, Marek."

"Then what are you going to do?" I ask him, a little nervous at the idea of having him just sitting there watching me. I rather enjoy it when he's Tristan, but I suspect I'll find it unnerving when he's Gilles.

He puts his finger to the side of his nose, and says confidentially,

"I'm going to investigate, of course," and I blink. I was sure he told me he was done with all of that.

"I intend to have a word with that new apprentice Marcel's got out there, Luc What's-his-name."

There's a brief interlude, in which all the stakes and all of the dowels drop from my hands with a clatter.

Tristan puts down the wands, and he gets down on his knees next to me as I make a show of picking up the scattered items. What I'm really doing is trying to keep him from seeing the panic on my face and thinking, *this can't be happening. This can't be happening.*

Let's just say, it's a complication I didn't anticipate.

After we've gotten everything gathered up and we're on our feet facing each other again, I stand there clutching my bundle for a while, not making any move to get going or saying anything. Without looking up at him, finally I ask miserably,

"Whatever *for*, Tristan?!" hoping that he'll attribute the quaver in my voice to my dislike of his investigations in general.

Tristan looks over his shoulder, as though to make sure Gilles and Pascal are out of earshot. Then he pulls me aside a little further and looks down at me with a serious expression.

"I didn't want to upset you, Marek," he says gently. "Rumor has it the boy's been claiming that *his* father was *your* father's friend. He may know something about what happened to him."

There's another brief interlude, in which I feel all the blood drain from my face. It must be puddling somewhere down around my toes, and my lips feel too numb to say anything.

"*Tristan* ..." I finally manage, and from the pleading in my voice he must know I'm going to try to dissuade him, because he interrupts me by putting one of his hands over mine.

"I may not be able to do anything about your father's murder, Marek.

Believe me, I've tried my best. But I won't have failed you entirely, if I can find out the truth about your father's accident. If this Luc boy's father really was your father's old friend, he might be the only one who can tell us. The only one besides Master Guillaume, that is. Would you really prefer me to go and ask *him*?"

I can see Tristan's bent on doing it, and nothing I can say will dissuade him. So I bow my head and I let Tristan lead the way through the maze of tents towards the shop, and although I'm touched by Tristan's determination, mostly I'm wondering as I go what possible words I can use to introduce my master to my erstwhile fiancé. Standing idly by and listening to Tristan grill Luc Fournier about Jan Verbeke is going to be excruciating. Maybe Tristan's right, though, and Luc *does* know something, and anyway, I suppose it's better than having him do it when I'm not there to hear what Luc says.

"Everything all right, kid?" Tristan asks me as we trudge along, looking back over his shoulder at me and noticing my sullen frown. "Taran's not bothering you again, is he?"

"No, not him." I tell him. "No more than usual."

"There! What did I tell you? My warning to him in the garden did the trick," he replies, his satisfied tone shading into one of Gilles's. "I told you I knew what I was doing."

I let the comment pass. I'm too nervous to respond, and sarcasm is always lost on Gilles.

When we get to the shop, for one blissful moment I think that Luc's not there. He's not at the workbench where I left him this morning, and although the pile of shafts he was supposed to be smoothing is in something of a disarray, I can't really tell if he's done any work on them. They don't look any different than they did this morning, which isn't surprising, since they were already virtually ready anyway.

I'm just casting a quick look into the corners of the tent and satisfying myself that Luc is nowhere to be seen when Marcel notices us loitering around the workbench. He comes over to join us, and seeing us surveying the mess in front of us, he says a little grumpily,

"If you're looking for the Fournier boy, he's out back somewhere unloading wood from the supply wagon. I figured that'd be a safe enough job for him," and I can't help feeling a little sorry for Luc and his lack of skill. Just not nearly as sorry as I'm feeling for myself.

It takes us a while to find him. When we head around back to the supply wagon, I don't see Luc anywhere. I'm content not to look for him too hard, but when Tristan asks one of the workmen tossing freshly cut logs down out of the wagon about him, the man motions with his head towards a nearby line of diminutive storage tents.

From the nearest one a loud ruckus is coming, and my heart sinks. I can hear the commotion over the clatter the heavy logs are making as they crash down into an unruly pile at our feet, and even over the general din of activity around the pavilions and of construction floating out to us from the periphery of the yard. This noise is quite different — it's not the usual booms and shouts of labor. This shouting is sustained, more like cheering mixed with squawking, and what sounds strangely like the flapping of wings. It's a most uninviting sound, but when Tristan thanks the man and strides over to duck inside, I have no choice but to follow.

As soon as I stick my head into the little tent, I find it so filled to capacity that following Tristan inside isn't easy. I've got to push and shove, and even then it's hard to squeeze my way through an assortment of burly, red-faced men who are packed into the tight space like herrings in a brine barrel. From the way the men are all pushed up against each other and gesticulating wildly, if I weren't grasping onto the back of Tristan's cape with both hands I'd surely have already gotten separated from him. There must be over three dozen men crammed in here, none of whom appears to share the Journeys' enthusiasm for bathing.

To make matters worse, they're all shoving each other back flush against the sides of the tent, now surging forward eagerly and now jostling back against the canvas, alternately trying to get a better view and to stay out of the way of a frenzy of beaks and claws that's occupying the center of the tent.

"Cock fighting! How disgusting," Tristan mutters, pulling me disturbingly far into the center of the tent behind him and ignoring the two small but fierce gamecocks that are indeed lunging and flying at each other with a flurry of wings. They're locked in deadly combat only inches away, and I'm so much smaller than the other men I have to hope the cocks don't think that Tristan is shoving me into the ring with them.

"So, which one is he?" Tristan demands, turning his back on the spectacle and striking a pose as he surveys the crowd of scabrous sportsmen before him with displeasure, and I can't help but feel that his, too, is a rather dangerous position. Not because I think the men will attack him. Although they look like they want to, they must know he's a Journey, and they don't dare. But they might not have to, since by chance Tristan is wearing Gilles's peacock outfit again this afternoon and I rather fear him turning his back on the roosters, lest one of them should confuse him for a competitor and take his feathered cape as a threatening display.

"I don't see him, master. Let's get out of here," I say, but Tristan doesn't pay me any mind, since it's obvious I can't see anything. Even if I weren't too short, I've buried my face against Tristan's shoulder after getting one good look out of the corner of my eye at the so-called 'sport' that's under way. The chests of both cocks are already shredded and dripping with blood, yet two men who must be the owners of the birds keep prodding them with sticks anyway, urging them to slash at each other with vicious curved metal spikes that have been fitted onto leather cuffs and tied over the natural spurs on the backs of their legs.

Instead, Tristan clears his throat, and over the roar of the men and the screaming of the birds, he demands loudly,

"I say, gentlemen! Which one of you fine fellows is Luc Fournier?"

"That's 'im, right there!" one of the men laughs, kicking the nearest of the roosters so that it momentarily flies our direction and ricochets with a squawk off one of Tristan's boots. This is met by a chorus of riotous laughter and swearing, while another man who must be the owner of the bird gives Tristan a piece of his mind, replete with colorful expletives. I'm beginning to reconsider my assumption that these men won't dare to beat a Journey, so when Tristan quips,

"Come, come! There's no call for *fowl* language!," I tug at his sleeve.

"Come *on*, Tristan," I'm hissing, "Gilles will kill you if you get cock's blood on his favorite tights. And if it's your *own* blood, he's not going to like it either," when I spot Luc.

He's on the opposite side of the tent, among a group of thugs dressed in the garb of Kingsmen. With his hunched shoulders and his soft, rounded face with its slightly wide-eyed and vacant expression, he stands out like a sore thumb. He's spotted me, too, and I can't pretend I haven't seen him, since just as Tristan's eyes follow the direction of my gaze across the tent, Luc gives me a tentative, friendly little wave. Either the boy really is the best actor I've ever seen, or he's much too naïve to be let loose on the guild grounds. I'm going to have to have a serious talk with him about the dangers of gambling.

Having succeeded in locating Luc, Tristan makes short work of hustling him out the back of the tent. As I slip out after them, one of the rougher-looking men calls after us,

"Sneaking off, Fournier? Don't think I'll forget. When *my* bird wins, you'll still owe me, despite your fancy Journey friends," and I fear it's too late to keep the men from taking advantage of him.

Once we're clear of the rank air of the tent, Tristan wastes no time in setting about questioning Luc about my father (well, actually, he *does* waste a little time, since the first thing he does is elbow me in the ribs and say, "*Phew*, Marek! There's only one word for the atmosphere in *there*, eh? But I'm not a man to use the same joke twice"). He's pretty blunt about it, and he doesn't bother to explain himself, which from my perspective is just as well. I'm eager to get this over with.

To my immense relief, Luc shows no signs of being surprised by Tristan's questions. He just looks puzzled and a little star-struck that a Journey in all his splendor is deigning to talk to him. He gives every appearance of being too simple to wonder why my master is so curious about the now long-dead Jan Verbeke, and it doesn't take Tristan long to discover that Luc doesn't know much more than the usual rumors about my father's Journey days.

Even what he has heard is spotty, to say the least.

"Didn't your father *ever* talk to you about Verbeke's accident?" Tristan finally demands of him, sounding exasperated.

"You mean when he fell off his horse, right in the middle of his butts competition?" Luc replies, and I shake my head.

"It was *clouts*," I think, but I don't correct him, and it doesn't really matter, since this was all Luc had heard about the accident anyway.

By this time I'm motioning with my head to Tristan as if to say we're wasting time, and we should be on our way. Not even the mention of my father's name has sparked the faintest flicker of recognition in Luc's eyes, or ruffled the benign and slightly benighted expression on his face. But even though he really doesn't seem to know much about my father's past, there are a few things he could say about the Verbeke family in general that I'd much rather he didn't, although I'll confess. I've been so busy worrying that Luc might be jogged by the conversation into remembering *me* that I haven't really stopped to think too hard about what else he might tell Tristan. It's only starting to occur to me that there are quite a few other things I know for a fact that Luc could tell him that would be very hard to explain.

Sure enough, just when I think even Tristan is tiring of trying to squeeze information from such an unpromising source, the conversation takes a dangerous turn.

Tristan sticks out his hand to Luc, to offer him a dismissive parting shake. I'm rocking eagerly forward on my toes in anticipation of bidding Luc a most welcome farewell myself, when Tristan pauses, and asks him casually,

"So, what was your father's connection to the guild, anyway?"

"My father?" Luc says stupidly, almost as though he's forgotten he had one. "Why, none," and Tristan stops in his tracks.

"None? Then how did he know the master?" he inquires, for some reason not letting go of Luc's hand.

"Master Guillaume? He didn't, that I know of. Not personally. In fact, I don't think they'd ever met."

"Wait a minute," Tristan frowns, pulling Luc a little closer to him. "If your father didn't know Master Guillaume *at all*, then how did you get this gig? It's pretty obvious you're no fletcher."

"I told you, it was because of Jan Verbeke. He was a great favorite of the master's, everyone knows that. The master really loved him, and I was going to be his apprentice."

"*You?*" Tristan demands, with a sputter. "You, the apprentice of Jan Verbeke?" and I rock back so far on my heels, I almost fall over backwards. Too late, I see where this might be leading.

I tug on Tristan's sleeve and interject hurriedly,

"We really should be letting Luc get back to work now, Tristan," just as Tristan says,

"And just how did you manage *that*, if I may be so bold as to inquire?"

Before I can do anything to stop him, Luc replies happily,

"Well, you see, it's like this. Verbeke needed somebody to marry his daughter, and I was going to be it."

Tristan's eyes bug out. He clears his throat, and shifts position. And when he's composed himself, he strikes one of Gilles's studiously casual poses, plucking at the lace of one sleeve, while my heart sinks like a rock to the bottom of my chest. I feel it going down, down, down, to settle somewhere just below my navel, as Tristan says carefully,

"If you don't mind, could you repeat that?"

"I was engaged to his daughter."

"His daughter?" Tristan echoes hollowly.

"That's right."

"Jan Verbeke's *daughter?*"

"Yes."

There's a pause, in which I seriously consider telling Tristan I'm going to pop back into the tent to see how the cock fight's coming along. He's doing such an excellent job of copying Gilles's studied imperturbability that I have no idea what he's thinking, and I'm both dying to know and dreading to find out.

Finally, Tristan repeats slowly,

"So, you're telling me that Jan Verbeke has a daughter."

"Obviously," Luc says, looking like he's beginning to think Tristan's the one who's a little slow.

"I see. And just where is this daughter *now?*" Tristan inquires, and I shuffle a few steps closer to the flap of the tent.

"*That* is a mighty interesting question," Luc muses, cocking his head to one side as though this is the first time he's ever wondered about it. "I don't rightly know," he says. "But I've got my ideas."

Luc is still looking at Tristan with an open and slightly dopey look on his face, and his voice sounds just as soft and shy as ever. It must be my own anxiety that makes me think I hear the faintest hint of a sly undertone to his last comment.

The hairs on the back of my neck stand on end anyway, and I start to feel horribly afraid.

"What do you mean, you don't *know?*" Tristan is now demanding incredulously. "How can you *not know* the whereabouts of your own fiancée?!"

"She disappeared about the same time as her father, didn't she? Everyone assumes she's dead," Luc explains defensively, so cowed by Tristan's imperious manner that he's almost whimpering, and I must have imagined the coldness I thought I heard from him a moment ago. It doesn't give me much comfort, though, when I picture Tristan rallying all the boys to scour Louvain, to help *me* find out what happened — to *myself*. I have a terrible feeling, too, that we're about to hear Luc's 'ideas' on the matter, and that they're going to be unpleasantly close to the truth.

Before I can complete the thought, as anticipated Tristan is already giving Luc an impatient look that prompts him to continue.

"You know, everybody thinks whoever done for her father probably did for her, too," he says. "Me, *I* don't buy it. I bet she's still around, hiding out somewhere. That's what *I'd* have done, if it'd been *my* father who got thrown down a well."

"You mean, you think she could be around town somewhere," Tristan queries, a little sarcastically (at least, I'm hoping that's what I'm hearing). "Hiding out in a convent or working in some field, or in a disguise in the market square, peddling bread?" He raises his eyebrows, and then he turns to me with studied casualness, and asks,

"Marek, what do *you* think about it?"

"I think I hear Marcel," I say, just as Luc scoffs,

"Nah. She can't be doing *that*. Anybody who'd met her would be sure to recognize her."

"And why is that, pray tell?" Tristan inquires, and I shrink back a step or two until I'm standing almost directly behind him, as though this way I could block out what Luc is about to say.

Luc looks up, and right at me over Tristan's shoulder. He cocks his head to the side again. And then he says:

"She has a bunch of hideous scars all over her face."

At just that moment Marcel does appear, sticking his head out of the shop tent to summon Luc back to work. Another load of wood has arrived and his absence has finally been noticed, but it's too late for me. The damage has already been done, and while Tristan gives Luc a pat on the back by way of thanks for his information and bids him adieu, I'm standing rooted to the spot, while one thought pounds through my head like the blows of a hammer on a white-hot anvil:

Luc knows. He knows. He knows!

And now Tristan knows it, too — that all this time, I've been lying to him.

Sure enough, before I can fully process what's just happened, Luc is turning away and Tristan's hand is gripping my upper arm, hard.

Soon Tristan is propelling me forward, and it's all I can do to stay on my feet as I try to keep up a stumbling trot along beside him as he pulls me roughly away. He's striding purposefully towards the row of pavilions that separates us from the guild yard beyond, and I can only guess where he's taking me — *back to his room, to question me? Straight to Master Guillaume?* I'm not thinking straight, and my mind is too fuzzy even to try to figure out how I can hope to explain why I never told him that my father had a daughter.

A daughter, with scars on her face.

Just when I think it can't get any worse, while the shop is still visible behind us and Luc is still fumbling his way inside it, right as we're about to pass behind one of pavilions in front of us and out of sight, in afterthought Tristan turns back for a moment, and calls out,

"Hey, Fournier! This daughter of Verbeke's. Does she have a *name?*"

I trip over my own feet, and Tristan has to jerk me upright. I'm still clutching Tristan and leaning heavily on him when Luc stops, and turns around. There's a pause that's so long and agonizing that despite myself I glance up from where I've buried my face against Tristan's sleeve.

Across the space between us, Luc looks me full in the face.

"Well, of course she does," he says.

And then — he hesitates.

"M ... m ..." he hums, and I have no idea if he's just murmuring in thought to himself, or he's about to come out with my name.

I can almost hear the slow cogs in his brain churning, and I'm holding my breath. That little pause seems so long, I have to fight down a hysterical urge to blurt out "Maybe it's *Melissande,*" thinking a bit bitterly of how I've been so worried Tristan would find out about *that*.

"It's funny, though," Luc finally says, staring vacantly at my petrified face. "I can't quite remember exactly what it is."

My legs are like porridge as Tristan drags me around the corner of the nearest tent. He's got the front of my tunic balled up in his fist, just the way Taran did that first day in the alley, before he punched the living daylights out of me. And in a way, I'm glad of it. Otherwise, there's no way I'd still be on my feet.

I have no idea what Tristan's thinking. But I can imagine it, and there's a horrible queasy feeling in the pit of my stomach that has nothing to do with hard boiled eggs. For the first time since the night of that awful Roxanne affair last year, Tristan must be genuinely and truly angry with me. And I hate myself that instead of thinking how I'm going to explain the truth to Tristan, I'm frantically trying to come up with more lies.

It's no more than I'm expecting, then, when as soon as we're out of sight of the shop, Tristan shoves me roughly back against the wall of the tent.

Then he collapses heavily against it himself, and he doubles over.

And then he bursts out laughing.

"Oh mercy, Marek!" he wheezes, "I didn't think I was going to make it. I could hardly contain myself! Can you believe the *gall* of that clown? What a lousy liar!" he exclaims.

Tristan's let go of my shirtfront, and I feel myself sliding down the canvas of the tent. I could be a big glob of porridge someone's exploded against the wall, oozing down to puddle on the ground in a lumpy, shapeless mess. When I put both hands up to cover my face, Tristan must think I'm trying to stifle my own amusement, because he slides easily down next to me and leans his head back against the tent pole, still laughing.

"What a monumental joke!" he chortles, slapping my leg. "It's really too,

too marvelous. And *you*! I could tell you were struggling. How in the world did you manage to keep a straight face? Imagine! Trying to tell *you* that you had a sister you didn't even know about."

He jostles me with his elbow, and I try to summon a chuckle for him. My throat's too dry to do anything more than gag, so he continues himself:

"Why, I'd bet my life his father didn't even know your father! It was all a bare-faced lie, just to get himself hired on here. And that stuff about *scars*. What a stupid mistake!" He shoots me a look that's half apologetic, half conspiratorial. "It's true that half of Louvain is scarred *somewhere*, but it's obvious where he got that idea from, isn't it? I mean, it can't be a coincidence that he bolstered his story with that little detail, right while he was staring you in the face. No offense, of course, kid," he says, and he shakes his head in disbelief. He's thoroughly enjoying himself.

When I still can't say anything, he gives me another playful poke in the ribs.

"Man, was that *rich*. Watching him try to deceive you, about your own father! I had half a mind to tell him just who he was trying to peddle his lies *to*, I can tell you that. Can you imagine if we'd told him the gig was up, and that he was actually *talking* to the son of Jan Verbeke? It's a mighty good thing you played it cool, though, Marek, and that you didn't give yourself away, to a boy like that."

Fortunately for me, Tristan doesn't seem to expect a response to any of this, since I know what to say even less than I know what to think. That red-hot hammer is still pounding away against my temples and my mind feels like a twisted, molten mess. I'm not even sure when it fully registers that miraculously, Tristan hasn't believed a word Luc's said.

And although I can't bring myself to laugh at him, now I'm not at all sure what to believe of Luc myself.

It's true that scars are a common enough sight in Louvain, and Luc certainly didn't seem to recognize mine *specifically*. And really, I hate to say it, but to my great good fortune, it's painfully obvious that the lad is a few candles short of brilliant.

I've dodged another arrow — the second one today (or maybe the third, or fourth — at this point I've lost count, and don't even get me started on how many it's been this week). It would be a lot easier to convince myself that the threat of Luc was behind me, though, if Tristan could stop going over it all and chuckling about it to himself.

"What do you say, little brother?" he suddenly exclaims, sitting up eagerly like he's just had a fabulous idea. "Should we let Gilles and Pascal in on this? You know, bring 'em around with us, and question him again?"

"Let's not," I say.

"I suppose you're right," he sighs, settling back again and sounding surprisingly serious all of a sudden. "And listen here, kid. I know you've got to work with him, for Marcel's sake. But watch yourself, and otherwise steer clear of him, understand? He's plenty dangerous."

"Dangerous?" I echo, feeling a prick of worry again.

"He's a damned clever liar, Marek. You saw the smooth way he spouted all that rot, without batting an eye. And that innocent act of his! It was pretty convincing. Oh, he'd never have fooled *me*, of course, even if I hadn't known the truth. I've met the type before, you see — an opportunist, through and through! But he could easily fool a more gullible man," and he pauses, letting me know that ironically enough, in this scenario he thinks the more gullible man is *me*. "Innocent, my foot! He's just plain bad news — a shirker, and a gambler, and I don't just mean cock fights! He's in for bigger stakes, and I have no doubt he's utterly ruthless."

I don't pay much mind to most of this, of course. Tristan's always trying to pretend he's some kind of 'man of the world,' with much more experience than I have, and I know how much he enjoys it. So I simply nod and let his portrait of Luc Fournier as some sort of criminal mastermind restore some of my good humor. But not all of it, and soon he's adding one last warning that's impossible to ignore.

Tristan's now getting to his feet, and once he's reached down to pull me up next to him and as I'm dusting off his peacock's feathers for him, he says sternly,

"I must insist that you promise me you'll watch out for him. I can see you don't believe me. So remember this: he went to *Master Guillaume*, and brazenly spouted a fabricated story. I ought to know: a boy who'd dare do that will dare just about anything."

All the way back inside, I'm worrying anew about Tristan's own reckless streak, and I'm wondering if he's right that Luc actually spoke to the master personally. For obvious reasons, I'm hoping quite fervently that he didn't. Or at least, I'm hoping that if he did, he didn't see fit to mention his missing fiancée to him.

I may not have sat myself down at the masters' table, the way that Tristan did. But it now occurs to me that maybe I'm the one who's been sitting in the *siege perilous* all along, ever since I dared to come to Saint Sebastian's — and I just didn't realize it.

CHAPTER THIRTY-THREE

By the time we're back in Tristan's room and I'm helping Tristan off with his things, the residual knot of anxiety that's been churning in my stomach since yesterday afternoon isn't just back. It's grown from the size of an acorn into a towering oak tree, and instead of extricating Tristan from his clothing, once or twice I get him hopelessly tangled up in his borrowed finery. What if someone *else* around the guild confirms to Tristan that Jan Verbeke had a daughter — but who would that be? We lived in isolation, away from Louvain, and even with local gossip to consider nobody talks much about daughters. I doubt any of the veterans that hang around the place ever knew of my existence.

But the men who came that night to kill my father certainly did.

I feel just like one of those little toys I loved as a child, a whipping top kept in constant motion by blows from an accompanying string. I'm spinning out of control, and I have no idea from which direction the next stroke will come, or what it will be: another run-in with Taran, or humiliation from Aristide? A fright that Tristan will decide to question Luc again, or that the boy himself will suddenly remember something? Or maybe Master Guillaume will simply finally get around to punishing Tristan, for impersonating him.

All I know is that a crisis is coming. I can feel it, as though I've been building up in fits and starts ever since our return to St. Sebastian's towards some culminating catastrophe, and by the time I've gotten Tristan out of the feather cape, the cap, and his leather jerkin, I've started imagining all sorts of things. Chief amongst them is the fear that Luc has *already* said something to the master, and that what I'm really doing is waiting for Guillaume to get around to punishing *me*.

I wonder how long it takes to prepare a proper St. Sebastian's style execution.

I'm sure the worst has happened, when right as I'm bent over trying to get enough leverage to pry off one long, blue boot for Tristan and I'm picturing the scene (Frans with his tin drum, giving a tearful drumroll as Master Leon marches me out into the yard with my hands bound behind my back; the Journeys lined up in a semi-circle with their squires sullen beside them, pressed on all sides by a horde of sweaty veterans thirsting for my bloodletting; Master Guillaume giving the order, and a leering Master Bernard lunging forward at the front of the pack, eager to strip the clothes off my back with his huge, rough hands, and give my head the first *whack*), all at once the Journey corridor is thrown into chaos.

First comes the sound of men shouting outside in the hallway. Then comes the clattering of heavy, booted feet. Before I can straighten up in alarm or meet Tristan's eyes, someone's pounding heavily on the door. It flies open immediately, to let the burly Master Bernard burst in. He looks exactly as I was just picturing him, and he's got two equally goonish veterans right behind him. Out in the hallway beyond, more men are pounding on the other boys' doors and filling the Journey corridor with stomping and yelling, and everything's in turmoil. Tristan barely has time to exclaim, *"my good fellow! What's all this? Hey, watch the ponytail, buddy,"* before Bernard grabs us both by the back of our necks and gives us a shove out the doorway, bellowing right in our ears,

"Out, out! Everybody out and on the butts, *now*! Master's orders. All Journeys and squires to the line, double-time!"

With that, we're herded into the hallway and hustled roughly along, while all down the corridor a motley crew of equally beefy veterans rousts out the other boys who happened to be in their rooms. Ahead of us I think I hear Remy's reedy voice raised in protest, while somewhere behind us Gilles is demanding loudly,

"I say, gents! No cause to get physical. What in the blue blazes is going *on*?"

If he gets any answer, there's too much commotion in the hallway for me to hear it. I don't really need an answer anyway. It's all too obvious to me what's happened, as there can be only one reason why Master Guillaume is summoning us all so suddenly and so forcibly:

Whether purposely or by accident, Luc Fournier has outed me.

And unless I'm sorely mistaken, the punishment for girls here at St. Sebastian's is a good, old-fashioned bludgeoning.

As we all stumble out through the stables and onto the field under the veterans' relentless prodding, my legs have turned to porridge again.

There's so much confusion that nobody's bothered to line up properly, since nothing like this has ever happened while I've been at the guild — with the possible exception of the morning we were told of my father's murder, but the thought doesn't give me much comfort. We're all mixed up together, Journeys and squires, and luckily for me I'm wedged in tight right between Tristan and Falko, or I don't think I'd be managing to stay on my feet. It doesn't help that all the other boys seem nervous, too, or at least keyed up and on edge; they can all sense something out of the ordinary is coming, and at St. Sebastian's, 'unusual' is rarely good.

Only Falko seems oblivious to the suspenseful atmosphere. While the last boys are stumbling out and making their way over to the place where we've formed up a disorderly line, he leans across over my head and whispers loudly to Tristan, pointing down at my master's one bare foot,

"Hey, DuBois! Giving your flexible appendages a little air, huh? Well, if you're trying to measure up to Gilles, you're only halfway there! *Ha!*"

Tristan doesn't laugh. I doubt he's worried about getting in trouble for his inappropriate attire, or lack thereof, however; a thought that's occurred to me has probably occurred to him, too — that while the master's doling out punishments, maybe he'll finally get around to paying Tristan back for catching him sitting at the masters' table.

The unprecedented summons has come right while many of the Journeys were preparing for a pre-competition bath or changing after an afternoon of practicing. So Tristan's not the only one in a state of partial undress. Falko's own shirt is hanging open off his big shoulders, both Gilles and Pascal are bare-chested, and Jurian must have already been in his tub, since he's all wet. And he's buck naked. *Stark,* as Gilles would say, although it doesn't seem to be bothering him any. In fact, he's the only other boy besides Falko who seems fully at his ease. When I sneak a glance down the line at the row of agitated faces, instead of standing at attention, Jurian is making a show of prancing and posturing, virtually strutting in place.

"Where's old Guilly?" Tristan whispers back, more to me than in response to Falko, out of the corner of his mouth. His eyes are darting back and forth alertly, and he's right.

There's no sign of Master Guillaume anywhere.

Instead it's Masters Leon and Poncellet who are standing off under the archive eaves, watching as the men hustle us out and waiting for us to come to attention, or just watching us sweat. They're in identical positions with their arms crossed over their chests, and Master Leon looks even sourer than usual, if such a thing is possible — like he's spent the afternoon sucking on a rotten egg. For some reason, it scares me more that although Poncellet actually looks rather amused, even he seems to think the situation is serious enough that he's trying to keep a straight face.

I open my mouth to answer back to Tristan, "maybe Master Guillaume isn't here, because he's looking for his *bludgeon,*" but no sound comes out. By this point I'm so scared I don't have the will to close my mouth again, so I just let it hang slack, and by the time Master Leon catches sight of Jurian's antics and he steps forward to address us, drool is dripping down my chin and my teeth have started chattering.

"For God's sake, Jurian!" Leon barks at him. "Go inside, and get dressed! And what the hell, just stay there," just as Tristan whispers across me again.

"Hey Falko, who's that out in the garden? Isn't that your buddy, old Hardouin?" he asks, and I sway into Falko.

It's worse than I'd thought!

The master's summoned no less than Hardy the Hammer Hardouin, to see that I'm bludgeoned up good and properly, right into the ground.

"Say, I think you're right!" Falko chirps happily, forgetting to whisper, and as we all wait while Jurian trots off the field and disappears into the stables with a cocky wave and a grin, Falko puts up his hand as though to hail the huge, cloaked figure who is indeed visible standing right on the other side of the creaky old garden gate.

"It *is* Hardy!" he exclaims, "I wonder who that short guy is he's got with him?," only to drop his arm again hastily when Master Leon glares at him.

"Shut *up*, DeBruyn! And the rest of you boys, at attention please!" Master Leon snaps impatiently, and there's a pause as he waits for all the boys to assume the requested position to his satisfaction. I'm still slumped against Falko, though, and when Master Leon clears his throat and begins his formal statement, quietly I slip my hand into Tristan's.

But what comes out of Master Leon's mouth is so not at all what I'm dreading that at first I can't process it.

"It has recently come to my attention," Leon says, his voice sounding surprisingly sarcastic, given the circumstances, although I suppose the tone is simply second nature to him. "*Very* recently, that one of you boys left something of his behind at the castle, during our stay at Brecelyn's this winter. One of Sir Hugo's men is here today to identify the boy in question, and to reunite the, er, *item*, with its rightful owner. I'm sure you'll all remember him *fondly*. He's requested to have a friendly little word with you boys himself. So with no further ado, I'll turn things over to him."

Here he pauses to cast us all a supremely withering look, and I can feel the boys shuffling around a little in confusion. Forcibly hauling us all out onto the field like this is a mighty strange reaction to a stray possession, and in my own confusion, for a moment I think Leon might be talking about Meliana's journal, even though *that* little item we took *away* from the castle.

Then Leon frowns, and he nods gravely to a pair of veterans stationed on either side of the garden gate. The men accordingly swing open its little wooden door to let the cloaked figure enter, who from the size of him can hardly be anyone but Hardy the Hammer Hardouin. The hood of his cape is shielding most of his face, but there can be little doubt in anyone's mind that under the cloak is the giant of a man who beat Falko to a bloody pulp in the market square and then later befriended him.

To my immense relief, he doesn't appear to have his massive war hammer with him at present. But he's not alone; a smaller, similarly cloaked figure is indeed with him, just as Falko indicated. It rouses my curiosity, since by this point it's beginning to sink in that whatever is going on, it's not about me, and I don't see how anything having to do with Hardy can possibly be about Tristan, either.

So I straighten up and I watch curiously as Hardouin ushers his huddled companion forward. The masters, and all the veterans, too, are standing so stiffly and acting so squirrelly as the second man steps onto the field that as my panic recedes, I'm really starting to wonder what's happening. Even from here, I think I can see old Poncellet's mustache twitching.

Hardouin takes up a position on the spot recently vacated by Master Leon, and when he's dragged his companion up next to him, he throws off his own hood. He would be an imposing figure under any circumstances, because of his sheer size. Today his expression is impressively fierce, and at first he doesn't say anything. He just takes one good, long look up and down our ragtag line, sizing us up with an intimidating glare. From the scowl on his face, it's pretty obvious he doesn't like what he sees.

Then he snorts, and he yanks the hood off of the little man standing beside him.

There's a collective gasp.

Some of the boys even take a staggering step backwards, as though shrinking back from some atrocity, and next to me I can feel both Falko and Tristan involuntarily flinch.

It's not a man.

It's not even a boy.

It's a *girl*.

A girl, on the guild grounds.

"Oh, *geez*," I hear one of the boys exclaim under his breath, "No wonder Guilly didn't want to be out here for this!," even though I doubt any of us has a clear idea yet of what's actually happening.

"This, boys, is my *daughter*," Hardouin announces ominously.

Then he reaches over and yanks the cloak off the girl entirely.

There's another collective gasp, even louder than the first.

"*So*, which one of you good-for-nothing, low-life, degenerate scumbags is the rightful owner of THIS?!?" he demands furiously, gesturing down at the girl's waist, and next to me, it's Falko's turn to sway. Only he's so big, we both almost go tumbling over sideways. So there's a moment or two while we're sorting ourselves out before I get a really good look at exactly what is it that's so stunned all the boys, and what Hardouin is now so accusingly gesticulating down *at:*

an unmistakable bump, low and tight, right in the middle of her abdomen.

I recognize it for what it is immediately, of course. And what's more, I'm pretty sure I recognize the *girl*, too, even though I only saw her once. It was on the morning of our last day at the castle, when we squires were all heading out together to the wagons with Falko and we ran into a gaggle of giggling girls — girls among whom we all assumed one must have been Falko's winter indiscretion.

"WELL?" Hardy's demanding again, and down the line somewhere I hear Armand hiss,

"Oh, mercy!" and I know he's recognize her, too. But when Hardouin whirls around in his direction and snaps,

"Who said that?!" Armand has the sense to keep quiet, and nobody dares say anything else or even move a muscle as Hardy continues to rage.

"I put it to you again, 'gentlemen'! Who is the father of this baby?! I am *not* leaving here until I've got the culprit in my hands. Not even if I have to go down the line, and beat each and every one of you senseless!"

Nobody doubts the massive man will do it. From the looks of him, he'd probably enjoy doing it anyway, just for the hell of it. So while Hardouin's rant goes on in this vein, somehow without moving his lips at all Tristan manages to mumble to Falko under his breath,

"That's who you were fooling around with at Christmas?! Are you crazy, or did you have a death wish?" and Falko mumbles back,

"Well, I didn't know she was his daughter, did I? Not until *now*."

By this time Hardouin's started stomping back and forth up and down the line, looking each boy in the eye and trying to stare him down. Next to me poor Falko has started to tremble, and badly; just like the day he fought Hardy in the market square, if he were wearing any armor, I'm sure I'd hear his knees knocking together with a clang. But I can also tell he's struggling with his better nature, and I fear it's going to get the best of him. Any minute, he's going to step forward and confess. He'd surely already have done it, if he didn't know first-hand what it was like to be pounded by Hardy's hammer straight into the ground. Without taking my hand out of Tristan's, I slip my other hand into his, and I give it a little squeeze to urge him to keep quiet. I mean, I feel awfully sorry for the girl. But if Falko's natural sense of chivalry gets the best of him now, he's not going to live long enough to fail Firsts spectacularly.

Falko squeezes my hand back so hard, I have to bite my lip not to cry out. He doesn't let go when Hardy comes past him down the line, hardly bothering to stare down his 'good buddy' Falko. And he doesn't let go as Hardy passes on, not bothering to look much at me, either, and makes his way down the rest of the line. To my dismay, he does linger for an uncomfortably long time on Tristan, long enough to make it obvious he's heard plenty of rumors about his reputation as a ladies' man, but it doesn't take the big man long to realize that nobody's going to be foolish enough to confess. So soon he stomps back over to his daughter, pushes up his sleeves, and he prods her forward. When he croons into her ear loudly enough for us all to hear,

"Okay, honey. Don't be shy! Go on, and point the scoundrel out," Falko's hand is so slick with sweat I could be grabbing a wet trout.

483

The girl steps forward reluctantly, and it must be so humiliating for her that I don't know which of the pair I feel sorrier for — the girl who's being forced to condemn her former lover in this public fashion, or my friend who's about to lose his life.

The others must be thinking the same thing, since as the girl begins to make her way slowly down in front of the line, all the boys have hung their heads — in part as though already in mourning for Falko, and in part to avoid having to meet her eye. If nothing else, they're probably rightly afraid that looking up at the wrong moment could be taken as a sign of confession, and give the girl leave to single them out.

When suspense gets the better of me and I risk sneaking a glance up in the girl's direction, however, to my surprise I see she looks anything but shy. She's got a defiant expression on her face and an intelligent look in her eye, and from her plucky demeanor I suspect she's plenty used to dealing with her father's rages. Her cheeks are red and she's terribly embarrassed, that's for sure. But as she makes a show of going slowly down the line and looking the boys over in much the way her father did, I can tell she's also thinking hard.

She goes past Pascal, and Gilles. She passes Rennie, and a whimpering Frans. She, too, lingers a moment in front of Tristan, and my heart stops.

And then she's in front of me, hardly pausing or bothering to look me up and down, and I fear my hand might really break in the vice of Falko's hand. For a split second as she goes by, her eyes meet mine, though, and it's funny. It must be my imagination, but I think something passes between us — a moment of understanding between girls, caught up in circumstances.

Soon she's moved on to Falko. When she looks the poor boy right in the eye, Falko sways again, and now it's not just his hand that's sweating. Rivulets of the stuff are pouring down his temples to soak the open collar of his shirt, and more sweat is dripping from his hair down the back of his neck.

Then he lifts his foot. He swallows so hard I can hear it, and I know he's just about to step forward valiantly and own up to his misdeed, when just like that the girl shakes her head — and moves on.

After that, she makes her way purposefully down to the opposite end of the line.

"That's him," she announces firmly, grinding to a halt and pointing out in front of her.

For one insane moment in which the whole field tips sideways, I think she must be pointing at Taran; I can't really see what's happening, since next to me Falko is now reeling in a mazy, circular motion that's blocking out my view of most of the field.

Tristan must think it, too, because as I'm craning my neck wildly to see past Falko down the line, he mutters,

"Man, he really *can't* keep it in his pants, can he?!"

She's not, of course — although at first, the boy she has fingered seems to me equally unlikely.

Of all people, she's pointing right at Aristide.

I guess it makes some sense. He's one of the few boys who's fully dressed, and sumptuously so. Even if the girl didn't already know who he was from our time at the castle, it's got to be obvious that he's filthy rich.

It's a pretty clever move, and I give the girl credit. She's probably heard that the Journeys are usually as close as brothers. But if she thinks Aristide is going to cover for a friend, she's going to be sorely disappointed. From the way most of the other boys have all started shuffling around, I'm sure they're all thinking the same thing.

Imagine our surprise, then, when instead of hotly objecting as we're all expecting, Aristide simply inclines his head in an almost regal gesture of acceptance.

He steps forward with a sort of apologetic grin that still manages to be mixed with a healthy dose of arrogance; it's just the sort of feigned sheepishness meant to convey more pride than regret, and we all watch in stunned silence as he takes the girl's hand, looking inordinately pleased with himself. Making a little bow, he lifts the tips of her fingers lightly to his lips and gives them a genteel kiss. It's either the bravest thing he's ever done, or the stupidest.

Then he turns to Hardy, who's now staring at him with an expression on his face so sour it could rival one of Master Leon's. And when the huge man glares down at him, and with his massive hands on his equally massive hips, he demands,

"So, any last words?," Aristide clears his throat. Then he says manfully,

"My dear sir, you look like a frightfully intelligent chap! Shall we retire to one of the masters' offices, to discuss a financial arrangement I think you'll find highly to your advantage? Let me assure you, *I* can be extremely generous. And if you're as smart as you look, I do believe *you're* about to become extremely rich!"

"Son," Hardouin exclaims warmly, his entire demeanor transforming as he slings an arm heavily around Aristide's shoulders, "That is *exactly* the sort of thing I was hoping you would say."

Without further ado, the two of them head off inside arm-in-arm, although it's not entirely clear whether Hardouin is giving Aristide a paternal embrace or keeping his head in a firm grip to ensure that he doesn't try to get away.

Once they're out of sight, with a snort of relief Master Leon gives a quick signal to one of the veterans to escort Hardouin's daughter safely off to await her father out in the guild chapel. As soon as the girl has disappeared back through the gate, next to me there's a massive thud as Falko's knees finally give way under him.

He crashes to the ground with a moan, his impact raising an impressive little cloud of dust.

Master Leon was right in the middle of issuing a curt dismissal. When he hears me coughing and he looks over to the spot where Falko is now swooning around in a kneel on the ground and trying clumsily to get up, he cuts his remarks short to bark in disgust,

"And somebody, take DeBruyn to the lavatory, and give him a thorough washing! He's sweating like a plow horse, and he's covered in dirt. For the love of Saint Peter! For such a tough guy, he's awfully sensitive to the heat."

Armand accordingly steps forward to help Frans hustle his still-swooning master off for the much-needed bath, but I'm still feeling too dazed by the turn of events to make any move to help them. As soon as the masters themselves have all gone in, it's in something of a fog that I follow Tristan and the other remaining boys out to the garden to hold court, where the order of the day is sure to be a lively discussion of Aristide's recent activities.

We haven't had time to do much more than settle in when Jurian strolls out to join us, now fully dressed.

"So, boys. What'd I miss?" he drawls, and there's such a confusing babble as the boys all talk over each other in their eagerness to be the one to tell him what's just happened that it takes a long time to convince him that we're not trying to put one over on him.

We haven't been out in the garden long before Aristide himself joins us. He's come to terms with Hardouin remarkably quickly, although I suppose it isn't surprising. He'd be unlikely to refuse a man like Hardy just about anything.

I am surprised that he'd want to put in an appearance now, though, since he has to know that we're all out here talking about him. And I'm even more surprised by the remarkably buoyant mood he's in. Even if it weren't for the public shame of it, he's surely just had to agree to the outlay of an outrageous sum of money. But it's undeniable. I never thought I'd use the word of Aristide, but as he steps out onto the grass from beneath the portico with all the flourish of an actor taking the stage, he's positively radiant. He's got a huge grin plastered on his face, and from the way he wastes no time in taking over the conversation, swaggering and bragging, you'd almost think he was glad he's been caught out by old Hardouin. At least, now that the cat's out of the bag, as it were, he can't seem to wait to share all the details of his affair with anyone who'll listen.

"We started up at Christmastime," he tells us loudly, sitting down backwards on one of the little chairs and straddling it in a stagey way that suggests he's going to try to hold forth in the manner of Tristan. "Not long after *your* poetry contest, DuBois! I think it must have been my entry that won her over," he says, preening, and it's all so unlikely that I almost snort.

When I cast my mind back to that night at Brecelyn's castle, though, I have to concede that although I can't recall what Aristide's note said exactly, I do remember thinking at the time that his poem was surprisingly sweet.

"We were together on and off all winter, and none of you boys suspected a thing! Not even when I almost got caught out in the middle of the night, *by the girl's own father* — and that idiot DeBruyn unwittingly came to my rescue!" he declares, and I realize uncomfortably that he's talking about the night *he* caught *me*, reading Meliana's diary.

Mercifully he's got bigger things on his mind this afternoon than tormenting me, so he just keeps going without bothering to mention me.

"It was easy. I'd go along and fetch her from her room at night, see, and we'd sneak out together to the hayloft in the stables or to the armory. Sometimes I'd even ride her through the woods on *your* horse, Lejeune, out to Brecelyn's chapel of St. Sebastian! It seemed fitting, under the circumstances. Mellor may have had the idea of using it as a trysting place *first*, but I bet *I* used it more often!" he crows, looking around him expectantly.

"And who'd have thought Gilles and *Marek* here would be frequenting the place, *too?*" Jurian poses rhetorically, but thankfully nobody's listening to him.

It's obvious Aristide thinks congratulations are in order, and he's so puffed up with pride he seems to have forgotten that fathering a bastard is not something that all the boys are likely to appreciate — particularly not my master. Indeed, throughout Aristide's oration Tristan has been unusually silent, and he's now starting to get one of those dark looks of his. I'm sure it's not helping his mood any that right on the other side of the garden gate a group of veterans is crowded around and haggling loudly with Poncellet, and over all the other voices, now and then the old master can be heard exclaiming lazily, *"Pay up, men! The whole lot of you who bet it was going to turn out to be* another *one of Slick's!"*

Gilles isn't looking much different. It's probably less out sensitivity to his friend's feelings than because Aristide is bragging about having taken his horse without permission, or maybe it's simply because his hated rival is now claiming the kind of the attention that's usually reserved for him and Tristan. But he looks almost as fed up with Aristide as Tristan does, and so when Aristide crows,

"It may have cost me a fortune, but it was worth it! And at least I kept my head, if you know what I mean," Gilles interrupts to admonish him.

"Pretty careless of you, to get that poor girl pregnant," he says coldly. "Not to mention most ungentlemanly. You should at least have had the decency to take suitable precautions."

"I assumed she was taking them, naturally," Aristide sniffs. "Don't most girls?"

"Some do, some don't," Gilles says noncommittally. "Not all girls work in a brothel, Ari. Besides, if you mean tonics and the like," he adds, and my ears prick up, "I'd not let a girl of mine use them. They're too risky."

I can't help it. My eyes flit to Tristan. When Gilles's words don't seem to mean anything to him, I catch myself darting a sharp glance around the garden for Taran, to see what effect the mention of tonics might be having on *him* — having forgotten for a moment that the subject of babies in general (and of fathering bastards in specific) is so distasteful to him at present that he never joined us out here in the first place.

As I'm looking around, out of the corner of my eye I notice Falko slinking out through the side door of the great hall to join us. He's clearly had his bath, as he's looking clean and fresh. But he's sporting an awfully hangdog expression, and he doesn't come out any further than the cover of the portico, preferring to lurk in the shadows behind the climbing jasmine and from there to cast ashamed little glances out at all the boys, particularly at Tristan.

Falko's still fiddling with a stray vine and looking pathetic when Aristide finally decides he's had enough of Gilles. He goes off inside in search of better company, his news having received a colder reception in the garden than he anticipated. As he's leaving, Rennie chortles,

"That'll teach him not to be so cheap next time! I bet the whole thing *did* cost him a fortune. Much more than if he'd just stuck to frequenting brothels," and unfortunately for Rennie, Aristide hears him.

He turns back, his face red with fury, and he retraces his steps just far enough to reach out one long arm and give Rennie a stinging slap across the face. Nobody's much surprised by it; Aristide's not one to let an insult slide, particularly from a man he considers an inferior. But I'm sure Rennie isn't the only one who is taken aback by what Aristide then says to him.

"Watch it, squire! You're talking about the *mother of my child*, and you'd do well to remember it. I'll hear no ill spoken of her in my presence. Do I make myself clear?" When he looks around the garden challengingly, nobody dares answer him, since he sounds entirely serious. I'd never have thought Aristide the type, but he almost sounds chivalrous. Then he smooths down the front of his jerkin as though satisfied, and he turns to back Rennie.

"Cast aspersions on the lady's character again, and it won't just get you a slap. It'll get you a thorough beating."

With that he stalks off, and it's not until after he's long gone and not even the echo of his boots on the flagstones of the portico is audible any longer that Rennie ventures to exclaim,

"Well, I guess that means he doesn't know she was also fooling around with Falko!"

A few more minutes pass, in which the only sound in the garden is a mournful rustling coming from behind the jasmine.

No one breaks the silence, until finally Tristan says shortly,

"All right, Falko. You can come out now," and the big guy lumbers obediently forward.

"Dash it all, Tristan," he grumbles bashfully, obviously feeling more sensitive to his friend's likely feelings about a boy who'd be careless enough to father a bastard than Aristide was. "I was just so damned *lonely*, thinking my girl was in love with another chap." He casts me a pleading little glance, and I suppose it's only fair he'd look to me for help, since I'm the 'chap' in question. But if Falko thinks I'm going to jump into this conversation, he's got to be crazy. "And you know what they say about seeking a little physical comfort, when you can't have the one you really want ..."

"So," Tristan cuts in, as Falko's voice trails off hopefully. He crosses his arms, and fixes Falko with a stern look. "Did Aristide just claim your baby, or not?"

Falko drops his eyes.

"I don't know," he mumbles. "I don't *think* so. I mean, I *was* fooling around with her. But I didn't think I let it go as far as all that."

"What do you mean, you don't *know*?!" Gilles scoffs. "Either you went far enough for it to be possible, or you didn't."

"Oh, uh, *right*," Falko puffs. When nobody says anything and it's clear from Tristan's expression that he's still expecting an answer, Falko shifts around a little in place, hitching up his trousers. "Right-*o*," he blusters. "Yessiree, in*deed*y."

We all watch while Falko purses his lips and makes a show of gazing off into the corner of the garden with his head tilted to one side, as though considering carefully. His eyebrows contort through such an impressive array of positions that would be pretty hilarious, too, if the circumstances were different. And if both Tristan and Gilles weren't still staring at him so icily.

The boys let him sweat it out for a while, until Gilles finally takes pity on him.

He gets up with a sigh, and he slings an arm around Falko's shoulders, in much the way that Harduoin recently did to Aristide.

"Come along and step into my office, and let Papa Gilles explain everything," he says soothingly, steering his big friend gently but firmly back into the shadows of the portico, no doubt to give him a belated lecture on the finer points of the birds and the bees, since by now it's clear enough that for all his crude talk, Falko's not entirely sure how far 'far enough' actually is. And I'll admit it. Instead of feeling sorry for Falko, when I think of how he tormented me in the mess hall over the illuminated page Father Abelard gave me, I can't help feeling a little fed up with him. Clouters may be able to keep their big mouths shut, but the same can't be said of their trousers, apparently. That, and for a moment, I'm actually tempted to ask if I can join them, since it's a topic about which I, too, am plenty ignorant.

When Gilles and Falko return a few minutes later, there's such a huge smile on Falko's face that if he grinned any wider, he'd surely get a cramp in both cheeks.

"Nope!" he chuffs, positively beaming. "*Not* mine! Nope, nope, nope! *Not-a-chance.* No-sir-ee. Couldn't be! And that's a 100%, proof-positive guarantee," he declares with a delighted air of finality. By now most of the other boys have started making their way inside to tidy up for supper, and so Falko gives one last relieved chuff, and he stumps off back inside after them happily, rubbing his hands together and with only the slightest hint of a man making a hasty retreat.

As the garden slowly empties of its occupants, Tristan and Gilles make no move to leave. So I stay sitting where I am, too, on the grass beside Tristan's chair, and none of us says anything until we're all alone out here.

From across the little table at which they're both seated, Tristan and Gilles exchange one long look. Then when Tristan raises one eyebrow at him inquiringly, Gilles says dryly,

"I'd put the odds closer to 60-40."

"We'll find out in about four months' time, give or take, I reckon," Tristan agrees grimly, both boys obviously of the opinion that Falko's newfound knowledge has come too late for any certainty on the matter. "That is, when the child comes out either with a beak like an eagle, or the size of a heifer."

"In *that* event, I suppose the girl *could* claim it takes after its *grandfather*," Gilles says carefully.

The temperature must be dropping, because I don't think it's my imagination that the atmosphere in the garden is starting to feel a little chilly.

When Tristan makes no reply, Gilles raises both eyebrows a little. From the way the corner of his mouth is twitching, I think he's trying not to smile, and without looking up, he says almost to himself:

"Yes, our boy is mighty lucky Aristide shares his taste in women. A smarter man would have never dallied with a lady's virtue so carelessly. Not unless he was counting on pawning off any inconvenient consequences on another lover who more closely resembled him."

"If there's an implication in there, *friend*," Tristan says icily, "you'd do well to remember that I'm the one now in possession of a trusty rapier."

At Tristan's tone Gilles looks up sharply, looking genuinely surprised. "Oh, I say, old man!" he exclaims, almost as though he'd forgotten that Tristan was listening to him — and that Tristan and Taran share a father from whom they've inherited a few striking similarities, despite their obvious differences — distinctive features like their thick black hair, dark eyes, and slightly cleft chins. "I thought we'd hashed this out already. Of course I wasn't talking about *you*," he declares bluntly, and I have to believe him. Something else is on his mind, so I don't think he means it as a slur, either, when he adds,

"I was talking about a *clever* man. In generalities."

We sit a little longer, both boys apparently lost in their own thoughts.

But the air out here isn't getting any warmer, so it's not long before Gilles gets up with a satisfied stretch to make his own way indoors.

Before he departs, Gilles looks down at me to declare with a wink,

"So, squire! Looks like there was no mystery about that handkerchief we found out in Brecelyn's chapel, after all! I was right all along. It was just Aristide's."

Even after Gilles is long gone, Tristan makes no move to leave. He's barely shifted position since talking to Falko, even, and he looks so grave, I really wish I knew exactly what he was thinking. There are so many things that could be bothering him, I don't know where to begin: Melissande's baby is surely one of them, and Falko's is another, and he can't have liked Gilles's parting dig about the handkerchief. But I have a feeling that what we're both really thinking about most is our own fathers' behavior. So when I finally venture to say to him,

"You *are* going to forgive him, aren't you, Tristan?" I'm not entirely sure who I mean.

At first he doesn't answer.

"I'm in no position to judge him, am I, Marek?" he finally says bitterly, and I don't want to think about all the things *that* could mean. So I change the subject, since Gilles's parting comment has gotten me thinking.

"Master, can I ask you something?"

"Seems to me you just did," he replies, his mood showing little sign of having improved since the departure of Gilles. When he sees how serious I look, though, he sighs and says,

"Shoot, kid. Ask me anything."

"It's about Luc. You know, Luc Fournier, from the shop this morning."

"Him?" Tristan frowns, looking surprised, and from his expression, unpleasantly so. "I told you, Marek. He's bad business. Stay away from him. Maybe I should have a talk to Marcel and get you out of instructing him."

"It's not that," I reply, shaking my head, and feeling a little guilty about letting Tristan form such a negative opinion about him. "It's that I've been thinking. If Master Guillaume loved my father so much that he'd give Luc a job simply to honor his memory, how could he have been involved in killing him? It doesn't make sense to me."

"I don't know. A guilty conscience, maybe?" Tristan says dismissively, pretty obviously not wanting to discuss the matter any further. After Gilles's comment about the handkerchief, he's in no mood to have me poke any more holes in what's left of his tattered theory.

"Why don't you ask *Gilles* about it?" he says sarcastically, getting to his feet. "He seems to think he's clever enough to find an answer for everything."

"About that," I continue. "Gilles *is* a clever man, isn't he, Tristan? Or at least, he certainly *thinks* he is," I say deliberately, and Tristan looks down at me inquiringly.

There's just no good way to say it, and my timing couldn't be worse. It's sure to upset Tristan further, but Firsts is *the day after tomorrow*, and Pascal's set to make his proposal right in the middle of it. It's now or never, and forever hold my peace. Tristan and I are now standing close together and there's no one else in the garden, so I just blurt out to him,

"Oh master, do you think Ginger could *already* be pregnant?!"

If I've been thinking maybe Tristan's suspected something similar all along, I find I'm quite mistaken. He looks thoroughly taken aback to hear such a suggestion, particularly from me.

"Heavens, Marek! Falko's one thing. And *Aristide*'s another thing entirely. But surely you can't think *Pascal* capable of such a thing?"

"That's not what I meant," I say, and when I won't meet Tristan's eye, he gets my implication immediately.

"Oh, *no*. Surely not," he says firmly. "Gilles is a gentleman."

"They seem to be the worst offenders," I say dryly, but Tristan just shakes his head.

"That night, when he rode Ginger to the convent," I press. "She was starstruck, and Gilles was, well, *Gilles*. Irresistible! It would have been easy for him to take advantage of the situation, and you have to admit it. He *was* gone for an awfully long time, and they were alone in the woods. And, *er*, we know they had a blanket."

"Sorry, kid," Tristan says firmly. "If it were anyone else, maybe. But Gilles wouldn't believe the worst of me, so I won't believe it of him. Even if I could believe Gilles would be such a cad to a lady, he'd never do anything so low to Pascal. He loves him. They may have had their quarrels, but he'd never do anything really to hurt him."

He sounds so sure and the topic is so obviously distasteful to him that I have no choice but to drop it and to try to believe him. It didn't escape my notice, though, how carefully Tristan said he *wouldn't* believe it, rather than that he *didn't*, and *something* is wrong with Pascal's engagement, I can feel it.

I have no doubt Gilles loves Pascal, better than any brother. Yet I'm also sure that he's still in love with Lady Sibilla, and that he's not forgotten how Pascal pursued her behind his back all winter. Fooling around with Pascal's new interest would be an obvious way to pay him back in kind, and it all fits too well for me to dismiss it entirely, and after this afternoon's line-up, let's face it. I'm no longer sure I really know what *any* boy is capable of doing.

I'm just not convinced, and as we make our way inside, I have the disturbing feeling that recently all my idols have been falling, and what's running through my mind is a phrase of Armand's that I now find more worrisome than ever:

"*For love, a man is capable of doing just about anything.*"

At the very least, I sincerely hope that the secret Tristan's been sharing with Gilles, the one he's gearing up to tell me, isn't that there's a 60-40 chance Melissande's baby really could have been his.

CHAPTER THIRTY-FOUR

Against all odds, mess that evening turns out to be a joyous affair. We've entered the final countdown to the competitions, and with them now so close the boys were likely to be wound up anyway. But the energy stirred up by the afternoon's unexpected line-up is still flowing through our veins, and if the thought that Firsts is finally right around the corner weren't enough cause for celebration, Aristide's delight at finding himself a father-to-be is so undeniably genuine that even the most reluctant boys can't help getting caught up in it.

It has to be admitted, a more cynical boy might suspect some of Aristide's delirious good cheer is put on to save face after being so publicly caught out, and simply to annoy Gilles. But when the meal is winding down and Aristide sweeps up onto one of the benches with his tankard raised to proclaim his affection for the girl in a move that could only be in imitation of Tristan, even my own master is eventually won over.

It doesn't hurt that as soon as the masters had vacated the hall for the evening, Aristide instructed Armand to nip back to his room to fetch a half a dozen bottles from a private stash of his own so that the boys could toast him in style, and the wine is flowing freely. The stuff is so strong that after just a few sips the mood at the table's turned exuberant, and I'm already feeling tipsy.

"A toast, gentlemen!" Aristide is now booming, to all appearances thoroughly enjoying his chance to play the romantic lead for the evening. "To my lovely lady, Swanhilda!"

"*Oh, dear me, no! Not seriously?*" Gilles whispers, in one of his typically audible asides. But Swanhilda does indeed prove to be the girl's improbable name, and when Armand leaps to his feet with a rousing cry of "To Swilda, lads!," we all join in, even Gilles — although much of Armand's enthusiasm probably has less to do with happiness for Aristide than with getting a little of his own back with Pascal. For once his own master's done something with which Pascal's can't compete, even if it is something dubious.

My own levity tonight isn't just from the wine, or even because I secretly find the news about the baby rather exciting and sweet (and no one can deny that the effect it's had on Aristide is nothing short of miraculous). What's now coursing through my veins more potently than any wine is an intense feeling of relief. It started the moment Falko hit the dust, out on the field. Fueled on by alcohol and by the boys' raucous laughter, it's been accelerating rapidly all evening. The terrible sense of foreboding I was feeling all day has turned out simply to be building up to some folly of *Falko's*! I've been foolish to think that timid, mild Luc Fournier posed some sort of threat to me, and best of all, Gilles is surely right:

The handkerchief was just Aristide's.

Master Guillaume is strange, all right. Sadistic, even. But for all his casual cruelty I haven't wanted to think him a villain, and at least Luc Fournier's arrival has proven to me that the master *did* love my father. I'm certain of it.

Our best competition yet is coming, one Tristan can't fail to win. All my anxieties old and new have been miraculously swept away in time to allow me fully to enjoy it, and I'm reveling in the feeling it gives me — well, all my worries but one, naturally. But he's sitting at the far end of the table, and I manage to ignore him.

"I'll claim the boy, of course, as soon as I'm back on my estate," Aristide is now declaring, typically assuming that the baby is going to be male and apparently not noticing that he's as good as admitting that even he doesn't think he's got a chance of ending up in Guards. "And I'll fix it with my father to have both mother and child moved close by, so that I can see to it that he's raised properly."

He says it so matter-of-factly, he must assume his father will have no problem with his son openly keeping a mistress. No doubt he's right, since Aristide probably inherited his lax moral code from him. But I actually find it rather touching, and so I raise my cup and call out an approving *"Hear, hear!"*

Then I catch a glimpse of Tristan's face, and I lower my cup guiltily.

"What's your *wife* going to say about that, when your father finds you one?" Gilles asks dryly, and when Aristide snaps back,

"What concern will it be of *hers*? She'll just have to put up with it," any warmth I was beginning to feel for Aristide cools instantly.

"If *you'd* ever loved anyone other than yourself," Aristide continues pompously, "you'd understand how I feel. Nothing on earth could induce me to give her up."

"Oh, *yeah*? What if I were to tell you —" Rennie starts in laughingly, until Armand gives him a judicious kick in the shins under the table, and he wisely decides to keep the rest of the thought to himself — possibly because he notices Falko glowering at him and slowly clenching one of his big fists. Or maybe it's because at the far end of the table, Taran gets abruptly to his feet.

Aristide is too wrapped up in himself to notice the stirrings of tension at the table, made more acute by the fact that I'm not the only boy who's had too much to drink. From the expressions on some of the others' faces, though, they've begun to realize that the topic of preferring another woman to your wife is unlikely to sit well with a boy whose own mother had to put up with a husband who kept a mistress. And who openly claimed the bastard he fathered on her. Not when said bastard is his father's favorite. And not when he's currently sitting at the same table with him.

He's going to like it even less, if he suspects that the half-brother in question has recently been cuckolding him.

Without a word to anyone Taran proceeds to stalk straight through the side door and out into the portico. And when Remy scrambles up and out in imitation of his master, I'm not sure why, but it's not long before we're all getting to our feet to head outside after them. It's probably just the wine muddling me, but it all feels familiar, like somehow following an angry Taran out into the garden has become some sort requisite pre-trials routine.

I think it's only right at that moment that it really begins to sink in:

Firsts is only *one day* away, and it's funny. After waiting for them for so long and obsessing about them so much, I now feel like somehow they've managed to sneak up on me.

Outside in the garden, the air is crisp enough to be sobering, despite the balminess of the evening. A drowsy bee or two is still bumbling around in the vines and somewhere out in the stables an owl is hooting softly among the rafters, and the atmosphere is so different out here from the stuffiness of the hall that for a moment it's disorienting. I stumble as I step out from under the portico, but it's not because I'm drunk, or because my eyes haven't adjusted. It's something else entirely that brings me up short: a moon so full and so low in the sky that it seems to have perched itself precariously atop the diminutive spire of the guild chapel to spy down on us — a moon so full and heavy with moonlight it's positively *pregnant*, and it's bathing the little space in a pale glow so beautiful it's almost painful.

The last time I saw a moon like that was out in Brecelyn's snow-strewn clearing, and I come to a full stop for a moment, gazing up wide-eyed at it. I'm unsure whether I'm enthralled by it, or sickened — even before Gilles nudges me as he goes past, to say sarcastically,

"Looks like your *lovers' moon* has followed us, eh, Marek?"

I'm spared from having to answer by Rennie, who comes stumbling out behind me, only to crash right into me.

Gilles seats himself at the rickety table nearest to the garden gate, where soon he's occupying himself in vigorously shooing away the old dog Popinjay. The ancient mutt usually follows after Tristan, but he's been as confused by the boys' switch as the rest of us, and lately he's taken to dogging Gilles's steps, quite literally — no doubt thrown off by the scent of Tristan's clothes on him. While Gilles prods the animal disapprovingly with the toe of one boot, Pascal excuses himself to practice his proposal behind the rosebushes, and I look around for my own place to take a seat.

The other boys have taken up lounging positions around the garden's periphery, sprinkling themselves here and there among the greenery, and in the moon's unearthly light they look so flawless and unreal they could be statues, temporarily brought to life by the moon's magic. It's as though now with the witching hour upon us they're slowly freezing back into their accustomed positions, and in front of me Tristan in particular has flung himself down dramatically at the base of a tree in the middle of the grass, where he's now reposed most decoratively. He's in much the same place and pose where I sat with him the other day, our heads together and sharing confidences, and as always my first inclination is naturally to join him.

Tonight, I hesitate. An equally impressive figure is perched directly across from the spot, with his back resting up against a pillar of the portico and as frozen as marble in the pale moon's light. Although he, too, is sitting stone still and he shows no sign of being inclined to look my way, I can't help thinking of how he caught me out here so recently, to all appearances telling my master his secrets.

That feels like a long time ago now, though, and when I glance over at Taran's profile, he's got such a faraway expression on his face that I doubt he's thinking about how he came upon me fondling Tristan under this very tree and apparently laughing about wounding him. Or even about me or Tristan at all, and how much he hates him. With Aristide still babbling away merrily about babies, there's only one thing he could possibly be thinking about.

The bright moon is casting deep shadows across Taran's features, and he's staring up at it so fixedly that it now seems to me as though it's leaning down specifically to him, eager to share a confidence with him. And when I risk darting a glance his direction, Taran does look awfully serious, that's true. He doesn't look sad, though, exactly, and I suppose it could just be the midnight shadows deceiving me. But it looks more like he's thinking over something intently, something that's troubling him, and I have to wonder if the competition isn't finally getting tight enough that it's starting to worry even him.

After all, Pascal was right — there's no beating Gilles at wands. And thanks to the boys' transformations, Tristan has improved at the skill drastically. Maybe there's no beating a 'Gistan,' either (or *is* it Trills? *Goodness, I really have had too much to drink!*), and Taran's right to worry. At least, he looks like something so heavy is weighing on him that I can't help wondering uncomfortably if the wound I gave him might not really be hurting him.

It certainly didn't impede him from grabbing me in the archives, though, did it? No, he wasn't hurting any *then*, that's for sure, and with Firsts so close I can't let myself feel conflicted. I force away the memory of Taran saying, "I won't just lose. I'll be *thoroughly humiliated*," and when Tristan puts out a hand to motion me down next to him, I march over and plop down decidedly beside him, albeit rather gracelessly.

I nestle in next to Tristan, and I pretend Taran is just another decorative statue. I drink in the jasmine-scented air and the feeling of companionship all around me, and I fill my mind with thoughts of only one thing: anticipation for the coming trials and the unveiling of the boys' joint trick.

It's just the kind of night we always seem to get right before the trials, the kind that encourages introspection, and I know I'm not the only boy who's thinking of the competitions. So it's hardly surprising that before long a somber mood has fallen over us all, just as though it really were the night before Firsts, come one day early. Maybe it's because this year we're all so ready for the trials, or because we've waited so long for them to start up again. But when Jerome pulls out his lute and begins to tune it and Charles readies his voice to accompany him, the impression is complete.

Soon a feeling steals over me that's familiar, too — a sensation I always get right before the trials that something's coming to an end, a sensation that's bittersweet. Tonight the sweetness of Tristan's coming triumph is so sharp I can taste it, but it doesn't make the bitterness any easier to swallow, knowing which two boys will be gone by this time next week.

Jurian's sprawled out in one of the chairs next to Gilles, the faery light illuminating his golden head and making him look impossibly handsome, and needless to say, I have mixed feelings about knowing he's about to leave. I'll not miss his sly innuendos, that's for sure, or his frequent jokes at my expense. But I will miss just looking at him. I wonder what will become of him, but I'm not too worried. Like a cat, he's sure to land on his feet.

Falko is another matter entirely.

When I first arrived at St. Sebastian's, I think I hated him the most. Now I can't imagine the place without him. The thought of the big guy setting out to face the wide world all alone is almost as upsetting to me as if it were about to happen to me, and to Tristan. I wonder, too, how Jerome and Charles must be feeling, watching the others preparing for the competitions and knowing themselves already out of it. But tonight as I look around the garden, in place of my usual pre-trials jitters what I feel most is strangely at peace. With both my favorite former Journeys here with us again I can lie to myself a little and tell myself that Tristan was right: what's been lost *can* be found, and somehow the boys I love the most will always find their way back to the guild, and to me.

"Feels awfully good, doesn't it, kid?" Tristan asks me, shaking me out of my thoughts as I stir around next to him, and for a moment I think he must mean his shirt. He's wearing the bronze tunic that goes with Gilles's peacock outfit, and it's so soft and luxurious that it does feel awfully good against my cheek. I know he's really talking about the trials, though, even before he says,

"To be so ready, so early," and I can only agree.

"It's going to be your best performance yet, master. A masterpiece."

"It'll be the last one that's easy, Marek. So we might as well enjoy it," he says, and although his tone is light, I know he's serious. After Firsts we'll have our work cut out for us, and this may well be the last trial Tristan can pass at all, let alone win. And so as Jerome plays and Pascal paces amongst the rose bushes, murmuring the words of love we squires helped pen for him, Tristan and I sit with our heads together, whispering; we dare not talk about the boys' trick, in case any of the others are listening — Jurian, for example, has notoriously sharp ears — and we don't try to guess what the tests will be, either, since it's bad luck this close to the trials and we don't want to jinx it. Instead, I tell him all about the maneuvers we've been working up in squires' squad for our group retrievals, even though I've already told him everything, and he seems so calm and relaxed, I can't help asking,

"Tristan, you *are* ready, aren't you? For wands, I mean."

Tonight he's dressed quite simply, despite the expensive tunic he's wearing. He's not sporting either a jerkin or a vest, or anything with brocade or ruffles. The only extravagance besides Gilles's shirt is a pair of tights with one brown leg and the other white, paired with short boots of the same two solid colors but worn on the opposite feet, and it's all so plain I'm surprised the things are even Gilles's. He's smiling down at me with his head bare, and even through Gilles's clothing I can see my old Tristan — the light, laughing boy full of easy charm who came like a vision from above to rescue me — and it makes me a little nervous, since now he's supposed to be Gilles. But he just grins and laughs,

"But of course, my lad! In*dub*itably."

We stay out like this late into the night, lulled by the wine and the music, and by the luminous moon's spell. It's one of those rare hours at the guild that I love the best, when the spirit of friendship overcomes the boys' rivalry, and for a while Poncellet even drifts out to join us, lending more of a sense of occasion to our moonlit gathering, since he rarely joins us out here, and for once he doesn't seem inclined to talk, even about himself. He just leans up against a pillar of the portico, puffing on a little clay pipe and smoking some rancid weed he claims he got somewhere on a crusade (although he told *me* he'd never been out of Ardennes), and staring up at the moon in a way that makes me wonder if he isn't thinking about de Gilford's wife, and all of her sons who look exactly like him.

He looks as moonstruck as the rest of us, and luckily the cloying aroma of his pipe is too far away to reach me, and he's so silent that I hardly notice when later he taps it out and wanders back inside again. I'm too busy sitting back and letting the evening soak in with all its beauty.

I'm so contented and happy, nothing can spoil the intoxication of the evening for me; not even that giant eye of a moon staring down at me out of my peripheral vision. Or even the memory that it brings on, of Gilles's voice saying "somewhere, there's a *man* who's suffering. Suffering, from unrequited love." As the night wears on, I simply nestle up closer to Tristan and I ignore it, content to be caught up in the strange night's power and getting drowsier and drowsier, until I'm not thinking about the trials or any of the boys, or even about anything — not even when once or twice my eyes stray over to Taran, and in the dark I think I see him running one finger lightly across his lips.

I'm hardly paying any attention to Gilles, either, as he's staring out contemplatively toward the place where Pascal is pacing among the rosebushes. So I only really notice that he's being unusually quiet much later, when the long, lazy evening is winding down and the moon has come down so low in the sky it seems about to crash down right on top of me.

My head's lolled back against Tristan's shoulder, and I'm listening to Jerome's tune and to Tristan's desultory voice and I'm probably already half asleep. My mind is blissfully empty, when in letting my gaze rove idly around the garden, my half-closed eyes come briefly to rest on Gilles's. We contemplate each other for a moment across the flame of his candle, and it's probably just a coincidence that it's only at this moment that Gilles gives old Popinjay a rest, and with the toe of his boot, he prods me instead.

From the look on Gilles's face, I'm fully expecting him to make another annoying comment about the moon. And I think he almost does, before thinking better of it. Instead, he shifts around a little on his seat, and he calls over to Jerome, who's latest song has just come to an end.

"Play the *Wands* song for us, won't you, my good fellow?" he demands, in an odd tone that's nothing like his old one, or one of Tristan's, either.

"That old chestnut?" Aristide scoffs. "Don't listen to him, Jerome. Give us something livelier. That's too depressing, and I'm in the mood to celebrate," and there's a general murmur of agreement.

"It's a *classic*," Gilles sniffs. "It's one of my favorites, and no one can deny that the occasion is entirely appropriate."

No one can think of an answer to that, so although I think none of the others are in the mood to hear the song, Jerome inclines his head and begins to strum out a few soft chords that do sound rather melancholy.

I'm not eager to hear the song, either. I've heard it before, of course, since Gilles is right and it is a classic. At least, it's one of the old guild songs everybody knows, and I can vaguely remember my father singing it to Jules once or twice around the fire on a winter evening. I can't remember how it goes, exactly; it's been a long time since I heard it. I really only remember enough to suspect that I'm not much going to like it. Gilles's demeanor as he settles back to listen would be enough to tell me so, since he's now looking over at the place where Pascal's voice is still drifting back to us from among the roses with an unreadable expression.

Sure enough, as soon as Jerome nods his head and Charles's deep baritone accordingly rings out in the garden, the only good thing I can say about the song Gilles has proposed is that it turns out to consist only of a few short stanzas.

"*In a clearing in the forest
there stands a willow tree,*" Charles croons, and I don't like the song already. But I tell myself with Gilles suggesting it, it could be worse. It could be about a stump.

"*Beneath its bending branches
you used to wait for me,*" Charles warbles on.
"*But your heart is as fickle
as clouds that ride the skies,
for oh my faithless lady,
you believed all their lies!
Why did you give ear to idle rumors,
slurs that I was fancy free?
Or trust in the opinions of others
over your own experience of me?
How often have I proved noble,
more than worthy of esteem?
Oh, why didn't you remember:
things aren't always what they seem?*"

My head swivels around and I look sharply over at Gilles; it's obvious now where he got this line of his. But he's not looking at me, and I don't think he asked for the song to tease me. And as Charles begins the next stanza, I have to wonder why he did. Despite cutting his hair (and some of his affectations), Gilles is still a wands man. So maybe it's as simple as that.

But I doubt it.

I feel myself blushing in the dark, and I look furtively around the garden to see if anyone is looking at me, embarrassed by the thought that the reproachful words of the song could somehow be meant for me. Of course, no one else is thinking about me in connection with the song. It's a love song after all, and their heads are full of thoughts of the trials, or of their own amours. So I suppose, given the way he feels about me, it's only natural that the one boy who is staring at me intently from across the little patch of grass is Remy.

I can't tell if the moonlight is making him romantic, or if he's thinking about what happened between us in Brecelyn's clearing, when we found Taran's broken arrow and he begged me not to tell. But I bet he knows I kept that promise about as well as I've kept my promises to his master, and with the moon casting long, distorting shadows across his face he looks older than usual, and more serious. Hard, even, and a stray thought pops into my head, that it's odd Remy's never held my low opinion of his master against me. In the strange light that's making everything look so different, it suddenly strikes me as incredible. Where another boy would hate me for it, instead Remy loves me.

It must be the alcohol confusing me, since soon Armand nudges Remy and the two of them start whispering about something together, to all appearances quite happily. But as Charles's rich tones fill the garden, I can hardly bear to hear any more of the song, or to think about what Remy's *master* must be making of it, and it takes all my willpower to keep myself from looking directly over at him.

St. Sebastian's is our family,
and a merry band were we,
until I found you with another,
with my own guild **brother** —
Tell me, was that kiss
just to **punish** *me?*

Before Charles can finish the line, Taran's already on his feet. He's gotten up even more swiftly than he did from table, and just like then he turns heel and without a word to anyone he disappears into the darkness of the portico, no doubt heading inside to bed.

Nobody much seems to notice; abrupt departures are nothing unusual for him, and the boys are too spellbound by the magic of the evening to pay any mind to him. Even Remy doesn't seem to mark it, since Armand is now pestering him with some nonsense about ghosts, and the two of them are quietly arguing about it.

Nobody, that is, but me. As soon as Taran is on his feet, in the same instant I've sprung up, too, almost as though we were connected by an invisible string. And without a thought for what he or anyone else might think about it, in a flash I dash recklessly across the garden, and I run after him.

I catch up with Taran behind the vines, and as Charles is belting out the last lines of the wretched song, I'm pulling Taran back frantically by his sleeve.

"When all my trials are over,
dig my grave beneath that tree,
with a wand as my marker,
inscribed for all to see:
No one ever loved her more,
or did more for her than me."

Taran turns to peer down at me in the dark, and as the words of the song hover in the air between us, we stand there in the portico, so frozen for a moment that again I think we could be statues in a niche, hidden from the view of the others in the garden only by a thin veil of leaves.

"Taran," I stammer breathlessly, "Taran, I ... oh, Taran, I don't, *I don't* ... I, oh, *Taran.*"

And then I'm in his arms, and I'm kissing him.

Or he's kissing me, most violently. I don't know how I got there — if I grabbed him, or he grabbed me.

I don't really care, since his arms are tight around me and I'm swimming in moonlight, up through the clinging vines that are sweet with scent and trembling right along with me. The blood in my veins is liquid fire and it's moonbeams, and as I drink Taran in as deeply as I longed to do that day in the archives, his kiss is moonlight, too, and it's fire and I'm drowning in it.

As abruptly as it started, it's over.

Out in the garden the boys' voices raise in laughter at some joke or other, and at the sudden sound my eyes fly open.

Taran's nowhere to be seen.

I'm still sitting out in the garden, with my head on Tristan's shoulder and my back up against the base of the tree.

It was just the moon playing tricks on me, and I dreamed the whole thing.

I straighten up, and I wipe away the drool that's been puddling from the corner of mouth onto Tristan's shoulder self-consciously. I'm burning in the dark, as disoriented as if my feet had been suddenly pulled out from under me and all the breath knocked out of me; I'm only vaguely aware of Tristan now drawling amusedly over my head,

"It's dashed *ungrammatical*, too, isn't it? It really should be 'no one did more for her than *I*," and as the boys all laugh again, I struggle back to reality:

I've been slumped out here under a tree drunkenly slavering over Taran, while he's surely back in his room, lying face-down on his cot with his face buried in that sea-foam green veil of my sister's.

But I don't let it upset me unduly.

I really don't.

On a night like this, anyone can slip. I *am* a little drunk, and no one can control what he thinks in his sleep. Besides, I've already admitted to myself that I'm in love with him.

The full moon comes around only once a month; by morning it will be gone, and with it all its cruel fantasies. So I force myself to settle back into enjoying what's left of the evening, and I think I manage it pretty admirably, although some of its charm has understandably palled for me.

What stays with me the longest isn't the humiliation of it, or even annoyance at myself that I haven't really managed to forget about that almost-kiss of Taran's, since it's not hard to figure out what inspired the dream. It's the chastising words of Gilles's song. And it's that the feeling I had in my dream that there was something I was desperate to tell Taran is still lingering — only now that I'm awake, I'm no longer sure exactly what it is.

With the competitions starting up again in earnest, I know I'll never really have a chance to thank Taran for saving me on the tower, or find a way to tell him that I no longer think quite so badly of him. But I have a niggling feeling that whatever my dream-self was about to say to Taran there under the vines was something more than either of those things.

Gilles interrupts my meditations not much later, by giving me another meaningful prod with the toe of his boot. When he proceeds to drawl down at me sourly,

"A *lovers' moon*, indeed! What a pity, Marek, it's turned out all along just to be *Aristide's*," all I can do is agree.

And with that, I'm more than ready to go in.

I cast one last baleful look up at the brilliant moon. It's so huge and bright, it could be the eye of our Saint himself, keeping tabs on me. So I lift my arms in that motion that's like I'm aiming to shoot down the moon, and as I follow my master inside to get some much-needed sleep, I grumble to myself,

"If you *had* to give me a test, Sebastian, did it have to be such a hard one?"

CHAPTER THIRTY-FIVE

The next day finds me up bright and early, and on my way out to the shop to check on Luc Fournier.

I'm in a fine mood this morning, as predicted. The moon is down and outside the sun is rising on what's sure to be a glorious day, and all that's left over from last night is a growing sense of excitement for the trials, and a bit of a hangover.

Even better, I've got the whole morning to myself. All official drills have been cancelled to allow the Journeys to prepare for the impending trials as they see fit. In Tristan's case, that's sure to mean sleeping for most of it. I'm to be free all day, which means I won't have to worry about dealing with my master's clothing, or lack thereof — not even his competition attire, since after we were mobbed during our St. Sebastian's day procession back in January, Gilles generously took it upon himself to have entirely new costumes commissioned for all the Journeys. They've already been delivered, and I've got Tristan's crimson-lined cape spread out flat across the foot of an empty cot, next to my own shorter, matching one. The master's generously given us permission to wear the costumes from our St. Sebastian's day show tomorrow, as part of our 'squires' squad' solidarity — everything but the little felt caps, and I can't really blame him for drawing the line at that. I've got everything pressed and polished, burnished bright and laid up in readiness, and I plan to spend the whole day lost in the pleasures of checking over Tristan's equipment obsessively and daydreaming about the trials, since for once I'm not being eaten up by anxiety over them. I've only got one little task left to do today, and even that is entirely pleasant.

As I was pulling on my boots, while most of the other boys were still abed, one of the kitchen boys popped into barracks to deliver a note for Pascal from the masters, informing him that crossbow bolts had been added to our competition equipment lists at the last minute. It can only mean that Master Guillaume has also agreed to a request floated on behalf of our club by Taran, that we squires be allowed to carry our crossbows out to the line with us during the trials. It's probably just for show, to add a little color to the proceedings and as an advertisement for next year's crossbow competitions, or something similar. But just the thought that I'll have my crossbow with me tomorrow is fueling my high spirits, and I'm brimming with anticipation. Firsts are *tomorrow*. I can hardly believe it.

I've got plenty of bolts in stock, and picking up the ones necessary to complete the new inventory will be the work of mere minutes. So there's no real reason for me to be rushing out so early to do it, except that I'm too antsy to sit still. Besides, Pascal's the only other boy already up and dressed. If I hang around barracks, I'm sure to get roped into wasting the day listening to him practice his proposal, and I'm eager to get out before the others wake — particularly Remy.

I have a vague memory of him staring at me from across the garden last night with an intensity that was disturbing, even for him, and for his own good, I know the time has come to have a firm talk with him. It's long overdue, and it'll be the kind thing; I have better reason than most to know how painful unrequited love can be, when it's allowed to linger. And what it feels like not to get a kiss, when you've been longing for one all evening. I'm just not looking forward to the confrontation, and there's no way I'm going to do it before Firsts; I've waited too long for the trials and too much is at stake for me to let my head to be anything but clear going into them. The last thing I need is to be reminded of last night, out in the garden.

I duck out hastily, while the other boys are just starting to stir and before Pascal can hail me over, and I trot briskly down the hallway, intent on raiding the sideboard for something to deposit inside Tristan's door for him to eat later. But when I round the corner into the corridor where the big sideboard stands, to my surprise I spot Taran.

He's leaning restlessly up against the wall, looking down and now and then giving the leg of the sideboard an impatient little kick. Taran's rarely out in the hallways this early, and I don't remember ever having seen him lingering at the sideboard. He doesn't have to; Remy's too solicitous. It looks a lot like he's waiting to waylay some luckless boy while there's not much of anyone else around in the hallway; if that boy happens to be me, I'm in no hurry to let that happen.

I draw back hastily, before Taran can see me. If he is waiting for me, I know why, and I have no intention of suffering through a stilted apology from him now for that kiss he almost gave me. I can practically hear him spouting *"it was a terrible mistake"* or *"nothing like it can ever happen again, do you understand me?!,"* and I don't want to hear it. I'm not going to spend the morning letting Taran make himself feel better about what happened in the archives in a way that's sure to make me feel a whole lot worse about it. So I retrace my steps, thinking that this would be an excellent time to get started on gathering up those crossbow bolts, and anyway, I want to see how Luc is doing this morning. Now that I've put aside my misgivings about him, I've started to feel sorry for him.

Luc will hardly be expecting me, since it's the day before trials. I'm pretty sure he'll already be there, though, even though it's awfully early. I know what it's like to be new to a place where you feel you don't fit in, struggling to do a job for which you are unprepared and ill suited. He'll be trying to make up for his lack of skill with a show of diligence, and it'll be fun to surprise him.

As I head down the corridor past the masters' offices and out across the yard, I'm so excited about the thought of striding out in front of the crowds decked out in my crossbow gear (and about having eluded Taran, too), I'm even humming snatches of the *Wands* song to myself, and musing about possible mottos for the master's crossbow contingent. After everything I've been through since that terrible morning in Brecelyn's forest, today I feel like I could do anything — slay a dragon, shoot a dozen apples off Tristan's head — even compose a motto, in Latin. Tomorrow is going to be even better, the culmination of months of effort; if you'd told me back when I was lying face-down on the floor of Brecelyn's chapel that Tristan would be heading into Firsts with a shot at edging out his rival, or that I'd have made an uneasy peace with Taran sure to benefit all the squires, I'd never have believed it. It gives me a little guilty pleasure, too, to picture Luc up in the stands, unwittingly cheering on the squire who once had nothing more to look forward to than becoming engaged to him.

When I slip inside the shop tent, Luc's already there, as I knew he would be. He's dutifully seated at a workbench with an array of fletching tools spread out in front of him, although he doesn't seem to be doing anything with them. I can't say I blame him. I doubt anyone's told him how to use them. He's just looking around the tent worriedly, and as soon as he spots me, he breaks into such a huge smile that I can't help smiling back, wondering how I could have thought I had anything to fear from him.

The grin Luc's giving me as I come up to join him is so big and dazzling, in fact, it could almost be one of Tristan's. I'm doubly glad I decided to come out so early, since it's obvious that nobody else is going to pay any attention to him, and it hasn't taken me long to see I was wrong about one thing: Luc doesn't look at all surprised to see me. He's been anxiously on the look-out for my arrival, and it would have been a shame to have disappointed him.

I hasten over to join him, and after we exchange a few awkward pleasantries, I let him help me add the necessary crossbow bolts to an assemblage of equipment I've already got piled up next to the boys' exhibition materials, ready to be transported over to Tristan's pavilion tomorrow morning. I thoughtfully add Pascal's crossbow to his similar stockpile of Gilles's equipment, and as I work through the list of new items with Luc, I make it an opportunity for a lesson. He's got to learn the properties of different weights and lengths of arrows sometime, and this morning his bright and eager mood matches mine and he's full of questions. Not about fletching, admittedly, but about the trials, and I can't blame him for that, either. He's a local boy and he's grown up with them; it's only natural he'd be excited about them. Still, it gives me a thrill of pride that he's so delighted to be getting an insider's view of them, and it's all so flattering, it doesn't even strike me as odd me that what seems to have caught his imagination the most is the timing of everything.

We pass a pleasant morning in which I probably do more bragging about my master than instructing, and Luc is gratifyingly interested in all the details, even in little points of organization that I'd hardly have thought to ask myself. It's only after an hour or two have passed that I realize I've not actually taught him anything more about how to fletch an arrow; still, I consider it a day's work well done. We've gone over Tristan's gear and my own so many times and so carefully that even I have to be satisfied. By the time my stomach's started growling loudly enough that I can't ignore it any longer, Luc is starting to overcome his timidity, and I'm beginning to think that on closer acquaintance he may yet prove more intelligent than I've been giving him credit.

I stay on with Luc a little longer — just long enough to give him the hastiest of lessons on the rudiments of working a nock into a shaft, and to be absolutely certain that any loiterers around the sideboard have had ample time to clear out. Then I dust off my hands, and before I take my leave of Luc, as I watch him fiddling inexpertly around with his knife against the butt end of an arrow, I ask,

"You'll be okay out here by yourself for a while, won't you?," and Luc looks up.

He looks around, and not seeing Marcel anywhere, he says,

"Uh, actually, Marek, would you mind taking a detour to come with me past the stables, on your way back inside?"

When all I do is look at him questioningly, he drops his eyes and mumbles,

"I've been storing my stuff out there, in an empty stall. And you see, it's like this. I've got something I want to give you. A little something, to thank you. It isn't much, but I think you deserve it. I was really hoping you could use it, during the competitions."

He says it so shyly, he could be offering me a token, and at the thought I almost laugh out loud. It's so sweet, I can't help but be touched. So I give him a little nod, not trusting my voice, and soon we're heading off together companionably across the yard. As we go, eventually I ask him,

"What is it, Luc?"

"It's a *surprise*," he replies happily, and he looks so full of gleeful anticipation about it that I don't press him, not wanting to spoil it for him.

All's quiet in the stables at this hour; it's past time for the work crews to arrive, and there's nary a stable boy in sight. The only sounds within are the gentle blowing and stomping of animals, moving around in their stalls. Only a few slivers of daylight are coming in from gaps up under the rafters, and the air is so musty and rank as we enter that I sincerely hope Luc hasn't been resorting to sleeping out here. But I don't say so, and I don't say anything as I follow Luc inside. I simply trot along behind him, letting him lead me down the dank and dusty central aisle, until Luc motions me toward one of the darkened back stalls.

It's Taran's old hideout, and I can't help balking. When I pull a frown, Luc says conspiratorially,

"I'm probably not supposed to be in here," and he takes hold of my upper arm. His grip is surprisingly firm and soon he's propelling me forward, eagerness making him bold; whatever he's got for me has gotten him so excited, I'm starting to get pretty curious. Curious enough to let Luc hustle me into the shadowy stall unresisting, even though I've started to feel a little odd.

With the other stalls all so overcrowded, it seems strange that this one is standing cold and empty. And when Luc then says,

"Don't tell anyone! You won't tell on me, though, will you, Marek? No, I don't think you will. I can tell, you're good at keeping *secrets*," the hairs on my forearms bristle, just as though I were becoming frightened.

"It's back there," Luc says, motioning toward the far corner of the stall, and he steps aside with a gesture that urges me to take a few steps further inside past him. It would be silly to refuse, after coming this far with him — although now, I'm reluctant. I feel like a character in a fairytale, stepping into a cave — and he's a giant, blocking the exit.

It's so pitch black in the shadowy corner of the stall that at first, my eyes can't adjust to the lack of light, and I don't see anything. Nothing but piles of moldy straw, anyway.

"Where is it?" I ask.

"Look *closer*," he says, and as he says it, he comes up behind me so close that I take another involuntary step forward.

As I do, Luc suddenly puts both his hands on my shoulders, guiding my attention down toward a spot in the stall's innermost corner. I bend forward toward it a little, and I peer down. And at first, I still don't see anything. I don't see any sign of the possessions he was talking about, either.

Then I see it.

There *is* a little canvas bag, lying on the straw. From the flat way it looks, whatever's in it must be awfully small.

"I told you it wasn't much," Luc says apologetically, when he sees I've finally spotted it. And when I hesitate, without letting go of my shoulders he takes another step up closer behind me, so that he's virtually on top of me.

In a voice low and thick with anticipation, he urges,

"Go on, open it."

I don't feel anything inside the little bag when I do bend down and pick it up.

And I don't feel anything inside it, as my fingers work open its drawstrings. There must be something in there, though, because I can feel Luc stirring around expectantly behind me.

Then I put my hand inside.

"It's empty," I say dumbly.

My hollow words hang in the still, murky air. There's no other sound in the stall, except for the buzzing of a fly. And Luc's rapid breathing, hot and moist on the back of my neck.

Somewhere behind me a voice I hardly recognize whispers into my ear, "Surprise, *Marieke*."

He says it so softly, I barely hear it. The words trickle down my spine like drops of icy water, and at first all that registers is how different Luc's voice sounds. It's low, deep, and male, tinged with triumph and thick with amusement. So I'm already afraid, even before I realize the full significance of what he's said.

Luc's not just called me by my old name. He's used it as a threat.

I whirl around, my heart pounding — only to shrink back at the sight of Luc's face. The shy, gentle boy from the shop is gone. In his place a cool and confident man is now towering over me, his sly eyes glinting with delight in the weird half-light.

"You didn't recognize me," I say stupidly, and he laughs. Of course he did.

"Did you really think I could forget a face like *yours*?" he says, raising one eyebrow archly and taking a step toward me, just for the pleasure of forcing me back. "I recognized you the *first* time I saw you — at your St. Sebastian's day exhibition. Why do you think I came here? I know an opportunity when I see one."

He leans up against the side of the stall, his impressive bulk between me and the door, and he watches me with an amused smile while I try to recover from the shock of what he's saying enough to process it. But his lips are thin and they stick to his teeth, and with everything about his big frame now radiating power, all I can do is feel confused and panicked.

"I rather expect that's something we have in common," he declares lazily, and he's caught me so off guard, for a desperate moment I let myself hope what he's saying is that he came here when he recognized me in order to help me. "As it happens, I owe money around town. A lot of it."

"You can make a g-good living from fletching," I stammer shakily, even though the thought of working with Luc now makes my stomach give a nauseating flip. "And you can count on me!" I add, trying to rally. "I'll help you learn the ropes, and you'll get the hang of it, eventually. Why, you're sure to settle in nicely, once you quit gambling." I'm rambling, nervously tripping over the hay in an effort to inch toward the stall door, when Luc cuts me off coldly.

"Fletching!" he spits, shifting his weight forward just enough to signal that I'd be wise to stay in my place. "I don't want to be a *fletcher*," he says scornfully. "Surely not even *you* can be as naïve as all that."

"What *do* you want, then?" I manage to ask.

"Goodness! There's no need to look so tragic. Me? I'm just looking to get out," he says. "I'm for Meuse, the first chance I get. Only there's the matter of a few unsettled debts. And I'll need a stake. A man can't show up in the big city with an empty purse."

"I don't have any money." My throat so dry, it could be stuffed with straw. "And neither does my master."

"Ah yes, *him*," Luc purrs. "Such a taste for fancy clothes, and no money? What a shame! And he looks so *good* in them. Got yourself a pretty little set-up here, don't you? So many *perks*." He draws out the word in a way that leaves no question that he's figured out I'm in love with Tristan — or at least that I'm in lust with him.

It's all happening so fast, I'm not at all sure what Luc's getting at. But when he drawls,

"And *so* many privileges! Free run of the guild buildings, not to mention access to all those rich boys' rooms," I must be starting to have an inkling, since my mouth flies open in protest.

Before I can plead with him or voice an objection, Luc shoots forward. For such a large boy, he's surprisingly agile.

"No more games!" he snaps. "We've had our fun, our little charades. But I know who you *really* are. You're an imposter and a liar, and I've heard the rumors. Everyone knows you're a thief. So tomorrow during the competitions, while all the Journey rooms are standing empty, you're going to steal something for me. Something *big*. Then you're going to put it in that bag I gave you, and you're going to bring it right back here to me. Shall we say, during the interval before the exhibitions? That should be perfect timing."

Halfway through Luc's speech, I start trying to push past him. But Luc simply shoves me back with one hand, almost playfully, but with easy power, and horribly, he looks like he's enjoying himself.

"Luc, *please*. You've got it all wrong. I'm not really a thief."

My voice is the barest of whispers, and I must sound pathetic. But Luc is unmoved.

"Really?" he drawls. "That's unfortunate." Then he gives me one last shove. "Guess what?" he says darkly. "You are now."

He steps back, his head cocked to one side as though to assess from a better angle the effect he's having, clearly finding the look on my pale and sweaty face terribly gratifying.

"Ah, don't take it so hard!" he chuckles, in a way that suggests he thinks the tears now threatening to trickle down my cheeks are all just an act. "And cheer up. I'm not looking to horn in on your operation. Come through for me and I'll be out of your hair in no time. What's left of it! It should be perfectly safe. From what you've told me, the veterans on guard duty won't question a squire's presence in the Journey hallway on competition day. And if they do, you can simply tell them you're fetching something for your master. The way I see it, I'm doing you a favor. It's awfully considerate of me to coincide my little request with the trials, when there'll be so many strangers milling about. It's perfect cover, and who knows? Once the theft is discovered, maybe you won't even be suspected."

"If I'm seen in the Journey hallway, it'll be remembered," I protest, hating that I already sound like I'm going to do it.

"Then don't get caught! Or steal from one of the masters, or don't wait for tomorrow, and take something tonight. What do I care? *You* figure it out. You owe me. One score, for your dear old fiancé! For old times' sake. Consider it your *dowry*. So if you know what's good for you, you'll stop arguing, and start thinking — thinking about what you can take, and about what's *at stake*. Because if you don't come through for me tomorrow, I'll air your dirty secrets, and you don't want that. Not when you've made such a comfortable little nest here for yourself."

"You wouldn't denounce me, Luc, would you?" My throat is so dry now I'm barely able to force the words out. "The penalty. It's *death*."

"Should have thought of that sooner, eh, *Verbeke*?" he replies coldly. "But I'm not bloodthirsty," he grins, looking a lot like he'd enjoy nothing better than opening up my veins and taking a big drink. "And I wouldn't have to do *that*, now would I? All I'd have to do is tell *your* master. He seemed mighty keen to learn the whereabouts of Jan Verbeke's daughter. I have a funny feeling the last thing you want is for him to find out."

With that Luc reaches down and picks up the canvas bag from where it's fallen onto the hay at my feet, and he dangles it over my hand.

"So, what's it going to be?" he demands, although after threatening to reveal me to Tristan, he knows there's nothing I can say. All I can do is hang my head, ball up the little bag tightly in my fist, and stumble out of the stall with it.

I can feel Luc's eyes on me, watching me go, and when I've reached the stable's big double doors, he calls out,

"Oh, and *Marek*. Just in case you're thinking of bolting, here's the thing. Running off can't save you this time. If you disappear on me, I'll go straight to the masters. Better yet, I'll go straight to *your* master, and I'll tell him what really happened to Marieke Verbeke."

CHAPTER THIRTY-SIX

I emerge from the darkness of the stables into the bright light of morning in a daze and my stomach fluttering with panic, to find that I was right.

It is a glorious day.

The sky is impossibly high, and out in the garden I can hear birds chattering to each other among the rosebushes. It would be lovely to spend the rest of the morning sitting in the shade of the jasmine vines and listening to their song, and before me our practice field lies open just as invitingly. Out on the far field, the flaps of colorful canvas pavilions are waving to me in the breeze as though beckoning me over merrily, and from beyond the line of the old wall I can hear the sounds of tinkering and hammering, telling me that Charles is out there somewhere hard at work building his forge, yet surely happy to take a break for a while to sit and chat with me. But I can't move from the spot, and my eyes move over all of it unseeingly.

I've let my identity be discovered by a boy who is anything but noble, and there's not a thing in the world I can do about it.

The funny thing is, I don't even feel afraid.

How could I?

I'm far too numb to feel anything.

I stand immobile, framed by the open stable door behind me, and I let my eyes rove over every inch of the guild complex and I drink it all in, trying to memorize it like the face of a friend I might never see again. *I wonder where I'll be, when the master finishes his tower?* If I'll ever see the magnificent buildings he's got planned. Maybe by then I will be out in the garden, next to Baylen — six feet underground.

Even that sounds like an awfully sweet fate, compared to what will really happen if Luc follows through on the worst of his threats. I'll be thrown out as carrion for dogs and birds, to rot out behind the wall on unconsecrated ground. Tristan will be disgraced into the bargain, and instead of avenging my father, I'll just have made him a laughingstock all over again. I've been so foolish and so careless, right now the indignity of ending up being eaten by old Popinjay seems like a fitting end.

My eyes stray out toward the treetops of the greenwood that borders St. Sebastian's, and I picture it, stretching out for miles all around. In my mind's eye I can see its shady glades, and the little meadow where the abandoned windmill stands. I imagine running through it as it must be now — a sea of poppies, each one redder than the last. But without Tristan, the old windmill holds no refuge. It's just a moldering pile of lumber, and I'm not really thinking about running away. Luc's already made it perfectly clear I can't do that.

Maybe he wouldn't really denounce me to the master if I fled; he'd have nothing to gain by it, and with me gone, he'd have no way to prove his claims. But he might, and I'd be a fool to test him. He's going to watch me like a hawk, and if I refuse to steal for him or try to run away, he'll at least tell Tristan the truth, out of pure spite. I'd rather really be dead than have him do that, and if I were to disappear without a word of explanation on the eve of the competitions, what of Tristan then? It would be a betrayal he'd never understand. With no squire and abandoned by his best friend, he'd surely fail. If I run, Tristan will be out — it's as simple as that.

I don't know how long I stand there, lost in frantic, extreme thoughts and letting them get more and more dramatic. But at length I tell myself I've got to calm down and pull myself together. Indulging in self-pity isn't going to help me, and I've been in tough spots before, haven't I? And I managed to think my way out of them.

Besides, Luc isn't here to get me in trouble. If he were, he'd already have done it. He just wants money. If I get it for him, he'll be gone, and good riddance. So I try to convince myself I'm overreacting. It's a setback, that's all. A complication. Maybe Tristan was right, and I've got to toughen up. There are plenty of men and boys like Luc in Meuse, and if I'm headed there myself, I'm going to have to get used to having my wits about me.

One big score. For a clever boy, how hard can that be?

Still, the thought of stealing from the guild makes me break into a sweat, and I have no idea what it could be.

When I turn around, Luc's long gone. I circle around through the yard to go inside anyway, not wanting to step back into the stables, eager to retreat back inside where Luc can't follow. As I go, I tell myself anything I have to suffer as Marek is surely better than being Luc Fournier's *wife*. But as I make my way to the sideboard to retrieve Tristan's breakfast, all the while scanning the hallways for valuables, I'm also muttering to myself,

"I'm not a thief. *I'm not a thief!* I don't want to be a thief."

It's not really stealing, though, is it, if it's done under duress? I just don't let myself think about the fact that if I get caught, the consequences will be the same, no matter what the circumstances.

After scavenging what I can from the dregs still on offer on the sideboard and depositing it outside Tristan's door for his breakfast, making sure not to wake him, I spend the rest of the morning scurrying up and down the long guild hallways, feeling miserable and popping my head into rooms and peeking in through doorways. I can't go back to barracks. I don't dare let myself run into any of the boys, in the state I'm in. I can't even check on my master, and that's the hardest thing — that, and the feeling that Luc's trapped me inside my own guild, and the walls I've always found so protective now feel suffocating.

All through noon mess, I'm distracted. Tristan's already deep in conversation with Gilles and Jerome when he shows up and he sits down at the opposite end of the table, absorbed in a lively discussion with them about flexible appendages. He's had no opportunity to see anything amiss in my manner, and I suppose Luc was right about one thing. Maybe I should be grateful that tomorrow's trials are providing such a perfect excuse for my agitation, since nobody else seems to suspect that something more might be on my mind, either. I do my best to join the boys in their breathless, happy banter, but I'm also looking around the main hall, appraising all the contents, sizing up their value.

The room is still virtually empty; most of the usual ornamentation has yet to be unpacked, and it'd all have been too big to take unnoticed anyway. The only thing in the room worth enough to satisfy Luc is staring down from the wall at me, giving me a mocking expression: the painting of St. Sebastian. It's the one thing I'd gladly rip off the wall and hand over — if it weren't so massive.

Between Pascal's proposal, his ongoing feud with Armand, and the boys' own preoccupation with their masters' chances in tomorrow's trials, the squires have all got their own problems. So the only boy at our end of the table who notices my agitation is Remy. He's always sensitive to my moods, and he keeps flitting a nervous hand around my shoulder and tittering out solicitous questions.

"If it's Tristan's exhibition you're worried about, it's not too late. If you tell me what it is, I can help you tweak it," he says at one point, meaning to be helpful, so I know I shouldn't do it. But I can't help snapping at him,

"Worry about your own master, Remy! Because for once, the trick *my* master does is surely going to beat his."

Nobody else at all has any reason to think that something other than the trials could be distressing me — nobody, but Taran. Throughout the meal I feel his gaze on me, as though he's trying to read me. Only I don't dare look down the table at him. So I don't know how he reacts, when at one point I break under the pressure. I feel like I'm drowning in a sea of boys and I can't get a breath, and during an unfortunate lull in the conversation, I gulp for air with a loud sound like a strangled hiccup.

Making a joke of it, Falko calls out down the table, "Hey, Taran! Better give Marek another great big hug. Sounds like he's choking again!"

All I know is, it upsets Remy. He spends the rest of the meal darting looks back and forth between me and Taran, clearly worrying that his master has started harassing me again.

Once mess is over, I'm out of the hall like a shot. I don't even wait for Tristan. I just dash off as soon as he stands up, pretending I don't hear him calling. And I don't wait for Remy, either.

He comes scampering after me anyway. To my surprise, he doesn't pester me with questions. But from the determined set of his jaw, he intends to stick to me like a cocklebur in a mangy goat's fur, and he must have figured out I'm in imminent danger of being cornered by Taran. I can tell he's trying to help me keep from getting caught alone with him, and any other day, I'd probably be grateful. As it is, it's horribly frustrating. Luc's given me precious little time to accomplish my task for him, and I can't do it with Remy following me. I spend a harried half-hour trying to slough him off, and I manage to ditch him momentarily out in the vestibule, but Remy's damned fast. He catches me up as I'm circling back out through the kitchens, and it takes all my ingenuity and all my speed to lose him again, this time by hiding behind a tree, out in the garden.

As soon as Remy's gone, I head straight into the chapel. I doubt even prayers could help me now, but it's worth a try, and more than anything I need a quiet place to think. If nothing else, I've got to figure out what I'm going to steal. And how I'm going to avoid getting caught in the process.

I know which boy I'd prefer to rob, no question: Aristide. Only I've recently been in his room, and I didn't see any possibilities. Whatever valuables he has, he's got them well hidden. Besides, if something should go missing from *his* room, I might as well just lop off both my hands and hand them over, since he won't waste any time in accusing me of the theft (and rightly). So I let myself in through the chapel's little side door beyond the rosebushes and I make my way down the center aisle to one of the front pews, where first I pause to kneel and say a dutiful prayer, hating myself that as I do, I'm also looking around to see if there's anything in here I could pilfer.

Nobody much is in the chapel at this time of day. Now and then the guild priest wanders in, shuffling around behind the altar to ready the necessary paraphernalia for tomorrow's opening ceremonies, and an occasional serving boy or two ambles past, trailing a desultory broom along the floor, but for now I have the place virtually to myself.

I'm all alone, and today the vaulted nave of the little church feels as cold and as lofty as a long-forgotten tomb. My nerves can't take it, and I know I can't count on having the place to myself for long. Sooner or later, some of the Journeys will surely be coming in to say their own pre-competition prayers. So when I spot a narrow opening deep in shadow between the back of the wooden confessional booth and the stone wall of a side aisle, soon I'm slipping into the inviting little gap.

I can only wedge myself into the little hidey-hole with difficulty, but the uncomfortable snugness of the space is almost as welcome as the thought that not even Remy could think to look for me here. It's so warm and close, I could be crawling into the safety of a mother's arms, or back into my father's tight embrace.

I stay there most of the afternoon, cramped and sweaty and uncomfortable, as I think through my options. It's pretty easy, since there aren't many of them. I think about my father, too, about how I wish he were here to help me, and how glad I am he never had to know what kind of boy he almost welcomed into our family. I think about all the choices I've made since he died, the good and the bad. And I second-guess all of them. But the more I think about it, the more I know the one thing I can't regret is coming to St. Sebastian's, whatever the consequences. If I hadn't been with Tristan on the tower at Thirds, there would have been no one there to save him.

But I also know I've been kidding myself.

I can't steal from my friends, or from my guild. I can't undo the good I've done for my master, by letting Luc make me into a thief. Even if no one ever found out about it I'd be a disgrace to my father's memory, and a disgrace to myself. And if I'm caught, I know exactly what my exposure and my death will look like, don't I? I spent a very vivid hour yesterday afternoon picturing it.

From my hiding place, out of the corner of my eye I can just see the gruesome little statue of St. Sebastian that stands on the altar at the front of the church. It's been hovering on the periphery of my vision, not very subtly seeming to grow larger and larger, as though trying to force me to give it my attention. Now I shift around a little so that I can peer down the central aisle, and I stare at it.

I take in every detail of its arrow-riddled body and its gaunt, agony-contorted face. There's no sudden flash of light, no radiant vision. Dust motes hang motionless in the streams of afternoon sun coming in from the windows high under the chapel rafters, and the stubborn little figure doesn't move at all, but I'm not surprised. I'm not looking for another sign. I already know what the immobile little figurine has to tell me. His wooden lips aren't moving, but even from here, I can practically hear him whispering to me,

"Nobody said it was going to be easy."

I can't run. And I won't steal. But I do have to do *something*, and the Saint and I both know there's only one thing it can be.

I'm going to have to beg Taran for his assistance. He already knows my secret, so he's the only one who can help me.

It's not going to be at all easy, though, I can guarantee it.

It's already hard, just thinking about it.

The hardest thing about it is that I've known all along I was going to have to do it.

And that Taran will surely agree.

I WAIT IN MY HIDING SPOT BEHIND THE CONFESSIONAL A LITTLE longer, listening for sounds out in the chapel, and steeling myself to seek out Taran. My heart is thumping and my upper lip is beaded with sweat, but now that I've decided on a course of action, what I'm actually feeling most is a rush of relief. If anyone can deal with Luc, it's Taran, and how bad can it be to ask him?

It's going to be awkward, certainly. Taran's sure to make me grovel, and I'm no doubt in for plenty of judgmental frowning and arm-crossing, not to mention a lot of expletive-laced exclamations of *'Oh, for Pete's sake!'* and *"I told you so,"* and *"how in the hell did you manage to get yourself into such a bloody mess!?"* But it's going to be a heck of a lot better than being bludgeoned to death, and when I remember how Taran went after the boys who beat me last year, I also think he's going to be rather protective, and indignant on my behalf. And it's funny. But after everything we've been through together lately, underneath it all I think we're even sort of starting to become friends. I just wish I didn't have to ask Taran for another favor before I've thanked him properly for the last ones, and when I'm surely in for a humiliating lecture about keeping my hands to myself.

How I wish now that I'd just kept that expensive veil of his! But at least I know he's got something he can give me to hand over to Luc that won't really be stealing, and since it's already supposedly missing, it'll raise no questions.

As I've been thinking, now and then there's been an occasional scuffle on the flagstone floor beyond the confession box, and a periodic creaking of its wooden doors, as one of the priest's acolytes moves around in the cubicles, preparing them for use or retrieving something from within. All's quiet now, though, and it's been a while since I heard the soft clicks of the little doors signaling that the attendant was closing up the box and he's long departed. The coast is clear, so I shift around onto my hands and knees, in preparation of crawling out of my hiding spot and heading straight off to find Taran. Now that I'm resolved, I feel like I can't stand to have the matter of Luc Fournier hanging over me for one more second.

It's trickier to back out of the tight space than it was to wedge myself into it, however, and to get myself turned around, I have to press my head up flush against the back wall of the confessional.

At the very moment when my cheek makes contact with the wood, right into my ear a loud voice trumpets,

"ARE YOU READY TO CONFESS?"

I lurch sideways, and I'm lucky there isn't enough room back here for my head to go much of anywhere — otherwise I'd surely have knocked myself out, I recoil so hard against the stone wall opposite, only to rebound right back up against the confessional. For one dizzy moment before my head clears, I'm sure it's the wrathful voice of God Almighty, demanding my penance for lurking in his chapel. Only it's not much better.

It's the *guild priest*, and the terrifying note in his voice wasn't really anger. It was just impatience, amplified by coming straight through the wood. The man wasn't tidying up the confessional earlier; he was simply going in. And what's more, there's a boy in there with him, in the adjoining cubicle. He's been sitting in there silently for the last five minutes, waiting for the boy to begin.

I deliberate for a moment, debating whether to sit tight and wait the reluctant boy out, or risk creeping away unnoticed while both he and the priest are still within. My nerves were already shot, but now they're paper thin, and I curse my own foolishness. *Why in the world did I think it was a good idea to conceal myself behind a confessional?* Getting caught sneaking out from behind the box will surely get me marched straight into the master's office, and it's not just awkward to overhear another man's confession. It's a sin, and I've got to find Taran, right away. I've wasted too much of the day already.

I shift forward tentatively, testing the waters and preparing to make a furtive exit, while the priest says more gently,

"This isn't the first time you've come in, only to do nothing more than sit. Whatever's on your mind, I guarantee you'll feel better, once you've been reconciled with it."

And that's when a deep, troubled voice replies,

"Forgive me, Father. I do have something to confess. Something *big*. But there can be no reconciliation. What I've done is unforgivable. At least, I'll never forgive myself for it."

It's *Taran*, and I freeze. There's no way I could make myself move from the spot now, even if I wanted to. Even if listening to his confession means risking eternal damnation. From the sound of it, Taran's about to confess to *shooting* Tristan. And to do that, he's going to have to tell the priest the whole truth about exactly what happened.

"I'm listening," the priest says, and I press my head up closer. I'm listening, too, with every fiber of my being.

There's another long pause. I'm pressing my ear up against the wall so hard that I'm getting splinters in my cheek, but that's not why it's agonizing waiting for him to speak.

Finally, Taran's harsh voice rasps through the wood,

"I forced myself on a girl, against her will."

"Mercy!" the priest exclaims, sounding shocked. "That *is*, uh, *unpleasant*," and I get the impression he's only managed to stop himself from saying 'unforgivable' at the last second.

To say I'm feeling shocked, too, is an understatement.

Taran's confessing to *molesting* Melissande. Every horrible thing Tristan said about him out in the windmill that day was nothing but the truth, and Tristan was right. It *is* worse than attempted murder, and even hearing it from Taran's own lips, I don't know how I can believe it. I don't think I could be more stunned if Taran sprouted wings and flew right out the chapel window.

There's another brief pause, while the priest composes himself.

"Taking a lady's virtue," he says gravely, "that *is* a sin, and one not to be taken lightly. The sanctity of the connubial couch —"

"*What?!*" Taran interrupts, sounding thoroughly taken aback. "What are you talking about? I'm not talking about any, er, *couching*," he says scornfully. "I'm *talking* about a kiss."

"A kiss?" the priest asks blankly.

"A kiss," Taran confirms. The priest sounds so confused and Taran so pompous that I almost laugh out loud. Only it isn't funny. Taran's not confessing to molesting Melissande. He's talking about kissing *me*, in the archives. "Er, *kisses*. It may have happened more than once," Taran clarifies, and all at once the stuffy little space I'm wedged into becomes Taran's hot little room; he's pulling back my hair and I'm opening my mouth, and as his mouth comes down on mine, I'm suffocating and I'm drowning.

"A kiss?" the priest repeats again, sounding a little bewildered. "It's hardly chivalrous, I'll grant you. An offense, indeed. But it doesn't sound so terribly serious."

"It's not just the kiss *per se* that's so terrible," Taran says, sounding agonized again. "It's the motive behind it."

"Ah, yes. Lust! That old beast." The priest makes a *tsk*ing sound with his teeth, sounding relieved to be back on familiar territory. Before he can wax lyrical about the dangers of lust, however, Taran interrupts him again.

"*Lust?!*" he explodes disdainfully. "Who said anything about *lust*? I didn't kiss her out of *lust*. I *did* it to punish her, in a moment of anger. I did it out of hatred."

"Mercy!" the priest exclaims again, for lack of anything better. Taran doesn't seem to notice, and I can hear him shifting around in the cubicle. When he continues, from the muffled sound of his voice, his head must be buried in his hands.

"No, that's not right either. I *don't* hate her. Not really. I don't hate any girl! I *won't*. I promised myself a long time ago that I'd never treat any woman with anything but courtesy. And anyway, what I really feel for her the most is pity. She's had it rough, I know. And her father! — well, I can't speak of that, not even here. But *damn* it! She's been a thorn in my side, from the moment I met her."

"I see," the priest murmurs soothingly, sounding like he doesn't see at all. I wish I could say the same.

519

Spurred on by the priest's soft commiserations, Taran continues vehemently,

"See? *See?* You don't *see* anything. How could you? The whole situation is unthinkable. Outrageous. *Intolerable!* She's used my own code of honor *against* me and made me party to deceit. I'm so tired of shielding her, of keeping her dirty secrets. I'm sick to death of it! Oh, I've tried to free myself of her, I have. *Believe* me. But she wouldn't stay at that convent, would she? And there's just no other decent way to be rid of her. Maybe it's not her fault. Maybe she's just doing what she thinks she must, for her father, and I can respect that. Admire it, even, if the circumstances were different. But she's been nothing but a humiliation to me from start to finish, and so ... so ... ugly. So yeah. When I kissed her, well, I wasn't exactly myself. But I won't make excuses. At that moment, I *did* hate her. I was so furious, I could have killed her!"

"I see," the priest repeats gently; he's had his fair share of experience with overwrought boys, and he clearly assumes Taran is exaggerating. I'm not so sure.

Taran must have his head in his hands again, since I can barely hear him muttering to himself,

"It's been weighing on me, ever since it happened. Even before the boys started teasing me. And that blasted song! *Don't* tell me Gilles didn't request *that*, just to needle me! But it's true. I *have* wanted to be noble, and I have been proud of it! Only instead I've been treating girls shamefully. Even if she did suggest it herself, well, she wasn't expecting what she got, was she? And the worst of it is, I can't explain myself to ... to ...*uh*, to anyone! I'm not allowed to speak," and then for a while all I can make out are random words like *that little* and *gladly* and *throttle her*, which come out so garbled that for a moment I almost imagine he's saying, *"that little glass bottle of hers,"* but when the priest gives a cough, Taran pulls himself together and says more clearly,

"It doesn't help that she's been throwing herself at my own damned *brother*, every chance she gets. I can't really explain. The situation is complex."

"I'll bet," the priest says, in a tone that makes it obvious he's heard plenty of gossip about the Mellor brothers; he must think Taran's been talking all this time about Melissande. "But a kiss," he probes, even more gently. "It's a strange sort of punishment, wouldn't you agree?"

"I *may* have had some thought of getting a little subtle revenge on someone else, into the bargain," Taran admits. "And of, *er*, making someone jealous. As I said, I wasn't thinking clearly."

"Another woman! I suspected as much," the priest says knowingly, leaving little doubt that he's also heard the rumors about Taran carrying on with a light-fingered mistress.

"Yeah, well. *She's* in love with him, too," Taran says shortly, not bothering to correct the priest's assumption that he's talking about a lover and not now about his own fiancée.

"Forgive me, son," the priest says shrewdly. "To tell the truth, you don't sound very penitent. Whatever's really on your mind, don't you think it's time to tell me what it is?"

There's another long pause.

"Possibly I *have* been having some trouble with lust," Taran finally says sheepishly, and when the priest doesn't respond immediately, I can imagine him rolling his eyes. Everybody knows all about Melissande's baby; it's been the talk of the guild.

"That's not all it is, though, I swear it," he continues hastily, sensing admonition in the priest's silence. "Not for *me*. If it were, I could resist it! I don't know how to describe it. But when we're alone together, er, *intimately*, I'm sure I can feel something more there between us. An understanding that needs no words. Maybe I'm just deluding myself, and yet — sometimes it's so strong, I think she must feel it, too — a sort of unspoken sympathy, underneath it all, even when we're arguing."

"Can I give you a word of advice, son?" the priest says soberly. "A wild oat or two, when a man is young. That's one thing. But I shouldn't have to remind *you* that adultery is serious. I've visited the lavish little chapel in Meuse paid for exclusively by selling your own father indulgences."

"Don't you think I know it?" Taran bursts out. "Don't you think *I* think about *that*, every single day? Isn't it the thought of being an even bigger cad than my father ever was the very thing that's stopping me from taking a shot at happiness?! Well, that, and the fact that it's pointless. She as good as told me so herself, didn't she, when I practically begged her this winter to run away with me? She'll never leave him. So *don't* get me started on Tristan. Even God himself would forgive me, for pounding in *his* head."

"Trapped with one girl, in love with another, and a bastard brother right in the middle of it," the priest says musingly. "As it happens, I was once in a similar situation myself."

"How'd *you* get out of it?"

"I became a priest."

There's another pause, longer than the rest.

"Yours is a tricky situation, my boy," the priest sighs, with a note of finality; he's clearly decided that Taran is working himself up into a lather, and it's best not to encourage him further. "So reflect on it. Apologize for the liberty, and get the girl's forgiveness. Or better yet, avoid the girl entirely, until after the competition. That should be easy enough! And if I were you, I'd confine your rivalry with your brother to archery," he declares, and he rattles off a list of verses for Taran to recite in penance. Before he takes his leave of the box, the priest adds sternly,

"For tomorrow, you need a clear head. There's a lot riding on your performance, after all, and ..." he lowers his voice confidentially, as though

521

he doesn't want even God to overhear what he says next, "as it happens, I've staked an entire year's wages on the outcome myself! If I were you, I'd forget all about girls, and concentrate on winning."

His confession thus over, I wait where I am while Taran mumbles through a rather long selection of prayers, hearing the deep hum of his voice but not really listening. After he's done and I hear the sound of his side of the confessional opening, I wait some more, until I'm sure he's gone. Then when I can't stand it any longer, I burst out of my hiding place, my limbs numb and my muscles so stiff they're hardly working, and I stumble out into the garden, desperate for some fresh air.

I stop underneath the tree, and I lean up against it to take a few big, gulping breaths.

I'm not mad at Taran. I never should have heard his private thoughts, and I already knew how he felt, didn't I? His words may have been cruel, but they weren't anything I haven't thought a dozen times myself. If anything, I can't help but be moved by how agonized he sounded over Melissande. Still, I can't deny that hearing them hurt, and now I have no idea what to do, or where I'm headed.

All I know is that I won't be asking Taran for his help.

I'd rather really be a thief, before I have to do that.

It's only after I've taken a few more deep breaths that I notice Tristan.

He's sitting silently at one of the little tables near the vines, and to all appearances he hasn't noticed me, either. He's decked out to the nines in one of Gilles's flashiest outfits, but he looks about as miserable as I feel and he's staring down unseeingly at his hands, twisting Gilles's big ring absently on his finger.

I go over and sit down on the chair across from him in something of a daze, and when he doesn't look up, I know what he must be thinking about even before he says,

"She's not coming, Marek. She's not going to be there, to see me do to the trick."

I don't bother asking him where he got his information. All I do is grunt. The last thing I'm in the mood for right now is a discussion about Melissande and how wildly in love everyone is with her.

We sit there for a while, each lost in his own thoughts, and although neither of us says a thing, it's comforting. Companionable, even. My heart is aching and so is his, and back there in the chapel, I don't know what was worse: hearing Taran claim the very relationship with Melissande that I was just thinking I shared with him myself, or finding out that all winter, while I've been angry at Taran for not being a noble boy, Taran's felt the exact same way — only *he* thinks *I'm* the one to blame for it. Only now I've got a problem much too big to let myself dwell on Taran's bitter confession. I'm in deep, deep trouble, and Tristan's my best friend. He's the only boy I can

always count on. I don't know why I keep letting myself forget it. So after a while, I ask him quietly,
    "If I were to ask you for a really big favor, would you do it, Tristan, without asking questions?"
    "I suppose that depends on what it is."
    When I can't bring myself to answer, finally Tristan looks up and gives me one of his best quizzical expressions, à la Gilles. All I do is hang my head, and when a hot tear slides down my cheek, Tristan says gently, in his old voice:
    "Of course, Marek. What is it?"
    "I need to borrow Gilles's ring."
    It's so huge, it's fit for a king. If it won't satisfy Luc Fournier, I don't know what will.
    There's no other way to say it, and Tristan's eyebrows shoot up. But he doesn't say anything. He simply gives the ring a few more twists around his finger, as though he's thinking about it.
    Then he twists the ring right off, and he presses it into my hand.
    "Are you really going to hand it over to me, just like that?" I say, incredulous. I was sure he would argue with me. "It's worth a fortune. If I lose it, you can never repay it."
    "I trust you, Marek. Implicitly," he says, "Don't you know I'd trust you with my life? With anything," and I feel even more miserable. But I'm out of options, and so I take the glittering jewel from him.
    "Care to tell me why you need it?" Tristan inquires carefully, as he watches me palm the ring.
    "Not today," I reply dismally, and I tuck it down into the safety of my waistband.

THAT EVENING, IT TAKES A SMALL ARMY TO GIVE TRISTAN A PRE-trials bath thorough enough to meet his newly exacting standards. All the squires except Remy lend a hand, and Gilles props one hip up against the side of an empty tub to oversee the task in a way that would be entirely reminiscent of Rennie's makeover, if Tristan weren't already starting out so clean and handsome. The whole time the boys are keeping up a steady stream of lively banter, but I'm not listening to any of it.
    With all the candles flickering and wet sponges sliding over Tristan's slick body, I'm thinking back to the night before Seconds, when I bathed Tristan alone in his room — back when it was just me and him against the world, and I miss it, a little. But this is appropriate. We're going to be part of a team tomorrow, and the truth is that others have already been helping us, for a long time now. So I'm also thinking back to the night I lay on the floor of

Brecelyn's chapel, feeling hopeless, and Gilles offered me a helping hand. And I'm thinking of his big ring, in my waistband.

There's going to be hell to pay when I have to tell Tristan that I've lost it. But I promise myself I'll work like a dog every day for the rest of my life, if I have to, to pay Gilles back; I just hope Tristan was telling me the truth when he said he'd forgive me anything, and by the time he's climbing out of his tub and the others are slowly dispersing, I've come to a decision.

Although it may be an imperfect one, I've found a solution to my immediate problem. Tomorrow is going to be our triumph, mine and Tristan's, the culmination of long, hard months of effort and determination, and of endurance through heartache and disappointment. After thinking all winter that Tristan was surely headed for elimination, it's going to be our sweetest victory yet. I'll not let worrying about Luc or pining after Taran rob me of my enjoyment of it.

Still, when Tristan takes the towel I've been holding to dry his hair and I notice that Armand hasn't left the lavatory (he's been over at a washbasin, using Aristide's straight razor to scrape some peach fuzz off his face, in the hopes that stubble will make him look more like a clouter), as he wipes off the blade and prepares to depart, I forestall him. And I ask him to stay, to give Tristan a haircut.

"Come on, master!" I urge him. "Let Armand give you back your old look, for the competitions. You don't need the trappings any longer. You've mastered the wands attitude, internally." When I take the field with him for his best competition yet, I want him to be Tristan, not Trills or Gistan. And so I add,

"You heard Gilles. It's just *hair*," and laughing, he agrees.

While Armand fetches his scissors, Tristan wraps the towel around his middle and settles himself on a low stool, and soon moist curls are falling in a halo on the floor around him. Before long my old familiar boy has emerged out from under the shadow of Gilles, and I can't say I'm sorry to see that ponytail go. But when neither of them is looking, I bend down and pluck up one of Tristan's dark locks, and I tuck it down into my waistband. It's going to be *my* best competition, too, and if I'm to carry a token, it should be Tristan's. But I'm also not a fool. If somehow things go wrong with Luc tomorrow, I know I'm going to have to run away, and risk hoping Luc was bluffing that he'd expose me anyway. At least this way, I'll have something of Tristan to take away with me.

When Armand's done, Tristan reaches up a hand to feel around his head. "How do I look, boys?" he asks, with a grin.

"Perfect, master! Just like your old self," I say, just as Armand says,

"Yeah, just like Samson, after a date with Delilah," and I have a moment's qualm. Maybe Tristan *does* need the trappings. That was the boys' whole plan for getting Tristan past wands, wasn't it? Tomorrow Tristan will be dressed in his usual regalia; the longer hair was going to be the only thing he had to make him feel like Gilles. But I needn't have worried.

"*Fab*ulous," Tristan drawls, standing up with a languid stretch and tossing the towel dismissively aside. Then he saunters out of the lavatory buck naked, and when he struts all the way down the Journey hallway and back to his room that way without any shame, I can see there's still plenty of Gilles left in him to last through one more day.

CHAPTER THIRTY-SEVEN

"So, how do I look?" the handsome boy in front of me asks, as I pin a silk-lined cloak to his shoulders the next morning. "Do I pass muster?"

I stand back and cock my head to one side to look him over, as though surveying him critically. It's Frans, standing next to his cot in barracks and bobbing from one foot to the other like a jittery little bird. He's wearing Pruie's hastily-altered performance costume, and I have to say it still looks a few sizes too big for him. But nobody will notice from the stands, and he looks so smart, I mean it when I say,

"You're perfect! Only can you run in those?" I point down at his feet; his boots are about two sizes too big for him, too, since the only dress pair we could find was an extra one of Pascal's. "You can wear your old ones, you know, if you have to."

He considers for a moment. "It should be okay. I stuffed the toes with scraps from the alteration, and Pascal gave me a few of Gilles's old handkerchiefs." When I can't help grimacing, he hurries on, "I am glad, though, that we'll be retrieving as a team."

The poor boy does look petrified; his mobile little face keeps shifting between abject fear and palpable excitement, and he's twisting his hands together in a way that can't help reminding me of myself on the morning of Firsts last year. All the same emotions are bubbling up in me, too, despite my determination to enjoy myself, and so when Frans gathers up my own costume and puts it into my hands, saying,

"You'd best get ready yourself, master," before I head out of barracks with it, as much for my own benefit as his, I tell him,

"We'll have each other's backs out there today, and it's going to be bloody fantastic! And Frans, remember — when you step out in front of the crowds with the boys for the first time, it isn't as good as you imagine." Frans cocks his head, and I grin. "It's *better*."

By now some of the other squires have wandered over, so I look around and demand,

"Am I right, boys?!" and in answer we all give a cheer for squires' squad. It's such a beautiful moment, it can't even ruin it when Remy chimes in,

"And three cheers for *my* master, for arranging for it!"

"Going somewhere?" Remy asks me a moment later, when he sees me gathering up a handful of items from my bedside table and adding them to the pile of clothing in my arms.

"Just to Tristan's room," I say. "Why?"

"No reason," he replies, still eyeing the items, trying to see what they are. "That the money, Marek?" he asks, catching sight of Luc's little canvas bag. Last night, I borrowed what few coins I could from the other squires without raising too many questions. "What are you going to use it for?"

"It's just a little insurance," I tell him, giving him the same explanation as the last three times he asked me about it. I'm sure it's all going to be fine, but I figured it wouldn't hurt to have some coins in my pocket — on the off chance that I do end up having to make a sudden run for it. "Tristan's out of funds, and I want to be able to get him some refreshments, between the tests."

It's not a very good lie, since most of the booths will treat us if they know it's for the Journeys, but Remy doesn't call me on it, and really. It's just a few pennies. I don't see why Remy's so curious about it.

When I get to Tristan's room, I find him already up and in the process of dressing. He looks like he slept as little last night as I did, but I take it as a good thing — a sign that he's as excited about the trials as I am.

"Ready, master?" I say by way of greeting, as he steps out into the hallway. "Ready, for your best competition yet?"

"It's going to be a great day, Marek," he agrees, to my surprise reaching up to attach his cloak to his shoulders all by himself. "It's going to be *our* day, I'm sure of it."

"Yours, and Gilles's?"

"Yours and *mine*, kid!" he laughs.

I make short work of it to dress while Tristan waits out in the hallway; some of the others have started gathering, and I can hear Tristan laughing and talking with them out in the corridor. Even through the closed door, I can feel the charged atmosphere typical of competition mornings starting to build, and once I've got my performance gear on, my mood soars — particularly when I strap on two new pieces of equipment, ones I've never worn in the trials before: a black leather shooting bracer, and a leg quiver to hold bolts for my crossbow.

Then I add the finishing touch to my ensemble, by tucking an array of tokens down into my waistband: Tristan's lock of hair, Gilles's ring and the little canvas bag of Luc's, now filled with pennies, and last of all, the little wooden mouse that Taran carved for Remy.

I can't just leave it behind. Even without it, my waistband feels overstuffed and lumpy. But it's all I have of Taran, and despite everything, I can't bear the thought of leaving here without taking something of him with me.

When I rejoin Tristan out in the corridor, he's leaning with one shoulder up against the wall, and in his full regalia and with his freshly cut hair, he looks exactly like he always does on competition mornings — gorgeous, charming, athletic, my old familiar Tristan. It's what I wanted last night, but now it makes me nervous, since today he was *supposed* to be Gilles. When he sees me stepping out into the hallway in my costume, he flashes me one of his lazy grins, and that one wayward lock of his hair falls forward across his brow. So I reach up and grab it, and for once, I smooth it back off of his forehead.

"Just for today, okay?" I tell him, just as Gilles comes out of his own room and comes over to join us.

He leans up against the wall on the other side of me so that I'm framed by the boys in the open doorway, and I almost laugh out loud at the thought that they could be a pair of matching ornamental doorposts, but it's true. Lounging there languidly side-by-side but opposite each other, the boys are so similar in looks and in attitude now that they could be twins, and my confidence surges. It *is* going to be the best competition yet. It's going to be our day, and more. It's going to be a triumph of teamwork.

"Any last words of advice, my friend?" Tristan asks, and when Gilles cocks his head to the side, for a moment I think he's going to come out with one of his flowery statements. Instead, he looks Tristan in the eye and says simply,

"Hit the wands."

Tristan laughs, taking it as a joke, but to me, it isn't very funny. Gilles is right. No amount of style and poise will help Tristan any, if the others all hit the wands and he doesn't.

"Come on, there's still plenty of time. Let's hit the lavatory, and get properly perfumed up," Tristan says, slinging an arm around Gilles's shoulders. "And where's Pascal? Isn't he ready?"

"He's probably already in there, being sick into a bucket," Gilles replies.

I'm spared from finding out by the appearance of Frans. While we've been talking, he's come scurrying into the hallway to knock on Falko's door. Not finding his master within, he's come over to hover anxiously on the periphery of the boys' conversation.

"I can't find him anywhere," he tells us worriedly, when Tristan draws him over and asks him what's the matter. "His room is empty. His cot's not been slept in, and wherever he is, he's not dressed yet for the trials. His regalia is where I left it last night, laid out on the foot of his bed."

"He's likely ridden out to your uncle's farm, Frans," Tristan says, "to fetch Roxanne along to watch him go out in glory. Unless I miss my guess, you'll find him out on the exposition grounds, hanging around the ladies' boxes," and when Frans looks nervous about heading over to look for his master in the crowds by himself, I offer to go with him. I'm fond of Frans, and Falko, too, and this morning the lavatory is sure to be nothing but humid and malodorous. But mostly, Taran's also just emerged from his own room, holding the pitcher that goes with his washbasin and looking a lot like he didn't sleep much last night, either.

When he catches sight of us, he stops. And maybe it's my imagination. But he looks right past the others and straight at me, and his mouth starts twitching. Unless I miss my guess, Taran's got something he's itching to say to me, badly enough he might not care if he does it right in the middle of the crowded lavatory. And maybe I'm not mad at him for what he said yesterday in confession. But this is *my* day, and I'll be damned if I'm going to start it off by suffering through an apology from Taran for that kiss in the archives.

Frans and I step out of the guild building proper and straight into a madhouse. I'm no stranger to the chaos of the competitions, but this time Master Guillaume has pulled out all the stops. The yard is overflowing with men — Kingsmen in red uniforms, veterans in St. Sebastian's black, and a hodgepodge of workmen, all of whom are yelling — and to judge from the number of wagons clogging up the yard, the master hasn't given the construction crews the day off. To make things worse, half the men are mounted, and from the looks of it, nobody's sure who's in charge. Before we've managed to dodge our way across the yard and out through the postern gate, we're almost run over by the white gazebo, as a team of men struggles it out into the L'île-Charleroi road.

Out in the street, it's even more packed. The road's been closed from the alley south of the guild all the way north to Porte L'île, to allow the Kingsmen to move their camp temporarily off the exposition grounds and pitch their tents out here. More of both Kingsmen and veterans are stationed by moveable barricades of the kind we use to mark off the competition field set up at either end of the road, where they're trying to keep people out and direct the flow of traffic, to little avail. If Master Guillaume was worried about the crowds, he needn't have bothered. It's still early, yet townspeople are already swarming everywhere, and there are so many spectators now arriving, they must be pouring in from all over the country. After the tough winter of plague, people are eager to be entertained. Either that, or Master G's vigorous program of promotion has paid off, since I notice quite a few people with flyers advertising Pascal's proposal clutched in their hands.

We follow along in the dusty wake of the rolling gazebo, letting it forge a path for us through the crowd, and before long we're weaving our way between the booths out on the exposition grounds. There look to be at least twice as many stands as usual, and now and then Frans can't resist stopping to gawk at them. But time is wasting; I've still got to bring over all of Tristan's equipment and the components for the boys' joint trick, and if Falko's wandered off among the concessions, it's going to take forever to find him.

Luckily for us, as soon as we've skirted around the competition field far enough to have a clear view toward the bleachers, we spot Falko right where we expected to find him. With his shoulders, even out of his regalia he's unmistakable. He's standing next to one of the boxes, chatting with the ladies already seated within, and he's not alone. A boy almost as big as he is stands next to him; Falko must have brought his former squire Pruie along to accompany Roxanne, who's standing between them. I can tell it's her from the fact that she's holding Falko's hand, although on her head she's wearing a long veil which obscures her face and covers her head entirely. They've apparently just arrived, since as we approach, Falko's in the process of introducing Roxanne to the girls in the box, who I now see are none other than Lady Sibilla and Ginger.

We hasten over to join the group, and for a moment there's a merry babble of confusion as I try to introduce Frans around to the ladies while also greeting this collection of old friends appropriately. I'm particularly glad to see Pruie, and from the happy cluck he gives when I hug him I think he recognizes us, too, despite still not being able to say much of anything. Roxanne likewise greets us warmly, although it must be our voices she recognizes; I'm not sure she can see much through the thick veil she's wearing. From up close, I have to say it looks a little odd, but it's understandable. After almost being stoned this winter, Roxanne can't risk showing her face in Louvain — not when she's currently supposed to be residing in heaven — and frankly, wearing it is probably going to make watching her lover's performance today much more enjoyable.

I doubt anyone will be looking at Roxanne, though, or noticing anything unusual in her attire. Not when she's seated next to Sibilla and Ginger. Both girls are dressed in matching silk dresses so blindingly white that the morning sun is glinting off them like a beacon; ships at sea could surely see them from miles out, and perched on their heads are identical wreaths of full-blown pink roses. Not only are these garlands enormous, but the color of them clashes unfortunately with the vibrant red of the girls' hair, which is hanging loose down their backs and interwoven with a veritable garden of smaller white blossoms. They look both impressive and rather ridiculous, and Lady Sibilla in particular seems to be attracting a small swarm of bees.

The outfits have obviously been designed to coordinate with the boys' cloaks for the big proposal, since Gilles's color is white (and, I suppose, to match the gazebo). I hadn't realized that Gilles and Sibilla were to be part of the betrothal performance, though it makes sense. Someone will need to escort the pair and stand up with them, and it will add to the drama. But the strangest thing about it is that instead of looking annoyed at having to wear the uncharacteristic outfit, Lady Sibilla is positively beaming. There's no other word for it. And either she's stifling in the tight bodice and voluminous skirts of her dress and the roses on her head are giving her an allergy, or else she's blushing furiously. She looks terribly flushed, actually, and I'm surprised. I wouldn't have thought she'd be so excited about the engagement of her servant.

"I do wish Meli was going to be here, to see the proposal," Sibilla sighs, when I sidle over to exchange a few pleasantries with her, and for a moment, I'm taken aback. I'd forgotten that Melissande sometimes goes by her mother's nickname.

"Where is she, anyway?" I ask.

"Meuse, I think, with her father. And that man, de Gilford. Something about a royal hunting party. Daddy's rather put out that he wasn't invited," Sibilla replies, nodding toward a dour man a few boxes down, closer to the judges' table. He looks so much like a younger, beefier Sir Brecelyn but with red bushy hair and eyebrows that he must be Brecelyn's brother and Sibilla's father.

"Everyone's disappointed she's not here," Ginger says sweetly, as I turn to take her hand and kiss it. "So many of the boys have been by, to ask about her."

"That big thug of a fiancé of hers, in particular," Sibilla puts in sourly. "He's already been past here *three times*, pestering us with questions. So demanding! And shockingly rude about it."

"Is that him?" Roxanne asks, joining the conversation as Falko helps her up into the box to take a seat next to Ginger, and pointing a finger off in the direction of the concessions. "That big boy, leaning up against that booth and staring at us? Staring at *you*, Marek."

"No," I say, in a small voice, as Sibilla exclaims, "Insolent! Just *look* at that expression."

It's not Taran. It's Luc. And Roxanne's right. He is lounging against the back wall of a cider booth and watching us.

"Who is he, then? He seems to know you," Ginger asks, and I'm spared from having to answer by Falko.

"*Him!*" he snorts, turning to look at Luc over his shoulder. "Ladies, *look away*. By all means, do *not* encourage him. Tristan tells me he's a wrong 'un. Why, the other day, he even caught him cock fighting! Disgusting."

At this there's an indignant gurgle from Pruie, and when even some cooing noises from Falko can't seem to calm him, Falko finally gives in to the frantic little pleas Frans has been making.

"Come on, buddy," Falko exclaims, slinging an arm around Pruie's shoulders and letting Frans lead them both off toward the guild, so that Falko can dress for the competition. "Let's go find you somewhere safe to wait out the trials. Somewhere with some soothing animals," he says, and soon the three of them are disappearing into the crowd, and I find myself momentarily alone with the ladies.

I've still got to arm myself, and to carry over Tristan's equipment. But Luc's slinked off and Roxanne's gotten into an animated conversation with Ginger, and I've been feeling guilty that I never had a chance to talk to Sibilla alone during our winter stay at the castle. Now's my chance, since the other girls aren't listening. So I sidle over closer, and swatting away a stray hornet or two, I lean up next to Sibilla against the box's railing.

"So," she demands bluntly, without any warning. "Are you still in love with him?"

Caught off guard, I gush back,
"More than ever!"

It's embarrassing when I have to add, "Only, *er*, not the same one."

"Yeah, *tell* me about it," is all she says. But she's making an odd noise, like she could be coughing up some phlegm. If I didn't know better, I'd swear she was giggling.

Before either of us can ask any questions, there's a commotion on the far side of the field. A crowd of veterans stationed at the barricades near the Journeys' tents have started calling out enthusiastically, and up in the stands, the spectators already seated near the top of the bleachers are coming to their feet. There's a big flurry of dust rising from across the open competition space, and even over all the whooping and hollering, I hear the pounding of hoofbeats.

All at once, out of the cloud of dust a lone rider emerges. He's mounted atop a massive white steed, and as applause rings out from the stands, the boy on the horse thunders out into the arena, racing up and down across the open field while urging the crowd into further peals of applause by standing in his stirrups and holding a rapier aloft over his head. It's Gilles, making an entrance. I should have known it would be him, since he's the only one who could get away with it.

He gallops once or twice more back and forth, stirring up the crowd into a frenzy. And then without breaking speed, he charges straight toward us. It's only when he's almost about to crash the huge stallion right into the bleachers that he pulls up sharply, reining in the big horse so hard that it rears up with a dramatic whinny directly in front of the place where Lady Sibilla is sitting. The early morning sun is directly behind him, glinting off the rapier he's still waving around and streaming all around him, blurring his outlines, much as it did to Tristan when I first saw him on the garden wall and I thought him a divine apparition. And I have to say, Gilles does look heavenly as he slides easily to his feet, struts over, and with a grin almost as blinding as one of Tristan's, he takes Sibilla's hand in his and bends over it to give it a kiss with so much panache, not even Poncellet in his prime could have outdone him.

He's got one unruly lock of hair hanging down rakishly across his forehead, one of Tristan's lazy smiles on his face, and with that little sliver of his eyebrow missing, he looks devilishly handsome. At the sight of him, Lady Sibilla is speechless. Her eyes bug out, and she looks like she's having trouble breathing. And when Gilles then looks up, raises one eyebrow, and without any hint of his usual drawl, he exclaims with a cocky wink,

"Top of the morning to you lovely ladies," with no further ado she falls straight over backwards. She's fainted dead away, poor dear, and I can't say I blame her. I don't think it's the heat and the dust, or even her tight bodice, however.

It slipped my mind entirely to warn her about Gilles's transformation.

Gilles gallantly pretends not to notice. He examines his fingernails while Ginger, Roxanne, and I quickly revive her, and he waits until we've gotten Sibilla seated back upright, with her garland back on her head in more or less the right position, before he continues.

"Do pardon the intrusion! But I simply could not wait to present my gift for the be*auti*ful bride," he declares, making a sweeping gesture toward the horse once Sibilla's recovered, and it really is generous. A stallion like that must have cost a fortune. "A magnificent creature, for a magnificent creature," Gilles purrs, moving over now to kiss Ginger's hand, and then Roxanne's, though the whole time he's still making eyes at Sibilla. He's flirting shamelessly, but Sibilla seems to love it. She's tittering away and using a husky voice that she must think coquettish, and it's all rather embarrassing. But I'm glad, and watching the two of them bantering away, I can't help feeling happy for them. I was right, back at the castle; you'd have to be a fool not to see that Lady Sibilla is head over heels in love with Gilles now, and that he's as crazy about her as ever.

"Are you both ready and *eager* to do your parts?" Gilles asks smoothly, catching sight of one of the flyers announcing the engagement in Ginger's hand. I've yet to see one of them up close, so I lean over, trying to read it. It all seems rather vague; just a lot of flowery nonsense about a 'mystery proposal' sponsored by the Marquis de Chartrain, and a promise of a spectacle. I don't see what I'm most looking for: Ginger's name, since I've been reluctant to admit to her that I don't know what it is. It's been a bit awkward, actually; I can't just call her by the boys' nickname for her. But I don't see Pascal's name on it, either.

"Yes, yes, *eager*," Sibilla agrees, frothing a little, and I exchange a few more polite pleasantries with Roxanne and Ginger while Gilles and Sibilla have their heads together, exchanging increasingly arch quips with each other that all seem to be heavily laced with innuendo. This goes on for quite a while, until Lady Sibilla seems to be almost on the point of hysteria, and until Pascal appears, hovering over a ways away in front of the judges' table, keeping back shyly but waving his hand now and then trying to get his master's attention. It's getting late, and we've still got to bring over our masters' equipment.

Catching sight of him, Gilles declares,

"Come now, Marek. Let's away! The hour is advanced, and it wouldn't do, would it, for the crowd to see the bride and groom too close together before the proposal? It would be *such* a pity to spoil the surprise of it, for everyone," and for some reason, Lady Sibilla titters.

Gilles swings himself back up onto his horse, and with a promise to take the wedding gift safely back to the stables, he plucks me up onto the saddle in front of him and he rides me back across to the Journey tents with him, leaving Pascal to trot along on foot behind us.

The little visit with the ladies took longer than I would have liked; some of the boys are by this time out in front of their individual pavilions or mingling with their sponsors, and the bleachers are filling. Even the double ranks of Kingsmen and veterans stationed around the perimeter of the field are having trouble keeping the crowd back behind the low barricades, and troupes of jugglers now dot the field. As we wend our way between them, I can see Pascal and I are going to have to hustle to get everything carried over from the guild, but I'm glad we took time for the interlude. Ginger's sure to make a stunning bride, and I must say she looked remarkably poised. There was nothing wrong with her at all that I could see, and from the shy little glances she was casting over at Pascal, I'm sure the two will make a most happy couple. Pascal and Ginger; Falko and Roxanne; and from the looks of it, Gilles and Sibilla — I can't be anything but happy at the prospect of so many happy endings.

It's a good omen, a sign that everything will come out right today, that Gilles is a trustworthy friend and ally. And if there was something slightly off about some of the things that Gilles and Sibilla were saying to each other, well, that's probably because I've never understood flirting. So as Gilles slips me down from the big bridal horse outside Tristan's tent, I tell him,

"Good luck out there today, *master*. You were right! With you and Tristan working together, a happy ending is positively guaranteed, for all of us."

"Luck, my boy, has nothing to do with it," Gilles replies, reaching down to give Pascal a jovial slap on the back before he rides off to return the horse to the stables. "Mark my words, boys! Today, everyone will get exactly what's coming to him."

I'm sure Gilles means this to be encouraging, but as soon as the big white horse moves away, over Pascal's shoulder I see Taran standing outside his own pitch-black tent. His arms are crossed and he's staring out toward the ladies' box with a scowl on his face, looking a heck of a lot like he'd like to take a dirty shot, at someone.

By the time I've taken enough trips back and forth with Pascal to bring everything over from the workshop and deposit it in the boys' tents, I've worked off a little of my pre-trials nervousness. But Pascal's as jittery as a jackrabbit. Seeing Ginger in her get-up hasn't improved his nerves any; he's been zipping through the crowds with his loads so quickly I can hardly keep up with him, all the while muttering snatches of his proposal to himself under his breath. I'm not eager to hang around outside the tents with him or to wander out among the booths, so I'm glad that we've cut it rather close: the bleachers are overflowing, the crowds are surging forward to find a place along the barricades, and while a crew of veterans is escorting the last of the jugglers off the field, up at the head table Master Guillaume is now conferring with the panel of judges in a pose that looks as though he's about to get things underway. Firsts is finally upon us, and it's time to join my master.

I give Pascal one last hasty encouragement by way of parting, saying, "Gilles is going to be outstanding today, my friend. Enjoy it." When this fails to calm him, I add, "Don't worry. Ginger's going to be enormously proud. And, er, *you* saw him earlier. Gilles hardly paid any attention to her. It's obvious Sibilla's the one he's after. Why, he probably arranged the whole proposal, simply to impress her. And from the looks of it, it's working. You have your speech memorized, right?"

He confirms that he does, but he still looks glum. "It's a good speech. Thanks, by the way, Marek. But it's just some purple prose. I can't compete with a knight in shining armor."

"Good thing you don't have to, then!" I tell him, giving him a quick pat on the back. "Besides," I add, making a joke of it, "It could be worse! You could be up against the *Knight of the Dirty Shot*," and with that, I duck inside Tristan's tent.

Tristan's right on the other side of the canvas. He's been looking out through the tent flap, his crimson-lined cloak hanging down behind him, and I almost run into him.

"*There* you are, Marek! I was beginning to think you were going to make me do this one alone."

"No, master. Not today. Not ever," I say back, babbling a bit and hoping it's true, and hoping he didn't overhear my last comment.

Tristan doesn't notice. He's looking back out through the opening in the tent, no doubt towards the empty place in the ladies' box next to Sibilla and Ginger.

"Shouldn't you be picking some lint off your cuff, or something?" I ask him, trying to distract him; it doesn't take much to see that he's brooding over Melissande's absence every bit as much as Taran is. And that he's nervous.

Why didn't I see it sooner? He's been trying to hide it all morning, and I curse myself for leaving him to stew alone for so long in the tent, and even more for insisting on that blasted haircut. I should have known Tristan *does* need the trappings. He's always needed them. Only now it's too late. His hair won't magically grow out again, and there's no time to run back to the guild, ransack Gilles's room, and come back with his peacock blue tights for him to wear them under his trousers. Without Melissande in the stands, I can't just run over and get him another token.

Outside, there's a flurry of bugle blasts, followed by Guillaume's voice raised to address the crowd. The master is always long-winded, and today he's sure to drone on longer than usual; even through the canvas of the tent I can hear him launching into one of his speeches about rising Phoenix-like from the ashes. There would be ample time for one of my flowery speeches of encouragement; they've become something of a tradition with us, and I've been looking forward to giving Tristan one of them. But I didn't really expect Tristan to *need* it, and the way he's started jiggling one leg in a very non-wandsmanlike fashion has started to alarm me. None of the bland platitudes I can think of to spew at him are having any effect, either. Instead, he keeps reaching up absently to touch the back of his head, as though feeling around for his now-missing ponytail.

"Wait right here, master," I say, rather ridiculously, since the trials are about to start and Tristan can't go anywhere, "and, *uh*, could you bend down for a minute?" But I've had an idea, and before Tristan can ask me what I'm doing, I've slipped his St. Sebastian's medal from around his neck and darted out of the tent with it.

I make quick work of my errand, keeping low and skirting around behind the row of Journey tents to slip into Gilles's white one. In a flash I'm back, and what I'm holding in my hand now is Gilles's veteran's medal on its golden chain. After that first day, out of sentiment the boys have been wearing their own medals, but Gilles has graciously let me switch his out again for Tristan's.

"See this, master?" I tell him, as I undo the clasp and I string a second medal onto it. "Gilles is now wearing your St. Sebastian, but I kept this one, your St. Margaret. You know, the saint who blessed you with her kiss, when you were wounded in Brecelyn's chapel. She promised she'd see you safely through the trials, and she's never going to leave you." At this, Tristan smiles, and when the hint of a blush rises to his cheeks as he lifts a finger to his lips, as though remembering it, I hurry on, before I can start blushing, too.

"And this," I point to Gilles's medal, "this is our patron, St. Sebastian. The one who's always been at your side, only in a slightly different form! A golden saint, for a golden boy. Wear it over your heart, to bring out your inner wands man. Don't you see, master? You don't need to copy Gilles. Calm, poised, assured — brave, and stylish. You've always had that boy inside you. How else could you have done all the things you've done at St. Sebastian's already? And I don't just mean in the trials. Living here all these months, in the shadow of your brother; facing up to him every day, and never letting him see how he affects you?" It's all true, although I have a funny feeling as I continue that I'm also talking a little about myself. "It hasn't been all an act! That boy you've been pretending to be — nonchalant, unflappable — nobody's that good an actor. Maybe you don't know it, but I do. You're stronger now. You're better. But not because you're pretending to be Gilles. Because you've been *practicing*. You don't have to fake it today. You're as good at wands as the rest of them. You can give the best of them a run for their money, if you just go out there and relax, and enjoy it!"

"Oh, I fully intend to, little brother," Tristan declares, bending his head to let me slip the golden chain around his neck, almost as though I were knighting him. "Only you're wrong about one thing, Marek. I *am* that good an actor!"

With that, Tristan leaps up in one smooth, fluid motion, and as he rolls his shoulders and gives a languid stretch, he looks more than ready to 'be the wand.'

"I wasn't really nervous, kid. But I could tell *you* were. And I know how much you enjoy giving me these little pep talks. I didn't want to disappoint you," he drawls, and I don't know or care whether or not I believe him. But I find I've changed my mind. I'm glad to be about to take the field with Gistan and Trilles, and Gilles and Tristan — all of them jumbled up and working together, we're going to sweep the competition. We spend those last few seconds waiting to be called out to the field just standing there on either side of the tent flap in companionable silence, holding hands across the little space between us and grinning like fools at each other.

A flurry of applause rises from the bleachers. Master Guillaume is done with his preliminaries, and once a single bugler begins to blow the fanfares on his horn that are a summons to the Journeys, it's Poncellet's silky voice that rings out, calling out in turn the names of the six remaining competitors. With Royce and Baylen dead and de Gilford absent, the role of master of ceremonies has fallen to him, and even at the top of his lungs, he sounds as amused as ever. Soon I hear him shouting,

"*Ladies* and Gentlemen, I give you the inimitable Gilles Lejeune, wands master extraordinaire *and* the Marquis de Chartrain! He dazzled you last year — can he do it again? And look who's with him! Squire Lover Boy. Ladies, prepare to swoon this afternoon, when you hear the proposal of this silver-tongued devil!"

Either Master Guillaume instructed the man to pour on the theatrics, or Poncellet's taken it upon himself to be insufferable. But I hardly care, since his announcement can only mean one thing: we're not to be called out in alphabetical order as usual. Taran's convinced the master to agree to an order of our own devising, though I have no idea how he's managed it. I doubt Taran told the master anything specific about our plans for squires' squad.

We're to be lined up so that Pascal and Armand will be at opposite ends of the line, with Gilles closest to the stands and Aristide the furthest. Next in from each end will be Jurian with Rennie and Taran with Remy, leaving me and Tristan and Falko and Frans right in the center, with Falko next to Taran. The arrangement is both practical and ingenious, designed to set up the retrieval maneuvers we've got planned while also keeping the boys who hate each other separated. Still, I can't help but be pleased that it's going to end up leaving Tristan and me right in the middle. Not only will ours be the most prominent place on the field, but sandwiched between the plague-weakened Jurian and the battle-battered Falko, Tristan can't help but shine by comparison.

If the masters are following our requested order, we're to be called out after Jurian. So when I hear Poncellet announcing,

"Don't let his beauty fool you! Lean, strong, and as tough as they come! He's one to beat this day, gentlemen," I know Tristan's next, and I can't help myself. I cross to him quickly, and I hug him tight around the middle, as hard as I can. In response his arms fold affectionately around me, and I swear: even through the thickness of his regalia and all my own gear, at last there's no space at all between us, and everything is right about the picture we make together.

"I give you Tristan *DuBois*, and his squire, *Marek* Vervloet," Poncellet booms, and from the way he draws out our names, as Tristan and I emerge from our tent I almost expect the old master to add, "a matched set of pseudonyms!" But of course he doesn't, and when he doesn't add anything else at all, I'm not sure whether or not to be happy about it.

We plunge out into the brilliant light of morning arm-in-arm, and everything about that walk out to the line lights up my senses: the dizzying crowd, its shouts and cries filling air that's high and fresh after the closeness of Tristan's tent all around us, and the rumbling of feet stomping against the boards of the bleachers; the bright row of tents behind us, and the cloaks of the boys already on the line before us, flapping in the morning breeze like pennants with the boys' colors; the overpowering aroma of flowers from the festive garlands, of food from the stalls, of horses and men and of the press of perfumed bodies, mixed with the scent of bow oil that's filling my nostrils. Heightening it all is the thrill of my own excitement, under the stifling weight of my costume, with my leg quiver bristling with bolts and Tristan's great yew bow on my shoulder, glinting in the sunlight — and above it all, the roar of the crowd lighting a fire in my belly. It's all there again as I take my place on the line with Tristan, and as I drink it all in, reveling in it, I'm flying so high I don't even care that one of the faces in the crowd must be Luc Fournier's, and that if he's watching me, it's with amusement. I'm about to be the best I've ever been, and there's nothing Luc or anybody else can do to stop me.

As we take our stand on the line and wait for the others, Tristan scans the crowd, for a moment looking as dazed and overcome as I am. Without taking his eyes from the stands, he says to me,

"It's really happening, Marek. I can hardly believe it! We made it through," and it should be funny, since the trials haven't yet even started. But I know what he means.

With the sun at our backs and the competitions underway, our long, hard winter is finally over.

"Journeys," Poncellet cries, strutting back and forth in front of us while stroking his mustache, and addressing the boys in a voice loud enough to reach the stands. For once he's in proper regalia, but from the expression on his face he's trying hard to stifle the urge to call the boys some of his rude appellations. "I direct your attention downfield. Observe the men now in the process of planting one two-inch wide willow wand before each of you, at a distance of 250 paces. These are your marks, for the first test." He makes a sweeping gesture in our direction. "Squires! Step forward, and take a bow," he commands, and we accordingly advance and twirl our capes. "Now, show these good people what you have in your masters' quivers!" We each lift out five arrows, every one marked with our masters' colors.

"Men," Poncellet continues, as we step back into line, "your first test today should be familiar. I'm told it resembles almost exactly the first test of your First trials last year —except, of course, for the different target and greater distance, requiring elevated shooting. You will each loose five flights of five arrows, for a total of twenty-five shots at your respective wands. Speed will count as much as accuracy, so squires, be quick. Your masters cannot begin their next round until you return with their arrows." He pauses, letting the instructions sink in, and then he adds in a lower voice, so the crowd can't hear him,

"And boys. The targets should be spread out enough to avoid any misadventures. But I don't think I need to tell you that the master will *not* look kindly on any boy who accidentally hits a squire."

I'm not so sure about that; after last year, probably some of the people in the crowd are hoping for more of that kind of excitement, and the master's watchword for this year is *desperate times call for desperate measures*. With Falko's faulty aim, this test almost seems designed to ensure some sort of mishap, since Poncellet is right. It is almost exactly like the boys' first test last year, and it's clearly meant to be a race.

Even if the master doesn't intend to sacrifice any squires for the sake of a little added drama, I'm sure he is expecting it to send us into a panic, particularly us slower boys, since the retrieval distances are damned far. Instead, we're all grinning at each other. It's going to be perfect for the performance we've got planned, and it's going to look fantastic.

Even better, as Poncellet makes his way off the field, Tristan is eyeing his rather distant wand with apparent satisfaction. He looks so calm and relaxed as he stretches and flexes, it's easy to picture him barefoot and bare-chested, in nothing but Gilles's peacock-blue tights, more than ready to float an arrow up high and light, just as though he really were Gilles's alter ego.

"What do you say, my friend? Ready to give Guyenne and Mellor a run for their money?" he calls down to Gilles, and I have no doubt at all that they're going to do it.

Throughout these preliminaries, I've been doing my best to avoid looking down the line directly at Taran. What with the space between the boys and with Tristan, Frans, and Falko all standing between us, it's been relatively easy. Even without looking, though, it's impossible to miss the fact that Taran's in a foul mood this morning. He's sullen and distracted, and maybe he's just upset that Melissande isn't here to watch him. But he didn't look like he was paying any attention while Poncellet was describing the test, and now he's just standing there stonily in place, staring out in front of him, not looking at the crowd or at the target. When I do cast a glance in his direction, I can see a muscle working in his jaw, and whatever he's thinking, it isn't about playing to the audience. There's no way Taran can fail to pass today. But if Taran keeps it up this attitude, for the first time I let myself think that Tristan might really have a chance to best him. It's what I want, isn't it? It's what I *need* to happen. So I mutter to myself under my breath,

"*Just don't think about him,*" and I don't ask myself if it works. This time, it has to.

Poncellet's already trotted off to the side of the field, and when he calls out, "At the ready, men! Draw, aim, *shoot,*" I can't let myself be distracted. Before I've even handed Tristan his first arrow, Taran's nocked and loosed his own, and although I can't say he gave it much style, his arrow hits his wand dead center. Tristan's still fitting his arrow onto his string, in no apparent hurry, and I turn all my attention to my master.

"That's it. No need to rush," I encourage him, readying the next arrow. "It isn't a race. Not really," but I needn't have bothered. All Tristan's days of imitating Gilles have paid off, and as he sweeps his bow upward in the graceful arc needed for the distance, he's as fluid as Gilles ever was. I watch as his arrow hovers for a breathless moment at the top of its arc, so high and light as to be positively joyous, and if his arrow doesn't quite strike the wand in as impressive a position as some of the others, it *does* hit it, and that's all that matters.

"What a beauty, DuBois!" Gilles calls from down the line, already wafting up the last of his own arrows, and as the boys laughingly cry out encouragements to each other I watch Tristan take the rest of his shots, feeding him his arrows, fletch first, nice and easy. At first, I think the spectators don't know what to make of the boys' attitude, since they're supposed to be in fierce competition. But the boys are being so entertaining that the crowd begins to join in, getting into the spirit of it and calling out encouragements of their own. Before long there's an energy flowing between Tristan and Gilles, connecting them to each other in a way that's so infectious, it pulls the audience into rooting for the two of them, as a team, just as I predicted.

Gilles finishes first, with all his arrows nestled close together in the center of his wand. It's a fantastic showing. Aristide and Taran, too, finish quickly, with Tristan only a little behind them. Better yet, just like them, Tristan hasn't missed any of his shots, and while the boys wait for Jurian and Falko to finish their first round, Tristan and Gilles keep up their loud banter, designed to encourage the crowd to judge each other's performances as all the more impressive.

"Think you could have grouped your shots any closer, Lejeune?" Tristan calls down to his friend, and Gilles calls back, "Possibly, if *you* could have given your shots any more style," and I hug myself with joy, wondering how I could have ever suspected Gilles of being anything other than an ally.

His comment was exactly what was needed to draw attention away from the fact that Tristan's own arrows are spread out more widely than either Aristide's or Taran's — and that two of them are so close to the bottom of his wand that they could almost qualify as narrow misses. Out of the corner of my eye, I can see Master Guillaume sitting at the judges' table, and I wonder what he's making of it. None of the squires have left the line, to begin their retrievals. It was supposed to be a race, and nobody's acting like it. But I suppose he simply assumes that none of us wants to risk having Falko kill us, since from what I can see, he isn't managing to hit a wand with any of his arrows — except the last one. Only it doesn't hit his own wand. It hits Taran's.

I do think I see the master half-rise out of his seat a moment later, when as the crowd is still laughing at Falko, Taran steps forward. All the boys are done with their first round, and it's time for squires' squad. It's a moment I've both been waiting for and dreading, and we're just going to have to hope that the master loves it, if the crowd does — *after* the fact. Still, my heart is beating fast as Taran turns to face the line, and in a loud voice he barks,

"Squires, on your marks!" and as one, Armand, Remy, Frans, Rennie, Pascal and I all step forward to assume the starting stance we've been practicing: one foot forward, arms stretched out in front of us toward our targets, and eyes fixed on Taran.

We hold the pose for a moment, just long enough to be dramatic, as Taran holds up a hand and looks up and down the line, to make sure we're all in position. And then he looks back down the line in my direction.

For a moment, his eyes lock on mine.

It's just for an instant. But in that instant, all the days of practicing at squires' club with him come rushing back, all the hours spent planning this, together — all the bickering and the worrying and the fighting, and the heat of the archive fire. I'm not thinking about the feeling of his finger, lightly tracing a line along the inside of my wrist, or even of his lips, opening against mine in an obliterating kiss — a kiss I heard him tell the priest was fueled by pure hatred. At least, not consciously. I'm thinking about how we put our feuding aside, for the pure love of archery.

Taran's *supposed* to be calling over to Pascal, to instruct him to lead us through our retrieval. But now there's an energy connecting the two of us together, and for the first time this morning, Taran's frown has disappeared and he looks almost boyish. And when he opens his mouth, I suppose it's in a command to Pascal, as we planned it. Only he's still looking at me, and I guess I get as caught up in the moment as he is. Because when he cries out with a gesture in what seems to be my direction,

"Squire, are your men ready?"

I hear my own voice answering back,

"Squires' squad is ready, master!" and I take one step forward as Taran steps back, and I take over calling the cadence.

"Gentlemen, on *my* order!" I shout, leaning forward further in my eagerness. I take a quick look up and down the line, to see all the boys now with their eyes fixed on me, bodies taught, ready to sprint, and although Pascal's rolling his eyes, I think he's secretly relieved, and like all the boys, he's grinning. With no further ado, I cry out,

"First men, *go!*," and Frans and I dart forward, running side-by-side at the swift, steady pace we've been practicing, making sure to stay parallel to each other, with our short, colorful capes fluttering behind us merrily.

We're keeping up a regular stride, matching our footfalls in perfect unison in a way so reminiscent of our St. Sebastian's day show that it doesn't take the crowd long to figure out it's on purpose. Soon everyone's clapping and stomping along in rhythm with us, and when I estimate we've covered about a fourth of the distance, I raise an arm up over my head and I call out loudly,

"Second men, *go!*" From the cheer that goes up from the stands, I know that behind me Rennie and Remy have taken off from the line. They're faster than we are, and their pace is faster; I can't see them, but when we reach the halfway mark, they should be halfway to closing the gap between us.

"Last men, *go!*" I cry, and I picture what it must look like, as Armand and Pascal, too, speed from the line, the fastest of us all, and moving the fastest.

If we've calculated it correctly, from above in the bleachers it should look fantastic: a carefully orchestrated *V* of squires, arranged in a purposeful formation and all with their colorful silk-lined capes streaming behind them, a *V* which then slowly collapses into a single line, when we all reach the wands at the exact same moment. It may not be as elaborate as our show, but instead of the chaos that would have ensued if each man had been left to himself, we surely look skilled and professional, just as Rennie suggested. It's our way of letting the faster boys shine without shaming us slower ones, and most importantly from my perspective, without letting my lack of speed ruin Tristan's chances.

I close my eyes, feeling the breeze in my hair and my cape fluttering behind me, and with my legs working hard beneath me, for one disorienting moment I'm running through Brecelyn's woods, running towards my goal — running towards Taran. Maybe it's because of that grin he just gave me, I don't know. But I blink my eyes open and the field snaps into focus: I see Tristan's wand in front of me, and for once I'm positive I'm running in the right direction. The sting of that morning will always be there, and the pain of rejection. But now I know I wouldn't go back into those woods again, not even if things could be different, not even if Taran could love me. I could never have been happy if I'd abandoned Tristan or betrayed my vow to Saint Sebastian.

I feel a surge of triumph, and I revel in it — in the dust under my feet and the camaraderie with the boys, since if this really had been a race, it would have been an unmitigated disaster. And with the audience urging me on, I make my peace with everything that happened this winter. *This* is the picture of Taran that's right with me in it, too; this is the role that's right for me at St. Sebastian's, and I run faster. Who cares about making Journey? I'm a squire, and I'll take friendship over romance any day. It's something we can all share, and it's the love that's lasting.

We all wait for each other at the wands, too, until each squire has gathered up his master's arrows. Remy and I even help Frans round up some of Falko's, which takes some time, since except for the one Falko put into Taran's wand, he overshot his mark with every single one of them. Then we line up again, and we do it all over again on our way back. We keep up this routine between each flight of arrows, mixing up the order a little to change up the formations, and on the last retrieval we spice things up by weaving between each other on the way back to the line, while tossing the arrows back and forth to each other as we're passing. By the time the first test is over I'm thoroughly exhausted, but I couldn't be happier. The crowd loved it, and when Poncellet runs out onto the field and calls out,

"Let's hear it for squires' squad, everyone!," I get the impression the audience enjoyed watching us almost as much as they did the Journeys.

Best of all, out of twenty-five shots, Tristan only had three misses.

CHAPTER THIRTY-EIGHT

Back in the tent, I help Tristan unpin his cloak and I give his shoulders a quick massage.

"What about that, eh, squire?" he says to me with satisfaction. "Only *one* behind Aristide. Can you believe it? And I'm two *up* on Jurian! Gilles, of course, was flawless." I notice he doesn't bother to mention Falko. "And Taran! Did you see him? He was even more graceless and lackluster than usual."

"He didn't *miss*, though," I put in, but Tristan just crows,

"He didn't win any points with the crowd, by refusing to play up to them. I wonder what's eating him?" I don't bother suggesting that Taran, too, is upset that Melissande is missing his performance. Tristan is still pretending to believe that Taran doesn't really care about her, and I wouldn't bring her up anyway. "Why, the only time the old boy looked at all animated out there was for your squires' part in it. He must have been enjoying sticking it to the master, as payback for making him spend his afternoons training you boys rather than doing his own practicing."

I don't answer this, either, and not just because I don't like having our squires' formations described as *sticking it to the master*, since I was rather hoping that Master Guillaume would like it. Before I can start worrying that there might be some price to pay for all of our teamwork, however, Tristan is already chuckling,

"And *you*! You were wonderful! Why didn't you tell me you were going to be the star of it? I can hardly believe old Mellor allowed it."

"It was supposed to be Pascal, actually. I just sort of got caught up in the moment, I guess," I confess, and Tristan laughs harder.

"You really *are* a bloody pain in Taran's neck, aren't you, kid? How fantastic."

"He's probably just nervous," I say, changing the subject.

"Nah, Taran doesn't get nerves. That would require having feelings. No, it's something else. Oh well, who cares? It's to our advantage, and you know what? I'm beginning to think you've been right, Marek. About this plan of yours. Can you believe it? I was in *last place*, all winter. But if Taran keeps up this dour mood of his, by the end of the day I'm sure to be ahead of him."

Tristan's in too good a mood himself to obsess over Taran, and I'm feeling good enough about how the first test went that I don't object when Tristan suggests I pop out to bring back some pints of ale so we can toast our successes. I'm not eager to wander out among the booths alone, but it should only take a second.

I don't make it more than a few paces before I run into a brick wall. I'm already exclaiming fondly but a bit rudely, "Hey, watch it, big guy!" when I look up, and I see it isn't Falko.

It's Taran, hovering so close to Tristan's tent that he can only be out here waiting for me to come out, or debating with himself about coming in.

I pull up short in surprise. He's caught me off guard, and I must still be flying high from the success of our performance — because instead of shrinking away from him, without thinking I step closer. Putting one hand on his chest, I start babbling,

"We did it! We really did it, didn't we? Squires' squad! I wasn't sure we'd get a chance. That it would work, with the tests the master was setting. But it all went beautifully!"

"It could have been better," he says shortly.

"Better! How could it have been *better*? The crowd seemed to think we were pretty impressive."

"You were late, with your calls from downfield. Pascal and Armand almost couldn't catch up with you. And you didn't wait for Frans on the way back. I *told* you to match his step, or you'd outrun him."

"It was those blasted oversized boots of Pascal's he's wearing," I counter, gearing up to have one of our arguments and Tristan's ale forgotten. Only when I look up into his face and I find I've still got my hand on his chest, I suddenly remember how our *last* argument ended. And that he's been trying to corner me ever since, wanting to apologize for it.

Sure enough, before I can go on, he cuts me off with a curt,

"Could you just *shut up* a minute, and listen? There's something I need to ask."

I'm tempted to tell him that any apology he might make in his current mood will surely not win him much redemption. But after the success of squires' squad, I know I owe him something. And although I *do* want Tristan to win, I don't want it to be because Taran feels guilty for a kiss I taunted him into giving or because his shoulder is hurting, and I know I'm going to have to suffer through forgiving him eventually. But I'll be damned if I'm going to let him do it now, in the middle of the trials, and besides, over his shoulder I've just caught sight of Luc, leaning insolently against one of the barricades and watching us with interest from a distance. So when Taran turns his head to see what I'm scowling at behind him, I duck under his arm and I'm off like a shot, disappearing into the crowd and calling back,

545

"First, you'll have to catch me!"

It's a juvenile trick, but effective. Taran's such a stickler for the rules he'd never stray far from the Journey pavilions between the tests, certainly not to chase after another Journey's squire.

Once I've dodged my way between enough booths to be sure Taran's no longer visible behind me, I slow my pace and regain my composure. Luc's a nuisance, but Taran's something else entirely. I *cannot* let thinking about him distract me, but it's a heck of a lot easier not to feel guilty that I've masterminded a plan to defeat him when he's not standing right in front of me.

It takes a bit of wandering between the booths to find the one from the Vendon Abbey. I've never seen the exposition grounds so crowded, and as I push my way through the unruly throngs around the popular vendors, it's hot and noisy. Hands keep reaching out from all directions, some to shove me roughly out of the way, and others to clasp me on the shoulder and offer congratulations. But eventually I spot a grey and white awning, under which a large figure in a monk's habit is standing. Brother Benedict wasn't enthusiastic about me returning to St. Sebastian's, but he won't begrudge me some ales on the house, surely.

As I draw closer, I see that the figure in the monk's robe is tall and thin and ascetic-looking. It isn't Benedict, it's Father Abelard, and he's staring out toward the bleachers with a frown on his face, almost as though he too had been hoping to see someone there and he's been disappointed. *What, is everybody moping over Melissande's absence?* I think to myself, even though I know that's ridiculous.

"Did you see us? What did you think, Father?" I exclaim eagerly, after I've rushed up to him and essentially pounced on him, giving him a bit of a fright, actually.

"There you are, Mar— uh, Marek!" he exclaims, once he's recovered enough to give me a proper greeting, and after sending a boy around to the front of the booth to fetch some ales for me, he says,

"I don't know, it all seems rather dangerous, child. But you and your young man do make a good team, I'll grant you. I'm glad he's here, looking after you."

"Actually, *I'm* the one looking after *him*," I reply, and I'm about to launch into a description of my strategy to have Tristan and Gilles work together, when Abelard continues,

"Such a fine boy. Yes, I've liked him ever since he you brought you to the abbey. He does still owe us quite a bit of money, though, for breaking down the cloister doorway." It takes me a moment to realize he's been talking about *Taran*, and when I do, I open my mouth to protest.

For some reason, what comes out of my mouth instead is a mumbled, "*The Ballad of Taran and Marek*," and before I can correct his assumption or ask him any questions, the old monk looks off over my shoulder and declares,

"And look, here he comes now. Goodness! He looks rather angry."

I don't waste time turning to look. With a hasty word of thanks for the drinks, I scamper off as fast as I can go in the opposite direction. I'm skittering around the corner of a tinker's tent with the mugs of ale in my hands sloshing wildly when Taran cuts me off. *Tricky bastard!* He's skirted around from the other direction, so just when I think I've lost him, I run right into him.

"Oh, no you don't! *Damn it!* Where's DuBois? He's not in his tent," he demands, grabbing my upper arm when I try to sprint off again and offering no other preliminaries.

"I don't know! Where's Remy?" I croak back, even though it makes no sense. I can never think straight when Taran's so close, and I know what's coming. All I can think is, *if this is Taran's idea of atoning for bullying girls, he's going to need a lot more time in the confessional.*

"I sent him back to the guild, on an errand," Taran says, and when I open my mouth, he grunts, "Time is wasting. Just give me a straight answer for once, will you?"

There's nothing for it, and after Abelard's reminder of Taran's heroism in saving me, I know I have to give Taran what he wants. So I squeeze my eyes shut and muster my courage.

"*Please*, Taran. Don't. *Don't* apologize to me. Not now. I don't want to hear it. Can't it wait? Or better ... forget about it! I have," I lie. "There's nothing to forgive, anyway."

All he does is snort.

"Apologize? To *you*? Why should I?" he demands, and my eyes pop open — just in time to see Remy bustling up to join us.

Right behind him is Master Bernard. It doesn't take much to guess that Remy's enlisted him to help him find his master, and when the big man sees us to all appearances lounging around drinking in the shade of the tinker's booth, he wastes no time in barking at us to get back to our tents. Taran's got no choice but to obey, and at Remy's rather breathless arrival, I pry Taran's fingers from my tunic, saying,

"We shouldn't even be talking to each other, in the middle of trials. After all, you and my master are rivals," but Taran just snorts again.

"There are things more important than the trials! So *don't* think you're going anywhere, until you give me a straight answer. *Did* DuBois send that letter, or not?!"

"Letter?" I blink. "What letter?"

"A *letter*," he repeats, grabbing back the sleeve of my tunic and giving it a frustrated little shake, even though it must be obvious from the look of sheer surprise on my face that I have no idea what he's talking about. "A letter, *to the castle.*"

When this, too, fails to elicit anything from me but more confusion, and with Remy now tugging on *his* sleeve, Taran drops my arm. With a frown, he gives one of his irritated sideways head stretches. Then he says,

"Huh, and here I was, thinking you two told each other everything."

With that he stalks off, still jerking his head as he goes, with Master Bernard striding along purposely behind him, leaving me to make a hasty escape of my own.

I haven't made it far, though, before Remy darts back over to me. With a quick glance over his shoulder to make sure Taran's well out of earshot, he says,

"Best if we keep our masters away from each other until the tests are over, Marek. My master isn't himself this morning, and, *uh*," he lowers his voice, as though he's reluctantly letting me in on a terrible secret, "he has a bit of a temper."

"What's eating him, anyway?" I ask, too curious to make a sarcastic remark and feeling a niggling of worry. I should have known it wouldn't be something about me that's gotten Taran so rattled, and I'm still feeling confused and flustered by our odd little encounter. But Remy just frowns.

"I don't know! He just keeps muttering about a letter."

We hastily fix it up between us to make sure our masters stay away from each other until the competition is over, though before we part ways, I can't help asking,

"Er, Remy. Taran doesn't happen to have a brick in his tent with him, does he?"

I think I mean it as a joke. But if Taran's gotten it into his head that Tristan's still writing love letters to his fiancée even after everything that's happened, I hate to think what he might do — even in the middle of the trials. It doesn't make me feel any easier, when I think of Tristan saying to me upon our return to Saint Sebastian's,

"If *he* comes after *me*, all bets are off," just as though he's been certain all along that Taran's eventually going to do it.

WHEN I GET BACK TO OUR TENT, I FIND TRISTAN BACK FROM AN impromptu visit to Gilles, and Jerome has joined him, Gilles having apparently sent him along to help keep Tristan in character. They're sitting next to each other on camp stools; Jerome's strumming his lute and Tristan's removed his boots, and he's wiggling his toes in time with the music, limbering up his flexible appendages for the next round of shooting. I can't complain, since Tristan looks relaxed and happy, and he and Jerome are singing along to the tune in merry unison. Appropriately enough, they're singing the *Wands* song, and I come in just in time to hear them warbling out,

"Did you do it, just to *punish* me?"

"Hey, easy there, Marek!" Tristan exclaims, when I've shoved one of the tankards of ale into his hand rather abruptly, and he sees me swilling the contents of mine sloppily.

"We've got two more tests to get through, and I need a squire who's sober," he laughs. "Slow down, kid, and enjoy it."

I know he's right, and I am enjoying myself. I really am. But the tensions of the day are starting to get to me, and I need some courage. I'm not sure if it's because of Taran or Luc, but the truth is that I'm feeling as jumpy as hell, and although I am glad Tristan's holding up so well under the pressure, his composure is making me feel a little flustered. I'm not used to having him be the one who has to keep *me* calm and encouraged. It doesn't help when a big, burly man suddenly barges into the tent right behind me, and for a moment, I think it's Taran; knowing him, he would choose the worst possible moment to burst in and have it out once and for all with my master.

It's Master Bernard, come to inform us of the equipment we'll need for the next test. Usually, the thought that we're about to take the field again would make me more nervous, but so far I've been finding the interval more stressful than the actual tests.

When Bernard is finished rattling off his instructions, he turns to me and says,

"And squire. You're to bring out your crossbow, with your three smallest bolts for it in your leg quiver."

Over our mugs Tristan and I exchange a glance, and Jerome stops playing. I can't believe it. Letting us carry our crossbows out to the line is one thing. But specifications for bolts means the master is going to let us shoot them.

"Can you give us a hint about the nature of the test, master?" Tristan asks, and Bernard just scoffs.

"I'll tell you this much. It's something with *birds*."

When Tristan, Jerome, and I all start laughing, I'm sure Bernard has no idea what to make of it. I'm not even sure why I'm laughing myself, since I don't really like the sound of it.

This time, there's no fanfare to call us out to the field. Not long after Master Bernard leaves us, one of the kitchen boys dressed up smartly in official-looking livery appears at the opening of the tent, beckoning to us to follow him. He shushes Jerome when he starts to strum a chord to punctuate our departure, and the crowd, too, is hushed as the boy leads us out across the field and over to the same places on the line that we occupied for the first test. Tristan has his own bow slung over his shoulder, since I'm carrying both his big quiver and my own crossbow.

We soon see why. In front of each Journey, there's a wand of ridiculously slender proportions planted upright and only about 100 yards from the line — significantly closer than is typical for wands shooting. At the top of each wand, there's a little horizontal crossbar, like a tiny wooden perch. And on each of these makeshift perches a pure white dove is seated. Some of them are gently cooing. Others seem to be asleep. All of them are nestled in comfortably, and the veterans stationed along the bottom of the bleachers to keep order now have their hands up in a gesture to the audience to keep quiet, presumably to avoid disturbing the creatures. When we get closer, I see what look like short lengths of twine attached to the wands, and it doesn't take much to figure out that the birds have been tied by one leg to their perches.

"Something with birds, indeed!" Tristan whispers to me gleefully. "Marek, I do believe we're in our element."

"It's a good thing Pruie's not in the stands to see it," is all I can think to say back, since Tristan's right. The birds are essentially live popinjays, meant as targets. Pruie's not the only one unlikely to appreciate this set-up. It can't appeal to Taran, and I'm not very happy about it, either. Because the reason that the wands are so close and that we squires have been told to bring out our crossbows has to be because we're going to be the ones who have to shoot at them.

Sure enough, soon Poncellet's strolling back out onto the field, making a show of tiptoeing as he gets closer to avoid startling the birds, and explaining the test in an exaggerated stage whisper to both us and the audience.

"As you can see, men, you Journeys each have five arrows. Five chances to hit your wand, and it won't be easy! These are narrow marks indeed, and you'll want to aim near the top of your wand, if you really want to sway it — and you do! Because the master wants wands in motion, and because *your* job is to send your dove flying as high as you can up into the air. Once your bird is up as far as its string will allow it, *your squire* has three bolts to try to down it. You will be scored mostly on your own ability to launch your bird in as few shots to your wand as possible. But a solid hit to the dove by your squire will certainly enhance it — and make a tasty stew later, for dinner! Is that clear?"

We all nod. It is simple, and I should be pleased. I'm the best shot with a crossbow of all of the squires, and probably the only one who's had any practice at all on a moving target. What's more, since the boys are to take their shots at their wands one at a time, when it's Tristan's turn, I'll have my moment. It'll be the chance to shine that I've wanted, to be the golden boy — the boy who makes the shot that everybody is talking about in the Journey trials. But I don't like the idea of shooting the bird, and next to me I can hear Frans whimpering a little. The poor boy has had woefully little time to practice with his crossbow, and down the field I can hear Pascal groaning. He's right in front of the ladies' box, and there's virtually no chance he'll hit his dove, either. Today we're supposed to be a team but there's no way I can help them, and I have the grace to feel a little guilty that I spent more time during squires' club bickering with Taran than giving them all crossbow lessons.

As it turns out, Frans is spared the humiliation of missing. Instead of having the Journeys take turns in the order of our line-up, Poncellet moves back and forth behind the boys, tapping each one on the shoulder in accordance with gestures from Master Guillaume. Falko's first, and he misses the wand with all five of his arrows. His dove remains blissfully snoozing atop its perch throughout his turn, thus sparing Frans from the embarrassment of having to try to hit it.

Armand's not so lucky. When Poncellet taps Aristide next, I'm surprised. I'd imagined that the master was picking the order to save the best for last, in his typical fashion, so I was expecting Jurian to follow Falko. But as I watch Armand fumbling around to get a bolt into his crossbow, I realize nervously that the master *is* arranging the shooting order based on his expectations. Only this time, he's arranging us based on his expectations of the *squires*.

Aristide hits the wand with his second shot. It's a glancing shot but it's right at the top, and when his dove flies up into the air with a squawk the crowd erupts in applause, waking the other birds and causing some of them to stir on their own perches. Nobody's pretending to keep quiet any longer; everybody's shouting at Armand, urging him to shoot the bird, and he tries valiantly. But three bolts isn't very many, and frankly thirty wouldn't be enough for him ever to hit it.

There's a brief interlude after Armand's stepped back into line, head hanging, while we wait for all the birds to settle back on their wands after all the racket — the one Armand was shooting at included. It proceeds to sit there with its feathers puffed up and looking pleased with itself for the rest of the test, almost like it's mocking him. And I do feel sorry for Armand. But his master is one of Tristan's main competitors, and if the bird is mocking Aristide, too, I can't be sorry about it.

Jurian is next, even though Rennie is much better with a crossbow than Pascal is. But I doubt Master Guillaume has ever bothered to take much notice of Rennie, and the whole time that Jurian tries to hit his wand, I can sense Pascal getting increasingly nervous. He, too, thought that Gilles would be next, and he's eager to get his own turn over with, since it's certain to be ugly. He's dancing from foot to foot down the line while Jurian makes his slow, lazy shots, one after another missing his target. Jurian's really taking his time, and as always he looks magnificent in motion; he's fluid and effortless, almost like he's not even trying. But the plague took its toll, and he seems as surprised as everyone else when he finally hits the wand with his last arrow.

Rennie, however, is ready. He fires off his bolts as soon as the bird is in the air, hitting his mark with his last shot also — sort of. At least, he shoots off some of the dove's feathers. After all the other squires' misses, it's enough to get him a cheer, and I'm glad. This is surely his last competition, and he deserves it. It can't be doing much for Pascal, though, who's rightly assumed that he's next. And that he can't hope to be spared having to take a turn, since there's no chance that Gilles will miss. But then a funny thing happens. As Gilles fits his first arrow onto his bowstring, I call down the line,

"Come on, Pascal! You can do it," even though I know he can't, and next to me Rennie chimes in,

"Yeah, come on, Squire Lover Boy!"

Pretty soon everyone in the stands is chanting, "*Lover Boy, Lover Boy,*" and Pascal is calling out over all the noise, "Oh, I'm going to hit it, all right!" and he sounds so determined and he looks so handsome, I think everyone watching must believe him. It wouldn't be the first time an audience assumed that a boy's shooting matched his looks. And at that moment, Gilles lets loose.

Pascal has lined up Gilles's five arrows point-down in the ground next to his master, and Gilles grabs them up one at a time with lightning speed. He then proceeds to bombard his wand with them, each one whacking squarely into the top of the wand even though the first hit was enough to set the reed to reeling and the bird to flapping like crazy. He does it so fast and so hard, at the barrage of arrows the poor dove goes into a frenzy. Before Pascal can so much as lift his crossbow into position the bird has broken free of its string, and it's flying off over the bleachers to safety.

Even so, Pascal is so caught up in making a good showing in front of Ginger that he trains his crossbow on the bird as it dips and wheels over the audience. There's a horrible moment, when the bird veers toward the ladies' boxes and I think Pascal's going to put a premature end to his marriage by shooting his bride in the stands before even making his proposal. Luckily, Gilles restrains him, and even better, Pascal's apparent eagerness convinces the crowd that he would have certainly succeeded in hitting the thing, if the bird hadn't eluded him. They give him a rousing round applause for his restraint for good measure.

Now it's down to just me and Tristan, Taran and Remy. As Poncellet comes down the line toward us, I'm not sure where to hope that he's heading. It would be an honor for me to go last, for Guillaume to deem my skill greater than Remy's and to have Tristan's turn be the culmination of the test. But it would mean that Tristan has to follow Taran's performance, and that's usually not a good thing. Watching Taran shoot always unnerves him, and maybe Taran's not himself today. Maybe he *is* preoccupied and angry. But he hasn't missed yet. So when Poncellet passes behind Tristan without stopping, I'm not sure what I'm feeling.

As soon as Poncellet taps on Taran's shoulder, it's obvious what everyone in the stands is feeling. Taran may not have wowed them today, but he's still one of their favorites. I can almost feel everyone collectively leaning closer; they expect big things from him, although I'm not sure what more he can do than Gilles did, since the test is relatively simple. The crowd falls hushed again, holding its breath, and I find I'm holding my breath, too, and all the boys have turned to watch Taran. That is, all the boys but Tristan. He's examining his fingernails.

"What's he doing?" Tristan whispers to me out of the corner of his mouth, a few minutes later.

"Nothing," I whisper back, while some of the other Journeys start moving around, and Jurian gives a purposeful cough or two. "He's just standing there."

It's true. Taran's just standing stock still, not lifting his bow, staring downfield at his wand with a frown.

"What's he trying to do, up the anticipation?" Tristan whispers again, incredulous.

"No, I don't think so," I say, staring down at Taran's wand, too, with a slightly sick feeling in the pit of my stomach. "I think he's going to refuse to shoot it."

Now we're all staring down at Taran's wand, and there's a tension on the field that's partly radiating out from Taran himself, and partly coming from what we're all thinking:

Taran could never bring himself to shoot and miss on purpose. But if he shoots the wand, the bird will fly into the air, and Remy will kill it.

He's gripping his bow so hard, I half-expect Gilles to drawl, "that's not a *stump*, you know. If you squeeze that bow any harder, you're going to break it," and from the way Taran's knuckles are standing out white where they're wrapped around the bow's shaft, for a moment I fear he might actually snap it. It wouldn't be the first time.

"*Shoot* the wand, *master*," Remy finally hisses. "Shoot, or we'll be forfeit."

And so Taran takes his shot. An excellent one, right up under the perch, and I don't think it's my imagination that he was aiming for the string. But Gilles was right; you can't break a string with a bodkin point, even with a direct hit. The dove flies up, its wings silhouetted against the sky, only to be shot down a second later by Remy. He gets it in one, and as the bird falls like a stone to dangle lifelessly at the end of the twine, even over the roar of the crowd I can hear Remy saying,

"It had to be done, master," and I don't blame him. He had to make up for his master's hesitation, and he did.

He shot the dove right through the eye.

I'm trying hard not to see the dead bird as I hand Tristan his first arrow. The master's saved *us* as his best for last, so the pressure is on, and it's time for us to step up and be spectacular. I can't let sentiment stand in the way of that, and even if Taran didn't do anything to play up to the crowd, his turn was dramatic. It's going to take something big to beat him, after both he and his squire hit their marks with their very first arrows.

What's worse, Tristan knows it, and for all his efforts, he can't hide it that now he's nervous. After all, the wand really is outrageously narrow. I'm all out of speeches; all I can think of is *'be the wand,'* and Tristan's never found the phrase anything but annoying. Now it would be absurd, since it would be hardly inspiring to picture being a wand with a bird perched on top of it, or with a dead dove dangling from it. So when I notice Jerome out of the corner of my eye, still lounging with his lute outside Tristan's tent, I figure a little drama of our own might be in order. I beckon him over.

It takes a few pantomimed gestures and a reluctant nod from Master Guillaume to get Jerome to trot out onto the field.

It takes a few more insistent gestures to get him to start playing his lute, softly strumming one of the tunes he used to set the right mood for the boys' joint practices. As he does, I tell Tristan,

"There's no rush, master. Nice and easy," and I take him through some of the stretches he learned from Gilles, much to the audiences' entertainment, since Tristan makes quite a show of it. From down the line Gilles gives him an appreciative whistle, encouraging the ladies in the crowd to admire Tristan's physique. I don't let it go on too long; just long enough to loosen Tristan up and to remind the audience how extraordinarily good-looking Tristan is, without making Master Guillaume too angry, and it works like a charm. Tristan's first shot at the wand really is a thing of beauty; he's elegant, flowing, poetry in motion — he gives one of Gilles's effortless Lejeune upswing draws, with some of the bang of his own at the release — but he misses the wand. So I tell him,

"That's it, master! That was pure *Gistan*. Now on this next one, let's show 'em *Trills!*"

With a grin, Tristan swings up his bow in a motion even more sweeping than the last one, and when he releases, his arrow flies from the bow, straight to its target. It's a beautiful shot and it hits dead center, right at the top of the wand, and I can't hesitate. As soon as Tristan's dove is on the move, soaring upward, I swing up my crossbow. It's loaded and ready, and I follow the bird with my eyes, looking for the killing shot. I mean to aim for its heart. I really do. I know I have to shoot it.

Only I can't bring myself to kill it. After Taran hesitated, it feels too much like shooting the little merlin. And I can't miss it. So I adjust my aim, and I shoot it in the wing.

"I'm sorry, master," I say, as the bird flaps and gurgles, jerking at the end of the twine.

"That's okay, squire," Tristan says. "You hit it. That has to count for something."

We watch it for another moment or two, while the crowd gives us a rather lukewarm round of applause, until the bird stops struggling and falls still, hanging upside down from the string and blinking.

"You could still make it, Marek," Remy calls over to me. "You've got two bolts left, and now it's an easier shot. A static target. Try again, and this time you won't miss!"

He means to be kind, and after his own shot he can afford it. But I'm sure everyone in the bleachers can hear him, I want to cry out and tell everyone that I missed the dove on purpose. Only I can't do that, and what's worse, Remy's right.

I could shoot again. And I'm sure I could hit it. But shooting the bird again is the last thing I want to do, and now it would simply look ridiculous. Particularly if I missed it. Only now everyone is staring at me, and I don't know what comes over me. Instead of raising my bow for another shot, I drop it in the dust and I run out to the wand, and I untie the little bird. Then I wrap it up carefully in the hem of my tunic and I carry it gently back to the line with me, much to the amusement of the audience.

I'm sure I'm making a fool of myself, but by the time I get back to Tristan some of the more sentimental in the crowd have started to make sympathetic noises. I even think I hear a few *'oohs'* and *'awws'* coming from some of the ladies when Tristan bends his head down over mine and reaches out a hand toward the bundle in my hands, as though he's assessing the bird's wing; it doesn't hurt that he surely makes a most handsome picture, with that one unruly lock of his hair falling fetchingly across his forehead in the process. We must make a rather sweet sight and the appreciative murmurs of the audience increase, until finally one loud female voice rises up from the stands in a quavering and agitated warble,

"It's not *dead*, is it?! Oh, what a terrible omen, for the wedding!"

It's Lady Sibilla, and encouraged by her reaction, Tristan sweeps his cloak from his shoulders. Then he takes the wounded creature and gently wraps it up in it, and he makes a show of inspecting it carefully.

"Ladies and Gentlemen," he announces triumphantly, *"it lives!"*

We bring the test to a close by parading off the field with the bird still cradled in Tristan's arms, having first promenaded with it past the boxes to reassure the ladies of the dove's survival and to proclaim it an excellent portent for the upcoming nuptials. As we go, the crowd gives Tristan the first standing ovation of the day, as much for his tender heart as for his brilliant shooting.

CHAPTER THIRTY-NINE

"What a stroke of genius, Marek! Pure *genius*," Tristan laughs, as soon as we're back in his tent and he's handing the bird back to me. "A crowd loves nothing better than a show of sentiment. We must have won back whatever points we lost for our misses, and even better, we showed up Mellor and his little rat for the thugs they are in the process! Whatever made you think of it?"

"I was actually just concerned for the dove," I admit.

Tristan helps me transfer the little bird onto one of the cloths I use to wrap his bow, since he'll need his cloak for the rest of the competition.

"Do you really think it will be okay, Tristan?" I ask him, once we've wrapped the bird's wing to hold it still against its body.

"Sure, kid. But its wing is broken. It'll take time to heal, and you can't keep it in barracks. What in the world are you going to do with it?"

I must give him a pleading look, because he furrows his brow and he makes a show of thinking about it. "All right, I'll tell you what," he says at length. "Pruie's here somewhere, right? After the tests, we'll give the dove to him. He can take it back to the farm with him. It can be a friend, for Buboes."

"And in the meantime, it can stay here?" I ask, and he agrees. He even helps me fix up a little makeshift nest out of more cloth for it to rest in, and he's being so understanding about the bird that I have to tell him,

"I could have hit it, Tristan. With that first shot."

"It's a good thing you didn't!" he laughs back. "Otherwise, we'd never have outshone that lucky shot of Remy's."

At just that moment, Remy pops his head into the tent.

He's come to check on the little patient, and as I lead him over to show him the bed of cloths we've made for the dove, Tristan takes the opportunity to duck out the back way, 'just to stretch his legs.' I suspect he's actually going over to Gilles's tent again to gloat with him about how fabulously they're both doing, and that's probably a good thing. It'll keep him in character, and besides, he can't stand Remy.

After Tristan's gone, Remy and I chat about the dove for a while. When he makes no move to leave, I sense there's something more on his mind. I can almost feel him trying to figure out how best to broach the subject.

"Tristan's doing really well today," he finally says casually. "You should be pleased," and I can tell he's just trying to prolong the conversation. He seems pretty nervous, more so than usual during the trials, and I suppose it could simply be because for once, my master is giving his master a run for his money. But from the way he keeps darting glances from the front tent flap to the back one, I get the impression he's worried that Tristan might come back — and that his own master might arrive to confront him.

"Your master is doing well too, of course," I tell him. "Like he always does."

"You know as well as I do Taran's off," Remy replies sullenly.

"It's probably just the stress of competition," I offer, but Remy shakes his head.

"It can't be that. Not with the exhibition he's got planned. It's incredible. It's sure to be the best of the competition," he says, giving me a sidelong look from under his lashes in a way that makes me suspect that this is why he's really here. It wasn't concern for the dove that led him to our tent. He must really be worried about Taran's standing, to be indulging in a little psychological warfare. I don't take it amiss. We're good squires, and we've both got to do whatever we can to help our masters. So I just grin and play along, and I say back,

"Wait until you see the trick *I've* come up with for them, I mean, for Tristan! It's going to be incredible, too. If I do say so myself, it's going to be *unbeatable.*"

We both laugh, as though it's all been a good joke, but I can tell that Remy's still worried. He gives the little dove one last pat, and with his errand accomplished, he departs, saying over his shoulder to me as he lifts the front tent flap,

"You know, it'll never fly, with its wing broken."

A broken wing is a heck of a lot better than a shot through the eye, but I don't say so. It must have cost Remy something to say it, too, since I'd be a fool not to know this is his way of warning me to keep my eye on Tristan, without having to say anything bad about his master. It's sweet, but it also gives me an uneasy feeling; it always seems to be just when I'm beginning to think better of Taran that all the other boys start warning me against him.

"I'll keep my eye on it, I promise," I assure him, just as Tristan himself comes in through the back flap.

"You promised what, Marek?" he says, once's Remy's gone.

"I promised him that for once, you're going to beat his master!" I reply, and it's not a lie. After all, I'm pretty sure that this is partly what Remy and I were really saying.

"It *is* all going to plan, isn't it?" Tristan says. "Only let's not count our chickens — or doves, as the case may be — before they're hatched! Master Guillaume always saves the worst test for last. I have to say, though, I'm looking forward to seeing what he's got for us! It must be almost time for it. I can hear the crowd outside getting restless."

He moves over to flip back the front flap of the tent to look out, and instinctively I reach out to stop him, for a moment letting my imagination run away with me and picturing Taran standing right on the other side again, ready to confront him. But there's no one there, and when Tristan just stands silently looking out past the field and toward the bleachers, his handsome face in profile against the midmorning light in that way that always makes him look like a romantic hero, I hear myself asking him,

"How did you know, Tristan? That she wasn't coming?"

It's the wrong time to ask. But it's not the first time I've wondered if Tristan's secretly been communicating with Melissande and if Taran suspects it — suspects *something*, anyway, since I can't be the only one who overhears things in the narrow guild hallways. But Tristan just says absently,

"What? Oh, Auguste told me." Only Auguste can't read, and when I press him, he admits,

"I may have bribed him to let me have a first look at all of Mellor's correspondences."

"Was that wise, master?!" I groan, and Tristan just chuckles back,

"Wise? Heavens, no! Deadly dull is what it was. But informative." He winks. "Come on, kid! Looks like the judges are back at their table. We'd better get my cloak reattached."

Tristan sounds so calm and poised, like he's finally genuinely in the relaxed mood he's been pretending to be in all morning. He really is looking forward to the next test, and that's what matters. So I keep my thoughts to myself about him reading Taran's mail, and I don't bother bringing up that Taran might have gotten the wrong idea about it. Only my hands are trembling a little as I pin his cloak back to his shoulders, plucking off a few stray feathers in the process. I'm not thinking about broken wings or busted heads, or what's likely to happen between the boys once the tests are over. The last test surely will be the hardest, and if it's more challenging than the last, it's going to take more than a gold chain and some attitude to see Tristan safely past it.

To make matters worse, as I shift around to adjust Tristan's cape, I feel Gilles's ring digging into my stomach. As soon as this third test is over, I'll have to meet Luc Fournier. As good as it will be to be rid of him, I can't say I'm looking forward to it.

"YOU'RE NOT NERVOUS, ARE YOU, SQUIRE?" TRISTAN ASKS ME, AS the call for the final test goes up.

"A little," I confess, as we duck out of the tent and take the field together. "You?"

"Nah," he says, stopping on the line to shake hands with Falko on one side and Jurian on the other, as we take our place between them. "A wands man is always ready for anything."

I hope that extends to explaining to Taran about intercepting his private letters, but I don't say so. Out of the corner of my eye I can see old Poncellet over at the judges' table, and the last thing I want to do now is to imagine Tristan getting an arrow welt burned into his abdomen by an angry clouter.

"Good Lord, boys! What do you make of that?" Tristan exclaims, getting a good look at the field in front of us. "It looks elaborate enough to be something of yours, Marek."

"Looks like the master's planting a forest," Falko declares, while Jurian drawls,

"Whatever it is, it looks exhausting."

I have no idea what to make of it, either.

Out on the field in front of us is a sea of wands. There must be over a hundred of them.

It has to have taken a crew of veterans forever to cut them all, and even longer to position them. They aren't planted in the ground the way wands usually are. They're standing free and balanced in an upright position on little squares of wood that are acting like bases, and although the wands are squarer in section than is customary, I can't imagine how much work it took to get them all standing in that fashion. About twenty of them are lined up in front of each Journey, one behind the other, with the closest of them about 200 paces distant. For the boys, that's not too difficult a shot, but I don't see what they're supposed to do about the rest of the wands, since they're lined up so exactly and so close to each other that each wand blocks the view of the ones behind it. It does look a lot like a forest, and the only boy who seems at all happy about it is Gilles.

"Have you ever seen so many wands?" Falko calls over to Tristan. "There can't be a willow tree left around St. Seb's in a three-mile radius."

"The old boy looks like he thinks he's died and gone to heaven," Jurian agrees, nodding down to where Gilles is indeed in raptures, although I'm not sure whether it's because of all the wands, or because he's so close to the bleachers that he's sidled over beneath the ladies' box and started flirting again with the Lady Sibilla.

"Journeys, Judges, Squires, Esteemed Audience, Blushing Brides and Bridegrooms!" Poncellet booms, swaggering out onto the field to explain the last test. "For the final ordeal of the day, I give you — wands, *in motion!*"

He makes a sweeping gesture out toward the wands behind him, and he laughs, since they're all standing there motionless and static. There's something more to it, and it gives me a bad feeling. For the old master to be looking so forward to what's coming, it can't be anything but excruciating.

All those wands. The sight of them probably should be reminding me of the fantastic joint trick that the boys have planned. Instead, the set-up has started to remind me of *Taran's* wands trick *last year* — the one in which he shot down a whole line of wands in record time, without missing a single one of them. Twenty wands each, more or less. With that many targets, I'm pretty sure that no amount of beautiful shooting is going to count for more than actually hitting them. Unless Taran starts missing, no matter what mood he's in, by the time this round is over he's sure to be ahead of us.

Tristan must be thinking the same thing. He nudges my shoulder, and with a wink he says,

"Don't worry, kid! After this, we've got *your* exhibition! Mellor won't know *what's* hit him."

Tristan sounds so confident, I should be pleased. And I am. Only he's made his comment so loudly that the other boys have all heard him, and over his shoulder I can see Taran standing stock still and staring out in front of him with a deep scowl on his face. I can almost see a dark cloud gathering over his head, and I fear Tristan's comment is going to stir him up into one of his impossible-to-beat, rage-fueled performances.

There's no time to respond before Poncellet's launching into his instructions.

"The test is simple, men. But that does not mean that it will be easy," he's now saying. "Your goal is to set off a chain reaction, by hitting the first wand in the line of wands in front of you so that it falls directly backward and knocks over the wands behind it. You will receive five points for each wand which topples as the result of that first single arrow! Then, once you've made a solid hit and your wands are falling, you are to *keep shooting* at them until they hit the ground — at that first wand, and at any wands that are falling behind it! Any wand that's moving is a fair target, and each hit you make to a wand in motion will land you another point. What's more, if all your wands aren't knocked over, you may shoot at the wands that remain standing, to try to set more of them in motion — but you won't get any points just for shooting a wand that's static. You see, men, for this test you will get points two ways: by toppling the most wands with the fewest arrows, and for hitting as many wands as you can while they're still in motion; a crew of veterans will be standing along the sidelines to keep count for each Journey. Good luck, men! You're going to need it. It will take an extraordinary shot to get that first wand to fall in precisely the right direction to bring down all the wands beyond it."

"That's impossible," a reedy voice objects. It's Aristide, and he's just saying what we're all thinking. "You can't hit a wand *again* before it falls to the ground. Not at these distances. And as for setting off a chain reaction. That depends as much on how they're set up as on how you hit them."

"Precisely!" Poncellet trills. "And that's why before you Journeymen commence shooting, you will all send your squires down the field, so that they can adjust your wands until they are aligned to your liking. We must give the squires their moment, mustn't we?" he purrs, and with a stroke of his mustache he's gesturing us squires out to the field and slinking back to the judges' table.

"Ugh, what is this? Payback from the master, for teamwork?" Rennie grumbles, once we're out among the rows of wands and the one he's trying to reposition for Jurian falls over for the fourth time in as many minutes. I'm sure he's right, since we've barely gotten started on the task and it's already pandemonium.

Everyone's shouting and gesticulating at once, the Journeys from the line and the squires from the field, and the wands are so precarious that they're ready to fall at the slightest touch. Moving them even slightly without knocking them all over is virtually impossible. Tristan's got his arm out in front of him with his thumb up, and he's sighting down it and waving me to the right and to the left with his other hand as I dart from wand to wand, trying to follow his gestures to make the necessary refinements. At one point, when Rennie accidentally backs into me, causing me to stumble and knock three of Tristan's carefully positioned wands over with a clatter, over at the judges' table I think I do see Master Guillaume watching with satisfaction. But maybe he's just pleased with all the spectacle, because the audience is loving it.

Instead of laughing at us as I expected they would, they've gotten caught up in it, and they're all calling out to the squires of their favorite Journeys, trying to help us by shouting out advice from their elevated point of vantage. They don't know our names, so they're addressing us by our masters' names or by our colors; over all the noise I think I hear the guild priest shouting at Remy, but there's too much chaos to make out much more than the occasional *"hey, more to the right, Lover Boy!"* Even the veterans now taking up positions on the field to keep count for the boys once the shooting starts can't resist chiming in from the sidelines, and it's actually pretty fun, even though it is nerve-wracking; I never expected us squires to get so much attention, and my heart is already soaring when I hear a loud voice call out *"Marek!"* over all of the others. I just have time to think with a rush of excitement, *somebody* does *know my name!*, when I realize it must be Luc. He's right in the front row, grinning at me.

By the time I've rejoined Tristan with his wands all precariously positioned to his satisfaction, my nerves are raw and my heart is pounding.

Even before Armand and Frans are back to the line, there's another loud fanfare and Poncellet is crying out,

"Gentlemen, *loose your arrows!*"

It takes us all off guard. We'd been assuming that the boys would take turns, since even shooting one at a time it's going to be hard to see what's happening. Instead, it's a free-for-all, and before I've gathered my wits

561

enough to shoulder Tristan's quiver or pull out an arrow for him, Gilles is already shooting.

A roar goes up from the crowd, since with one arrow Gilles has sent his first wand straight over backward, and as each successive wand falls in a perfect chain reaction, even out of the corner of my eye I can tell that Gilles is still shooting like a madman, hitting plenty of the wands as they fall for good measure. That's fine by me. We were never going to outdo Gilles at wands. But Aristide's also already shooting, and Taran, too; with no birds involved and his annoyance at Tristan fueling him, he's not hesitating this time, and there's to be no time for one of my little exchanges with my master before the test this time. Gilles is already almost done, and we haven't even started. And so as I thrust an arrow into Tristan's hand, I say to him,

"To hell with flair, master! Just hit some of the damned wands!"

Soon Tristan's shooting, and Falko's shooting, and Jurian, and the sky is filled with arrows; the colorful bands on the shafts are swirling and everywhere wands are falling, and I have no idea how anyone can possibly be keeping track of what's happening. All I know is that both Gilles and Taran set off a reaction with their very first arrows, but before I can start worrying about it, Tristan makes a solid hit. His first wand goes over backward, and we're off.

The field narrows down to just me and Tristan, and I feed him the next arrow, nice and easy. And then the next, and the next — one after the other, as each falling wand reveals another wand behind it — some taking down other wands with them, others falling off to the side at an angle, and some arrows missing entirely. And I'll admit. I don't really know how many tries it takes Tristan to get all his wands to fall, or how many of them he manages to hit while they're still in motion. But I doubt anyone in the stands can tell, either, and the whole thing is so exhilarating that it doesn't matter. Tristan's putting on one heck of a show, as are all the boys, and with Gilles and Pascal now calling down their encouragements to us, it almost feels like we really are all of us working together. Let the master think what he wants, but as the last of the wands falls and the audience comes to its feet, to me it feels a lot like a masterpiece of teamwork.

As the audience dies down and I come to my senses, I see to my surprise that there is one long line of wands still standing. Poor Falko is still shooting. With his injured shoulder he can't draw nearly as quickly as the others. He's thoroughly exhausted and he's hurting, and as he's fumbling to nock another arrow, his shoulders are visibly drooping. An awkward silence has fallen over the field, as we all watch him. The crowd is silent now, too; they're all still on their feet, shuffling a little, as though everyone is only just now noticing that Falko's not managed yet to hit even one of his wands. Missing that single wand in the previous test, that was one thing. It was extraordinarily slender. But failing to hit even one wand

MASTERS

out of twenty will mean complete humiliation, and he's only got a handful of arrows left.

"You can do it, master," I hear Frans telling him encouragingly, and pretty soon all the Journeys and squires are adding their voices.

"Come on, DeBruyn," Jurian calls over to him. "Don't go down without a fight," and I feel tears forming in my eyes as Falko lets the arrow in his bow fly toward the wand, only to overshoot it. Falko's too magnificent an archer to end his Journey days with such an embarrassing failure. It's a cruel reward for his valor in the marketplace, and it's even worse that nobody in the audience is hissing or booing, as though they've already all given up on him.

A few more listless arrows later and it's clear Falko's all but given up, too. He's just playing out his turn, trying to get it over with, while Frans hands him his arrows and hops back and forth from one foot to the other. After a rocky start, the little guy's now awfully fond of his master, and finally Frans can take it no longer. With a little cry, he thrusts another arrow into Falko's hands and then he darts off down the field.

"Hey!" Falko cries, "Come back! I'm not done yet." But Frans isn't listening. He's got his head down, and before Master Guillaume or Poncellet or any of the other veterans can stop him, he's run all the way out to the first wand in Falko's row and he's pushing it over. As it falls backward, Frans yelps,

"Shoot, master! Now, *now*! You can get 'em in motion, I *know* it!" And then he scampers off as fast as he can, head ducked and his hands clasped over his head, as Falko lets loose, encouraged by his squire's grand gesture.

At Tristan's urging, I step over to feed Falko the rest of his arrows while Frans hot-foots it toward the sidelines, and as Falko pushes himself with one last heroic effort, for a moment his old power and panache are back — the ghost of his former invincible self, going out in a blaze of glory. It's a beautiful sight, though I'm not sure if he actually hits many of the falling wands. I doubt it.

But he does hit something. As Frans comes circling back around to join his master, Rennie is the first to see it: there's a big fat arrow sticking out of the toe of Frans's boot.

"Good Lord, he's shot him," Jurian exclaims, at his squire's outcry. "Not another one."

"He's not just *shot* him, boys!" Aristide crows, sounding more gleeful than upset about the fact that Falko's probably just crippled his squire. "He's pulled a *DuBois*!"

The rest of us gather around in concern, but Frans just reaches down and pulls out the arrow. Then he waves it over his head with a grin, brandishing it for the audience. Fortunately for him, the boots he's got on are much too big, and the only thing with a hole it in is one of Gilles's handkerchiefs that was stuffed down inside of it.

The crowd rewards him with a cheer, and he's earned it. We all know it was an outrageously dangerous thing to do for his master, since it was just dumb luck that Falko didn't actually kill him. So Armand and Pascal hoist the little fellow up onto their shoulders between them, and all of us squires fall in behind to carry him around the field in honor of his heroism.

It's the first time Armand and Pascal have worked together since they started feuding over Gilles's haircut, and on our second time past the bleachers, the Journeys join us. Master Guillaume doesn't object, even when Charles jumps down from the stands to join them. The audience redoubles their applause when they see it, rewarding Frans for turning tragedy to comedy and touched by the sight of the handsome former Journey's affection for his brother, and I think the only thing they would have enjoyed better is if there really had been a more serious accident.

CHAPTER FORTY

Things finally break up when the master calls the Journeys over to the judges' table. For once, Guillaume is giving the boys their exhibition order in advance. With wands involved, each squire will need some lead time if he's to have the materials ready as his master's turn approaches, particularly since the master is hoping the boys have taken his advice to heart and made their tricks suitably elaborate.

I hang back with the other squires while the Journeys receive their orders, watching a troupe of jugglers who are making a show of tossing around some of the wands now littering the field as part of their performance. The jugglers are still at it when the boys rejoin us (luckily enough, since otherwise we squires would have been made to clean up the wreckage), and as we all head back toward the Journeys' tents together, Tristan and Gilles have their arms around each other's shoulders, just as though they were already the day's big winners. They lead us in a longer route than is necessary, circling around below the grandstands while waving into the audience, then past the far end of the field near the barricades, to treat the standing-room crowd to a good look at them for good measure.

"And how are you feeling, dear boy?" Gilles says to Pascal, over his shoulder. We're passing the place where the white gazebo is parked, waiting to be rolled out for his proposal.

"I think I'm going to be sick again, actually," Pascal warbles.

I know how he feels. Tristan's through the main tests. He's done really well — maybe even better than I could have imagined. I'm still pumped up with energy from my own part in everything, and I'm elated. Only we've just passed the bleachers, and the place where I'm sure I saw Luc Fournier earlier is empty. He's already out in the stables, waiting for me.

Back in his tent, I ask Tristan about the exhibition order while I work up some courage for my meeting with Luc. As expected, Falko and Jurian are to be first, followed by Aristide, Tristan, Gilles, and Taran. I'd have preferred for Gilles to be before Tristan, so that Tristan could be the first of the boys to jump in on the other's trick. But as usual the master has put the Journeys in an order that reflects his expectations of their performances, and there's no way I could have really thought the master would expect more of Tristan at wands than of Gilles, and I have to be content with it.

"That's good, master! Really good. You boys are right next to each other, and that's what matters. And the master's put you *after* Aristide! That should count for something. Even without the trick, you must be only a wand or two behind him."

"Better than that, surely! After your stunt with the bird, I'd say we're tied," he protests. But when he doesn't say anything else, I know he's thinking what I'm thinking. The master's put Taran dead last. Even *after* Gilles.

I do my best not to hear the master's voice murmuring,

"*He's the best shot that's ever been at St. Sebastian's.*"

But it isn't easy.

Tristan hasn't mentioned it, and I haven't either — but the hard line of his mouth and his furrowed brow tell me that he knows as well as I do the one thing I haven't wanted to let myself think all winter: that just passing today isn't enough. If Tristan can't outdo Taran now, when the playing field is level and the skill is a neutral one between them, he'll never convince the judges that he deserves to beat out Taran for Guardsman.

What's more, he'll never believe he deserves to, either.

I've been lying to Tristan, and to myself, right from the beginning. Seconds isn't the crucial test this year. It's this one, and the deciding moment is coming up in just a few minutes. The only thing good about it is that it makes it easy to convince Tristan to accompany me back across the street to the guild, to pray to St. Sebastian.

I'm not sure why I suggest it. Tristan's never one to want to wait out the intervals in his tent, and I guess I just want his reassuring presence with me as long as possible, because I'm getting nervous.

Not about trick — at least, not about the *doing* of it. It'll take some set-up and I'm anxious about getting back in time to help with it, but the trick itself isn't really all that hard. Like Poncellet advised, it just *looks* impossible. All we can do is wait and see if it will be enough to sway the masters. And I'm not too worried about my solution to the Luc problem, either. Gilles's ring is sure to satisfy him, and he's an opportunist. As soon as it's in his hand, he'll be off for bigger things. But it is going to be mighty unpleasant to have to face him alone again and to hand that ring over, and the stress of it all is starting to get to me. I won't feel at ease again until both the boys' trick and my meeting with Luc are over, and I don't much like leaving Tristan unattended, either. It wouldn't do for him to be seen too much with Gilles before the exhibition; as it is, Master Guillaume probably already suspects something. It would be even worse for Tristan to do something more to antagonize Taran. The last thing we need is for things to come to a head between them right while the boys are doing their exhibitions, with all Louvain watching. I figure the chapel is the safest place for him.

Why, oh why did I agree to meet Luc in the middle of the trials? Why didn't I seek him out and give him Gilles's ring last night? He'd be halfway to Meuse by now, and I'd be out in front of Tristan's tent, enjoying the first boys' performances. But I was too surprised and flustered to argue with him, and I guess it's simple: I can try to deny it, but the truth is I'm afraid of him.

My hands have started shaking as Tristan and I make our way in fits and starts through the crowds in the L'île-Charleroi road, stopping now and then as townspeople reach out to shake Tristan's hand or slap him on the back in congratulations, and when I try to talk to Tristan, all I can do is stammer. He's assumed I'm nervous about the trick, and so as we dodge our way into the yard through the postern gate, I try to encourage him about it.

"Remember, master. Pascal and I will have it all set up, and you'll step up to start your trick. And then Gilles will run up from the sidelines, shoot out the first dowel, and then you'll be off — him setting the wands free, and you shooting them in motion. And then we'll set up and do it all over again, switching roles, for his exhibition."

"I know the plan, Marek. I've only done it about a hundred times. Don't worry, kid. It's going to go just fine. It's going to be perfect," he assures me. Only his voice catches a little on *perfect*, and I know he's disappointed. He's always wanted to be the one to jump in first, to be the boy who makes the grand entrance.

"Look at it this way," I say, once we've crossed through the great hall and we're coming out under the portico at the edge of the garden. I stop and turn to him, and I put a hand on his chest, in the way I did to Taran earlier. "Gilles is in first place. That's fine! More than fine. It *is* perfect. We were never going to beat Gilles at wands; nobody is. And maybe you're not in second place, yet. But when you boys go out there and do that trick together, Gilles is going to pull you up into second place, right behind him. That was the whole plan, from the beginning! So if it's Gilles who gets to make the surprise of it, that's okay. You're a team, and sometimes teamwork means letting someone else have the big moment."

"You're right, Marek, as usual," he says, and he slings an arm affectionately around my shoulders, as though to lead me toward the chapel. "Wands is Gilles's specialty, and I can't be selfish. But when it's butts, M. le Marquis had better step aside. Hey, aren't you coming in with me?"

I haven't budged or taken my hand from the front of his jerkin.

"Prayers should be done alone," I tell him. "And, uh, there's something I forgot, out in the shop, for the exhibition. Wait in there for me, will you? I'll be right back. What I have to do will only take a minute."

He agrees easily, as I knew he would. As he turns to go, for a moment I clutch up the front of his shirt harder, and I say,

"Say a prayer for me, too, won't you? And one to St. Margaret, while you're at it."

When he smiles down at me one of those old, lazy smiles of his that lights up the whole garden, although the veteran stationed at the door in the garden wall is watching us, I step in quickly and I hug him tightly, even though I promised myself I wouldn't do it.

I WATCH TRISTAN CROSS THE GRASS AND LET HIMSELF INTO THE chapel through the little side door amongst the rosebushes, just long enough to make sure he's really going to go inside and not cut back around to the concessions. And then I can't put it off any longer. Time is passing, and Luc is waiting for me. So I screw up my courage and I make my way out the rickety garden gate and onto the butts, and I circle around to the stables.

I skirt nervously past some veterans hanging around next to the water barrels, but nobody tries to stop me or questions what a squire is doing going into the stables. Luc was right about that; I do have the run of the guild, although as an apprentice I'm sure Luc's had no trouble getting into the stables either. I know where I'll find him — in the back stall, where the shadows are the deepest. I can already sense his presence there as soon as I cross over the threshold, even though except for all the animals, the stables appear to be empty.

There's nary a stable boy in sight; Luc must have chased them off, and as I make my way down the musty aisle between the overcrowded stalls, I imagine him enjoying prolonging my discomfort, as though he could know just from my scars how much I hate horses. Even over all the sounds of hooves shuffling and stamping against the packed dirt floor, bridles jangling, and a few stray chickens clucking, I think I can hear Luc's eager breathing.

The big white horse Gilles was riding earlier has the second-to-last stall in the row all to itself. It's standing with its head bent down over the low wall that divides its stall from the very last one, and when I reach it, sure enough Luc Fournier is there, lounging against the partition near the animal's head and languidly petting it. It's a carefully arranged tableau; I'm sure Luc hastily moved the inhabitants of the last stall into other overcrowded compartments, and he's staged his stance to look like he's fully relaxed and casual. But I can sense that he's tense and impatient, and as he watches me letting myself into the stall with him, he says,

"Ah, there he is! The hero of the hour. Or should I say *she*? For a moment there, I thought you weren't coming."

"Of course I came. I want to help you, Luc. Truly," I stammer, and I prepare to launch into an incoherent phrase or two about wishing him well in Meuse that I've been composing for myself between here and the garden.

Only Luc is not interested in hearing anything. He's noticed the bulges in my waistband.

"That the bag?" he demands, his greedy eyes glinting. He shoves the horse's nose away and takes a step toward me. I step back. I've barely had a chance to say a word, and I'm already retreating. At the sight of Luc's raw, angry face, flushed and sweating, the little flicker of fear that was jumping in my belly has grown into a raging fire, and before I can fumble the ring out of my waistband, Luc's hand is there, snatching out the little canvas bag and hefting it as though to assess the weight of it. My mouth dry as he opens the bag and pours its feeble contents into his hand.

"Wait, Luc. I can explain," I try to tell him. "That's not what I brought for you. It's not what you're thinking."

But Luc isn't listening. Before all my words are out, he explodes,

"Is this a *joke?*," and he clenches his fist around the pennies.

And then he punches me, low and hard, right in the middle of my abdomen.

It's just one quick jab, only a fraction of what he's capable of doing. But it catches me unawares, before I can steel myself for it, and I double over in surprise and pain.

Pain, mostly.

My head swims, and all my breath leaves my body. I stumble a few more steps backward, until I hit the back wall of the stables and there's nowhere more for me to go, and Luc steps forward to tower over me. He's so close I can't get any air, and I couldn't speak anyway; the pain is too intense and a warm, sick feeling is spreading through my gut that's partly fear and partly the feeling like something inside of me has ruptured.

Luc grabs me by the chin, thrusting my head up and pushing it back against the wall. He leans down over me with a look of pure fury on his face, until our noses are almost touching, and I know I'm about to get another punch before I've had a chance to recover from the first one.

It's another swift jab, just like the first one.

I clutch my belly and I open my mouth; something liquid slides out — saliva, or bile, or blood, I don't know — all I know is that I've got to say something, to tell him I have something better for him. Only with all the wind knocked out of me, my mind is no longer functioning. I've been too stunned by his sudden attack, by the pain and the violence of it — too paralyzed by a sudden, irrational fear of showing Luc the ring, of how he might react to it. Tristan was right; there *is* something wrong with Luc, and nothing about this meeting is going how I thought it would. As he gives me another rough shake, rattling my head against the boards behind me, all that comes out is,

"Luc, Luc. What *happened* to you? You were a nice boy."

"God, you really are a fool! Nice? I was never *nice*." And he punches me again, harder. A rush of pain sweeps up my body. I cry out, and the horses

569

and mules in the stalls around us stamp in their stalls, agitated. "I've been dying to do *that*, ever since we met. I thought I warned you then that I'd bite you back, if you tried to cross me."

"Your *father*. My father," I groan. It's all I can manage. Luc just laughs.

"The great Jan Verbeke! Being *his* apprentice, that might have been something. I was willing to try it, while my father was alive. For his sake. Even if it meant marrying *you*. Even if it meant having to look at your *face*," and he pulls back his fist, as though he's going to drive it straight into my eye. But when I cringe, he drops his arm and laughs harder.

"Come on, *Marek*. I thought you were a tough guy. Why don't you fight me?" He jostles me a little, and I can see he wants me to try it. But I can't, and not just because I know he'd enjoy it. There's no way I could hope to fight him off. My limbs have gone numb beneath me, and it's taking all my strength not to pass out.

"No?" Luc says in mock disappointment. Then he leans in closer. "What *happened* to me? Your father *died*, and *my* father died, and they left me with nothing! And maybe you weren't listening. But I owe people money. So let me tell you how it's going to be. Since I'm such a *nice guy*, I'm going to give you one more chance. You've got until the start of the exhibitions to bring me what I asked for. I'm going to let you up, nice and easy — don't be stupid enough to try anything! — and you're going to march inside the guild building proper, right now, past the veterans stationed outside the archives, while I wait here for you. I'll give you about five minutes. If you're not back by then with something worth a king's ransom, I'll go across the street and I'll announce that you're a girl, that you're Jan Verbeke's *daughter*, to Master Guillaume himself! Don't forget for one minute what I'm holding over your head."

"If I do, you'll leave?" I whisper, letting one hand sneak up to finger Gilles's ring, where it's still tucked down tight in my waistband. "You'll leave, and never come back?"

I came here to give him the ring, so I should just do it. Luc's not bluffing and I'm out of options. Only when I look up into Luc's face, one glance at his shrewd, vicious expression is enough for me to realize too late that not even Gilles's ring can save me. My instinct not to hand the ring over wasn't irrational, it was the right one — because the moment Luc has it, I'll be a liability to him, not an asset.

Why didn't I think it sooner? Then *he'll* be the thief, and of a Journeyman's jewel that's worth a fortune. He can't risk having me tell on him once he can be caught with it. He's been planning to kill me all along — just as soon as I've given him something of value.

No, giving Luc Gilles's ring won't save me.

It'll seal my death warrant.

My heart is beating fast, thumping a beat in my breast that's racing almost as fast as my mind is calculating. As soon as Luc lets go of me, I know where I'm headed. I'll go dutifully inside the guild — and then I'll run out the back way. I'll run straight to Taran. He's right across the street somewhere.

"So many questions!" Luc says, his mouth twisting into a smile, as though he's seen the hope of escape on my face, and he's amused by it. "If I were you, I wouldn't waste any more time in small talk. You've got a job to do, and quick. But first," he grins, "I'm going to give *you* a lesson — not to come to a rendezvous empty-handed! Don't worry. I won't leave a *mark* on your face. It's already so decorative, and we don't want your master asking any questions."

He hits me again, this time driving his knuckles sideways into my ribcage. Now he's holding nothing back, and I cry out at the blinding, searing pain of it. Worse even than the agony in my side and the pain still burning in my belly is the sudden rush of fear — overwhelming, welling up inside me, taking over my senses — as the reality of what's about to happen hits me. I'm to have no chance to run, after all, and Luc doesn't know his own strength. I can't take another punch. I've had more than I can take already. The lesson Luc's going to give me now — there's no way I'll survive it.

What a fool I was, to try to handle Luc by myself! To think that I could talk my way around him, like this was some kind of adventure. Like I was Tristan. *Why didn't I listen, when Tristan tried to warn me? Why didn't I swallow my pride, and just ask Taran to help me in the first place?*

Luc raises up that huge fist of his, one more time. He holds it up high over my head for a moment, poised for another blow, and he lets me get a good look at it, enjoying his power. He's still holding onto the front of my tunic, but now he lets me slide a little down further against the wall, and as I do, I rasp out one last plea to him to see reason:

"Luc, p*l*ease. You're going to kill me."

What strength I had is gone, and there's nothing in the stall I can use to defend myself. All I can do is stare up at him as he pulls back, preparing for that punch, and wait for it.

As I do, my vision blurs, and over his shoulder I see a huge black shadow rising up from the stall behind him. I know what it is. It's death. Slaver is forming at the edges of Luc's mouth, and it's too late to fight or flee, or even to offer him Gilles's ring. Luc's past caring about the money; he's going to vent his rage on me for everything he thinks he's suffered, or maybe he's simply read it on my face that I'll run straight for help if he lets go of me — and damn the consequences. All I know is that this punch is going to be my last one, and in the distance, I can hear a roar going up from the audience out in the bleachers. The exhibitions have started; all the boys will be back on the field.

Tears well up in my eyes, and a dozen thoughts race through my mind in a single instant. I've faced death before, on Brecelyn's tower. Only then, I'd thought I was ready. It felt like a fitting end. Now everything is unfinished. I'll miss seeing Tristan's and Gilles's incredible trick, the one I devised for them. I'll miss Tristan's victory, and it hurts as much as any broken rib. But then Luc's fist is coming hard and fast toward me, and there's no room for anything but stark terror, and a sudden, violent wish, a wish as desperate as any I've ever felt — a wish that Taran were here with me.

Not to save me. Just to be with me. Just to feel him one last time wrap his arms around me.

Time has slowed around me, as I wait for Luc's fist to connect. When it does, everything happens at once. Luc's aimed for my stomach, and by chance his knuckles graze my waistband, right where I've got Gilles's ring.

"Ho, ho!" he crows, pulling his punch short and fishing the ring out with rough, grasping fingers. "What's this!? Holding out on me, eh, Verbeke?" he cries, gloating as he shoves me down onto the straw and holds up Gilles's ring triumphantly.

Only I'm not looking at the ring. My eyes are riveted on Luc, as two huge hands snake around his neck from behind — and begin to squeeze.

Luc's eyes bulge out.

They roll back in his head.

His mouth opens in a choking gurgle, and I watch in horror as he claws at the fingers now digging into his throat, throttling the life out of him.

Froth flies from Luc's lips. His tongue lolls out, and all the while he's wildly kicking around in the straw, flailing and thrashing and making awful sounds. But he was caught too off guard to put up an effective fight, and as gruesome as it is, I'm too shocked at the sight to look away from his distorted face as it drains of blood only inches in front of mine, while in the distance another boisterous cheer rings out from the grandstands.

Then, horribly, he goes slack. Just when I think he must be dead, the big hands release him, and Luc Fournier falls to his knees onto the moldy pile of straw beside me.

A boy even bigger than Luc is now standing over us. All I really see of the hulking boy is a vague, blurry outline, because both he and I are staring down at Luc's body next to me where he's sputtering and gagging, as I try to process what's happened — although it's obvious enough. The boy now towering above us came climbing over the partition wall between the stalls in answer to my desperate pleas, and he's just choked Luc half to death.

More than half, by the looks of it.

Flies are buzzing around Luc's head as he coughs up a trickle of bile; his eyes are bloodshot and his face and tongue are bluish, and his hands are clutching at his neck and tearing at the collar of his shirt, as though he's still struggling to suck air into his crushed windpipe. He's almost too terrible to look at, and I fight down a wave of revulsion to keep from being sick myself. But I can't help it. What I feel most is desperately glad that he's now lying in the straw convulsing, with his hands not on me but on his own neck.

I gaze up, into the face of my rescuer. Our eyes meet, and while Luc continues to gag and gurgle between us, we share a long, solemn look.

Then he reaches down a hand and pulls me shakily to my feet — a hand that shows all the tale-tell signs of having suffered in the plague, and that's missing the tip of one of its fingers.

Pruie must have been sitting in the neighboring stall the whole time, quietly communing with Gilles's bridal gift for Ginger and the other animals.

I lean heavily on my big friend, and I let him steady me for a moment. Then I prod Luc with the toe of my boot.

"Get up! Get up, Luc, and get out." When Luc looks up at me, his eyes red and his pale, puffy face incredulous, I can tell he can't believe what's just happened, and I sway a little. I'm not sure I can believe it, either. But I continue as bravely as I can; my side is throbbing and my head feels like it's spinning, but someone has to say something, and it isn't going to be Pruie.

Besides, Luc's now glancing up at Pruie's broad, impassive face, and looking as petrified of Falko's former squire as I just was of *him*. And I hate to say it. But I can tell Luc's thinking something close to what Falko said of Pruie himself, that he's 'not quite right anymore, *in the head*,' and that it's scaring him even more than Pruie's incredible clouter's strength. So I say coldly over him,

"We *are* nice boys, so we'll give *you* one chance. Take the ring and run all the way to Meuse, and never look back. And if you stop to breathe a word about me to the master or to anyone else, *I'll* expose *you* as the thief you are, and you'll have to answer to my friend again into the bargain."

As though to punctuate my words, Pruie rocks forward a bit on his toes, and it doesn't take more than that. Without a word, Luc scrambles out of the stall so fast, he hardly bothers to get upright. He's still coughing and gagging, and as he stumbles his way out of the stables, I collapse back against the wall, trying to will down the throbbing in my gut and to summon some strength and courage. Pruie and I stand there in silence, eyes locked, listening to the sounds of Luc's departure and to my own belabored breathing, until the worst of the pain has subsided and I've gotten myself under control, a little.

"He won't come back, will he?" I finally say, once I'm sure Luc is gone. I'm not sure how I expect Pruie to answer, but my head is pounding and I need a little assurance, and in response, the big boy shakes his head, clucking out a noise that sounds a bit like a reassuring hen. He looks perfectly calm and a little confused, the way he has ever since he suffered from the plague, and I'm not sure how much he really comprehends of what's just been happening; maybe not much more than that Luc's 'a wrong-un' who likes cockfights, as Falko told him. But I know my old friend is still in there somewhere, and there's something in his expression that seems to me to be trying to tell me something.

And that's when it dawns on me that Pruie overheard my whole conversation with Luc.

Every single word of it.

What's more, something in the depths of his gentle, vacant eyes tells me that he heard *everything*, and that he understood it.

As if in confirmation, Pruie takes a step closer. An almost confidential look appears on his features, and he puts one huge hand softly on my shoulder.

He opens his mouth, his expression serious.

He looks me right in the eye.

Then he says,

"*Buboes.*"

From the solemn way he says it, I know I don't have to worry that Pruie will tell anyone my secret — and not just because he still can't say anything more than the name of his chicken.

CHAPTER FORTY-ONE

The sound of another fanfare in the distance brings me around. Out on the exposition grounds, Aristide must be starting his trick. That means Tristan is next. I've got to get back across the street as quickly as possible. There will be time for me to think about what's just happened, later; all that matters now is that Luc is gone. If he's smart, he's on the road to Meuse already, and one look at Pruie's huge hands, now dangling limply at his sides, tells me that I'll never see him again. I can't imagine how much strength it took Pruie to throttle a man the size of Luc even though he's missing half his fingers, and it's the one thing Luc didn't anticipate, a thing a boy like that would never take into consideration — that I might have made real friends here, and I say my own silent cheer to myself. It's the second time today that squires' club has saved me.

But when I try to step forward, I sway, and my knees buckle underneath me. My side is killing me and I'm still queasy, both from shock and from Luc's punches. I brace myself against the wooden wall of the stable for another minute and I gulp in some fetid air, and I will down the pain still blazing in my stomach. I've had worse, I tell myself, even though I probably haven't. I'm not going to miss the boys' trick, not now — not for anything. Not if I have to crawl across the L'île-Charleroi road on all fours, or slither like a serpent.

Any minute Tristan will be doing *my* incredible trick. For that I could run all the way to Meuse, even if Luc really has broken every one of my ribs.

"Come on, Pruie. Let's get you back to Roxanne," I say, after one more deep breath. I can't leave him here. His lucid look is gone, and maybe I imagined it. Now he seems confused and agitated, and I doubt there are enough chickens in Louvain to soothe him. So I hustle him out and across the yard with me, and no one stops us. The veterans who were stationed outside earlier are gone; they've probably migrated over to watch the exhibitions themselves, and the men on the wall have no reason to pay any attention to a couple of squires.

We're halfway across the L'île-Charleroi road when we run into Armand

and Remy, running in the opposite direction. Frans is tagging along behind them, and from the looks on all their faces, I'm sure both Falko's and Aristide's tricks were disasters.

"What happened?" I ask, pausing to catch my breath and clutching my side. "Where are you guys going?"

"*There* you are, Marek!" Armand exclaims, not listening to my questions. "Pascal is frantic! We're looking for *you*. Where in the heck is Tristan?!"

"What are you talking about?" I demand, in between wheezes. That's when I notice with a rising sense of alarm that the boys are all too agitated themselves to wonder about my condition, and for some reason, Frans is carrying Tristan's massive yew bow and his quiver. And that if Armand is standing in front of me, Aristide's trick must be over.

Either I was too focused on being beaten by Luc to hear all of the fanfares, or maybe nobody at all cheered for Falko, but I've miscalculated. That blast of the bugle wasn't for Aristide's turn.

It was for Tristan's.

"He never came back to his tent after the third test." It's Remy, sounding nervous. "What were you two doing over here, anyway? Where *is* he?" he says, as Armand cuts in urgently,

"Pascal's out there right now, setting up for Gilles. He sent me to find you. He said to tell you that it's not too late, and that he's stalling. He said you'd know what he means."

And I do. Tristan's *missed* his own turn, and it's all my fault. I told him to wait for me out in the chapel. He must still be there now, expecting me to come and fetch him. I should have known he wouldn't be able to hear the bugles through the chapel's stone walls! Now I've got precious little time to find him and get him back across the street. If Tristan doesn't do a trick at all, he'll be out. I've got to get him back, so he can jump in on Gilles's.

I point Pruie in the direction of the grandstands, and with one quick, tight hug of gratitude, I send him on to rejoin the ladies. Then I turn heel and I run back towards the guild chapel as fast as I can, with both hands wrapped around my battered sides to brace them and with the other boys following along behind. We hustle back across the yard, down the guild corridors, and through the main hall, and I'm already feeling apprehensive, before I think to ask Remy,

"What are you doing here? Shouldn't you be getting ready to set up for Taran?" and he replies,

"Taran's not back yet, either."

"Back from what?" Armand demands, as we come out into the garden. But even before Remy can respond, I fear I can guess the answer.

"He always prays before his exhibitions," Remy says tremulously, but I doubt he does. Taran must have come over here looking for Tristan, wanting to pester him with questions.

I can't have been with Luc that long, although at the time it felt like an eternity. And I'm sure Tristan and Taran *do* have a lot to talk about. But they've never had a conversation long that didn't come to blows, so I'm already worrying that I might not be the only boy who's just been taking a beating by the time we all burst into the little chapel.

Even so, I'm not prepared for the sight that greets us as soon as we fling the chapel doors open. I'm probably still in shock from my encounter with Luc, and so light-headed that I'm hallucinating. But at first, I can't make sense of it. I've been fully expecting to find the boys scuffling. To find them rolling on the floor, even, finally brawling it out over Melissande in earnest.

Instead, the chapel is still and silent. And at the very center of the chancel, two handsome boys in cloaks are illuminated by a beam of light, both so unmoving and so artfully arranged that they could be posing for a scene in a passion play, or a giant icon, come to life.

Tristan's lying at the foot of the altar, unconscious. And Taran's kneeling next to him, bent over by his head, like he could be praying for him.

Only he doesn't look very pious. He's scowling.

And he's holding a bloody brick in his hand.

"Oh, mercy!" Armand hisses, right in my ear, sounding a lot like he's having second thoughts about becoming a clouter.

We've all screeched to a halt, me in front with my hands up as though to hold the others back, and the others behind — all no doubt frozen in a tableau of astonishment; somewhere behind me, I can hear Armand muttering "man, not *another* dirty shot!" and Remy softly whimpering,

"You *know* Tristan provoked him! It's not what it looks like!"

Nobody asks what 'it' is. Nobody has to, since what it *looks* like is that Taran's come up behind Tristan while he was kneeling at his prayers and bashed him over the head with one of the stones left over from the wall demolition. We've caught him red-handed, with the weapon still hot in his hand — the very brick he's been carrying around for weeks, itching to use it on my master.

"Thank God," Taran says matter-of-factly, looking up at the sound of our arrival. "It looks fresh. It must have just happened."

I'm the first to react, and soon we're all rushing to gather around Tristan.

"It's not bad. Just a hard enough blow to knock him senseless. He's already starting to come around," Taran's continuing, standing up and moving aside as Armand and I crowd forward. "But he's going to need a bandage."

He doesn't sound the least bit guilty or apologetic, and he doesn't offer any explanation, either, although he surely heard the boys and he must know what they're all thinking, even his own squire. He just stares down at Tristan with a frown, his knuckles standing out white around the bloody brick still clutched in his hand.

"It must have been a thief," Frans squeaks, sounding tense, and Remy picks up on the suggestion. While he gently pries the brick from his master's

577

hand, both he and Frans start murmuring about all the pickpockets and footpads in Ardennes, even though we all know that nobody from outside could have snuck into the chapel without any of the veterans seeing them, and even though Gilles's expensive gold chain is still hanging around Tristan's neck.

I'm hardly listening. By this point I've gathered Tristan's head up into my lap and I'm running my fingers through his hair, partly looking for a wound, and partly trying to revive him. He's already moaning softly, and although there is a nasty cut somewhere right above his hairline, Taran's right. It doesn't seem too deep. The blow wasn't mean to hurt him seriously, just to incapacitate him for a little while. I can't help thinking, *just long enough to make him miss his trick.* Only I don't care what happened. Right now, all I care about is fixing it. There will be time for explanations, later — I know there has to be one. Taran can't have really come up behind an unsuspecting Tristan and hit him coldly over the head. The boys must have been fighting — although it didn't look like it. All I can think now is that I've got to get Tristan up, I've got to get him back across the street. There's still time. There has to be. It just can't end like this. It can't be all over for us here on the chapel floor, and not out on the field.

"You don't have a length of fabric on you *today*, do you?" I ask Taran, without any sarcasm. I just need something to bind Tristan's head. But even if Taran does have Melissande's veil stuffed down inside his quiver, he didn't bring it to the chapel with him, and the place is so austere there isn't even a cloth on the altar that I can shred.

"I can fetch something from the great hall, or get one of the veterans to help," Remy offers, as Taran says seriously, "someone needs to tell the master," but I shake my head. Fresh tears are forming in my eyes, tears of frustration and rage. First Luc, now this: everything that's happened is threatening to overwhelm me, but I'm not ready to give up yet.

"There's no time for that! I've got to get him up, now. I've got to get him back, before Gilles's turn is over. Before it's too late. Before he's *out*."

"Marek," Remy starts to say gently, just as Frans gives a little cry. He slaps his forehead, and as we all watch, he pulls off his one of his boots. He's still got some of Gilles's handkerchiefs stuffed down inside it. Soon I'm wrapping a white cloth around Tristan's brow, and as Tristan's eyes start to flutter open, Armand says shrewdly,

"Remy, you'd better get him out of here."

Taran hasn't moved. He's still standing next to Tristan, wordlessly watching as I tend to him. But now when Remy tugs on his sleeve, imploring him,

"Come away, master. There's nothing more we can do here. We've got to get ready for our own trick," Taran lets his squire lead him off. I don't know whether he looks back at us over his shoulder or not, as I lean over to press my cheek against my master's, and I start to babble to him in a voice thick and urgent with concern,

"Tristan! Tristan, can you hear me?"

Without opening his eyes, at last Tristan mumbles back, "Is that you, St. Margaret?"

"It's *me*. Marek," I tell him as his eyes come open, and Armand and I help him up into a sit, propping him against the altar. "Master, are you all right?"

"Where am I?" he asks, sounding so confused and disoriented that I almost expect him to say, "*Am I in prison again?*" the way Gilles did after Taran hit *him* in the head.

"You're in the chapel, at St. Sebastian's. You were praying, and you took a nasty blow. But you're okay now. You're going to be all right." I don't mention Taran. I don't know why. I'll figure out what I think about it all, later.

"I think I remember," he says, coming to his senses and reaching up to the makeshift bandage around his temple. "At least, I remember blacking out and falling forward; there's enough incense in here to make a whole army keel right over! Hey, wait a minute ... I was praying for the success of our *trick*, wasn't I?! So what are we doing, sitting around here? It must be almost time for it!" he exclaims, and he starts getting to his feet.

When he stumbles from the effort and for a moment his eyes flicker closed again, I come to my senses. My stomach's burning and my side's throbbing, and Tristan is reeling, his blood already soaking through his bandage. It's over, and for Tristan's sake, I have to accept it.

"It's too late, master," I say, steadying him and resting my head on his shoulder, and trying to will away the sensation that the future we've worked for so long and so hard is slipping through our fingers. "Gilles's turn must be almost over. Besides, you're in no shape to stand, let alone shoot. But you're alive, and I'm alive, and that's all that matters." I hug him as tight as I dare, and I try to mean it. After all, it's true. Only every part of me is hurting, the disappointment sharper even than the pain, and I'm sure Tristan can feel it radiating from me.

"To hell with *that*!" Tristan cries, squeezing me back briefly, then putting me out of his arms. "I'm not out *yet*, by Saint Sebastian! I'm going to do that bloody trick of yours, Marek, or die trying. At least I'll go down fighting! I'll be damned if I wedged myself into peacock-blue tights and frilly shirts and wore my hair in a blasted ponytail for nothing!"

Before I can argue with him or do anything to stop him, Tristan's grabbed up his bow and his quiver from Frans and he's out the door, at first stumbling and swaying, and ricocheting between the doorposts as he crosses over the threshold. Then he's running full tilt down the portico, and I'm running right behind him. He's still in shock, and so am I, and before long he's moving so fast it's all I can do to keep him in sight.

He barrels through the guild hall, then out into the yard, and even with the stabbing pain in my side I manage to keep pace with him until he's crossing the street — pushing aside the crowds and forcing his way through with his bow held aloft out in front of him. His quiver is slapping wildly against his shoulder, the arrows rattling around in it with a clatter, and his makeshift bandage is already so askew that fresh blood is dripping freely down his forehead. He looks for all the world like a bat flying out of hell's mouth with his black cape flapping behind him, and as he cries out to clear the way before him, he's making a terrible racket.

I catch up with him on the exposition grounds, where the denser crowds impede his progress. I follow on his heels as long as I can, clutching onto the back of his cape as he plows his way forward, only to lose him again in the press around the barricades, when the unruly throng surges closed behind him. Nobody wants to miss a moment of Gilles's trick, and from the cheers that are going up from the spectators who can see out to the field, he must be well into it. I'm not sure *how* he's doing it — whether he's shooting out the dowels himself, or Pascal is loosening them for him manually — but from the sound of it, whatever he's doing looks just as fantastic as I'd imagined it. Only I'd been hoping for Tristan to be the most fantastic thing about it, and the trick must be nearly over. It'll almost be crueler to come so close only to fail now than if we'd just stayed in the chapel.

I only realize Armand and Frans are with me once I've jostled my way up to the barricades, and I'm looking anxiously over one of the waist-high barriers and out to the field beyond. Tristan's nowhere to be seen. *How is that possible?* He was in front of me.

I'm on the sidelines, only a short way from the line at which Gilles is stationed. Pascal is already way down the field, near the last of the wands; he's got a little knife in his hands, and I see with a surge of affection that he's been cutting the strings that hold the wands in the bent position. Bless his heart! It would be a lot easier simply to shove out the dowels, but he hasn't wanted to give away the mechanics of the trick. He's still hoping that Tristan will show up to jump in, and so is Gilles. It only takes a moment to see that they're both stalling.

Gilles is now stretching and strutting and getting the crowd to clap for him, while Pascal makes a show of holding up the knife and gesturing to the crowd, as though encouraging them to urge him to cut another wand free. It's a terrific performance, just what the master ordered, and that could be all it is. Except that I can see them scanning the barricades, looking for Tristan and looking worried, and it's been going on for so long, the master is getting impatient. He signals to the buglers, and when they blow a blast on their horns, Pascal has to set another wand in motion. And as it springs up into the upright position, Gilles has to shoot at it.

Even in my agitation for Tristan, I can't help straining forward. This is *my* trick, and I lean over the barrier as far as I can, to watch with a catch of my breath to see if Gilles will hit it while it's still moving. Of course he does, and it's a beautiful shot. Gilles hasn't let Tristan's absence ruffle him, and with a rush of pride I'm cheering along with everyone else when I see it. Only now there's only one wand left — the one with a second wand balanced on top of it.

"Where *is* he?" I cry, just as Armand grabs my shoulder and points downfield.

He's not pointing out toward the open arena. He's pointing into the crowds behind the barricades, down past the row of Journey tents, to a place midfield where there's a commotion among the spectators. I know it's Tristan even before I can see him, and somehow he's acquired an entourage of veterans who are clearing a path for him. Clever boy! He knew the trick would be almost over, so he's circled straight around to come out onto the field at the far end of it.

"Oh, Armand! He'll never make it!" I grip the railing and lean over as far as I dare despite the pain in my ribs, straining to make out what's happening. And now the bugles are sounding again, and Pascal's cutting the string, and as the last bent wand springs upright and sends the wand balanced on top of it tumbling high into the air, my heart is in my throat as Gilles sends up his last arrow.

It's a shot so high and light, it looks like it could hang there at the top of its arc all day long, and into the evening — like he could be aiming to replace the moon with it. But now my heart isn't soaring with it. It thuds down into my belly like lead, and I can feel all the burning in my gut and every pain in my ribs, and my lungs are so heavy I can't breathe at all, as everything that's happened since the last test catches up with me.

"It's going to hit!" Frans suddenly squeaks excitedly, his wide eyes on Gilles's arrow. I'm sure he's right, but I can't even bring myself to watch it. It's our last glorious moment of competition at St. Sebastian's, and Tristan isn't part of it. Even in my wildest fears for what might go wrong for us in the competitions, that Tristan would miss his own exhibition never occurred to me. I've already started groaning,

"He's out. He's *out*," when Frans squeals,

"No, *look*, Marek! He's jumping *in*," and a voice rips the sky.

It's a huge, reverberating cry.

It thunders across the field and ripples through the bleachers, and when I hear it, the hairs on the back of my neck stand on end — not in fear, but with a thrill that shoots through me, and my heart's back up in my throat — because the voice is Tristan's. He's now running full tilt for the barricade, about three-fourths of the way down the field.

"*FAST!!*" he roars again, that archer's signal that he's about to shoot, and in front of him the crowd parts as if by magic, startled by his warning cry and forced aside by the rough hands of the veterans accompanying him. He's holding his bow up and out in front of him, and as he dashes forward, he's nocking an arrow.

He doesn't slow down when he reaches the railing. Instead, he takes one mighty leap — and he jumps right over it.

In that one perfect second when Tristan's legs are stretched out in opposite directions and his cape is flying out behind him like a streaming pennant, while he's silhouetted against the sky and he's sailing over the barricade, he bends his bow in a huge, sweeping motion, and looses his arrow. I've never seen anything like it. He really could be a bat, a winged devil or an angel. To me, he's like a god — the young Apollo himself, come to life— and from the astonished cries of the spectators, nobody else has ever seen anything like it, either.

The only thing more glorious than the sight of Tristan as he pulls back his bowstring and releases is the sight of his arrow. It flies from his bow while Tristan is still suspended in mid-air, its red bands spiraling as it soars up straight and fast over the field, and if you told me that today those bands really were Tristan's blood, I'd believe it. I've seen that shot, once before: that glorious shot, the red arrow following the white. So I think I'm the only one in all of Louvain who isn't stunned, when instead of aiming at the wand, Tristan shoots Gilles's arrow right out of the sky.

Tristan lands on his feet with only the slightest of stumbles, and as he hits the ground, he's still running forward. It's happened so fast, that last wand is still tumbling end-over-end upward; it's time for the grand finale, although nothing the boys do now could top what's already just happened. Everyone in the stands is on their feet, too, cheering like crazy, and even over at the judges' table everyone is standing. Master Guillaume himself looks thunderstruck, and as Tristan darts forward, pulling out another arrow from his quiver and nocking it, I doubt the master could pull himself together in time to order Tristan to stand down, even if he wanted to. The only person in the entire crowd who looks composed enough to stop the boys from completing the trick together is Poncellet, but he's too busy laughing.

"Just like we planned it, eh, my friend?!" Tristan calls downfield to Gilles, as he kneels down swiftly into the striking pose he's been practicing.

"Not at all, dear boy!" Gilles calls back, "a million times *better!*" and they both shoot — Gilles first, Tristan second, so that with a *twang* and *pluck* and a satisfying *thwack thwack*, their arrows hit simultaneously, and they bring down the last wand together.

At some point my legs must have given out beneath me. At least they're no longer holding me up, and as Tristan's been getting to his feet, I've been hanging onto Armand and Frans, who are supporting me between them. Tristan's standing in the middle of the field, his bow held triumphantly aloft and his head dripping blood, while the crowd goes wild. He couldn't look more heroic, and when Gilles comes running downfield to embrace him, I'm overcome with emotion. It's a mixture of everything I've felt all day — every high and low rolled together into a dizzying kind of elation, but I can't describe it. I don't think there's a word for it, even in Latin.

Pascal's spotted me on the sidelines as he's dashing back out to join his master. So he changes course and he runs over, pulling me into such a fierce celebratory hug that he pulls me right over the barricade with him.

"Where in the heck *were* you guys? Oh, who cares! That's got to be the best exhibition that's ever been at St. Sebastian's!" he gushes, and I couldn't agree more. It *was* better than if Tristan had never been late, and what's more — it was the impossible arrow-downing trick, as I'd originally imagined it. Only I don't think Tristan was forced into it by circumstance. From the grin on his face as he embraces Gilles and the two of them bask in the applause that's still ringing out all around us, I have a feeling Tristan's been planning to down Gilles's arrow all along. He just wanted to surprise me with it.

When Tristan's finished taking his bows in a way that makes it clear to the audience that this was all really *his* trick, there's a brief interlude in which I help Pascal reset the field so the boys can do it all over again, this time as Gilles's turn, with Gilles shooting out the dowels and Tristan hitting the wands in motion. It's a little tricky, since we've got to retie the twine to the dowels, and now that Pascal's cut them, the strings are shorter. Luckily the wands are supple enough to make it possible, and the success of his unbelievable aerial shot gives Tristan the strength to hold up long enough to run through it. They do the whole stunt again, although when they get to the last wand, Gilles doesn't try to shoot down Tristan's arrow. He probably wants to try it, but the boys are a team, and besides — Gilles is smart enough to know that nothing could outdo the drama of the way Tristan unexpectedly jumped in on him.

By the time the trick is nearly over, I've had time to recover from it some myself, but I'm still feeling light-headed and woozy. So I know how he feels, when as the last wand falls to the ground, so does Tristan.

He makes a graceful pirouette and sinks down onto the dust, arms out and face up. He's fainted dead away, and lying there splayed out in the center of his cloak with its crimson lining surrounding him like a frame and his hair tousled fetchingly across his bloody and bandaged forehead, he looks so magnificent and he gets such a sharp sigh of concern from the audience that I suspect he must be faking it.

I don't mind. The day is all ours, and Tristan has outdone himself. If he wants to prolong the moment, well, so do I.

We've more than earned it.

CHAPTER FORTY-TWO

Over at the judges' table, Master Guillaume has recovered from his own shock, and his dour expression is back. He signals to some musicians loitering in front of the bleachers to take the field as a distraction, and he bustles out determinedly from behind the table. As Pascal and I rush forward to join the throng of Journeys and squires, veterans and judges who are all hastening from different directions to converge on the recumbent form of Tristan, the master looks so displeased that Pascal whispers to me,

"You don't suppose one of the little dowels of wood *hit* him, do you?"

I doubt it. I'm pretty sure the master thinks Tristan's passed out on purpose, too, and I can tell he's torn between being pleased with the audience's reaction to the spectacle and thoroughly fed up with my master's theatrics. It doesn't help that when Pascal and I run up, Falko's already there, prodding Tristan's shoulder and blubbering,

"DuBois, DuBois! He's *dead*. Oh God, it's the curse! The curse of the *siege perilous*."

"So, what happened to *you*?" Master Guillaume demands not much later, pointing at Tristan's head as Tristan begins to come around (Master Bernard having thrown a bucket of water on him at the master's orders).

"How was that for *bang*, kid?" Tristan says, either ignoring the master or not hearing him, and looking around for me in the ring of faces peering down at him as soon as his eyes are open.

"It was stupendous, master! Unbeatable," I tell him, kneeling down to steady his head as some of the others help him into a sitting position, while Armand and Remy talk over each other to explain about finding Tristan in the guild chapel.

"It must have been a thief," Armand finishes, repeating the explanation the boys offered in chapel, while Remy murmurs a nervous assent. Frans doesn't say anything. Nobody mentions Taran.

"Did you get a look at the man? And what were you doing out of your tent?" the master asks Tristan.

"I don't know," Tristan replies, putting a hand up to his head. "I don't remember. I don't remember much at all, since yesterday. Even that's a little fuzzy."

"He was praying, for his trick to work," I say.

"Someone's trick worked, all right," the master says grimly, looking down at Tristan with such a grimace on his face that I briefly entertain the idea that Guillaume sent someone to the chapel with a brick himself. "A *thief*! At St. Sebastian's," the master mutters incredulously, "and at work *right in the middle* of the competition. I can't believe it."

There's something chilling about the way the master says the word *thief* that stirs up a little residual swirl of fear in the pit of my stomach. Maybe it's the way that some of the veterans crowded around glance my way as the master says it; Luc's not the only one who's heard the rumors about me. Surely no one would think I'd bash my own master over the head, would they? I'd have much easier ways to steal from him. So maybe it's really that the master doesn't look much like he's going to be convinced by Armand's explanation of what happened to Tristan.

I can't say I'd blame him. It sounds about as unconvincing now as it did the first time Armand said it, since Gilles's gold chain is glinting in the sun around Tristan's neck, where his shirt has come open. "Something must have scared the man off, before he could take it," Armand offers, and no one has to ask what he means. We've all been staring at the medal.

"Saint Sebastian," the master says firmly. "Guarding his own chapel." But he still doesn't sound very convinced, and I fear he's going to accuse Tristan of hitting *himself* over the head, simply to stage one of his shenanigans. Only then one of the veterans clears his throat, and that's when I notice he and the man next to him are the two who were standing guard outside the stables earlier.

"Actually, we may have already caught the man," he says, looking at his comrade and sounding nervous. It's such an unexpected turn of events that it takes me much longer than it should to figure out what they're talking about.

"What?!" the master demands. "Why didn't you bring this straight to me? Where is he? Take me to him."

"We didn't want to bother you with it, until after the exhibitions," the man says, but the master is already storming across the field and back toward the guild proper, growling *"tell me everything!"* and dragging the man by the sleeve with a sharp bark over his shoulder to Master Bernard to stay put and keep the entertainment rolling.

Nobody asks permission to accompany him. We all simply fall into step behind him, following the master as he hustles off the field, across the L'île-Charleroi road, and into the yard through the postern gate. With our matching cloaks billowing behind us as we hustle along, we must look like a black cloud trailing along in the master's wake. Falko and Gilles are helping to support Tristan between them, and I'm trotting along behind, wringing

585

my hands in agitation. I've only been able to hear snatches of what the veterans have been telling the master, as we hurry along behind them. Not much. Only it's enough to tell me that I probably haven't seen the last of Luc Fournier after all.

We follow the master straight past the stables, and just when I'm wondering where in the world we can be going, I spot him.

There's Luc, dressed just as he was earlier. Only now he's got a largish leather traveling bag next to him, and I don't know what to feel when I see him.

He's lying face down in the middle of the butts, with two big, fat arrows sticking out of his back.

We all come to a stop in a semi-circle around him.

"You see how it is," the veteran who's been explaining things to the master says, after we've all contemplated Luc's dead body for a long, horrible moment. He gestures toward the bag; a little wooden box is just visible, peeking out from the top of it. It's the set of tools the master gave to Marcel. "He came out of the stables, looking funny. So we followed him. We caught him red-handed, shoving stuff from the shop into that bag, along with his own belongings. When he made a run for it, we shot him."

The man says it flatly, as though it were nothing, and if I'm hoping Master Guillaume will object, I'm disappointed. He just nods, looking grim, and before he can say anything, someone asks,

"Who is it?"

"Roll him over," the master orders. I hadn't noticed that he was with us, but now Master Leon steps forward, and prodding Luc with the toe of his boot, he flips him over.

I can't look. We've all seen plenty of dead bodies, and after the plague, they should be almost commonplace. I've seen too many dead boys, and ones much less deserving of their fates. Only somehow, this one is worse. Maybe it's because try as I might, I can't wholly be sorry that he's dead.

"Hey, isn't that the new fletcher?!" Falko exclaims. "And what happened to his neck? It looks all red."

"Forget his neck! What about his *fist*? There's something in it," Jurian says, and he and Master Leon kneel down next to the body.

Despite myself, I press forward, as curious as the others. I've started to feel awfully sick to my stomach, but what I feel most is numb. I've been riding waves of emotion all morning, and I think I've used all my emotions up. Still I'm careful not to look at Luc's face, but Jurian is right. The fingers of one of Luc's hands are still curled, as though he died clutching something.

Master Leon gently pries Luc's fingers open, retrieves the item, and holds it up.

It's Gilles's ring. I'd forgotten all about it.

"How'd he get *that*, Lejeune?!" Master Guillaume demands. Next to me, Tristan looks down at his hand with a frown, inspecting it, as though he's remembering something. I hope he's not remembering giving that ring to *me*, yesterday in the garden.

"*I* was wearing it, master," Tristan says. He doesn't mention lending it to me. And maybe I'm not as good a judge of whether or not a boy is acting as I'd thought I was. But miraculously, I think Tristan really doesn't remember that he wasn't wearing the ring in the chapel. That brick he took to the head must have knocked the memory right out of him.

"Of course you were," Master Guillaume says sourly. Then he brightens. "Well, that explains it, men! The boy was a thief. I never liked him. A gambler, I hear," he says, pausing to look to Master Leon for a nod of confirmation. When he gets it, he continues, "Owed some men some money, I'll wager. So he followed DuBois into the chapel and struggled with him. That'd explain the state of his neck. No Journeyman of mine would let himself be robbed without putting up a fight! Either that, or some of the Kingsmen worked him over first, wanting their cash. Then he hit DuBois over the head, took the ring, and he thought he'd get away with it."

"What did I tell you about him, Marek?" Tristan murmurs, once the master's little speech is finished; he's rubbing his temple and frowning down at Luc as though he's still trying to process the master's words and remember what happened. "Of all the gall. Attacking a Journeyman! Attacking *me*. I can hardly believe it."

While Tristan is talking, I'm not sure what it is that makes me turn my head and look behind me. All I know is that when I do, I see Taran standing near the back of the pack, staring right at me.

We hold each other's gaze for a while, just long enough for it to grow uncomfortable, and for once I don't have to guess what he's thinking. He's looking to see if I believe the master's explanation.

I haven't had a chance to think about what we saw out in the chapel, to try to figure out what I think must have really happened. Maybe I haven't wanted to — because if Tristan and Taran were out there quarreling, Taran must know that Luc was never there. He's the only other person in all the guild besides me and Pruie with reason to know that Tristan can't have been wearing Gilles's ring when he went into the chapel, and he hasn't said a word about it.

"What should we do with him?" one of the veterans asks, as Master Leon hands Gilles back his ring and hands up the little wooden case of tools to the master.

"Leave him, until after. When the crowd's gone, we'll bury him, somewhere on consecrated ground. I owe his father that much. Come, men! That's that," the master exclaims, but he hasn't moved. He's still standing, staring down at Luc, his brows drawn tightly together and his lips pursed, and the expression on his face is so severe, he looks almost sad. For a moment, I think he's going to say something moving about the pitiable fate of boys who lose their fathers.

587

Instead, he says,

"Fool! He paid the thief's price, and more than paid. But deservedly. Mark my words. It was the Saint's own hand that guided those arrows. *Saint Sebastian's punishes his own,* and there is no room within these walls for sentiment. May the same befall any man who dares to break the cardinal rules of our guild brotherhood!," and before he turns away, he spits next to Luc's body.

I'm no longer looking back at Taran, but I'm pretty sure he's still watching me. At least, I feel *something* on the back of my neck, like the gaze of pair of intense eyes boring into me. It's not the feeling of a goose walking over my grave, though, that makes the hairs on the back of my neck stand on end, as each man in turn walks past and spits, just as the master did.

No, it isn't one goose. It's a whole gaggle of them.

"On second thought, men, take this miscreant, and dump his body over the back wall — quietly," the master is now ordering. "He can be disposed of properly, later. Right now, we've got a competition to finish, and it wouldn't do for anyone to see a local boy riddled with arrows lying dead around the guild. I don't think I have to mention that by no means is any word of this to make it across the street. We've saved the best for last, and we'd better get back to it before the crowd gets antsy."

I'm not sure if Guillaume means Taran's exhibition, or Pascal's proposal.

I'm not looking forward to either. But Gilles is slipping his big ring safely back onto his finger, and when Tristan slings his arm around my shoulder to lead me back across the street, declaring,

"So, there *is* some justice in the world, eh, Marek? Rough justice, to be sure. But I told you Fournier was no good, and now that his bad deeds have caught up with him, he won't be around to bother you any longer," I can't help but agree.

I can't feel glad about Luc's death, of course, and I know the memory of his distorted face will haunt me in my dreams. But it was him or me, and the others all seem to agree with the master that Luc got the end that was coming to him. If they were unnerved by the violent manner of it, they don't show it, and I'd be lying if I said I wasn't mostly enormously relieved. Now there can be no doubt that I've seen the last of Luc, and I say a silent prayer to St. Sebastian for his part in it, since I've decided that Master Guillaume was right. Saint Sebastian intervened, to save his squire. It's the only explanation that makes any sense to me.

BY THE TIME WE'VE ALL GOTTEN BACK TO THE EXPOSITION grounds, a crew of veterans has already cleared away the remains of the boys' joint trick. But the field isn't empty; I didn't notice at the time that Remy didn't come across the street with us, but he apparently stayed back to set up his own master's trick. As Masters Guillaume and Leon take their places at the judges' table and the rest of us gather around outside the Journey tents with the boys who've already completed their performances, Remy is putting the finishing touches on the set-up for Taran's exhibition. It's the only one left and Master Guillaume clearly expects it to be the highlight of the day, but I can't imagine how anything Taran can do could possibly top the drama that's proceeded him — unless like Sir Brumant from the legend, he spontaneously bursts into flames.

Pascal and Frans thoughtfully bring out some stools for Tristan and me to sit on, and soon all the boys are hauling camp stools out from their tents, too, and we all sit down in a line along the sidelines, watching as Remy does a few last tests and makes some minor adjustments. I watch him dispassionately, not feeling much of anything, even though I can see right away that Remy did get an idea for his master's exhibition that day out by the millpond, just as I suspected. It's annoying, but I'm not really bothered by it, since too much else has already happened, and it's finally starting to sink in: our trick *worked*. And I was right. It was unbeatable. Let the exhibition be fantastic. There's nothing Taran can do now to outrank Tristan. Not today.

Like most of the boys, this time Remy and Taran have built something for their performance. It's relatively simple, but I wonder when they had time to make it, let alone practice with it. It's a contraption that must have been inspired by the rotating motion of the old waterwheel. Only it's no more than one large, upright wand, with two more wands crossed at their centers in an *X* and attached horizontally to the main wand by a little rod that acts as an axle. This rod can turn, allowing the crossed wands to spin freely, like four arms of a windmill.

"Wands, in *motion*, only differently," Frans squeaks, scooting his stool up closer to mine excitedly. "Isn't that clever? Oh, I'm *so* glad it's turned out that *he* had no part in what happened in the chapel, aren't you?" he adds innocently, as Taran strides out to take his place at the line, as always looking regal and imposing with his solemn expression and his pure black regalia; after starting the year petrified of Taran, Frans has become unaccountably fond of him.

"*Hmm*," is all I reply, watching Taran myself through half-closed lids.

"Good lord! What do suppose the old boy's going to do with *those*?" Tristan demands with a laugh from the other side of me. Out on the field, Remy is now attaching little bags full of something to the four ends of the crossed wands. They look a lot like the bladders full of colored porridge we used to simulate blood during our St. Sebastian's day show, and they are — only instead of being identical, each of these bags contains a mixture of a different color: red, green, blue, and yellow.

"He's going to *shoot* them, obviously," Gilles drawls in answer from down the line, as Taran puts up his hand to quiet the murmurs of the crowd in a signal that he's about to start his trick. After Tristan's unbelievable shot, the audience is in a high state of anticipation. Everyone is waiting to see if Taran can justify his position as the final exhibition of the day and outdo Tristan. And I have to say, when Taran drops his arm and Remy accordingly gives one of the arms of the contraption a mighty swing, for one terrible moment I have a sharp jab of fear that maybe I was wrong, and that's exactly what's about to happen.

As Remy scampers out of the way, the arms of the makeshift windmill purr into motion, spinning remarkably fast. Instead of slowing down as they rotate, the more they turn, the more they pick up speed. Taran's lifted his bow, but he lets the contraption spin until the colors at the ends of the wands blur and it's impossible to see where one color ends and the next one begins. It's mesmerizing, and by the time Taran calls out to the crowd *"pick a color!,"* I've almost forgotten to be worried about the rankings. I'm too interested in seeing what's going to happen.

Even the other Journeys have gotten caught up in it, since Jurian shouts out affectionately,

"Mellor, you're madman! That's impossible," just as Falko cries, *"Blue! Blue!,"* having forgotten that Taran's his competition and he shouldn't be participating.

"Blue," Taran echoes, and he shoots.

A splash of indigo-tinted porridge explodes into the air. As soon as the crowd sees it, everyone starts shouting out colors.

"Green!" someone calls, louder than the others. So Taran shoots the green pouch, too, then the red, and the yellow — he hits them all on his first attempt, and it's not just incredible. It *is* impossible. He's essentially shooting blind, and I have no idea how he can be anticipating where the little bladders are going to be, but it can't be pure luck. It's harder even than Tristan's shot at Gilles's arrow, and he's just made *four* of them in a row.

As soon as Taran's done, all the Journeys are on their feet, applauding, and so is everyone in the stands. But the audience is clapping for all the boys, for the entire day of performances, for us squires, even, and Taran's trick went by so fast, I doubt anyone in the crowd really understood just how hard it was.

"Poor Taran!" Gilles chuckles, as he, too, claps politely, and he winks at Tristan as they both step forward to take another bow when some of the people in the audience point them out. Nobody's forgotten Tristan's unexpected entrance onto Gilles's trick or the impression he made with the sheer drama of it. No shot could top it, however difficult, and Tristan's not just prince for the day. He's the king. Not even Taran's superior skill was enough to topple him.

I should be glad. I should be exultant, even. And I am. It's exactly what I wanted. I'm here. Luc's gone. Tristan was stupendous, and despite a few nasty bumps along the way, in the end all our plans and all our hard work worked out perfectly. Only as I've been watching Taran take his turn, underneath my joy for our victory, I've been growing increasingly upset and uneasy.

Out of the corner of my eye, I can see Gilles's ring, flashing in the sunshine. It's winking at me, teasing me, telling me that Master Guillaume's reconstruction of what happened to Tristan in the chapel can't have been correct. Not entirely.

It made perfect sense. It all fit, and it explained everything. And sure, Luc *was* a thief and he *did* owe money. But he didn't get that ring from Tristan, he got it from *me* — while someone *else* was with Tristan in the chapel. Someone no one else now has any reason to suspect, someone who's gotten away with bashing my master over the head with impunity.

Taran's still standing in the middle of the field, a magnificent figure in St. Sebastian's garb, without a spot of color to relieve the midnight of his costume. A big, magnificent beast, just as I once thought him. And while the cries and shouts of the crowd still ring out all around us, I know that what happened between the boys in the chapel has been obvious all along — glaring, even. I should be standing here and hating Taran — hating him, with every fiber of my being — for following Tristan to a secluded place and then venting his rage on him. I'm the only one who knows that Luc couldn't have been the culprit. And let's face it. We *did* catch Taran red-handed, with the brick still warm in his hand. What makes it worse is that despite everything that happened this winter, against my better judgment I'd let myself start thinking better of him again.

The only the thing is, I don't believe it.

I don't know why I'm so sure of it. But I'm absolutely, positively certain that it wasn't Taran who hit Tristan in the chapel, and all I really feel looking out at him now is that same desperate urge I felt out in the stables, to run straight onto the field and throw my arms around him. There *are* plenty of thieves and footpads in Louvain, and everyone's seen Tristan wearing that big ring. Any number of people — one of the veterans, a Kingsman, maybe even the guild priest, protecting his bet — could have had the thought of divesting Tristan of it. Taran's arrival must have scared off the real attacker, just as he said.

And that's only the beginning.

I know it's irrational, that it doesn't make any sense. But I'm so certain of his innocence now when all the evidence is against him that I just can't believe Taran's *ever* tried to hurt him. At least, as Gilles might say, *not in private*. Taran never took a shot at Tristan out in Brecelyn's woods at all, not even by accident. Not the first one that missed. Not the second. It wasn't Taran who wounded Tristan at the hunt. I'd stake my life on it.

No, Taran didn't do *any* of it, and all this time, I've been accusing him falsely.

Somehow, I've made a terrible mistake.

CHAPTER FORTY-THREE

"Ready, dear boy?" Gilles trills, as a drumroll of the kind that usually announces an execution starts up from the direction of the bleachers.

It's time for Pascal's proposal, the grand finale of the day. If the preparations that have been underway ever since Taran exited the field are any indication, it's going to be a spectacle of unprecedented proportions, exactly what Master Guillaume ordered and the perfect send-up for an unprecedented day.

No one in the stands has left, and all of us Journeys and squires have remained lined up on our stools, too, sitting and watching as a team of twenty mules gets hitched up to the front of the gazebo, while a crew of reluctant-looking veterans equipped with buckets strews rose petals all around the arena, in and around the troupe of acrobats in rosy-pink unitards which has been keeping the audience entertained. That is, all the boys except for Gilles. He went off to the stables, and now he's back, seated astride the white horse and reaching a hand down to Pascal. Both boys have traded their black exhibition cloaks for pure white silk ones, and they've got wreaths of flowers similar to the ones Sibilla and Ginger are wearing perched on their heads. I notice that between the time I confronted Luc in the stables and now, someone's even braided flowers into the horse's mane and tail.

At the sound of the drums, from somewhere behind the Journey tents dozens of white doves suddenly take the air, and the mules lurch forward. Two stable boys in short white robes are leading them reluctantly toward the center of the field, as they slowly drag the white wooden gazebo along behind them. It rolls past with a rattle and a clatter that's audible even over all the drums and the fanfares that are now also blaring. Inside it are Lady Sibilla and Ginger, looking radiant, even though they're clinging onto the pillars of the gazebo to keep from falling over. I see both the bride and the groom are to have an attendant even for the actual ceremony, to add to the pageantry — and no doubt so that Gilles can be justified in hogging more of the attention.

Sure enough, instead of slipping off the horse's back to let Pascal up in his place, Gilles pulls Pascal up onto the steed behind him. Then while the gazebo is getting settled into position, he proceeds to prance them around the structure a few times in a wide circle, waving to the crowd and causing havoc for the stable boys who are trying to get the mules unhitched and out of the way. When the buglers run out of breath, Gilles gestures to Jerome to pluck a lively tune for them on his lute, and he keeps the horse in motion, high-stepping back and forth in front of the bleachers as though displaying the groom to them, even after Poncellet materializes to make a preposterous speech clearly meant to help prime the audience.

The old master's supposedly giving the lovers' backstory, although he clearly doesn't know either of their names or anything about them, and what I can hear of it over all the hoofbeats and the merry catcalls from the crowd and the laughter of the boys, it sounds a lot like some of Poncellet's usual tripe about himself, although at least he doesn't make any mention of a seraglio.

"Gosh, I didn't know Pascal fought at the battle of Crécy," Rennie is saying, when the last of the mules has been driven from the arena and Gilles finally prods Poncellet with the point of his rapier and signals to Jerome to cut the music. There can be no more stalling.

A pallid Pascal slides off the back of the horse while his master slides off the front, and the crowd falls into an expectant silence as they mount the steps of the gazebo together. I've had my doubts about the whole affair, but the boys look so handsome and the ladies so lovely, and Gilles has done nothing today but prove himself to be a most loyal ally. I can't be anything but happy that Pascal is about to get his happy ending, and all of us squires have naturally gravitated together in nervous excitement for our comrade.

All eyes are riveted on the four white-clad figures now shyly coming together in the center of the gazebo, under a bower of roses. At least, Pascal and Ginger look shy; Gilles is strutting forward, chest out and looking like he's fully enjoying the moment, and for her part, Lady Sibilla looks so puffed up with joy her dress seams might burst at any moment.

"The old gal looks about ready to boil over," Rennie whispers, snickering, as Remy warbles,

"Isn't it *romantic*?" He's sidled over next to me and he's now squeezing my hand in excitement. "Oh, can't you just picture Taran and Melissande there, too, for *their* wedding?"

I don't say anything, although I can picture it well enough. The last thing I want to think about right now is Taran, and I know both he and Tristan can picture it, too — that they *are* picturing it, in fact, since we're all standing pretty close together and I'm sure they've heard Remy. It's not a comment that's likely to make either of them pleasantly nostalgic, however, since to my knowledge the only one who's kissed Melissande passionately in a gazebo is Tristan, not Taran — and that kiss is surely what's been fueling the worst of the speculation about the paternity of Melissande's lost child.

I do hear *someone* sigh, though, when Gilles goes up first to Sibilla, and taking her hand in his, he bows over it and plants a genteel kiss on her fingertips. Only I think it's Armand; I'd all but forgotten that he, too, got a kiss at Brecelyn's gazebo, and from Lady Sibilla.

And that Gilles surely thinks the boy who got Sibilla's kiss that day was Pascal.

I think I only finally figure out what's happening, however, when Gilles steps back quickly with an exclamation of "the beautiful bride, ladies and gentlemen, and her handmaiden!" and I see that Sibilla is now practically wheezing, and she's gazing up at Gilles with open adoration.

Lady Sibilla thinks *she's* the bride. And that the man she's about to become betrothed to is Gilles.

It's a little cruel but harmless bit of payback, for Sibilla's original preference of his squire. No wonder she looks so giddy and elated! She thinks she's not only about to get one of the most handsome men in all Ardennes as a husband, but also the richest.

It *is* cruel, though, and I feel a sharp pang of sympathy for Lady Sibilla. When she finds out she's not the bride, it's going to sting, terribly, and I wonder if Gilles has any idea just how much this stunt of his is going to hurt her. After all the flirting they were doing earlier, surely he can't be so blind as not to see that she's now madly in love with him.

Only I'm wrong entirely.

Sibilla *is* the bride.

And now Gilles is draping an arm around an astounded Pascal's shoulders and propelling him with a shove forward towards her.

My mouth falls open. All around me, the other boys start swearing softly, as with a swirl of his cape Gilles thrusts Pascal's and Sibilla's hands together, and then he grabs an astounded Ginger by the elbow. With no further ado, he leads Sibilla's handmaid stumbling off down the stairs with him, calling back to his squire as he goes,

"And now let's give *Lover Boy* and his Ginger-haired beauty a little privacy, shall we?! I'm sure they want to be alone for the actual avowal."

He leaps back up onto the white horse and pulls the stunned girl up in front of him (it doesn't take much to see that she, too, like Sibilla was under the impression that Gilles was to be the bridegroom, and she's not at all pleased to find that *her* Pascal is about to become betrothed to her mistress). Then he dashes off with her, while she's looking forlornly back at Pascal over her shoulder.

Poor Pascal! He just stands there twisting his hands together while they ride off, letting the dust settle and staring wide-eyed and petrified at an equally horrified and formidable-looking Sibilla. She's glaring across the arena at Gilles's receding back with an expression that says if she had a bow, she'd be shooting it.

"Goddamned plucky bastard!" Jurian mutters. "What in the devil is the lad supposed to do now?"

But there's nothing either Pascal or Sibilla can do. Neither can object or back down now. As Gilles said, it's all too deliciously public.

"Maybe Gilles is being sincere," Rennie offers dubiously. "I mean, Pascal *was* chasing her ladyship most of last winter. And she does have red hair."

It's true enough, and I might even have believed it, if it weren't for all of Gilles's talk about a 'clever man.' And if he didn't have such a supremely self-satisfied look on his face as he rides off past us, like a cat that's just swallowed a big, fat rat and couldn't be happier about it. It *is* dashed clever, too, since everything he's said about the bride does fit Lady Sibilla, and no one can prove that he meant to be purposely deceptive about it.

"He'd better do *something*," Aristide drawls. "Otherwise, it's going to start to be insulting."

He's an unlikely person to be worried about a lady's sensibilities, but I guess his own romance has made him soft-hearted, and he's right. Pascal's been standing up there trembling and looking a lot like a rabbit about to succumb to a nasty case of plague for much too long, and even he must know it. So when at a gesture from Tristan Jerome plays an encouraging chord, Pascal pulls himself together. With one long, pleading look over at us squires, he clears his throat.

As soon as he does, Armand groans, "Oh, *mercy!*"

"What? You didn't think she was going to marry *you*, did you?" Rennie demands, assuming like the rest of us that Armand's simply overcome by the sight of the only girl he's ever kissed getting engaged to his best friend.

But Armand shakes his head. "Uh, boys. I think he's going to go ahead with the speech he's *already* got written. You know, the one *Marek* wrote for him."

"It's not going to make any sense," Frans titters.

"I know! But there's no time for him to come up with something else, and besides, *look* at him. He's too nervous."

"I didn't write *all* of it!" I protest.

I know it sounds crazy. But even after everything that's already happened, I think it's one of the lowest moments of the day, standing shoulder to shoulder with all the boys as Pascal warbles out at the top of his lungs the first line of his speech:

"I've loved from the moment I first saw you, on the garden wall!"

It goes on and on like this, and I have no idea what Sibilla can be making of it. None of it fits her in the slightest. I doubt she cares; she looks like she's trying not to rip the garland off her head and beat Pascal with it. She's got the poorest attempt at a smile plastered on her face that I've ever seen, and as Pascal's voice trills out a long, melancholy list of raptures over her supposed attributes that are so inappropriate for her that they are bordering on insulting, I'm pretty sure she's snarling. But I'm not really listening. I've heard the speech before, and I know the descriptions don't sound that much like Ginger, either.

They sound a lot like Tristan.

Tristan is standing right next to me, and I can't help wondering what he's making of it. I'm not sure why I didn't think about how it would all sound sooner; I guess I wasn't picturing us all listening to it with Armand's reminder that *I* wrote most of it hanging over us.

I don't dare look around. I keep my eyes plastered on the gazebo, because I also know that Taran is somewhere not far behind me. I can sense him back there seething, and I force away the memory of him telling the priest how much my disgraceful behavior toward Tristan disgusts him. Even without looking at him, I'm sure he can tell exactly which lines I contributed, and I don't know why, but the gushing phrases inspired by my master sound even worse to me when I think of all the terrible ones I've been flinging at Taran all winter.

It's not until Pascal is choking out a particularly bad line that I break, and I turn my head, to see how Taran's taking it:

"Why, any other's kiss would be a *punishment* — nay, a torture!"

Taran's not looking at me. He, too, is standing as stiff as a board and staring out with his eyes fixed on the gazebo, and I should have known he wouldn't be thinking about me. He's probably still picturing Melissande there under the roses with Tristan, because his mouth is set in a hard line and he's not moving a muscle.

When at last Pascal drops to one knee, grabs Lady Sibilla's hands in his, and cries out with a feigned passion bordering on hysteria,

"Marry me, and I will always be your defender! A St. Sebastian's man can make no greater vow than this: *I'll take an arrow for you!,*" then Taran *does* whip his head to look in my direction.

When his eyes lock on mine, I've only seen a look as accusing and as piercing once before — from the top of Brecelyn's stairs on the night Melissande lost their baby, and there's only one thing at all good about it.

Well two, really.

One is that Pascal's speech is over.

The other is that I'm pretty sure I no longer need to worry about suffering through an apology from Taran for that kiss in the archives.

After that, the gazebo is rolled away and a fuming Lady Sibilla whisked back to join the large, squat man in the stands who must be her father. A shaken Pascal rejoins us, and I think the worst thing about the whole sorry affair comes as the crowd begins to disperse and we're all trudging back to the guild to recover. When Gilles comes trotting up to congratulate his squire, Pascal hangs his head, shakes his master's hand, and thanks him for it.

CHAPTER FORTY-FOUR

"He set you up, you dolt!" Armand hisses, as we're all filing into the main hall later that evening. He's been pestering Pascal to admit it ever since the proposal, and he's still at it as we take our seats, all of us squires sitting in solidarity together at the end of the Journey table. It's surely Frans's last meal with us, and Rennie's, too, and Pascal needs company to keep up his spirits. But Pascal's been refusing to hear a word against his master.

"I played fast and loose with a lady's affections, and I'm reaping the consequences," he sighs. "How was Gilles to know I could be so fickle? I shall simply have to make the best of it, for her ladyship's sake."

He sounds so glum about it, nobody mentions the obvious: that Sibilla didn't look too thrilled to be marrying him, either. Pascal's determined to put on a brave face and to celebrate his master's victory, since no one doubts that Gilles has won the day, and after all the trials and tribulations of one of the longest competitions on record, I'm eager to help him do it.

It's been a day of soaring highs and stunning lows, and I can't help but feel for Pascal and for Lady Sibilla, and for the boys and their squires who will soon find themselves cut from St. Sebastian's. I'm sure we'll all be suffering some serious fallout from the day's events in the weeks ahead, myself included. But after all my agonizing over Tristan's ranking through the long months of winter, the best high of them all is coming: the official announcement of the standings. Tonight, it seems to me that we all have permission to make merry, even though two of the boys are about to be out; we've all known which two they'll be for a long time, and for his part, Jurian is toasting the boys quite happily, and openly talking about his plans.

"Don't worry about me, boys. I'll be around," he tells us, when Tristan asks him where he'll go. "As it happens, I hear there's an opening for a huntsman at Sir Brecelyn's castle."

I do worry a bit about Falko. I'm not sure he's entirely accepted that he's failed, even though Frans has been regaling us at our end of the table with a whispered account of Falko's disastrous exhibition. I don't think Falko's been refusing to face the obvious because he's so sad about losing Guards, however. When I said my goodbyes to Roxanne earlier, handing the wounded dove over to Pruie with a very heartfelt *thank you* in the process, I'm pretty the sure the reason Falko was looking upset wasn't embarrassment over his wretched performance. He knows full well that when he leaves Louvain, he can't take either his girlfriend or his former squire home with him. But after more cups of wine between us than I care to count, Falko himself is feeling fine and the atmosphere at table is so exuberant, I'm feeling too fantastic to focus now on Falko's future.

All our long months of practicing and planning have paid off, and big. Gilles will be in first place, but Tristan's incredible leap into Gilles's exhibition can't have failed to pull my master up into second place. Our Trojan horse of a trick worked exactly as planned, and more — in that moment when Tristan stood bandaged and bloodied with Gilles's downed arrow at his feet, he overshadowed them all, even Gilles the undisputed wands master. And if I do feel a prick of guilt at the memory of Pascal sneering *"don't you mean cheating?"* on the night I came up with idea for it, it's only a little one. Taran's surely passed, too, even if the boys did gang up on him.

He's sitting down at the far end of the table, where I don't have to look at him. Predictably, he's the only boy who's making no effort to join in or enjoy himself. Instead, he's digging into the tabletop with his little knife, not saying anything, and it's surely an indication of his mood that he's brought it with him despite the master's prohibition. But I can't think about Taran now. I don't feel guilty about helping Tristan beat him; that's my job as squire, and I have to look to my own future. But every time I hear the tip of that knife jab into the table, I have a flash of gouging at Taran's broad back with the tip of his broken arrow, and I feel more than guilty — I feel queasier than I have all afternoon, which is saying something.

By the time the meal is winding down, the boys are all raucously toasting weddings, or at least girlfriends. Gilles is keeping up such a steady call for drinks in his squire's honor that sound so delighted and sincere, either I'm getting tipsy or maybe the old boy really *does* think Pascal and Sibilla are still in love with each other. Jurian is happily toasting Rennie and the swineherd's daughter; Falko is drinking to Roxanne, Aristide to his Swilda, and even Tristan is joining in, the happiest of the lot — drunkenly toasting Taran and Melissande, albeit rather ironically.

It seems to be getting under Taran's skin, and that's probably the point of it. Something in the tone of Tristan's voice, though, makes me suspect he might be picturing battling his way up to the gazebo out in Brecelyn's garden and snatching Melissande away on a white horse, right in the middle of her wedding to Taran. But if he is, tonight I'm too happy to care. My mind is too full of another heroic image of my master, one that really did happen:

Tristan, silhouetted mid-air, downing Gilles's arrow. Today my master did a trick that was unbeatable, and *I'm* the one who came up with it for him.

All that's left to crown the day is the formal announcement of the final standings. The boys have already been celebrating their win, hard — and I've been helping them do it. So have plenty of the others; as soon as the festivities were over, Gilles tapped one of the casks of wine he bought from Brian de Gilford, and half the guild crowded into his room to join us in a round or two, at one point or another. There's been a party atmosphere in the corridors all afternoon, fueled by the best of Sir Brecelyn's stolen vintage, and it's still going strong here in the main hall.

Now Gilles is wearing his wreath of roses from the proposal, and as Master Guillaume rises at the head table, glass of port in hand, to address us, Gilles pulls out the wreath that Pascal was wearing and plops it down on Tristan's head. It's so reminiscent of Firsts last year, when Tristan won Melissande's garland, that a shiver of anticipation snakes up my limbs when I see it: Tristan as Gilles, Gilles as Tristan, tonight with the matching wreaths adorning them, they look so alike and so aglow with victory that they could be twin divinities. With the wine warm in my blood, I feel so awash in the pleasure of it I can hardly contain myself, and I'm feeling plenty pleased with myself, too, and with the crowning achievement of our dirty little word, *teamwork*, even before the master calls for attention.

"Gentlemen! Quiet, please, for some important announcements," Guillaume begins, once we've all risen a little raucously to our feet at a gesture from Master Leon. "After careful consideration, given the unrest on our borders and the growing uncertainty of the international situation, as a show of good will I have decided to send a contingent of veterans to Meuse under the command of Master Bernard, first thing tomorrow morning. These men can assist the Kingsmen in keeping civil order — in an unofficial capacity, certainly. And although I'm sure it's an unnecessary precaution, he will also be coordinating with Brian de Gilford and with Sir Hugo Brecelyn, so that our men in Meuse can be on hand to assist our own Guard in the unlikely event of foreign activity. There will be extra pay and perks, of course, for service; any men wishing to sign up, please speak with Master Leon after mess to get your orders. I mention this now, because it might be a tempting opportunity for those of our Journeymen who are soon to find themselves without other employment."

There's a pause of the kind that's usually filled by a sarcastic whispered comment from Gilles. But tonight Gilles seems to be mulling over the master's words with a slight frown, not finding them very amusing, and instead it's Taran's voice that whispers hoarsely across the table.

"Hey, DuBois. *Did* you write a letter, or not? A letter, to the *castle*?"

I can't believe he's going to do this *now*, in the middle of Master Guillaume's announcements. He must know Tristan's about to outrank him for the first time and be furious about it. Only the strange thing is, he doesn't sound angry. He sounds worried.

When Tristan just gives him a blank and slightly drunken look, Taran whispers louder,

"A letter to the castle *at Meuse*. To our *father*, about your theory that the regent is in danger."

When this, too, is met with no answer, Taran sticks the tip of his knife into the tabletop, harder. And in a voice that sounds so tight I'm sure it's costing him something, he says,

"Maybe you should have."

Master Guillaume is talking again before Tristan or anyone else can say anything, and he's already well into a long string of platitudes about service to the guild before I figure out what Taran's saying. *I should have known that something Taran would think more important than the trials wouldn't be anything to do with girls at all!* He's not been preoccupied all day worrying about the whereabouts of his fiancée, but of her *father*. And from the sound of it, he was more convinced by Tristan's theories than he's been letting on.

Of course he was!

He's known for certain all along that he wasn't the one who shot at Tristan in Brecelyn's forest.

"Enough of politics!" the master's now continuing, his tone turning jovial. When he then gestures to us to resume our seats and reaches down for a sheet of parchment lying next to him on the table, I let the motion sweep aside everything from my mind except sweet anticipation for what's coming; I'll worry about Taran, later. It's not as though I didn't already know I was going to have to have a reckoning with him.

"Let me congratulate you all on a show-stopping Firsts, one Louvain will long be talking about!" the master cries, his voice rising an octave higher, and all around me I can feel excitement building in all the boys, until they must be almost as excited as I am. "I asked for wands in motion, and men, *I got them!* After today's unrivaled performances, it can come as no surprise to all of you that for the *second time* in guild history, we have a tie for first place."

Here Guillaume pauses again for effect, but by now the room is reverberating so loudly with the stomping of dozens of boots, the cheering of men, and the pounding of tankards against the tabletops that nobody's whispering. Everyone is whistling and yelling, me louder than anyone. This is our moment, now, the one I hardly dared let myself dream of all winter: Tristan's and Gilles's, and mine and Tristan's.

"Or that one of the men at the very top of the order is our very own marquis in residence, Gilles Lejeune!" the master booms. "Rise, Gilles, and receive your well-deserved approbation! And take that thing off your head."

Gilles leaps up onto the bench and takes a sweeping bow, wreath in hand.

He's already reaching down to pull Tristan up next to him, when the master continues,

"And for his unsurpassable performance in the exhibitions, it is my pleasure to announce that the Journey in first place with him is, of course, none other than the invincible *Taran Mellor!*"

The silence that follows this statement is so deep and so awkward, it's worse even than the one that met the master's announcement of Taran's engagement.

Gilles is still frozen in place, one hand reaching down toward Tristan. Tristan is frozen in place, too, with his hand reaching up to Gilles's, and I feel like the blood in my veins has turned to sludge and it's stopped circulating entirely. Across the table, Taran's sitting stock still with a frown on his face, as rigid as a pillar, and everyone else in the hall has stopped moving, too — even the guild dogs are uncharacteristically silent. There's one long moment in which nothing at all happens, except that old Popinjay slinks under the Journey table.

"Not to mention, of course," the master adds, with a great, big smile — after having let the silence stretch out long enough for everyone but him to find it uncomfortable, "his exceptional and selfless work with his squad of squires."

None of the Journeys says anything, nor any of the squires. Not even any of the veterans at the surrounding tables, as Gilles climbs down from the bench with a frown.

"Get up, son, and take a bow," the master prods, since Taran's still not moved a muscle either, and when at length he rises halfway out of his seat and nods his head so stiffly his neck could be made of iron, we all remember to clap for him. And I guess after the initial shock of it, it makes sense.

After all, his trick *was* remarkable. We should have known that the masters would look past the theatrics and judge solely on the archery, although Guillaume's little jab about squires' club proves he's also getting some malicious pleasure out of it. I remind myself that the plan was from the beginning for Tristan to be in *second* place, and that's what's happened. Only I didn't expect it to be second place *behind* Taran, and I can't help it. It's a huge disappointment, but I tell myself I'll get over it.

Only then the master calls the next name.

And it's Aristide's.

Another confused silence falls over the room, deeper even than the last one. This time it makes no sense at all, and nobody bothers to cheer for Aristide. He doesn't even bother to get up. It makes even less sense, when before anyone in the room can fully process this announcement or make any reaction, a moment later the master is calling out with glee,

"And in a respectable fourth, Jurian Legrand!"

Tristan's at the bottom of the order, above only Falko.

It's so incomprehensible, so unforeseen and so unexpected, it takes me a full minute at least to realize what it means. Even then I'm not sure it would have sunk in, if I didn't look down the table at Tristan and see the look on his face.

Tristan is second — *to last*.
That means he's out.
It's over.
It's over, just like that.
We're out of St. Sebastian's.

TRISTAN'S NOT THE ONLY ONE WHO LOOKS STUNNED BY HIS ranking. I'm not exaggerating when I say that every face in the room is stamped with an identical expression of pure disbelief. Every face, that is, except for the master's, and I feel so numb and cold and everyone in the hall is so unmoving, we could have all been frozen by a magician's curse or turned to stone by some mythical monster. Only the monster is up at the head table, taking a big swig of his port.

It's so blatantly unfair that before long a rumbling starts up from some of the back tables, and soon it's not just the veterans who have started grumbling. It's all the Journeys and all the squires — even Taran. It's not the way he wanted to win; he told me himself that giving Tristan a public trouncing was going to be the best day of his life, and he's just been robbed of it.

The master's essentially stolen Taran's own victory out from under him, and I even think he's about to protest. Maybe he would have, too, if Jurian didn't beat him to it. As the grumbling at the Journey table grows louder, Jurian gets to his feet.

"Master!" he cries, practically shouting to be heard over the swell noise of angry voices. "I don't understand. I thought last year's rankings weren't going to count. Tristan was magnificent today. He was better than I was. I don't deserve to beat him. I *didn't* beat him. And that shot at Gilles's arrow. It was spectacular."

"True, true," the master croons happily, rocking forward on his toes as the voices in the hall die down to hear what he's going to say about it. "What a shot! The crowd *loved* it. It was the highlight of the competition, a real showstopper! We can all be most grateful to Master DuBois for that. *Un*fortunately," Guillaume coos, his mouth curving into one of his thin smiles, "he *missed* his *own* turn, didn't he? So that shot counted as part of Lejeune's performance. For his *own* exhibition he scored a zero, since he was forfeit. Rules are rules, Jurian. And I'm afraid there can be no exceptions, even for extraordinary circumstances. We always follow the rules, here at St. Sebastian's."

There's nothing Jurian or anybody else can say to that, although he

MASTERS

knows as well as I do that's not really Master Guillaume's reason for failing my master. He sounds too gleeful about it, and the situation is surely so unique that Guillaume is free to do as he wishes. If the master chose to count the shot for Tristan, no one would question it.

As Guillaume's been talking, he's reached out one hand to rest it on the back of the empty chair next to him, the one once occupied by Master Gheeraert. Now it's lingering there while the master drums his fingertips against it lightly, and Jurian has to sit back down in his own place on the bench, muttering under his breath,

"*Sodding sadist.*"

It's all so cruel, no one makes a joke about the cursed siege perilous — not even Falko, although for once it'd be damned appropriate.

But maybe Falko really doesn't notice the gesture of the master's. He's been too busy trying to process the knowledge that he, too, is out. Unbelievably, this seems to have come as an even greater shock to him than that the master has just snatched deserved victory out of Tristan's hands. The poor boy looks like he's been blindsided, and he's not the only one.

It's been a day of extremes, no question. I'd thought I'd been thoroughly drained by them. That I was all out of emotions. I'd thought it was over, and that I'd come out on top. But Tristan, *out*? Of all the things I feared today, of all the things that happened and the ones that didn't come to pass, this isn't just the one thing I never anticipated, the one thing I didn't think could happen. It's the thing I've been dreading more than any other since I first came to Saint Sebastian's. To say that I've been blindsided by it doesn't begin to cover it.

Now all the emotions of the day come rushing back, the highs and the lows mixing together and washing over me in a dizzying confusion, while all the places where Luc's fists connected start to throb anew, and then some. And maybe I am a little drunk. But I'm not prepared. I'm not prepared at all, and the only thing worse than how I feel myself is the way my master looks. Tristan is simmering with such fury, I think he might really combust spontaneously.

I have a sudden, violent urge to rush up to the masters' table, grab that wretched empty chair, and hurl it against the painting of Saint Sebastian, hard enough to smash them both to pieces and to bring that horrid painting down. I feel desperate and helpless enough to try it, and I might even have done it — done something foolish, anyway — if out of the corner of my eye, I didn't see one of the men who put an arrow into Luc Fournier's back. And if I didn't know in my heart that what's just happened doesn't really have anything to do with Tristan sitting at the master's table. After what happened to Luc, I'm willing to bet that the master never saw that midnight stunt of Tristan's, that he never even heard about it. It was just a shadow I saw that night, out in the hallway — because if the master had seen Tristan in Gheeraert's chair, he surely would have shot him on the spot. The truth is

603

so much simpler. Master Guillaume has always hated Tristan, and he's indulged him long enough. I can tell just from the expression on the master's face that he was going to fail Tristan today, no matter what.

Either that, or the master really won't tolerate teamwork at Saint Sebastian's. I should have listened to Pascal when he tried to warn me. I should have known the master would be harder to outfox than a citadel full of Trojans.

Having achieved his revenge, Master Guillaume takes one last, long draught from his cup and sets it down with a deliberate, satisfied motion, and he makes his way out of the hall. No one else has moved, and through it all, Tristan's been staring down in front of him. His hair is hanging down over his eyes, masking them, but even so, I can see bitter tears forming in them, tears he's struggling not to let fall. All his muscles are clenched and his whole body is quivering. So I'm not surprised, when right as the master passes behind the Journey table, Tristan jumps angrily to his feet. I am plenty alarmed, however, since he looks wild enough to risk a dozen arrows in the back for the pleasure of pounding Master Guillaume's head to a pulp against the hard guild pavement.

There's a horrible moment, when Tristan is standing face-to-face with the master, eyes blazing and his fists clenched, and all the other Journeys stand at attention, in solidarity with him — and I'm absolutely certain that Tristan's about to launch himself at Guillaume and try to throttle him, in the way the boys have done to each other so disturbingly often.

Before I can croak out the cry of *"don't do it, master!"* that's rising in my throat, instead Tristan takes one threatening step forward, and with a strangled oath, he thrusts Pascal's wreath of flowers back down onto his own head. With all the righteous indignation he can muster, he spits at the master's feet — just the way the master did, next to Luc Fournier's body. His head held high, Tristan then turns heel and storms out of the hall with his crimson-lined cloak flashing behind him, making a grand exit, while I scramble to follow after him.

Before I can climb my way out over the bench, Master Guillaume comes up behind me to block me.

"You boys will be staying on, of course," he says, putting one hand on my shoulder and the other one on Frans's and giving us both an avuncular jostle, seemingly unaware that we might care that he's just gutted both our masters. "There's a vacant place for a fletcher's apprentice for you, lad," he nods at Frans, "and Vervloet. I still need your help with the crossbow contingent."

The strangest thing about it is that Guillaume looks genuinely taken aback when I shake my head.

"I'll be leaving with my master, *master*. And as for the crossbowmen, I can give you their motto now. *Where you lead, I follow*. Have one of the boys put *that* into Latin."

From the look on the master's face when I shrug off his arm and push past him to run out of the hall after my master, I can tell Guillaume is shocked I don't intend to stay at Saint Sebastian's. What's more, that he's upset about it.

Only not as upset as I am. Because I *do* want to stay on. I want it more than anything. At the thought of leaving St. Sebastian's, right now I feel like I've never been more miserable about anything.

AN HOUR LATER FINDS US SITTING OUT UNDER THE STARS WITH our backs against the embankment of the far butts: me, Tristan, Falko, and Frans.

"I can't believe it! *Me*, out," Falko's saying, for about the millionth time. I don't blame him. I still can't believe it, either. "Oh, I *knew* it," he mumbles. "I didn't hit a wand all day, did I? I just didn't *know* it, if you know what I mean."

"All our plans, for nothing," Tristan agrees dismally, kicking a pebble in the dirt with his foot in the dark. "You know what the worst of it is, kid? I really wanted to be a Guardsman."

"I know you did, master. And you'd have been a great one."

"There's a joke, Marek! What a couple of Guardsmen we'd have made. A master who won't kill a man, even if he's an assassin. And his squire, who can't bring himself to shoot a bird."

"Yeah, well, Taran didn't want to kill the dove, either," I remind him, while Falko grumbles,

"*I'd* have shot the damned thing, if it'd just held still. And if my shoulder weren't so messed up," he admits grudgingly.

"Why do you suppose Mellor hesitated?" Tristan says bitterly. "Surely he's gone hunting dozens of times. It can't be the first bird he's ever shot. And that hawk of his must have killed plenty of doves in its day. He looked a proper fool. What a sodding hypocrite."

"It was doing it *like that*, I think," Frans offers. "A sitting duck, *er*, dove, as it were." I don't bring up the fact that Taran's hawk is dead, or that it's probably partly why shooting the dove bothered Taran. Or the fact that Tristan's never wrapped up a wounded bird in his cloak and brought it home from a hunt, either. Tristan's already saying,

"Besides, we all know he has no qualms about shooting a *man*," and I don't know if he's thinking of the arrow in his own side or Taran's shot that killed the second assassin on Brecelyn's tower. I don't want to think about any of it, of how badly I've been misjudging him.

"What'll you do, Falko?" I ask the big guy, leaning my head for a moment on Falko's shoulder and missing him already.

"I don't know. Never thought about it," he says gruffly. "The master'll surely give us a few days' grace, though, *eh*, DuBois? To make a plan, and figure things out."

But Tristan won't hear of it. We're to start packing up first thing in the morning, and when Falko suggests that they go to the master together to ask about staying on as veterans in another capacity, Tristan shakes his head. I don't blame him. Hanging around after he's been cut to oversee certifications or the like would make Tristan miserable, even without the mortification of having to beg the master for it, and it would be too much to ask him to watch from the sidelines while his brother wins it all. Whatever I may think of Taran now, he's been training his entire life to defeat Tristan and he's sure to revel in it, and Taran's not the only one who would make a point of rubbing his victory in Tristan's face. I even suspect Master Guillaume would let Tristan stay on just for the pleasure of watching him suffer the humiliation of it.

"What *will* we do, master?" I ask Tristan, once Falko and Frans have gone in.

"I don't know yet, Marek. But to start with, I guess you can stop calling me that."

"Never, master," I say, and now I rest my head on *his* shoulder, and he puts his own head heavily down on mine.

It's a wonderfully warm night, and the sky is filling with stars. But I don't look up at them. It's a night like the one of our St. Sebastian's day show, and I can still remember how I felt lying in the wreckage with those stars hurtling down on top of me and knowing I'd never be a Journey. I can't imagine what it's like now, for Tristan. It's the same kind of bitter defeat after the expectation of victory from which my father never recovered.

After a while, though, he laughs. "You can't say I don't know how to fail with style! And that shot. It *was* good, wasn't it?"

"The best."

"How'd I look, lying there after?" He flashes me a grin. I knew he was faking it!

"Incredibly handsome, master. As always."

There's another long silence, in which Tristan lets his head rest against mine more heavily. And when I feel moisture on my cheek, I know he used up all his courage for acting. I don't think I realized how much Guards meant to Tristan until this moment, or how much I wanted it for him. What makes it more unbearable is knowing that he'd already resigned himself to losing back at Brecelyn's castle, only *I* built him up again so high that he's had to fall even harder.

"She wasn't there, Marek," he whispers, his voice catching. "She didn't see me. And now I'll never see her again."

"I know, master." Once I would have been glad at the thought of it, but not tonight, and instead I feel my own tears falling. I think he really loves her, and I know she loves him, too, and tonight I feel like I've been

misjudging everyone. I imagine poor Melissande alone and lonely in that cold castle, and I want the happy ending for them both more than ever, the one I'll never get for myself. So after a pause, tentatively I hazard the question,
"Have you been writing letters to her, master?"
"No, of course not," he replies. "Not that I haven't wanted to," he adds, when he senses me frowning. "But I've caused her enough trouble."
"You *did* have some plan about her, though, didn't you master? Maybe it could still work," I press, and to my surprise, he hangs his head — and laughs.
"Shall I really tell you, Marek? All right, why not? It's too late for the scheme now, and anyway, it was always just a fantasy. If Seconds was clouts and I was sure I'd be out, Gilles and I were going to liberate Melissande from her father's castle, old Poncellet style."
What he really means is that Gilles was going to help him sneak into Sir Brecelyn's manor, abduct Melissande, and convince her to elope with him.
"Tristan, that would have been suicide!" I tell him, for the first time tonight starting to think that getting cut before Seconds might not be the worst thing that could have happened to him.
"Yeah, well. We were never really going to do it," he says, but I'm not sure I believe him.
"I just wish she'd been there to see it," he sighs. Then he continues with the air of a man pulling himself together, "Ah, well! I expect she'll hear all about it from Lady Sibilla, and *you* were there. That's what matters. And I went out with a bang! That's something."
"And at least we'll miss poor Pascal's wedding," I agree. "That's something else."
We stay out together for a while longer, sitting in silence on the hard ground with our backs against the butts and our cloaks in the dust, until the air begins to grow chilly. At length, Tristan says,
"I think I'll talk to Master Leon in the morning, about that contingent of veterans. See if they'll let us tag along."
I don't bother replying, since Tristan isn't asking, and to me, it sounds horrible. With Master Bernard in charge, it's sure to be a motley crowd of thugs with no other purpose than to roam the streets of the capital looking for Kingsmen to brawl with, but there's no point in saying so. I already know anything likely to appeal to Tristan for us to do next is going to sound just as unpalatable, and there's nothing I can do about it. Particularly not when he continues, his tone turning serious,
"I *did* want to be a Guardsman, for my own sake, Marek. But I was also going to use the position to find out something about your father. I was *going* to help you get justice for him. I made myself a promise, and now I can't keep it. Maybe in Meuse, we can still learn something. It's as good a place as any, to reinvent ourselves."

607

I can see he really means it, so I hug him tighter, even though the thought of what lies ahead fills me with dread, and I make a promise of my own. There's something I have to do before I leave here, something for myself. If Tristan's serious about leaving the guild in the morning, it has to be tonight. I've put it off too long already.

CHAPTER FORTY-FIVE

It's well past curfew when I say goodnight to Tristan outside his door, but I don't let it worry me. We've already been cut, and there's not much more that the master can do to us. I wait a beat or two to make sure that Tristan's settled in for the night, and then I dart back to barracks, to fetch the thing I need. Soon I'm back, knocking on another boy's door.

When there's no answer to my light rap, I bang on it, until a grumpy and groggy Aristide cracks his door open.

"Marek? What the hell? Do you know what time it is? If you've come to complain about the ranking, you can't expect me to try to do something about it."

"Here," I say, shoving the handkerchief of his that Gilles and I found into his hand. "Take it. Now that we all know what you were doing out in Brecelyn's chapel this winter, I figured you might want this back."

"Seriously? You're banging on my door at this hour, over a handkerchief?" he says, taking the cloth with a frown and looking confused, like he was already fast asleep and I've woken him. When he starts to shut the door, I lean my shoulder against it.

"I want something in return. The notebook." I put out my hand for it. "I want you to give it to me. Right now."

"Fat chance! Are you mad? Why in the world would I do that?" he sneers, shoving me back and starting to swing the door closed in my face.

I stick out my foot to block it.

"It's my last chance to read it, Ari. And I think maybe you're nicer than you pretend. At least I'm betting you've got a heart in there somewhere. Enough of one to understand why I can't leave here without knowing everything that's in that diary. Because," I take a deep breath, "Jan Verbeke was *my father*."

Aristide's eyebrows shoot up, but he doesn't say anything. Then with a snort he gives me another shove backward, harder than the first, and he slams his door shut in my face. I consider banging on his door again, but it's pointless and I've already turned around and started trudging back to barracks with my candle when Aristide's door opens again. He must have been fetching the notebook from its hiding place, since he's now holding out Meliana's diary in his hand.

"*Enjoy*, Woodcock," he says, shoving it into my grasp and disappearing back inside his room before I can thank him. After the door's already clicked closed, I hear him muttering, "and whatever you do, *don't* bring it back again!"

I have a feeling that what's really motivated him to hand the diary over isn't sentiment, but the thought of those two big arrows, sticking out of Luc Fournier's back. It's not a thought I'm eager to dwell on, either, as I make my way further down the dark hallway with the stolen notebook in my hand.

I take the journal along with me to the Journey lavatory, where I sit down with it in one of the boys' empty bathtubs. I prop my candle in a pool of wax on a stool next to me, and in its dim glow I flip through the little book's pages, until I come to the place in it where I think I left off.

It's a little hard to be sure, since the last time I was reading the book, Aristide was chasing me down the hallway. I *do* remember that Meliana was right in the middle of urging my father to follow her into the guild chapel, and the thought of reading about my father's sexual exploits from the point of view of his lover is excruciating. The thought of getting shot in a Journeyman bathtub by a sleepy veteran who might stumble in to relieve himself is even worse. But I can't leave St. Sebastian's without knowing once and for all the whole truth about my father. I won't have kept all my vows or promises to him, either, but if I leave the guild tomorrow without learning all I can, I'll never forgive myself. Tonight, I'll read the diary to the bitter end, no matter how difficult, even if Master Guillaume himself walks in and catches me with the journal in my hands.

Only once I've found my place and started to ease myself back into the story, I find there's only one page left:

I let a hint of my old, flirty tone creep in, just enough for us both to know what I really had in mind, what was surely going happen, the moment I was alone with him.

I could tell he was going to try to resist ... so for good measure I pressed myself up shockingly close against him. And when his eyes flashed in response, I knew I had him.

Only it wasn't lust, it was anger.

"We can have nothing to say to each other, Meliana," Jan replied, looking down at me like he was only just seeing me clearly. "Or should I say, Lady *Meliana? It's funny, but I don't think we ever really did. At least, there can only be one thing left to say between us, and that's goodbye."*

I watched Jan Verbeke stalk back into the guild hall where I couldn't follow him, and I knew he wouldn't be coming back. He'd not be waiting for me in the garden again. He was done with me.

I threw myself down on the ground, plunging my skirts into the mud where the boys' boots had churned it up. I tugged at my hair in rage, tangling it into snarls, and it was all I could do to keep from howling. How dare Jan Verbeke spurn me! Who did he think he was? I was right, he's a nothing. A peasant. By all rights, he should have been the one doing the begging. Good riddance to him, the ungrateful louse! Let him have his stinking cottage. He can rot there, for all I care. I'm better off without him. I should be glad to be rid of him.

I should be. But I'm not.

I don't know how long I lay there, huddled under the tree and sobbing, before I realized I wasn't alone. Someone was hovering in the corner of the garden, watching me. One of the boys spying, probably, witnessing the whole wretched scene, or waiting for an opening for himself. One of the poor slobs who'd sell his right arm to have the kind of chance with me that Jan had just rejected.

I raised my head, and I saw I was right. Across the garden a face was contemplating me, soft with concern at the sight of my tears. But underneath, his eyes were blazing with desire. I straightened up, and with some effort I managed to reward him with a crooked smile. It wasn't just a reflex. Everyone else wanted me. Why, there was one right in front of me who'd have done anything to have me. I was gorgeous. Irresistible. I could see it in his eyes.

I'd show Jan Verbeke — show him that he can't throw me over. I wasn't thinking straight. I just wanted Jan to be sorry, when I gave the prize that should have been his to another. So I got slowly to my feet, smoothed my hair, and wiped my eyes. Then I made my way over to my stunned admirer, and I held out my hand invitingly. I led him into the waiting chapel without a word. When I pulled him down onto the cold stones of the chapel floor on top of me, he couldn't believe his luck. But there was no joy in our coupling for me. It was cold comfort.

… What a fool I've been! A careless, stupid fool. Of all things, I've gone and gotten myself pregnant. And it's all Jan's fault! If he'd just been willing to play along, if he hadn't flustered me, I'd never have gotten myself into this predicament. Or at least, the child would be his, and that would be an entirely different matter. I just needed a little physical comfort to soothe my ruffled feathers. I deserved that much, didn't I? And I was no virgin, at least not technically. But I'd always been careful. Now I'm in a real fix. What's worse, now my whole future rests in the hands of that fool Jakob.

That's it. That's the end of the diary. There are no more sheets, just some jagged edges near the book's interior binding, as though the last few pages have been ripped out.

"What, you again?" Aristide demands, when minutes later I'm banging on his door again. "I thought I told you not to bring that cursed book back again."

"Where's the rest of it, Ari?" I ask, flipping open the book and pointing. "Where are the missing pages?"

"How should I know? The book was like that when I got it. I thought *you* had them."

Aristide could be lying, but I don't think so. I doubt he cares enough about it. But after what I've just read, to say that I care is an understatement. Whatever else was in that diary, I *have* to find it out.

To make matters worse, while I'm standing there feeling stymied and my mind whirring, Aristide reaches back into his room. Soon he's thrusting the handkerchief I just returned to him into my hand.

"I *told* you so at the time! This isn't mine. Red thread! How *gaudy*," he snorts, rolling his eyes, but I'm hardly listening. I'm already disappearing down the hall and letting myself into Tristan's room.

I close Tristan's door softly behind me and I kneel next to his cot, prepared to shake him awake. But I find he isn't sleeping. He's lying on his back in the dark, his arms folded underneath his head and his eyes open, staring up unseeing at the ceiling. He doesn't react at my entrance, not even when the halo of my candle illuminates his profile, and I don't know why. But his vacant stare and dry eyes seem worse to me than if I'd found him in here crying.

I put the candle on the floor and I rest my head down on his chest, and when all he does is fold his arms around me, we stay like that for a while in silence. Under my ear I can hear his heart beating in his chest, and a heaviness settles over us like the weight of a blanket. Now it's not the burden of unspoken words pressing down on me, but the weight of both our failures, and of the heaviest loss of all — the loss of Saint Sebastian's. Tristan must think it's like the night of our squires' show, when I came in search of comfort to tell him I would never be a Journey, since after a while he throws back his covers to let me to crawl in with him. But I shake my head, and I tell him what's really brought me.

Tristan may have been half asleep when I entered. By the time I finish telling him that I want him to borrow Gilles's big, white bridal horse and ride me on it out to the Vendon Abbey, he's wide awake.

"If we get up at the crack of dawn, I can get to Father Abelard before his duties. I promise it won't take long. And we'll be back in time for you to talk to Master Leon, if you really want to," I implore. "I can't just leave town without saying goodbye, after the way he and the monks healed me." By this point Tristan's sitting up and running both hands through his hair. When he gives me a shrewd look, I don't want to lie. So I admit,

"And there's something I need to ask him. Something about my father. I can't leave Louvain without knowing the answer. I can't wait any longer to find it out."

"You might have asked this any other day, Marek. Why now?"

"It's hard to explain. But it's important, I swear it. Trust me, master. Just one more time."

To his credit, Tristan doesn't press me for an explanation, which is lucky;

now is not the time to tell him I've been keeping the existence of the notebook a secret from him. It's *really* not the time to tell him that I just don't know any longer if the girl he loves is *my* sister, or his own — or that I owe it to Taran to tell him, if it turns out that all this time he's been engaged to his own half sibling. Tristan may keep a few secrets from me, but he also lets me keep my own, and it now occurs to me that any other boy would surely have blamed me for his failure, since I'm the one who convinced him to go alone into the chapel and to put his trust in teamwork. Not Tristan. He's never mentioned it.

"You really want to do this? To ride all the way to the abbey, on horseback, in the dark?" When I nod, he considers a moment. Then he laughs.

"Why wait 'til morning, then? Anything's got to be better than lying awake in this cell all night."

After a brief interlude in which I hug him as tightly as my battered ribcage will allow me, I gather up our traveling cloaks while Tristan has a quick word with Gilles, and soon we're riding out through the postern gate of the guild and into the woods together on Lady Sibilla's wedding present.

Nobody stops us, although by now it's long past midnight. Tristan's out, and he can do as he pleases. Or maybe the veteran on duty at the gate feels sorry for us. Tristan was robbed today, and everybody knows it. Even the Kingsmen still camped out in the road let us pass by them unmolested, and as the horse under us picks its way along the path through the woods beyond by moonlight, I keep up a steady stream of mindless babble, as much to keep Tristan from asking any questions as to distract myself from how excruciating it is to ride after the beating I took in the stables. We're taking the circuitous route, through the forest, and I want to keep my own mind off how we'll be riding out along this same path tomorrow, leaving St. Sebastian's for good, never to come back again — and I don't want to think about the *last* time I made this ride, either: unconscious in Taran's arms, slung across his saddle.

When at length we come out of the woods into the open space in front of the abbey, Tristan helps me slide down off the tall horse's back. Then he leads Gilles's mount away in search of a comfortable place to wait, leaving me to circle around alone behind the cloisters. Tristan's promised to let me talk to Abelard alone and he's as good as his word, as always.

I find my way easily despite the dark, although it's been over a year since I last made my way like this around to the spreading chestnut tree at the base of Father Abelard's window. When I pick my way through the tall weeds and come up close enough to feel its bark in my hands, the old tree looks bigger than I remember, and I hesitate.

Marieke had no trouble scrambling up this tree. Even with sore ribs, it should be even easier for Marek. That's not the problem. It's just that if Father Abelard doesn't have the answers I need, I'll have to admit defeat. I'll

613

never know the truth about Melissande, or what really happened to my father.

It's just last-minute jitters, and I shake them off. I reach out and clasp my hands firmly around the truck of the tree, and I start climbing.

SCRAMBLING UP THE BIG TREE IN THE DARK IS A STRANGE sensation, at once deeply familiar and completely alien, as though the girl who used to know every foothold of the way was someone else, a stranger. And maybe she was. The last time I climbed this tree was a lifetime ago. But it's not long before my body falls into its old rhythms and I'm shimming up the thick trunk faster even than Pascal when he went up the tree outside Sibilla's window for a kiss at the convent.

Once I'm perched precariously on the big limb outside Abelard's window, I pause again. Father Abelard is a notoriously light sleeper. He used to tell me he slept with one eye open, on the lookout for demons, and I believe it. So I say a prayer that he's having one of his wakeful nights; I'd hate to cap the wretched day by scaring the old monk to death. Then I reach out and give the weatherbeaten shutters in front of me three sharp raps, followed by a low whistle between my teeth in imitation of the call of a thrush. It's my old signal to the monk that I'm outside.

It isn't long before there's a shuffling from inside, and through the warped shutter's slats I can make out a faint glow moving about, as Father Abelard calmly lights a candle from an oil lamp hanging on the wall and carries it toward the window. I should have known it would take more than a midnight visit to ruffle Abelard; after the way I turned up here at the abbey as a half-dead boy in Taran's arms the last time, it would probably take quite a lot for me to surprise him.

Soon the shutter in front of me is creaking open. I lean back against the trunk of the tree to let it swing past me, as the candle emerges out the window at the end of a thin, boney hand. Abelard's gaunt face next appears out of the gloom, peering through the dim light at me. I know better than to grin at him; he'd think I was a demon, for sure. So I give him a solemn nod, and he stands aside wordlessly to let me swing myself over the sill and into the little cubicle beside him.

"I suppose it's too much to hope that you've finally left St. Sebastian's," he says by way of greeting, surveying my squire's costume with displeasure. "Is that your remarkable young man you've got with you?" he asks, peering out over my shoulder to a place in the distance where Tristan can just be seen lying under a beech tree.

"Yes. No. Not yet. And if you must know, it's another one," I tell him, and when he rolls his eyes, I cut him off before he can ask me any more questions by plucking the little journal out of my waistband.

Then I open it to the page with the sketch of Meliana Brecelyn on it, the one that's virtually the same as the one on the marred illumination he gave me the last time I was in this room with him, and I hold it out between us so that the picture of the blonde woman is face-up in the candlelight.

"Tell me about her, Abelard," I demand. "Tell me everything you know about St. Sebastian's."

Abelard stares down at the book in my hand, frowning. When he doesn't take it, I thrust it out in front of me further, in the same accusing way I once did to Tristan with the illumination in front of Brecelyn's fire. But I can't keep my hand from trembling, and at my insistence Abelard reaches out and takes the diary from me gingerly, as though it were still as wet as his copy of the picture was on the day he gave it to me. As he does, his hand is trembling, too. It could be just from old age. But I don't think so. So I say more gently,

"Oh, Abelard! Don't tell me *you* were in love with her, too?!"

He's silent for so long and his expression is so dour I'm afraid I've angered him with my blunt question.

"There's a difference between love and lust, Marieke," he finally says.

"I know that!" I reply, sounding more indignant than I intend. But I'm not sure I do. At least, I'm not sure I know what it is.

Abelard's not moved, nor looked up from the little book in his hand. So I sit down on the edge of his hard, spare cot, and putting a hand on his sleeve, I urge him,

"Tell me about her, Abelard. Please. It's time. Tell me about Lady Meliana Brecelyn, and about my father's accident."

At the name, Abelard twitches. It's an involuntary move somewhere between a startle and a shudder, and he shoots me a quick, shrewd glance. I gesture toward the cot next to me, giving it an encouraging little pat, and after a moment the old monk sits down heavily next to me.

"The priest, the one disgraced at the convent. That was you, wasn't it?" I ask, and he nods to confirm it.

We sit in silence side-by-side for long enough that again I think he isn't going to respond to my request. But just as I'm casting around for something more to say to prod him into speech, he reaches down under the thin straw of his mattress, and he pulls out a fistful of loose sheets of parchment. From the size of them and their jagged edges, they can't be anything but the missing pages from Meliana's notebook.

"I knew there must have been a diary," Abelard says, handing the little stash over. I notice he doesn't ask me how I found it; he must believe in providence as much as Brother Benedict. "At the time of her ladyship's death, I was in Sir Brecelyn's employ, saying masses for the family out in his private chapel. I found these with her body when she died, and I thought it best to remove them. But I couldn't bring myself to destroy them. I see you've already read part of the story. Here, child," he says, holding the torn pages out to me. "I guess it's time you knew the rest of it."

I take them from him carefully, since they seem terribly fragile and crumpled, and while I smooth them out, Abelard turns the diary over in his hands, leafing back to the beginning of it. And then we exchange a look, and we both bend over by the light of his candle, and side by side, we read — him the diary he's never seen, and me the missing final pages of it.

It took me a while to figure out what was happening. At first I thought I was just sick and miserable over my falling out with Jan, though it didn't take me long to see that things weren't as bleak as I'd been painting them.

I was sure I could figure out a way to get Jan back, given the opportunity. But I was right. After that afternoon, Jan stopped coming into the garden. He took to going straight into the guild through the stables to avoid me. Then before I could figure out a way around it, I realized that on top of everything else, that pitiful encounter in the chapel had left me in real trouble.

My immediate problem, my burning problem, was Jan. I wasn't worried about Hugo. I knew I could fool him easily enough. It would be easy to get him between the sheets any time I wanted, and he's so gullible, I doubt he'll count out the months. And Jan might eventually forgive me for marrying Hugo, once I could make him understand about the money. But he'd never forgive me for letting Hugo have his way with me before the wedding, once he figured it out. And if he suspected that Hugo wasn't the father ... well, I just couldn't let that happen.

I considered getting rid of it. Mother knows some herbs that can be boiled off and ingested to induce the necessary fever, but they don't always work, and they're risky; one sip too much, and the fever can be fatal. I had a better idea, anyway. All I had to do was convince Jan the child was his. Then I'd never have to worry about losing him. He's one of those honorable types, the kind who'd never leave me if he thought I'd given him a child. It was perfect, really. If I could get Jan to lose control just once, I'd have him for life. But how was I to get back in Jan's favor, and get him to go further with me than he ever had before, when he wouldn't even talk to me? I didn't have even the usual four months or so until I started showing. Thirds was already fast approaching, and I knew then as well as I know now that once the competitions are over, Jan will be off to Meuse and out of my reach. So there was only one thing I could do. For a boy like Jan, the only way to win was total surrender. So I'd tell him I'd marry him after all. In his joy at winning me over, he'd fall right into my arms. I could always tell him I couldn't get out of my contract with Hugo, after.

My first attempts to reestablish myself with Jan were less than successful. I couldn't get anywhere near him. You'd even have thought Guillaume was working in concert with him to thwart me, the way he was always turning up with a bark and a scowl whenever I tried to slip out onto the field. Undaunted, I set my mind to finding other ways to get at him. Access was my real problem. Finally one day I managed to get past Guilly by letting myself in by the postern gate, the one that opens onto the L'île-Charleroi road. Father has a mounted exhibition planned for Thirds, and there was a chance Jan might be out riding.

My luck held, and Jan was out in the far pasture. But he wasn't alone. That wretched groom's daughter was with him, sitting on a fencepost and watching him. I had no choice but to wander over to join her, and even my rudest comments weren't enough to drive her off. I couldn't afford to be subtle. I had to work fast. It was damned awkward, and I'll admit I was rattled by having that horrid girl in my way again. I didn't need her interference wrecking my hard-won opportunity.

In the end, I couldn't make any headway. They both ignored me, intent as they were on cooking up some trick to wow the crowds.

"Is that the best you can do?" the girl was calling out, as I approached. Jan was attempting to stand up on the back of the horse as it trotted by, not very successfully. He dropped back into the saddle as he went past, giving me only the most perfunctory of nods.

"I suppose you could do better?" he laughed to the girl, who turned up her nose and sniffed.

"Ah, I've got a great trick. If I were competing, I'd put you boys to shame. Get off, and I'll show you!"

Jan was just trying to annoy me, but he slid off the horse and let the girl clamber up in his place. Then he continued to ignore me, leaning up against the post next to me but not saying anything, and making only noncommittal grunts to my forays at conversation while we both watched the girl go through a ridiculous series of maneuvers to end up hanging off one side of the horse.

"Now what?" he called out to her merrily as she bumped along.

"Now, I'd shoot! Upside down!" she called back triumphantly, mimicking bending a bow with her arms. It was all too silly. Oh, I'll admit she can ride well. She was raised in a stable, wasn't she? Probably suckled in a stall, along with the donkeys.

She pulled up again and trotted back over, saying,

"It wouldn't be hard, with a little practice. If you timed it perfectly, so you were shooting at the right point in the horse's motion, just as its gait tossed you in the air, it shouldn't affect your aim too much."

"That's absurd," I said, seeing my opening. "Jan doesn't need any childish tricks. He'd be a fool to try something that risky, when he's sure to win."

"Jan's no coward," the girl replied, bold as brass. "He'd do it, just for the hell of it! Wouldn't you, Jan?" and to my immense annoyance, Jan just grinned and asked to see the trick again. After a while I had no choice but to leave, when I spotted my father coming around the corner of the stables in the distance. After that, every time I tried to slip through the L'île-Charleroi gate, Guilly was there on the other side waiting for me.

It was only a temporary defeat. I saw another chance not much later, and ever since I've been hard at work on a new plan that's sure to solve my problems. My opening came about two weeks ago, when Father mentioned at supper that he's commissioned a famous artist to come from Antwerp to do a painting of St. Sebastian to hang in the guild hall. It's to be a massive canvas, and the master painter is bringing along a number of apprentices to do the rough work. I wasn't paying that much attention, until my father added that one of the boys would be pressed into service to pose as the young saint. And that the boy in question was to be Jakob Mellor.

I started in on my father that very night. Wouldn't it be a lovely idea to commission a painting of me, as a wedding gift for Hugo? I could pose for it alongside Jakob, with some of the apprentices working on my portrait at the same time as they work on the guild picture. I had a delightful conceit in mind, too: me, as Helen of Troy, in front of the walls of Troy, depicted as Hugo's castle. Those could be painted in later, and it would be more than fitting. A little private joke, since it's a story all about an adulterous love affair, isn't it? And a beautiful woman. The most beautiful woman in the world.

It was all too perfect. I'd have an excuse to be inside the guild daily, if only out in the outbuildings where a makeshift studio's to be set up for the project near the far pasture. But it would be a foothold inside the walls, and even if I couldn't use posing for the painting as a way to skulk around and see Jan, I knew I could make good use of my time. I needed something foolproof, and fast. And I knew the rules of love from reading my Capellanus. There was only one thing that could get me back on track with Jan in the time left to me: jealousy. The oldest trick in the book.

...It's all worked out exactly as I imagined. Father agreed, and things have been progressing nicely. If I play my cards right, all my plans should finally come to fruition this very day. Getting poor Jakob all hot and bothered has been easier than stirring up that old fool of a priest. It's been as much fun, too. I mean, Jakob's an idiot, but he's got a splendid body, and the outfit they have him posing in, it's no more than a tiny rag. All I have to do is look at him in it and he's chomping at the bit. But this afternoon, at my connivance, Jakob's gotten Jan to promise to come by for a visit, to see how the work's coming along while the painters take their midday break. I've got to be ready to strike. I'll only get one chance at it.

...Well before the appointed hour, I settled myself onto the stool in front of the painters' easels where I've been posing out in the hot little makeshift studio. As I did, I pulled the bodice of my green dress down as far as I dared and prepared for work. I'd been so eager to get started that I was early, though I could hear the painter's apprentices in the back closet, sorting through paints and preparing their pallets, and it wasn't long before I heard Jakob's unmistakable voice ringing out a boisterous greeting, as he entered through the back and set about stripping down to don his own skimpy costume. I licked my lips, partly to get them looking luscious, and partly because I really was looking forward to what was coming.

When the painters came out carrying their equipment and found me already perched on my seat, I gave them a gracious nod of greeting. If they were surprised by my early arrival, they quickly covered for it. I'm usually quite late. I can't really be expected to be stuck in there, immobile, with the likes of them all afternoon, can I? And stringing Jakob along — that really only requires a matter of minutes each day. But I was pleased with how my portrait was looking, and my plan was shaping up so nicely that when Jakob followed them out, clumping along and struggling to keep his dirty little rag of a costume in place, the dazzling smile I gave him was entirely genuine. After all, if everything went as planned, I knew it would be the last time I had to put up with any of them. The painters could finish the rest of my picture from memory; they couldn't possibly forget what I look like.

As soon as the painters set about their work and the session got underway, I gave Jakob the full treatment. I was sitting primly on my stool, and after a shyly gruff greeting, Jakob slung his arms over his prop: a rough-hewn structure with an upright post and a crossbeam to hold up his outstretched arms, which the painters are to fashion into the likeness of a tree on the canvas. We weren't supposed to move, of course, but I'd arranged things so that we were posing next to each other, with Jakob turned so that he was essentially staring right at me, and me with a slight cock of the head that would let me look at him, too, when I wanted to.

I usually worked up to it gradually, but today I started right in casting Jakob long looks from under lowered lashes, ones that worked slowly up and down his body, exposed as it was in all its glory. The poor boy tried his best to keep up a steady stream of his usual blustery conversation. But whenever I let my eyes linger on the pathetic thread of a loincloth clinging precariously to his groin, he couldn't help it. His fatuous remarks were punctuated in turn by that awful chuffing noise he makes or by inadvertent high-octave hisses. I made a game of it, seeing just how low my eyes had to wander to elicit a chuff or a squeak, and before long, I could almost get a little tune out of him, much to the barely disguised amusement of the boys behind the easels. Of course, all that squirming and wriggling just put Jakob's costume in greater danger of sliding off, and pretty soon I barely had to look at him at all, luckily enough. My neck was starting to get a cramp. It was all too easy, but I didn't feel sorry for him. He'd been flirting with me shamelessly for weeks, leaving little doubt about what he wanted, even though he knew I was engaged to Hugo; I told him so myself, every time he made one of his clumsy passes.

By the time I got up to take one of my stretches and to move around to see how the paintings were progressing, Jakob was putting on such a show that even the apprentices were having trouble keeping straight faces. I made a point of skirting around to pass so close by Jakob that I brushed up against him, and after all my ogling, it was almost enough to put him over the edge. When the accustomed hour for our midday break arrived and the apprentices finally draped a moist cloth over their pallets to head outside for some air, I knew Jakob was more than ready. The scaffolding he was draped over was clattering so much and his legs trembling under him so unsteadily, the little wooden box of a room we were in was shaking harder than an unevenly loaded wagon on a bumpy road full of potholes.

"We'll leave him to you, miss," one of the bolder painters said to me with a smile as he made his exit.

"I know exactly what to do with him," I smiled confidently back. And as soon as they were out the door, I slid off my stool, ready to make good on my statement.

I didn't have time to play around. If Jakob had done his part, Jan would be showing up at any minute.

I'd come prepared. I was wearing two ribbons in my hair, pretty red things, but as strong as wire. As I sauntered over to where Jakob was straightening up and stretching out his limbs, I pulled one of them off, untangling it from my golden curls.

"Poor thing!" I cooed, sidling up and reaching out a hand to rub his biceps. "How tired your arms must get, holding them up like that so long!"

"Aw, it's nothing, Meli," he grumbled, blushing. "I'm strong as an ox, look!" and he tensed his muscles until they were bulging. They really did look like meat, and despite his abbreviated costume, he was already sweating.

I circled around behind him, moving my hands up to massage his shoulders, and simpered into his ear,

"Still, it can't feel good. And I do so want you to feel good, Jakob. What do you say? Do you want to feel good?"

I took the strangled grunt he made as an affirmative, and I grabbed up one if his hands. Quickly I stretched it out and draped it back up over the fake tree limb behind him, holding out the ribbon as I did with a flourish. Then I tied his arm at the wrist to the tree, using a double knot. Before he could protest, I said silkily,

"See? Isn't it clever? Now you won't have to waste your energy holding up your arms. You can save your strength for more pleasing tasks ..." And I giggled.

While he was looking confused and giving his bound hand a trial tug, I grabbed up the other one, stretched it out in the opposite direction, and tied it up, too.

"There! Isn't that better?"

All he could do was gurgle.

I skirted back around in front of him, trailing my hands lightly up the inside of his outstretched arm as I went, and he strained at his bindings, giving the scaffolding under him an impressive rattle. But they held fast.

"It's no use, Jakob," I purred, looking him over where he was splayed out wide and helpless in front of me. "You're my prisoner. Whatever should I do with you, I wonder? You've been terribly, terribly naughty."

"Mercy, Meli!" he groaned, as my hands started to roam over his chest.

"Why Jakob," I made a little tsking sound between my teeth and swayed in even closer. "Surely mercy is the last thing you really want me to give you."

He lurched forward, as though he was about to dive head-first into my cleavage, and the scaffolding shuddered about a foot forward across the floor with him. I slipped out of his reach, and as his head lolled back and the muscles of his chest shuddered beneath my fingertips, I moved in again and groped my hands against him harder.

"In fact, it's *you* who has something I want," I murmured. "But I can't quite seem to find it. Now, now, let me see ... where *can* you be hiding it?" and my hands crept lower, as though I was searching him for a misplaced item.

He'd given up any attempt at conversation, and as I continued to fumble around on his body, moving slowly lower and pretending to search around as I made purring noises, his head was rolling from side to side and his arms were pulling at his bonds, and he was moaning and gnashing so much he was basically foaming at the mouth. It was really terribly entertaining.

It was no game, though. It was a careful calculation, and the whole time I was keeping a sharp lookout over his shoulder toward the entryway behind him. Sure enough, before long and right on schedule, Jan appeared in the open doorway. Jakob's body was between us, his broad back to the door and shielding my actions from Jan. And so as soon as I saw Jan crossing over the threshold, I leaned in and whispered in Jakob's ear, too low for Jan to hear,

"I do believe I've found it!" and I thrust both hands firmly under Jakob's loincloth. And squeezed.

"Argh-grrumphf!"

With a huge roar, Jakob lunged. In an impressive show of strength, he burst through his bonds and hurled himself on me like Samson on an unsuspecting Philistine, and we both went crashing onto the floor with a resounding thud, as his wooden tree came tumbling down on top of us.

It all came off even better than I'd hoped. As I rolled around under a wildly groping and grunting Jakob, Jan rushed forward as I knew he would, to save me.

It took quite a while for Jan to pull Jakob off me. I'm not sure he'd have managed, even, if I hadn't snuck in a judiciously aimed knee or two in the midst of all our flailing. Finally, Jan disentangled us, jerking Jakob off to the side with an oath, and yelling,

"Get the hell off her, Mellor, you flaming idiot!" and lifting me to my feet again. But Jakob didn't let me go that easily. He started hurling abuse at Jan, and soon their heated words turned to blows. Before long it was the two of them that were rolling around on the floor, scuffling and cursing each other, and basically fighting like cats and dogs. It was perfect.

I patted down my hair and straightened my skirts, and I stepped around them to take my leave. My work was done. But I didn't go far; that was only step one. Once outside, I pressed myself up against the wall next to the open door, where I could hear everything going on inside and wait for Jan.

I couldn't make out exactly what Jan was saying. His voice wasn't as penetrating as Jakob's. But even from one side of the argument, I could tell things were going as expected. Jakob kept bellowing out things like, "Ha, you just want her for yourself!" or "What's the matter, Verbeke? Can't stand it that she prefers me?" and "Oh yeah? Hypocrite! You'd give your shirt for a little 'use' like that yourself!" You know. The usual stuff.

By the time they'd exhausted each other and called each other every name in the book and then some, I'd started to get tired of waiting. Jan had responded so satisfactorily, I could barely contain my anticipation. I could almost taste Jan's kiss on my mouth already, and after going without it for so long, I couldn't stand to wait one more second.

Eventually I heard Jan coming out again, leaving Jakob lying in a heap behind him on the floor, and I hastily prepared myself. Jan's lip was bloody and he had a hideous frown on his face, and when he came out through the door, he was so furious he went right past me without seeing me. I had to grab him back, to get him to notice me.

"Jan," I said breathily. "Oh, Jan! I knew you still loved me! You must, to be so jealous," and I tried to pull him to me.

He pushed me away roughly.

"This was all your doing, wasn't it? I should have known."

Then he did lean in, his face close to mine, but he didn't look at all like he was about to kiss me. Instead, he said deliberately,

"Listen to me, Meli. I'm warning you. Leave that poor boy alone."

I could see he was still terribly angry. I knew he would be. That was all part of the plan. And I knew just how to fix it.

"You can't think I'd ever be seriously interested in a boy like Jakob?" I laughed, pouting my lips prettily. "I just had to show you, Jan, how much you still care! To get you to listen. I have something to tell you. Something important. Something that's going to make you happy."

When he took a step backward, almost as though he was recoiling from me, I rushed on urgently,

"It will be different now, Jan, I promise! It'll be as you wanted. You can have it all your own way. I'll break with Hugo. I'll marry you instead. I'll even stay with you here in Louvain, if that's what you want. Anything, everything, just as you say. There, that ought to please you. That ought to settle things! Come now, let's be friends again. More than friends. Come with me, somewhere, now Jan, and let me show just how friendly I can be."

Throughout my speech, Jan just stood there staring at me. I waited for a slow smile to break across his face as what I was saying began to sink in, as he realized the concessions I was making.

"You can't be serious."

He said it flatly, and if anything, his expression got harder. I didn't understand. I'd given him everything, and it wasn't making any difference. I'd miscalculated somehow.

It was so not what I was expecting, I didn't know what to do. So I panicked.

I pulled down my dress.

"Jan, Jan. You can't resist this, can you?" I demanded huskily.

And he sneered. Literally, he sneered at me, as he reached out quickly and yanked my dress back upward again, choking out,

"For God's sake, Meliana!"

At just that moment, Jakob staggered out through the doorway next to us. My dress was only halfway up, and Jan's hands were still on it. It must have looked like Jan was in the process of pulling it down eagerly, and as soon as Mellor saw us, his eyes went wide and he let out a strangled cry. He turned tail and ran off sniveling across the yard, holding up his hastily donned breeches with one hand and wiping his bloody nose with the other. What a baby.

"Damn it, Jakob, wait!" Jan called after him. With a grimace at me, he shoved my dress back at me and turned to rush off after him, but I grabbed him back.

"Let him go, Jan!" I cried, clutching his sleeve, my dress still down around my waist. "He doesn't matter! He's nothing. Nothing matters, nothing but you. But us."

I know I sounded hysterical and my hand were clawing at him, but I couldn't stop myself. I had to catch him back. There wouldn't be a next time.

"Jan, listen!" I shrieked. "I'm saying I'll marry you, that I want to marry you," and this time, I really meant it. I was ready to do anything. I couldn't lose Jan. I can't. "I'll live in a hovel with you, or a cave, and wear rags, if that's what it takes!"

I must have looked maniacal, grasping at him and sobbing and trying to hold up my dress. We struggled there a moment longer, until Jakob had disappeared into the guild and there was no hope for Jan of catching up with him. Then Jan went still. His arms that had been trying to extricate himself from me fell limp, and he turned back to face me. For a moment he looked down at me with a look that was completely empty, as he clenched and unclenched one fist. Then he finally said, "I can't believe I was ever dazzled by you, that it took me so long to see you for what you are."

"And what's that, Jan?" I asked tremulously, trying valiantly to sound a little flirty and still clinging to a hope that he was going to say something that would put everything right.

"What are you, Meliana?" he replied coldly. "I think, you must be the ugliest girl I've ever met."

And he walked away, just like that.

Now it's late. A single candle is burning on my bedside table, a puddle of wax pooling around it. Its flame is stretched out long and thin where it's burned down low to expose the wick, and the shadows it casts in the oversized mirror propped up on the table in front of me are long, too: a spidery web of lines across my face like a hag's wrinkles. I've been sitting here unmoving, not eating or sleeping and with my door locked, for three days. I haven't stirred for my mother's pleas from the hallway, or my father's threats.

It's Thirds tomorrow at St. Sebastian's. Jan's last day.

Even in the dim light, my eyes look puffy and blotchy, my face drawn and gaunt. My hair's an unkept mass, hanging in a tangle around my shoulders. My brush sits idle on the table, close at hand, but I don't pick it up. I just keep staring at my reflection. And I do look ugly, just as Jan said. What does it matter now? Jan won't even look at me.

Next to my brush, I've got another weapon. It's a slender little knife, a pretty thing with an inlaid handle. A weapon for a woman. But the blade is sharp enough. When I bend over it and its surface reflects my face back to me, the sheen on its metal in the faint glow of the candle is warm and inviting. I pick it up and turn it over in my hand. It offers so many possibilities, and I've considered all of them.

I thought of using it on myself. I was ready to do it. I'm no coward. It wasn't even the thought of letting Jan beat me that stopped me. It was the thought of him living on without me. Even now, I can't bear to lose him. But I can't sit by and watch him win, either. When I think of that scornful look he cast down at me, I won't endure the shame of sitting spurned in the bleachers, I won't sit idly by while he performs to the crowds. Doing that miserable girl's trick.

Jan, Jan! I love him still. I can't have lost him. Does he think I'll just let him go off to Guards? All his talk about being a country boy, does he think I don't know what that was? Empty threats, to punish me. While he's off to glory in Meuse, am I to stay here, saddled with a swollen belly and an idiot for a husband? Does he think he can really leave me behind? No, I'll never let that happen.

Even now, as I'm writing, pen in one hand, I pull my dress down slowly with the other, just as I did that day. For a moment, I contemplate my breasts in the mirror. How can the sight of them not have moved him? He'll be sorry, when I use them to move another. It's a pity to mar the perfection of them, but I'll leave one intact — a lure while the other will be a goad, and I'll lead Hugo on just like a donkey, with a stick and a carrot. I'll grasp one round, gleaming globe in my hand, and I'll dig my fingers into it as hard as I can.

The pain will be agonizing. But I'm done with crying, and I can't use half-measures. I've got to be sure that livid bruises, lurid yellow and purple things, will spring up by morning, early enough so they'll be ready when I waylay Hugo on his way to the competition grounds. I'll not let Jan win. But I'll not lose him, either. I'll not lose at all. It's not too late. It's not too late to win.

I'll tell Hugo tearfully how Jan and I have been secret lovers for weeks, behind his back. How Jan seduced me, made me promises, and then refused to marry me after he'd gotten what he wanted. I'm sure Mellor's already told everyone what he thought he witnessed. So when I show Hugo my bruised breast, the evidence of what happened to me when I tried to resist Jan's advances, he'll do anything I ask of him. There's no hatred like that for a former friend, for a fallen idol. Hugo'll be putty in my hands. Just a little slice, that's all it will take, I'll tell him — to give me my honor back, to humiliate Jan, the way he's humiliated the both of us. And if Hugo has doubts about my story later, well, the proof will come in nine months' time, won't it? I'm glad now that I've not done anything about Hugo, that I've made no effort to cover myself with him. The child growing inside me can still be used to my advantage. Why not? It should be good for something. And if Hugo doesn't have the guts to weaken the straps of Jan's saddle, I'll do it myself.

Jan will lose. He'll be disgraced. Let's see how aloof and superior he is then! But mostly, he'll have to stay. And I'll be there, to pick him up. I'll forgive him. I'll comfort him, when that miserable girl's trick backfires on him, and he sees how foolish he's been. Oh, I'll be so sympathetic! And he'll need me. He'll come back to me, in time. He'll not be too good to fall in with my plans, then.

Yes, Jan will come back to me. He'll be mine again. He has to be. I won't lose him. I can't. I'll never give him up.

We must sit for a long time in silence before I notice that Abelard's finished reading Meliana's diary, and that I, too, have finished reading the last of its loose pages. I've been lost in Meliana's story, steeling myself to hear the grisly details of my father's fall. But I've come to the end of it, and I'm grateful. I'm to be spared suffering through that vicious girl reveling in my father's accident, or maybe even she was too horrified by what happened to write about it. She couldn't have known he'd end up getting trampled. I guess she only meant for him to fail. When I look up at Father Abelard and he bows his head as though in confirmation, I know that this time, there really isn't any more of it.

"Was I right to show you, child?" Abelard asks, placing a boney hand on mine where they're clasped tightly around the rumpled pages in my lap.

I nod. It's all I can manage. I mean, I knew the story would be ugly. I just wasn't expecting it to be revolting.

After all that's happened today, I should have reached the saturation point long ago. I thought I had, when I heard that Tristan was out. I didn't think even hearing hard truths about my father could make me feel anything more. I'd figured out much of the miserable story already, hadn't I? The rough shape of it.

It hits me hard anyway. If nothing else, it brings fresh grief for my father flooding back, and with it, grief for Tristan's failure — bitter grief for them both, robbed of their triumphs by deceit and treachery. But I am glad I know the truth. I've wanted to know what happened to my father for so long that finally finding out is a weight off my shoulders. I'm not at all sure what I feel or what to say, though, and not only because of Abelard's confession of his own shameful part in the story.

"She didn't win, though, did she, Abelard? Not in the end," I finally say, not raising my eyes from his hand where it's clasped over mine. "My father never did go back to her. He never worked for Brecelyn."

"No, child. Your father was one of the lucky ones," he agrees quietly. "He had a narrow escape."

We sit in silence for a while longer, each lost in his own thoughts, as the phrase hangs in the air between us.

The story is so awful, it takes a long time for me to take it all in. It takes even longer for a new emotion to begin to stir in me, underneath my sadness. Slowly, unmistakably, it grows, getting stronger and stronger.

My father never touched Meliana! He behaved honorably. He *was* honorable. Oh, he was a typical boy, a vain and posturing Journey, to be sure. But he was also the noble boy I've always thought him to be. The image of him I had tucked up in my mind through all the years of my childhood has been washed free of taint, almost as though he were himself a square of illumination that I've been carrying around in my waistband, marred with ink.

I look down at the notebook in Father Abelard's hand. I imagine I can see Meliana's face peering up at me, jeering at me from under a black stain, and I have the grace to feel repentant, too, and ashamed. I let manipulative lies sway me, I let rumors and suspicions cloud my memory of my father. I'd lost faith in him, when I should have trusted in my own experience of him to tell me what kind of man he was.

What makes it worse is that it's the second time today I've had the exact same realization.

It's a testament to how much the story's affected me that it takes me even longer to see the thing that I really came here tonight most hoping to learn. And this time, the emotion it brings with it is unequivocal. It's not just joy. It's elation.

My father is innocent of begetting Melissande. He's not her father. But neither is Jakob Mellor.

Melissande isn't related to me by blood, or to Taran or Tristan either.

625

To say that it's a huge relief is an understatement. Now I can be glad I never voiced the terrible suspicion to either of the boys. But my emotions must still be all in a jumble, because after months of worrying that Melissande might be my sister, I'm actually a little sorry now to find out that she's not.

"Oh, Abelard!" I exclaim, only just noticing that the pages from Meliana's journal haven't really answered the question of Melissande's parentage, at least not fully. The boy in the chapel that day — he could have been anyone.

"I guess I'll never know who Melissande's father really is," I say, and the old man shakes his head sympathetically, giving my hand another pat.

"You don't think," I venture, "that there's even the *slightest* chance it could have been Jakob Mellor?"

It doesn't seem at all likely from the story. But after having come this far at midnight, I might as well be absolutely certain, although I know it's unreasonable to expect the monk to have all the answers.

"No," he says, shaking his head, and I roll my eyes inwardly, thinking back to just how inaccurate Brian de Gilford's description of Tristan's and Taran's father was. There was nothing reluctant about the young Jakob Mellor. Or subtle, either.

I get slowly to my feet, and with a stretch of my limbs I prepare to take my leave. Somewhere outside a bell's started tolling, and a glimmer of light is coming in through the open window. Morning is breaking, and I've got to get back to Tristan.

I reach down to give Abelard's hand a last squeeze of thanks, and as I make my way across the room, I wonder if perhaps Brian de Gilford could be Melissande's father. Somehow, I think I'd like that.

"What did happen to her, Abelard?" I ask, almost as an afterthought, and pausing at the window. "Whatever became of Lady Brecelyn?"

"She died, not long after Melissande was born."

"Childbirth, I suppose," I nod absently, turning back to the window and slinging my leg over the sill. "Probably trying to give Brecelyn an heir."

It's common enough. My own mother died that way, giving birth to me. And let's face it. The danger of childbirth is a subject that's still fresh in my mind, after what happened to Melissande's baby.

But Abelard shakes his head. And when his answer comes, it startles me so much that I lurch forward, and only a quick grab at the trunk of the tree in front of me keeps me from falling out of the window.

"I found her lying dead out in Brecelyn's chapel of St. Sebastian. Strangled, with those pages stuffed down into her mouth. Her neck had been snapped clear in half."

It's so shocking, I can't be anything but horrified. Brecelyn must have proven harder to fool than that scheming girl bargained for.

There's nothing I can say, so with a shudder I clasp the branch in front of me in preparation of climbing down. As my hands close firmly around its smooth bark, though, in my mind I see a pair of large, rough hands, snaking around a neck — and squeezing; Brecelyn's hands, squeezing around the little merlin's neck, and I lose my grip. It takes me a moment to fumble around and right myself, and I'm still perched precariously halfway out on the limb and rubbing my sore side when a last question occurs me, the most important question of all.

I can't believe I was going to leave without asking it.

I lean my head back into the room with an exclamation, and Abelard looks up from where he'd been staring into his lamp's flame. I put one hand down to the little book now tucked back into my waistband.

"Abelard, why *did* you give me that page of illumination? Don't bother to deny it. I know you did it on purpose."

To my surprise, a cornered look flickers across the old monk's face, like he's been caught on the brink of his own narrow escape. As preposterous as it sounds, for a moment I even think he's casting around for a lie to tell me.

Then he sighs. His expression transforms into sheepishness, and when he replies, he sounds tired.

"Why did I give it to you, Marieke? I guess I thought you deserved to know the truth. And I've always felt a little guilty. Because in a way, I helped cause your father's accident."

At my puzzled frown, Abelard sighs again.

"Jan wasn't Melissande's father, child. And neither is Jakob. *I* am."

I guess I should be shocked. But I think I'd already figured it out, about halfway through the story.

In the wake of this confession, poor Abelard looks so frail and so alone that I scramble impulsively back in through the window, and I throw myself into his arms. I've never done anything like it, and at first I'm not sure how the old monk is going to react. But after only the slightest of hesitations, his arms fold gently around me and his head comes down to rest on the top of mine, just the way Tristan's always does when I embrace him.

"I've always loved you like my very own, Marieke," Abelard says softly, sounding unbearably sad. "I couldn't do anything for her. I couldn't help her. But you're so strong," and I'm surprised by the adjective. It's the last one I'd ever use for myself. "Why did I give you that picture? It's foolish, I know. But I hoped that it would help you. And I think, I even hoped that somehow, it would help her, too. That maybe one day, you might meet her. That you'd remember the picture and you'd befriend her. That you'd help her find a way to bear the burden of beauty without becoming like her mother."

"I did, Abelard! I *will*," I promise him. "And Melissande *is* beautiful. Truly. Only she's nothing like her mother."

He gives me one last squeeze and puts me gently from him, and I make my way back to the window. I think it's almost to break the solemn mood that's fallen over us that I turn back toward the room one last time, once I'm poised again on the limb, halfway in and halfway out the little window.

627

"And that funny little girl," I say lightly, from my perch in the tree. "Whatever happened to her?"

"Don't you know, Marieke?" Abelard asks, a smile appearing on his face for the first time this evening.

For once when someone says this to me, I do.

"But she was beautiful!" I protest.

"And who was it who told you that?" Abelard chuckles, and I get it. There was really only one person who always told me my mother was beautiful.

I make my descent down the old chestnut tree in a daze, as dawn breaks around me. After all the revelations of the day, who would have thought there could be time for one more, one more unexpected than any of the others? But there's no doubt that this one surprises me as much as any that preceded it.

As it turns out, there *is* such a thing as a boy who prefers a defiant look.

My own father was one of them.

CHAPTER FORTY-SIX

I find Tristan fast asleep under the beech tree. He's spread his cloak out on the ground and he's lying on top of it, with the edges of it folded up over him on both sides like wings. His still longish hair is tousled against his cheek, and in the soft morning light his face glows as smooth and as white as marble. He could be a statue, an effigy from an old story about a sleeping youth ravished by the dawn, and I hate to wake him. I have an urge to bend down and give him a fond kiss on the forehead myself.

Instead, I give him a stiff prod with the toe of my boot. Back at St. Sebastian's everyone will be waking soon, and we've got a long ride ahead of us.

"Gads, Marek," he exclaims with a languid stretch, apparently forgetting for a moment that he no longer needs to pretend to be Gilles. "These monks must be chatty fellows. I do believe we've been here all night!"

He springs to his feet, seemingly as spry and as refreshed as if he'd spent the night on a featherbed and not on the hard, damp ground. After giving his cloak a shake and carefully plucking off a stray piece of hay or two, he makes quick work of saddling up the horse again, and it's not long before we're on our way.

We don't talk much on the ride back. Despite appearances, I know Tristan's mood must still be fragile, since this morning he still doesn't demand any explanation for dragging him out at midnight. His only inquiry, as he leads the horse past the brewery yard and waves a lazy hand at a few of the monks who've started to wander out to tend the garden stretched out beside it, is to ask,

"So, did the old boy provide any *illumination?*" and I shoot him a quick glance, wondering if he's figured out that the illustration of mine that he threw into Brecelyn's fire must have come from Father Abelard.

But Tristan is all innocence, and when I just give a noncommittal murmur, he doesn't press for details or attempt to draw me into conversation, and that suits me fine. I've got plenty to think about, and I want to have time before I get back to the guild to mull over everything I've learned.

In all, I should be pleased, and I am. The big question of Melissande's father has finally been answered, and although I'm sad for Abelard, I can't be anything but glad to find my own father absolved of direct involvement. I have to be even gladder to find that Melissande isn't the boys' sister, either. But as we make our way into the woods, I'm also feeling dissatisfied, a little.

It sounds ridiculous, but I know I've been hoping for a long time that understanding my father's past would help me safeguard Tristan's future. My father's story has always seemed such a perfect parallel to Tristan's, I really thought hearing about it would tell me what our next move should be! Or at least help me figure out what really happened between Tristan, Melissande, and Taran. But the parallel I was expecting wasn't there at all. Jealousy was the cause of my father's accident, but it wasn't as I'd thought. It wasn't jealousy between Journeys. Not really. My father's old enemy wasn't one of the other boys.

I couldn't have really expected my father's story to tell me who shot Tristan, though, could I? It's irrational, I know. But I'm disappointed anyway.

As the big shocks of the story Abelard's shared with me sink in, I'm also finding plenty to disturb me in its smaller details. In particular, I have a sudden flash of pulling down Melissande's veil to reveal my breasts in the hopes of tantalizing Taran, and I have to thrust it quickly away.

As we go deeper into the woods, the more the resonances between past and present swirl around in my mind. When I try to grasp them and make sense of them, though, the more elusive they become, slipping and sliding until I'm not sure what they mean, if anything. But they keep coming back to me, and unlikely as it seems, I begin to get the feeling that there *is* a message for me in my father's past somewhere. It's not strictly parallel to the boys' story, true, but there are definite similarities. It feels relevant, somehow. But how?

I can't possibly believe that *Melissande* shot Tristan, or that she put Taran up to it. Melissande would never do anything so awful. Her condition can't have had anything to do with Tristan's wounding, either, since she couldn't have already been pregnant. I can't see Taran being someone else's fool, the way Brecelyn was Meliana's, and anyway, I'm certain now that Taran never aimed a single shot at Tristan. Still, Gilles's words float back to me, *things aren't always what they seem*, and there are plenty of things about Tristan's accident that still need explaining. If nothing else, that broken arrow of Taran's that Remy and I found out in the bushes tells me Taran *did* shoot at *something* — and he missed. There has to be an explanation for that, and I can't shake the feeling that my father's past does hold a clue for me. I'm sure of it.

I just don't know what it is.

Tristan's been putting on a brave face, but he's had a rough night, no better than mine. As we ride along, he's still struggling to make sense of everything that's happened, too, and I know he's as worried about the future as I am. So when at last he breaks the silence by asking, "Tell me about it," I readily comply.

In the broadest of strokes, I confess to Tristan about finding the notebook at the castle, and I tell him Meliana's story. Understandably, I do some judicious editing. I can't bear to go into all the details of the tale again so soon, and I don't tell him about Melissande's father, since Abelard's secret isn't mine to tell. For obvious reasons, though, most of my omissions involve Jakob Mellor.

At first, I think Tristan is a little annoyed at me, when I have to confess that the embroidered handkerchief wasn't the only thing I found out in Brecelyn's chapel and neglected to mention to him. But my story is so awful, by the time I finish, he just asks,

"You all right?"

"I don't know," I admit, shaking my head. "You?"

"I don't know, either." He doesn't elaborate. He just waits patiently, sensing there's more I want to say.

"I wish I'd known, Tristan," I finally tell him. "I wished I'd known while my father was still alive. All this time, I've been wrong about him. Unfair. I thought our life together out here in the country was a sign of his defeat. But it wasn't. It was the life he wanted. It was his triumph, in a way. I wish I could tell him that I loved our life, too. I wish I could tell him just how sorry I am."

I close my eyes and I picture my father, laughing up at a young girl perched above him in a tree. A girl who looked a lot like me.

"I think I finally understand him, Tristan," I say softly. "It wasn't his accident that shattered my father, or that wretched girl's schemes. It wasn't a broken shoulder that changed him from the boy he was at St. Sebastian's into the man I knew. It was a broken heart."

Tristan's silent for a while, and I know he's thinking about Melissande. I'm having a little trouble keeping my thoughts from wandering myself. But then after a while Tristan says,

"There's something else bothering you, too, isn't there, kid?"

Tristan knows me awfully well.

I take a deep breath. This confession is even harder.

"All this time, I've been wrong about Brecelyn, too, Tristan. I've been wasting my time hating him."

Tristan stirs behind me in the saddle, surprised, and I don't have to see him to picture him raising his half-eyebrow at me inquiringly.

"He's not really to blame for my father's accident." Behind me, I sense Tristan's eyebrow sneaking higher. "Oh, I'm sure he did wield the knife. But his wife put it into his hand. He was just a pawn. Brecelyn was as much a victim as my father was."

"You still think he killed your father, don't you?" Tristan protests. "You can still hate him for that. Or don't you think any longer that it was Brecelyn's voice you overheard that day, mocking your father as he died?"

"Oh, it was his voice, all right. I'm sure of it. He shot the arrows. Brecelyn did kill my father. But he's not my father's killer, if that makes any sense."

"Not really," Tristan says mildly, and I take another deep breath.

"It's time I faced it, Tristan. You were right, about everything. Brecelyn did hate my father. But the plot that got my father killed, the plot to kill the *regent* — Brecelyn can't have been the one who was really behind it. Brecelyn's no mastermind. He's not a leader. Somebody who knew about Brecelyn's past and about his hatred for my father must have manipulated him, just like Meliana did. Somebody who *is* a leader. Somebody who was plotting the whole thing, from inside St. Sebastian's."

Neither of us says anything, since all I'm doing is repeating Tristan's own theory back to him. Besides, it's been obvious enough from the very beginning. It's just never made any sense, and I haven't wanted to believe it. But the time has come for me to say it out loud, and it's hard. Almost as hard as it was to admit to myself that I'm in love Taran (and there's no way I'm telling Tristan *that*). But I guess I've always known there's a thin line between love and hate.

I fish around in my waistband for a moment, and I pull out the handkerchief that Aristide returned to me and I hold it out.

"And now we're *leaving*, Tristan. Master Guillaume will never have to pay for what he did to my father. He's never going to pay for anything. He's going to get away with it."

"Never say never, Marek," Tristan replies solemnly, taking one hand from the reins to put it over my hand, and covering the big red G, he squeezes in a gesture that's a comfort but also a promise. "Who knows what the future holds? It's a new day, and don't forget. I swore I'd get vengeance for your father, and I will. Only the master *is* a clever man, and we've got to proceed with caution. If there's anything I've learned from being Gilles, it's that revenge requires patience. But I swear to you I'll get it in the end. And when I do, it'll be for the *both* of us."

This time I don't make the mistake of thinking Tristan isn't serious, even when he adds with a laugh,

"I'll tell you what! I'll become a knight errant, and it can be my quest."

We ride on, toward the sunrise, and toward our one last day as St. Sebastian's men. We're both exhausted, and so I settle myself back heavily against Tristan and I let my mind go blank. I need to conserve all my energy for the difficult tasks ahead: packing up all our things, into my old traveling bag. Folding up my blanket one last time back in barracks, and saying goodbye to my old cot. Saying goodbye to all the squires and to the Journeys who are left, and facing down Master Guillaume in the process. Then there'll be heading out again, for good — and figuring out where in the world Tristan and I can think we're going, and if there is a place outside the walls of St. Sebastian's where Tristan and I make sense.

But there's one task more than any other that I'm dreading. It's the hardest one of all, and if I think about it now, I'll break.

Figuring out how to say goodbye to Taran.

And how to tell him once before I go, how I really feel about him.

"Say, Marek," Tristan asks me, cutting into my thoughts and his voice deceptively casual, "Did Father Abelard happen to mention anything about *my* father?"

"A little," I admit. It's risky, given the mood Tristan's in. But I venture to add, "I kind of liked him, actually. He reminded me of Falko. Only, uh, *more so*, if you know what I mean."

"It figures," is all Tristan says.

SNEAK PEEK OFFER!

Guards: the Archers of Saint Sebastian IV is COMING! Don't miss the exciting final installment of the Archers of Saint Sebastian Tetralogy. You can request a complimentary sneak peek into the first chapter by visiting the contact page at www.jeanneroland.com ... *and a plea:*

    If you enjoyed *Masters*, **please consider leaving an honest review of the**

SNEAK PEEK OFFER!

book on Amazon or Goodreads. Independent authors like me depend on ratings from readers like you to give us visibility. Your support is greatly appreciated, and if you can think of anyone who might like the series, please do recommend it! 'Word of mouth' is my marketing department.

I'd also love to hear from you; getting messages from readers telling me that they enjoyed my books or just chatting with me about them is my greatest reward for writing, it makes my day and sharing my world with others is my whole reason for publishing! Visit me at www.jeanneroland.com to tell me what you thought of Masters, or if you have questions or other comments, and if you're interested in keeping up with my latest projects, please consider signing up to get my newsletter.

A NOTE FROM THE AUTHOR

The Archers of St. Sebastian I, II, & III are more fiction than history, and it would be more appropriate to say that this story was inspired by late medieval Belgium than that it actually takes place there. There was never a principality called Ardennes; although the forested region of the same name is undoubtedly real, the country at the heart of this story, its institutions, and its attitudes are all fabrications. The Louvain in this story is not Leuven; that city lies well to the north of my fictional Ardennes, whose borders I imagine as corresponding roughly to those of medieval Wallonia. The real towns and rivers of this region, too, have been altered to suit the story, and even the basic topography of southern Belgium as it is described in my book is probably more convenient for my purposes than it is accurate.

Likewise, although there were many longbow and crossbow guilds throughout northern Europe during the 14th century, my archers' guild of St. Sebastian, its operation, inhabitants, and competitions are all the products of imagination. Nonetheless, I have endeavored to avoid glaring anachronism in the telling of my tale whenever possible, and to present an image of medieval archery that is detailed and compelling. But I have also continued to take it as my guiding principle that the needs of storytelling should always trump the demands of strict historical accuracy, particularly when it comes to language. For the basics of medieval archery, fletching, and hunting, I relied heavily on *With A Bended Bow: Archery in Mediaeval and Renaissance Europe* by Erik Roth, Spellmount Publishers Ltd., 2012; all errors, misrepresentations, and flat-out embellishments are of course my own.

It would be disingenuous, however, if I did not admit that the glorious city of Bruges provided the inspiration for this story. Indeed, the seeds of it were planted long ago, on an idyllic afternoon spent wandering lost through the backstreets of Bruges with my father, searching for a park purporting to contain a statue of Jacque Brel's Marieke (the Judy Collins version of the

A Note From The Author

song being one of his all-time favorites). I still have the picture I took of my father once we finally tracked down our quarry, holding the statue's hand and pretending to skip along with it — just as there is a picture of a youthful me, sitting in Bruges's archers' guild of St. Sebastian earlier that same day, and staring up at a beautiful painting (it's published at the end of *Squires*). I had the great good fortune to revisit Bruges this past summer thanks to the generosity of my fabulous sister, where it was with great joy that she and I recreated that long-ago picture with the statue of Marieke; I'd like to think that my father was there with us, in spirit.

ACKNOWLEDGMENTS

Whereas writing *Journeys* was the greatest adventure of my life and writing *Squires* was a close second, writing *Masters* has been one of my greatest ordeals. At many points I despaired of ever finishing it, and I can't say for certain that I ever fully tamed this magnificent beast. I think I kept trying to make it something that it didn't want to be, something I thought it should be, instead of letting it unfold in all its unruly glory; I've come to love it and I hope my readers all will, too. Perhaps this is one that just has to grow on you — or maybe sneak up on you!

As with the first two volumes in this series, to list all of the people who helped me along the way would be a true impossibility; as Marieke might say, the task has gone from 'just possible' to impossible, and so I won't pretend to try. Those of you who read a draft of the first two books, offered advice, listened to me talk about them *ad nauseam*, or provided much-needed emotional support, you know who you are and again I thank you from the bottom of my heart. If you also read a draft of this book and stayed with me through yet another agonizing creation process, you have surpassed the designation of champion and have achieved hero status!

As always, my inner circle remains the same, and I cannot omit giving special thanks to those who are the knights at my creative round table: first and foremost, my super-sister Sue, to whom *Squires* is dedicated; let no other sit in her chair, for it is my own *siege perilous*! Mimi, my first and best fan, and always my best reader; it was she who got me over the finish line on this one, and as always, if this book is good at all, it is largely because of her assistance. And of course Sam, my most unflagging cheerleader — she was the first to love this one, and it is because of her that a certain event didn't get cut from this story; it is these two steadfast muses to whom this volume is dedicated. If it were not for them, this book would surely still be running wild! I also owe a special thanks to Laura and Nadine, who constantly prove that old friends are the best ones, and to my dear friends Melissa and Naomi.

As always, I owe an even bigger thanks to my family, both here and in Greece — a debt of gratitude that has now grown so large I can never pretend to repay it. Thank you, my dear husband S, for putting up with me! Thank you, my wonderful twins V and C, for hashing out ideas with me and cheering me on so tirelessly — and I would be remiss if I didn't also mention my author friends who have encouraged me and helped me spread the word about my series in the writing community on X/formerly Twitter.

However, this time around, I want to thank most of all my dedicated readers. To everyone who took a chance on an unknown author and picked up the series, please know how deeply grateful I am! Putting out my debut novel was petrifying, but finding such a wonderful group of people with whom to share it has made the experience richly rewarding. If you read *Journeys*, I thank you! If you went on to read *Squires*, I more than thank you! And if you wrote reviews, rated the books, or connected with me and cheered me on via social media and/or helped to spread the word about the series in any way, I can never express all of my gratitude. I have a file on my computer into which I have copied and pasted every single encouraging reader comment I have ever gotten, and I cherish each and every one of them.

In particular, I want to thank the wonderful group of people who regularly comment on my author Facebook page and who have unflaggingly cheered me on there. I dare not try to list everyone by name, lest I inadvertently miss someone, but you all more than any others have encouraged me not to give up and to keep writing, and I cannot wait to find out what you all make of this installment!

Finally, I will end in the same way I always end my acknowledgments, because those to whom I owe the greatest thanks and debt of gratitude will never change. And so once again I thank my mother, for being an exemplary model of what women can achieve, and my father, for never losing the ability to see the world through the lens of childlike wonder, and for teaching me that a life filled with passions and lit by intellectual curiosity is the best life possible. If anyone ever embodied Socrates' phrase *"not to live, but to live well,"* it was he.

ABOUT THE AUTHOR

Roland hails from northern California, where she spent most of her youth lounging at the pool, soaking up the sun, and daydreaming. She had a key ring that read *I'm running away to join the circus*, and her favorite moment of the day was when the local movie theater went dark, and the slogan *escape to the movies* appeared on the screen. As an adult, her passions include all things melodramatic and beautiful — everything from classic movies, British romantic poetry, ancient tragedy and epic, to Italian opera. She is now a professor of Classics in a small midwestern town, where she lives with her Greek husband, her fraternal twins, and a Bernese Mountain Dog named Mr. Franco Corelli.

facebook.com/jeannerolandwrites
twitter.com/booksbyJeanneR
instagram.com/jeannerolandwrites

ILLUSTRATION CREDITS AND CITATIONS

All illustrations in this book were created for Nepenthe Press using Canva fonts and graphic elements licensed under the Canva Pro license, illustrations and vectors licensed under the Shutterstock standard license, Herculaneum font, and public domain artwork for which source files are Open Access or have been made available under a Creative Commons license. A comprehensive list of all the source files used herein is as follows:

Cover: Canva Pro graphic elements (arrow, arrow hole, poppies, frame) and fonts, plus the following artwork: *"Flowers by a Stone Vase,"* Peter Faes (Flemish, 1750–1814), ca. 1786, Oil on wood, 20 x 14 7/8 in. (50.8 x 37.8 cm), Bequest of Catherine D. Wentworth, 1948, , in the Metropolitan Museum of Art (MMOA) AN 48.187.737, OA Public Domain image, web accessed at https://www.metmuseum.org/art/collection/search/436290 on August 27, 2023 **(background image)**; *"The Martyrdom of Saint Sebastian,"* Workshop of Gerard van Honthorst (Netherlands ca. 1623), oil on canvas, 101 cm (39.7 in) by 118 cm (46.4 in), Centraal museum, Utrecht, Public Domain image web accessed on August 27, 2023 from https://commons.wikimedia.org/wiki/File:Saint_Sebastian_from_the_workshop_of_Gerard_van_Honthorst_Centraal_Museum_31722.jpg, cropped **(inset)**. Both paintings are in the Public Domain in their countries of origin and other countries and areas where the copyright term is the author's life plus 100 years or fewer.

Title page:
"Willem Tell met handboog," August Claude Simon Legrand, after a painting by Lambert, print on paper, France ca. 1775-1815, Rijkmuseum Object Number RP-P-1922-641, Open Access Public Doman image, web accessed from the Rijksmuseum online collection on August 27, 2023.

Dedication: *Doodle Red Poppies*, Shutterstock ID 1238279428, by Ollisia.

Section divisions: Canva Pro graphic element (scrolls), plus the

643

Illustration credits and citations

following artwork: **Part one**: *"In the Woods,"* Asher Brown Durand, 1855, oil on canvas, 60 3/4 x 48 in. (154.3 x 121.9 cm), Gift in memory of Jonathan Sturges by his children, 1895, in the Metropolitan museum of art (hereafter MMOA), AN 95.13.1, Open Access Public Domain image web accessed from the MOMA online collection at https://www.metmuseum.org/art/collection/search/10790 on August 27, 2023. **Part two**: *"Zwijnenjacht,"* Charles Aubry, 1836, print, Rijksmuseum Object number RP-P-OB-41.272, Open Access Public Doman image accessed from the Rijksmuseum website collection on August 27, 2023. **Part three**: *"Dood van Adonis,"* M. Martinet, engraving after a painting by Pietro Bianchi, Rijksmuseun Object number RP-P-1998-736, Open Access Public Domain image accessed from the Rijksmuseum website collection on August 27, 2023. **Part four**: *"Still Life with a Vase of Flowers and a Dead Frog,"* Jacob Marrel, 1634, oil painting, Rijksmuseum Object number SK-A-772, Gift of H. W. Mesdag, The Hague, Open Access Public Doman image accessed from the Rijksmuseum website collection on August 27, 2023.

Chapter headings:

Canva Pro graphic elements (all vectors and graphics are from Canva Pro except those explicitly listed below), plus the following artwork: *"Poppy flowers collection on white background,"* Shutterstock vector ID 386473642, by Stockakia;*"Medieval Bow 3D illustration on white background,"* Shutterstock ID 1810862491, by PixelSquid3d, *"Hunting arrows collection,"* Shutterstock ID 194942657, by Tribalium 88; *"Different mice,"* Shutterstock ID 1484129015, by A788OS; *"Set of predatory bird cute adult falcon cartoon animal design birds of prey character flat vector illustration isolated on white background,"* Shutterstock ID 1817468843, by Alfamaler; *"Quiver and arrows,"* Shutterstock ID 517555045, by Elsbet. Shutterstock ID 194942657, by Tribalium 88. *Doodle Red Poppies*, Shutterstock ID 1238279428, by Ollisia.

Guards placeholder cover: Canva Pro graphic elements and *Hunting arrows collection,"* Shutterstock ID 194942657, by Tribalium 88.

Jeanne Roland and Nepenthe Press logos: created by Miblart.

Made in the USA
Columbia, SC
30 September 2023